CYCLOPS

THE BICYCLE THIEF
HOW CYCLOPS GOT HIS GROOVE BACK

Writer: Lee Black • Art: Dean Haspiel • Color Art: Jose Villarrubia
Letters: Jeff Eckleberry • Production: Randall Miller • Editor: Sebastian Girner
Editor in Chief: Axel Alonso • Chief Creative Officer: Joe Quesada
Publisher: Dan Buckley • Exec. Producer: Alan Fine

MARVEL
Spotlight

visit us at www.abdopublishing.com

Reinforced library bound edition published in 2012 by Spotlight, a division of the ABDO Group, 8000 West 78th Street, Edina, Minnesota 55439. Spotlight produces high-quality reinforced library bound editions for schools and libraries. Published by agreement with Marvel Entertainment, LLC. The stories, characters, and incidents mentioned are entirely fictional. All rights reserved. Used under authorization.

Printed in the United States of America, Melrose Park, Illinois.
052011
092011
♻ This book contains at least 10% recycled materials.

Library of Congress Cataloging-in-Publication Data

Black, Lee.
  Cyclops / writer, Lee Black ; penciler, Dean Haspiel. -- Reinforced library bound ed.
    p. cm. -- (X-men: first class)
  ISBN 978-1-59961-947-7
  1. Graphic novels. I. Haspiel, Dean. II. Title.
  PN6728.X2B57 2011
  741.5'973--dc22
                          2011013928

All Spotlight books are reinforced library bindings and manufactured in the United States of America.

THE BICYCLE THIEF
OR: HOW CYCLOPS GOT HIS GROOVE BACK

Writer: *Lee Black* • Art: *Dean Haspiel* • Color Art: *Jose Villarrubia*
Lettering: *Jeff Eckleberry* • Production: *Randall Miller* • Editor: *Sebastian Girner*
Editor in Chief: *Axel Alonso* • Chief Creative Officer: *Joe Quesada*
Publisher: *Dan Buckley* • Exec. Producer: *Alan Fine*

Special Thanks to *Jen Ferguson*

The End

A Smithsonian Nature Book

The Great
Gray Owl

Phantom of the Northern Forest

ROBERT W. NERO

Photographs by **ROBERT R. TAYLOR**

Smithsonian Institution Press, Washington, D.C.

Library of Congress Cataloging in Publication Data
Nero, Robert W.
The great gray owl-phantom of the northern forest.
(A Smithsonian nature book)
Bibliography: p.
Includes index.
Supt. of Docs. no.: SI 1.2:OW4
1. Great gray owl.   2. Birds—Manitoba.   I. Title.
II. Series: Smithsonian nature book.
QL696.S8N47   598'.97   80-607110
ISBN 0-87474-672-8

Cover   Free again! A newly banded owl in full flight looks for a suitable distant perch.

Frontispiece   When an owl is annoyed or anxious, the bristly feathers surrounding the bill are spread.

Dedicated to John T. Emlen, Jr., professor, mentor, and friend

Contents

Foreword, 8

Preface, 10

Acknowledgments, 12

1. **A Beginning**, 15

2. **Out of the Woods**, 28

3. **An Owl in the City**, 37

4. **To Catch an Owl**, 44

5. **An Elusive Bird**, 57

6. **The Species—A Closer Look**, 69

7. **Short Days and Long Nights**, 85

8. **Feathers on the Snow**, 94

9. **A Time of Change**, 101

10. **A Nesting of Owls**, 113

11. **In Search of Nests**, 123

12. **Nest Builders**, 135

13. **A Different Race of Creatures**, 148

Bibliography, 157

Index, 163

Foreword

The Great Gray Owl stands near the top of every serious bird watcher's most-wanted list. On their periodic forays south into the northern United States, these huge, pale-eyed phantom visitors from the boreal forests bring forth a rush of binocular- and camera-laden voyeurs who study, photograph, and record their every move; subsequently, the owl's quizzical face peers forth from nature magazine covers and stories are told and retold.

In the past such incursions resulted in spates of trophies or specimens displayed in game rooms or deposited in museums. In more recent years, however, a network of telephone information centers has alerted bird watchers to the owls' occurrences south of their usual haunts and has meant that many more persons could enjoy the silent winter visitors. Nevertheless, few scientists have studied their habits on the breeding grounds and little was known of their home lives.

What studies there were, especially in North America, had generally been fortuitous, the result of chance finds of convenient nests. But scientist Bob Nero of the Manitoba Department of Natural Resources and photographer Bob Taylor from Winnipeg doggedly and successfully pursued their quarry in the spruce-tamarack bogs near the United States-Canadian border over a number of years. Their anxious listening for deep hooting and hopeful waiting for the great birds to come winging silently back to the nest for a new season were rewarded. Their work began in earnest—and this book is the result.

Owls have persistently charmed, fascinated, and awed mankind for aeons, and their nighttime calls have struck terror into the superstitious as harbingers of danger or even death. Unlike most birds, owls can look you straight in the eye; their flat faces and large eyes impart an almost human aspect to their physiognomies. The owl was a symbol of wisdom long before Athena's Little Owl first peered defiantly from the tetradrachm, and even today children recite an ode to the "wise old owl." As we learn more about their habits, some of the owls' mystery vanishes, but our fascination persists.

The Great Gray Owl's diet of forest voles hardly seems adequate for such a formidable, long-winged predator, but under its long, dense feather coat lurks only a modest body, hardly bulkier than those of its more temperate cousins, the Barred Owl of North America or the Tawny Owl of Eurasia. Unlike its relatives in the genus *Strix*, it is not entirely nocturnal, but can hunt actively during the day, providing many more hours for it to capture prey in the forest. Also, nesting begins before the trees leaf out, so that, even in the cool early morning hours, there is relatively good light in the forest. These circumstances, and an accessible nest, made it possible for Nero to study the birds' behavior and for Taylor to make his superb photographic record. Furthermore, because of their remote forest habitat, the owls hadn't been exposed to humans and were thus remarkably tolerant of observers. The female incubated the eggs or brooded the young, and the male regularly brought food to the nest, even when Nero and Taylor were visible.

Great Gray Owls must also be competent night hunters, for many stay in the far north all winter, when days are short and few small mammals emerge from beneath the snow. Then the owls' ability to hunt by sound guides them to prey under the surface, where even their keen night vision is of no use. The large facial disc, rimmed with remarkably modified feathers, concentrates sound into the owl's highly directional ears. Cruising silently through the forest, the hunter scans the snow for faint sounds of activity. Broad wing tracings in a soft white blanket of newly fallen snow found by Nero vividly record the tragic end of an unsuspecting vole which thought itself secure in its burrow under the snow.

Over a period of years, Nero and Taylor and their collaborators have pieced together the story of the home life and annual cycle of the owl. It is a fascinating account of adaptation to a special way of life. I first heard of this project in 1975, when the American Ornithologists' Union held its annual meeting in Winnipeg. Nero and Taylor showed the AOU members an early version of their film on the Great Gray Owl; several hundred ornithologists, professional and amateur alike, were held in awe at the trustful nature of their subject. We watched the female take a vole from the male and feed it to the downy white young. And we marveled at the capacity of the chick's maw as it labored to gulp down whole a rodent nearly its own size.

Bob asked me then about the Smithsonian Institution Press and other possible publishers for his study. I encouraged him to submit his manuscript. The result is this book, which now makes the Great Gray Owl one of the better understood large owls and should stir even wider interest among birders for catching a glimpse of one on their next southern foray when winter food becomes scarce in the boreal forests.

George E. Watson, Curator of Birds
National Museum of Natural History
Smithsonian Institution

Preface

Had a different title been used for this book, say, "Gray Owl of the North," some would have assumed that here was yet another biography of "Grey Owl," that semi-mystical Englishman-turned-Indian who carried woodland lore from Canada to England's royal family. That devoted conservationist, despite his Indian-given name, was no particular friend of the owl, which he called "a detestable bird whose name had been imposed on me only on account of my nocturnal habits."

Grey Owl's unkind comments about his namesake probably reflect an older, almost universal view of owls as mournful creatures of darkness, usually of ill omen, an attitude frequently expressed in poetry and prose. Typical is this phrase from "To the Owl" by Robert Burns: "Sad bird of night, what sorrows call thee forth, to vent thy plaints thus in the midnight hour?"

More recently, and in keeping with a changing view of owls, author August Derleth commented: "The lore of owls, I am inclined to think, takes too little notice of such intelligence as the owl surely has; the bird merits a wider appreciation and some course in public instruction designed to teach mankind something more of his way of life."

"Intelligence" may not be the correct word for the behavioral flexibility and learning capacity exhibited by owls, but otherwise I can agree with Derleth's viewpoint. A Long-eared Owl, taken as a fledgling and kept in our home a year for study, taught me that owls are sensitive, playful birds. Changes in its posture and facial appearance gave evidence of a variety of moods, from relaxed docility to aggression and fear. It taunted both our sleepy, old cat and our slightly puzzled spaniel, aggressively hopping across the carpet daringly close to them, one feathered foot in front of the other, while leaning backward in readiness for escape should either target arouse itself. Muzzle flat to the floor, the dog's main responses to the advancing bird were cocking his eyebrows or flaring his nostrils; the cat's twitching tail suggested a greater emotion, but both seemed to accept the advancing owl as something to be endured, if not appreciated.

Daily I engaged the owl in a hunting game, tossing a tightly rolled ball of yarn onto the floor while the owl watched expectantly from its perch on the curtain rod. Then followed a pause while we watched each other to see which would make the first move, and then a quick dash downward by the owl as I simultaneously reached out for the ball. If I got it first, the owl returned to its perch, shaking out its feathers and readying itself for another try. When it succeeded in snatching up the ball it gave a pleasant cackling call, as close to triumphant laughter as I dared attribute to it, while flying a circular course through the living room and kitchen, back to its perch, the ball clenched in its talons.

The close observations made possible by that captive bird later provided useful insights. When I moved to Winnipeg in 1966 I had no special interest in raptors and had never seen a Great Gray Owl. All I knew about them was that they were rare. I first saw them in 1968 and found them to be captivating birds. Since then I have observed them every year, winter and summer, day and night, in Manitoba and adjacent Minnesota. No other species has so preoccupied my time and attention. This unique species is as much a part of the northern coniferous forest as loon, raven, wolf, or moose.

Almost unseen in some years, at other times they have been relatively common. My colleagues and I have been privileged to see and handle unusually large numbers of Great Gray Owls. We have studied them under more diverse circumstances than can be described. What has impressed me most is their range of expression, their variety of mood and behavior, and their relative docility. It has been not so much a study as a pursuit, but it has been greatly rewarding.

It has not been my intention to describe all the events we experienced or to document all the data we obtained during the period of our study. Technical reports of our joint findings are in preparation for publication in suitable journals. Rather, this book is meant to provide, in addition to a basic account of the natural history of the Great Gray Owl, an opportunity for the reader to share in our experiences.

One has to stop somewhere, and in the main, observations and data in this book do not extend beyond July 30, 1979.

Acknowledgments

For constant companionship in the field and mutual pleasure in studying Great Gray Owls from 1968 to 1980, I am especially indebted to Herbert W. R. Copland, an experienced birder, born and raised in Winnipeg. The good and bad events that Herb Copland and I have shared would make a memorable story. His good humor, patience, and enthusiasm provided invaluable support to our field work. Beverly Copland kindly consented to her husband's participation. Robert R. Taylor, naturalist and free-lance photographer, really got me started on owls. Bob Taylor's photographs, which add so much to this book, reveal his technical skills, and his experience in working with owls. The many hours of assistance given me by my son, Redwood "Woody" Nero, are a rich part of my owl years. His younger brother, Brook, also assisted me.

Raymond Tuokko is a Winnipeg resident, but his folks live near Lac du Bonnet, in an area practically surrounded by Great Gray Owl habitat. From the day I first met Ray on a highway where we were looking for owls, he has actively shared our interest in this bird. Ray's records, observations, and tireless field efforts have been a valuable asset.

Spencer G. Sealy, ornithologist at the University of Manitoba, who arrived in Winnipeg in 1974, soon found himself caught up in our quest. His energy and questioning spirit lent important support to our efforts. K. Michael Collins, working under Spencer toward a Master's degree in zoology, began a two-year study of the Great Gray Owl in 1975. Few of his findings appear here because his thesis is not yet complete. However, I have described a few situations in which we were both involved.

Inspiration and encouragement were provided by Dalton Muir, a Great Gray Owl fan and photographer with whom we spent many hours at an active nest.

Many people provided assistance and information, but special thanks are due the following: Kathleen S. Anderson, Eugene F. Bossenmaier, Soren Bondrup-Nielson, Daniel F. Brunton, Paul M. Catling, Fred Cooke, John Christie, Calvin Cuthbert, Alice Dennis, John Donald, Kim Eckert, David L. Evans, Carl Feilberg and family, Don G. Follen, Sr., Ken Gardner, Robert E. Gehlert, W. Earl Godfrey, David R. M. Hatch, John C. Hellson, Stu Iverson, Paulette J. Henson, Nils Höglund, C. Stuart Houston, Ross D. James, Patricia A. Knipe, Gerry McKeating, Katherine A. McKeever, Heimo Mikkola, William Nakka, Clarence E. Nordstrom and family, Albert F. Oeming, Marianne Page, Al Peden, Richard M. Poulin, Philip B. Reader, James R. Salt, W. Ray Salt, Vere H. Scott, William Sitar, Jack Steinbring, Robert Stitt, Betty Struthers, Jack and Irene Tuokko, Wayne Tuokko, Brian Turner, Jens Wahlstedt, Sam Waller, Ed and Marg Ward, Jon Winter, and Andrew Yakiwchuk.

Grants in support of field work were received from the Seven Sisters Falls Wildlife Association (Manitoba), the Manitoba Naturalists Society, and the Frank M. Chapman Memorial Fund (American Museum of Natural History). Financial support was received as a gift from Al Graham, a former fellow employee with a special fondness for owls. Some support was received initially from the Manitoba Museum of Man and Nature.

From fall 1978 onward, the Manitoba Department of Natural Resources, in which I have been employed as a wildlife specialist since 1970, provided invaluable travel and sustenance support. For this service I am especially grateful to Richard C. Goulden, Director of Wildlife. Information and assistance were received from many of my fellow employees. Regional staff of the Department contributed numerous observations and rendered many useful services. Regional accommodations of the Department were made available to us over the entire period of the study. Immigration and customs officers at Canadian and United States stations at the Manitoba-Minnesota border points of South Junction and Middlebro, Manitoba, rendered many useful services.

Sherryl B. Wilner did much of the typing. Inga Storgaard and Fritz A. Lindberg kindly provided a translation of a Swedish publication.

For critical and helpful comments on an early draft of the manuscript I am indebted to Carol A. Scott. Her enthusiastic response provided incentive when it was badly needed. Special thanks are due Vene Parnell and Mary Ann Rodewald for their insightful and supportive perusal of a late draft. Many hours were spent by Linda L. Safir who skillfully and energetically applied her pen to several drafts. Certain passages owe much to her fine judgment.

I am grateful for comments on the manuscript received from referees for the University of Wisconsin Press and the Smithsonian Institution Press. I am especially indebted to staff of the latter organization for assistance in bringing this book into being, particularly Edward F. Rivinus and Hope Pantell.

In writing the text I have drawn extensively upon the literature, especially in respect to the Great Gray Owl, relying on accounts by ornithologists, birders, and naturalists. Credit is given to authors for cited material, and references are listed in the bibliography. The maps were prepared by Horst Schell.

Finally, I am grateful to my family and particularly to my wife, Ruth, for extended support during the past twelve years. Without her understanding and forbearance it would not have been possible to devote so much of my time to watching owls and writing this book.

1

A Beginning

In a mature stand of trembling aspen beside a massive granite outcrop, long before leaves are out, shadowy figures slip silently back and forth, building a nest high in a weathered old aspen tree. Sleek, bluish-gray Goshawks pile twig upon twig in an upright triad of limbs; many twigs fall to the ground, but day by day the nest grows in size until a compact, interwoven mass eighteen inches across and nearly as deep has been formed. Before the young will have left the nest in midsummer there will be a wide array of colorful feathers beneath it—American Robin, Blue Jay, Common Flicker, and even larger birds falling prey to this species. Fast and powerful, the red-eyed Goshawk is a specialist in capturing forest birds and mammals. With its broad, fan-shaped tail acting as a rudder, it can steer adroitly through thick stands of trees, efficiently pursuing Ruffed Grouse.

Through summer and fall the Goshawk family feeds on woodland birds, reaching out over a wider area with each passing week. In late summer, hordes of migrating birds, intent on foraging in advance of the next night's long flight, are easy prey. In autumn, migration over, the woods are suddenly still. Last year, snowshoe hares and Ruffed Grouse provided an abundant fare, but in this season they are scarce. Driven by hunger, the Goshawks finally move southward into new, distant lands. Two months later, in a woodlot eight hundred miles to the south, the male Goshawk is shot from a perch by a hunter seeking cottontails. A week later, the female Goshawk is shot in a nearby farmyard as it makes a second pass at a flock of wheeling pigeons.

For two years the nest in the aspen grove is unoccupied. In the third year, late in February, a Great Gray Owl, drawn to the aspen woods and adjacent farm fields by an abundance of meadow voles, flies to the snow-covered nest. In the next few weeks it returns again and again, hooting softly in the cold night, and eventually attracting a mate. So the Goshawk nest, deserted for two years, becomes a center of activity for another season, another species.

A hunting male on an aspen branch. This Great Gray Owl is so intent on a mouse beneath the snow that it is barely aware of the photographer. The fine tips of its tail feathers identify the bird as immature; by size it is a male (smaller than the female in nearly all owl species).

In early June 1964 ornithologist David F. Parmelee was told about a nearby Goshawk nest by a friend, Philip B. Reader, whom he was visiting about ten miles north of The Pas in north-central Manitoba. This chance remark led to a visit to the nest—and to the surprising and exciting discovery that instead of Goshawks, it was occupied by Great Gray Owls! It was a first for both men, although Reader, a woodsman and trapper, had lived in that area for most of his life. Parmelee reported: "The mate, after first announcing his arrival by hooting softly, flew from the muskeg directly to the nest with a small rodent. Upon presenting the prey, he quickly flew back to the muskeg on perfectly silent wings and disappeared only to return a short time later. Both birds were decidedly tame—almost indifferent to our presence."

This was only the second Great Gray Owl nest recorded for Manitoba, the first having been found nearly two hundred miles to the south in mid-May by birder Ed Robinson. I learned about the nest at The Pas late in 1964 when Dave Parmelee submitted a nest record card to the provincial museum. Each year thereafter, at my request, Phil Reader checked the nest, but it went unused, and I began to wonder if I would ever see a Great Gray Owl. Then in March 1968 Reader spotted owls near the nest tree, and in April he sent news that the female was on the nest, apparently incubating! In mid-April Robert R. Taylor, then photographer at the Manitoba Museum of Man and Nature, took a crew to the nest site. The group, which included the late Jack D. Herbert, director of the museum, was led to the nest by Reader. Several loads of equipment were carried in through heavy, wet snow, and a tower was erected to support a camera level with the nest. In mid-May 1968, when there were three young in the nest, another trip was made from Winnipeg to The Pas, and I went along, anxious to see my first live Great Gray Owl.

The nest was in the crown of a tall aspen poplar tree in a mature grove of aspen surrounded by black spruce-muskeg. Several leafless, adjacent dead aspens gave the site an open aspect that surprised me. I had expected to see this bird nesting in deep shade, not high up in open sunlight. Upon our arrival, the female left the nest, restlessly moving from one branch to another, gliding lower with each move, finally settling on a snag twenty-five feet high and about fifty yards from the nest tree. At first she faced us, blinking and looking down so steadily she made me uncomfortable. After we arranged ourselves on logs and became quiet, however, she turned her head away, looking toward a bank of spruce trees. With head lowered and back feathers slightly elevated, shifting from one foot to another, she seemed impatient, hooting softly at regular intervals and occasionally emitting a nasal call. Suddenly, as if guided by her voice, the male came flying out of the woods, heading directly toward her. Briefly clinging to the same perch, large wings spread for balance, he gave her a vole, then turned and fled back into the woods. Without a glance our way, the female, vole in bill, flew up into the nest tree, landing on the edge of the nest fifty feet above us. I watched through binoculars with great interest while she fed the vole to one of the nestlings. Though the food exchange sequence passed all too quickly, and would be witnessed again and again, this first view of it was thrilling, and well worth the 500-mile drive from Winnipeg.

Now, with the female at the nest, the young stood up, downy heads visible, calling repeatedly, a nasal, rasping "*Sherrick!*" While we awaited the next visit of the male, Pileated Woodpeckers called from a nearby nest in a large, dead aspen bole; a Common Goldeneye Duck unexpectedly sped through the trees heading for another nest cavity; boreal chorus frogs shrilled almost constantly from pools of meltwater on the forest floor. Sip-

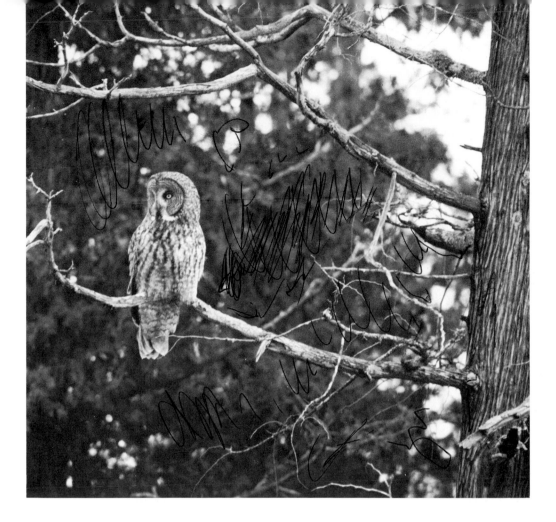

ping hot tea freshly brewed by Phil in a tin pail over a small fire, we congratulated ourselves and gratefully toasted our host. We conversed quietly, seldom taking our eyes off the nest. Finally, with a renewed calling by the female and young, the male arrived again! This time he flapped heavily up to the nest. Scarcely had he landed before the prey he brought was plucked from his bill by the female. Seconds later he dropped away from the nest, sailing off out of our sight through the spruce.

The female, when not brooding or feeding the young, perched at various places in the vicinity of the nest tree, usually on a conspicuous branch or snag. When a light breeze ruffled the long feathers on the back of her head and neck, it looked as if she had a mane; backlighted by the sun, the rippling feathers were luminous. When preening her breast or neck plumage, she would bend forward and seize a feather at its base with her bill, then

slowly draw her bill along the entire length of the feather, raising her head with each smooth stroke. She exhibited a surprising agility when doing this. Though all birds preen, it was pleasing to see the owl doing it. It suggested that she was completely relaxed in our presence.

For the next three days we eagerly studied and photographed these owls, which, for the most part, seemed barely aware of our presence. Once, in later afternoon, the female flew down into shrubbery beneath the trees and we thought she was hunting. But no, she had gone to bathe in a pool. A quick splashing was heard, a moment later she landed on the upright roots of an overturned tree and proceeded to dress her plumage. As she vigorously shook out her wet feathers, her dark, shadowed outline was suddenly surrounded by a spray of sparkling drops of water.

When we stood beneath her and imitated the squeak of a mouse, she would

Above: An owl driven from the forest by hunger sits on a fence post. Falling snow and low light levels bring owls out of the woods into city backyards in search of prey.

turn her head and stare down at us for a moment, bright yellow eyes steady and unwavering; then she would slowly turn and look back toward the nest, and toward the woods where her mate moved on his distant hunting forays. Other birds were of little concern to the owl, though when a soaring Red-tailed Hawk, out of some aggressive fancy, gave a shrill scream and suddenly swooped at the nest, the brooding female, without leaving the nest, gave a loud hoot followed by several rapid and softer notes. Late one evening when the female was away from the nest, a flock of eleven migrant Whistling Swans flew by over the nest tree. The young owls, evidently responding to the sound of the swans' wings, stood up, crying with hunger, mouths wide open as if they expected to be fed.

Wanting photographs of the male bringing food to the female at night, Bob Taylor fastened a remote-controlled camera and flash unit to the top of the tower. He and I sat nearby in the cold night, looking up in the general direction of the nest, relying on vocalizations by the female as a signal to trigger the camera. The male came four or five times, mainly in the early part of the night. When the electronic light flashed, we caught a tantalizing glimpse of the nest—owls, nest, and branches momentarily illuminated. After each photo was taken, Bob patiently climbed the metal rungs of the tower to advance the film for the next shot. Later, looking at the night photos, we found the exercise had been a success. One photo revealed unexpected prey, a wood frog dangling in the male's bill. Best of all, the photos showed owls with fully expanded pupils for night vision. This gave them large, dark eyes, a softer look than we had known.

In early June we returned to the site for a final visit, having been told that the family had disappeared. It was an empty scene. The nest, now just a bundle of twigs, and no longer the focal point of activity for a pair of owls, was of little interest. We managed, however, to find two of the young, locating them by listening for their rasping hunger calls. Both were several hundred yards from the nest tree and on low perches. But where were the parents? They should have been in sight, hooting and showing annoyance at our presence. Though we stayed near the young owls until past midnight, no adults appeared nor did we see them the next morning. By now both young were weak and, though we force-fed them, they died before the day was over. We finally and reluctantly concluded that both parent birds were dead. The presence of a line of new marking tape right past the nest tree suggested a survey party may have encountered the adults. With young on the ground nearby, the owls would probably have been attentive, perhaps even aggressive. Had they been shot, we wondered, for trophies?

We took the dead owlets along for museum specimens and, thinking it would be a long time before we would see Great Gray Owls again, returned with some disappointment to Winnipeg, far from owl country; or so we thought. That winter, however, to everyone's surprise, large numbers of Great Grays unexpectedly appeared in forested lands not far east of the city. Suddenly we had owls at our doorstep! Before winter was over we were to see more owls than had ever previously been reported in the province. As many as twelve were seen in one day along the Trans-Canada Highway thirty to seventy miles to the east of Winnipeg, and two owls even appeared in the city. Weekends and evenings were spent looking for owls to photograph, trap, count, and just watch, but there was never time enough. We estimated that a hundred owls were present that winter in southeastern Manitoba and northern Minnesota. Though there had been reports of invasions of owls in earlier years, nothing of this magnitude had been observed.

It was overwhelming. Suddenly we had owls in an amusing variety of situations and often close at hand. Great Grays hunted from perches a few feet off the ground, dark bodies prominent against a snow-covered landscape, taking little notice of our presence. Those birds we captured for banding were handled with respect and admiration. In hand, Great Gray Owls are even more imposing; once they ceased struggling, these owls bore our prodding and stroking with haughty disdain. Only after they were released and had flown up to the nearest tree, when they turned and stared back at us, did we sense their annoyance; with a great ruffling of feathers, they rid themselves of our alien touch.

Is it any wonder that my interest in this species has continued to this day? The opportunities to keep looking for owls were too good to resist, and I soon found myself heavily involved in a search for more information about owls in this region. The following winter a much smaller number was observed in essentially the same area; however, a concentration was found just south of the border, in Minnesota, in April 1970, an observation that led to the discovery of an active nest. Thereafter,

from 1968 to 1980, my friends and I concentrated our efforts in extreme southeastern Manitoba and adjacent Minnesota.

The country roughly west of Lake of the Woods and south of Lake Winnipeg became our main study area. Though Winnipeg sits on a vast, intensively cultivated plain, suitable Great Gray breeding habitat lies as close as thirty miles eastward. Here, a band of black spruce and tamarack-muskeg country a few dozen miles wide and a hundred miles from north to south lies adjacent to the rocky Precambrian Shield region. The western margin of this boreal forest lowland is bordered with aspen parkland. Wherever the soil in this area is suitable for agriculture, and sometimes where it is not, the land has been cleared and farmed.

In this area, not far from a metropolitan city of more than half a million, with patience and luck it is possible to find Great Gray Owls. Retiring by nature, fond of deep, secluded woods and bogs, these birds are unseen in many years. Following an increase in population, or when food is scarce, they emerge from the forests in search of prey. A mixture of old burns, cleared forest, marginal cropland, abandoned fields, grassy meadows, pine and

By night and day, an emigrant owl looks over unfamiliar fields and woods.

A tense moment in pursuit of an owl: one man is ready with a net, the other with rod and lure, as a bird approaches. The trick is to keep the lure (an artificial mouse) moving just fast enough so that the owl chases it until the bird is close enough to net. Capturing and banding Great Gray Owls under appropriate scientific permits is an essential way of gathering information on population size, movements, age and sex ratios, and other biological data.

Banding an owl. It is important to hold the bird's feet tightly, ever watchful of the long, sharp talons, while a numbered aluminum leg band is attached as a permanent means of identifying individuals.

spruce woods, bogs and streams, the area attracts moose, wolves, Common Ravens, Gray Jays, and many other boreal forest animals.

What is most curious about this southern range is the occurrence of owls in relatively sparse forest cover. Stunted spruce-tamarack stands, not much more than thirty feet in height, for example, would hardly seem to be suitable Great Gray Owl habitat. And yet, birds have nested in this kind of cover, close to roads and logging operations, a far cry from the usual habitat with which the species is so often associated. Is there a relationship between southern tamarack bogs and spruce-tamarack muskegs of the north? Wet tamarack stands east of Winnipeg, for example, are similar in many aspects to the northern transition forest. Robert Stitt, a university student who spent the winters of 1976–77 and 1977–78 trapping in the "great, empty muskegs" west of Moosonee, Ontario, at the southwest corner of James Bay, wrote me that he found the Great Gray Owl the "most frequently seen" of the four species occurring there (Great Horned, Hawk, Boreal, and Great Gray Owls). Although conspicuous in some situations, Great Gray Owls can remain hidden even in the heavily cutover and often burned forests typical of southern Manitoba. Indeed, the transitional aspect of many tracts of forest, altered by fire and cutting, may make these sites especially attractive to owls.

But the area is also divided by several main highways and numerous side roads, many parts are logged continuously, and much of the area is intensively used for recreation in summer and winter. Perhaps nowhere else on the continent are their breeding grounds in such close contact with so much human activity.

Through intensive searching, mainly in winter, spring, and early summer, we discovered that Great Grays were regular residents of this area. Even in years when few were seen, we heard birds calling late

at night. This resident population of owls, as we gradually came to understand it, became the focus of our attention.

Made aware of our excitement about owls, many people watched for them with us. Customs and immigration officers, Royal Canadian Mounted Police (RCMP), conservation officers, naturalists, and the general public became acquainted with our studies and interests through posters, newspaper accounts, occasional lectures given in schools and community centers, and through personal contact at every opportunity.

Our search for owls led us into many out-of-the-way places, and in this way we became acquainted with many interesting people. Farmers, loggers, tradesmen, housewives, and children were our informants and friends. Many pleasant hours were spent talking about owls and other subjects with people for whom these woods were familiar grounds. And as we exchanged confidences, so too we exchanged information. Once, reaching the end of a small road that led to a little farmhouse close to spruce-tamarack woods, we chatted with the gruff owner, an unshaven, older man wearing a tattered parka and black rubber boots. After telling him why we were looking for big owls, we asked if he had seen any. In broken English he told us that for several days during the bitter cold weather of the previous week, one had come each day to sit on the power pole beside his house. Yes, he said, it looked just like the owl in the photo we showed him. He thought it was hungry, because it had been a hard winter, with lots of snow and few mice. With evident sincerity, he argued that the government should help feed wildlife in winter, including hungry owls.

Another day, we drove several miles along a narrow logging trail. Neat stacks of freshly cut spruce logs stood about the edge of a large clearing devoid of all but a few spindly tamaracks and low heaps of spruce boughs. Seeing a man in rough clothing working beside a machine, we parked and walked over to talk with him; the cold air was redolent with the sharp, pleasant scent of spruce and cedar. When we asked about the presence of owls, we were given a hard look and firmly told that no owls would be shot by us or anyone else in his presence! We hastened to explain our interest in owls and then shook hands all around in support of his point of view.

One cold morning on the Trans-Canada Highway, Bob Taylor and I saw a police car with a flashing red light coming up behind us, and we anxiously asked each other what we could possibly have done. We pulled off the road and stopped, and were stunned (and relieved) when the RCMP officer shouted that we should follow him back the other way because he had just seen a Great Gray Owl! Following his lead, we did a fast turnaround and sped down the highway behind our excited escort. I don't recall if we caught that owl or not, but I well remember the incident. That kind of cooperation from someone we had spoken to twenty minutes earlier in a coffee shop is a good example of the response we got from people when we told them about our project.

Frequently, upon making enquiries, we were invited in to warm ourselves or to share a meal. The enthusiasm with which the members of a family would tell us about owls they had seen made these enjoyable events. Oh, there were other kinds of people as well! I won't forget the pretty, well-spoken woman who told me she had indeed seen a really big owl sitting in a tree near the barn, "one of those big gray fellows; it sat right out in the open, tame as could be . . . how I wished I had a gun . . . it would really have looked nice stuffed!"

Below: An owl with a painted tail hovers over a shadow-striped snowbank. Spray painting the tail feathers of banded birds makes it possible to identify banded and unbanded owls in a winter population. Painting is a temporary marking method, lasting until the tail feathers are shed in summer.

Opposite: Hunting the hunter—two men with owl-catching gear in hand try to get closer to an actively hunting bird in the woods. Trapping and handling seem not to have much lasting effect on Great Gray Owls; banded and tail-painted birds may be hunting again within minutes after their release.

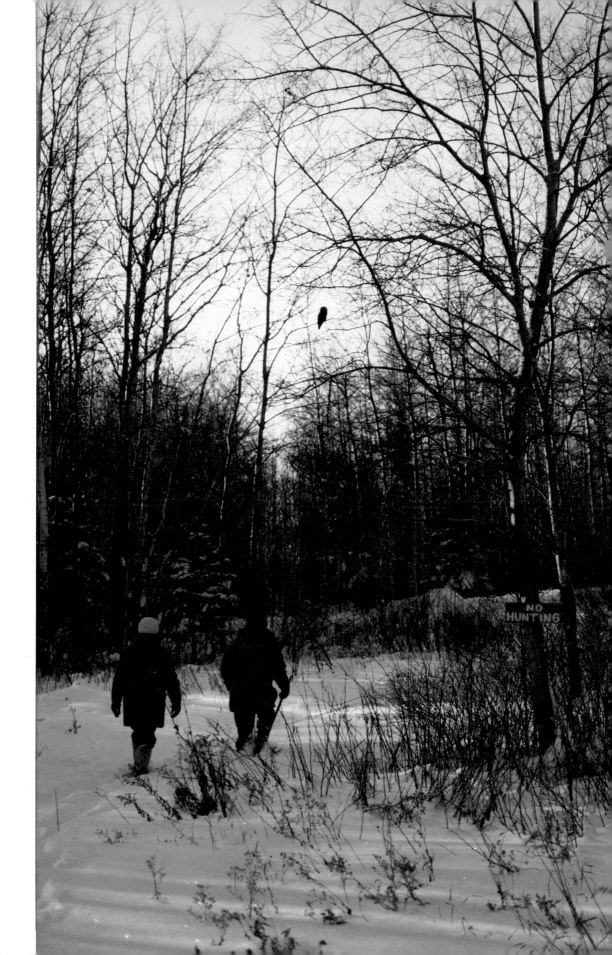

2

Out of the Woods

Characterized by trees, shrubs, and numerous other plants that are green in winter as well as summer, the boreal forest is adapted to a short growing season. Evergreen—*what a wealth of impressions that name brings forth. Compared with the brown, muddy fields and drab vegetation that appear with spring in southern parts, the evergreen world of the boreal forest is a revelation. Beneath the snow the forest floor is carpeted in green. Feather mosses, club moss, Labrador tea, bunchberry, and a host of other green plants lie beneath the embracing arms of pine, spruce, fir, and cedar; all are chlorophyll machines perpetually in gear, ready to take advantage of daylight once winter loosens its hold. On the coldest day in midwinter, though their trunks are iron-fast and their veins immobilized with cold, the evergreen forests stand heavy and lush with foliage.*

There is comfort in the heavy mass of spruce that surrounds us as we ski through the woods, comfort in the absence of wind, and in the close contact with winter birds that approach us with curiosity. A flock of Boreal Chickadees, briefly pausing in their prying inspection of limbs and twigs, repeatedly call: "Dee-dee!"—fluttering about us when we softly squeak to draw them close. Gray Jays, light as down and fluffed out like thistle heads, come to visit us, dropping down in slow, almost motionless glides, then loosely hopping from one perch to another, whistling and chattering.

Though it is thirty degrees below zero, a sudden, sharp sense of springtime bird song halts us: a Pine Grosbeak in cheerful red plumage, perched on a wiry black spruce spire, delivers his sweet, flutelike call. How, we wonder, do these winter birds find enough food to sustain themselves? Moving lightly and quickly, they seem without cares; but they are constantly on the move, seaching for food as they go through the forest, and this is part of their adaptation to long, cold winters.

Few other birds that nest within the boreal forest of North America have been sought so energetically by birdwatchers as has the Great Gray Owl. According to the American Birding Association (which numbers more than 3,000 members in North America), the Great Gray Owl is the sixth most wanted bird on the continent. Occasionally, these birds wander in winter outside their usual range to southern parts of Canada and the northern United States. When the news gets out, enthusiastic birders may travel hundreds of miles in hopes of seeing one of these owls.

In the winters of 1965–66 and 1968–69, for example, a few Great Gray Owls in the Ottawa area attracted hundreds of birders from all over the eastern United States and across southern Ontario and Quebec. In the winter of 1977–78, when large numbers of owls appeared in the Duluth, Minnesota, area, hundreds of birders from many midwestern states drove there to see Great Gray, Boreal, and Hawk owls. Great Gray Owls made headlines in the winter of 1978–79 when several birds appeared in New York State. During the same period, unusual numbers were seen in the New England states and especially in southern Ontario and Quebec. Close to forty Great Gray Owls were recorded on Amherst Island in the St. Lawrence River near Kingston, Ontario. A thousand birders from as far away as New Jersey, Maryland, and Texas came to Amherst Island that winter. Several happy birders were able to see both the eclipse of the sun and Great Gray Owls, which were present in considerable numbers east of Winnipeg in late February 1979.

A single Great Gray Owl that appeared on January 22, 1973, at Gill, Massachusetts, and lingered on at the same farm until mid-March, attracted the attention of an estimated two hundred eager searchers each weekend and ten each weekday. Conservatively, perhaps three thousand people looked for this one bird, and two thousand saw and enjoyed it! How is one to measure the value of such a bird? In 1978 the United States government published a set of postage stamps bearing illustrations of four species of owls: Sawwhet, Great Horned, Barred, and Great Gray. That the Great Gray Owl should have been chosen despite the several more common species of owls in the United States is an indication of its appeal.

The thrill that invariably accompanies a Great Gray Owl sighting is shared by neophyte and experienced ornithologist; it is related to this bird's general scarcity, its great size, and its boldness. Few birds look upon people with the apparent calm stoicism of Great Gray Owls. Perched for hours on a roadside tree or telephone pole, they are unmoved by hundreds of passing vehicles; a noisy snowmobile passing directly underneath an owl may not even draw a glance; at times, dozens of photo-hungry naturalists may approach within yards without flushing the bird. Filled with my own impressions formed during many hours in the company of Great Gray Owls, I can appreciate the reactions of other people who have encountered this species.

Commenting in the *Winnipeg Tribune* on a bird that appeared in the city in November 1959, nature columnist Angus H. Shortt noted that it "showed a great deal more concern about a passing train and aeroplanes flying overhead, than about the bird watchers standing only a few yards away." And, after observing wintering birds in the Alymer, Quebec, area in 1966 amd 1969, Ronald Pittaway and Daniel F. Brunton wrote: "The Great Gray Owl is absurdly tame. If the bird doesn't feel like flying, it *cannot* be moved (short of being shot!). Repeatedly, one of them has flown directly past observers, within inches of them without changing its direction or course whatsoever. It is often the case that the bird is difficult to interest in even looking in the direction of the observer."

Observing a winter vagrant near Ded-

Below: Almost close enough to net! Blood on the bill of this owl, gliding in after a lure that has just been cast to capture it, shows that it had taken real prey minutes before this picture was made.

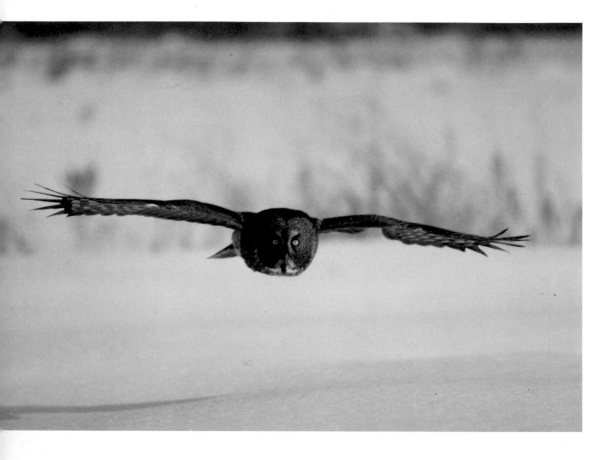

Opposite: An owl flies down off its perch on a telephone pole toward the live mouse beside the net. A responsive bird may be caught in less than a minute.

ham, Massachusetts on February 7, 1904, Francis H. Allen reported in an ornithological journal: "I was attracted to the spot by a great clamor of Crows and soon found my bird perched on a low limb of a white pine in open mixed woods. It held in its claws a dead and partly eaten crow. . . . The owl seemed perfectly fearless of me, but showed nervousness when the crows cawed near by, and followed with its eyes the flight of the single crows that flew over its tree from time to time. I drove it about from tree to tree with snowballs. It flew low and always took a rather low perch—from ten to twenty feet from the ground, and usually on a large branch of a pine tree, near the trunk, though twice it alighted on the very top of a red cedar. I could get as near as the height of its perch permitted and was frequently within twenty feet of it during the hour or two that I spent in its company."

Naturalist-farmer Archibald D. Henderson, writing in 1923 about his experiences with these owls on their northern Alberta breeding grounds, remarked: "The Great Gray Owl is not at all a wary bird and always permits a close approach. All that saves him from extermination in the settled districts is the fact that he is seldom seen away from the heavy timber which is his home." That it still retains its peculiar, inherent fearlessness in the presence of man is shown by a recent successful nesting only thirty miles southeast of Edmonton, Alberta. Visiting the nest, which was "within a mile of one of the most heavily used public beaches in central Alberta" on May 5, 1972, Norbert G. Kondla, who discovered the nest, wrote: "Both adult birds were constantly present and seemed quite unafraid of the mob of observers. . . . Despite the large number of observers on May 5 and many subsequent visits by other observers, the owls managed to raise two young. . . ."

John Christie, a Winnipeg birder, found an even more unlikely nesting in 1979.

Great Gray Owls had successfully occupied a conspicuous nest twenty-five yards from the edge of a road. There was little traffic, but the nest site was only two miles from a main highway. My first reaction on seeing the nest was one of disbelief. It had been built on top of a large "witches'-broom," an abnormal growth of twigs in a tight mass resulting from infestation by the parasitic plant mistletoe. The nest, probably built by a Red-tailed Hawk, was about twenty-five feet above ground in a nearly dead balsam fir, surrounded by low willow, alder, spruce, and tamarack, and knee-deep water. Only a few people knew about the nest, and it was kept secret in hopes of seeing it succeed despite the precarious situation. Fortunately, it did succeed. On June 30 we banded two fledged young and the female, and watched them move off safely into adjacent aspen woods.

Few people have been privileged to see the Great Gray Owl at its nest. The periodic emigrations of Great Grays are periods of hope for birdwatchers, the best chance of seeing one being when these owls come out of the boreal forest, hungry and lean, though still massive in their grayish-brown coats. F. Napier Smith, in a letter in the *Montreal Daily Star*, eloquently described such a meeting in late afternoon, February 12, 1928, near an island in the St. Lawrence River not far from Montreal:

"The wind came in gusts out of the north, driving little clouds of snow along the surface of the river, but despite the icy blasts and the bleak position of its outlook, the Great Grey, apparently a female, sat at perfect ease in her luxuriant coat of feathers . . . when I first viewed her, she blended softly with the neutral grey background of the bare hardwood trees on the island. But as I came alongside the island, she stood out boldly against the opalescent wintry sky, the abnormally large, round head giving the bird a top-heavy appearance. . . . At a distance, the bird appeared to be of a solid grey color but at fifty yards or so, in the sunlight, the mottling of the feathers was discernible, although I was unable to detect the small lemon yellow eyes without field glasses. . . . If she appeared huge in the stunted tree growth she looked a veritable 'eagle-owl' as she flew toward the Verdun shore, alighting some 150 yards away on a rise in the ice . . . the large wings and tail and dark coloration emphasizing her size as she skimmed over the surface of the snow."

In cold winter months when they occasionally visit settlements, Great Grays take to TV antennas, houses, barns, telephone poles, fenceposts, and various other man-made perches as freely as if long accustomed to these things. Few raptors have rested with such impunity on so many peculiar perches or so close to man, but Great Gray Owls move into settled areas as unconcernedly as swallows. David Lambeth, a North Dakota birder visiting southern Manitoba in late winter 1979, wrote that he could hardly believe that Great Gray Owls could be "as common and conspicuous as Red-tailed Hawks."

Some things defy explanation. For ten years we never saw an owl perch on a powerline or telephone wire. Then, on December 2, 1978, we saw one fly through trees to land on the lowest of several telephone wires. There were a few seconds when we weren't sure it would maintain its balance, for the wire was swinging and the bird was teetering back and forth, tail spread wide and swinging forward, but it managed to balance itself and sat quietly as we drove by. Thereafter, to my continued amazement, throughout the winter on numerous occasions, we saw birds perched on wires. Moreover, we received reports from several observers who saw them in similar situations and even a hundred miles from our main study area. When a bird landed on a wire close to a pole, or on a heavy cable, it had little difficulty balancing, but those birds that chose to land on a single-strand wire midway between poles went through some vigorous contortions to bring themselves to a standstill. Overnight, it seemed, Great Gray Owls had acquired a new habit.

At The Pas Ed Johanson, a resident with a landscaped yard, described to me how one winter a Great Gray Owl came for weeks and sat for long periods on top of a pole near a bird feeder just outside the picture window. It paid little attention to birds at the feeder, and presumably was after mice attracted by sunflower seeds. At other times it perched on garden stakes and preyed on mice at a backyard compost heap. These large owls have also appeared in yards far from their breeding habitat. For people used to seeing robins or meadowlarks, the sight of a huge owl in the daytime is a spectacular event. Not far from Winnipeg, a housewife photographed a Great Gray Owl through a window. The color photo she sent me shows the owl perched in a tree close to the house.

Great Gray Owls seem to be attracted to people, just as is the Gray Jay, an opportunist always on the alert for food. Still, something else brings jays close to us. I tossed part of a sandwich onto the snow one day for a jay perched near my car, then sacrificed a cookie, but to my

surprise the jay ignored the food. When I
left the car to go off through the woods,
however, the jay followed me, flying along
and perching just overhead. Curiosity—or
what? Great Gray Owls sometimes sit and
watch woodcutters at work in the forest
as if they enjoyed man's company—or are
they perhaps awaiting mice driven out by
fallen trees?

One acquaintance told me that on November 20, 1978, while out moose hunting near Lac du Bonnet, Manitoba,
wearing the prescribed uniform of white
coveralls and a blaze-orange cap, he was
followed for half an hour by a Great Gray
Owl. The bird kept close to him as he
moved from one stand to another, sometimes perching on stumps as close as ten
feet. Robert Stitt found Great Gray Owls
"very tame and curious" near Moosonee,
Ontario. On December 22, 1978, he wrote
to me as follows:

"Upon returning to camp at dusk I saw
the outline of a Great Gray Owl ahead of
me near our camp, which is in a narrow
band of spruce along the river bank levees
in this part of the country. At this point I
was in open muskeg. I hurried into camp
on the possibility that there was sufficient
light for photos. On reaching camp I discovered 3 of the birds very close to our
tent. One of the birds seemed very curious
and at one point was walking down a
limb over my head and making low hooting calls. There was insufficient light for
photos so I went back out to the open
muskeg to check a marten cubby which I
had passed upon first seeing the owl. The
distance back out to this cubby was approximately 100 yards. One of the owls
flew this distance and perched at the top
of a dead spruce at the base of which was
my cubby. As I was kneeling down repair-
ing the cubby I could look straight up and
see the bird directly above me, peering
down on me. This was quite an interesting experience for me. When I returned to
camp, and was moving about getting
wood, water, etc., the owls were moving

from tree to tree and showed interest in
what I was doing."

Heavy-headed and long-tailed, a Great
Gray has a shape unlike that of any other
bird. Perched in the open or outlined
against the skyline, its characteristic form
can be identified almost as far away as it
can be seen. Close up, the round, silvery-
gray face and conspicuous white neck
stripes are distinctive. Owing partly to the
heavy feathering of the head and neck, the
bright yellow eyes seem small and close
set. Even though it looks like the big bird
it is when perched, the size of its wings
when it takes flight is still surprising.
Spanning nearly five feet, the broad wings
expand with ease, flapping deeply as they
send the owl off with a rush, giving it, as
more than one observer has noted, a heronlike appearance in flight. Upon landing
on a new perch, the wings are carefully
folded into place, and again one sees the
familiar, blunt-headed silhouette of the
Great Gray Owl.

For several years we had all accepted
the fact that Great Grays occasionally
landed and perched in awkward situations, sometimes with tail askew or one
wing out, as a consequence of a branch interfering with normal posture. This sometimes is the case, but watching a female
owl perched in a willow bush one April
morning in 1979, I suddenly realized that

the bird was deliberately keeping one wing spread in order to maintain its balance on the slender branches. When the owl changed position, it closed its wing, but when it began to slip, it put one wing out on top of the willow twigs, thus keeping itself upright. That revelation also brought to mind Jens Wahlstedt's report of a Great Gray Owl that nested successfully in 1973 on top of a tall birch stump: the bird constantly supported itself on this unusually small nest platform by resting one wing on a protruding strip of bark.

Despite its bulky appearance, broad wings, and long tail, the Great Gray is a masterful flier, remarkably fast and adept. At times it suddenly brakes in midflight, wings flopping loosely as it wheels about, quickly changing course to pounce upon a mouse unexpectedly popping out of the grass. With wings only partly spread, it can move its wing tips in a rapid, shallow manner like a falcon, quickly attaining high speed. We noted that a bird gliding with wings fully extended, occasionally would partly fold its wings, thus immediately increasing its speed. I have seen owls fly through dense stands of trees, through passageways seemingly too small to admit a bird of this size, abruptly closing their wings to slip through a narrow space, then spreading them out again when clear. They can also time their wingbeats to avoid striking trees.

The most noticeable aspect of their flight behavior, however, is the slow, almost effortless glide with which they move from one perch to another. With a dive off a perch and a few powerful flaps of its wings, a Great Gray is capable of gliding onward for hundreds of yards, silently skimming on broad, outstretched wings across meadows and openings in the forest. An occasional flap or two serves to maintain forward momentum, change direction, or help it rise up to a perch, but otherwise it moves as a shadow. As described so well by Dalton Muir: "Its wings are thick and deep for slow speed flight. It prefers to glide great distances on set wings, close to the ground through the galleries between trees, seldom flapping and steering with obvious tilting with its long, broad tail . . . a vivid demonstration of the efficiency that can be achieved by a perfectly formed aerodynamic shape moving at a speed just sufficient to keep airborne . . . [it] has perfected low speed, silent, manoeuverable flight as a way of life."

Albert F. Oeming of Edmonton, who had carried out an extensive publicity campaign to protect Great Gray Owls in Alberta in the 1950s, also noted the unusual flight manner of these birds: "They were slow, measured and soft, giving the bird an eerie wraith-like appearance as he glided through the great shadowy trees. Although dusk was imminent, if he had been 'as blind as an owl,' as the story goes, the lingering light would have had him crashing into twigs and branches—for his wings were huge billowing sails They were of such a size as to seem clumsy for life in a dense forest, but he missed branches by a fraction of an inch, making skillful use of this equipment evolved through the ages."

Kapten Wahlberg, observing a female at a nest forty miles north of the Arctic Circle in Sweden, commented on this same aspect: "When she flew with slow lissom strokes between the trees, I thought it very curious that she did not collide somewhere. This is a bird as big as a male Golden Eagle . . . and it was quite amazing to see her flying low in that rather thick wood."

Occasionally their wings do strike branches or twigs, but because the pinions are so soft and flexible, no serious harm seems to result. My observations of birds with one or more broken flight feathers, however, suggest that accidental collisions sometimes cause damage.

One winter day when we were attempting to capture a barely visible owl that was screened by tree branches next to a road, I was startled to see the owl respond to a lure by flying directly through the branches instead of flying around the tree. In its haste to get at the lure, it crashed straight through the branches, snapping off twigs as it came. We caught the bird, and were surprised to find it undamaged. There is another situation in which owls seem reckless about the state of their feathers. Nesting females, when badly upset by the presence of a dog, often go into an astonishing display, hurling themselves onto shrubbery and thrashing their wings against boughs with such force that one would think their flight feathers would break.

In low light at dawn or twilight, the course of a Great Gray Owl's flight is difficult to follow as it glides through shadows and groves and against dark spruce clumps. Even while watched, it may suddenly disappear, but if one follows its line of flight, the eye may catch its flapping wings at some distant point as it reaches for balance on a precarious perch. Once it has gained its balance and is still, it is again easily lost to view, for the woods are full of owl-like shapes.

3

An Owl in the City

Day and night the owl crouched and listened, but the forest was still. Occasionally its attention was drawn to a faint rustle and sigh, as if some hidden vole had suddenly let out its breath. Then the great round head turned down toward the ground, its ears measuring every remote shifting sound beneath the snow. It had not eaten in two weeks.

So it began to move, drifting farther and farther from its natal grounds, searching constantly for the sounds of prey: the pitch-pipe squeal of aggression, the squeak of excitement, the steady, grating gnawing of tiny teeth. But everywhere it went, across snow-covered fields, through open woods, down a tree-lined rivercourse, it found only cold silence.

Often, in the daytime, Black-capped Chickadees and other winter birds chirped and whistled notes that brought the owl to attention, eyes gleaming, but it stayed perched while they flitted past, twittering faintly as they disappeared into woods or field. Once, long before daybreak, a brown shrew skittered across a snowdrift like a leaf in the wind, and at once the owl swooped, snapped it up without landing, and sailed up to a perch. Its bill opened, and in one gulp the shrew was gone.

Driven by hunger, the owl moved onward, drifting over fencelines, skimming beneath power lines, flapping over a cold, bleak cemetery to land in a lone tree. But in the whole area nothing moved. Streets, houses, blocks of human habitations expanded in its vision, and were absorbed as novel but meaningless patterns. Before the sun rose, a strange hum became an insistent drone, strange, confusing sights and sounds of cars and trucks moving in all directions, surrounded by vaporous clouds, gradually overwhelming its senses.

Starving, reduced to a remnant of its normal weight by many days of frantic search, its eyes lost their shine, its movements lessened. Perched on a tree in the middle of the city, shocked by a great rumbling, hissing, and metallic shrieking, the owl subsided, sinking deeper into itself. Sleep, the sleep of hunger, drew it slowly into a stupor. It blinked occasionally when sudden sharp sounds struck its ears, but soon it was motionless, eyes closed, feathers fluffed out, hunched on a limb, lost in an unknown world.

While at the office during a midafternoon snowfall on January 10, 1975, I received news of a supposed Great Gray Owl seen in an older, established residential district in Winnipeg. It seemed unlikely because there had been few reports of Great Grays anywhere that season. However, the caller, John Badertscher, said he had positively identified it. Though it had since disappeared, somewhere among houses and streets, it was just the excuse I needed to leave the office early on a Friday afternoon.

While I dashed home to get a net and some live mice, Herb Copland and several other birders went to try to find the owl. Forty minutes later we were all standing in the snow looking at a bona fide Great Gray Owl dozing on the trunk of a misshapen elm, only ten feet off the ground, beside a garage in a back lane. We hastened to try to capture the bird before it disappeared again, using a live mouse and

a landing net, but we couldn't rouse it. After letting the mouse loose on the snow, I made squeaking sounds, scratched on the side of the garage, and muttered a variety of comments to the owl, but it wouldn't open its eyes. It was frustrating. Then it occurred to us to use a ladder, and net the owl where it sat, apparently asleep. A ladder was found beside someone's garage and we were soon in position. But suddenly, when another person came running up to see the action, the owl spread its wings and flew away, heading straight down the lane, looking bigger than ever against a background of two- and three-story houses, garages, power poles, and a multitude of wires. We watched with dismay as it narrowly skimmed a wire, then glided low down the length of the lane, swerving upward at a cross street over the top of several moving cars. In a moment it was out of sight, and we weren't sure which way it had turned. Seven birders again scattered to search for the owl. Traffic, which at this hour was heavy on all streets, plus the heavy snowfall, made it difficult to get about, and we weren't certain we would see the bird again.

Half an hour later, however, after disconsolately combing five city blocks, and rapidly getting cold and tired, I discovered the owl hunched on a post, eyes tightly closed, on a low porch about fifteen feet from a young man who was vigorously sweeping snow off his car. So short of breath I could barely speak, I pointed out the owl—which he hadn't noticed—and urged the astonished man to keep an eye on it while I ran back to my car for the mice and net. "What'll I do if it flies away?" he asked. "Just tell me which way it went!" I shouted back while hurrying off through the falling snow. A few minutes later I was back at the scene and, while my new acquaintance watched with broom in hand, I quickly walked through the soft snow up behind the owl and dropped the net over it. After a brief struggle I had its feet firmly held, then freed it from the net, folded its wings and cradled it against my chest, meanwhile giving a running explanation of our interest in the bird and its habits. Then, clutching net and mouse cage, and carrying the owl upright in the crook of one arm with the top of its head against my chin, I happily set off to my car. A trio of schoolboys passed me on the sidewalk along a busy street, doing a double take and then stopping to argue over whether the bird was alive or not, one of them insisting he had seen it blink its eyes. I left them wondering, and hurried on. Several minutes later a delighted group of birders gathered about to photograph the bird and watch the banding operation.

That evening the owl was subjected to a lot of disturbance. After it was photographed twice by local newspapers, we measured, weighed, and color-marked it. It seemed only slightly alarmed by the flash of the electronic lights, people talking, and the warm, dry new surroundings, maintaining a steadfast staring expression, and making little effort to move so long as its feet were held firmly and it was kept in an upright position. Though we hadn't intended to confine it for long, a week passed before we were able to release it. Our plans had been to hold it overnight and free it in the morning in suitable habitat east of Winnipeg, for we doubted that it would survive long in the city. Unfortunately, the first blizzard of the season struck the region that night, keeping us snowbound for forty-eight hours, unable to get out in the country until the following weekend.

Later, we learned that the owl had been sighted at noon, on the day of its capture, by twelve-year-old Becky Walker while she was going home from school for lunch. Walking down a lane she and two friends were startled when, coming from behind, a small cat ran close beside them on one side while a large, gray owl swooped by on the other side, only a few feet away. The owl landed on a post and the cat escaped. Later, eleven-year-old Betsy Badertscher found the owl perched in a nearby tree and told her parents about it, and thus it was reported to us.

The first time Great Gray Owls were reported in Winnipeg was the winter of 1922–23. The late Harold Mossop, a well-known Winnipeg naturalist, told me that that winter, when he was a teen-aged boy and a keen birder, he had seen possibly twenty owls while on his way to school and while hiking about in wooded sections of the city on weekends. In 1966, in an account of the event in the *Winnipeg Free Press*, he recalled: "an invasion occurred in the Winnipeg area when, because of their lack of fear of man, numbers were shot by irresponsible gunners." One Great Gray Owl from that period exists as a scientific study skin in the collection of the Riveredge Foundation in Calgary, Alberta. The specimen was col-

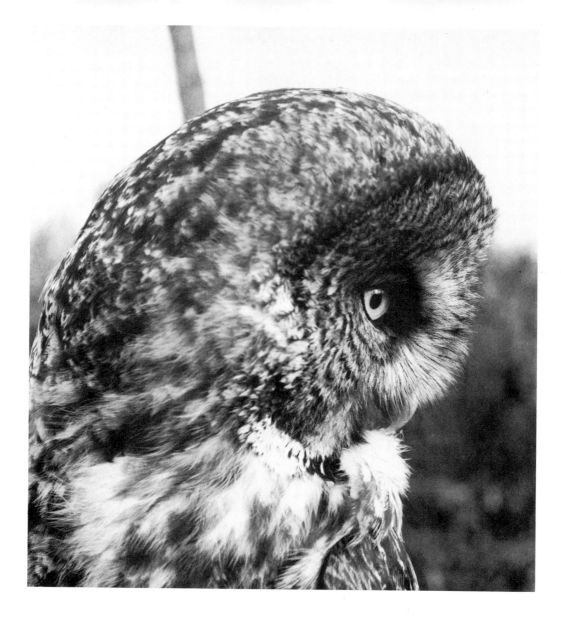

lected on October 30, 1922 (about four weeks before I was born), in the Charleswood section of Winnipeg where I now make my home!

Not until 1959 was another Great Gray reported in the city. Found near Omand's Creek on November 21, the "big bird stayed in the vicinity throughout the day and was seen and photographed by several local ornithologists," according to an item in the *Winnipeg Tribune* by Angus Shortt. What was possibly the same bird was found a month later suffering from gunshot wounds in Charleswood (!); not long afterward it died in captivity. The bird had been discovered by fourteen-year-old Jorma Jyrkkanen, whose family had re-

cently arrived in Canada from Finland where his father had seen Great Gray Owls. His parents recently informed me that at the time Jorma had found the owl he was already caught up in nature study. Now he is a biologist!

Though our owl evidently had been in the city for at least two weeks, having been seen by other persons, it was in reasonably good condition. It weighed slightly under two pounds, a fair weight for what we judged to be a male bird, but it came to us with an empty stomach—at least it cast no pellet until the day after it had eaten a white laboratory mouse. The little regurgitated lump of yellowish hair and bones found beneath its perch the next morning showed how fast digestion takes place in raptors.

It sat quietly on its perch for hours while we watched television, all of us occasionally glancing over at this novelty in the house. Keeping the owl in captivity gave me a good opportunity to watch it closely. That first weekend, especially, when traffic was at a standstill and we were kept indoors by a blizzard, I sat in comfort with notebook in hand, studying my uncommon subject. It was an entertaining and instructive situation. I learned that the width of its head and neck changed as it raised and lowered its feathers. Depending on its mood it alternated between rapt attention and withdrawn indifference. At times, it tipped back its head and was motionless; it seemed then to be listening to distant sounds, responding to some mechanical sound in the house—the hum of a refrigerator motor or a dripping faucet—as if reminded of some more normal sound of significance. When it shook out its plumage, hunching forward, raising its wings slightly and ruffling its feathers, it gave an impression of composure; thus, its comfort-shake never failed to make me feel better for seeing the owl relaxing. It called infrequently, mostly when we first entered the room in which it was kept, giving a low, mellow *"hoo-hoooh!"* Sometimes it gave this in response to imitations of its call or when the dog or cat suddenly appeared. Whether this was in greeting or in defiance we could not tell. Some of the pleasure in the close relationship I enjoyed with this owl may be seen in the following notes made at the time:

"I could spend hours looking at this bird, seeking to further understand its compelling appearance and behavior. It is a beautiful bird. It sits on a cedar stump in the middle of the family room, tethered by a leather thong. It is twenty-four hours since it was so rudely captured and it has just taken its first meal: two chunks of fresh beef and a dead white mouse. It takes these items directly from my hand, glaring at me all the while with pale yellow eyes, but with little hesitation. Now it seems more relaxed. Last night, when I showed the owl to the surprised family, our trembling dog and the electrified cat, it was docile and unalarmed, permitting itself to be stroked endlessly, almost as if in a trance. Only when I repeatedly pushed my head toward its face did it show any alarm or aggression; then it hissed, and clacked its bill, snapping the lower mandible against the curved upper bill. Finally, it turned its head sideways and nibbled and pulled at my hair, literally preening. Each time I pushed the top of my head toward its face it stretched out its neck, tilted its head and nibbled rapidly along the scalp through my hair, occasionally holding and pulling gently in the hair—a curious behavior. Only when it suddenly seized the edge of my ear, pinching hard, did it hurt me at all. All this while, it also held its wings out from the body, normally a sign of aggressiveness.

"Sitting four feet from the owl, able to watch it closely, I am less able to fathom the bird or my feelings toward it. It watches me as steadily as I watch it, unmoving, except for its eyes: occasionally the nictitating membrane, a semitransparent 'third eyelid' found in all birds, flicks downward from the upper and inner corner of each eye. This gives a startling effect, like a wink without closing the eye, but mostly its eyes are steady and arresting. It is difficult to avoid staring back at the owl. For an hour now we have watched each other, though at times the owl looks off to one side slightly, or briefly closes its eyes by bringing the lower lid up, or else it squints, closing both eyes until the merest slit of yellow shows. Surprisingly, when, without making any other movement, I open my eyes wide, the owl at once opens its eyes too. But it seems to want to sleep; gradually its attention wanes, its lower eyelids slowly come up, the pupils contract, and the eyes are finally almost closed. But when I turn a page, or merely turn my head, it opens its eyes wide again. It is much aware of me even when it appears not to be."

The indifferent and calm state of the Great Gray Owl in captivity is nicely illustrated by an experience related by Alex G. Lawrence in a nature column in the *Winnipeg Free Press*, on March 15, 1928. This, his first view of a Great Gray, occurred in Winnipeg in 1911 "when one of these huge owls was placed on a perch in a drug store window, together with a notice asking if the bird were alive or stuffed. There was a large crowd in front of the window, some members of which stated they had seen the bird move, although it had every appearance of being a stuffed specimen. The owl remained absolutely motionless; not a tremor was noticeable, not a blink of an eye, not a single sign of the bird's breathing; it displayed not the slightest interest in the crowd pressing against the window, and finally, it paid no attention to any scratching on the woodwork, a trick to which a caged owl will nearly always react.

"After ten minutes' steadfast gazing at the bird we were convinced that it was a stuffed specimen, when suddenly the bird sprang to life, stretched its wings, turned its head and yawned amidst the laughter of the crowd. Doubtless many readers will remember being 'stung' by this bird's statue-like posing."

That incident is reminiscent of James Thomas Field's poem "The Owl-Critic," in which a young man in a barber shop delivers a long harangue about the poor workmanship of an owl perched on a shelf. " 'Do take that bird down; have him stuffed again, Mr. Brown!' " he exhorts. Then follow several verses in which the faulty arrangement of all parts of the owl, including its glass eyes, are pointed out by the self-declared owl specialist. The poem ends with the owl arousing itself and suddenly getting down off its perch.

Presumably Lawrence's drugstore bird had been captured in midwinter, possibly even within the city, though he did not say, and was no doubt as hungry and desperate, reduced to conserving its strength, as the bird I kept in our home. On its second day in captivity, our bird again readily accepted chunks of raw beef that were held out before its bill, seeming to recognize these items as food, or responding to the gesture of something held out before it as had been the case throughout its nestling and juvenile life. When a House Sparrow that died overnight in our bird feeder was offered to the owl, it was seized and held by one foot; when I came closer, the owl threatened me, spreading its wings, snapping its bill and glaring intently. Defending the sparrow, still clenched tightly in the talons of one foot, it crouched low on the carpet, covering its prey.

Over the next few days, as it consumed more food, and multi-vitamin capsules concealed in meat, the owl become increasingly aggressive and restless, pulling at its leash and flapping about on the floor around its perch. Left alone, it seemed to spend all of its time trying to free itself. I never knew where it would be when I entered the room after an absence. Once free of the leash it might be perched on the couch, on the back of a chair, or on the bookcase; or, if not free, it was often tangled in its leash. As I neared it to untangle it or to capture and refasten it to the leash, it would rear back with a fierce look, snapping and hissing and flapping its wings. It seemed more and more uncomfortable and unfriendly; clearly the time had come to release it.

Just a week after we had brought it indoors, Herb Copland, Bob Taylor, and I drove fifty miles east of Winnipeg and down a winter logging trail until we reached a black spruce-muskeg site where Great Grays had previously been seen. It looked like a suitable place to release our bird, and we hoped that it would soon find companionship among its own kind.

Though everything was covered with soft, flaky, newly fallen snow, on the sides of drifts in an open, grassy area we found mouse trails and burrows of mice, a heartening sign that the owl would find prey in the vicinity.

Carefully untying the owl's tether for the last time, I held the bird while its portrait was taken against the wintry backdrop of dark spruce. Finally, and with some reluctance, I gave it a gentle toss and it was on the wing. Its broad wings beating heavily at first as it sought to gain momentum, the owl moved rapidly across the snow-covered clearing, heading straight toward a dead tamarack, a lone, leaning pole that seemed to have immediately caught its attention. The owl swooped up onto the pole, landing with graceful precision right on the tip, flapped its wings twice to steady itself as the pole swayed, then folded its wings and was still. . . . Suddenly it was all owl again, wild, beautiful, free. It gave a heavy comfort-shake, ruffling and settling its plumage, and we knew it was back in its own world. It turned its head about and stared briefly toward us, then left its perch and steadily flew off toward the nearby bank of spruce trees, lifted easily over their ragged tops, and was lost to sight.

4

To Catch an Owl

— Excerpt from a letter to the author from Mrs. Elsie Carlson, Pine Falls, Manitoba, February 20, 1974.

"I was looking from my kitchen window in our mobile home which is nestled in a bluff of trembling aspen (poplar) and birch. . . . I noticed a black object near a fence. The background was all deep snow and the black object aroused my curiosity. My husband and I then both observed the black object with a pair of binoculars. The object suddenly took the shape of a large bird and it seemed to be struggling. It was much too large to be a raven so I decided to investigate further.

"I strapped on my snowshoes and with a rabbit snare and stick to hold this bird away I went to help him. When I got to him I was afraid that he might decide to bite me. I snared his head but while I was busy doing this he got me by the hand with the claws from both feet. My woolen gloves were no protection I can assure you. My next thought was, what do I do now in this predicament! With my free hand I took the stick and put it next to his feet. He removed his claws from my hand (which really hurt and was bleeding) and sank his claws into the stick instead. Then, with my hand that was not wounded I grabbed both his feet above the claws, and held him upside down while I attempted to free his wing from the barbed wire. . . .

"At this stage of the game it would be safe to say that my heart was beating about as fast as it could. I didn't want to injure the owl any more than he was, but it was necessary to pull his wing free of the wire. Finally I did free him and then turned him away from me, and he fluttered away about 10 feet. He then turned around and looked at me. I turned around and walked home to nurse my hand.

"I got in touch with the local conservation officer who captured the owl the following day. I learned from the officer that the owl had followed me most of the way home. Neighbors tell me that the owl had been in this area for the past two weeks and had no fear of buildings, houses etc. . . . You may wish to note that my rescue of the Great Gray Owl was an ordeal for both of us, for I am 70 years of age."

To gain information on Great Gray Owl population size, movements, sex and age ratios, and other biological data, we attempted to capture every bird we could find. Most were caught in winter when they were conspicuous and responsive. Operating under appropriate scientific permits, during the past twelve years we captured 171 full-grown adults and banded 49 nestling or fledgling birds—a total of 220. The figure astounds me; six years ago I would never have believed that we would reach that number. (The first Great Gray Owl ever banded in North America was captured only thirty-two years ago, in January 1947, near Toronto, by Gordon Lambert.)

From 1968 to 1973 inclusive, we banded only seven grown birds, but from 1974 to the end of June 1978 we banded sixty-nine. In the winter of 1978-79 we banded an unprecedented eighty-eight owls. Of the forty-nine young banded, forty-five were banded from summer 1974 to June 30, 1979. In less than eight months, from December 2, 1978, to July 8, 1979, we banded 110 birds (all in southeastern Manitoba), thus doubling our total. In the winter of 1979-80, an additional fifty birds were banded.

Our success in more recent years was due to the presence of large numbers of birds, improved capture techniques, and a greater effort. For example, in the winter of 1978-79, Herb Copland and I were in the field every weekend from November 26 to April 16, traveling as much as five hundred miles in a day. That winter was one of the longest and coldest ever recorded for Manitoba. On exceptional days we were able to band four to six adult owls. The length of time it took us to capture one varied from a few minutes to two hours or more. Owls were taken at all times of day, from earliest light to after dark, with a few unsuccessful attempts made at night. Weather conditions varied from dense fog (in mid-April), rain and snow, to bright sunlight. Generally, more birds were seen on calm, dark, cloudy days, often during a light snowfall. Early morning and late evening were also prime times. On windy days owls usually were difficult to find.

It took us at least thirty minutes to process a bird. That was the time spent from the moment of arrival back at the car to the release of the owl, including banding, measuring or describing twenty or more features, and recording in detail the state of molt. We also spray-painted the tips of the tail feathers twice, drying the feathers separately under the car heater both times (and, incidentally, leaving smears of paint on various parts of the car). We carefully avoided getting paint on the undertail coverts.

By painting the tail feathers (red, yellow, or green) we could tell which birds we had already banded, making it possible to identify banded and unbanded birds in a winter population. The ratio of marked to unmarked birds enabled us to estimate the numbers of birds in an area. Unfortunately, local wildlife photographers found our painted birds less appealing. Painting the tail is a temporary marking method. By June or July the paint will have faded or the tail feathers will have been renewed. It didn't seem to have any effect on the behavior of the birds, and more than one tail-painted bird was later found at a nest. The aluminum, numbered leg band, which we put on each bird, is a permanent means of identifying individuals, but the bird has to be captured (or found dead) for the band number to be read. A few breeding females, captured at the nest at the time we banded their young, were marked with brightly colored plasticized-nylon wing tags, one-inch-wide strips fastened in a loop around the base of each wing. It would take birds an hour or two to get used to the tag, but eventually they preened the tags into suitable position and thereafter bore them with little effort or signs of annoyance. These tags, which had identifying marks on the end, made it possible to follow the movements of individual birds from summer through winter.

They were sometimes retained for a year or more. I always felt a little reluctant to attach tags to birds. Obviously, it's a slight hindrance. But we've watched them raise their families successfully, apparently undeterred by the bright ribbons. In January and February the sight of a bird bearing a colored tag provides extra reassurance and unusual excitement, the additional information obtained from individual recognition of the owl making it all worthwhile.

We captured owls by a variety of techniques. For trapping birds in winter, we relied for the first several years on a standard bal-chatri trap, a small, wire-screen cage large enough to hold a live laboratory mouse, meadow vole, red squirrel, or House Sparrow. The cage is covered with upright, monofilament nylon slip-nooses set to catch the toes of the owl. Attracted to the live lure, an owl lands on the cage and is supposed to become en-tangled in the nooses. One noose pulled tight on a toe is enough to hold an owl; a weight attached to the trap prevents the bird from flying away. Sometimes this works well, but I have seen a trapped owl break a noose and escape. At other times I have watched helplessly and with disappointment while an owl repeatedly hopped about on the cage, trying to get at the lure, without getting caught.

Once, an owl hovered over a trap containing a red squirrel, inspecting the lure, and then flew away. On another occasion, a startled owl flew quickly away when a House Sparrow in a trap suddenly fluttered its wings. We soon decided that small rodents worked best. Laboratory mice were used most often. Although meadow voles are better able to withstand exposure to wind and low temperatures, we found them difficult to keep in captivity. Our most effective trap animal was the short-tailed shrew, hardier and even more active than meadow voles, but not easy to find in winter.

Later, we used trapping methods that yielded better results, our most successful technique having been inspired by three published reports. In the first, Marilu L. Madura vividly described, more than twenty years ago in Wisconsin, how she lured a Red-tailed Hawk down from the sky by pulling a dead mouse some distance across a meadow with a length of fishline. Hiding in some nearby brush and hoping to lure the bird in for a photograph, she patiently waited for the hawk that daily hunted over the site. When it finally came into view she pulled the line, making the mouse jump out of the grass, whereupon the hawk swiftly spiralled down, following the mouse as she frantically continued to pull on the line. The hawk seized the mouse with one foot, when close to the observer, and then jerked the fishline from her grasp. "It was with a feeling of consternation that I saw with riveted gaze the long fishline, the captured mouse, and a few spears of dry grass in his talons trailing behind him."

That story had stayed with me all these years and was recalled upon reading a report by Daniel Brunton and Ronald Pittaway, who used the stuffed skin of a meadow vole towed by hand on a white string to lure Great Gray Owls wintering near Ottawa. The owls "would approach within an arm's length of the observers," they noted, to attack the moving skin. Brunton's field notes follow: "Got a bird to react to mouse-on-a-string; bird saw specimen on snow and immediately flew over to it, hovered briefly and dropped onto it, legs extended and wings folded over its back. When the specimen was pulled from the owl while it was still on the ground, the bird pursued it, taking 4 to 6 foot leaps across the snow, wings flapping, totally concentrated on the specimen. It chased it approximately 15 feet until I fell, then it grabbed it and attempted to fly off; a brief tug-of-war, then it released its grip and flew over to a small aspen from which it continued to stare at the specimen. The procedure was repeated and the owl attacked again when the specimen was very close to me—it apparently had no perception of my presence. The owl hit the specimen when it was about 2½ feet away, and only then it looked at me . . . with an expression that could only be described as shock and indignation! I attempted to catch the bird, but could only manage to grasp its wing

briefly. The owl flew off to a nearby sapling and stared intently back at me."

The mouse-on-a-string technique was adopted by Bob Fisher in October 1973 to study hunting behavior of a Hawk Owl in Alberta. To lure the owl, a white string was tied around the neck of a dead meadow vole which was then thrown out and retrieved by hand. "From 50 yards away," Fisher wrote, "I managed to attract the owl's attention to the vole by alternating quick movements with short pauses. The owl immediately flew to within 20 yards of me. Within 10 seconds it swooped down without a flap of its wings and, with both legs extended, landed on the back half of the vole. The owl, 8 feet in front of me, was holding its wings out as if balancing itself. I pulled on the string; at this movement the owl struck the vole's head with two sharp thrusts of its beak. Then it picked up the vole with its beak and flew into the forest."

When a large concentration of Great Grays appeared east of Winnipeg in the winter of 1974, I decided to try to build a better mouse. A reasonable facsimile of a fat meadow vole was made from a piece of wood covered with artificial fur from a hat; a piece of shoestring for a tail, an eyescrew at the other end—and there it was, an artificial mouse for fishing for owls! A bait-casting rod and level-winding reel with braided nylon line provided the means for throwing and retrieving the lure.

The first time I cast the lure at a Great Gray was on a bright, cold morning in February; it was minus 20 degrees Fahrenheit, but the air was still and the white landscape sparkled. We found our first owl perched in a frost-covered tree a hundred feet from the road, hunting intently. It paid no attention as I walked a few steps from the car, motor running, my son Woody and our springer spaniel looking out open windows. I cast across an open drift, and while the lure was still in midair the owl left its perch. With rapidly beating wings it came straight toward the lure, which now was sliding smoothly along on top of the snow. I reeled in line as fast as I could, but not fast enough— the owl swooped low, snatched up the lure, and turned away with its prize. I let some line run out, but finally had to jerk the lure free. This made the owl lurch in flight, but it turned and landed on a nearby tree. After a moment, while the owl watched closely, I made another short cast, letting the lure fall on the snow for a moment. Nothing happened. But as soon as I set the lure in motion, the owl came straight toward it, made a pass over it, turned on one wing, dropped and pounced. Again I had an owl on the end of my line, and once more reluctantly pulled the lure away. By then my fingers were numb with cold, though I was greatly enjoying myself.

Over the next two hours I cast the lure at four more owls with equal effect. The sight of the lemming-sized bait moving up and down snowdrifts like an over-sized, running vole, zigzagging between weed stalks as I teased it along, seemed to release a strong attack stimulus. I reeled fast or slow, watching the owl and trying to hold its attention by varying the lure's speed and action. One owl came down to the lure more than a dozen times, recklessly darting in as compulsively as a pike.

We used this technique for trapping owls for three months, leading a responding bird into a large throw-net laid flat on the snow and operated by a second person. Once an owl was sighted, the net was set out on a flat drift and the net operator crouched at one end of it, usually up to his waist in snow. The lure was then cast across the net and retrieved at a measured pace so that the owl would follow it and drop down onto or beside it in the middle of the net. A responsive owl would launch itself from its perch, fly rapidly toward us with continuous flapping, and then, for

the last several yards, approach in a smooth glide, eyes blinking rapidly as if to clear its vision as it neared the lure. At times the owl would veer off, but when things went right, the owl would suddenly be on the snow and in the net, flapping and kicking.

Since we were often casting for owls perched in trees beside a main highway, we sometimes slowed traffic, receiving curious looks from passing motorists. There were some disadvantages to the technique—it's almost impossible to use a rod and reel unless barehanded, and it's a miserable job trying to untangle a snarled line in subzero weather with an owl sitting nearby and one's companions impatiently waiting for the crucial cast. On those days I often had cold fingers and a short temper.

Though we had seen owls fly off after distant prey on the snow, we were still impressed when birds two hundred yards or more away from us responded to the lure the moment it began to move. On one occasion, when we were preparing to trap a distant owl, I stood at the back of the car, letting out some line to rewind on the reel to ensure a good cast. In the process, the lure fell to the road at my feet. At once the owl left its perch and flew rapidly toward us. When it swooped in at me, I whirled about, trying to keep the lure away from the bird, which flew around me, almost touching the car with it wings. Meanwhile, the rest of the crew looked on, stunned by the action. The owl flew off and, of course, couldn't be attracted again. Thereafter, though it seemed silly, I usually kept the lure in my hand or concealed at my side when approaching a bird.

All this while, another technique was available. Al Oeming had demonstrated a method on television in March 1974. He placed a live laboratory mouse on the snow, and when a Great Gray Owl flew in to get it, he captured it like a butterfly with a large fish-landing net. In late

After setting a Verbail pole-trap, the author walks off carrying a rod and reel. Note the artificial mouse used as the lure.

March we tried his technique, using a nineteen-inch-diameter net with a two-and-one-half-foot-length handle—and it worked! One man with a net and a live mouse could capture a bird by himself. There were quick and immediate results, though not every bird responded. The main problem was the mice; at times in cold weather they wouldn't move enough, huddling in a ball, or suddenly darting off across the snow and out of reach of the net, so that a few owls got free meals.

It is an exciting game to play. Set the mouse loose and wait, motionless, watching the owl. Sometimes the least movement of the mouse, one turn, is enough to set an owl peering and craning; another move by the mouse and here comes the owl! Several rapid flaps of its wings, then a steady glide, bright yellow eyes staring fixedly, low across the field, straight in to the target. With the mouse less than four feet away and the approaching owl seeming to stare straight into one's eyes, it is almost unnerving. The bird looks huge when still far off, and one has to learn to wait for the critical moment—wait for the gliding owl to land beside the mouse and close its wings—then, quick, in one motion drop the landing net over it!

Great Gray Owls coming in to our live mice invariably landed close beside them rather than upon them, so the mice usually escaped injury. This manner of approaching prey was observed under more natural circumstances. One day, for example, an owl flew far out over an open field in pursuit of a vole scurrying on top of the snow. Gliding after it on set wings, the owl landed near the erratically moving vole, folded its wings for a second, then simply hopped onto its prey. Although a vole out on top of the snow is especially vulnerable, this sort of leisurely attack may relate to a bird's needs, a hungry owl probably making a more direct approach. Some owls picked mice off the snow without even pausing in flight.

Especially intriguing was the way in which Great Grays at times, with feet ex-

tended, slid in along the top of the snow behind the rapidly moving lure. By thus skidding on the surface of the snow they were able to catch the lure, and they probably take prey in this fashion when required. Though the birds are almost always in complete control of their movements, a hunting Great Gray Owl was seen taking a tumble late one winter evening. The owl swooped down upon a mouse running on the snow, reaching for it with both feet extended. Just as it struck the mouse it evidently caught a talon in the snow crust or on some hidden object, for the owl suddenly toppled forward with wings still extended, its momentum sending it somersaulting two or three times. But it held fast to its prey and finally flew off as if nothing unusual had happened.

A few years later we acquired a larger fish-landing net, using it to take owls pursuing the cast lure or coming in to a live mouse. It is oval-shaped, twenty-four inches wide and thirty-two inches long, with a fifty-eight-inch handle. This makes it feasible to net birds while they are still in the air, approaching, passing by, or even swerving away. It takes experience to judge when a bird can be safely netted and, because we didn't want to risk injuring a bird, sometimes we deliberately let one slip by. Once an owl lifted out of Herb's reach at the last moment, flew behind us and then returned, darting past me, stretching out one foot toward the lure that was lying on the handle of the net. I was speechless, and the bird flew right past Herb's head as it left. Herb was still motionless, waiting for the bird to return to its perch, to make another pass at the lure.

Even if the owl isn't captured, the sight of it sailing in at close range is impressive. When it hovers nearby or veers away, its flapping wings are noiseless, even when within arm's reach. Skimming by with feathers in immaculate order, it has a remarkably trim appearance. Only the flat, forward-directed face looks anomalous, at odds with the otherwise streamlined form. What a contrast between this beautiful bird and the same struggling, disheveled creature in the net!

Working as a team, we followed a general pattern, first trying to attract an owl with the cast lure, often netting it directly. At other times the cast lure served to bring an owl closer to us so that we could try other methods. If a bird failed to come in on the cast lure, the person with the net would take a live mouse out of his pocket (where it was kept comfortable with a handwarmer) and place it on the snow, or, better, on a white cloth-covered board. A long period of trying to seduce the owl with a live mouse was sometimes necessary before the owl would fly down to be netted. If this didn't work we still had bal-chatri traps, and often dropped these on the edge of the road from the slowly moving car when trying to get a shy bird. In the winter of 1978–79 we obtained a Verbail trap, a neat device that supplemented the bal-chatri. Invented in the 1920s by biologist Vernon Bailey, the Verbail could be fastened onto a bal-chatri or attached to a pole set nearby as a perch for the owl. When an owl landed on top of the treadle, this triggered off a tightly flexed spring wire that would in turn quickly draw a cord noose about the bird's feet. We found it to be a safe and sure method of capturing Great Gray Owls. The trick was to get them to land on top of it. Now when we're out looking for owls we travel with a full load of gear: live mice in warm boxes, bal-chatris, the

Verbail, nets, casting rod and lure, and banding equipment. Upon sighting an owl there's a certain amount of scrambling to get things in hand, and more than once owls have quietly disappeared while we were getting ready.

I can recall numerous stories of adventure or misadventure in connection with capturing or trying to capture owls. We spent some long hours, for example, digging our vehicle out of snow-filled, hidden ditches. We also had problems with flat tires, barking dogs, curious motorists, birdwatchers eager to see the action, and snowmobilers.

One sunny day we stopped to try for an owl seen ahead of us, perched on a utility pole. We barely had time to get our equipment out when suddenly a snowmobiler appeared, speeding toward us along the line of poles, certain to frighten the owl away. We ran ahead to the edge of the road and I made a hasty cast while Herb was still getting himself in position with the net. The owl left the pole when the lure started moving, just as the snowmobiler reached the same pole. It was a race between the two; we could see both the owl gliding toward us and a spume of snow from the noisy machine coming up behind it. Despite the potential distraction, the owl kept right on course. Seconds after Herb netted it, the snowmobiler pulled up alongside us to see what we were doing.

Another day, spotting an owl hunting from a stump in an open field about a hundred yards from the edge of a highway,

Pursuing the lure: the sequence of photos on these two pages offers studies of intense concentration and determination!

we stopped and made a cast. As I started reeling in the lure, the owl leapt off its perch, flapped heavily several times, and headed directly toward us. Just as it set its wings in a glide, it was joined by a second bird, equally intent on the lure. Where the latter bird came from we had no idea; all we could do was marvel at the spectacle of two Great Gray Owls side by side, wing tips almost touching, round faces fixed on the moving lure, gliding rapidly toward us. Herb netted the nearest bird, the other swerved up and over us at the same time

and settled in a nearby small tree, where we caught it a few minutes later.

Sometimes we captured Great Grays with a wire snare on the end of a long pole, thus taking a few winter birds and females at nests after the young were well grown. Capturing an owl with this technique can be an agonizing experience: trying to raise the delicate snare up through branches and twigs to the perched owl before it moves away, desperately manipulating it into position over the bird's head—all this, while the owl is moving its

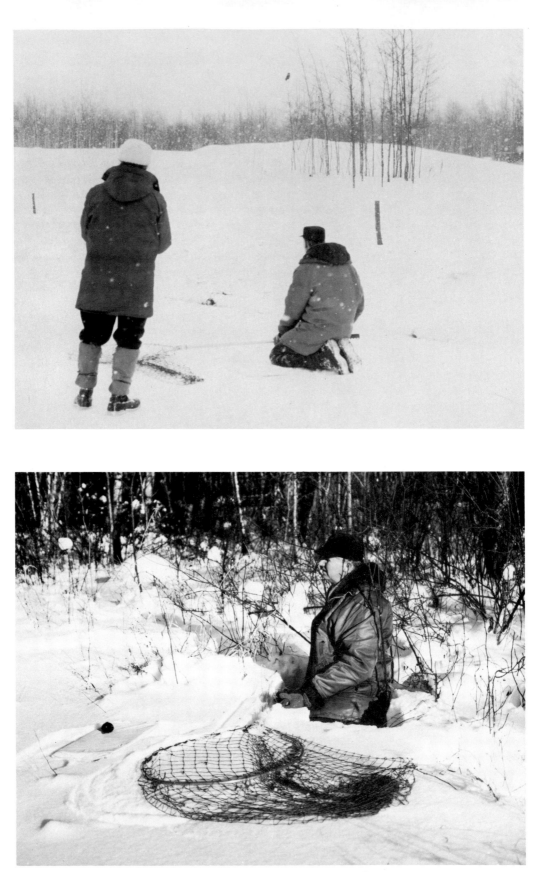

Herb Copland is ready for action. Note the live mouse near the net.

Inch-long talons are a good reason for keeping a firm grip on the owl's feet as it is banded.

head about in annoyance each time the snare brushes against its feathers. One minute the bird is aloft, perched, balanced, magnificent, out of reach, staring downward or across the forest; then when the snare is pulled, the owl suddenly is brought down, wings flailing. One rushes forward to secure it, to keep it from hurting itself, to undo the snare, to restore some of the bird's lost dignity, rearranging its feathers and cradling it to bring it to a quiet state. The whole affair sounds appalling, but little harm is done; owing to an abundance of feathers on the neck, the wire seldom draws tight.

When a bird is trapped, by whatever means, one must control it, holding the feet tightly and always being watchful of the talons, gathering in the wings against the body. The talons, being long and sharp and quick to close, can produce painful punctures and scratches. An owl is insecure except in flight or when properly perched; the constant flexing of its toes when it is being handled is probably due to the bird's need to hold onto something, rather than aggressive behavior. Occasionally, an individual will snap its bill and try to bite. Such birds, recorded as "a biter and struggler," frequently nipped at me with their bills and seldom stopped struggling, making it difficult to carry on our work. These were more often adult females, which are generally more aggressive in nature than males; but occasionally an adult male or an immature bird of either sex would show similar behavior. I was impressed by the strength of their legs, which have a heavy musculature. At times, when the bird shoved its feet forward, or tried to, I had to exert considerable force to keep it in position against my body.

Once held properly, legs grasped firmly in one hand, wings tucked in and the body embraced and upright against one's chest, most Great Gray Owls are relatively tractable. They submit to being stroked, and indeed seem to enjoy having their "ears" scratched just as a cat or dog does. Gentle probing with a finger deep into the feathers behind the ear opening sometimes causes them to tilt their heads sideways, suggesting a favorable response to grooming, a remarkable behavior for a freshly captured wild animal. Most of the owls I've handled have been surprisingly docile. It's difficult to resist caressing and nuzzling one of these beautiful, warm, soft-plumaged birds. Though perhaps a sentimental gesture, burying my nose deep in the side of the big feathered head gives me pleasure. The smell is of warm feathers, a pleasant scent.

Trapping and handling a bird didn't seem to have much lasting effect. Sometimes we watched birds for fairly long periods after they were released, and generally their behavior appeared normal. One marked bird, taken in the Verbail trap, two weeks later responded strongly to the cast lure, once even picking it up and flying away with it. One owl, captured via the cast lure and net technique, pursued the same lure as if it had never seen it before, only forty minutes after being released. In this case I tested the bird only because she stayed near us and kept right on hunting; it was evidently a hungry owl.

I suspect it is mostly hunger that drives Great Gray Owls to respond to our lures, making them almost totally ignore us in their urge to take prey. A resident of The Pas, John Donald, told me that on several occasions when he encountered Great Gray Owls, to amuse his children he threw a mitten onto the snow, bringing the owl down close. Another friend, less acquainted with this species, tossed his wallet out the car window late one winter evening to see what would happen. He told me he was surprised to see how close the bird came; it actually landed on the wallet for a brief moment. I told him he was lucky the bird didn't carry it away! Sounds, as well as objects, attract them. Once, in good light, while we stood by our car, squeaking to draw the attention of a Great Gray Owl to a mouse in a balchatri trap, a second bird appeared. Evidently attracted by the sound, it flew toward us, suddenly stopped short and pounced on a lump of brown ice in the center of the highway. It sat for a few seconds foolishly looking at its mistaken prey before flying away.

Winter banding draws to a close in late March or mid-April when, with the melting of snow, small rodents are more readily available, and owls have returned to distant nesting grounds, or are busily engaged at nest sites back in the woods. The number of owls to be found out in the open rapidly decreases, it becomes increasingly difficult to approach those that one does find, and they become much less responsive. Suddenly, winter is over.

5

An Elusive Bird

By what powerful alchemy have the northern coniferous forest and its inhabitants been brought to the present artful arrangement? By what magic do snowshoe hares suddenly cover the forest floor, providing a rich bounty that moves a hundred systems, and then as suddenly disappear, leaving hungry predators desperately searching for food, running and flying, fleeing to far places, and dying?

Perhaps the owl knows. Itself a creature of bog and forest, the Great Gray Owl has shared in the slow, cold death and eventual rebirth of northern woodlands. Watching the silent struggle of plants and animals moving northward after the crushing ice masses reshaped the land, the owl became part of the fragile network, adjusting to the ebb and rise of a tide of small rodents, themselves responding to subtle forces. A bird of mystery, the Great Gray Owl bears in its aloofness some of the remoteness of the vast northland; its plumage the color of lichens and weathered wood; its soft hooting, part of the wind.

Hare and lynx, caribou and wolf, mouse and owl—in no other region is there such a precarious arrangement of cause and effect. Something tips in the balance and a million conifers produce a burden of cones, feeding nuthatches, crossbills, squirrels, voles, and mice, and these in turn are food for predators, furbearers, animals important to man. Another season, and the failure of the cone crop sends waves of birds far outside their normal range.

In the balance of things, an owl, a mouse, a single plant entwined in the decayed roots of a toppled spruce, may be part of the answer. The explorer, the scientist, the poet, pondering these problems, must look everywhere, must enquire of all the creatures that live in these woods—the woods of the Great Gray Owl.

British explorers during the North American fur trade era discovered both the Great Gray Owl and its nest. The species was described first by John R. Forster in 1772 on the basis of a specimen sent to England in 1771 by Hudson Bay Company factor and naturalist Andrew Graham. At the time, Graham was at Severn (then Fort Severn or Severn House), which is at the mouth of the Severn River on the west coast of Hudson Bay in northwestern Ontario, about seventy miles from the Manitoba-Ontario boundary. Graham received many bird skins already "stuffed and dried" by Indians and obtained inland, but it is not clear how the first Great Gray Owl specimen seen by any interested white man came into his possession. That he saw other Great Gray Owls, and in the flesh if not alive, is clear from his remarks that "some only weigh two pounds one quarter, others three pounds."

Fifty-four years later the first nest known to science was found by Sir John Richardson at Great Bear Lake. The indefatigable Richardson reported: "On the 23rd of May [1826], I discovered a nest of this Owl, built on the top of a lofty balsam-poplar, of sticks, and lined with feathers. It contained three young, which were covered with a whitish down. We got them by felling the tree, which was remarkably thick; and whilst this operation was going on, the two parent birds flew in circles round the objects of their cares, keeping, however, so high in the air as to be out of gunshot: they did not appear to be dazzled by the light." Richardson must have been intrigued by the owlets, which survived the fall, for instead of turning them into scientific study skins he kept them alive for two months, no mean feat under the conditions of their expedition. The first behavioral observation of young of the species is his brief comment that "they had the habit, common to other Owls, of throwing themselves back and making a loud snapping noise with their bills, when any one en-

tered the room in which they were kept." Rather laconically, he adds that after keeping them that long "they made their escape."

Richardson and William Swainson (the latter an ornithologist who collaborated with the physician-naturalist on their joint 1831 publication) gave a remarkably good account of the distribution of the Great Gray Owl in Canada, especially considering the paucity of information available at the time. They noted that the species "is by no means a rare bird in the fur-countries, being an inhabitant of all the woody districts lying between Lake Superior and latitudes 67° or 68°, and between Hudson's Bay and the Pacific. It is common on the borders of Great Bear Lake; and there and in the higher parallels of latitude it must pursue its prey, during the summer months, by daylight."

The Great Gray Owl (*Strix nebulosa*) occupies a vast circumpolar range, being resident across the coniferous forest belt of Eurasia and western North America at both low and high elevations. The Eurasian subspecies (*Strix nebulosa lapponica*), paler and more strongly streaked than its North American counterpart, resides in northern Norway, Sweden, Finland, and the Soviet Union. Initially thought to be a separate species, it was long known as the Lapland Owl or Lapp Owl. In Russia it has been called the Wood Owl, Bearded Night Owl, or Bearded Owl, the last two names owing to the small patch of black feathers beneath its "chin" or bill. When common names for subspecies were in vogue, this race was identified as the Siberian Great Gray Owl. The North American subspecies (*Strix nebulosa nebulosa*) has been known in the past as the Cinereous Owl, Great Cinereous Owl and Sooty Owl—references to its grayish-brown color. It has also been called the Speckled Owl, the Spruce Owl, and the Spectral Owl. Edward H. Forbush, speaking of the former scientific name of the species, noted: "*Scotiaptex nebulosa,* the name which systematists have given the Great Gray Owl, certainly is descriptive of this bird. Freely translated it runs thus—'The gray eagle-owl of darkness.' "

In fact not a bird of darkness, but a bird of light, the Great Gray Owl is distinct among its kind, being the only species among the eleven in the genus *Strix* that is not primarily nocturnal. The noticeably small eyes of Great Grays are undoubtedly an adaptation for daylight hunting, a feature evolved during the origin of the species in the circumpolar Arctic region long before the Ice Age. It is, incidentally, the only species of the genus that occurs in both the Old and New Worlds. Numerous aspects of form and behavior, achieved through a long period of time in forested regions in extreme northern latitudes, are a heritage carried by both geographic races. Though divided into two separate populations, North American and Eurasian birds have retained almost all features in common, hence, for the most part, can be treated as one.

Though it occurs northward to the northern limit of dense evergreen forests on both continents, the Great Gray Owl's range in Europe and western North America extends far southward. Its known North American breeding range runs from central Alaska and Canada south in the western mountains to central California, northern Idaho, western Wyoming and Montana, extreme northwestern Minnesota, and south-central Ontario. There is an apparent extra-limital nesting record for extreme northwestern Wisconsin. In Canada, the heart of its North American breeding range, it breeds in most of British Columbia, northern and central Alberta, northern Saskatchewan, all of Manitoba except the extreme northern and southwestern parts, and Ontario west of James Bay; though it likely breeds east of James Bay and into Quebec, there are few summer records for that large region.

Great Gray Owls occur across a large and varied region on this continent, ranging from stunted, transition forest in the Hudson Bay Lowlands to subalpine and montane forests from Alaska to California and Wyoming. Birds occasionally venturing out on the tundra undoubtedly have feasted on lemmings; others have roamed quietly on the edge of meadows above timberline at high altitudes. But it is with the northernmost forest cover that these birds are most closely associated.

Like many other owls, the Great Gray lays its eggs in nests built by other species, such as crows, ravens, and various hawks. Accordingly, its nests naturally vary considerably in height, shape, durability, and in the habitat in which they occur. In Alberta their preferred nesting habitat is considered to be stands of mature poplar adjacent to muskeg country. Islands of black poplar or aspen poplar amid a sea of spruce and pine are probably attractive nesting places for birds that build large, stick nests. The dominant tree species over much of the northern range is black spruce. And even on wintering grounds, sometimes miles from known nesting range, black spruce-tamarack forests are seldom far away. There also is good evidence that the deciduous tamarack or larch, which often accompanies spruce, occurring as islands within spruce stands, along wet margins or as extensive stands, may be especially important as breeding habitat.

Considered common in eastern Siberia, the Great Gray Owl is scarce in Europe and much of its North American range. Still, these owls may be more abundant than is generally believed. Scandinavian workers have amassed a great deal of information on the species, having recorded more than one hundred and thirty nests. According to Heimo Mikkola, a Finnish ornithologist who has long studied the species, the most dense concentration of breeding Great Grays has been observed in northern Finland.

Despite its large range in North America, only a little more than a hundred

The North American breeding range of the Great Gray Owl is indicated by the shaded area; the hatched area is where this species occasionally occurs in winter.

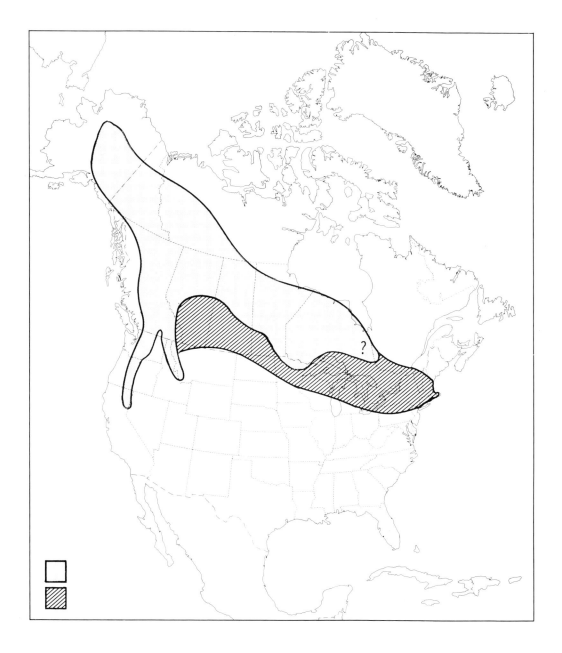

Great Gray Owl breeding distribution is within or close to the boundaries of the Boreal Forest Zone.

nests were found in the 150 years after Richardson's discovery of a nest at Great Bear Lake. Sets of eggs—egg clutches—in museums provide the largest number of nest records. Early naturalists took the eggs from almost every nest they discovered, but this aspect of scientific collecting would have had little effect on the overall population. The majority of the nests were found in Canada, especially in Alberta.

Owing to its dependence on small mammals for food, this species suffers severely when its prey declines, at times undergoing starvation or making lengthy migrations into southern Europe. Thus, its numbers fluctuate according to local conditions, making it difficult to arrive at overall population estimates. Similar conditions operate to some extent in North America, owls occasionally appearing in numbers in southeastern Canada and adjacent United States.

How many Great Gray Owls are there in North America? The range of the species is so large and there is so little information available regarding its density that it is difficult to estimate their abundance. Judging by our experience in Manitoba and Minnesota, I believe that there may be upward of fifty thousand. Many people will think this figure is too high for a species considered rare or uncommon. But we have learned how secretive they can be when nesting, how seldom seen except at the nest site. We have seen concentrations of winter birds of fifty or more in a relatively small area, and our evidence suggests that these are mostly local birds, from good breeding habitat within thirty to fifty miles. Much remains to be learned about the species, not the least of which is population density and abundance.

Ready wanderers, quick to leave nesting grounds when prey is scarce, and likely to nest elsewhere should they find prey and suitable nest sites, there is evidence that Great Gray Owls have an attachment to their original breeding sites, or at least the general area. Two marked females that bred successfully in Manitoba in 1978 were seen on numerous occasions during the following winter within a mile or two of their nest sites. In Sweden, as reported by Wahlstedt, three adult females banded at nests in 1973 used the same nests the following year! Their habit of remaining on the breeding grounds in years of poor food supply and simply not breeding shows an adaptability to declining prey species as well as a means for sedentary existence. Occasional irruptions may result from a combination of years of good reproductive success followed by abrupt prey declines. Ecologist Charles S. Elton, it should be noted, included the Great Gray Owl as a member of several boreal forest species exhibiting this characteristic pattern.

Writing in 1927, Forbush gave an over-simplified explanation of the appearances of Great Grays in the New England states: "When the northern forests fail to produce cones for winter food for small arboreal birds; when deep snows cover the runways of mice, and grasses and weeds that feed ground-birds and when bush rabbits and ptarmigan are scarce in the northern wilderness; then we may expect an unusual invasion of Great Gray Owls."

High populations of owls, scarcity of food due to low numbers of small mammals and other prey species, icy crusts, or unusually deep snow may account for appearances and concentrations of owls within the breeding range as well as in adjacent areas. Occurrences of owls hundreds of miles beyond their normal range, however, are less easy to understand. What compels them onward, flying slowly over open terrain, across alien country? Is it hunger alone? Or do they have an inherent urge to move, released by some of the factors mentioned above, that drives them outward from their

breeding grounds? Is there, perhaps, some biological advantage to this movement that at times leads them astray, into inhospitable areas, into cities and towns, where many eventually perish?

One of our young birds, banded in May 1976 as a nestling about fifty miles east of Winnipeg, was found dead on a roadside in extreme southeastern Minnesota, about twelve miles from the Iowa border. That is about four hundred and sixty-eight miles in a straight line from the nest site. Presumably the bird hadn't left the natal area until September, for until then it should have been a weak flier. Douglas Butler, a motorist who found the remains of the bird in mid-March 1977, wrote me that he thought it had been dead for three to four weeks. In five months or less, then, the young owl made that extended journey. On the other hand, another young owl, banded in the nest by us in 1978, was struck by a car in mid-October of that year, less than a mile from the nest site.

In the winter of 1978-79 unprecedented numbers of Great Gray Owls appeared in southern Ontario and Quebec. I was told that at the peak in January and early February there were about forty birds in the Toronto vicinity, and an equal number near Kingston on Amherst Island (where nine were seen in one tree!), and eighteen or so on the adjacent mainland. About fifty were reported in the Ottawa vicinity, where, over the course of the winter, many were shot or starved to death. During that same period, numerous sightings were made in upper New York State and New England. That same winter, Great Gray Owls were seen in abundance in southeastern Manitoba, with perhaps a hundred birds occurring in an area described by a circle with a diameter of forty miles, centering some seventy miles northeast of Winnipeg. From December through April, Herb Copland and I captured and banded eighty-eight owls in that area. Large numbers had been observed in a portion of that area in the winter of 1973-74, when we trapped fourteen birds, and again in the winter of 1977-78, when we took thirty.

Birds appearing in winter far from known breeding range, such as those in New York and the New England states, are clearly emigrants, displaced birds. Their origin is unknown, but there is little doubt that they are far from home. The appearance of the owls in winter in southeastern Manitoba is less unexpected because this area is within their breeding range. Active nests over several years, occasional recaptures, and especially sightings of color-tagged females that bred successfully in the area emphasize the point that the wintering population east of Winnipeg consists of both resident and nonresident birds.

Although the estimated numbers present in winters of high populations in Manitoba are impressive, I think that these birds can be accounted for by movement of owls from nearby breeding grounds. Areas of concentration for these birds were ideal hunting sites, consisting of open, grassy fields adjacent to woods. A high meadow vole population in 1978-79 undoubtedly contributed to the unusual number of owls. The ratio of resident to nonresident birds is unknown, but nonresidents could be coming from adjacent breeding habitat that stretches for hundreds of miles. So there is little reason to think that Manitoba birds are coming any great distance.

Birds appearing in Duluth and southern Ontario and Quebec could be coming from not-too-distant breeding grounds, for

Not at all amused, a captive bird glares at its captors. Though owl "faces" are less mobile and expressive than those of mammals, because the former lack the complex facial musculature, some range of expression does exist.

suitable habitat lies not far from these areas. What is not known is the population density of Great Gray Owls on those more remote breeding grounds, let alone in our more accessible study areas. Birds may be coming in some cases from great distances, but one need not necessarily look too far in northern Canada for a source of birds appearing in southern Canada and adjacent United States.

Conspicuous appearances of Great Grays during periods of emigration (related to over-abundance or food shortages or both) may lead to misinterpretation of population size. Actual populations may be much higher, or lower, than estimated on the basis of winter appearances. This species can occur regularly without being particularly obtrusive. Like most owls, they are generally retiring, keeping to remote or dense woods and avoiding man. Except at active nests or during critical winter periods when they are forced to hunt during daylight hours, their presence in an area may go unnoticed.

There is no reason to believe, on the other hand, that Great Grays occur uniformly throughout their range. Numerous water bodies, vast stretches of open bogs and stunted trees to the north, and even-aged, dense stands of spruce and pine elsewhere are likely devoid of resident birds. Moreover, in large regions of apparently ideal habitat there are few summer or winter records. The species likely varies locally in abundance, increasing and decreasing from time to time with rodent population fluctuations and other limiting factors. Changes in habitat through extensive clear-cutting of trees, for example, or extensive forest fires, undoubtedly also affect its numbers and distribution. Archibald Henderson suggested that in Alberta the species flourished during low density populations of other raptors, an abundance of vacant nests providing maximum opportunity for selection of suitable sites. Great Gray Owls did well when raptors such as Great Horned Owls, Goshawks,

and Red-tailed Hawks diminished, following declines in numbers of snowshoe hares and grouse, the prey species on which they most depend. It must be presumed, though, that there was a fair supply of small rodents in those areas where Great Grays nested.

Despite many more observers in much of its North American range, there has not been a corresponding increase in observations of this species. Though there is evidence of recent nesting in Saskatchewan, the last recorded Great Gray Owl nest was found there in 1949. This, despite the fact that C. Stuart Houston, M.D., an enthusiastic birder by avocation, has had a wide network of cooperators searching methodically across the province for nesting raptors since 1958. Up to 1979 Dr. Houston had banded an astonishing 2,885 nestling or fledgling Great Horned Owls (his specialty) at 1,248 nests. The scarcity of breeding Great Gray Owls and relatively few winter records for Saskatchewan suggest that the population in that province is low compared to Manitoba. At present Saskatchewan has far less tamarack-bog habitat than Manitoba; this may be the reason for the striking difference in population levels in these regions.

More than three dozen nests have been found in Alberta, yet this species has been considered scarce and "even close to extermination" by some Alberta ornithologists. Henderson found thirteen nests between 1913 and 1922 near his home at Belvedere (collecting all the eggs in nearly every case!). For the next thirty years, however, he found none. From 1950 to 1955 Al Oeming and several companions "travelled 36,000 miles over every conceivable type of terrain and using every imaginable means of navigation. . . . Thousands of trappers, loggers, Indians and other woodspeople were interviewed. . . ." Eventually two nests were discovered. Oeming concluded that the Great Gray Owl in Alberta was a vanishing species, though writing in 1955:

A male owl feeds a female on a curved bough in a tamarack forest. Sometime between January and April, as part of courtship behavior, a male brings food to a female for the first time, thereby establishing a close relationship with her. He continues to feed her during courtship, egg laying, incubation, and the development of the nestlings—who must also be supplied with prey by the male.

The female has taken the mouse from the male and is about to gulp it down. From this moment on, the pair bond is assured.

"Recently the Alberta Government passed an Act protecting all the hawks and owls in the province. In such protection rests the Great Gray Owl's last chance of survival. Education of the public, strict observance of the new law, and preservation of suitable nesting areas may yet ensure the continued existence of this rare, beautiful and beneficial owl." Oeming's forecast now appears reasonable, for between 1970 and 1974, north and northwest of Edmonton, two dedicated birders, Edgar T. Jones and Robert E. Gehlert, found nine Great Gray nests.

The discovery of twenty-six Great Gray Owl nests, and good evidence for several other recent nestings, in a small region of Manitoba and adjacent Minnesota from 1970 to 1979 shows that the species is doing well in this area. This is not to say that the species is not rare. By comparison with many other birds, Great Gray Owls are indeed uncommon, but perhaps no more so than other northern coniferous-forest-dwelling raptors such as Hawk Owls and Boreal Owls.

6

The Species—A Closer Look

Standing on a road in Great Gray Owl country late on a cold, damp April night we throw back our parka hoods and listen. Across the starlit bog a chill sits on all the black spruce huddled shoulder to shoulder, their irregular heavy heads just perceptible on the horizon. It is still. We wait and wait, and then, there! a faint, soft, almost booming sound. A long series of regularly spaced hoots, all on the same note, then speeding up while dropping in volume, leaving us uncertain when the last note has sounded. In a moment, again, the distant call, an emphatic "Hoo-hoo-hoo-hoo," unhurried and deliberate, at the close faintly echoing over the bog. From another direction comes a reply, at first soft, mellow, each note carefully drawn, a decisive message from a second owl.

It is remarkably quiet . . . it is too early for frogs, and apart from a distant Great Horned Owl no other birds are active. We shuffle about, speaking quietly, staring out into the night as if we thought we could see them, listening for another call. Then it comes, much closer, and now each note is heavier, somehow intense, perhaps huskier or more rasping than before. We sense a greater meaning in the calls, now coming one right after the other, the two owls evidently responding to each other, declaring their territorial boundaries. "Hoo-hoo-hoo-hoo!" exclaims each bird in turn, and on what thread of meaning, what fine tuning, what peculiar vibrancy of the calls their interrelationship revolves we do not know.

For us, listening in the night has a dreamlike quality; we stand stiffly hunched, envisioning owls silently flying from perch to perch, following each nuance of sound in each other's calls. When the calls finally cease, a calm stillness falls upon us. Having found what we sought, we stamp our feet, speak softly, and nod agreeably, then hurry to the warm confines of the car, on to the next listening post.

Life on the forest floor provides a food base for Great Gray Owls. The red-backed vole is an important prey species.

Below: Newly hatched chicks rest their heads on a remaining egg. Considering the size of Great Gray Owls, the eggs are surprisingly small—little more than two inches long and less than that in width—not even as large as a hen's egg.

A clutch of four eggs is about average for Great Gray Owls, but in years when prey species abound, the female may lay more. While most owl eggs are round, those of Great Grays are ovoid or conical.

Their light weight enables Great Grays to perch almost anywhere. This one is on the bent tip of a spruce tree.

"Strix capite laevi, corpore fusco, albido undulatim striato, remige sexto longiore, apice nigricante"—so begins John Forster's Latin description of the Great Gray Owl, published in 1772, more than two centuries ago. A more informal and appealing description was given in 1960 by a Saskatchewan farmer, Clifford Law, whose land lay adjacent to Great Gray breeding grounds: "The most conspicuous features of the Great Gray Owl are its large round head and its very dark feathers. The width of the owl's head would be between five and six inches at the base. Because of the thick head feathers, the face looks flat and sunken." The large, round head and circular facial disc are features characteristic of the genus.

Up to thirty inches in length, with a tail a foot or more long, and a wingspan up to five feet, the Great Gray is a large bird. As Richardson noted: "the *tail* is wedge-shaped, consisting of twelve feathers, of which the outer ones are more than two inches shorter than the middle ones: it is very concave below."

A taxidermist, after looking over a specimen killed at Wickford, Rhode Island, on March 25, 1883, concluded: "Taken all in all, it is the most bird for the least substance we ever examined." This apt statement has since been repeated almost verbatim by several authors. Arthur C. Bent wrote that "in bodily bulk it is exceeded by the snowy and great horned owls and is but little larger than the barred owl; its long wings and tail, its large, round head, and its long fluffy plumage make it seem much larger than it really is." Great Grays weigh roughly two to three pounds, females generally being heavier than males and occasionally weighing up to four pounds. Body weights also vary with a bird's condition, emaciated individuals falling as low as three-quarters of a pound.

In owls of nearly all species, females are larger than males, but the sexes are otherwise similar in appearance. Although some observers have stated that female

Great Grays are darker than males, there is much individual variation, pale and dark birds of both sexes being known. When a pair is seen together, the size difference between the sexes is readily apparent, but single birds are difficult to identify. Even in the hand, though there is a size difference and some as yet undefined facial features that help differentiate the sexes, their measurements overlap, and sexes cannot always be identified with certainty. Throughout winter, because of long exposure to sunlight and abrasive forces, the feathers of older birds are usually brownish or beige in color, in contrast to the truer gray color of younger birds in fresh plumage. This is particularly noticeable in the tail, which may be badly worn at the tip, and in flight feathers of the wings. The worn, faded tail feathers of an adult female, who may have spent much of the summer exposed on a nest, may appear markedly paler than the rest of her plumage, standing out even at a distance. Primary and secondary feathers are often lighter and browner than the rest of the plumage; if viewed with binoculars (or in a photograph), one may discern new, dark feathers among the old. Even in summer, old and new flight feathers may be apparent.

After recovering a known-age, banded young owl, and then handling a large number of birds in the winter of 1978–79, we became aware of plumage features whereby birds hatched in one season could be separated from older birds from late summer through April. Young birds generally have grayer or darker plumage; although varying individually, their plumage appears overall as one color. Their primary and secondary feathers and tail feathers are alike in age and color. On this basis, along with additional features, subadult owls can be recognized almost as soon as captured. Of the eighty-eight birds captured in the winter of 1978–79, roughly one-third were identified as young from the previous summer.

We recorded the appearance of each flight feather in both wings and the tail in more than a hundred Great Gray Owls. This large body of data has yet to be analyzed. At present, I can say that the molt pattern is complex and not fully understood!

Because birds lack the complex facial musculature of mammals, their "faces" are less mobile and hence less expressive. Nevertheless, some facial expression is possible. In owls, especially, with forward-facing eyes and unusual development of certain facial feathers, a considerable range of expression is achieved. There is a vast difference between an owl peering sleepily through half-closed eyelids and one staring menacingly with fully open, round eyes. Even changes in the size of the pupil, notable in owls because of an almost instant response to changes in light level, occur in different moods.

Owls typically have a foreshortened appearance, as if the face had been flattened to bring the eyes onto one plane, thus achieving binocular vision. Completing the characteristic owl face is a circle of feathers surrounding the eyes. The latter aspect is related to development of acute hearing. Nearly all birds have specialized feathers called auriculars or ear coverts on the sides of the head behind the eyes. The stiff coverts protect the opening to the inner ear while offering minimal resistance to sound waves. In owls, where hunting by sound is a particular specialty, extensive and enlarged ear coverts, supported by a fleshy flap, are fanned out around the eyes. Supporting this auricular flap and forming a semicircular trough nearly surrounding each ear opening is a dense wall of stiff feathers with flattened quills. The disc is a sound-gathering device, contributing to the remarkable hearing ability of owls.

Hudson Bay factor Andrew Graham astutely commented as far back as 1772 on the peculiar structure of the feathers covering the external ear openings in the Great Gray Owl: "In examining the external ear which is very large I observed a

As this late evening silhouette of a bird on a fence post shows, the Great Gray Owl's white "chin stripes" are visible even in poor light.

An aerial display at twilight. With the sun at tree level, an owl glides into the picture.

Great Gray Owls, which typically use stick nests built by hawks, crows, ravens, and other species, may begin hunting for nest sites as early as mid-February. The male plays an important role in finding a suitable nest, but the female probably makes the final choice.

range of short brown feathers. All the other feathers within the circle are grey with obscure bars of black, stiff and very thinly furnished with webs similar to hair by the peculiar direction of providence, for without this provision the perception of sounds would be very difficult in a bird so remarkably full of plumage.''

A greatly enlarged facial disc, extending far above the top of the cranium, partly accounts for the large head of the Great Gray. The ear coverts are concealed by softer feathers radiating out from the eyes and marked by six or more brown concentric rings on a gray background. The disc forms a nearly complete circle, the center of which lies midway between the eyes. Each half of the facial disc is slightly concave and angled backward. In the Great Gray, especially when relaxed or dozing, the upper half of the disc may be moved forward over the eyes, giving a heavy-browed effect. In this position, with lower, pale gray-colored eyelids raised in sleeping attitude, the eyes seem deeply set with the owl's head.

The color of the bill of grown birds varies in puzzling fashion from ivory to pale olive green to bright yellow. Olive green is the color most often recorded, both in summer and winter. At first I assumed that an increasing amount of yellow pigment indicated advancing reproductive condition. Some January birds had vivid yellow bills (retained in some study skins). I changed my mind, however, after noting that birds with young had bills that were pale olive green with a marked ochre-colored cere or base and ochre-colored rictus (fleshy edge of inner bill). The ochre color, so prominent in breeding females, was generally not noted in winter birds. Some birds in winter had a bill that was pale olive green or yellowish, with an ivory tip, and a dark olive green or blackish base! Clearly, there is more to be learned about bill color in this species.

Rictal bristles, modified feathers at the base of the bill, are found in many species. They are especially large and prominent in owls, extending up and between the eyes. In Great Grays, the rictal bristles appear as two opposite-facing crescents partly surrounding the eyes and usually concealing all but the tip of the bill. Because these feathers are light colored or even white in this species, they stand out boldly and are a distinctive part of the facial plumage. When an owl is feeding or preening, the feathers of the lower half of these white crescents are usually raised, exposing the entire bill. This frees the bill for action and also helps to keep adjacent feathers from getting soiled. During aggressive situations, the bristles about the bill are fully erected, giving the bird a more fearsome appearance.

In all birds the bill acts as a substitute in carrying out tasks rendered with forelimbs in many animals, including nest building, grooming, handling food, and manipulating eggs and young. The delicacy with which such tasks are performed serves to remind us of the numerous functions of the bill. An owl's bill is thus more than a device for seizing prey. In the Great Gray, prominent tactile bristles surround the bill and eyes, doubtless assisting the bird in a wide range of activities, much like the whiskers of a cat. Bending far forward to turn her eggs or to check the conditions of nestlings, or to dissect a mouse, the female's sensitivity is undoubtedly enhanced by sensory bristles. Jens Wahlstedt thought that perhaps the bristles or "brush feathers" of the female played a role in stimulating a young owl to open its bill and snap at food.

Bill-snapping, in which the lower mandible is forcibly thrust against the upper, producing a click or snap, is commonly given by most species of owls in aggressive or defensive situations, functioning as a warning sound like the growl of a dog. Close observations of a captive Great Gray Owl revealed that the sound is produced when the lower bill or mandible is thrust forward beyond the bill tip, pressed against the tip and then slipped back off to snap against the upper bill. Even young nestling Great Gray Owls bill-snap when handled. In trying to bring females in range of our snare we usually prodded the young birds, eliciting bill-snapping until they were too tired to respond. In June

1979 I learned that imitating the sound, in this case tapping one stone against another, worked even better! A harsh, hissing sound is often given under similar circumstances. Bill-snapping and hissing occur in both young and adult Great Grays, appearing in nestlings at an early age.

A defensive, crouching attitude commonly observed in Long-eared Owls and some other species, in which the back feathers are raised, the partly spread and raised wings are held forward, and the tail is spread, while the bird snaps its bill and hisses, has only occasionally been observed in the Great Gray. Al Oeming, who photographed a female Great Gray in this posture, mentions that it did this when a Red-tailed Hawk was diving at it, and when a dog was present at the nest site. An immature female owl kept by me for two weeks in November 1977 showed this defensive behavior on several occasions. It displayed the posture while perched on the back of a couch, in response to the sudden appearance of our full-grown English springer spaniel. The appearance and approach of our cat elicited even stronger display. In addition to bill-snapping and hissing, the wings were spread and lowered, the head was brought down (and directed toward the dog or cat), and—most striking of all—the scapular feathers were fully erected. However, the wings, although partly spread, were not raised and brought forward as in the typical Long-eared Owl display. On approaching a tree with an active nest in Saskatchewan, the female being on the nest and the male on a limb nearby, Clifford Law noted: "When I was about twenty yards from the tree with the nest, the owl sitting on the limb lowered its wings, ruffled its feathers and started to snap its beak." Nothing like this was seen by us, the male being fairly shy in most cases. This points out the variability of behavior in the species. An apparently similar display was observed in Finland. Erkki Pulliainen and Kaleni Loisa reported that "The male Owl defended its

While the attentive female shelters her brood from the sun, a downy owlet begins gulping down a whole vole, which had been delivered to the nest by a male.

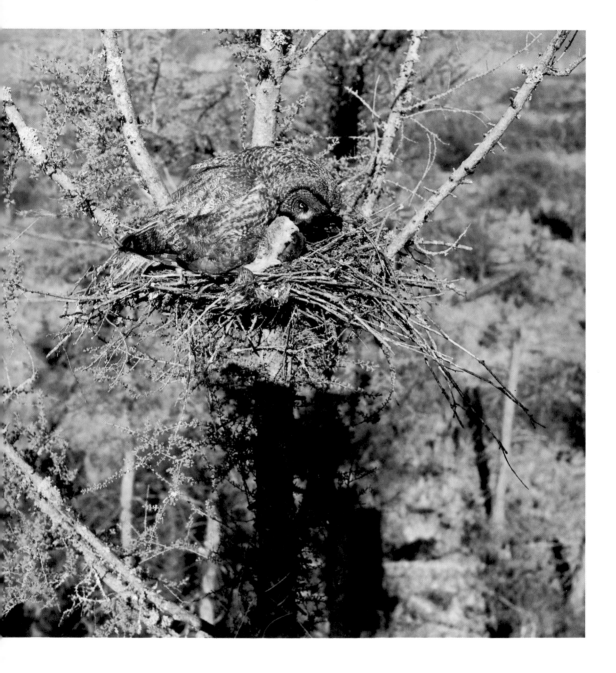

A few days after this photo was taken, the nest collapsed, probably as a result of the pushing and shoving of the young. The still flightless owlets dropped safely thirty-five feet to the forest floor. Within a few days, they were able to climb up into nearby trees. The male continued to deliver food to the young while the female remained near.

nest against an attacking Goshawk by spreading its wings and ruffling its plumage."

In the Great Gray Owl, normal roosting behavior provides fairly effective concealment. Perched close to the trunk of a mature aspen tree, a Great Gray blends so well as to be almost invisible. With head lowered, eyes closed, and facial discs "folded," the face is divided by a vertical dark line that matches streaks on the tree trunk. The streaked plumage of breast and belly are equally suitable camouflage patterns. There is another feature of Great Gray plumage that may also function in concealment. It is a trait found in many other species of owls. Owing to a diffuse pattern on the sides of the head, neck, and especially the upper breast, these areas seem out of our focus, whether viewed in life or in a photograph. The effect is partly the result of light penetrating semitransparent feathers. In the Great Gray there is a charcoal-gray and black pattern; never quite distinct, the shadowy, grayish tones blend smoothly together.

Most owls have a patch of light-colored or whitish feathers at the base of the chin. Usually these feathers are exposed prominently during the upright concealment posture; this disruptive color pattern effectively interrupts the darker form of the vertical body. In the Great Gray Owl the white patch, which is separated into two bars by blackish feathers in the middle of the foreneck, is almost always fully exposed. Law thought that at a distance the feathers looked like a "white moustache." These feathers are glossy white in both sexes. Because they reflect so much light, on a dark day or late in the evening they often may be a means for identifying the species. This distinctive feature of Great Gray Owl plumage may also function as a species recognition signal. Some observers have reported that the white patches are larger in females than in males. Others have noted individual differences in this character; the supposed differences may

A sleeping owl perched close to the trunk of an aspen poplar practically disappears from view.

partly be related to the bird's behavior and the extent to which the white patches are exposed.

The delicate pattern and subtle colors of its plumage can best be appreciated by looking at Robert Taylor's photographs, taken of several individuals under a variety of light conditions. An additional feature is the occurrence of a white margin on the outer scapulars or shoulder feathers, a trait shared with several species of owls. In some individuals this white mark is pronounced, appearing as a definite stripe at the base of each wing.

Great Gray Owls, like other birds, groom or preen, stretching in all directions as agilely as contortionists to reach nearly all parts of their plumage with bill or foot. By running feathers through the bill, dirt is removed and the complex interlocking structure of each feather is maintained. To reach its throat feathers an owl bends its head sharply forward, then, wagging its head from side to side, works its bill down the length of each feather. In methodical fashion it straightens and arranges feathers of the breast, back, and wings, occasionally reaching around to the rump, raising the feathers that overlap the base of the tail and vigorously rubbing its bill into this area. An oil-secreting gland at the upper base of the tail provides a dressing for the plumage. When the gland is pressed an oily substance oozes out and is transferred to the bill and thence, in the course of preening, to the feathers. It is a vital process. When the thin, oily film on feathers is exposed to sunlight, some of it is changed to vitamin D. Through subsequent preening a small amount of this altered oil is ingested, thus providing birds with a substitute source of this needed vitamin. Owls have relatively large oil glands, even compared to waterfowl. Owls need to sun themselves and so we may sometimes find them on the edge of woods, perched with closed eyes, facing toward the bright sun.

On one occasion only, I saw a Great Gray Owl "sun-bathing." This curious reaction, whereby an individual rigidly holds its head or body at an angle to sunlight, has been reported for a wide range of birds. The bird I saw was a female brooding young on June 2, 1970, in a high, exposed nest in northern Minnesota. For almost a minute, while I watched from less than twelve feet away and at the level of the nest, she held her head sideways to the sun, with her bill open and her eyes closed.

An owl preens its face with its talons, lifting one foot to clean all about its head and bill. Sometimes the feathers of the ear region are attacked as vigorously and audibly as when a cat scratches behind its ear. Undoubtedly, feather lice and other parasites occasionally provoke a bout of irritated scratching, just as fleas annoy dogs and cats. Extended preening of the whole body often follows head scratching. After preening, a Great Gray, like most birds, gives a comfort-shake to adjust its plumage, shaking itself heavily, then ruffling its head feathers.

Development of especially long talons has not eliminated the necessary manual dexterity that owls require to carry out a variety of tasks, notwithstanding that the bill is used for this purpose in many ways. Watching a Great Gray Owl in our family room feeding itself, I was surprised to see how it handled small food items. With talons closed, the owl used its knuckles, that is, the joints at the base of the talons of the two anterior toes, to pick up and hold small pieces of meat, raising the foot to transfer food to its bill.

Feathers of all owls are relatively soft-edged, reducing the sound of their movements. Because of this, when hovering over prey they may be able to hear better and are less likely to be heard. Great Grays, specialists in the pursuit of small mammals, have feathers that are unusually soft and their flight must be nearly noiseless.

A tail feather from a Great Gray Owl provides a lesson in beauty and adaptability. Twelve inches long and two and one-half inches wide, it is a reminder of the large tail of this relatively small-bodied bird. The feather's light weight is impressive; despite its size, it floats to the floor when dropped, and it lifts with the slightest breath. Considering the function of the tail, an individual feather is remarkably soft and flexible. Mottled grayish brown, with alternating light and dark bars, it appears denser than it is. When pressed against a printed page the letters show through clearly, even through the darkest parts, and the grayish-white bars and spots seem almost nonexistent. The central two tail feathers, which are longer and usually grayer (or brown, if faded) than the others, are nearly transparent, colored objects being visible through the vanes even when held eight inches away.

Great Gray Owl body feathers also are exceptionally long, a feature noted by Ernest S. Norman, a Manitoba farmer, who reported: "One morning in February, 1918, I noticed an unusually long and fluffy feather hanging in a willow bush near my barn. I at once knew that it was that of an owl, but had never met here any species of owls with such tremendously long feathers. Several days later the puzzle was solved, when, in broad daylight a Great Gray Owl (the first one and only one that I have seen) flew to a shade tree in front of our house. It stayed around for several weeks after that."

Great Gray breast feathers may be more than nine inches long. They are highly filamentous for most of their length, bearing long, downy plumes except for the distal inch or two. Though the filaments or plumes arise laterally from the feather shaft, as do the vanes, they are extremely light and airy, floating off in all directions as if repelled electrically, giving the feather a cylindrical form. They move freely, responding instantly to the least movement of air, trembling and swinging

about like the feathery appendages of some sea animal. Thus, even the contour feathers provide a remarkable degree of insulation. It is this downy aspect as much as the distinctive color and pattern that makes it possible to readily identify feathers from a Great Gray Owl.

In spite of their heavily feathered appearance, Great Gray Owls, as do most birds, have areas of the body surface that are featherless. These apteria, as they are called, include an almost inch-wide strip down the sternum to the vent, noticeable only after considerable parting of the abundant, downy bases of adjacent feathers. Even larger, though concealed by overlapping feathers, is an area under each wing, running from the neck and shoulder, across the side of the breast and onto the thigh. The under-wing apteria provide a significant means of losing heat. Overheated birds droop their wings, exposing their armpits, so to speak, thus helping to lower their body temperature through a cooling effect on blood vessels. On a warm day, adults handled for banding frequently do this after being released. It also is a sign of stress and distress, and a warning; a female, upset over disturbance of her young, may droop her wings prior to attacking. Heat reduction is also obtained through panting, a behavior often seen in nestlings as well as grown birds.

One day in mid-April 1979 we banded and released an owl in a large, open area with a few tamarack trees and some willows near the road. It was a dull, misty day and the ground was still covered with deep, wet snow. Upon release, the bird flew a short distance away, fluorescent-green tail gleaming, and landed on the snow. After standing for a few minutes, ruffling its feathers and staring back at us, it began walking across the snow, deliberately placing one foot before the other, moving with a heavy, waddling gait, not using its wings at all. Immediately I thought of the name given this bird by Indians along the Yukon River in Alaska;

according to zoologist William H. Dall (reported by Bent), the owl was called *nūhl-tūhl*, meaning "heavy walker." After a few minutes, posed motionless on the broad snowfield, the owl flew a short distance to another slightly elevated prominence, folded its wings, and again slowly walked about as if searching for something. When the owl repeated the sequence a third time, I was convinced the name was appropriate. If Indians saw Great Gray Owls walking on top of snow in this fashion, then I could understand their use of the name "heavy walker."

This incident also reminded me of an observation made of a wintering Great Gray Owl near Ottawa in 1969. Dan Brunton had followed a bird into a cedar thicket where it had gone, evidently searching for mice. His field notes record: "As I approached, the bird literally ran out from under the trees into the open . . . its tracks showed it definitely was running, one foot in front of the other. . . ."

Although its feet are small in proportion to its body size, one must remember that this is a relatively light-bodied bird. The feathers on the toes are lighter than in the Snowy Owl, but except for bare soles and three yellow scutes at the upper base of each talon, the feet are covered with short, dense, furlike feathers, undoubtedly an aid in walking or running on top of snow.

The owl kept in my home for a short period in November 1977 was so gentle I was able to let it perch on my bare fist; the bird rarely showed any inclination to tighten its talons. Thus I discovered that the soles of the feet were warm, a slight but oddly satisfying observation.

Like the Barred Owl, its close relative, the Great Gray Owl may be said to emit a hooting sound, but this statement fails to convey any semblance of the vocal capability of the species. It is doubtful whether written descriptions can properly portray the quality and variety of its vocalizations. A low, mellow hooting an-nounces the presence of the male, a series of regularly spaced notes of equal duration and interval and up to eight or twelve in succession, being the primary territorial song. Toward the end of a sequence the notes are given more rapidly and with decreasing volume. Reporting on a detailed study in Sweden, Wahlstedt describes this call, which he notes as being fairly weak compared to other species of owls, as a series of pumping sounds given about one and a half times per second. He observed that in certain body positions the tail wagged inward at each note. The call is reported to be audible under ideal conditions up to eight hundred meters. The male's territorial call may be given not only in early spring but also late in the breeding season in June and July.

Another call, used by both sexes and heard less often, consists of a series of double notes, given more rapidly (about three times per second according to Wahlstedt), and up to as many as a hundred times in one sequence. It is evidently a defensive or warning cry. It is weaker than the male's territorial call, carrying only about fifty meters, but it is given with great vigor.

A variety of rasping, screeching, cooing, or whistling calls have been described by several authors for both male and female Great Gray Owls. Probably most common is a soft mellow hoot or *Whoop!*, often given by the female on the nest as a means of communicating with the male. Hungry chicks give rapid, chattering, or chirping notes, a pleasant sound; when older they give harsh, rasping *Sher-rick!* calls. Wanting food for herself or, more likely, for her hungry young, the female calls softly or loudly: *"Sher-rick!,"* or gives an extended *"Shreek!"* Well-grown nestlings or birds that have left the nest may give the *Sher-rick!* begging call repeatedly. My observations agree with those of Valdemar Berggren and Jens Wahlstedt; reporting on a detailed study of vocalizations in the Great Gray Owl, they stated: "The female's call when fed by the male and during copulation is shown to be a reminiscence of the begging calls of the chicks and juveniles, and advertises the female's willingness to be approached by the male." This is the case in many bird species.

Somewhat similar vocalizations were given by the closely related Barred Owl during an apparent distraction display by a female with fledglings nearby, according to an observation described by David M. Bird and Jo Wright. Parmelee describes similar behavior for the Snowy Owl out on open tundra.

During alarm situations, the female often utters a loud, drawn-out sound that appears to be an extreme form of the begging call. And the strangest calls of this species are undoubtedly those given by the female during injury-feigning or distraction display. The greater the distress, the more extreme the calls. A loud, heronlike squawk or bark climaxes a series of notes ranging from vigorous hooting to high-pitched wails and squeals, all expressing great anxiety. This is probably the basis for many unusual calls ascribed in the literature to this species. (For a description of extreme distraction display, see pp. 130-31).

Vocalizations carry meaning not only in terms of specific syllables, but in intonation and strength as well. Thus, the numerous calls given by Great Gray Owls can, and do, vary according to different situations. In short, a wider range of vocal communication occurs in Great Gray Owls than is indicated here.

7

Short Days and Long Nights

It is twenty degrees below zero on a sunny day in January. Two feet of snow cover the ground. Near a spruce bog, a Great Gray Owl hunches on an aspen stub at the edge of an opening in the woods. Except for quick movements of its head, the owl is motionless, its mottled gray and white plumage blending with the pale and scarred bark of the tree.

Beneath the snow, fifty feet away, a little red-backed vole ascends a ventilation shaft, a frozen, crystalline tunnel leading to a small hole on the surface. Restless, it ventures from the warmer, burrow-ridden, leafy ground level to the icy, cold air above. The vole is surely dazzled by its first glimpse of the daytime world.

For the Great Gray Owl, patiently following each minute sound with gleaming eyes, the appearance of the vole has a galvanic effect. The owl launches forward with its powerful feet, wings unfolding with the precision of an umbrella mechanism, into a fast, steady glide that ends with a sudden downward pounce. One long, clawed foot arrives first, grabbing the vole securely; a swirl of snow particles shimmers momentarily in the bright light, then settles about the bulky, feathered creature.

For a moment the owl is motionless again, staring vacantly as it crouches with broad wings and tail outspread, flight feathers splayed upon the immaculate surface of the snow. Its ivory-smooth bill and bright, yellow eyes are like jewels set in dead wood. Sparkling snow crystals lie on the stricken vole's reddish-brown fur; locked in the owl's talons it is already dead, and a bright drop of blood, a crimson bead, lies in the snow beside it. Then the owl bends down, nips the vole sharply with its bill, brings its head up and swallows the warm, furry body with three gulps, saliva glistening along the hard edge of its bill.

Winter is a critical period for many animals. For Great Gray Owls, depending chiefly on small mammals—mice, voles, shrews—for food, availability of this restricted prey must be a significant factor in their distribution and movements. In Finland, according to Heimo Mikkola, these birds eat about four or fewer mice daily during summer months. Low temperatures of winter make greater demands on all organisms, however, and Great Grays probably eat far more in such periods. This is supported by W. Earl Godfrey's observation in the Ottawa district of one capturing and devouring five mice in half an hour. Probably, owls eat as much as they can catch, storing up fat against days when they are unable to get food. In exceptionally cold weather, time and effort spent searching for prey must be measured against the return. Staying close to good hunting grounds and resting for long periods, insulated by their heavy plumage, means saving energy, and reduces the amount of food needed to survive.

Faced with a scarcity of prey species, they can search for new hunting grounds, flying into new and unfamiliar country, settling down for long periods where mice are available, or making long, unsuccessful flights into areas where there are no mice. In the Scandinavian countries, on numerous occasions large numbers have perished from lack of food. Unable to find sufficient prey, faced with dwindling body reserves, they may become lethargic, appearing tamer than usual. Thomas Nuttall, the gifted English botanist and ornithologist, reported that Great Grays were ". . . occasionally seen in Massachusetts in the depth of severe winters. One was caught perched on a wood-pile, in a state of listless inactivity, in the morning after daylight, at Marblehead, in February, 1831. This individual survived for several months, and showed a great partiality for fish and birds." That owl, it may be noted, attracted the attention of John James Audubon. The great bird artist and

naturalist hurried to the scene, undoubtedly anxious to see his first live Great Gray Owl. One can still sense his disappointment upon finding when he arrived, as he noted later, that "it had died, and I could not trace its remains." Maurice Street, a meticulous birder, describes how a farmer in central Saskatchewan caught a weak and thin bird by hand in December 1955. Fed raw meat, "it became so tame it would follow him about the yard, even into his house. Unfortunately, it lived little more than a week."

Accounts of Great Grays feeding on carrion are few. In March 1974 a bird was reported eating fat and remnants of flesh from the remains of a butchered moose carcass in a yard close to a house in southeastern Manitoba. The bird seemed unafraid of people and paid little attention to two adult Saint Bernard dogs. This observation of carrion feeding is difficult to understand since there was an abundance of voles in the immediate vicinity; however, the snow was very deep at the time. For the same winter there is a report of apparent predation and cannibalism by an adult Great Gray Owl in Alberta. Bob Fisher observed one owl perched atop a still warm carcass of another that was slightly eaten. It was believed that the owl had attacked a weak or dying bird. Some Great Grays observed feeding on snowshoe hares and other large prey may have been feeding on road-kills. I have several reports of owls seen feeding on snowshoe hares caught in snares. It is not clear, however, whether in any of these cases the owl killed a struggling hare or was feeding on an already dead animal. In one observation, when approached by the trapper, the owl attempted unsuccessfully to fly away with the carcass, and was reluctant to leave. Robert Stitt wrote from Moosonee, Ontario, that he had found a hare completely removed from a snare. All that remained was a bit of hair and blood. Previously, martens had occasionally eaten snared hares, but he thought it unlikely a marten could consume an entire hare at one feeding. In addition to fresh marten tracks, he found a large feather from a Great Gray Owl at the site. At another time, Stitt, upon returning to his camp, saw a Great Gray Owl fly up from a spot near a pile of marten carcasses partly buried in the snow. At first the owl perched on a nearby ten-gallon gas drum, then flew away. One or two marten carcasses had been moved a foot or so away from the others, and there were wing marks in the snow. My informant presumed the owl had just begun scavenging. Ability to feed on carrion could help carry an owl through a period of food scarcity.

Although Great Gray Owls feed almost exclusively on small mammals, other prey occasionally are taken, for example, red squirrel, Norway rat, pocket gophers, moles, and weasels; duck, grouse, and songbirds. Still, I was surprised to find remains of an adult Sharp-tailed Grouse in a nest in June 1979. That's a heavy load, and I wonder how the male carried it to the nest, if indeed he brought the entire grouse. At the other extreme, a United States customs officer described to me how one night a Great Gray Owl pounced on a dragonfly fluttering about on the roadway beneath a bright light!

Despite the evidence that Great Gray Owls can capture small birds, the report of one collected many years ago with thirteen redpolls in its stomach is puzzling. I can't imagine a Great Gray catching that many active, sparrow-sized birds in one day. This particular specimen, a female, was obtained by Dall on April 11, 1868, near Nulato, Alaska, as noted by Bent. Perhaps the owl found a night roost or a flock of exhausted birds floundering in the snow after a severe coldsnap or snowstorm.

Recent published reports of Great Gray Owls being a threat to poultry strike me as an exaggeration of their known behavior. Thomas S. Roberts writes about a Great Gray Owl that killed two fowl by

entering a henhouse one December, but this appears to be a solitary and singular episode. I have several times assured local farmers or landowners that the large owl perched near their buildings was hunting mice, not house cats or domestic rabbits! On several occasions we captured a Great Gray Owl near a farm home, taking the bird indoors to demonstrate its docile nature and other characteristics. Even strong skeptics have changed their opinion of this bird after seeing one being measured at the kitchen table.

Attracting the attention of all observers who have watched these owls closely in winter, whether on their northern breeding grounds or elsewhere, is their ability to locate prey by sound alone. This capacity is most apparent in winter when owls are successfully capturing mice from deep beneath the snow, though it is of obvious advantage in hunting in heavy vegetation, in low light, and at night.

As often as not, when they turn those big heads they are simply directing their ears toward some intriguing sound, some faint scuttling in the grass. So their eyes sweep past us, seeming vague and unfixed as they concentrate on sound. Lacking their ability to probe beneath the snow, we are often puzzled by their actions. Late one winter evening we found a bird perched about ten feet high in a tree, engrossed in an event near the base. The owl stared down intently toward the blank surface of the snow, ignoring me as I carried in a live-trap to first a hundred, then fifty, and finally twenty-five feet. All the while, it paid scant attention to me, but kept peering steadily downward. After several minutes, during which the mouse in the trap, numb with cold and barely active, drew no response from the owl, I retrieved the trap. With some haste because of the growing darkness, Bob Taylor set out to try to capture the owl using a wire snare on the end of a long pole. To our surprise, he went right up to the bird and from directly in front of it began the difficult task of trying to fit the wire loop over its head. At that height and in the poor light, Taylor was unable to see the snare. An agonizing effort to bring the invisible snare into position followed; twice the pole bumped the owl's breast, but, absurdly, the owl paid no attention! When Taylor made a final, desperate attempt, the end of the pole hit the bird's bill. With a startled look, the owl shook itself, looked at his would-be captor as if suddenly seeing him for the first time, then unfolded his wings and flew off into the night.

When attempting to lure owls from distant perches we usually relied on a squeaking sound. With this we could get their attention, even from distances of a hundred yards or more. Law noted: "As the Great Gray Owl sits, slowly turning its head from side to side and sometimes looking straight down below it, we learn to know that it is picking up the sound of a mouse chewing up straw or grain. Silently it sails off its perch to a distance of about sixty yards, hovers over a spot for a few minutes and then drops suddenly down into the soft snow. After remaining motionless for a couple of minutes, it slowly raises one foot out of the snow with a dead mouse in its talons. The owl then proceeds to swallow the mouse whole, and after that it flies back to its perch or to another tree limb nearby"

Recent studies of hearing ability in Barn Owls have shown that this species can readily locate and capture prey in the total absence of light, relying on sound perception alone. Further, it has been discovered that they respond to a fairly specific range and type of sound, especially faint, rustling noises. So it should be no surprise that Great Grays can hear and locate mice beneath snow.

As reported by Law and others, the characteristic manner in which Great Grays capture prey beneath snow is by dropping down from a perch or from an almost motionless hovering position.

While hovering, the birds can look down almost between their feet. From this position they can get a good auditory fix on their prey. Usually, they then drop in a quick pounce, their long legs reaching down in readiness to seize prey. Godfrey noted that they did this with "legs extended fully, the thrust of the talons reaching to the ground under eight inches of snow." Brunton and Pittaway reported that a bird would hover "with legs dangling" and would then "crash into the snow and capture prey." As early as 1772 similar behavior was observed at Severn, Ontario, by Andrew Graham, who stated (and his observation was published almost verbatim by Nuttall fifty years later): "It chiefly resorts to the woods and fly [sic] in pairs living on mice, hares, etc. It flies very low yet seizes its prey with such force that in winter it will make a hole in the snow about a foot deep."

Our previous observations, and the above published descriptions of owls capturing prey in winter, gave little hint of the extraordinary behavior we were to see in owls hunting under deep snow conditions, especially in late winter 1973–74 and thereafter. Again and again, while we looked on with wonder, owls plunged deep into the snow in pursuit of prey, often briefly disappearing altogether. Typically, an owl would fly out from a perch, hover over the snow—apparently taking a final bearing on its prey—then partly fold its wings and plummet downward into the snow, sometimes vertically, at times at an angle. They did this so often and so successfully it would appear that this is an adaptation for preying upon small mammals in the deep, soft snow characteristic of northern forests.

The spectacle of these solemn-faced, relatively clumsy-looking owls sailing forth on their huge wings, then suddenly folding up and diving face downward into snowbanks astounded us. Much in the manner of terns, ospreys, and other birds that dive into water for prey, Great Gray

In this sequence, photographed at four frames per second, an owl fixes the location of prey under snow by sound, hovers, turns about, and plunges into the snow. It missed! Some idea of the speed of the dive may be gained from noting the position of the bird relative to the tree on the right in the last four photos.

Owls flung themselves into snow with the same carefree appearance. Observation and study of films and photographs revealed that though at times the feet were brought forward under the chin at the last moment, the plunge was often made with the feet well back under the tail, the owl entering the snow face foremost. The wings were closed at the last moment, but held out from the body so that they provided a brake, preventing the bird from going in too deep. Nevertheless, owls repeatedly plunged right out of sight, and occasionally remained below the surface for half a minute or more. Still, their wings, though not always visible to an observer, were usually on or close to the surface of the snow. Sometimes they emerged from the snow by raising themselves up on their spread primaries. Thus, the wings served not only to help absorb the shock of the plunge, but also to permit the bird to return to the surface.

Since Great Gray Owls have long legs, we wondered at first why they should have to exert themselves in this strenuous fashion. We finally decided that they were crashing down through soft snow to try for mice otherwise out of reach. The sudden and unexpected collapse of snow caused by an owl's plunge apparently demolished tunnels leaving a mouse or vole confused and cut off from escape. Once having plunged into snow after prey targeted by sound, the owls attempted to capture them with their feet. Often, when the back of an owl was above the snow we could see that it was making grappling motions, and foot and claw marks in the bottom of fresh holes gave a clear picture of this behavior. Their long talons permit an especially wide grasp, toes and talons spreading close to four inches fore and aft, doubtless a great assistance in making this kind of blind capture. By making a plunge and thrusting down with their feet, they could reach prey as deep as eighteen inches.

Owls that we saw capture prey often rested briefly, half-buried in the snow, then put their heads down to their feet, brought up a mouse with their bill and swallowed it with a few quick gulps. Dan Brunton noticed that they usually made a quick scan of the field around them for danger before proceeding to eat. After feeding, they frequently remained in the same place, at times with wings outspread, before returning to a perch. The appearance of an owl in this situation is aptly described by Earl Godfrey: "Once, in deep soft snow, the wings and bulky feathers were spread out over a surprising area, looking at a distance like a rug with an owl's head on it!" Brunton suggested that the spread wings could serve the owl as a glare guard, a means of reducing light reflected from the snow, and he thought it was done less often on cloudy days. Perhaps the dark gray or blackish feathers adjacent to the inner edge of their eyes serve the same function. In soft snow the outspread wings and tail also keep the bird on the surface, enabling it to rest. We couldn't always tell, when watching owls in action, if those that plunged out of sight were successful, but it seemed that a bird that missed prey flew up shortly afterward. Examination of some holes revealed a drop or two of blood, which we assumed to be evidence of a kill. On the other hand, on a few occasions when we saw an owl swallow prey, we were unable to find any blood in the hole.

Depth of plunge-holes varied, apparently depending on the total depth and softness of the snow, as well as the level at which the prey species were active. Where the major vegetative cover beneath the snow was alfala and, especially, sweet clover, meadow voles frequently fed at some distance above ground, judging by droppings and other evidence that we found in plunge-holes. The force with which owls plunged into snow could be appreciated by the degree of compaction of snow in the bottom of a hole. Inverted cone-shaped masses of crystallized snow almost a foot

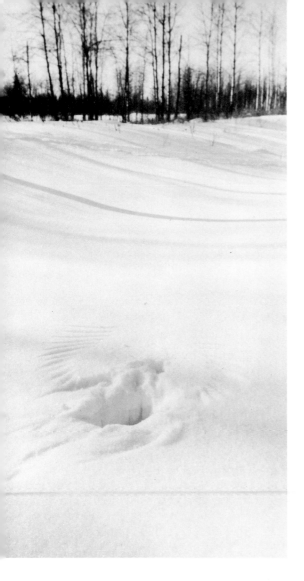

An owl has come and gone, leaving a distinct and lovely plunge-mark in the snow.

layer of snow on top of the crust preserved good impressions. At one hole, the wing length could easily be measured, and at five other holes an impression of an owl's face was visible, including in one case even the outline of the bill! These birds were apparently unable to break through the crust with their heads, or weren't trying, but in each instance they had been able to break through with their feet. The manner in which they plopped their faces against the crust made us wonder if the heavy facial disc feathers might not also provide protection for snow plunging.

Once we saw an owl, hunting along a line of utility poles a half-mile from any trees, plunge face-downward onto hard-packed drift snow beside a road. When the owl struck the snow it crumpled up and was still; I was sure it had broken its neck, for the bird had made no impression on the hard surface. A moment later, however, it raised its head, stood looking about for a second or two, then flew back up onto the pole.

Sometimes a successful bird would sit in the snow for a minute or more after swallowing its prey, and one bird had its head out of sight for a measured forty-five seconds. In late winter and spring, when occasionally the snow was wet and heavy, a plunging owl would have some difficulty getting back up onto the surface. We often wished we were close enough to net them, for at times it appeared that they were stuck in the snow.

I didn't really notice until March 14, 1979, that when an owl made a vertical plunge, the wings were partly withdrawn at the last moment so that for the final five feet there was a rapid acceleration. I noted this under perfect lighting conditions and later determined that this was the usual case. Also, at times plunging birds went so deep even the wrists went into the snow, so that only the tips of the primaries and tips of the tail feathers stuck up above the surface.

thick were removed from some old holes.

We often discussed what the owls would do if and when a crust formed on the snow. After this happened, they continued, to our surprise, to dive into the snow, breaking through quarter-inch and half-inch crusts. In mid-March 1974, when there was a one-inch crust under two inches of fresh snow, we checked a number of fresh holes in a field favored by three Great Gray Owls. The snow depth over the field ranged from twenty-three to thirty inches. Plunge-holes in several cases were made by birds mainly using their feet. These holes went down as much as ten inches, giving an idea of the reach of their legs. But some birds, judging by the evidence, had plunged head downward, even through this crust, whole bodies going down six or ten inches. The thin

It is curious that we did not observe snow-plunging until February 7, 1974. We had watched Great Gray Owls hunting in winter on many days in previous years, but this behavior was not noticed then; thereafter, it was seen each winter when we found owls.

Whether shallow or deep, plunge-holes left by Great Grays almost always have distinctive, crescent-shaped marks left by the folded wings on initial impact, as well as a fainter pattern of the spread primaries where the bird braced itself to lift out of the hole. Often, an impression of the tail can also be seen. Where owls were regularly pursuing prey in this way, plunge-holes were abundant. Thereafter, we frequently identified Great Gray Owl feeding sites by these characteristic signs of their

A burrow opening in the snow. Mice, voles, and shrews burrow to the surface after a fresh snowfall.

presence, looking at roadside snowbanks while driving through owl country. Plunge-holes often can be identified after they are many days old and even after a light snowfall. We have since found these distinctive signs almost everywhere we have seen owls.

Nothing in our previous experience, however, had quite prepared us for the sight of 128 fresh plunge-holes along a mile stretch on one side of a road. It was a bright day in late January, five days after a snowfall, and the numerous impressions were conspicuous on the otherwise smooth, white surface.

Herb Copland and I once saw a Hawk Owl plunge into soft snow, apparently hunting prey by sound. Since Hawk Owl-sized plunge-marks are rare, even where these birds are frequently seen, this is presumably an uncommon hunting technique in this species. Ornithologist Richard Knapton told me he watched a hunting Boreal Owl repeatedly plunge into snow in a wooded area near Winnipeg. Both species have the capacity to do this, but evidently employ it less often than does the Great Gray Owl.

The small eyes of Great Gray Owls, relative to their body size, as mentioned earlier, appear to be linked to daytime hunting, presumably another trait associated with long daylength in far northern latitudes. Great Grays can see surprisingly well, even in bright sunlight over snow, and it appears that their visual acuity serves them well. In early February at midday we watched a Great Gray fly out

92

with rapid wingbeats over an open field for at least two hundred yards to pounce on what we presumed was a vole on top of the snow. Similarly, Brunton and Pittaway reported seeing a Great Gray Owl in February fly approximately two hundred yards to snatch up a small mammal on the snow, apparently having seen the prey from that distance.

Nevertheless, Great Gray Owls are usu- ally most active during periods of low light in early morning and late afternoon and evening. Dull, overcast skies and falling snow produce similar conditions, sometimes bringing birds out in numbers. Although strong winds tend to keep them in the woods, occasionally we have found a Great Gray Owl on an exposed perch, feathers ruffling in the wind like loose clothing, staring across open fields.

8

Feathers on the Snow

Reaching far out on swaying birch branches, a Ruffed Grouse snips off six more buds, each time with an audible snap, then, bobbing its head as it seeks to regain its balance, it stands upright, poised against the gray, late evening, winter sky. Throat bulging with brown, resinous buds, the grouse ruffles its plumage, then flies off, wings clattering against twigs. Making a fast glide into a nearby tamarack grove, it changes perches twice, then, as is its nightly habit in winter, quietly dives into a snowbank in an open space between two trees.

In early morning light a Great Gray Owl, hungry after a cold night spent motionless on its perch, blinks its eyes, shifts from one foot to the other, then shakes out its feathers. The gray hunter drops down and drifts on broad wings through the frosty air, then rises abruptly, settling lightly onto a favorite perch on the tip of a dead tamarack, watchful, listening, head turning from one point to another. The first chickadee calls, plaintive awakening notes, then the owl suddenly cocks its head downward, its whole attention brought to a focus on the blank surface of the snow. Snug in its overnight cave, the grouse stirs, nibbles at the snow, then pushes upwards, thrusting its head out into the daylight. Sighting the small, dark object, the owl at once pounces, seizing the grouse's head, but the unexpected thrashing of wings brings it off balance. Leaning back on its tail the owl struggles to right itself, then bends forward, crushing the back of the feathered head with its bill. For a few seconds longer the grouse's wings futilely pound the snow.

Intent on plucking its prey, the owl fails to hear the soft footfalls of a rapidly approaching lynx. Padding lightly across the snow, the cat springs while the owl's head is down. One quick bite amid a flurry of wings, and the lynx has made its kill. Ears laid back, it pulls and tears at the owl carcass, feathers drifting across the snow. It devours all of the owl's scanty flesh, shearing off the long flight feathers as, with head tilted, it chews the wings. Rubbing one great, furry paw over its face to rid itself of clinging feathers, the lynx then sniffs at the half-buried grouse. In one quick motion it seizes the grouse in its jaws, turns, and pads quietly away.

Few accounts are available regarding natural enemies of the Great Gray Owl. Oeming suggested that black bears climb to nests to prey on young raptors, but without referring to a specific example of predation on the Great Gray Owl. We saw what appeared to be old claw marks on limbs near an occupied nest, fifty feet above ground. The Great Horned Owl appears to be a fairly serious cause of mortality. Oeming described a case in Alberta where one apparently killed and ate a Great Gray Owl, and three similar cases were reported to him by a trapper. One was observed near Lac du Bonnet, Manitoba, January 10, 1978, feeding upon a Great Gray Owl on the ice next to a small island. When approached, the owl made threatening signs and attempted to fly off with its prey, but it was left alone. The next day it was discovered that the victim was an adult female banded by us a month earlier about eight miles southward. In March 1978 remains of a second Great Gray Owl were found about six miles away on top of fresh snow in a situation suggesting predation by another Great Horned Owl. On May 5, 1979, in the same region, old Great Gray Owl feathers were found beneath a man-made nest; I estimated they were from a young owl possibly killed in July 1978. Mallard feathers were found at the same site. Presumably the nest where the feathers were found had served as a feeding platform for a Great Horned Owl that had raised three young in a nest about three hundred yards away. At least two other man-made nests were used as feeding platforms by Great Horned Owls. When biologists John and Frank Craighead released a captive Great Gray Owl within the nesting territory of a pair of Great Horned Owls, however, it established a temporary range and was not molested by the resident birds. When snowshoe hare populations are high and nest sites are limited, the Great Horned Owl may be a strong competitor as well as a predator.

In the previous chapter I mentioned a possible case of predation by a Great Gray Owl. According to Alex Lawrence, a Manitoba taxidermist found the remains of a Great Gray in the stomach of a Golden Eagle. The same species was reported by Nils Höglund and Erik Lansgren as a possible predator on the Great Gray in Sweden. A Goshawk attacked and killed a Great Gray Owl in Finland in the summer of 1978; this unusual incident was observed by Antti Leinonen and reported to me by Mikkola. An adult Great Gray Owl found dead on a roadside near Lac du Bonnet, Manitoba, on April 11, 1979, may have been the victim of an attack by Common Crows. When I received the bird I assumed it had been struck by a vehicle, but upon preparing it as a study skin I found only a shallow puncture wound in the outer edge of one eye, just deep enough to penetrate the brain. The small hole in the skull was wedge-shaped and could have been made by a crow's bill. Common Crows were reported active in the vicinity. A month earlier, two local residents of the same area told us that one of two Great Gray Owls seen near their home had been harassed by crows early in the morning. This was the first day that spring we saw crows, and they were fairly abundant. In the previous winter, birder Ray Tuokko saw a flock of crows harass and drive a Great Gray Owl into the cover of dense spruce trees. Common Ravens, on the other hand, which are frequently seen in the vicinity of Great Grays in winter, have never shown any aggression toward them or hardly any interest in them.

Even on its breeding grounds the Great Gray Owl has probably always been subject to some mortality by man. As reported by ornithologist W. E. Clyde Todd in the early 1900s, this species was often killed by natives at Moose Factory on the James Bay coast: "Together with other owls, they are caught in pole-traps, set up in a conspicuous position, and all are used for food." Undoubtedly, the steel trap was used to take owls as soon as the early fur traders brought it into this country. Even today, Cree Indians living at Winisk on the Hudson Bay coastline of Ontario, about a hundred miles east of Severn, are reported to kill Great Gray Owls for food at every opportunity. Old Crow Indians of Alaska considered Great Gray Owls "not bad eating, while the slightly more common Great Horned Owls are not particularly good," Laurence Irving mentioned in a 1960 bulletin of the United States National Museum. Owls were seldom eaten, however, except when food was short. As recently as 1976, natives were given an open season on Snowy Owls in three wildlife management areas in Alaska.

Great Gray Owls have also been used by native people for other purposes. The skinned facial discs of Great Gray Owls seem to have had special significance. The stiff, flattened circlet of feathers was removed intact, together with the supporting skin, then the center portion was carefully decorated with beadwork, perhaps in imitation of an owl's eye, but sometimes with floral designs. Often only one disc, that is, the feathers surrounding one eye, was used, but occasionally both discs were sewn together. In 1969 I purchased two modern versions of these artifacts in a native handicraft shop at Churchill. One of them bore a beaded replica of the 1967 Canada Centennial design, an interesting example of acculturation. Both curios, it turned out, were made from owls shot by a Cree Indian in the winter of 1968–69 at Herchmer, ninety-five miles south of Churchill. There are reports that in earlier times Cree Indians attached these decorated discs to dwellings. They also were used as a decoration at the point of attachment of carrying strap "tump lines" for cradle boards.

Winnipeg wildlife photographer George Cotter told me he had observed a skin of a Great Gray nailed to the door of a Cree Indian house at Winisk, Ontario, in late winter, 1974, but no explanation was offered for the practice. And at Grand Rapids, Manitoba, in 1975, I was informed, a Cree Indian father hung a dead owl, apparently a Great Gray, on the door of his home as a kind of babysitter; so long as the owl was on the door his young daughter was afraid to go outside. This use of owls, and especially the preparation of owl facial discs, may be a cultural trait of some antiquity. The Ojibwa Indians of Parry Sound in Ontario, as reported by anthropologist Diamond Jenness in 1935, kept children indoors in the evening with an owl mask made from birch bark and hung outside the wigwam.

Once when Clyde Todd was in James Bay, the late Sam Waller, naturalist and museologist, gave him a Great Gray Owl facial disc skinned by Indians and obtained by him when he was teaching at Moose Factory from 1923 to 1930; Waller told me he thought that this was Todd's first record for the species in the region.

Great Grays also are accidentally taken, along with other owls, in traps set for furbearers. Mice and shrews scrambling about in search of bait on or near traps must lure many owls to death from starvation, exhaustion, or freezing. In the winter of 1926–27, of eighteen Great Grays brought to a taxidermist in northern Minnesota, almost all had been caught accidentally in steel traps set for weasels and other mammals. A trapper from that era told me that in some winters when mice and shrews were abundant and active, owls would eat the bait off his traps—worse, they would also eat his trapped weasels. Recently, biologists in Ontario found a dead Boreal Owl with its leg in a trap and a dead vole still clutched in its talons. A Manitoba trapper found a live Great Gray in a trap set for lynx, a dead Ruffed Grouse suspended above the trap serving as bait. Since one foot was frozen to the trap he severed it with an axe, thus freeing the bird. It flew up and

This Cree Indian artifact from Churchill, Manitoba, was made from a Great Gray Owl's facial disc feathers, the center portion decorated with beadwork on leather in imitation of an owl's eye.

Two sides of an owl's circlet of feathers were used in making this disc, which bears a replica in beads of the 1967 Canada Centennial design.

perched on its remaining foot in a nearby tree, seeming little disturbed by the harsh treatment. I have had reports of at least five other Great Grays caught in traps in Manitoba. In view of the number of trappers working with the range of the Great Gray Owl, trapping may be a mortality factor of considerable significance.

Owls, along with hawks and other raptors, have long been persecuted by man for various reasons: as supposed competitors for game or fur, as a hazard to poultry, as natural enemies or easy targets, and for use as trophies. Henderson noted in Alberta: "In 1914, I made a very diligent search for a nest of the Great Gray Owl, exploring every likely piece of timber for several miles around Belvedere, but without success. I saw a couple of birds but was unable to find a nest and almost came to the conclusion that their nesting here in 1913 had been accidental and might not occur again. I think one reason for my failure was the fact that a useless homesteader had located in my best hunting ground and amused himself by killing every owl and hawk he could and tacking them to the side of his shack."

Walter B. Barrows, writing about Michigan birds in 1912, noted: "Judge Steere, of Sault Ste. Marie, tells me that he has seen several specimens [of Great Gray Owls], more or less mutilated, hung up at deer camps in the woods in Chippewa and neighboring counties."

In 1955 Albert Oeming wrote as follows: "Few of North America's most travelled ornithologists have ever seen this continent's largest owl, the handsome Great Gray Owl (Strix nebulosa). Moreover, it is likely that even fewer will be privileged to see it in years to come, for the numbers of this species appear to be diminishing steadily.

"Less than twenty-five years ago the bird was not uncommon in the remote woods of Northern Alberta and throughout the rest of Northern Canada. When the coat of the Red Squirrel began to be used for fur, however, the situation changed suddenly and radically. This addition to the fur list led to the invasion of the great spruce forests of Northern Alberta by thousands of trappers. Since most trappers are imbued with a universal prejudice against owls, believing that all of them prey heavily on fur-bearing animals such as squirrels and so seriously reduce the potential profits of trapping, the Great Gray Owl was condemned along with the ubiquitous Great Horned Owl. As the Great Gray does not have the wary and suspicious nature of the latter species, it made an easy target for trappers' guns. Its decline in numbers was alarmingly swift. . . ."

Heaviest mortality occurs to Great Gray Owls during their irregular winter incursions south and east of their main breeding range in Canada. In the winter of 1842–43 seven were collected in Massachusetts. One can guess that in that early period others were killed but not recorded. About six dead ones were "exposed for sale in the Montreal markets" in the winter of 1876, all having been obtained either on Montreal Island or nearby. A "great flight" took place in southern Ontario and southwestern Quebec in 1889–90; as was typical of those days, many were shot for trophies, forty-nine being handled by two persons. The following winter a taxidermist in eastern Maine received twenty-seven dead ones. In the winter of 1922–23 Winnipeg was invaded by Great Grays; later, columnist Harold Mossop wrote that "numbers were shot by irresponsible gunners." A local birder who was active during that period recalled that after a Winnipeg taxidermist died, his stock of mounted birds was sold at an auction. There were a number of raptors in the collection, including several Great Gray Owls that were sold for twenty-five cents each!

During the winter of 1950–51 a taxidermist at Swastika in northern Ontario received thirty-six dead Great Grays by the end of January. An invasion in southeastern Manitoba and Minnesota in the winter of 1968–69 probably involved more than a hundred birds, as many as twenty reaching the Minneapolis-St. Paul area. Of twenty-four dead owls recorded that season in Manitoba, at least thirteen had been shot. For Minnesota, Janet C. Green noted: "many of the owls died before they were able to make the return journey." The following winter, numbers of Great Grays appeared in northern Minnesota; I found remains of eleven dead ones, more

than half of which had been shot. In 1972 an Alberta observer, William E. McKay, wrote: "A freshly killed Great Gray Owl was found along a road this winter near Rocky Mountain House. Whoever shot it took the time to cut off both legs and took them as trophies but left the owl near where it fell on the snow."

A heavy toll of wintering owls also is taken by collision with motor vehicles. Great Gray Owls fly low across even busy highways, ignoring passing vehicles, gliding slowly, clearly unaware of any danger. Apologetic drivers have brought in dead or crippled owls that flew into their vehicles "as if they were blind." One owl standing on the shoulder of a highway was struck and killed by a snowplow, much to the astonishment of the operator, who had expected the big bird to fly away.

From 1970 to 1979 I recorded forty-three dead owls in our area (not including the eleven I found shot or car-killed in adjacent Minnesota in early spring 1970). Of these, twenty-three were vehicle-collision casualties, four died of unknown causes, two were predated, two were electrocuted, one died after being caught on a barbed-wire fence, and twelve had been shot. One can assume that others were shot and carried away by aspiring taxidermists or trophy seekers. There is a recent report of an owl having been electrocuted in Alberta; after talking to Manitoba and Winnipeg Hydro-Electric employees about two found in our area in 1979, I am convinced that the toll from this source is higher than these few records suggest. Birds accidentally electrocuted on transmission lines are not as likely to be found as birds that die on highways.

Thanks to an enlightened and cooperative public and field staff of the Manitoba Department of Natural Resources, nearly all Great Gray Owls found dead in the province have been obtained by us for use as scientific study skins. These specimens, which have been positively identified to sex, have provided extremely useful information, and are permanently available for further study. Although the preparation of a study skin takes time (about three hours each, as I discovered in the course of preparing more than a dozen in the winter of 1978–79), the benefit to be derived from the specimen far outweighs its use as a mounted bird in someone's home.

Loss of owls through starvation and collision with vehicles can't be controlled, but shooting, which is still an important mortality factor affecting Great Gray Owls, needs to be eliminated. In many regions, despite legal protection, birds of prey are still being shot, either in righteous defense of game species, out of idle curiosity, or through ignorance. Present laws are relatively new, myths are difficult to overcome, and hawks and owls are relatively easy targets. Moreover, magistrates and others who rule on prosecutions, not knowing the value of raptors, often levy only minor fines. If hawks and owls were as numerous as grouse, perhaps it wouldn't matter so much. Ruffed Grouse populations, for example, are little affected by hunting, though hundreds of thousands are shot annually, for they are an abundant species with high reproductive rates. Except in cyclic lows, one can expect to find them everywhere in suitable habitat. Birds of prey, however, being on top of a food chain, are scarce, have low reproductive rates, and some are now rare.

For many people a hawk or owl is a wonderful creature, an element of the wild. But not for all. Everyone thrills to see a deer, but predatory birds generally don't seem to be admired in the same way. The words "predator" and "predatory" in themselves suggest a fearsome creature and an unpleasant kind of behavior. This partly relates to a misunderstanding of the role of the predator. A sentimental view of predation, colored by an unwarranted sympathy for the prey species, whether mouse or chickadee,

merely adds further weight to the myth. Just as the wolf has for so long been thought of as big and bad, so hawks and owls and other raptors have been looked upon as harmful and even evil. For many people there is something repugnant about one warm-blooded vertebrate animal killing another, an act considered much less acceptable than predation on butterflies or earthworms.

Herman J. Brown, a poultry farmer with lots of experience with avian predators, summed up his feelings about them in 1953: "It is well for everyone to know the capacity of these birds for harm, but I don't wish to give the impression that I am in any sense their enemy, or that any poultry grower should act against them without cause. During the years I spent alone [on a farm in northern Wisconsin] they and other animals were my chief source of mental stimulation and entertainment. No one with that experience could feel anything but an abiding friendship for them. Those Goshawks! In retrospect, the image of their savage perfection is worth a good many chickens."

Sportswriters and gun dealers, unfortunately, continue to refer to unprotected animals as vermin, using the terms "varmints" and "varmint-guns," thus extending the notion that animals are either good or bad. In the dictionary, however, "vermin" applies to any "mammals and birds injurious to game, crops, etc." This old definition hardly works any longer, for sportsmen are gradually learning the value of wolf predation on deer and are more than willing to pay the cost of grain eaten by Mallards. Despite this evolution of thought, however, many sportsmen still are reluctant to give up grouse to feed Goshawks, for so long have these and other raptors been identified as targets for "plinking."

Sportsmen also must learn that it is no longer fashionable to display mounted hawks or owls as trophies or decorations in dens. Now that raptors are protected there is no more reason for hanging them on our walls than songbirds or gulls. A mounted bird in a museum case or in a conservation exhibit has educational value. But the hawk, owl, or eagle displayed as a trophy is an anomaly, an artifact of the past. Today in Manitoba (and until 1979 in Ontario), in order to have a raptor mounted legally a permit must first be obtained, and a permit is issued only when it can be shown that the specimen will be used for educational purposes. Even if a person finds a dead hawk or owl (or claims to have found it), he is unable to have it preserved legally for private use. Thus, another incentive for shooting raptors has been removed.

Reducing illegal shooting is one step; getting hunters to appreciate and enjoy hawks and owls and other raptors is perhaps more important. This educational task should begin in the classroom. The task is of turning hunters into hunter-naturalists. Convincing a hunter to buy his first bird book may be worth more than selling a second one to a confirmed birder. Hunters need to realize that learning to recognize raptors is more fun and a better challenge than using them for targets. Being actively involved with wildlife and the outdoors, and often engaged in efforts to increase and maintain wildlife habitat, hunters are all potential naturalists. With binoculars and bird books so readily available, an additional feature of the sportsman's day afield may yet include watching hawks and owls.

Interest in rehabilitation of injured raptors has increased in recent years, with several centers or individuals now receiving birds from various sources. Those that can be brought to a state of normality are released; permanently disabled birds are kept for propagation purposes (with progeny being released to the wild), or turned over to zoos. Three injured Great Gray Owls have been turned over by us to the Owl Rehabilitation Research Foundation at Vineland, Ontario. To ensure the safe

journey of the first of these, an adult female owl with a broken wing, Mrs. Katherine ("Kay") McKeever of the Vineland center flew to Winnipeg. After several phone calls and considerable discussion with Department of Transport Officials, staff of the Winnipeg International Airport, and the flight crew of a major airline, permission was granted to take the bird on board the jet plane. Kay then changed her ticket to first class (because that section was empty), and bought a colorful baby sleeper outfit in which she tucked the owl. After carefully covering its face with a pink blanket, Kay boarded the plane, assisted by a stewardess. I have often wondered what the reaction would have been had any interested person between Winnipeg and Toronto lifted the blanket to look at the baby.

9

A Time of Change

On cold February mornings, frost-laden air lies heavy over the land. Against the early light of dawn every branch, every twig glistens with frost crystals. Old owl nests lie silent in the warped crowns of tamarack trees, exposed to any prying eyes. Though there is little protection from wind, snow, and cold in such a nest, this does not deter Great Gray Owls, who may be crouching upon eggs in a nest in mid-March. Crackling cold temperatures test the adaptations of this species to weather at northern latitudes.

Despite the low temperatures, the owls unknowingly respond to changing daylength, and certain behavior gradually changes, too. The male, instead of immediately swallowing a captured mouse, carries it to a nearby perch and sits motionless, staring quietly, prey hanging from its bill. It is a tantalizing sight for the female. Drawn to the same feeding grounds and perhaps competing for food, engaged for long periods in nocturnal bouts of hooting with each other and others of their kind, the pair has for several months reacted to each other aggressively and cautiously.

The sight of the dangling mouse releases in the female an ancient pattern—a curious mimicry of a hungry, young owl—shifting her weight deliberately from one foot to the other, bobbing her head and hooting softly, she begins chirping like an owlet. The male is mesmerized by this performance, hearing a sound he has not heard since attending a nest eight months earlier. He sits, watching closely as she flies toward him and lands on a nearby perch. Now they are closer than they have been all fall and winter. After some hesitation, for she is larger than he is, stimulated by the female's continued display, the male flies to perch beside her, closing his eyes as he leans toward her, holding out the mouse. With closed eyes and a slight mewing sound the female seizes the mouse. At the moment the female takes the mouse from the male the pair bond is formed or renewed.

The ritual of courtship feeding will be repeated again and again, strengthening the social bond. Many days will pass before there are eggs in a nest, but this crucial behavior determines their new relationship.

Pair formation, courtship, mating, and territoriality are among the least documented aspects of Great Gray Owl behavior. Earlier observations, although sporadic, indicated the existence of a considerable repertoire. In the past two years, especially, observations of captive and wild birds have helped to build a substantial, though yet incomplete, story of what happens. There is now evidence that aerial displays, mutual preening, and courtship feeding occur in this species.

Occasionally, in February and March, we have seen a Great Gray Owl capture a vole and then, departing from the usual pattern of winter feeding in which prey is eaten as soon as captured, carry it away in its bill and sit idly on a perch for a minute or two before feeding. This may be one of the first overt signs of breeding behavior in the male. Some time between January and April, pair formation and courtship take place. During this period the male feeds the female, thus establishing a close relationship with her.

In the Snowy Owl the sight of the male carrying a lemming provides stimulation leading to nesting behavior. As the courting male approaches with a lemming in its bill, according to Philip Taylor, it moves in a slow, undulating flight with wings raised in a V over the back. Parmelee has suggested that the number of available lemmings, and the rate at which the male can bring them to the female, work in some obscure fashion to initiate nesting and even to determine the number of eggs that the female lays! "When lemmings are abundant, the male places a goodly number of his catch beneath a favorite perch. Although we have never witnessed this piling up of lemmings by the male before the female, we have seen the evidence—upwards of a dozen uneaten lemmings scattered on the ground below a perch. At one perch we counted 26 lemmings in one heap!"

When small mammals abound, Great Gray Owls do well, raising large families

and tolerating others of their own kind as well as other raptor species at close range. In such years they may lay as many as nine eggs, though a clutch of four is about average.

Perhaps, as in the Snowy Owl, the female Great Gray Owl is stimulated to lay a larger clutch by the frequency with which the male brings prey; up to six dead voles have been found lying on the edge of an active nest. It also has been theorized that courtship feeding has important nutritive value; during the period in which the eggs are developing, the female's energy requirements are greater than the male's.

When mice or voles are scarce, only one or two eggs may be laid, or the birds may not nest at all. If there should be a shortage of food after the eggs have hatched, then the growth rate of the young may be greatly reduced and some chicks may perish. The rapid growth rate of nestlings under normal development requires an abundant food supply. Höglund and Lansgren have shown that five days after hatching, a young owl may have tripled its weight and at two weeks of age may reach five hundred grams, from about forty grams at hatching.

Great Gray Owls demonstrate their interdependence in nesting as well as food habits. They habitually choose an abandoned or vacant nest built by another species, hence their nests vary in size, location, and condition. In our region, Common Crow, Common Raven, Red-tailed Hawk, and Broad-winged Hawk nests are probably most frequently used. The height of nests occupied by Great Gray Owls ranges from eight to sixty-five feet above ground; in Scandinavia, nests have been found on low stumps and even on the ground. Despite published statements to the contrary, there is no evidence of which I am aware that Great Gray Owls add any nest material.

Unlike the eggs of most owls, which are round, the chalk-white eggs of Great

Grays are decidedly ovoid or conical, a characteristic perhaps of some advantage when laying in old, well-used nests that sometimes have an unyielding, level surface. For a bird of the size of the Great Gray Owl, the egg is surprisingly small, being a little more than two inches in length and noticeably less in width, not even as large as a hen's egg.

Probably some time prior to breeding, one or more nest structures, perhaps one used by the pair in a previous year, become focal points for their activities. We have evidence that Great Grays visit nests as early as mid-February, at least in mild winters in this region. Since egg-laying may begin here in mid-March or earlier, it should be no surprise to find birds looking over potential nest sites a few weeks in advance. Nest-searching behavior was observed by Henderson in west-central Alberta on March 19, 1915. Shortly before dark he found a bird in a nest and another perched nearby. The bird in the nest "made a deep booming sound and the one on the limb a kind of whistle. After about a minute the one on the nest flew away and its mate followed. . . . The Owls had not yet decided which nest they would use. They were merely house-hunting."

On April 20, 1974, Spencer Sealy and I found a pair of owls in the vicinity of two nests a few hundred feet apart. The female was bolder than the male and remained perched near the larger of the nests. Initially disappointed not to see her at this nest four days later, we found her instead in the second nest, lying low and motionless as if on eggs. We returned a few minutes later with tree-climbing spurs, but she was gone, and the nest was empty. Four days later we were even more surprised to find her sitting in the first nest incubating two fresh eggs!

Although the male may play an important role in finding nests, the female probably makes the final choice. Höglund and Lansgren noted of Great Gray Owls in Sweden: "To all appearances, the owls visit various nests and finally they decide upon one of them. The male calls at the nest, but it seems that the female is the one determining whether or not the nest can be approved. At the time of our visit [end of April 1961] none of the great gray owls had laid their eggs. Yet they were staying in the neighborhood of the nests, and some of them were even observed in the nests."

Defense of territories appears minimal, some Great Grays in Sweden, for example, showing a surprising tolerance and nesting as close together as a hundred meters. Possibly this depends on rodent abundance. When prey is scarce, the male may search for hours over a wide area. Maximum diameter of the range at a nest in Wyoming, as reported by the Craighead brothers, was one and a quarter miles. Where prey is locally abundant the male may find all he needs within a half-mile or less of the nest. Selection of a nest seems to be based in part on the presence of high prey population. Aggressive encounters on winter feeding grounds, in some cases far from breeding sites, may be understood partly in terms of competition for food. Since sexual behavior in this species begins early in the season, however, encounters in late February and March may have some sexual connection. On February 24, 1974, when we forced an owl to move back into a woods, a marked female sitting up high and watching about a hundred yards away at once flew toward it and they grappled, hitting feet together in midair. This was within a few hundred yards of a nest later occupied by the attacking female. A half hour before sunset at another locality a few weeks later, two birds, first seen flying about in wide circles, approached each other in an apparently aggressive manner. One made a pass at the other and then flew up above it. They briefly came together, tussled in midair, and tumbled down to the snow before flying off in separate directions.

We have heard and seen females soliciting males by begging for food, and on a few occasions the male of a pair has been seen capturing prey and then flying off with it while accompanying or following the female into woods. Two examples follow: On March 18, 1979, we watched a pair of birds actively hunting in bright light from 6:15 to 10:00 a.m. Neither responded to any of our lures; they seemed too engrossed in each other to pay any attention to us. Once, both birds perched a few feet apart on the cross-arm of a power pole. We returned later that evening and found them back out again, behaving in much the same way. For a long time the male sat on top of a pole, occasionally glancing down at two live mice in a bal-chatri trap. Then, as if on signal, as the female headed toward the woods, the male casually dropped off his perch, plunged into the snow, and emerged with prey in one foot. He flew directly after the female, both disappearing in approximately the same direction.

Late in the evening on March 24 that same year, we found another pair engaged in similar activity, and equally unresponsive to our lures. Both birds appeared to be actively searching for prey, particularly the male who was busily shifting his head about, scanning the snow. Within a few minutes he dove down, came out of the snow with a vole in his foot, and flew off to perch close beside the female. It looked as if we were about to witness courtship feeding, but they flew off into the woods, the female leading, the male still holding the prey.

On March 2, 1975, Ray Tuokko found a concentration of thirty-three fresh plunge-holes in woods within a quarter-mile or less of an old nest. Three plunge-holes were found close to the nest tree; no plunge-holes were found outside this locality. Apparently, a male, or a pair, had hunted successfully (judging by spots of blood at some holes) for a few days around a potential nest site.

Plunging itself appears to be a part of pair formation or courtship, in some cases being performed as display rather than functional behavior. There were times in late winter, especially, when birds seemed in a frenzy of plunging activity; when overly desperate plunges suggested something more than hunger as motivation.

The entire flight sequence, beginning with soaring out over an open area, hovering, and then at last dropping down into or onto the snow, was seen by us on several occasions under circumstances indicating a display function. We observed an aerial display of this type for the first time on February 19, 1978. A bird, presumed by size and behavior to be a male, was seen on several occasions in December 1977 on the edge of a woods adjacent to farmland. It was the same vicinity, if not the same tree, where a male had regularly perched in late winter 1974, prior to occupying a nearby nest. The new male was shy and retreated each time a car approached. As we neared it, the bird flew into the woods and out of sight. We parked about a hundred yards away and, as an experiment, I played a tape recording of the begging call of a female owl, one kept by me briefly the previous November. Almost immediately the male came back out. Upon my repeating the tape, the bird twice flew slowly over an open field in level flight, wings atilt. Without pausing it turned and slowly flew back onto its perch. Two or three times it looked back into the woods, even though the tape was still running. Later I glimpsed a second bird, presumably a female. I am convinced that the female begging call had elicited courtship display in a territorial male.

It is not always easy to tell whether a bird is seeking prey or just going through the motions. On one occasion, we had two owls in sight. One bird (the female?) had forced the other (the male?) out into an open area. The bird in the open acted, in some respects, as if it were hunting, flying out over the meadow, hovering, and then dropping down onto the snow, but it did this in a casual manner. When the bird performed a third or fourth time closer to us (and not coincidentally closer to the first bird), landing on a paved road, the display function became clear. The owl took a few steps as if searching for prey, then hopped up onto blocks of frozen snow on the edge of the road, peering and leaning forward excitedly as if it had prey in sight. The first owl, still in sight, clearly was the stimulus object, for when it flew away, the bird on the road in front of us flew off after it!

On March 3, 1979, two owls came chasing after the cast lure at about the same time. This led to a brief antagonistic flurry between the two competitors, followed by what could only be described as a bout of snow-plunging. The next day, despite the advantage of three witnesses to interpret actions of three owls in sight, we still were puzzled by events of a similar nature. It was an exceedingly bright, mild afternoon. Things began to get complicated when I cast the lure for the nearest bird. Its approach was cut short by a second, more distant bird that came in faster and drove the first bird off. The two circled above us in a brief flurry of broad, flapping wings, a silent, spectacular clash. Seconds later, the harassed bird (I thought, but not all agreed) began rapidly snow-plunging, circling, hovering, and dropping in casual, random fashion; hardly with any time to detect prey. Soon two, and then all three birds were doing this. None seemed serious about catching anything, at times merely dropping onto the snow, then looking about as if to see what the others were doing. We had difficulty keeping track of the birds' identities as they circled and crossed each other's paths, and we couldn't be sure of the sexes. Still, it was a moment of splendid confusion. It seemed evident that this was pseudo-hunting behavior, whether functioning as courtship, appeasement, or territoriality.

One of the most detailed observations of pair interaction was made late in the evening of March 11, 1978, by Ray Tuokko. He had observed a male and female on three weekends hunting in an area of open fields surrounded by aspen and mixed-wood forest. A slightly revised version of part of his notes follows:

The female, hunting in one field, caught a rodent after five minutes' observation. She continued hunting for ten minutes, flying in large circles or completely across the field, hovering and plunging. She then flew to trees near a road, and the male was noticed approaching from the opposite end of the field. He perched in a tree some distance from her, whereupon she flew toward him. He flew out to meet her as she neared his perch and "he chased her around the tree twice, then both landed in the same tree, with the female 10 feet lower and on the opposite side of the tree. They remained there about 10 minutes, occasionally shifting position. The male occasionally bowed and tipped his tail up as if he were anticipating a flight." Both constantly turned their heads in all directions as if listening to some unseen bird, or possibly responding to the observer.

Next, the female left her perch, immediately pursued by the male. "They proceeded in a spiral, flapping flight of about 20 to 30 feet in diameter. They circled about in this manner, gaining about 40 to 50 feet altitude. . . . I could hear their wings touching noisily during the flight, but there was no body contact. This flight was terminated by a steep descent to nearby trees." At this point, partly because of the failing light and distance, the size differences could not be discerned. "They remained perched for about 5 minutes, then commenced an undulating, circular flight amongst the trees, so that *I could hear their wings banging recklessly against branches.*"

A little later Ray moved toward where the birds had disappeared and found an owl he thought was the male. It was very alert and kept turning its head as if listening to distant sounds. The male then flew toward Ray and perched nearby, alternately looking directly at him and in the direction of the female. He thought the male was defending his territory, or at least placing "himself between me and the female."

Based on this extended observation of a pair, the next day (March 12) Ray built a nest nearby in a small spruce-tamarack stand. The nest was successfully occupied by Great Gray Owls that season, likely the courting pair seen by Ray, for no other birds had been using that area. One of three eggs in the nest hatched on May 13, indicating a probable first laying on April 14, just four weeks after the nest was constructed!

Preening is one of the strongest patterns evident in pair bonding behavior for the Great Gray Owl, and can be readily elicited from both sexes, and adults as well as sub-adults. Every grown owl I have tested has shown a strikingly similar response. All I have had to do is to get the bird's attention and then push the top of my head toward its face. This gesture of submission leads the bird to run its bill through my hair, gently nibbling along the scalp and often seizing and pulling on a few hairs. Even badly injured birds have shown this response, but it varies in extent, depending on the individual and circumstances. Usually, as soon as I offer a bird the top or sides of my bare head it at once alters its facial plumage, pulling back the facial discs, raising the rictal bristles, stretching its neck up to full length, and then tilting its head to one side with partly closed eyes. Then it preens. When it stops and withdraws, the behavior can be elicited again by pushing my head against its face. Between preening bouts it often maintains the whole peculiar attitude, in the extreme position holding its head tipped sideways. Usually the pupils are constricted.

It also frequently bumps its bill against my head and occasionally I return the favor, repeatedly bumping my nose against its bill. Even aggressive birds can be treated in this fashion—and I am convinced that this helps reduce their aggressiveness—although a recent nose bite has led to some restraint in my bill-to-bill encounters.

In 1954 Al Oeming observed preening in a pair of captive Great Gray Owls: "The male would fly to the female's stump and face her. Standing face to face with breasts touching, he would commence rubbing his beak over hers, at the same time uttering a faint droning or humming sound. Often he would circle her face with his beak in a similar manner. This was observed regularly for eight days and would occur at any time during the day or night." Recently, similar behavior was reported in the related Barred Owl; in the summer of 1972, John W. Fitzpatrick witnessed and photographed mutual preening or "allopreening" in two wild birds. As reported by him in an ornithological journal; "Most preening was directed at the edges of the facial discs and the feathers surrounding the bill. . . . Periodically owl A gave thin, high-pitched notes reminiscent of those of a small dog while preening and, more consistently, while being preened. . . . Allopreening . . . appears to function as a means of sex recognition in some monomorphic species, and it may, in addition, provide a ritualized mechanism for pair bond maintenance in species that pair for extended periods."

Signs of pair formation: male on the left, female on the right. Note the compressed plumage of the male and the fluffed plumage of the female. A few minutes later, the male caught a vole and, carrying it in his bill, followed the female into the woods.

The functions of allopreening were recently reviewed by Eric Forsman and Howard Wight. Their study, which included observations of this behavior in the closely related Spotted Owl, led them to suggest that allopreening is ritualized aggressive pecking or biting, appearing as a peaceful interaction between individuals.

Following a fortuitous irruption in late winter 1978–79 of Great Gray Owls into the Ottawa area far from known breeding grounds, preening was observed for the first time in the wild. Richard M. Poulin, an ornithologist at the National Museum of Canada, kindly consented to let me publish this key observation. As reported by him, by late February pairing seemed to have occured in some of these displaced birds. On February 27 at least four apparent pairs were observed, two pairs being in the same tree. Of these latter, one pair kept in "very close proximity to each other . . . [they] were seen to bend towards each other until they were noticeably horizontal. In this position they were seen to preen each other about the face and head. The smaller male bird was most active. . . . This preening and caressing . . . lasted between 15 and 20 minutes. We could detect no sounds associated with this behavior. . . . The preening occurred between 8 and 9 a.m. The weather was warm (2° C) with heavy overcast and flurries, little wind."

Highly perceptive and significant observations of preening (or grooming) and courtship feeding have been made of a pair of captive Great Gray Owls by Katherine McKeever at the Vineland, Ontario, Owl Rehabilitation Research Foundation. The female owl was a one-winged amputee from Manitoba (for *that* story see the last paragraph in Chapter 8, p. 100), in residence with Kay and her husband, Larry, since March 1977. Otherwise in excellent health, the owl moved about her sumptuous quarters by walking along a series of long perches. The male, a bird from Moosonee, Ontario, recovering from trap-injured feet, was introduced into a large, outdoor cage in late December 1977. In early February 1978, when the male had recovered sufficiently so that he could feed himself, the female was put in with the male. Kay's notes (spring 1978) are so marvelously descriptive that I have used almost her entire letter:

"Initially—that is, for about two days!— she was surprisingly aggressive towards him but on the morning of the third day I was astounded to see them sitting side by side—wings almost touching—and both looking as if they had ALWAYS sat together that way! It was later in the afternoon of the same day that I saw them grooming each other, the male making the first moves and sticking the top of his facial discs toward her at the level of her mandibles, with his eyes closed. She would lean towards him a little and groom the edges of his discs, with her eyes closed too. Then she would often groom herself, following this (or preceding it) by stropping her beak on the perch as if to wipe something off it!

"Later (i.e., several days) he grew bolder and would fly to her and groom her first, then bowing his head and inviting her to groom him. When they had been together for about two weeks, it seemed to me that if they weren't dozing they were grooming! He would lift one of her feet in his talons, without apparently throwing her off balance, and nibble at it gently—much in the same way that I have seen owls nibbling at their own toes, as if cleaning the base of the talons. Even though her foot was thus held out and up at a slightly awkward (to human eyes) angle to her roosting body, she usually kept her eyes closed. Sometimes she would chitter a little and he would then let go, so I took the chitter to be a mild protest.

"Another grooming action that I saw three or four times was the male 'combing' the breast feathers of the female with the talons of one foot. At such times, their bodies were turned towards each other on the pole perches, whereas in the foot-lifting and grooming routine, the female remained perched with her left flank to the male.

"I cannot say which one usually initiated the facial grooming because when I looked at them they were either asleep or already at it! However, from my observations it was almost always the male who flew to the female, if they were on different poles, and at such times he would approach her and make the first advances, usually by stretching out his face to her, with eyes closed, and either be groomed or nibble at her discs. On the other hand, she groomed him much longer than he groomed her, and at such times they were very close—side breast to side breast—and he seemed to have telescoped his body down to a very low height, eyes tightly closed, plumage half fluffed, while she towered over him, nibbling at the top of his head, the back of his head, his face and side neck and around his mandibles and ears. Often this was accompanied by contented little sighs and grunts, although

I couldn't tell from which owl they came—perhaps from both.

"In April (13th) I saw him up on the pole adjoining her favourite pole, with a mouse dangling from his mouth. He would put it down, hold it on the perch with one foot, pause, take it in his beak again, turn around a few times, look around (it didn't seem to me, specifically AT her) and put it back under his foot again. Eventually he would eat it, sometimes on the spot, sometimes flying off with it. Four days later I watched him lodge the mouse, with some care, at the confluence of the two poles and go away and leave it. I never saw her take it but it always was gone in about an hour's time. On April 19th he ran back and forth along her pole and the adjoining one, with the mouse hanging from his beak and FINALLY went right up to her and thrust out the mouse, eyes closed. She turned her head on the side so her beak was at right angles to his and closed her eyes as she touched the mouse.

"There was quite a bit of vocalization

At some time during the courtship period a nest is visited by the pair. The female sits on the nest for a few days, and may visit more than one nest.

in the preamble to the food transfer, almost all from him. It was a soft, low, series of one-note rapid hoots. Does she make this noise to remind him of the noise he makes when he brings it, thus triggering his action, or is there a paucity of available noises, and this one means bringing food—whether asking for it or offering it??? I haven't heard the female Great Gray Owl make this noise yet, but she hasn't been on eggs yet, or fed young.

"By April 23rd the male dangled the mouse and the female came to HIM and took it. By April 27th she came right to the platform where he sat and took the mouse. Later that evening I saw her pick up a mouse that was draped over the platform edge, and eat it. I have to assume that he put it there, although to my amazement, on the 28th, I saw *her* down at the food box taking a mouse for herself, and walking up one of the ascending limbs with it dangling from HER beak, and then saw HER tuck it into the niche of the two poles!! Meanwhile, HE sat on one pole and stared into space! Suffering mackeral!"

The act of mating has rarely been observed in the Great Gray Owl. Our only record is a brief observation made on March 27, 1971. The event took place in late afternoon during a light snowfall. We had searched unsuccessfully all day for owls, then suddenly saw one on the tip of a tall spruce near a farm house. A few minutes later it moved to a wooded creekbed near the road and began hunting. I approached it as it sat on a tree stump about twelve feet high. When I was within twenty feet of the bird, which turned out to be a female, she turned about, glared at me and aggressively snapped her bill several times before flying away. Later she was joined by a second bird, apparently her mate. The pair flew off together to an open field and just out of our sight. Hurriedly climbing on top of the car for a view, we saw the female (recognizable by a broken wing

feather) perched about fifteen feet above the snow on the tip of a dead, leaning tamarack pole with the male astride her, vigorously flapping his wings. At the same time, one or both birds gave a peculiar, rasping screech, audible though we were more than three hundred yards away. Shortly thereafter the male flew away and the female resumed hunting. Observers in Sweden heard copulating Great Grays give a "series of squeaking notes."

On February 28, 1978, conservation officer Ken de Graff observed owls in a sexual encounter about fifty feet away through the window of his home at Wabowden, 340 miles north of Winnipeg. This incident happened between 6:00 and 6:30 p.m. A pair of Great Gray Owls, which had been observed nearby for at least a week, were seen moving from one telephone pole to another. The male, which always flew first, then landed on the house, whereupon the dog barked at it. The male next flew into a tree, where shortly he was joined by the female. At that point the birds were about twenty feet apart on the same branch, with the female perched ten feet higher than the male. When the female flew, the male followed and, like a Raven, cupped his wings, braking and falling upon her in midair. The male dropped onto the female for a second; then they separated and flew off together. Nothing like this has previously been reported for this species. Presumably this was an established pair, the aerial contact indicating a strong sexual motivation by the male.

We have found fresh feathers in nests visited by owls from mid-February into May. Prior to egg-laying, a female may visit more than one nest, accidentally losing several feathers, making us uncertain which nest she is going to choose. This habit seems so common, we think the presence of two or three nests built in close proximity provides additional nesting stimulus. Since Great Gray Owls begin laying as early as mid-March, when temperatures are frequently low, the insulative quality of plumage is important in keeping eggs warm. The female's well-developed brood patch is the source of heat. This bare, highly vascularized area, from which a handful of feathers have been shed, is about three and a half inches wide, extending from the upper breast and shoulder region to the vent. A thin layer of feathers, drawn from the developing brood patch, sometimes lies beneath the eggs and may provide some insulation.

Maintaining eggs at close to ninety-eight degrees Fahrenheit, when the temperature may be as much as thirty or forty degrees below zero, also requires close sitting. The persistent attendance of the female is a behavioral trait of significance to successful incubation. Unlike waterfowl, the females of which surround their eggs with down and other nest material when they leave the nest, there is no covering for owl eggs, nor hardly any opportunity to fly off from brood responsibilities.

The incubation period for a Great Gray Owl egg is about thirty days, but the period from laying of the first egg to hatching of the last egg laid may be from thirty to fifty days, depending on the size of the clutch and the interval at which eggs are laid. We found an egg-laying interval of three days, but it is reported by others to range from three days to an extreme of twelve.

For two and a half months, from the moment the first egg is laid, through incubation and development of the nestlings, the female is on or at the nest. Depending on weather and temperature, she may sit on the nest for twenty-four hours daily, despite snow and cold, wind and rain. When her offspring are able to maintain their own body temperature, she may leave them once a day for a few minutes respite. To keep up the female's strength and energy, to keep eggs and nestlings heated, and the latter fed, the male must bring a copious supply of food to the nest. Each day he must capture prey to feed the rapidly growing young, as well as his mate and himself. Before the young are two weeks old he may be bringing a dozen or more voles daily.

The male owl's diligence in hunting and bringing prey, no less than the attentiveness of his mate, is evidence of the continuing strength of the pair bond. The relationship that began in late winter, arising out of mutual preening, courtship feeding, and mating, provides family stability that lasts through summer and into autumn.

10

A Nesting of Owls

At dawn in early summer in the spruce woods, singing birds produce a medley of sounds as pervasive and constant as a running brook. Murmurs, whistles, lisping conversational notes, ringing musical tones intermingle as patterned light beams through mist and boughs. Each stirring song proclaims a new day.

In the midst of these sounds a soft, mellow hooting comes from high in a tamarack. In the rising orange light, a female Great Gray Owl slowly pivots her head toward a distant grove, then calls again, without opening her bill, giving three measured hoots. The downy head of a nestling owl pushes up beside her, chirping anxiously, hungrily tossing its head back, its bill open. Out of the deep shadows comes a gliding form; on set wings the male owl slips across an opening in the trees, suddenly rising abruptly to perch on the tip of a slender snag. The female watches intently, motionless, as the male bends its head down to pick up a mouse held in one foot. A moment later the male springs forward, flaps its wings heavily, then steadily glides toward the nest tree. He swoops upward effortlessly, his momentum carrying him precisely to the edge of the nest, mouse swinging in his bill. With no change of expression, the female leans toward the male and seizes the mouse, both closing their eyes at the moment of contact. A moment later the male turns and plunges off the nest, gliding rapidly away through the forest.

Though the young owls bob and weave about, pushing out from under her wings and breast, the female methodically snips open the mouse, holding it with one foot, then eats the stringy entrails. Using her bill, she delicately feeds bits of bright flesh to one or more of the owlets until the mouse is consumed.

The sounds of other busy birds still ring in the forest, but now the owls are quiet; the female shuffles about, adjusting herself upon the nestlings. Calmly turning to face the sun, now bright above the ragged spruce tops, she blinks several times, settles lower onto the nest, closes her eyes to slits, and is still.

In earlier days Great Gray Owls and their nests or eggs were often collected as soon as they were discovered. One of the first nests found in the United States, together with three fresh eggs, was sold by Henry Halvorson, a trapper, to amateur ornithologist Per O. Fryklund for three dollars. The nest was discovered in northwestern Minnesota less than a mile from the Canadian border on April 4, 1935.

In those days of ornithological exploration, naturalists with collections like Fryklund's were contributing to knowledge of birds. Museums were building scientific collections and specimens were in great demand. Fryklund paid Halvorson a dollar for each Great Gray Owl he shot, about ten being taken by the latter from this area over several years. A bird shot on April 25, 1926, had a well-developed brood patch, suggesting the bird had been incubating. In 1933 Fryklund found enlarged ova in another bird. Thereafter, he had urged Halvorson to try to find a Great Gray Owl nest.

When we visited Henry Halvorson in 1975, though it was forty years since he had found the nest, and he was seventy-three years old, he still clearly recalled the event. As he explained, in those depression years three dollars was a considerable sum. Halvorson, who had been making his living from trapping, set out that early April day on skis to check his traps. As he approached a grove of mixed conifers, two agitated owls flew out to meet him. He soon found their nest, which was about ten feet above ground, in some closely grown tamaracks. Both birds attacked him when he climbed up to get the nest, flapping their wings about him, hooting, and plucking at his hat. Carefully placing the nest and eggs in his packsack, he then skied away, followed for a short distance by the owls.

Sitting in the Halvorson home, looking at photos of Henry as a youthful trapper standing in front of a cabin draped with pelts of wolves, fox, and mink, gave us

some insight into the period of that earlier nesting. Listening to his account of the event, we briefly shared in the discovery. We also talked about a more recent discovery, a second nest found only about five miles east of his nest site and studied by us in 1970.

My attention was drawn to this area by a Winnipeg physician, Henry T. Dirks, who reported seeing eight live Great Gray Owls along a two-mile stretch of highway on April 1, 1970. Owls had evidently been attracted here during the winter by an abundance of voles. Unfortunately, a heavy toll was taken by shooting and collision with vehicles; over the next several weeks I found the remains of nine owls. Since some of these had died much earlier than the eight reported by my informant, there may have been two dozen or more owls in this vicinity. Two were salvaged as museum specimens, but the others were worthless. Soggy and dismembered, their remains were a sorry sight. On my first visit to the area on April 11, I saw a dark, moving form in a distant tree that I was sure was an owl. So it was, but an old, dead one, caught on a branch, one wing hanging down and flapping pathetically in the breeze.

Logging operations adjacent to the highway during the winter just past had left a large clearing in which a few tall tamaracks remained. One of these, not more than a hundred yards from the edge of the highway, held a large, conspicuous nest. Since I had just found three dead owls and hadn't seen a live one, I gave the nest only a cursory glance. A few days later, to my disbelief, customs officer Clarence Nordstrom phoned to say "a big owl" was sitting on that same nest. That weekend Bob Taylor and I drove to the site and, even before we stopped our car, we could see the large head of a Great Gray Owl on the nest!

We sat for some time, enthusiastic at seeing our second Great Gray nest, but worried about its survival. The nest, about

This nest and its occupant—high in a tamarack tree in April—could readily be seen from an adjacent busy highway. Goshawks probably built the nest the incubating owl is using.

thirty-five feet up in a tree that had few branches, was exposed to the elements as well as to every passing motorist. The logged-over area seemed bleak compared to the distant groves of spruce and tamarack; in all, the nest site seemed a poor choice. Later, we contacted customs officers on both sides of the border, explaining the value of this nesting, and with their cooperation established a watch on the nest. At our request, the local conservation officer spoke with those people thought to be responsible for the shooting during the previous months, and he also regularly patrolled the area. Eventually, numerous local people became aware of the nest and our interest in its welfare. The generally protective attitude that

soon developed surely helped save the nest.

A phone call in early May to Dalton Muir in Ottawa, telling him about the nest, brought immediate action. Although Muir had photographed many kinds of owls, the Great Gray was a species he had seen only as a rare winter visitant. Taking a leave of absence from his job, in a few days he was in Winnipeg with a trailer loaded with a wooden, portable observation tower. A little later, with Herb Copland's assistance, a forty-foot tower was erected within ten feet of the nest tree. The incubating female proved to be imperturbable, remaining on the nest during construction of the tower. When a small branch blocking the photographer's view

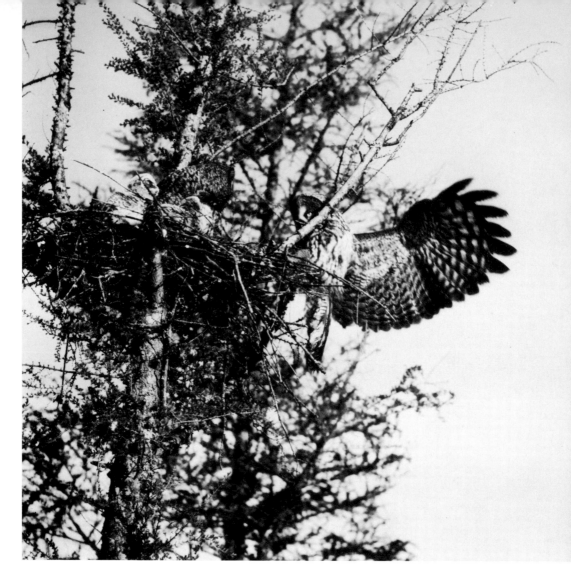

of the nest was sawed off, the female
tugged vigorously at the saw blade with
her bill, without leaving the nest! It was
soon found that the blind was unnecessary; the female paid us little attention,
and the male brought food despite our obvious presence. At times the persistent
photographer even had to prod the nest
with a pole to make the relaxed female
open her eyes. We were at the nest site on
twenty-two days between May 2 and July
29. Muir was there for the longest period,
living in a tent in the bog, photographing
owls day and night.

From the vantage point of the tower,
perched level with the nest and less than
ten feet away, we sat face to face with the
mother owl. We could also study details
of the food exchange. The male's delivery
of prey was fast and direct; swooping up

the edge of the nest, landing hard on his
usual perch, he seemed always impatient
to depart. Often, before he had folded his
wings he was offering prey to the female.
Both closed their eyes briefly when the female took the food from his bill.

Muir observed that "the female, in order to grasp the food, turned her head
sideways and delicately took the carcass.
Only when the hen had a firm grip and
pulled, did the male release his grip. The
sideways grip of the female appeared necessary to the successful transfer of the
food, because several times the female attempted to grasp the mouse without turning her head and each time the transfer
was awkward or the mouse was dropped
altogether." Sometimes the female failed
to respond at all; then the male, looking
about nervously, dropped the prey on the

edge of the nest or flew away with it, sometimes perching in a nearby tree and devouring it.

Hatching of the first egg in this nest occurred shortly after the tower was installed. Muir noted that the female was restless and squirming about, in contrast to her former immobility. A "barely perceptible squeaking" from a young bird emerging from an egg was heard at this time. With the hatching of the young, the male brought more food. Though he saw us almost daily, he still remained wary. On some occasions the male's hunting behavior was initiated by calls from the female, and possibly from the young. When not hunting, he was often dozing quietly on a branch, sometimes cocking his head to follow the progress of a nearby vole. On one occasion I watched while he sat in this manner for fifteen minutes. When the female called from the nest, he at once began actively hunting. Moving quickly from perch to perch on low stumps, peering here and there as he moved, within three minutes he captured a meadow vole and hurriedly carried it to the nest.

Voles were abundant in the area and we frequently saw them scurrying about. Little effort seemed required by the male to obtain food, and he mainly hunted within a quarter-mile or less of the nest. Usually, when the male caught prey he flew off, carrying it in one foot. Before flying to the nest, however, he stopped to perch in a tree, landing and balancing easily on one foot, and transferred the vole to his bill. Thus, when he approached the nest, the vole would be dangling from his bill. Peak feeding activities were from 4:30 a.m. to about 8:30 a.m., and from 4:30 p.m. until after dark, but on cloudy days, and sometimes even on bright days, the male might bring food at any time. The midday period, however, was usually an inactive time. Feeding at night was observed with the aid of a large spotlight powered by eight car batteries. Although the bright light lit up the nest and much of the sur-

rounding area, it seemed to have no effect on the birds. During the several times all-night vigils were maintained, the owls were relatively inactive from about 10:30 p.m. to 2:30 a.m. At other nests, when there was a food shortage, we found that the male was forced to hunt at all hours of the day and night.

When the young were small, the female fed them small portions of flesh, but within two weeks they were gulping down whole meadow voles and other rodents. The way in which the young were fed was closely observed by Muir, who reported: "The significance of the sideways turn of the head during food transfer became apparent when the hen fed the young. Small, downy, and blind at first, the young could only extend their heads through the hen's breast feathers, open their mouths and beg with a whimpering squeak. The hen tore off tiny pieces of flesh from the mouse and placed her curved beak directly into the gaping mouth of the young, at right angles to it. On contact with the hen's beak, the young owl clamped its mandibles on each side of the hen's beak and pulled back. Only when this right angle contact was firmly established did the hen relax her grip and allow the young to withdraw the morsel of food. The process was carried out gently, with great patience and evident concern."

Long after the young were good-sized, the female continued to shelter them from the elements. Her persistent attention was well demonstrated one day in June when it rained. The female closed her eyes as the rain increased, hunched lower over the young until she was almost flat on the nest, covering them completely, while drops of water ran down and off the end of her tail. By the time the rain had stopped, her plumage was thoroughly soaked and disarranged. Her head looked like a wet mop, and she shook it several times as vigorously as a dog. Then, with the dry young beginning to squirm out from under her, she stood up and began to preen. By ruffling and shaking her plumage, standing up in the warm breeze and preening her long breast feathers, her plumage was soon restored to normal.

When the young were about three weeks old the nest collapsed, possibly as a result of the growing belligerence of the young. Frequently we saw them pushing and shoving each other, and once one dangled briefly by one foot, hanging over the edge of the nest. Three of the four young survived the thirty-five-foot fall, including the youngest and smallest, but one of the larger owlets disappeared. Since we weren't there at the time, we can only guess what happened. Höglund and Lansgren have suggested that young Great Grays leave the nest before they are fully fledged, voluntarily leaping down from even tall nest sites, in order to escape from the heat of the sun shining on the open nest. Observers at other nests have noted that owlets when two weeks old may walk out onto adjacent branches, returning to the nest and the warmth of the female for the night.

Wahlstedt, studying a nest in northern Sweden, reported that the female was never seen in the nest except during a hot day or a heavy rain when she returned to the nest to shelter the young. Otherwise, she watched the nest and young from a nearby tree, while the male fed the young directly. The food supply was good and sometimes the young were overfed. "On several occasions it was observed that those young which climbed out on the branches of the nest tree became so satiated that they fell into a deep sleep. They lay on their stomachs, crosswise on the branch, with head and tail hanging helplessly down toward the ground. They very much resembled seasick people hanging over the railing of a boat. At times they took so careless a position I was much afraid they would fall down to the ground while asleep" [translation].

On our first visit after the nest fell, we found the young birds on the ground and on low perches near the nest tree, but within a few days they were able to climb up into trees. Like parrots, these downy owlets hitched themselves upward with their strong feet, hooking their bill or biting into the bark for purchase, or reaching over a branch for a higher grip. Their short, poorly feathered wings served to balance them as they slowly progressed upward. They climbed most effectively on slanted trunks, but they were able to go up straight trunks if there were enough close branches. Over the next two weeks, though they were unable to fly, we would find them as high as twenty feet in spruce and tamarack trees, increasingly farther from the nest tree. According to Thomas C. Dunstan and Steve D. Sample, young Barred Owls climbed in trees to heights of up to forty-seven feet.

Pellets, regurgitated lumps of indigestible material, are cast up by all raptors. Feathers, claws, fur, and bones, whatever isn't digested is neatly compacted in the stomach and ejected from the mouth. Great Gray Owl pellets, up to three inches long and about an inch in diameter, were often found and collected. Analysis of their contents later identified the prey being taken. As expected, based on what we had seen the male bring to the nest, meadow and red-backed voles were most common. When the young owls were small and eating mainly flesh, they cast no pellets, but later, when they ate whole voles, their small pellets were ingested by the female, which helped to keep the nest clean. Few pellets were found beneath the nest, but a heap of pellets was found beside a low stump by a pool where the female evidently bathed. Some of these pellets contained chalky excrement, evidence that the female had also eaten the young owls' feces. At later stages, the owlets forcibly ejected feces over the edge of the nest.

We rarely saw owls cough up pellets, but one day, watching an owlet that had left the nest, I had a good view of the proceedings. One of the larger young, stand-

A moment of rest at midday for a female and the large nestlings.

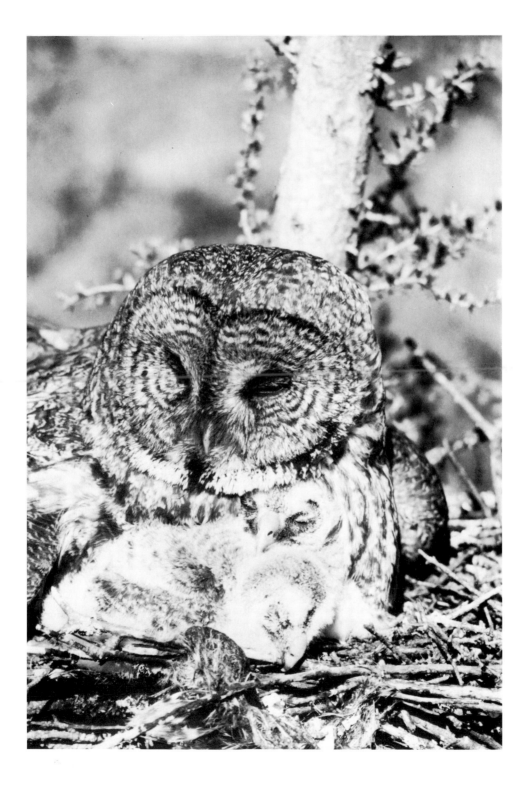

ing upright on a branch, with neck extended upward, gave a few, quick, jerking movements that presaged the arrival of the pellet from the stomach. Gaping widely as the pellet appeared in its mouth, the youngster, instead of dropping it, held it in its bill for a minute or two— as if it didn't quite know what it had and was unsure whether to drop it or swallow it—before letting it fall. I retrieved the pellet and found it was coated with a thin layer of mucous, a slick, membranous envelope that obviously made it easier to regurgitate. The shiny coating dried rapidly, but long afterward was still discernible. The pellet, like most, was blunt on the lower end and slightly tapered on the upper, taking the shape of the proventriculus where it had been formed.

With the young out of the nest, the male delivered food directly to the two older young, and they responded to his appearance by giving loud begging cries. He continued to do all the hunting, the female remaining near the young. When the young showed signs of distress upon being handled by us, the female often perched nearby. Once, she perched so close I captured her by simply reaching out and seizing her feet. Banded and released a few minutes later, she dropped to the ground, turned around and glared at us, ruffled her plumage, and then flew away. Five minutes later she was back on the same perch close beside me, watching closely while the young were being banded.

A few times the female took dead prey off the end of a branch held out before her. The first time, she seized a vole with her bill, flew off about a hundred feet to another perch, chewed on the vole, tore it apart by holding it under one foot, then dropped it. Half an hour later when she was perched about eight feet above me, I offered another vole to her in the same way. This time she plucked it off and soon gulped it down. I tried this again a week later, first holding a vole carcass on a stick in front of the female, then, when

she failed to respond, walking over and offering it to one of the older young. Incredibly, the female came winging in from about fifty feet away and, without pausing in flight, flew over the owlet and snatched the vole off the stick. She landed nearby on a higher perch, shredded the vole, and then carried off a portion, which she fed to the youngest owl, the latter having remained in her particular charge. She then returned and ate the remains she had left on the perch.

Long afterward I discovered that this was not the first time someone had fed a mouse to an owl in this manner. Napier Smith, encouraged by an old woodsman one day in May 1915, enjoyed a similar experience with a nesting male Hawk Owl near Ottawa. When a freshly killed "field mouse" on the end of a stick was held out to the bird, which was perched on a twelve-foot stump, the owl "stopped squealing and cocked his head from one side to the other, giving him such a droll appearance that I laughed aloud. On my advancing the mouse to the top of the stump, almost touching him, he opened his beak and gave a slight squeal; for a moment his pupils contracted, the yellow irises appearing enlarged, then, like a flash, he snatched the mouse from the stick with his claw. The next moment he was off with the mouse as buoyant as a feather, squealing as he flew through the woods."

A few minutes after the female took the dead vole off my stick, the male, who had been feeding the two older young, flew in with a vole in his bill, landing on a long, slanted pole several feet below an owlet perched near the end. The male walked up the limb toward the young, placing one foot before the other, wings upright for balance. Just as he reached the owlet, the female flew in from some distance, landed on the tip of the pole, causing it to sway, reached over the young owl's head and snatched the vole from the male's bill! At once she turned and flew off, carrying the vole over to feed to her young charge. It all took place in a few seconds and was a beautiful sequence to see as well as a further example of parental solicitude. Except for her special care, the young owl might have perished. Still, our observations agree with those of Höglund and Lansgren, who note that "it is probably a general rule that those young which get left behind in development will succumb sooner or later."

The sight of a dead vole evidently is a strong stimulus to a hungry owl. At one nest, we had placed three fledglings on a low limb to attract the female. As usual, the young owls were aggressive toward each other and to us. To test their feeding response, I held a dead vole by the nape in my lips and approached one of the larger, bill-snapping owlets. It immediately focused its attention on the vole, and, when I leaned close, tipped its head slightly to one side, then took it from me and gulped it down. I tried this at another time with an undernourished but grown young owl found in Winnipeg in November. Within a few days this bird gave begging calls whenever I entered the room in which she was kept to feed her. On three occasions she took mice from my mouth, always first gently nibbling on the mouse, then taking a firm hold and pulling until I let go.

The close relationship we felt with the nesting female changed abruptly the day her level of tolerance was breached. While I was trying to replace a struggling owlet on a branch above my head, the female suddenly attacked me, knocking off my cap and glasses, and sending me to my knees. Though frightened by the unexpected blow, I suffered only a minor scratch on my cheek. Later, when I was carrying the young owl to another location, the female slammed into the back of my head and neck, knocking me flat on my face. It was a shockingly strong blow to come from such a light, heavily feathered bird.

At Bob Taylor's insistence, I caused the female to attack three more times, holding a young owl while it flapped its wings and snapped its bill. The first time, the female came in so fast I threw myself down on one elbow to avoid her, and it appeared she had tried to strike the young. To ward off the female at the last moment, in order to protect both the young and myself, I then held a branch in one hand. Again she attacked, diving fast and low, and this time she struck the branch with one wing. We soon stopped photographing the diving owl, for it was clear that one of the three of us could get hurt.

At the nest, in our experience, the female is the aggressor. Moreover, her aggressiveness toward us seemed to be a response to distress signals from the young, rather than identification of humans as potential enemies. We were seldom attacked unless we were harassing the young. Since the female alone incubates the eggs and broods the young, her attachment to the nest is stronger than that of the male.

The tolerance so often shown by the female may be mainly an indication of her strong bond to the clutch or brood. Sometimes a female on a nest may even permit herself to be touched or pushed by hand. Similar strong broodiness is found in a variety of birds, e.g., bitterns, rails, falcons, and bluebirds. With continued visits to a nest, the incubating owl may show increased tolerance. But as the owlets increase in age, the female may show signs of agitation during nest visits. One learns to watch her behavior closely to reduce the amount of disturbance and to avoid being attacked. Her posture, facial expression, and vocalizations all provide signs of varying degrees of annoyance. When her wings are held out loosely and downward, when her bill is fully exposed, when she is standing upright, then it is time to be careful. Individual owls vary in behavior, but it pays to be wary. An owl that has permitted an observer to raise her off eggs one day, may later unexpectedly launch an aggressive attack. Brooding owls can be dangerous.

Höglund and Lansgren reported of Great Gray Owls in Sweden: "As a general rule the female was the most savage and defended nest and young many a time so frantically that it was difficult to make a close examination of the nest. In most cases it was necessary to use a mask for the face to protect from serious injuries. . . ." Wahlstedt, observing at a nest in Sweden, reported that on one occasion a male came flying in with a vole for the young while the female closely watched two observers beneath the nest tree. The male took no notice of the observers and flew directly to the female to give her the prey. The female became very irritated at this and buffeted the male so hard with her head that he lost his balance and had to take flight, in the process dropping the vole.

The male occasionally tried to lure us away, especially when the female uttered strong distress calls. He was usually relatively quiet and unobtrusive, and we had to look for him some distance from the nest. When approached, the watching male turned and flew off low and heavily, sailing just above the shrubs or suddenly dropping low, almost to the ground, an attractive ruse that impelled one to hurry after him. When we caught up with him we found him sitting on a perch, looking back over his shoulder and watching us. When we got closer, he fled again, but it was a conspicuous flight, and there was little doubt that this was distraction display, behavior serving to lead us away from the nest.

Our close contact with the adults was lost once the young could fly. Each time we found the young birds deeper in the woods, and when we approached them they flew away. We saw the three young for the last time at the end of July, locating them by listening for their loud calls. In addition to giving the food-begging call,

they occasionally gave a double-noted barking sound. They were fairly noisy, and called repeatedly, especially when a parent bird flew by, but they also responded to each other. On one occasion they flew from point to point until the oldest two were only ten feet apart and about forty feet from the youngest. Though out of the nest for seven weeks, they were staying together. By this time their wings and tails were fully feathered, but they still had downy heads and necks. I found one youngster being harassed by several birds, a mob scene involving a Common Flicker, Blue Jay, Gray Jay, and several Black-capped Chickadees. The owl flew off clumsily when I approached, flapping away with legs dangling, and made an awkward landing on a branch.

So we left them, apparently being fed by one or both parents, still not more than an eighth of a mile from the nest tree, but well hidden in a deep stand of tamarack. Their survival seemed assured, and we were not surprised to hear that a group of three Great Gray Owls, presumably this brood, had been seen in the general vicinity as late as September.

The length of time the young are dependent upon the parents for food is uncertain. I think they may be fed for three months or longer after leaving the nest, and social ties may endure even after the young have begun to forage for themselves. Two Great Gray Owls were seen in midmorning on October 1, 1978, in a heavily forested area in west-central Manitoba; they were heard hooting for half an hour before they were sighted. One bird, flushed from the ground, landed in a tree and hooted, whereupon the second owl flew in and perched above it. The latter hooted about six times, then both birds flew away. Parent and offspring? Nestmates? Whatever the case, two or more Great Gray Owls sometimes seen in close association in winter may be evidence of a continuing family bond.

11
In Search of Nests

There is a time between winter and spring which, for a searcher of owl nests, is ideal for roaming through woods and bogs. It varies in length with each season, but is never long enough. It is that time when the snow has almost disappeared, when insects are scarce, and when it is possible to see far ahead through the leafless trees.

Then the first pale green aspen leaves begin to flicker, and in a week this fresh color is spread across the tops of trees. Though we rejoice in the addition of color to the landscape, the growing leaves restrict our vision.

For many days after the aspens have leafed out, however, we can still see through the leafless tamaracks. But one warm day the first needles appear, emerging in tufts from tiny gray nubbins on each twig, and overnight there is a new fullness. At first merely a haze, a pale brush of green, the tamaracks quickly thicken with new growth, even though the needles may be less than a quarter-inch in length. Once the soft, feathery needles have fully emerged, the search for nests in tamarack bogs is a slow process. The hope of finding another nest, however, is strong incentive, and we have plodded through bogs in June and even into July.

In summer the bog is many shades of green, different tones in sun and shadow. The carpet of mounded, soft sphagnum moss, the leaves and stems of a multitude of other plants, all are green, and all reach out lovingly for the sunlight that streams down through the trees. In the humid heat the bog is like a greenhouse, and the liquid calls of Connecticut Warblers and Ovenbirds add to a growing sense of being in some tropical region. The feeling is enhanced by the sight of a colony, a grove of showy lady's-slippers. Like gaily colored feathered wands from a carnival thrust into the sphagnum mat, these waist-high, exotic plants rise from papery, pale green, furled leaves. They stand at the peak of flowering, startling white and pink voluptuous blossoms poised in the filtered light of this lacy, green retreat.

The edges of open bogs, rich with sedges and grasses, provide good habitat for meadow voles.

The two years following the much-studied Minnesota nesting were disappointing in that, despite intensive searching, we were unable to find an active nest. In 1973, however, we found a nest with a single, half-grown owlet. Encouraged, we searched even harder the following year, and managed to find three nesting birds in early stages of egg-laying and incubation. In 1975 we failed to find an active nest, but in 1976 we had four nests under close observation. Since two of these were in Minnesota and two were seventy-five miles northwest of Winnipeg, we were kept busy. In the next three years we had eight, two, and ten nests, respectively, for a total of twenty, all in Manitoba. We suspect that birds nested in Minnesota in 1979, but we simply ran out of time to check. Accounts of the discovery of nests from 1973 to 1976, and subsequent events, provide the main basis for this chapter. A final portion covers some unexpected activities at three 1977 nests.

In mid-June 1973 a report of a Great Gray Owl seen carrying prey led Robert Taylor and me to search for a nest in a bog about fifty miles east of Winnipeg. Relying on this one brief observation as certain evidence of a nearby nest, Bob and I spent most of a warm afternoon looking in this wet and tangled spruce-tamarack bog. We clambered over deadfalls in spruce stands, splashed through open areas of sedge, and looked carefully in two small islands of mature aspen, searching every tree for a nest, and listening for sounds of hungry young owls. It was soggy underfoot and sweltering; we constantly brushed away blackflies, mosquitoes, and sweat, meanwhile pushing onward, moving slowly from one grove to another, looking in every habitat type. Caught up in the excitement of the chase, we persistently searched, occasionally stopping to rest and briefly examine some bright bog flower.

Three hours later, when Taylor called to me from some distance, I had had enough

excitement and beauty. I finally found him in a grove of small tamarack, leaning against a tree and looking exhausted. I sank down upon the nearest trunk and tiredly asked where we should search next. Grinning, he motioned upward. I leaned back and was surprised to find myself looking at an owlet standing on a nest, not fifteen feet above us. The nest had been found! Hastily, I wiped my steamy glasses, sweating face and eyes, then feasted upon the spectacle of the nestling peering fixedly down at us. "How did you find it?," I asked. "Just walked right up to it," was Taylor's simple reply. While we rested, we looked and listened for the adult birds, but not until I began to climb the tree to check on the nest contents did they appear, and then they were in sight only briefly. So dense was the tree growth in the vicinity of the nest tree that we couldn't see them unless they were perched close to the nest, but we could hear them hooting in alarm at our intrusion.

We blazed a quarter-mile trail back to the road and found ourselves about a half-mile from where we had begun our search—tired, wet, and thoroughly pleased with our success. Later, companions who visited this nest with us expressed surprise at the locality. From the road, the stunted tamarack seemed unsuitable habitat for Great Gray Owls. Even the nest, which was small and in a tangle of branches on a deformed tamarack, was unlikely looking. There wasn't much room for the adults to get in and out of the nest; later, we saw both male and female swoop in over the tops of the trees, and gained a new appreciation for their dexterity in flight.

The following year as well, this nest was again occupied. On a visit in late May, Spencer Sealy and I saw the female sitting low and tight to the nest, but she suddenly departed as we neared the tree. When she left the nest, a small, downy chick fell out, to our horror landing in a pool of water below. We hurriedly dried it off with a handkerchief and placed it in the nest beside an even younger chick and an unhatched egg. Quickly backing away, we soon were relieved to see the female return. She walked along a branch to reach the nest, peered into it, lowering and weaving her head from side to side as she scanned the contents, then carefully settled onto the nest.

Newly hatched chicks, snuggled up under the female's feathers or between her feet, can accidentally be carried out of the nest if the female makes an abrupt departure. This unnerving experience taught us that there is potential risk in visiting an active nest during early stages. Although Henderson reported that a female Great Gray Owl returned and sat on an empty nest a few minutes after he had collected the full clutch of eggs, we later had a bird desert after it had laid four eggs.

Ideally, nests should be observed infrequently and from a distance, though this limits what can be learned. When I fret about the effects of our studies on Great Gray Owls, however, I am consoled by the thought that while we are disturbing factors at a few nests, there must be many other owls nesting in unknown sites, completely undisturbed by man.

On a return visit a few days later to the nest mentioned above, Sealy, wary of the possibility of a similar incident, crept forward and beneath the nest before the female flushed. Again, when she left the nest a chick went out with her. With a quick lunge, Sealy managed to catch the chick in mid-air, but not before it had struck a small twig. Though we didn't realize it at the time, this bird, the last to hatch, was seriously injured, for on the next day we found it lying dead on the ground beneath the nest. The female was still in attendance, however, and the other two young were in good condition. Ten days later, we were dismayed to find that the skimpy nest had collapsed, and there was no sign of adults or young. Thereafter, we tried to keep nests in good repair, using wire screen to give them additional support if necessary.

At the third nest studied that year, two of three young successfully fledged. In many respects this nest was the most pleasant to visit and the easiest to observe. But it was so close to civilization we were always uneasy. Adjacent to farmland and not far from a road, the nest was reached by a short walk through an open aspen woods and over a granite outcrop where a few large jack pine grew. An old, compact nest about twenty feet above ground in the forks of a mature trembling aspen was the site chosen by this pair of owls. It was a site we had visited as early as February, for owls had been present here and in nearby farm fields throughout the winter.

Before the eggs had hatched, Bob Taylor erected a light, metal tower about four feet from the nest tree. When I climbed the tower in late May, the female flew off the nest when I was halfway up, aggressively snapping her bill and hooting while in flight. A newly hatched chick, barely able to hold up its head, and two eggs, one just beginning to hatch, were in the nest. A minute later, the female returned, flying in aggressively, landing hard on the nest and accidentally striking the chick with one of her talons. Although the blow knocked the chick over, it survived, but I felt guilty. Two days later, when two young were present and the third egg was well pipped, Taylor climbed the tower, photographed the female, who remained on the nest, then put out his hand and touched her to force her off the nest. (At another of our nests, studied intensively by graduate student Michael Collins, the female became so used to his presence she would permit him to touch her, and often she stayed on the edge of the nest while the nestlings were weighed on a balance scale set in the nest.)

We spent many relaxed hours at this nest, for these were elegant surroundings: moss and lichen-covered rocks, greening woods, and a clear view of the nest from where we sat on a grassy bank about thirty yards from the nest tree. On a warm day in late May with wildflowers in

bloom and birds in full song, this was an ideal situation. From one sun-warmed spot we could see anemones, violets, strawberries, blueberries, and saskatoons in full flower. Meanwhile, there was time to sort out the bird calls: Ovenbird, White-throated Sparrow, Swainson's Thrush, Blue Jay, Least Flycatcher, and Rose-breasted Grosbeak, a surprising assortment against which to listen for the soft hooting as the pair of owls kept in touch with each other. This was quite different from the tamarack bog sites of other nests where Myrtle and Connecticut warblers, Winter Wrens, and Gray Jays had kept us company.

In late June and July, long after leaves had obscured our view of the nest, a major infestation of forest tent caterpillars had an astonishing effect. The nest tree and surrounding aspens and shrubs of all kinds were denuded of leaves by hungry caterpillars, opening up the canopy and letting in light as in spring. At the height of the infestation, everything in sight was covered with the dark, striped caterpillars, a crawling mass that moved in all directions, even flowing across the nest and between the downy young. The droppings from thousands of caterpillars pattered on the forest floor like rain. The owls seemed to pay no attention to the hordes of caterpillars, the male bringing voles and the female feeding them to her offspring as usual.

Now, as the male was no longer concealed by foliage, we often saw him sitting in sight of the nest, but at some distance. Usually he sat for long periods with closed eyes, relaxed and silent, but he was attentive to sounds at the nest. Whenever we disturbed the female, he at once became alert and peered toward the nest. But, like other males we had observed, he never showed the aggressiveness of the female. At midday on bright days he often sought shade in which to rest.

The young grew rapidly, and by the end

of June were out of the nest and about a hundred yards away, perched on low branches and being carefully watched by the female. Late one evening we brought the young back to the vicinity of the nest tree The next morning we were at the site at 4:30 a.m., in time to see them being led off. The female lured the young chiefly by perching a little distance away and about five feet off the ground, repeatedly giving a muted *"wowk!"* or *"whoop!"* Upon hearing this call, the young scrambled along the forest floor, through a heavy growth of sedge, over fallen limbs and up on slanted trees. They climbed rapidly and capably, balancing with their small wings, and hopping "hand over hand" as they went upward. Though still less than a month old, they could leap across a space of two feet from one perch to another.

The male's hunting grounds were mainly the same open farmlands used during the winter. The female, trapped and color-marked by us, was a familiar bird. Both male and female had fed regularly on meadow voles taken through the snow. Now, in early summer, these same uncut alfalfa fields and grassy ditches still held considerable numbers of voles, and here occasionally we observed the male

hunting. On June 2, arriving at 4:55 a.m., we found the male already busy hunting, perched on a telephone pole beside the road. While Sealy went in to watch at the nest, I had the male constantly in sight until 6:12 a.m., when he flew off to the nest with a vole. During this entire period he hunted actively, flying from pole to pole, gliding over a field, dropping down and standing on the ground, peering about, hopping along, and several times pouncing unsuccessfully. Once he passed by me within forty feet in a slow glide, wings slanted upward like a giant Harrier, and again—while I stood motionless—he sailed past within ten feet!

The male's hunting urge on this morning seemed intense, as if nest, young, and mate, some combination of stimuli kept him compulsively trying to capture prey. At 6:00 a.m. he went down in a long glide onto the far end of the open field, stood nearly motionless for ten minutes while peering intently, then rapidly hopped about, making short pounces, jumping up with wings partly raised and striking hard at the ground. Then, having captured prey, he crouched over like a cat feeding, head down and back curved; twice he lowered his face to his feet. He stayed for a long time in this position, seeming in no hurry, and apparently enjoying his catch. This surprised me since he had seemed anxious to get food for the family. When finally he raised his head there was a vole in his bill. After a few seconds he flew off into the woods, arriving shortly thereafter at the nest where Sealy saw him give the vole to the female.

Another day, I found the male perched on top of a telephone pole in the same area at 4:30 a.m. Again, obviously busy hunting, he paid little attention to my presence. To my disappointment, for I had hoped to capture and band him, he showed little interest in a live white mouse that I let run about on the road directly beneath him.

Watching this great bird in bright daylight perched above me and flying slowly past, almost as if I didn't exist, was enthralling. I worried, however, thinking how small its chances of survival were. Absurdly bold, frightfully conspicuous; a ready victim of the automobile, an easy target for gunners. That this particular owl and his mate and family survived, as they did, was a matter of good luck.

Not all of our efforts to find nests were successful. On numerous occasions we vainly searched areas where there was evidence that birds were nesting. One day in June my sons and I saw a Great Gray Owl with a vole in its bill fly out of a roadside ditch and off across a heavy stand of spruce. More than ten man-days were spent searching in that area for an active nest. We finally concluded that the nest or young to which the bird had been flying must have been farther back in the woods than we were able to search. We did find, however, a large nest forty feet up in an aspen, apparently occupied by Broad-winged Hawks that circled and called overhead. I returned to the site a week later, driven by a hunch, and used tree-climbing spurs to check the nest. It was hot and humid and the air was thick with mosquitoes. In a way, although it

was a difficult climb, it was good to get above the ground. Although no Broad-wings were present, the nest had been lined in their fashion with fresh twigs and strips of old bark. Beneath the new lining I discovered old Great Gray Owl feathers, an indication that this nest may have been used by them in the previous year! With that in mind, we checked the nest each year, and in the spring of the third year were gratified to find it occupied by Great Gray Owls.

For several weekends in late spring 1976, Herb Copland and I heard Great Gray Owls calling at night from deep in a tamarack bog in northern Minnesota. One night my first attempt to start the owls calling elicited a clear chorus of wolves! Each time I hooted, the wolves shattered the night with their loud howling. When I tried to imitate the wolves, however, they remained silent. But almost every night we heard owls, and once one flew by almost overhead. Each day we searched in vain for a nest; it was tantalizing.

In mid-May we were encouraged by an especially long bout of calling. We listened to the low hooting, trying to fix in our minds the location of the calling bird. It had been dark when we began, but now, from a heavy cloud layer that merged with the darker forest came the moon— first a pale orange light along the edge of the cloud, then a warm red orb rising into the sky, and finally the round full moon, brilliant pearly gray. Standing on the roadside in the bright light, amused to see our shadows so clearly, we debated venturing into the woods in hopes of finding the bird. Reason prevailed (knowledge of the many deadfalls, interminable thickets, unseen dangers of dead limbs), sending us away some time after midnight.

Determined to find a nest, we returned the following weekend. What happened on that occasion may perhaps best be conveyed in the following excerpt from a letter I dashed off to a close friend shortly after returning to Winnipeg:

A fledgling sits on a log close to the forest floor. At four to five weeks of age, the flight feathers are well under way.

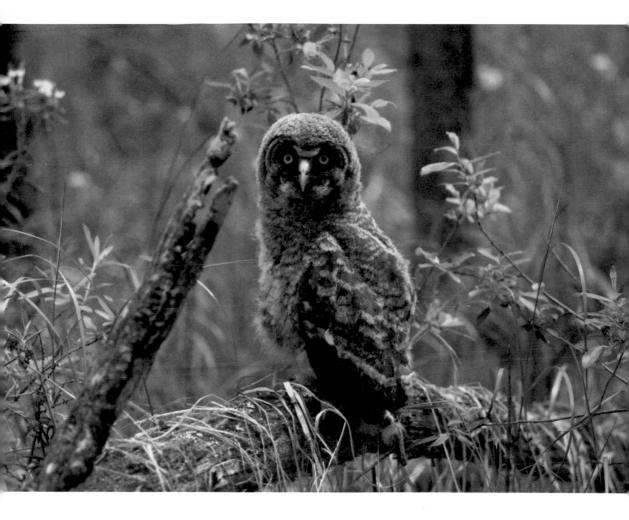

"Arrived home today, May 30, 4:30 p.m. after gruelling weekend, but happiness galore, result of finding another active (migawd) Great Gray Owl nest today. Persistent belief in analysis of observations during previous weekends (noctural seance, calls drifting back and forth from me to owl and vice versa) as full moon arose. Convinced that owls were on territory, Herb and I drove down there on Saturday afternoon, went into bog at 8:30 p.m. An hour later found male owl hunting; it came and snapped its bill and hooted at us—pure aggressive display on territory I said, and we hung about in woods until 10:30 p.m. forgodsakes—and I saw two beaver on dammed drainage ditch, slipped in and got wet but didn't care, it was so great for the owl to have come out and approached and snapped at me (as if I mattered!)

Went to bed late and arose early and sashayed back into the bog at dawn in the mist and heavy, heavy dew (especially on the equisetum, that stuff is made for dew, until one is soaked to the waist almost) and found the male hunting again in another mature tamarack stand, and this time we stood ever so long and finally saw it fly off with mouse in bill (which is sure indication of nest nearby) and trudged off and wandered about, with control man on point on cutline, and first I found two old empty nests, then another, and exhausted, sent Herb off on another round, while I stood and watched for the male. Herb about twenty minutes later gave a great shout and I responded in kind and then we met in woods and he had found the nest! and we went back and gawd there she was this gorgeous female with huge head and snapping bill while I climbed the tree first time ever, about twenty-five feet, branches breaking and almost fell but I have become a squirrel and clung and made it up and lo and behold an egg, another egg pipping, and a tiny chick! And down again, and away and watched her come back on the nest and then back-tracked a mile and a half through the tamaracks, few insects, but still hot and moist and lovely and a Mourning Warbler nest and a Song Sparrow nest, and mostly great clusters of pitcher plants and lady's-slippers and sphagnum and wet to the waist again and gawd how I loved it all. So a fifth nest for Minnesota and no one else knows where this faraway nest is and it is a great spot remote and most beautiful and we will check it again in three weeks or so and band the young and how you would love it!"

Three weeks later we found three young in the nest, attended by the alarmed female. While we lowered the young from the nest for banding, she remained perched on the tops of the highest trees in the vicinity. On our two later trips to the nest site, made in an effort to capture the female, she remained elusive. Even when we held the struggling young birds out for her to see, though much upset, she failed to come close enough for us to snare. She was by far the shyest female we had yet encountered at a nest.

Far less aggressive than any other female owl in our experience, she showed strong distraction display, especially when we brought a dog in to the site. This was an extra effort on our part to lure her within reach. We gathered the three young, which at this later date we found perched in trees within a few hundred feet of the nest tree, and placed them in a row on a low, horizontal limb. Then I urged my springer spaniel to bark, growl, and leap up toward the bill-snapping owlets. This created a considerable row and elicited a tumultuous display by the female. Uttering screams like a Red-tailed Hawk, mewing sounds, mournful hoots, and startling, heronlike squawks, the female flew down near us, flinging herself with widespread wings against low branches, seemingly in utter abandon. This display set the dog charging after her, drawn to the sight and sound of a bird floundering and flapping in low boughs. We were frightened, for at times it looked as if she could break her flight feathers, so violently did she thrash about. A moment later, as the dog ran toward her, she was upright and watchful, looking back at it. Then she flew off slowly, close to the ground, keeping ahead of the dog, before swooping up toward another perch. Each time she went through the same motions. When the dog was called off, the owl soon returned to a high perch as before, hooting softly, looking out across the forest and down at her offspring. When the dog was sent out again, the shrieking female dived down through the trees in a pell-mell, headlong plunge, flinging herself against boughs with flapping wings, repeating her display.

No matter how many times we tried, we couldn't get close to this bird. Despite her apparent abandon, whenever I approached with the snare-pole, she moved away or returned only to perch high above us. We couldn't think of anything else we could do to lure her within reach, and finally gave up.

I returned to the site again in early July, determined to make a final effort to capture the female. As my friends and I approached the site, we heard the female owl calling, and a few minutes later we found one of the owlets perched upright on top of a tall stump right beside the trail. The female circled above us on widespread wings, calling vigorously in alarm, while we searched for other young. In a few minutes I found a second owlet about fifteen feet high in a tree. I brought it down and carried it to a clearing, making it snap its bill and flap its wings in an effort to attract the female. She was much more agitated than she had been on previous visits and to my elation she suddenly landed on the top of a broken tree within range of my snare-pole. I quickly set the owlet down, reached for the pole and found that the snare wire was caught on a tiny twig. . . . I couldn't free it! And still the female sat and watched. In des-

peration, I wrenched the snare loose and although the wire loop was hanging crookedly, reached as high as I could and managed with considerable effort and shaking hands to bring the snare down over her head. Then I pulled her off the perch, bringing her flapping to the ground where I at once pounced upon the struggling bird, finally seizing her strong legs in my bare hands. In an outrageous feeling of triumph I raised her high and shouted aloud with joy and relief. I had her now and wasn't about to lose her. So, with the help of my friends (Karen Eastman and Charles Newell), we soon had her measured, banded, and marked. All the while, she just lay back in my arms, strong feet and sharp talons safely held out of the way with my two hands, blinking her wide eyes and occasionally giving deep glances at the owlet perched nearby. When finally I turned her loose, she landed not far off, great ruffled wings sagging, panting, a little overheated, but in a few minutes she was back to normal, perched high in the top of a tree, still keeping an eye on her offspring.

After gathering up our gear, we slowly made our way back through the tamaracks, taking more time now to admire various bog flowers and plants—orchids of several kinds, pitcher plants—and stopping to identify with delight a tiny nest with eggs of the Lincoln's Sparrow, a bird whose song we had heard on the way to the nest site. Our day was further brightened by the light, lilting song of a Winter Wren coming from a distant grove.

The following year, when we had eight active nests under observation, we found further evidence of the variable behavior shown by female owls. Some were wary and completely unapproachable, but one came right down to our level when we began to band her young; she was taken readily and gently with the snare-pole. We were able to bring her to the ground, slip the barely tightened noose off, band and mark her in a relatively short time and

A magical moment—the male delivering food to the female at a nest high above the ground. Both owls close their eyes briefly when the female takes the prey from his bill.

The male glides away from the nest after the female has taken the prey. He may doze on a nearby branch until a call from the female causes him to begin hunting again.

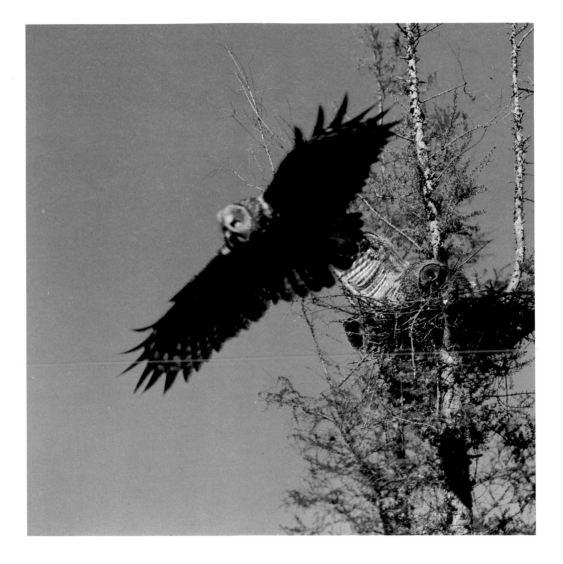

with a minimum amount of handling. A few minutes later she perched near us, colored wing tag conspicuous against her plumage, watching intently while we finished banding the young. When we left the site, it was as if she had never been handled by us; she flew up high to perch and call, giving weird distraction sounds, before eventually slipping out of our sight when we were some distance from the nest site.

At another nest, a female we had come to know as a fairly docile bird unexpectedly attacked me when I climbed the nest tree to bring down the young. Twice she struck me on the back of the head, giving me plenty of warning that her mood had changed. I pulled my cap down tighter, then, clinging with one arm to the trunk of the tree, tried to bundle one of the nestlings into a sack. At that moment the female flew directly toward me, coming fast across the nest with both feet held out before her, reaching toward my face with talons spread wide. I reacted without thinking, grabbing one of her feet in my gloved hand, then spent a few confusing minutes trying to bring her under control without hurting her or myself. I hung on to that one foot while she flapped her wings and struggled for balance, meanwhile clawing me with her free foot in the belly and on one thigh. It was a perilous moment, for I still had to hang onto the tree with one arm, but I was not ready to lose my hold on the bird. Meanwhile, my companion on the ground could only watch with alarm, repeatedly asking if I was all right. I soon had the poor bird tucked under my arm and was eventually able to grasp both her feet. After resting briefly I happily tucked her headfirst into the sack and brought her down for banding.

A few weeks later, visiting another nest to band the last young of the season, I again captured a bird by hand, but with much less effort. Although this was a shy bird, one that always disappeared from the nest each time we approached, even when she was on eggs, she invariably came back as soon as we climbed to the nest. On several occasions she landed on the opposite side of the nest and, apparently tame and unaggressive, watched closely while I was there. This time I was hoping she would do the same thing, and I was ready for her, having secured a firm foothold at the level of the nest. In a moment she came winging back through the trees, straight to the nest; just before she landed I quickly grabbed both her feet, brought her flailing wings together, and tucked her under one arm. Before taking her down to be banded, I clung to my perch, looking into that impassive face, into those gleaming eyes, trying in vain to glimpse something of the spirit of the large bird, now captive, soon to be ignominiously shoved into a sack. It was with some sadness that I thought of the several other times she and I had exchanged glances, looking at each other across the small width of the nest, when she stood aloof, free and untouched, bound to the contents of the nest.

12

Nest Builders

In spring, wandering alone through a cool bog to check a nest, I am at peace. Though the busy world rattles on, I have, in an hour's drive, rid myself of aggressive, screeching traffic, dusty city streets, and personal cares. Early in the season before mosquitoes have hatched, my sojourn is free even of those distractions, and briefly I can lose myself in what I fancy is the owl's world. The snow has recently disappeared, but under the dry top of the sphagnum moss there is still ice, and the water that splashes up from low spots is cold. Pushing along the well-worn trail to the nest, boots sucking in and out of the bog, my passage is noisy and labored, probably more than that of the moose, whose sign I see before me. Pausing to catch my breath, my mind is filled with the moment: the sound of my breathing, a sharp "Whit!" from a hidden thrush, the brittle bark of a tamarack branch to which I cling for balance.

Because this nest was used last year, we have already checked it a dozen times this season, each time hoping it would hold an owl. So I approach the nest site cautiously and peer with binoculars from some distance, standing beneath the green boughs of a cedar. But there is no owl on the nest; there is only a shaggy mass of twigs on a crooked branch. But since I have come this far, I might as well look in the nest itself.

Climbing the tree to the nest is routine by now, and familiar branches and knots support fingers, knees, and toes. A quick glance shows an absence of eggs. But wait, where last week there had been merely a lining of weathered tamarack twiglets, there is now a feather! One fresh, fluffy Great Gray Owl feather. A bird has at least visited here, and I picture it flying up to the nest, landing hard and balancing on the edge, eyes glaring fiercely, then springing away, led onward by other demands, one lost feather left in the nest—a sign to bolster my hopes.

Opposite: Once fed, the young owls settle down; hunger, or the next visit of the male to the nest, will bring them alert again.

This photo shows the food exchange between a male and female at a nest deep in a tamarack swamp. Note the quill feathers on the nearest nestling.

The female closes her eyes as a nestling seizes the prey.

Owing to their habit of using stick nests built by other species, Great Gray Owls must have a natural propensity for searching out and visiting deserted or vacant nests. Scandinavian ornithologists have noted that to keep Great Grays nesting in an area it is important to repair existing nests. Not only do nests naturally deteriorate, but the species has a peculiar habit of scratching deep into nests when inspecting them, sometimes digging right through the bottom. Moreover, a season of use produces further wear. Imitation or man-made nests, reasonably close duplications of natural nests, have been used by several species of raptors. Twice, in Sweden, Great Gray Owls used man-made nests.

After the collapse in 1970 of a natural nest from which Great Gray Owls fledged, we decided to try to elicit further nesting by providing a substitute nest. In July, using a wire-mesh frame for a base, we built a nest of twigs in a deformed tamarack about fifteen feet above ground. This was several hundred yards from the original nest tree in a nearby tamarack woods where the owl family was residing. We were hopeful that the nest would be used the following spring by the parents or their offspring.

Our expectations increased when, in early March 1971, we found signs that a Great Gray had visited the nest. A thick, compact mass of snow often forms on top of nests at this time of year and it was evident that the owl had removed a considerable amount of snow by scratching and digging, presumably trying to get down to the nest. A single feather frozen to the snow remaining in the nest identified the visitor. Despite this early visit, however, the nest went unused that year, possibly because of a dearth of mice and voles in the vicinity. Still, it was good to know that owls had found the nest and were interested in it. Encouraged by this observation, we built more nests here and northward for about sixty miles, particu-

larly where owls were seen in what we judged to be suitable nesting habitat.

Almost all our nests were built in tamarack trees, partly because nests in these deciduous conifers, we reasoned, must be more conspicuous from fall to spring than in other conifers, and because tamaracks are usually easy to climb. Where necessary, we drove in large spikes for climbing, or used climbing spurs, but in many cases we relied on branches alone. Nests were built at heights from ten to thirty feet. For a number of reasons, tamaracks are relatively easy trees in which to build nests. A tree with a deformed top makes a good nest support, especially where insect damage and disease have resulted in loss of the leader or tip of the tree, causing a growth of upright instead of horizontal branches. This ideal, basketlike arrangement makes the best support for a nest; simply cut out the dead tip, clear away a few branches, and the tree is ready to receive a nest. Similar sites, especially where the central limb has decayed, are often used by nest-building birds.

At first glance, a tree often has so many fine branches it is difficult to envision installing a nest. Sometimes it is necessary to climb the tree and make a closer inspection to ensure that there is adequate space for a nest. Once the decision is made, there ensues a vigorous trimming and alteration, clearing away unnecessary branches to open up the site. Large, dead branches, broken off the nest tree or from adjacent trees, are used to form a broad, thick base. Then smaller branches and twigs are added, tramped and packed down into a compact form about eighteen inches in diameter.

Much of this material has to be hauled up into the tree by rope, so the most effective operation calls for one person in the tree and another on the ground. In the final stage, fine sticks and twigs, crumbled by hand or broken and crunched underfoot, are added to form a dense lining.

Since Great Grays seem to prefer deep nests, I usually make a fair-sized depression in the center.

Where there were insufficient branches, a piece of wire screen was used as a base, and at times the sticks were wired onto the tree. Given a reasonably good nest site, it was sometimes possible to complete a nest in twenty minutes, but on at least one occasion it took two of us more than two hours to build one. A man-made nest doesn't usually look much different from a natural nest built by hawk or raven, but in choosing a nest site we also took into account the presence of nearby dead stubs for perches, and the nearness of old clearings and grassy places that would make good hunting grounds.

Finding a suitable tree usually took a lot longer than building the nest. Especially in winter, when many of our nests were built, we often spent hours driving about and hiking or skiing through woods, looking for the right tree. These winter excursions were enjoyable. Even at thirty below zero Fahrenheit it was pleasant exercise, at least on sunny days, though my teen-aged son, Woody, or Herb Copland, my usual companions, standing below in the snow and sending up tools and bundles or branches by rope, didn't always agree. Building nests in early spring or late fall, we finally decided, was much easier, though there were fewer weekends on which we could do this.

In the course of several seasons of building nests I gained a special fondness for the sturdy trunks and strong limbs of tamaracks, for their lichen-encrusted branches, friable twigs, and aromatic sap. Invariably, after a nest-building venture, I carried home some part of the tree—thin bark flakes, sticky twiglets, or tiny, round cones—on my clothing, in my pockets, or down my neck.

Although by January 1974 we had built thirty-five nests, none had been used by Great Grays. But we spent a lot of time each season checking nests, driving, walk-ing, climbing and, in some cases, just trying to find them. During this period, Red-tailed Hawks appropriated two of our nests, a Great Horned Owl used one as a platform on which to devour a snowshoe hare, and some predator finished off a red squirrel in another.

Reports in mid-April 1974 of Great Gray Owls in the general locality of our first man-made nest sent us to the area in a hurry. When we arrived at the nest site, we found the lining had been scratched out and twigs were scattered about on top of the snow. Several wet, bedraggled Great Gray Owl feathers were lying on the wire-screen bottom of the nest. I rebuilt the nest, adding branches to the edge and a new lining of fine twigs, carefully fitting them into position with silent, anxious hope.

Our next visit to the site was made on May 11. It was cold and raining lightly when we set forth across a clearing in the woods. Stumbling through the bog, both of us with misted glasses, Spencer Sealy and I stopped when still fifty yards from the nest tree. It was a wise move. Just barely visible through the dripping trees, the nest at first appeared to be empty. Great Gray Owls are usually conspicuous on a nest and we expected to see the owl's head protruding above it. We saw nothing; but, as we focused our binoculars, there was a movement, a wing lifted up, and then, to our delight, a Great Gray Owl slipped over the edge of the nest and away through the trees. She must have been lying flat in the nest.

We hastened forward, hardly daring to hope that there might be something in the nest. I scrambled up the trunk of the tree and was rewarded with the sight of two fresh white eggs, side by side. Shouting the good news to Spencer, I slid back down and we left right away so the female could get back on the nest. Considering how cold and wet it was, it seemed incredible that she had flown while we were still so far from the nest tree. Usually Great

Because Great Gray Owls have a habit of using vacant or deserted nests, rather than building them themselves, one way to keep the birds nesting in an area is for owl fanciers to repair existing nests or construct man-made ones. Here, the author hauls a bundle of branches up a tamarack tree during construction of a man-made nest in late winter.

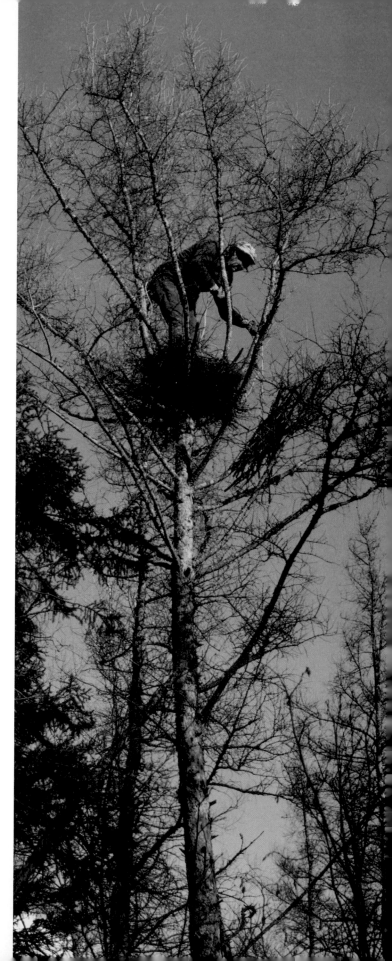

A female Great Gray Owl sits on a man-made nest in a tamarack bog in early spring. The twisted branches that provided support for the nest may have resulted from past infestation by larch sawflies.

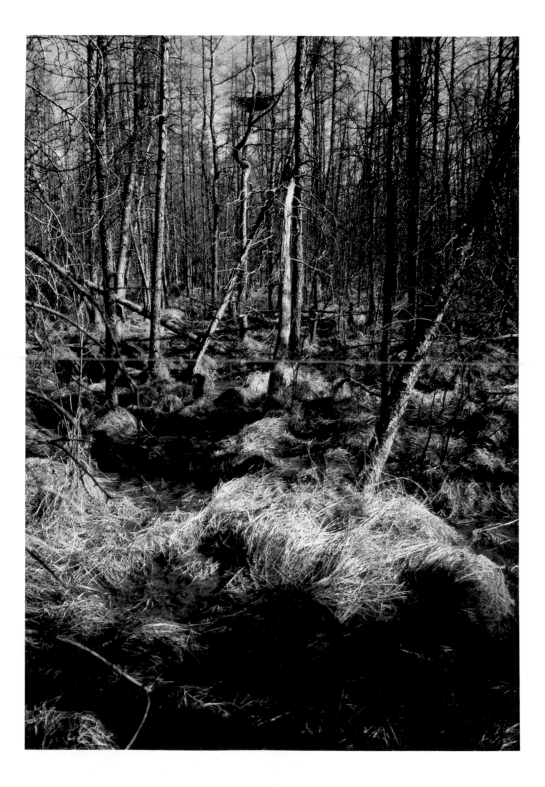

Grays sit tight to the nest, so we were afraid she might desert or the eggs get chilled. But, as we learned later, she came back, eventually both eggs hatched, and one youngster was successfully reared; the other disappeared. On a later visit, when we were able to observe the female more closely, we identified her as a bird that we had trapped, banded, and individually color-marked on March 30 within a quarter-mile of the nest tree. Thus, assuming it was the same bird that scratched out the lining of the nest in early March, this owl had been in the nest vicinity for at least two months.

This same nest, repaired and checked several times the following year, was found to have been visited by owls as early as mid-February. On April 1 we found a female on the nest, crouching low and watching us attentively as we approached. She stayed tight to the nest as we moved slowly forward, not flushing until we were within twenty-five feet of the tree. Although we were sure there would be an egg, there wasn't. There were several feathers, however, suggesting that she had been sitting on the nest for some time and that egg-laying was imminent. On our next visit, on April 3, we again found her on the nest, but this time we stayed far back, not wishing to disturb her during this critical period. From a vantage point several hundred yards away, we crouched amid small pools, sitting on damp mossy hummocks above the snow, but this soon proved uncomfortable. Finally, we arranged ourselves on an old tamarack log, breaking off the brittle, twisted branches so we could sit and watch in comfort. One time we saw her leave the nest, which was barely visible through the slender trunks and boughs, but she soon returned and settled down carefully, her manner suggesting she had at least one egg. Then she sank lower until only her head remained above the twigs that rimmed the nest. When I hooted softly, she swung her head about,

staring in our direction while we remained still, elbows on our knees, watching her every move through binoculars. Even at this distance we were wary of disturbing her, and remained motionless while she was looking toward us. Eventually we arose and departed in the cool evening, convinced that the bird was well established in our nest.

In time, four eggs were laid, but, shortly after incubation was underway, disaster struck. The parents were not to be found, and the four eggs were now only empty shells scattered on the ground, apparently eaten by Gray Jays. It was difficult to believe that the parents would have deserted the nest at this late stage. We guessed that either the male had been killed, forcing the female to desert, or else the female had been killed at the nest, either by a natural predator or by man. It was a great disappointment.

In mid-December 1975, inspired by the discovery of a few fresh Great Gray feathers hanging on twigs in fall and early winter in a tamarack woods close to a natural nest that had been occupied two years earlier, I invited a friend to help me build a new nest. This site was about fifty miles east of Winnipeg. It was a cold day when we set out, with about three feet of soft snow on the ground. Back in the bog it was dark and quiet, for it was a cloudy day. It was a new experience for my companion, who had not previously been in such habitat, and she was delighted to see dozens of White-winged Crossbills at close range feeding on tamarack cones. Cold hands and feet notwithstanding, she stood about in the snow while I searched for half an hour for a suitable tree. Then she patiently passed up to me the various materials I needed to build the nest. When the nest was finally completed, she insisted on climbing up to see the finished nest. With her soft mocassins, it was no easy feat to use the spikes I had driven into the frozen trunk. I was relieved when she had made her way safely back to the

A kind of third eyelid, the nictitating membrane sweeps across the eyeball from inner corner to outer, keeping the eye clean and moist.

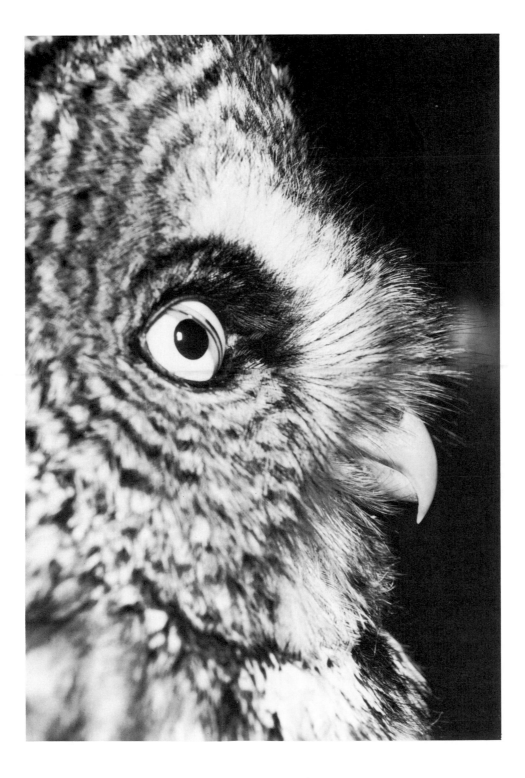

This fledgling is still largely in down plumage, but its semi-circular facial disc pattern is already evident.

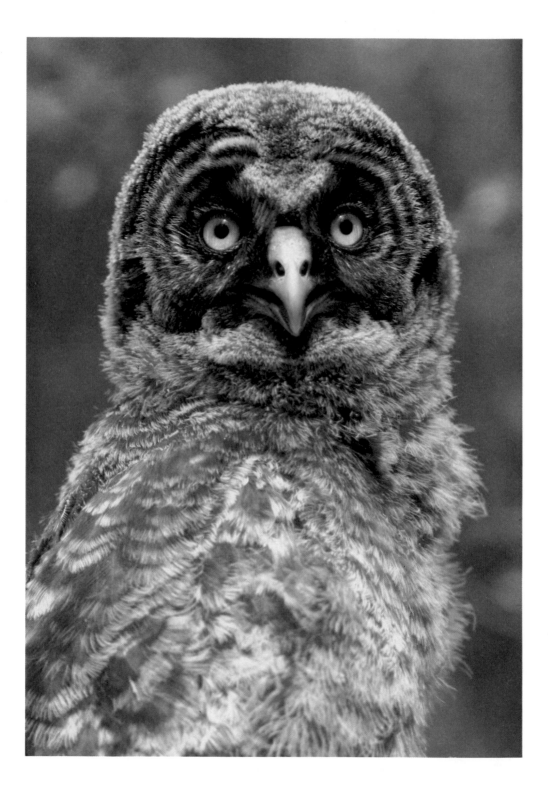

ground. Three hours had passed by the time we got back to the car.

The next time we visited this nest, in mid-May, it was warm, wet, and green in the bog. There were five downy young owlets in the nest, closely attended by a female. Built in mid-December, the nest had been occupied in early April, and here were the results! While we watched (my companion radiant at seeing her first Great Gray Owls), the male arrived with a vole, flew to the nest, gave it to the female, and disappeared over the tops of the trees.

My colleagues and I continued to build nests through the winter of 1975–76 and into spring, until we had more than fifty. In the fall and winter of 1976–77 we outdid ourselves. Ray Tuokko built an unprecedented thirty-six nests, often working by himself. I constructed another fourteen nests, relying on assistance from several people. This effort brought our total number of man-made nests to about a hundred. Of five nests that I installed in December along a three-mile stretch of road, three were occupied by Great Grays the following April. That season we had eight active nests, of which five were in man-made or reconstructed natural nests. In 1978 two of our man-made nests were used. In 1979, by which time we had built another thirty nests, we had ten active Great Gray Owl nestings. Of these, five were in man-made structures, and two were in rebuilt nests. To date, of thirty-two recent Great Gray Owl nestings, sixteen were in man-made nests, six in rebuilt nests, and ten in completely natural nests. In addition, our man-made structures were used by Great Horned Owls (twice), Long-eared Owls (twice), and Red-tailed Hawks (five times). Porcupines used a few for winter roosts, raptors used a few for feeding platforms, and one was used as a summer roost by a bat, probably a hoary bat, judging by the size of the droppings. Some of our nests have been up for five and six years, but have never been visited by Great Gray Owls (or any other bird, so far as we can tell). These nests are well constructed and in apparently suitable locations, but evidently some feature is lacking. Although a few nests built in aspens in upland sites attracted owls, the best response has been obtained from nests built in spruce-tamarack or tamarack bogs, often over water. Since most of our nests are fairly durable, we expect to be checking them for many seasons.

Probably there are many natural nests available to Great Grays over much of their range. After all, it doesn't take a pair of Broad-winged Hawks long to build a new nest. In many areas of suitable habitat that we examined, however, there was a scarcity or absence of nests; partly on this account we have continued to build nests for owls. Man-made nests, in any case, provide additional nesting sites, and may lure owls from less accessible places. In some areas, where natural nests are scarce, man-made nests could be a useful management technique.

On a few occasions, nests built by us in March and April were visited by owls a few weeks later. The quickest occupancy of a nest occurred less than four weeks after it had been built (March 12, 1979). This suggests that the birds found this nest shortly after it was installed. By finding one or two fresh Great Gray Owl feathers, or even a downy feather fragment caught on a twig, we could tell that an owl had visited a nest. This meant that an owl had not only discovered the nest, not merely looked at it, but had spent some time in it, crouched down and scratching, testing, making some judgment that only owls perceive. Thus, even after the nesting season is underway, non-breeding owls, or perhaps even a hunting male on his territory, quickly discover and visit new nests, possibly responding to an inner drive to catalog the location of nests well in advance of other seasons.

In our occupied Great Gray Owl nests we often find numerous tamarack twigs with the bark removed and the wood gnawed as if by a rodent. This is typical Great Gray Owl work. Protruding twigs that cause discomfort to the brooding female may be nibbled at over a long period in an attempt to remove them. In one nest, an owl's efforts to remove an offending twig evidently brought about the accidental trampling and loss of her eggs. However, in many successful nests small, loose twigs bear signs of nibbling, suggesting that owls find some satisfaction in this exercise. Perhaps it gives the female something to do during the long days on the nest. In some instances, the presence of a freshly nibbled twig is evidence, in the absence of a feather, that a Great Gray Owl has visited the nest.

Numerous visits are necessary to determine which nests are in use, to obtain egg-laying and hatching dates, and to band the young. Visiting a nest, however, provides more than an opportunity to gather information. Each visit is an adventure, exciting and sometimes offering unexpected delights. One early May day we were surprised to observe a male owl hunting in a small cattail marsh near a man-made nest in a spruce-tamarack bog.

When we neared the nest we walked with some apprehension because in April we had found the female on eggs, but we were aware that since our last visit she might have deserted. Upon our first, distant view of the nest, however, we could see the big, upright head of the brooding female. We moved forward, talking casually to reassure her, and she stayed on the nest, peering down at us with bright yellow eyes. Hesitating to disturb her, I tapped gently on the trunk of the tree, whereupon she flushed from the nest. Flying out over our heads, broad wings brushing against boughs, she flapped and then soared up to a high perch, meanwhile giving a soft alarm call and aggressively snapping her bill. I quickly climbed the tree, pulled myself up far enough to look over the edge of the nest, and found two white, downy young.

A few minutes after we withdrew, we saw the female return to the nest, land deftly on the edge, look down at the contents, then hop forward and shuffle about onto the owlets. When we saw that she was well settled, we headed out to the edge of the woods.

Hopes of finding a Sandhill Crane nest sent us into a nearby, nearly dry marshy bog, where in April we had seen a pair of cranes. The moment we walked out into the marsh, the strident clatter of crane voices rang out, and we saw the pair striding through the cattails and sedge a few hundred yards away. The female marched straight along, but the male circled about her, leaping up and flapping his wings. Close in front of us, at the same time, two loudly calling Common Snipe hovered with upright wings, circling over the vegetation. And two male Red-winged Black Birds, looking a little forlorn in the dry marsh, sang face to face.

And then, suddenly, we saw the *male* Great Gray Owl—upright and motionless, on a dead snag near the edge of the marsh, alert and actively hunting. It was the first time we had seen a Great Gray Owl in a marsh—the dark-plumaged bird contrasted strongly with the pale, dead grass and reeds. We slowly walked to within fifty feet of him, impressed by the rich brown and silvery-gray color of his plumage, vividly illuminated by the low evening light. From back in the woods the female owl called: a persistent, low, but penetrating single note. It seemed to stimulate the male. He moved from one black snag to another as if following a familiar route, peering intently from each perch. Finally, he dropped down out of sight; a moment later he came out carrying a vole in his bill. We followed his progress, lost him behind some willows, then saw him briefly as he headed into the trees toward the nest.

A few minutes later, while we were walking toward the cranes, the male owl reappeared, flew out to the same perch, and hunted intently once again, while his mate continued to call. At this moment, the cranes lifted and flew in tandem right over the owl, calling constantly, their loud calls echoing off the nearby trees so fast it seemed as if two pairs were calling. They flew off some distance, still calling as they went down somewhere else, leaving us alone with the hunting owl.

We stood still, charmed by the sight of the poised owl, reluctant to leave. As the sun lowered, the light seemed to become stronger, bringing everything into sharper focus. The owl flew to a new perch, where it was outlined against the pale sunset, and strongly back-lighted. Now its colors were indistinguishable; but light shone through filmy portions of its plumage, glowing brightly across the tip of the tail, up one side of the body, and around the margin of the head.

13
A Different Race of Creatures

On a day in early April, when edges of roads and woods are free of snow and dun-colored with last year's grass, I stoop to search for signs of mouse activity. Beneath clumps of old grass, I am pleased to find numerous damp runways and small, fresh, greenish droppings. The tops of newly arisen green leaves within the runways, freshly cropped by hungry voles, are further evidence. Nutrient-rich, succulent grass must be invigorating fare for animals that have survived the winter on dried stems and leaves. For early-nesting predators that depend on mice and voles for food, this activity has great importance.

I delight in the knowledge of all this fresh food out of sight beneath the matted grass, moving upward, drawn by the warm sun. I have visions of tiny, pink, blind mice clustered together in snug nests, nourished by sleek mothers fattened on this new vegetation. So I think: "Mice, grow! Reproduce—so that there will be plenty of food for owls yet to come." For not far away, in a cool, wooded grove where the snow lies more than a foot deep, I have seen a Great Gray Owl on a nest, covering her first egg.

A week later, the new grass leaves have pushed up through the old, and a light green color lies over all the dead grass. A faint buzzing of insects may be heard, and everywhere, the whistled calls of White-throated Sparrows. It is a busy time of year: willow catkins are emerging, leaves unfurling, the world is reaching out for sunlight, and in every thicket and hollow, birds are busily setting up territories, singing, and chasing with their special kind of madness.

Now the hen owl sits on three eggs, beside her a dead vole, excess food brought by her mate. Is he, I wonder, excited by the rustling and squeaking of mice and voles in shrubby meadows and grassy fields? Out of all the spring voices arising about him, the growing sounds of prey activity, their encounters, disputes, and hurrying feet, must be loud in his ears.

Focusing intently on prey, this owl is about to pounce.

It is not easy to write now that spring is here. At my desk, pen in hand, my mind wanders. I would rather be out in the still frozen bogs searching for yet another nest. We have looked in so many woods these past years it is bewildering to try to recall all the places where we have found or built nests. Each year is a new challenge. The sight of a nest, the shape of the tree that contains it, the surroundings—each situation is unique; and there have been more sites than I can easily recall. It is a group effort and between us, by quizzing and reminding each other of particular events, we manage to revisit almost every good nest each spring. Notebooks and maps help, but in the field there is a special delight as memory unfolds, as certain trees and landforms remind us of the direction to a nest.

Visiting known nests and searching for new nests each spring is a long, arduous task, and I often wonder where and when it will end. For how many more seasons will we do this? There are times when it seems senseless. And then, early one morning, after trekking a mile through the woods, following an old trail to a nest, led onward by broken saplings and faded colored marking tape, suddenly there is the nest, just as it was before. But wait, there is a new shape. Is that something on the nest? I fumble getting my binoculars into position, focus, and yes! The morning is ours, for a Great Gray Owl is there. And that is the incentive.

I still get pretty excited when I first see a Great Gray on a nest, and if it's one of our man-made nests, I can get fairly emotional. And why not? Owls can move over a lot of territory. A pair of owls moving into one of our nests is unusually satisfying. I feel like a surrogate parent—vain, jealous, protective, and should the nest fail, I am inordinately downhearted. But I ask myself the same question. How many more nests are we going to build? It's a long way to some of our artificial nests, driving and walking, and they need to be visited more than once during the season. We hardly have time now to check those we've already built. And yet, I keep thinking of special places, musing about certain sites in woods where I'm sure a nest would attract breeding owls. The urge to put up another nest is strong, to add one more nest to an empty forest, to try again to lure a pair of owls. Whatever the reason, science or pure enjoyment, I am likely to be there next April. The possibility of finding a nest occupied by a Great Gray Owl gives me all the excuse I need to wander in the bog.

There is no doubt that I have become charmed with tamarack bogs. The hours of fruitless stumbling and tripping over deadfalls, the swarms of blackflies and mosquitoes, the cold emptiness on some winter days—these are minor annoyances compared to the beauty of orchids and lush greenery, the songs of myriad birds, and the wonder of seeing Great Gray Owls at a nest site. Some readers may recall Aldo Leopold's story about the two Wisconsin farmers who, in their later years, took time to plant a truck-load of young tamaracks on their farm. After years of hard work, draining and clearing their land to survive, they realized they missed the wildflowers they used to enjoy, and so they struggled to replant a small tamarack bog. It is something I now can understand.

Today in Manitoba large tamarack-bog areas are being drained and cleared to obtain more agricultural land. Sometimes the peat is removed with bulldozers, but often it is burned off to expose the underlying mineral soil. In the best situations, where feasible, the peat is simply plowed into the underlying soil. But removal of peat by burning is still a widespread practice and peat smoke has become a highway traffic hazard. In many places, however, it is the peat that is sought. This resource is being dug up and shipped in plastic packages as far as the states of the Southwest for use as a natural mulch and fertilizer for gardens. So the organic debris accumulated during a thousand summers helps make flowers bloom in far-away deserts.

But peat has other values as well. The current energy shortage has given a new value to this substance. Next to coal, peat is America's second most abundant fossil fuel. It can be burned directly to produce power, and also can be converted into substitute natural gas. Half of the peat reserves of the United States are in Alaska, but the most readily accessible supply is in Minnesota, where there is an active program to develop peat for energy. Is peat mining likely to be a threat to Great Gray Owl habitat? (As I see it, some of the best habitat is in extreme southeastern Manitoba and northern Minnesota.) At the moment the answer is unknown, but replacement of peat is a slow process. In Minnesota, consideration is being given to the many values—including Sandhill Cranes, Great Gray Owls, and orchids—of these forested peatlands before they are released for commercial exploitation.

Until recently, the tamarack forest was of only marginal value to forestry, occasionally being cut for fence posts or firewood. On this basis, in Manitoba we have had some tamarack stands set aside for Great Gray Owl nesting sites. Now, however, trees are being harvested in southeastern Manitoba for paper mills in Wisconsin. According to foresters, good regeneration of tamarack is obtained by clear-cutting, and this is the present practice. If commercial use of tamarack forests cannot be kept on a sustained-yield basis, this may be a threat to Great Gray Owl breeding habitat. This new demand for the tamarack resource is not limited to Manitoba, but wherever tamarack is abundant and accessible.

Some observers report that in recent years, as a result of extensive tree clearing and other forestry practices, owl habitat in Norway, Sweden, and Finland has greatly diminished. Human activities in formerly remote regions over much of its breeding range in North America pose an ever increasing threat through shooting and an equally deleterious effect on elimination of habitat. In west-central Alberta, local observers report that during the past fifty years thousands of acres of habitat suitable for, and probably occupied by breeding Great Gray Owls, have been destroyed by lumbering, closely followed by the clearing of land for agriculture. At present, so I am informed, this destruction is spreading into north-central Alberta. The same observers report that in central and west-central Alberta, where Great Gray Owls frequently appear in winter to forage in open meadows for voles and shrews, heavy use of the same site by skidoos is apparently causing a reduction in microtine use, or reduction of the populations of these small rodents. At the same time, Great Grays, and other owls, are visiting these areas less frequently. There are also reports of widespread destruction of habitat in western and northern Saskatchewan by mining exploration crews. In the Lac du Bonnet area, northeast of Winnipeg, important winter feeding grounds are rapidly being lost to cottage site development. According to biologist Jon Winter, loss of mature old-forest habitat within the Great Gray Owl's limited range in northern California has put this species on the endangered list for that state.

Despite these pessimistic aspects, there is still a lot of habitat for these adaptable owls. In our study area, for example, I am impressed with the amount of potential breeding habitat. As I stand on the crest of a sandy, morainal ridge that rises above the boglands of southeastern Manitoba, there is habitat as far as I can see. Out over the tops of birch, aspen, and jack pine on the near slopes, out over the black spruce and tamarack, a blue veil reaches to the horizon. Mile after mile of muskeg, hundreds of square miles of habitat—homes for owls. With this vista before me, it is easy to forget the overall, broader concerns for habitat loss. I wonder how we should ever know this region? How we should ever determine how many owls find haven here? How we should ever know where owls are now established, female on nest, male nearby?

Moreover, there are some additional interrelationships here and elsewhere that warrant study. Owls eat shrews; shrews eat pupating larch sawfly larvae; the larch sawfly kills or injures tamarack (larch) trees. The tamaracks we choose to build nests in may have been deformed as a result of larch sawfly attacks. Infestation by larch sawfly caused suppression and massive die-offs in the past, across the range of tamarack in the United States and Canada, followed by the invasion and dominance of black spruce. Larch sawfly is still a major threat to tamarack. This is an area of investigation with possible implications to Great Gray Owl distribution, past, present, and future.

Loggers, trappers, cross-country skiers, snowmobilers, many know these woods better than we do, especially in winter, but few follow our trail, which is an intellectual and emotional one, a tangle, a bog, a journey, and an exploration of its own. In how many moments have I pondered the difficulties of ever knowing anything about this bird, this owl that so resists our efforts? Watching for owls in the early dawn, looking at the jagged tops of spruce and tamarack against the orange rising sun, I have thought of the many unsolved problems, the seeming insurmountability of really ever knowing the essence of this bird.

It will be many years before there are enough banded birds even in the small area in which we are working for us to learn much about them. How to identify local resident birds from northern emigrants? How to distinguish family groups? How to census this portion of their breeding grounds? How can we estimate their total numbers, and how will we be able to measure their population changes from year to year? How can we know the extent to which emigrant birds help sustain local populations? Against the obvious heavy mortality that this species suffers, is it the occasional influx of more northerly birds that maintains their presence

here? How far do owls range in those winters when they appear suddenly in strange places, like strangers still wearing their native garb?

Clearly, in some winters Great Gray Owls must come from more northerly breeding ranges, for often winter appearances of Great Grays coincide with irruptions of Boreal Owls and Hawk Owls, neither of which appears to breed to any extent in southeastern Manitoba. Movements of Great Gray Owls into southern Minnesota, Wisconsin, Michigan, and southern Ontario further support this idea. How to determine which owls are local birds and which are emigrants is one of the major problems.

On a local basis, much insight has been gained into the distribution and movements of owls, but probably the solutions to many problems lie in the analysis of information from a much broader region. Across the whole range of the species, a host of climatic and ecological factors act upon these birds. Studies now in progress in California, Oregon, Minnesota, and Wisconsin should shed considerable light on these aspects.

Radio-telemetry and other technological marvels of this space-age era may yet yield answers to questions that have intrigued us for years. The distant signal of a radio-tagged owl winging through the forest on moonlit nights could lead us to a nest, carrying us over unknown reaches of bogland. The same technique could reveal the duration of the family bond and outline the movements of young and adults, long after the nest has been left behind.

One day, a student shivering in a tent near a nest site in mid-February may see the courtship ritual of the Great Gray Owl. On some frosty dawn, with the woods aglitter with the first light, he may see the graceful posturing and hear the soft calls, witness with fresh insight what we have barely glimpsed. It will be a tough, cold task, but one day we may know what the owls do at night, where they roost, how they go about in search of nests, and how they behave when looking over a potential nest site.

What manner of bird is this? What is the explanation for its tameness? "Tame" is probably a misnomer. Unwary, docile, unconcerned with man? And yet at times it attacks man violently. Still, its seeming docility is one of its most noted characteristics. Is this trait related to its usual range in remote northern areas far from man? Boreal, Saw-whet, and Hawk owls are equally docile. So too is the Spotted Owl, the Great Gray Owl's closest relative in North America; a southern subspecies of the Spotted Owl, nesting in New Mexico, is reportedly equally as bold or docile. Many birds are unusually bold at the nest site. Perhaps it is the large size of the Great Gray that makes this aspect of its behavior especially noticeable. The Great Gray Owl's response to man is, really, an unknown quality of the bird, a feature that adds to its attractiveness.

Years ago, Thoreau wrote: "I rejoice that there are owls. Let them do the idiotic and maniacal hooting for men. It is a sound admirably suited to swamps and twilight woods which no day illustrates, suggesting a vast and undeveloped nature which men have not recognized. They represent the stark twilight and unsatisfied thoughts which all have. All day the sun has shone on the surface of some savage swamp, where the single spruce stands hung with usnea lichens, and small hawks circulate above, and the chickadee lisps amid the evergreens, and the partridge and rabbit skulk beneath; but now a more dismal and fitting day dawns, and a different race of creatures awakes to express the meaning of Nature there." He could, with that sentiment, have been writing about the Great Gray Owl.

However much is learned, there is some comfort, I think, in believing that the ultimate quality of a species, its essence, rests not in data alone, but in some impression in our minds, some subjective

An unwavering, steady stare that focuses past the photographer.

aspect. We probably can never really know any other creature fully. Though we catalog its comings and goings, measure and photograph its performances, count its numbers, and write endlessly about it, still, the true character of this "different race of creatures" eludes us.

In my own pursuit of the owl, I crave further understanding of its relationship to the spruce-tamarack bog and all it contains. What holds meaning for the owl? Being part of the bog, it relates to this environment in ways we'll probably never know. There are many barriers between us, but here I would venture. The owl has superior vision and hearing, but what does it perceive in its surroundings? When an owl drops down onto a mouse, does it notice the orchid blooming beside its feet? Or does it have visions of a nest, hungry young, or its mate? We say "it stares blankly," but we don't know what its visual world embraces. It hears everything we hear and more, but in what way? In sky, forest, flowers, and birds, we humans see patterns of light and color, hear a medley of sounds, perceive various elements according to our individual insights, sharing some, but not all. But ah! if we could perceive the world of the owl, what strange sounds and beautiful forms we might enjoy!

Bibliography

Allen, Francis H. "The Great Gray Owl near Boston." *Auk* 21 (1904): 278.

American Ornithologists' Union. *Check-list of North American Birds.* 5th ed. Baltimore, Md., 1957.

Angell, Tony. *Owls.* Seattle: University of Washington Press, 1974.

Audubon, John James. *The Birds of America.* Vol. 1. 1840.

Baird, Spencer F., et al. *A History of North American Birds.* Vol. 3. Boston: Little, Brown & Co., 1905.

Barrows, Walter B. *Michigan Bird Life.* East Lansing: Special Bulletin, Michigan Agricultural College, 1912.

Bell, Gary P. "The Owl Invasion of Amherst Island, Ontario." *American Birds* 33 (1979): 245–46.

Bent, Arthur C. "Life Histories of North American Birds of Prey." *U.S. National Museum Bulletin* 170, part 2, pp. 213–20. Washington, D.C.: Smithsonian Institution, 1930.

Berggren, Valdemar, and Wahlstedt, Jens. "Lappugglans *Strix nebulosa* läten." [The sound repertoire of the Great Gray Owl *Strix nebulosa.*] *Vår Fågelvärld* 36 (1977): 243–49.

Bird, David M., and Wright, Jo. "Apparent Distraction Display by a Barred Owl." *Canadian Field-Naturalist* 91 (1977): 176–77.

Blair, Hugh M.S. "Studies of Less Familiar Birds. 119. Great Grey Owl." *British Birds* 55 (1962): 414–18.

Blanich, Jo. "Summer Record of Great Gray Owls in Aitkin County." *Loon* 47 (1975): 188–89.

Brown, Herman J. "Bandits of the Pine Barrens." *Minnesota Naturalist* 3 (1953) 33–38.

Brunton, Daniel F., and Pittaway, Ronald, Jr. "Observations of the Great Gray Owl on Winter Range." *Canadian Field-Naturalist* 85 (1971): 315–22.

Buckner, Charles H. "Populations and Ecological Relationships of Shrews in Tamarack Bogs of Southeastern Manitoba." *Journal of Mammalogy* 47 (1966): 181–94.

Burton, John A., ed. *Owls of the World, Their Evolution, Structure and Ecology.* [Especially section on Great Gray Owl by Heimo Mikkola.] New York: E.P. Dutton, 1973.

Butler, Douglas H. "Great Gray Owl from Fillmore County." *Loon* 51 (1979): 46–47.

Clark, Richard J. *A Field Study of the Short-eared Owl, Asio flammeus (Pontoppidan), in North America.* Wildlife Monographs No. 47, Washington, D.C.: The Wildlife Society, 1975.

Collins, K. Michael. "Aspects of the Biology of the Great Gray Owl." Master's thesis (in preparation), University of Manitoba, Winnipeg.

Craighead, John J., and Craighead, Francis C., Jr. *Hawks, Owls and Wildlife.* New York: Dover Publications, 1956.

Dement'ev, Georgii P., et al. *Birds of the Soviet Union.* Vol. 1, Jerusalem: Israel Program for Scientific Translations, 1966.

Derleth, August. "Country Calendar: Autumn." *Passenger Pigeon* 14 (1952): 106–9.

Dunstan, Thomas C., and Sample, Steve D. "Biology of Barred Owls in Minnesota." *Loon* 44: 111–15.

Earhart, Caroline M., and Johnson, Ned K. "Size Dimorphism and Food Habits of North American Owls." *Condor* 72 (1970): 251–64.

Eckert, Allan W. *The Owls of North America.* Garden City, N.Y.: Doubleday & Co., 1974.

Eckert, Kim. "Invasion of Great Gray and Boreal Owls, Winter 1977–78." *Loon* 50 (1978): 63–68.

Elton, Charles S. *Voles, Mice and Lemmings: Problems in Population Dynamics.* Oxford: Clarendon Press, 1942.

Everett, Michael. *A Natural History of Owls.* London: Hamlyn Publishing Group Limited, 1977.

Ferguson-Lees, I. James. "Photographic Studies of Some Less Familiar Birds. LXIX. Great Grey Owl." *British Birds* 49 (1956): 26–27.

Fisher, Bob M. "Response of a Hawk Owl to a Lure." *Blue Jay* 32 (1974): 154–55.

———. "Possible Intra-specific Killing by a Great Gray Owl." *Canadian Field-Naturalist* 89 (1975): 71–72.

Fitzpatrick, John W. "A Record of Allopreening in the Barred Owl." *Auk* 92 (1975): 598–99.

Fleay, David. *Nightwatchmen of Bush and Plain.* [Australian Owls and Owl-like Birds.] Brisbane: The Jacaranda Press, 1968.

Follen, Don G., Sr. "A Probable Breeding Record of Great Gray Owls in Wisconsin." *Passenger Pigeon* 41 (1979): 53–57.

Forbush, Edward H. *Birds of Massachusetts and Other New England States.* Vol. 2. Norwood: Massachusetts Department of Agriculture, 1927.

Forsman, Eric D., and Wight, Howard M. "Allowpreening in Owls: What Are Its Functions?" *Auk* 96 (1979): 525–31.

Forster, John R. "An Account of the Birds Sent from Hudson's Bay." *Transactions of the Philadelphia Royal Society,* vol. 62. pp. 382–433. Philadelphia, 1772.

Godfrey, W. Earl. "The Birds of Canada." *National Museum of Canada Bulletin* 203. Ottawa, 1966.

———. "Some Winter Aspects of the Great Gray Owl." *Canadian Field-Naturalist* 81 (1967): 99–101.

Green, Janet C. "Northern Owl Invasion, Winter, 1968–1969." *Loon* 41 (1969): 36–39.

Grey Owl [Archie, Belaney]. *Pilgrims of the Wild.* London: Peter Davies, 1939.

Hausman, Leon A. *The Illustrated Encyclopedia of American Birds.* New York: Garden City Publishing Co., 1947.

Henderson, Archibald D. "Nesting of the Great Gray Owl in Central Alberta." *Oölogist* 32 (1915): 2–6.

———. "Further Notes on the Nesting of the Great Gray Owl." *Oölogist* 40 (1923): 126–27.

Höglund, Nils H., and Lansgren, Erik. "The Great Grey Owl and Its Prey in Sweden." *Viltrevy* 5 (1968): 363–421.

Houston, [C.] Stuart. "The Great Gray Owl in Saskatchewan." *Blue Jay* 15 (1959): 150–53.

Houston, C. Stuart. "Reproduction in Great Horned Owls." *Bird Banding* 46 (1975): 302–4.

———. "Recoveries of Saskatchewan-banded Great Horned Owls." *Canadian Field Naturalist* 92 (1978): 61–66.

Houston, C. Stuart, and Street, Maurice. *The Birds of the Saskatchewan River, Carlton to Cumberland.* Special Publication no. 2, Saskatchewan Natural History Society, Regina.

Irving, Laurence. "Birds of Anaktuvak Pass, Kobruk, and Old Crow." *U.S. National Museum Bulletin* 217. Washington, D.C.: Smithsonian Institution, 1959.

James, Ross D. "First Nesting of the Great Gray Owl in Ontario." *Ontario Field Biologist* 31 (1977): 55.

Jenness, Diamond. "The Ojibwa Indians of Parry Island, Their Social and Religious Life." *National Museum of Canada Bulletin* 78. Ottawa, 1935.

Jones, Edgar T. "The Great Gray Owl." *Blue Jay* 12 (1954): 8.

Konishi, Masakazu. "How the Owl Tracks Its Prey." *American Scientist* 61 (1973): 414–24.

Kondla, Norbert G. "Great Gray Owls Raise Two Young Southeast of Edmonton, Alberta." *Blue Jay* 31 (1973): 98–100.

Lambert, Gordon. "A New Species is Added to North American Bird Life." *Bird-Banding* 18 (1947): 129–30.

Law, Clifford. "The Great Gray Owl of the Woodlands." *Blue Jay* 18 (1960): 14–16.

Leopold, Aldo. *Round River.* New York: Oxford University Press, 1953.

Lindblad, Jan. *I ugglemarker.* [Owl-watcher.] Stockholm: Alb. Bonniers boktrykeri, 1967.

McKay, William E. "The Great Grey Owl." *Dinny's Digest* [Calgary Zoo.] 2 (1972): 16, 18.

McKeever, Katherine. *Care and Rehabilitation of Injured Owls.* The Owl Rehabilitation Research Foundation, Vineland, Ontario. Lincoln, Ont.: Rannie, 1979.

Macoun, John. *Catalogue of Canadian Birds.* Part 2. Ottawa: Geological Survey of Canada, 1903.

Madura, Marilu L. "Feathered Observations." *Passenger Pigeon* 14 (1952): 99–102.

Mikkola, Heimo. "Food of Great Grey Owls in Fenno-Scandia." *British Birds* 63 (1970): 23–27.

———. "Lapinpöllöjen joukkokuolema vuonna 1971." [Population crash of the Great Gray Owl in Finland in 1971.] *Suomen Luonto* 30 (1971): 177–79, 213.

———. "Owls Killing and Killed by Other Owls and Raptors in Europe." *British Birds* 69 (1976): 144–54.

———. *Der Bartkauz* [Great Gray Owl.] A Ziemsen Verlag, Witt L., Neve Brem-Buckereis no. 51. In press.

Mikkola, Heimo, and Sulkava, Seppo. "On the Occurrence of the Great Gray Owl (*Strix nebulosa*) in Finland 1955–68." *Ornis Fennica* 46 (1969): 126–31.

Mitchell, Bob. "The Great Gray Owl." *Wildlife Crusader* 15 (1969): 24–25.

Molhoff, Wayne J. "Great Gray Owl Distribution, Winter 1977–78." *Nebraska Bird Review* 47 (1979): 62–65.

Muir, Dalton. "At a Nest of the Great Gray Owl." *Nature Canada* 1 (1972): 20–22.

Nero, Robert W. "The Status of the Great Gray Owl in Manitoba, with Special Reference to the 1968–69 Influx." *Blue Jay* 27 (1969): 191–209.

———. "Great Gray Owls nesting Near Roseau." *Loon* 42 (1970a): 88–93.

———. "A Visit to a Great Gray Owl Nest." *Ontario Naturalist* 8 (1970b): 4–7.

———. "Additional Great Gray Owl Records for Manitoba and Adjacent Minnesota." *Blue Jay* 28 (1970c): 72–73.

———. "Spirit of the Boreal Forest: the Great Gray Owl." *Beaver* 302 (1971): 25–29.

———. "Great Gray Owl Impaled on Barbed Wire." *Blue Jay* 32 (1974): 178–79.

———. "Great Gray Owl Nests." *Manitoba Nature* 17 (1977a): 4–11.

——. "Great Gray Owls in Our Woods." *Wildlife Crusader* 23 (1977b): 10–12.

——. "Beware: Mother on Nest." *International Wildlife* 8 (1978): 12–15.

Nero, Robert W., et al. "Great Gray Owls Occupy Artificial Nest." *Loon* 46 (1974): 161–65.

Norman, Ernest S. "Additions to the Birds of Shoal Lake, Manitoba." *Canadian Field-Naturalist* 34 (1920): 154.

Nuttall, Thomas. "The Land Birds." In *A Manual of the Ornithology of the United States and Canada.* 2nd ed. Cambridge: Hilliard & Brown, 1840.

Oeming, Albert F. "In Quest of the Rare Great Gray Owl." *Canadian Geographical Journal* 73 (1955): 236–43.

——. "The Great Grey Owl." *Game Bird Breeders, Pheasant Fanciers and Aviculturists' Gazette,* August 1970.

——. *A Preliminary Study of the Great Gray Owl (Scotiaptex nebulosa nebulosa) (Forster) in Alberta with Observations on Some Other Species of Owls.* Master's thesis, University of Alberta, Edmonton.

Parmelee, David F. "Nesting of the Great Gray Owl in Manitoba." *Blue Jay* 26 (1968): 120–21.

——. "Canada's Incredible Arctic Owls." *Beaver* 303 (1972): 30–41.

Payne, Roger S. "How the Barn Owl Locates Its Prey." *The Living Bird* (1962): 151–89.

——. "Acoustic Location of Prey by Barn Owls (*Tyto alba*)." *Journal of Experimental Biology* 54 (1971): 535–73.

Pearson, T. Gilbert, ed. *Birds of America.* New York: Garden City Publishing Co., 1917.

Peck, George K. "Recent Revision to the List of Ontario's Breeding Birds." *Ontario Field Biologist* 30 (1976): 9–16.

Pittaway, Ronald, Jr., and Brunton, Daniel. "The Great Gray Owl—Fact and Fiction." *Trail & Landscape* 3 (1969): 94–97.

Pulliainen, Erkki, and Loisa, Kalevi. "Breeding Biology and Food of the Great Grey Owl, *Strix nebulosa,* in Northeastern Finnish Forest Lapland." *Aquilo Ser. Zoology* 17 (1977): 23–33.

Richardson, John, and Swainson, William. *Fauna Boreali-Americana.* Vol. 2. *The Birds.* London: John Murray, 1831.

Roberts, Thomas S. *The Birds of Minnesota.* Vol. 2. Minneapolis: University of Minnesota Press, 1932.

——. "Great Gray Owl, *Scotiaptex nebulosa nebulosa,* Nesting in Minnesota." *Journal of Minnesota Ornithology* 1 (1936): 65–66.

Robinson, Ed. "Found Nest of the Great Gray Owl." *Blue Jay* 12 (1954): 20.

Salt, W. Ray, and Salt, James R. *The Birds of Alberta, with Their Ranges in Saskatchewan and Manitoba.* Edmonton: Hurtig Publishers, 1976.

Saurola, P. "Artificial Nest Construction in Europe." In *Bird of Prey Management Techniques.* Edited by T. A. Geer. British Falconers' Club, 1978.

Sept, Duane. "Great Gray Owl and Whip-poor-will in Prince Albert National Park." *Blue Jay* 34 (1976): 164–65.

Smith, F. Napier. "The American Hawk Owl (*Surnis* [sic] *ulula caparoch*)." *Canadian Field-Naturalist* 36 (1922): 68–71.

Sparks, John, and Soper, Tony. *Owls, Their Natural and Unnatural History.* New York: Taplinger Publishing Co., 1970.

Stefansson, Ove. "Lappuggla (*Strix nebulosa*) i Norrbotten 1975–1978." *Norrbottens Natur* 34 (1978): 49–63.

Stewart, Robert E., et al. "Live Trapping of Hawks and Owls." *Journal of Wildlife Management* 9 (1945): 99–105.

Taverner, Percy A. "Great Gray Owl." (In General Notes.) *Auk* 29 (1912): 397.

Taylor, Philip S. "Breeding Behavior of the Snowy Owl." *The Living Bird, Twelfth Annual* (1973): 137–53.

Thompson, Ernest E. [Ernest Thompson Seton.] "The Birds of Manitoba." *Proceedings of the U.S. National Museum* [Smithsonian Institution], vol. 13, pp. 457–643. Washington, D.C., 1891.

Thoreau, Henry David. *Walden.* New York: New American Library of World Literature, 1942.

Todd, W.E. Clyde. *Birds of the Labrador Peninsula and Adjacent Areas.* Toronto: University of Toronto Press, 1963.

Tucker, James A. "ABA's 50 Most Wanted Birds." *Birding* 4 (1972): 189–90.

Turnock, William J. "Ecological Life-History of the Larch Sawfly, *Pristiphora erichsonii* (HTG.) (Hymenoptera: Tenthredinidae), in Manitoba and Saskatchewan." *Canadian Entomologist* 92 (1960): 500–516.

Tyler, Hamilton, and Phillips, Don. *Owls by Day and Night.* Naturegraph Books: 987 Happy Camp, Calif., 1977.

Vickery, Peter D., and Yunick, Robert P. "The 1978–1979 Great Gray Owl Incursion Across Northeastern North America." *American Birds* 33 (1979): 242–44.

Wahlstedt, Jens. "Jakt, matning och läten hos lappuggla *Strix nebulosa*." [Hunting, Feeding, and Vocalization of the Great Gray Owl.] *Vår Fågelvärld* 28 (1969): 89–101.

———. "Lappugglan *Strix nebulosa* i Sverige 1973." [The Great Gray Owl in Sweden in 1973.] *Vår Fågelvärld* 33 (1974): 132–39.

———. "Lappugglan *Strix nebulosa* i Sverige 1974." [The Great Gray Owl in Sweden in 1974.] *Vår Fågelvärld* 35 (1976): 122–25.

Walker, Lewis W. *The Book of Owls.* [Especially section on Great Gray Owls by Albert F. Oeming.] New York: A.A. Knopf, 1974.

Wechsler, Charles A. "Gray Ghost of the Boreal Forest." *Minnesota Volunteer* 36 (1973): 25–30.

Williams, Glyndwr, and Glover, Richard, eds. *Andrew Grahman's Observations on Hudson's Bay 1767–91.* The Hudson's Bay Record Society, London, 1969.

Index

Alaska, 59, 82, 87, 96, 151
Alberta, 32, 35, 59, 62, 65, 86, 95, 98, 103, 151
  government of, 68
Allen, Francis H., 32
Alymer (Quebec), 28
American Birding Association, 29
American Robin, 15
Amherst Island (Ontario), 28, 63
Arctic Circle, 35
Audubon, John James, 86

Bailey, Vernon, 51
Bal-chatri, 46, 51, 104
Barn Owl, 88
Barrows, Walter B., 97
Barred Owl, 29, 83, 84, 107
Belvedere (Alberta), 65
Bent, Arthur C., 72, 87
Berggren, Valdemar, 83
Bird, David M., 84
Black bear, 95
Black-capped Chickadee, 37, 122
Blue Jay, 15, 122, 126
Boreal Chickadee, 28
Boreal chorus frog, 16
Boreal Owl, 24, 29, 68, 92, 96, 153
British Columbia, 59
Broad-winged Hawk 102, 128, 145
Brown, Herman J., 99
Brunton, Daniel F., 28, 48, 83, 88, 90, 93
Butler, Douglas, 63

California, 59, 151, 153
Canada, 59, 62, 98
Caribou, 57
Carlson, Elsie, 44
Churchill (Manitoba), 96
Collins, K. Michael, 12, 126
Common Crow, 32, 59, 95, 102
Common Flicker, 15, 122
Common Goldeneye, 16
Common Raven, 24, 59, 95, 102
Common Snipe, 146
Connecticut Warbler, 126
Copland, Herbert W.R., 12, 38, 42, 45, 54, 63, 92, 115, 128, 139

Cotter, George, 96
Cradle boards, 96
Craighead, Francis C., Jr., 95, 103
Craighead, John J., 95, 103

Dall, William H., 83, 87
Dedham (Massachusetts), 29
de Graff, Ken, 110
Dirks, Henry T., M.D., 114
Donald, John, 56
Dragonfly, 87
Duluth (Minnesota), 29, 64

Eastman, Karen, 131
Edmonton (Alberta), 32, 35
Elton, Charles S., 63
Eurasia, 58
Europe, 62

Field, James Thomas, 39
Finland, 59, 77, 86, 151
Fisher, Bob, 48, 86
Fitzpatrick, John W., 107
Forbush, Edward H., 63
Forest tent caterpillar, 126
Forsman, Eric D., 108
Forster, John R., 58, 72
Fort Severn (Ontario), 58
Fryklund, Per O., 114
Fur trade era, 58

Gill (Massachusetts), 29
Godfrey, W. Earl, 86, 88, 90
Golden Eagle, 35, 95
Goshawk, 15, 16, 65, 80, 95, 99
Graham, Andrew, 58, 73, 88
Grand Rapids (Manitoba), 96
Gray Jay, 24, 28, 33, 122, 126, 142
Great Bear Lake, 58, 62
Great Gray Owl (*Strix nebulosa*)
  acoustical ability, 73, 87, 88
  agonistic display, 77, 105
  allopreening (mutual preening), 107–9
  apteria, 82
  banding, 23, 45, 56
  band recoveries, 63
  bathing, 17

behavior, 48–49
bill color, 76
bill snapping, 41, 58, 77, 128, 130
breeding grounds, 24, 32
brood patch, 111, 114
capture techniques, 45–56
capturing a female, 130–31, 134
capturing an owl, 39
carrion feeding, 86–87
caught on barbed wire, 44
chick, accidental loss of, 124–25
clutch size, 102
collision with motor vehicles, 98
common names, Eurasian and North
    American, 58
concealment behavior, 80
conservation of, 99
cooling methods, 82
copulation, 84, 110
courtship, 102–4
courtship feeding, 66, 67, 101–4, 109–10
density, 62
description of, 33, 59, 72, 73, 76–83
differences in sexes, 72
distraction display (injury feigning), 36,
    84, 122, 130–31
effects of capture, 56
effects of weather, 45, 93
egg shape and size, 102–3
electrocuted, 98
Eurasian race: *S.n. lapponica*, 58
feather traits, 82
feeding behavior, 117, 120
female aggressiveness, 56, 121, 122, 131
female attentiveness, 120
female behavior, 117–18
female boldness at nest, 126
female luring young from nest site, 127
female stealing prey from male, 120–21
first banded, 45
fledging behavior, 118
fledglings, 118, 122
food habits, 86, 87
flight ability, 34–35
growth rate, 102
gunning mortality, 97, 98
habitat, 59
hatching, 117
harassment by Common Crow, 95

incubation, 111–12
irruptions (incursions), 63, 86, 98, 108
length of family bond, 122
looking for natural nests, 149–50
loss of young from nest, 118
male feeds female, 17
male hunting behavior, 127–28
man-made nests, use of, 139, 142, 145,
    146
marking techniques, 45,
molt, 73
mortality by man, 95–96,
museum specimens, 21
nest at The Pas (Manitoba), 16–17
nest building, 102
nest desertion, 125
nest, first in Minnesota, 114
nest, second in Minnesota, 114–22
nest, first known to science, 58
nests, Alberta, 65, 68
nests, man-made, 106, 139, 145, 147,
    153
nests, number of, 59, 62, 65, 68
nests, early visits to, 138, 142, 145
nesting behavior, 138
nests, other, 125–34
nest site, 102
nest site selection, 103
nictitating membrane, 41, 143
nomadic habits, 62–63, 86
North American race: *S.n. nebulosa*, 58
number banded, 45
oil gland, 81
owl nest search behavior, 145
pair formation, 102, 103–106
peat mining, 151
pellets, 40, 118
perching on wires, 33
periods of activity, 93
plumage characteristics, 72–73, 76
population, 21, 24, 45, 59, 62–63, 64,
    65
predation on, 95
preening behavior, 17, 81
preening response to man, 41, 106–7
pre-fledging behavior, 118
prey, 62, 86, 87
protective coloration, 80
pseudo-hunting behavior, 104–5

range, 59–65
taking prey from man, 120, 121
rehabilitation of owls, 100
relationship to prey, 102
repeat use of nests, 62–63
response of captured bird, 66
response to man-made lure, 48, 49
Saskatchewan records of, 65
scientific collecting, 62
scientific names, 58
sexual behavior, 103–4, 110
snow plunging (to capture prey; in
    courtship), 88–93
subspecies, Eurasian, 58
subspecies, North American, 58
sun bathing, 81
specimens of, 58, 98–99
talons, 81
territorial behavior, 103, 106
territory (range) size, 103
trapping mortality, 96–98
twig nibbling, 145–46
use by Indians, 96
use of a wing for balance when
    perched, 34
visits to nests by birds, 110–11, 146,
    149, 150
visual acuity, 92–93
vocalizations, 40, 69, 83–84, 103, 122,
    126–27, 128
weights, 58, 72
winter concentration, Minnesota, 114
winter irruptions, 63–64, 65
Great Horned Owl, 24, 29, 35, 65, 69, 72,
    95, 96, 97–98, 139, 145
Green, Janet C., 98

Halvorson, Henry, 114
Harrier (Marsh Hawk), 127
Hawk Owl, 24, 29, 48, 68, 92, 120, 153
Henderson, Archibald D., 32, 65, 97, 103,
    125
Herbert, Jack D., 16
Herchmer (Manitoba), 96
Hoary bat, 145
Höglund, Nils H., 102, 103, 118, 121, 122
House Sparrow, 42, 46
Houston, C. Stuart, M.D., 65
Hudson Bay, 58, 73, 96

Idaho, 59
Irving, Laurence, 96

James Bay, 59, 95
Jenness, Diamond, 96
Jones, Edgar T., 68
Jyrkkanen, Jorma, 40

Kingston (Ontario), 29, 63
Knapton, Richard W., 92
Kondla, Norbert G., 32

Lac du Bonnet (Manitoba), 34, 95
Lake of the Woods, 21
Lake Superior, 58
Lambert, Gordon, 45
Lambeth, David, 33
Lansgren, Erik, 102, 103, 104, 106, 108
Larch sawfly, 153
Law, Clifford, 77, 88
Lawrence, Alex G., 41, 42, 95
Least Flycatcher, 126
Leinonen, Antti, 95
Leopold, Aldo, 150
Lincoln's Sparrow, 131
Loisa, Kaleni, 77
Long-eared Owl, 77, 145
Lynx, 57, 94, 96

McKay, William E., 98
McKeever, Katherine, 100, 108
Madura, Marilu L., 47
Maine, 98
Mallard, 95, 99
Manitoba, 16, 21, 45, 58, 62, 64, 82, 86,
    95, 100
    Department of Natural Resources, 98
    Hydro-Electric of, 98
Marblehead (Massachusetts), 86
Marten, 34, 86–87
Maryland, 29
Massachusetts, 86, 98
Meadow vole, 46, 48, 50, 90, 117, 118
Michigan, 97, 153
Mikkola, Heimo, 59, 86, 95
Minnesota, 21, 59, 62, 98, 114, 124, 128,
    151, 153
Mistletoe, 32
Montana, 59

Montreal (Quebec), 32, 98
Montreal Island (Quebec), 98
Moose, 24
Moose Factory (Ontario), 95, 96
Moosonee (Ontario), 24, 34, 86
Mossop, Harold, 39, 98
Mourning Warbler, 130
Muir, Dalton, 12, 35, 115, 116, 117

New England States, 63, 64
New Jersey, 29
New York, 63, 64
Newell, Charles E., 131
Nordstrom, Clarence, 114
Norman, Ernest S., 82
North America, 58, 59, 62
North Dakota, 33
Norway, 58, 151
Norway rat, 87
Nulato (Alaska), 87
Nuttall, Thomas, 86, 88

Oeming, Albert F., 35, 49, 65, 77, 95, 97, 107
Ontario, 29, 58, 59, 64, 96, 100, 153
Oregon, 153
Ottawa, 48, 63, 83, 108, 120
Ovenbird, 126
Owl Rehabilitation Research Foundation, 100, 108

Parmelee, David F., 16, 84, 102
Parry Sound (Ontario), 96
Peat, commercial use of, 151
Pileated Woodpecker, 16
Pine Grosbeak, 28
Pittaway, Ronald, 29, 48, 88, 93
Porcupine, 145
Poulin, Richard M., 108
Precambrian Shield, 21
Pulliainen, Erkki, 77

Quebec, 29, 59, 64, 98

Radio-telemetry, 153
Reader, Philip B., 16, 17
Red-backed vole, 70, 85, 91
Redpoll, 87
Red squirrel, 46, 87, 97, 139, 149

Red-tailed Hawk, 20, 32, 47, 65, 77, 102, 130, 139, 145
Red-winged Blackbird, 146
Rehabilitation of raptors, 100
Richardson, Sir John, 58, 62, 72
Riveredge Foundation, 39
Rhode Island, 72
Roberts, Thomas S., 87
Robertson, Ed, 16
Rocky Mountain House (Alberta), 98
Rose-breasted Grosbeak, 126
Royal Canadian Mounted Police, 24, 25
Ruffed Grouse, 15, 94, 96, 99

St. Lawrence River, 29, 32
Sandhill Crane, 146, 150
Saskatchewan, 59, 65, 77
Sault Ste. Marie (Michigan), 97
Saw-whet Owl, 29, 153
Scandinavia, 86, 102, 138
Scientific permits, 45
Sealy, Spencer G., 12, 124, 125, 126, 127, 139
Severn (Ontario), 88
Severn River (Ontario), 58
Sharp-tailed Grouse, 87
Shortt, Angus H., 29, 40
Short-tailed shrew, 46
Siberia, 59
Smith, F. Napier, 32, 120
Snowshoe hare, 15, 57, 65, 86, 95
Snowy Owl, 72, 83, 84, 96, 102
Song Sparrow, 130
Soviet Union, 58
Spotted Owl, 108, 153
Steel trap, 96–97
Stitt, Robert, 24, 34, 86
Street, Maurice, 86
Swainson, William, 58
Swainson's Thrush, 126
Swastika (Ontario), 98
Sweden, 35, 58, 63, 103, 110, 118, 122, 138, 151

Tamarack, commercial use of, 151
Taylor, Philip S., 102
Taylor, Robert R., 12, 16, 20, 25, 42, 81, 87, 114, 121, 124, 126
Texas, 29

The Pas (Manitoba), 16, 33, 56
Thoreau, Henry David, 153
Todd, W.E. Clyde, 95, 96
Toronto (Ontario), 45
Tuokko, Raymond, 12, 95, 104, 106, 145

United States, 29, 62
Verbail trap, 51
Verdun (Quebec), 32
Vineland (Ontario), 100, 108

Wabowden (Manitoba), 110
Wahlberg, Kapten, 35
Wahlstedt, Jens, 34, 63, 77, 83–84, 118,
    122
Waller, Sam, 96
Wight, Howard M., 108
Whistling Swan, 20
White-throated Sparrow, 126
White-winged Crossbill, 142
Wickford (Rhode Island), 72
Winisk (Ontario), 96
Winnipeg, 16, 21, 29, 38, 39, 63, 64, 92,
    98, 106, 114, 121, 124, 142
  Hydro-Electric of, 98
Winter Wren, 126, 131
Wisconsin, 59, 150, 151, 153
Witches'-broom, 32
Wood frog, 20
Wright, Jo, 84
Wyoming, 59, 103

Yukon River (Alaska), 82

This book was produced by Smithsonian Institution Press, Washington, D.C. Composed by Photo Data, Inc., Washington, D.C., in VIP Trump. Printed by Kingsport Press, Kingsport, Tennessee, on seventy-pound Warren's Lustro Offset Enamel Dull with Multicolor Textured endpapers. Casebound by Kingsport Press in Holliston B-grade Roxite, linen finish, and stamped in imitation gold. Designed by Elizabeth Sur.

By the same author

CHARLEMAGNE: FROM THE
HAMMER TO THE CROSS

THOMAS BECKET

LETTERS OF THOMAS MANN, 1889–1955
(*selected and translated with Clara Winston*)

THOMAS
MANN
The Making of
an Artist

New York 1981

ALFRED A. KNOPF

THOMAS MANN

MANN

The Making of
an Artist

1 8 7 5 ~ 1 9 1 1

Richard Winston

With an Afterword by

CLARA WINSTON

THIS IS A BORZOI BOOK
Published by Alfred A. Knopf, Inc.

*Library of Congress Cataloging in Publication Data
Winston, Richard.
Thomas Mann : the making of an artist, 1875–1911.
Includes bibliographical references and index.
1. Mann, Thomas, 1875–1955—Biography.
2. Novelists, German—20th century—Biography.
I. Title.*
PT2625.A44Z937 1981 833'.912 [B] 81-47515
ISBN 0-394-47171-7   AACR2

*Manufactured in the United States of America
First Edition*

Contents

1
Forebears and Childhood
3

2
School
22

3
Adolescence
37

4
Rambergstrasse 2
54

5
Italy
66

6
Forms and Masks
84

7
Buddenbrooks
102

8
The Army
123

v

Contents

9
Friendship
139

10
Fame
152

11
A Wider World
168

12
Courtship
178

13
Marriage
195

14
Theater and Novel
216

15
Highness
237

16
Tragedy in Polling
252

17
Death in Venice
264

AFTERWORD
by Clara Winston
281

NOTES
291

INDEX
315

THOMAS
MANN
The Making of
an Artist

1

Forebears and
Childhood

LÜBECK is water and ruddy brick, arcades and round towers, cobblestoned streets and gabled roofs. A humpbacked oval island lying between two rivers, the Wakenitz and the Trave, the city rises to what seems a considerable height above the flat North German plain. Two immense brick Gothic churches with enormous towers crown the central ridge: St. Peter's, the cathedral, and St. Mary's—the Peterskirche and the Marienkirche. The latter belonged to Lübeck's town fathers and was therefore called the Ratskirche. Its central location expressed the self-respect and assertiveness of the venerable city-state's merchants. In most of the cities of Europe the cathedral church, the bishop's seat, occupies the main square, often adjacent to or opposite the episcopal palace and other diocesan buildings. In Lübeck, however, the cathedral church has been consigned to the southern extremity of the city's north-south axis. The heart of the Old Town is dominated by the Ratskirche, in which Thomas Mann was christened, and by the Renaissance façade of the

Rathaus. Nearby, gateway to the center, stands the somewhat pre-posterous bulk of the Holstentor, with fantastic twin towers that might illustrate a Grimm fairy tale.

Even today Lübeck retains much of its Gothic or Renaissance character. Before the end of the nineteenth century a late-medieval atmosphere was more pronounced. What the building boom of the mid-century threatened to destroy, the antiquarian spirit simul-taneously tried to preserve or restore. The modernists—such citizens as Hagenström in Thomas Mann's *Buddenbrooks*—wanted to tear down the Holstentor, which had become an obstacle to traffic. But conservative pride in Lübeck's glorious past won out by a single vote in the Senate. The Free City provided funds for the restoration of the old gate, and the work on the Holstentor was completed in 1871, the year the German Empire was proclaimed.

The gables that lean over the streets of Lübeck, some severely straight, some stepped, some voluted in gentle baroque curves, attest to the city's kinship to Flemish and Dutch towns farther to the west. That relationship is corroborated by the canal, by the masts and smokestacks rocking gently on the water of the busy port, by the smells of waterfront, by the rugged features of the predominantly fair-haired population, and by the gutturals and dentals of the Low German dialect. But Lübeck's most famous son, the writer who was born there on June 6, 1875, preferred to see another analogy. The city that Thomas Mann used for the setting of *Death in Venice* re-minded him so strongly of his native place that he called it "Lü-beck's southern sister."[1] His understanding of the Queen of the Adriatic came to him by birthright, he maintained. At the Palace of the Doges he found once more the arcades of the Rathaus, where the self-confident burghers of Lübeck, among whom so many of his own ancestors were included, traded in commodities and stocks. Both cities lay on landlocked seas; and as Venice had once been mistress of the Mediterranean, Lübeck had ruled the Baltic. Merchants sus-tained the fame of both cities; but Venice traded in the pearls, silks, and spices of the East, Lübeck in the lumber, herring, and salt of the North. Necessities yield smaller profits than luxuries; the wealth of Lübeck never compared with that of Venice. And the wares men trade also influence their temperament—unless there is a pre-estab-lished harmony between certain wares and a given temperament. At any rate, the stolid, materialistic merchant prince of Lübeck could never have been mistaken for his mercurial, art-loving southern counterpart. But both were patricians, proud of their heritage, affirming commerce and merchant adventuring as an honorable way of life. And both cherished freedom—at least for themselves, though not necessarily for the lower orders.

Lübeck was eight hundred years or so younger than Venice, but still venerable enough to provide an aspiring writer with a sense of history and the right to identify himself with a tradition. As Thomas Mann wrote of the thinly disguised Lübeck he called Kaisersaschern in *Doctor Faustus:* "It was old, and age is past as present, a past merely overlaid by the present."[2] Founded in the eleventh century by a Christianized Slavic prince, Lübeck had suffered destruction and rebirth, then a tremendous flowering in the thirteenth, fourteenth, and fifteenth centuries. She became undisputed head of the Hansa, that curious association of cities, half empire and half conspiracy, which for so long dominated the trade of Europe. To live by the benefits of Lübeck law and to build in the Lübeck style became the ambition of dozens of smaller towns in northern Europe.

A special breed of merchant adventurer dominated the political and social life of Lübeck during the centuries of her ascendancy. At once hardheaded businessmen, daring sailors, and intrepid fighting men on land or sea, these Lübeck townsmen early wrested freedom from local overlords. They became virtual sovereigns in their own right, ruling their city as direct feudatories of the Holy Roman Emperor and negotiating with him on almost even terms. Long after the rise of nation-states had doomed such city-republics, the oligarchs of Lübeck strove desperately to hold the Hansa together. Theirs was "a last great rear-guard action . . . conducted not without gallantry,"[3] as their descendant was to write of his own efforts to stem the tide of history.

The Mann family had taken its place among the patricians who ruled Lübeck; but the Manns were not themselves *alteingesessen*, not old stock, not even North German. The family tree, as far as it could be traced, had roots in Bavaria, Franconia, and Switzerland. His ancestors, Thomas Mann recalled, were "Nuremberg craftsmen of the type that Germany has sent to the four quarters of the earth, even all the way to the Far East, as a sign that she was a land of cities."[4] Early Manns were peasants in Franconia, drapers in Nuremberg. Some remained in Bavaria; some, more restive and ambitious, left behind the hills and mountains of South Germany and sought out the northern "flatland." The first ancestor of whom the Manns had something more than the sketchiest knowledge was Johann Mann, born in Parchim on the Elbe in 1644. He became a town councillor in nearby Grabow and a member of the drapers' guild; it is recorded that he "stood very well" until he lost everything in a fire that raged through the city. But for the remainder of his long life "Almighty God provided him with his daily bread."[5] His son Siegmund settled in Rostock as a draper; *his* son, Jochim or Joachim Siegmund, initiated the chronicle in the family Bible in which these facts are set down, and on which Thomas Mann drew for the writing of *Buddenbrooks*.

Born in 1728, Joachim Siegmund, Thomas Mann's great-great-grandfather, was by his own confession something of a scapegrace who acquired a fervent piety as the consequence of several seemingly miraculous rescues that were accorded him. As a child he was nearly killed when a butt of beer fell on him at his sister's wedding. Three times he came very close to drowning. He grew up to be an unusually tough lad who did not shrink from the hardest work. Abandoning his father's trade, he became a merchant and brewer, and married into a family of shipowners and shipbuilders. His son made the move to Lübeck, where he shifted to dealing in grain—never far from a brewer's concerns. It was he who established the firm of Johann Siegmund Mann, Grain Dealing, Consignment, and Forwarding.

This Johann Siegmund—the Founder portrayed as Johann Buddenbrook, Sr., in Thomas Mann's first novel—came to Lübeck at the age of fourteen. A Lübeck merchant named Käselan had met him at the Rostock Whitsun fair and became so fond of him that he took him into his home as an apprentice. Later, in 1790, Käselan aided him in establishing his own business. It was Johann Siegmund's admonition to his son that Thomas Mann saw fit to quote in *Buddenbrooks* (where the language is deliberately archaized): "My son, work gladly by day, but undertake only such business that we will be able to sleep peacefully at night."[6] The novelist preferred to regard this as a moral precept, but the Founder's son, Johann Siegmund, Jr., took it as a warning against engaging in the excessively risky export business. That same Johann Siegmund, Jr., had, so early in the family's history, a bent for the written word. Instead of the laconic notations of births and deaths that had been the rule in the family Bible, he wrote a relatively elaborate "Sketches from My Life," to which year after year he added brief notes about his travels. The family tree given in *Buddenbrooks* was, of course, that of the Manns. Successive Manns copied the earlier records from the family Bible into a portfolio; Thomas Mann made use even of this minor item of family history in describing the old leather portfolio that Consul Buddenbrook takes from his rolltop writing desk.

A sense of family identical with the sense of history was early imbued in these descendants of the Rostock woolen draper. Both Heinrich and Thomas Mann would later write historical novels as a natural expression of their sense of "past as present." Heinrich Mann asks: "What have we to hope for when we come into the world? Nothing that could not be found in our blood. Nothing from outside; everything within us."[7] And whenever Thomas Mann made a formal accounting of his life, he spoke first of his heritage. His first major literary act was to explore the world of his immediate ancestors. And he returned to the theme again and again, trying to grasp the mysterious continuity of the flesh and the spirit over generations. Ultimately he found his deepest symbol for the participation of every child in the life of its forebears in the Castorp family's christening basin:

> There was Hans Castorp's father's name, there was Grandfather's own, there was Great-Grandfather's; then the "great" came doubled, tripled, quadrupled, from the old man's mouth, and the boy listened with head on one side, eyes fixed pensively, or perhaps only dreamily, lips parted in sleepy reverence, to that great-great-great-great—that sound of silence and slow time. Yet how it seemed an expression of a piously cherished link between the present, his own life, and all the long-buried past. . . . Religious feeling mingled in his mind with thoughts of death and a sense of history, as he listened to the somber syllable.[8]

Johann Siegmund Mann, Jr. (the Founder's son and the "original" of Consul Buddenbrook), lost his first wife after only six years of marriage.* His second wife, Elisabeth Marty, brought a Swiss strain

---

* Thomas Mann's handling of this material in *Buddenbrooks* suggests his attitude toward "real life." In the novel he shifts the loss to the previous generation. It is the Founder who makes a love match and records the "one brief year" at the side of his first wife (characteristically in French) as *"l'année la plus heureuse de ma vie."*

into the family. Her father, a grain dealer also, had been born in Glarus, Switzerland, descendant of a line of Swiss peasants, merchants, and armorers that could be traced back to the fourteenth century. The accidents of history first drove Thomas Mann into exile in Switzerland; but the affection he thereafter felt for the Swiss seems to have been stronger than an elective affinity, and when Europe was once more open to him he chose to go home to Switzerland rather than to Germany. His choice may also be seen as a return to the southern extremity of German-speaking lands, from which the Mann ancestors on both sides had originally come. Both Thomas and Heinrich Mann made much of the varied strains in their "blood"; the idea and the terminology were fashionable during the latter years of the nineteenth century. The twentieth century has learned abhorrence of racial theories; but families do hand down genes, impulses, ambitions, attitudes, traditions.

Great-grandfather Johann Heinrich Marty spent many years in Russia after leaving Switzerland, and he brought a certain cosmopolitanism to Lübeck and to the Mann family. Throughout his life he retained an attachment to his birthplace and used to visit Glarus almost every year, driving across the whole of Germany from north to south in his own coach. (That he kept a private coach was a sign of his luxurious ways.) When famine threatened Glarus in 1817, Marty took up a collection in Lübeck, Hamburg, Kiel, and neighboring cities. Within five weeks he had amassed "13,238 mark courant in various currencies, including louis d'or, carolines, Danish and Dutch gulden."[9] He sent this money to Switzerland to aid the needy.

By way of his daughter's dowry, Marty—whom Thomas Mann would portray as Lebrecht Kröger, the cavalier à la mode—also contributed a sizable number of "courant marks" to the firm of Johann Heinrich Mann. The rather ponderous calculations in *Buddenbrooks* concerning the sums added to or subtracted from the firm need no more be taken literally than the jeweled buttons of Lebrecht Kröger's waistcoat; but Elisabeth Marty was certainly a good match for Johann Siegmund Mann. Her portrait in *Buddenbrooks* could be painted from life, for she lived to the age of eighty. By the time she died, in the winter of 1890, Thomas Mann was nearly sixteen and moving on from "lyric-dramatic" poetry to experiments in narrative fiction.[10]

Thomas Johann Heinrich, eldest son of Elisabeth and Johann Mann, was born in 1840, and on his father's death inherited, at the age of twenty-three, the responsibilities and privileges of the head of the firm. An energetic and cultivated businessman, he early won and held the respect of his fellow citizens. "How often in my life," his son recollected in an address to his fellow townsmen in 1926,

> have I not observed with a smile that the personality of my deceased father was governing my acts and omissions, was serving as the secret model for them? Often I literally caught myself in the act. Perhaps some of you here knew him, saw him going about his life in this city, occupying his many offices; perhaps one or another of you recalls his dignity and good sense, his ambition and industry, his personal and intellectual distinction, his social talents and his humor, the affability which he used to practice toward the common folk, who were attached to him in the old and still entirely genuine patriarchal fashion. He was by no means a simple man, not robust, rather nervous and susceptible to suffering; but he was a man dedicated to self-control and to success, who had early achieved prestige and honors in this world—this world which was his, in which he had built his handsome house.[11]

The eldest son remembered his father as "young, gay, and carefree"—and indeed there is a picture of the father seated, holding five-year-old Heinrich between his knees. He is frozen in the pose that the long exposure times of the period required; but there is nevertheless an air of ease, confidence, and serenity in his erectness, and evidence of an affectionate nature in the way his hands lie gently on his son's shoulder and enclose the boy's arm. He is a strikingly handsome man with a bushy mustache of the type that has recently, a century later, come into favor again. Both of his sons would also wear mustaches throughout their lives, despite the radical change of fashion that took place after the First World War.

Heinrich Mann, as the father preferred to call himself, indulged in London suits and Russian cigarettes. Such tastes were not really exotic for a wealthy businessman in a seaport, but they showed a heightened discrimination. A similar fondness for rarity combined with solid worth governed his choice of a bride. She was a young lady who had just "come out"—only sixteen and a half when he first caught sight of her at a wedding party—and he found her exotic enough. Julia da Silva Bruhns was the daughter of a Lübeck planter who had established himself in Brazil, Ludwig Bruhns (1821–1895), and Maria da Silva Bruhns (1828–1856). Julia, who let her intimates know that her name was really Dodo and that she had called her mother and father Mai and Pai, was fond of saying that she had lived between jungle and sea for the first seven years of her life. Ebulliently, she told stories of plantation life in Brazil, of her grandparents' island paradise, of the carnival in Rio de Janeiro, of her black nurse and her father's black slaves, and of her encounters with a boa constrictor. On her father's side, however, she was descended from four generations of Lübeck merchants. Motherless since the age of six, she had been reared with the most fashionable young ladies of Lübeck in Therese Bossuet's boarding school (to which Thomas Mann sent his Tony in *Buddenbrooks* and Heinrich Mann his Lola in *Zwischen den Rassen*). Hers was a modified, tamed exoticism; and Heinrich Mann, Sr., was committing no act of folly or recklessness in taking such a wife. Still, he was making a love match, not a dynastic marriage; and that was somewhat uncommon in his circles in 1869.

In spite of her Latin mother and Brazilian childhood, Julia Bruhns was a thoroughly German young lady, raised in the pruderies, the sentimentalities, and the dutifulness of mid-century Germany. She had artistic yearnings, played the piano soulfully, and daringly "enthused" over a radical modern composer named Richard Wagner, whose galloping chords perhaps appealed to a lingering wildness in her nature, but whose romantic Teutonic strain reassured her that her alienation was only superficial. Perhaps she might have gone further in music if she had not, in her girlhood, had a falling-out with her music teacher. Fräulein Marie was gentle and patient in her teaching, and had a soft touch at the piano, for which little Dodo adored her. But the good relationship came to an end when Julia and her sister allowed their canary to die of neglect, for which Fräulein Marie savagely rebuked them.

Thomas Mann calls his mother "extraordinarily musical,"[12] but in North Germany in the late 1860s there was little that a young lady of good family could do with any artistic accomplishment. Like Gerda Buddenbrook with her violin, Julia Bruhns could never make of her devoted piano playing anything more than a social grace, of no greater consequence than her sketching or, in later life, her dabbling in writing.* In any case, the whole atmosphere of a girls' school was calculated to direct her toward marriage; and after her sister Mana's wedding she could think of little else. "I mustn't stay single, I mustn't be an old maid," she recalled thinking. Later she acknowledged that "in spite of all the good that life had given her she had too soon and too lightheartedly left her girlhood years behind."[13]

There was little danger that she would become an old maid. She was pretty, with the even features and square jaw of the far North, and she had the sparkle and flirtatiousness of the South. Related to *"tout* Lübeck" she delighted in the frequent balls and wedding receptions to which she was invited after her confirmation and her departure from the boarding school. Her Aunt Emma and Uncle Eduard saw to it that she had her fill of the amusements that a thriving Lübeck had to offer the young of the patrician bourgeoisie. Dancing often and well in her green tarlatan dress with white satin piping and a white sash, she was surrounded by young men who brought her flowers and paid her court. But she was capable of both flirting with and rebuffing them with the kind of pertness that Thomas Mann would ascribe to Tony Buddenbrook. She could decide impetuously that one young man had "overlarge side-whiskers, another popping eyes, a third a big red nose, a fourth flat feet, a fifth bad teeth, and so on." After insulting her would-be suitors she felt "dreadfully ashamed." Then, at the age of sixteen and a half, she encountered her future husband at several balls, and "her fate was sealed."[14]

But there was another side to her character, the soberer side both emphasized and exemplified by her father when he wrote to congratulate her on her engagement, his sentiments as stiffly conventional as his copperplate handwriting:

Rio de Jan°.
Feb. 4, 1869

My dear daughter Julia,
    This mail has brought me the glad news of your engagement to Herr Heinrich Mann;—knowing my children happy is for me the

---

* She wrote a memoir of her childhood, *Aus Dodos Kindheit*, as well as a novella, anecdotes, and a fairy tale; no doubt there were other short pieces that have not been preserved. In her girlhood she kept a diary.

best compensation for all the cares they have caused me. Dear Julia, you have often had the opportunity to judge your fiancé, and since it is actually you yourself who have given your hand to Heinrich I may assume that you hope to find your happiness with him.

Be assured of my blessing upon your connection with Heinrich, my dear child. May God shield you two and smooth the path of life for you both!

Uncle Eduard and Aunt Emma sound very pleased about the event, and we all cherish the hope that you and Heinrich will lead a happy wedded life. Your fiancé has all the qualities to make a girl happy, and it will depend upon you to requite his faithful love.

You with your great youth lack much experience and knowledge of practical life which are so necessary for happiness in the domestic sphere; but I am certain that sincere love for the husband of your choice will spur you to practice to the best of your ability the order, thrift, and domesticity that make every man in every condition esteem his wife. In marriage, dear daughter, there is sunshine and there are storms, but the latter pass all the more quickly the more sensible a woman is and the more she shows good character.

I have written to Uncle Eduard about your wedding and my arrival there, and with that I close, pressing you to my heart, my deeply beloved daughter.

J. Luiz G. Bruhns[15]

The wedding was celebrated on June 4, 1869, in the lavish style appropriate to the union of two substantial merchant houses. Invitations went out to all relations, poor and otherwise, and as at the wedding of Tony Buddenbrook, half the city came. For a short time after their marriage the couple lived with Heinrich Mann's mother in Mengstrasse 4, the house destroyed in World War II but since rebuilt and known to the world as the "Buddenbrook house." The following year Heinrich Mann rented an apartment on Breite Strasse, and there, on March 27, 1871, his first son was born and baptized Luiz Heinrich Mann.

Having founded a family, Consul Mann (he had been appointed consul for the Netherlands, like his father before him) bought a house the following year: Breite Strasse 36. But it was in a suburban villa rented for the summer that the Manns' second son was born. The date was June 6, 1875; the child was baptized Paul Thomas. "The planetary aspect was favorable, as adepts of astrology frequently assured me in later years," Thomas Mann commented in a curriculum vitae written in 1936. "On the basis of my horoscope they promised me a long and happy life and a gentle death."[16] In saying this, and in specifying that he was born at twelve noon, Mann was whimsically exploiting arcana to which he really gave no credence. Never one to believe unconditionally in science, let alone pseudoscience, he used astrology—as perhaps we all do—to assert his feeling of the world's being kindly disposed toward him.

One aspect of that generosity was simply his position in the family. He experienced the second child's advantages and disabilities; from his own statement, "My childhood was sheltered and happy,"[17] it is clear that the disabilities were outweighed by the advantages. His path was smoothed because his elder brother could lead the way —into literature if not into life; but the four-year difference in age was also a painful gap for the younger. In a letter written in the last months of his life Thomas stressed that he had always regarded Heinrich as *der grosse Bruder*—the phrase means both "big brother" and "great brother."[18] His respect for his brother remained even when disagreements over politics, literature, philosophy, and life style caused a public breach between them, and each attacked the other in print. For Thomas the "fraternal constellation"—*das brüderliche Welterlebnis*[19]—constantly influenced his life and thought. The current flowing from younger to elder brother was not so strong, although stronger than Heinrich imagined or acknowledged.

There was a familial as well as a fraternal constellation. Over the twenty years of their marriage three more children were born to Julia and Heinrich Mann: Julia, known as Lula, in 1877; Carla in 1881; and Viktor in 1890. The two sisters were the special favorites of the elder brothers. Heinrich in particular was deeply attached to Carla, a charming child when he was already a young man; her bohemian inclinations struck a kindred chord in him. The late-born son shared no part in his brothers' childhoods. Heinrich and Thomas were, in fact, so grown-up by the time he could speak that he ranked them with the adult world, calling them Uncle Heini and Uncle Ommo. For Thomas at fifteen, moodily enduring the *Frühlingssturm* of adolescence, the new baby scarcely existed. The accident of birth condemned Viko to live in the shadow, a *quantité négligeable* who in his own mind assigned himself a much greater role in his brothers' careers than he actually had. Nearly fifty,

Thomas Mann could write: "In the higher sense I have only one brother [Heinrich], you know; the other is a good fellow no one could quarrel with." But Viko, who shared some of his brothers' literary gift if none of their developed skill, resented this assigned role. At the end of his life he surprised his family by writing an autobiography, and there was an edgy emphasis to the title he gave it: *We Were Five*. There was one more Mann child, he seemed to be saying: the latecomer who trailed after his elders, always so outdistanced that he could not even summon up the hopefulness to cry "Wait for me!" In the end he wrote himself deeper into their counsels than the strictest truthfulness might allow.[20]

F A M I L Y photographs and scattered reminiscences afford only glimpses of Thomas Mann's childhood. Both the pictures and the recollections are somewhat stylized: a round-faced child watching warily the photographer's preparations, the boy of ten with his brother and two sisters, and so on. In one photograph the family resemblance among the three younger children is striking: the same rounded chin and firm lips. Heinrich, a remarkably handsome boy of fourteen, seems to show a touch of critical distaste for the whole proceeding. Whether by his own choice or the photographer's, he holds a book in his left hand, a finger inserted into the pages as if to mark his place. Thomas, in uniform, holds an ornamental whip that was perhaps placed in his hand by the photographer; but he has thrown himself willingly into the pose of a young hussar.

In his writings, both early and late, Thomas Mann subjected most of his references to childhood to literary stylization. In an occasional piece written in 1904 he recalled the "beautiful toys" he had had as a child. There was a store with a counter and scales, the drawers filled with groceries, the granary of exactly the same type as the one his father owned on the bank of the Trave. There was even a crane for raising sacks and bales; it was worked from behind the store by a crank. If this miniature shop did not stir the kind of ambition the father must have hoped for, it nevertheless helped to engender some of that respect for the merchant's vocation that is implicit in *Buddenbrooks*, explicit in "Lübeck as a Way of Life and Thought," and a recurrent theme in Mann's shaping of his life. Childhood influences can emerge in unexpected ways, very belatedly or not at all. The fact that he had possessed "a complete knight's armor of iron-gray cardboard, with visored helmet, tournament lance, and shield,"[21] did not make Thomas Mann into a writer of Gothic romances, any more than the puppet theater of his childhood made a playwright of him. But a fondness for the medieval remained, drawing added sustenance from the very streets of Lübeck which the aged writer conjured up with somewhat sinister overtones in *Doctor Faustus*. And in *The Holy Sinner*, written when he was seventy-five, he sportively manipulated the appurtenances and attitudes of chivalry for his parodistic purposes. As for the puppet theater, he later converted it into an element of his *imitatio* of Goethe, which became a sometimes jesting, sometimes overserious habit of his later years.

That puppet theater was already hallowed by family tradition, for it had belonged to Heinrich. The elder's toys naturally came down to the younger brother, or were appropriated by him—a sometimes painful and perilous descent when Heinrich had not yet relinquished a toy that Thomas craved. Heinrich long remembered the quarter-size violin that Thomas one day broke. Tensions between the two brothers arose early; but the puppet theater, the gift of Grandmother Elisabeth Mann, seems to have promoted amiable cooperation. Heinrich, who showed an early talent for drawing, enriched the stock of sets with many handsome backdrops. Together, the two boys created "strange music dramas"[22] that were performed before an appreciative audience of parents and aunts.

The puppet theater, for which Hanno Buddenbrook waits passionately one Christmas, also figures in the early story "The Dilettante" (Der Bajazzo). Here Thomas Mann, in a patently autobiographical vein and with the vividness of recent memory, has his narrator describe how he shuts himself up alone in his room to put on a performance:

My room was in the third story. Two gloomy portraits of ancestors with Wallenstein beards hung on the wall. I would draw the blinds and place a lamp beside the theater, for it heightened the atmosphere to have artificial light. Then I, as conductor, took my place directly in front of the stage, my left hand resting on a large round cardboard box which served as the sole visible orchestral instrument.

The performers would now enter; I had drawn them myself with pen and ink, cut them out, and fitted them into little wooden blocks so that they could stand. There were gentlemen in overcoats and top hats, and ladies of great beauty.

"Good evening, ladies and gentlemen," I would say. "I trust you are all well. I came early because there were a few matters to attend to. But it is about time to be going to the dressing rooms."

They went to the dressing rooms behind the stage and soon came back transfigured, in the gayest and most beautiful costumes, to look through the peephole which I had cut in the curtain and see if there was a good house. The house was in fact not so bad; and I rang the bell to let myself know that the performance was about to begin, lifted my baton, and paused to enjoy the sudden stillness that my gesture evoked. Then, in response to another movement, there sounded the low, foreboding roll of drums with which the overture began. I produced that with my left hand on the cardboard box. The trumpets, clarinets, and flutes came in; by shaping my mouth I gave an inimitable rendering of their tonal quality, and so it went until upon a powerful crescendo the curtain rose and the play began in a dark forest or a glittering palace hall.

I would mentally sketch out the drama beforehand and then improvise the details as I went along. . . . I drummed with my left hand, performed both song and accompaniment with my own voice, and with my right hand directed both music and acting down to the minutest detail. The applause at the end of each act was so enthusiastic that there were repeated curtain calls, and sometimes the conductor had to turn in his seat and with mingled pride and complacency bow his thanks.

Truly, when after such a performance I put away my theater, all the blood in my body seemed to have risen to my head and I was blissfully exhausted as is a great artist at the triumphant close of a production to which he has given all that is in him. This game remained my favorite occupation up to my thirteenth or fourteenth year.[23]

Thomas was so devoted to the puppet theater that he could not conceive the possibility of ever outgrowing its pleasures. Heinrich, at seventeen already experimenting with literary composition, took a mild revenge for the appropriation of the theater by teasing "Tommy." How absurd it would be for Thomas as a grown man to be sitting in front of the theater singing bass, he pointed out. But Thomas had already made the discovery that would permit him to

engage in his "curious game" for the rest of his life: that no props
were necessary. "With quiet satisfaction I became conscious of the
independent powers of my imagination, which nothing could de-
prive me of." He would awaken one morning deciding that he would
be an eighteen-year-old prince named Karl. "I clad myself in a kind
of amiable majesty and went about proud and happy with the secret
of my dignity. I could have lessons, be taken for a walk, or have
fairy tales read to me, without having to interrupt this game for a
minute; that was the practical aspect of it. Nor did I always have to
be a prince; my roles changed frequently."[24] Half a century later
Thomas's son Klaus (in whose honor Prince Klaus Heinrich of
Royal Highness was named) would record concerning his own childhood: "There were no 'games,' really: There was just one vast and
complicated phantasmagoria—a mythic system within the myth of
childhood, an elaborate cosmology. . . ."[25]

The myth-making impulse was nourished by an introduction to
mythology. The book, which had belonged to his mother, bore a
Pallas Athena on the cover, like the one presented to Hanno Buddenbrook for Christmas. Thomas learned many of the extracts from
Homer and Virgil by heart. He turned the gods and heroes into
characters in "the gods game" he had invented. The younger children of the family served as extras or props·

> As Hermes I hopped through the rooms with winged sandals of
> paper; as Helios I balanced a glittering golden crown of rays upon my
> ambrosial head; as Achilles I inexorably dragged my sister, who
> willy-nilly had to be Hector, three times around the walls of Ilion.
> But as Zeus I stood upon a small, red-lacquered table which served
> me as the citadel of the gods, and the Titans piled Pelion upon Ossa
> all in vain, so fearsomely did I flash lightnings with a red rein that
> had small bells sewn to it.[26]

The martial Achilles soon underwent something of a degradation;
he became the name of Thomas's "tenderly beloved" hobbyhorse.
Even in earliest childhood, it is clear, Thomas scarcely fancied himself in the role of the warrior. He was a dreamy child who preferred
listening to his mother's reading from Andersen's fairy tales and
from Fritz Reuter's dialect stories, or to her making music. He would
huddle for hours in one of the quilted easy chairs in the salon, with

its bright bay windows, while she sang songs by Schubert, Schumann, Brahms, and Liszt, or played Chopin on the Bechstein grand piano.

But those were the privileged hours; ordinarily his mother was the busy mistress of a great house. On the parquet floor of the Manns' ballroom, officers of the Lübeck garrison danced and courted the daughters of the local patricians. Young though she was, Julia Mann had to play her public part, had to assume a "representative"* role. This was all the more so after 1877, when her husband was elected to the Lübeck Senate, the ruling body of the Free City, and subsequently entrusted with increasingly important public duties. She was expected to give and to attend formal dinners of the kind described so elaborately in the opening pages of *Buddenbrooks*. The care of the children was entrusted to a nanny, a *Fräulein*; but the household was still sufficiently middle-middle-class (*bürgerlich*, Thomas Mann calls it) for the children to see a good deal of their mother.

The Mann children were also close to their grandmother, Elisabeth Mann, and were constantly running in and out of the ancestral home, Mengstrasse 4, in the shadow of the Marienkirche. Here they could escape for a time from the supervision of Idachen Springer, the Ida Jungmann of *Buddenbrooks*. Their visits were so frequent that Thomas Mann speaks of the "old family dwelling of the eighteenth century with the motto *Dominus providebit* on the rococo gable" as his "second home."[27] In "The Dilettante" Thomas Mann changed the motto "The Lord will provide" to "Pray and work," *Ora et labora*, but otherwise faithfully described his grandmother's home, with its large flagged hall, its white-painted gallery above, the columned vestibule, and the parlor with its "classical" wallpaper, white gods and goddesses against a blue background.

In 1881, with a fourth child expected, Senator Mann purchased the lot at Beckergrube 52 and there built a stately, "representative" residence for his family of six persons and the multitude of nannies and servants considered indispensable for the smooth running of a

---

* The English word *representative* does not normally convey the sense of the German *repräsentativ*, which generally signifies showing by one's conduct the position the world expects one to hold, representing the idea the world has of one. For practical purposes *representative* in this book will be widened to include both the English sense of "standing for some other person or group" and the German sense defined above.

bourgeois household at the end of the nineteenth century. Thomas Mann gently poked fun at this aspect of the servant problem (half the servants' work was created by the presence of so many servants) in Part Two of *Buddenbrooks*, when Betsy Buddenbrook suggests to her husband that a manservant is needed because the three maids cannot manage all the work. Betsy, whose parents lived on so lavish a scale, could not adjust to the relative frugality of the Buddenbrooks. Life imitates art; the situation depicted in the novel is, we may be amused to note, an anticipation of Thomas Mann's own household less than a decade later. Having likewise married an heiress whose parents lived on a lavish scale, Mann found himself a *Hausherr* responsible for an establishment with four servants.

T H O M A S M A N N attended Dr. Bussenius's private elementary school from 1882 to 1889. Since the records of this school have not been preserved, we have only his own testimony that from the first he "loathed school and was unable to satisfy its requirements."[28] Probably this was truer for his adolescence than for his years in elementary school; it was later, in the Realgymnasium, that he twice failed to be promoted.

He found compensation for the misery of school by the sea, the Baltic Sea. On his own testimony the happiest times of his childhood were the four weeks of summer vacation spent at the seaside resort of Travemünde. Here he had time for dreaming and indolence, satisfying a deep need of his nature. Here he could read whenever he liked, sinking into the melancholic romanticism of Theodor Storm, the fantasies and scientific curiosa of Adalbert von Chamisso, the bittersweet ironies of Heinrich Heine. Here he was free to lie in a beach chair and dream, to listen to music, or to stroll along the strand looking for amber. Recalling the summers of his seventh to his sixteenth year, he wrote at the age of fifty:

> That was the Travemünde of forty years ago, with the old Kurhaus in Biedermeier style, the Swiss chalets and the concert hall in which little Kapellmeister Hass, with flowing hair and gypsylike demeanor, conducted his crew. I would crouch on the steps in the summery fragrance of the beech tree, insatiably drawing into my soul music, my first orchestral music. It did not matter what was being played.

There in Travemünde, the holiday paradise, I spent . . . days of profound contentment, of wishing for nothing at all. . . . There music and the sea merged into one within my head and heart. And from this emotional and ideational conjunction something new was born: namely, narrative epic prose. Ever since, for me, the idea of epic has been linked with the sea and with music. I might even say that it is composed of them. . . . I like to think that the sea, its rhythm, musical transcendency, is somehow omnipresent in my books . . . the sea of my childhood, the Bay of Lübeck. In the final analysis I have made use of its palette, and if my colors have been found subdued, not luminous, the reason may be certain glimpses through silvery beechwood trunks of a pastel sea and pallid sky, upon which my eye rested when I was a child and happy.[29]

That was the experience recollected; but in the narration of Hanno Buddenbrook's waking to the joy of his first day at Travemünde, Thomas Mann, twenty-five years before he wrote the foregoing, had been able to relive his childhood paradise. Hanno wakes to "dazed and sleepy bliss; then he would be conscious that he was in Travemünde—for four immeasurable weeks in Travemünde." He lies still in indolent joy, listening to the sound of a man raking gravel paths, to the buzzing of a fly caught between the blind and the window-pane. This was the feeling of "quiet, well-cared-for, elegant repose which was the atmosphere of the resort."[30] In his short life Hanno loved it better than anything else; and throughout his own long life his creator also loved resorts.

Well cared for and elegant—the German bourgeoisie enjoyed its privileges during the last quarter of the nineteenth century. There were the endless and ample meals, the music in the mornings, afternoons, and evenings, the croquet, the visits to the stables. A child's dream, an eternity of twenty-eight days. There was supervision still, of course, for Ida Springer came with them to watch over the children and to make fun of those tourists who did not stay but merely came out on Sundays—"dayflies," she called them scathingly, to Thomas's delight. And everywhere was the sea:

But best of all was to go back to the beach and sit in the twilight on the end of the breakwater, with your face turned to the open horizon. Great ships passed by, and you signaled them with your handkerchief; and you listened to the little waves slapping softly against the stones; and the whole space about you was filled with a soft and mighty sighing. . . . How calm his heart felt, how evenly it beat, after a visit to the sea. Then he had his supper in his room—for his mother ate later, down in the glass verandah—and drank milk or porter, tasting strongly of malt, and lay down in his little bed, between the soft old linen sheets, and almost at once sleep overcame him, and he slept, to the subdued rhythm of the evening concert and the regular pulsations of his quiet heart.[31]

He loved sleep. There is a little-known essay of Thomas Mann's entitled "Sweet Sleep" which is a kind of prose poem in honor of Morpheus. Mann sings the praises of night's coming after the harassment, the pain, and the anxieties of the day, bringing the surcease of sleep to lave and soothe the quivering body like a gentle bath. "I recall having loved sleep and forgetfulness at a time when I still had scarcely anything to forget,"[32] he writes, and he recalls how this innate disposition became a conscious affect after he heard the fairy tale of the man without sleep. Sleep, night, the sea, death, became intricately associated, interchangeable, each flowing into the others in his conscious thoughts and in the unconscious currents that wind through his works.

The first day at Travemünde was as infinite as the sea itself; but the time passed relentlessly, and soon "the laden carriage stood before the door. . . . The thought of the rules and history dates which he had to get by heart had not lost its power to make him shudder."[33] The return to school could not be postponed. But for Thomas Mann as for Hanno Buddenbrook, school did not consist solely of intolerable lessons and tyrannical masters. His schoolmates meant a great deal to him.

2

School

AMONG the few school memories that Thomas Mann chose to evoke outside his fiction is one that may throw some oblique light on a few of his future interests as an artist and a man. Instinctively, he tells us, he sought out Jewish schoolmates. In his thirteenth year a rabbi's son named Ephraim Carlebach shared a classroom bench with him for a time. Tommy, as he was called both at home and in school, took pleasure in Ephraim's large dark eyes, his hair, and his name "full of desert poetry," although he also thought the boy "not so very clean." From the outset he had been intrigued because Ephraim was excused from the class in biblical history. Tommy, the inattentive pupil, remembered Ephraim gratefully for his helpfulness. In the tradition of the European schoolboy, for whom cheating is legitimate if one is not caught, Ephraim would keep the book open behind the back of the boy in front and "whisper the answers to me with incredible skill."[1]

Another vividly remembered Jewish schoolmate was the son of a Hungarian family named Fehér. His physical characteristics were "pronounced to the point of ugliness, with the early shadow of a mustache beneath a flat nose." Fehér's father ran a tailor shop on the waterfront below the Beckergrube, and Tommy would often walk home with his Hungarian friend, listening to stories of small gypsy circuses in Hungary. Fehér would sometimes run errands for his friend, making purchases that the gentleman's son did not know how to make for himself. In this way Tommy acquired his first real pocket knife. But the principal attraction was the Fehérs' extended family, the parents, children, children's friends, who joined in putting on performances of real dramas. They rehearsed *Der Freischütz*, which Tommy had seen as an opera, to give it as a play. Although he longed to take part, at least as an extra, he did not do so, "probably because for all my eagerness the shyness of a gentleman's son, social prejudice, inhibited my visiting the home of the Jewish tailor by the river."[2] After all the Manns were not, to use a famous line from *Tonio Kröger*, "gypsies in a green wagon."[3]

Both these Jewish boys shared that note of melancholy which Thomas Mann—himself scarcely a man of sunny disposition—believed had been "impressed upon this race by history." But there was another boy in *Tertia* (third form) whom Tommy remembered as the merriest of fellows. He was good-humored, kindly, lean to the point of gauntness, "so that his lips seemed to contain the only fullness in his outward appearance." The outer corners of his almond-shaped eyes were permanently crinkled from laughter. The somewhat senile arithmetic teacher had taken it into his head that the boy's name was Lissauer, although in fact it was Gosslar. "If Lissauer has the result, he may tell us," the old teacher would say. And Gosslar would smile forbearingly as he rapped out the answers to difficult arithmetic problems. For he was an expert in *Kopfrechnen* (mental arithmetic), that improving torture of nineteenth-century pedagogy. Such speed and sureness with numbers was sheer mystery to a bored and indifferent pupil such as Tommy. But Gosslar was not only a mathematical wizard. He was likewise drawn to less exact, if no less exacting, activities of the mind. "He showed an intelligent and unbiased interest, although mingled somewhat with irony, in the clumsy pomp of the ballads I secretly communicated to him, with well-founded trust. One of these dealt with the story of

Paetus and Arria (*Paete, non dolet*), beginning with the lines: 'Deep in Roma's darkest dungeon.' "[4] The easefulness of death, like the delights of sleep, were thus early formalized into conscious convictions. Possibly Thomas also read to Gosslar from his drama *Aischa*—the literary production that prompted him to sign himself, in the single extant letter from this period, "Th. Mann, Lyric-dramatic author."[5]

The predilection for Jews, thus early manifested, would continue into adult life: in his choice of friends, in his marriage, in his literary tastes, in his public positions. In 1907 he spoke of himself as a "confirmed philo-Semite,"[6] an attitude he shared with his brother Heinrich, who had come a long way in ten years. That was by no means a matter of course, for anti-Semitism was on the rise in Germany in the years before the First World War. In 1909 Adolf Bartels, the *völkisch* literary critic, announced his conviction that "the Mann brothers" were Jews, even though they themselves admitted only to a "Creole" admixture in their blood. Creole women were turning up with suspicious frequency as the mothers of German writers, Bartels commented acidly. As "evidence" for his thesis, Bartels adduced Mann's partisanship in *Buddenbrooks* "for the Jewish half-breed against the old patrician family," and his critical approval of such Jewish writers as Heine, Wassermann, and Bruno Frank. Even if Mann was not physically Jewish, Bartels concluded, he was inwardly a Jew. "In literary terms, at any rate, Mann belongs to the Jews."[7]

Even as he denied the critic's "charge," Thomas Mann announced his willingness to accept it. One did not reconcile racist professors by making professions of Germanism, he commented. At the same time he rejected attacks by the other side, the kind of attacks that continued to be made even after his death. He did not at all like "those dissimulators and artists at repression among the Jews who take the mere fact that someone does not overlook so striking a phenomenon as Jewishness as evidence of anti-Semitism."[8]

A philo-Semite as well as an anti-Semite might see hidden implications in Thomas Mann's almost obsessive references to the admixture of his "blood" (although that obsession had become a popular literary theme in the latter years of the nineteenth century). The Israeli scholar Kurt Loewenstein has attempted to track down the lineage of Thomas Mann's maternal ancestors, the da Silvas of

Brazil. A good many da Silvas of Jewish descent emigrated from Portugal to Brazil in the sixteenth and seventeenth centuries. Before the expulsions, the Jews in Spain and Portugal constituted a large part of the urban population; and after their forcible or voluntary conversions they intermarried freely with members of the Christian aristocracy. There are, consequently, some grounds for a presumption that a da Silva family in Brazil in the nineteenth century might have been the product of centuries of secret inbreeding, such as was practiced by the Conversos of Spain and Portugal, and that although Roman Catholic in religion, they retained some lingering elements of Jewishness. But as Mr. Loewenstein himself has pointed out, there is no way to prove such a presumption conclusively.

Thomas Mann overlaid his description of his childhood friendships with Jewish boys with the interpretation he in later life places on that early bias: "My relationship to Jewishness had an adventurous and hedonistic note; I saw it as a picturesque fact calculated to increase the colorfulness of the world."[9] And in the same context he reminds us of his introduction of a Jewish doctor into *Royal Highness*, and of his story about Jewish twins in "The Blood of the Walsungs." These characters would have been grist to Bartels's mill had he known of them; but *Royal Highness* had not yet been published at the time Bartels wrote the lines quoted above, and "Blood of the Walsungs" had been withdrawn just before publication—a last-minute act of caution that Thomas Mann was later to repeat under somewhat similar circumstances. He seems to have been sufficiently at ease with "the Jewish question" to express himself at times with a possibly inappropriate recklessness. With a modicum of ill will the short story, like his subsequent remarks on Jewishness in the article "On the Jewish Question," and like the Jewish characters in *Doctor Faustus*, could be interpreted as anti-Semitic. With good or ill will they could also be interpreted as Jewish self-criticism. Speculation on such a topic can be endless. But it "saves the phenomena" to speak of these varying but inwardly consistent views of Jewishness as emerging from the frankness of a truthful artist.

In his manhood Mann was attracted to Jews as artists, critics, impresarios, patrons, audiences. His own relationships with them were replete with ambiguities. He had been "discovered" by a Jewish critic, he pointed out; his lifelong publisher was Jewish; and many Jews had befriended and supported him. On the other hand, Jewish critics had often attacked him savagely, and there was one whose pen dripped venom whenever he mentioned Thomas Mann. In his boyhood there had been no such divisions, so far as we know; and Mann later concluded that he had been drawn to Jews by their "innate love for Mind—this love which quite often has made them leaders on man's sinful course, but which will always insure that the out-of-the-ordinary, the suffering and needful, the artists and writers, are indebted to them and remain their friends."[10] This solidarity of outcasts must serve us as the acceptable explanation, unless the probings of scholars should produce some unexpected revelations about sensed or known racial kinships.

O T H E R friends rise briefly out of the dimness of a childhood sometimes exploited for fictional ends, sometimes recalled in moments of sentiment, but never subjected to the orderly process of autobiographical reconstruction. In one of his brief sketches of his life Thomas Mann described his childhood as "sheltered and happy"[11] and preferred to say little more about it directly. Yet his fictional transmutations of childhood do not bear out this assertion. The pure joy of anticipation and of imaginative games is there, but in fulfillments there is always a note of further longing, of pain and melancholia, and a sense of the transitory that arose out of an awareness of time rare for children. Time, its subjective and objective nature, its variable human dimension, forms one of the great subjects of his works. At the end of his long life he distilled his views on it into the brief essay "In Praise of Transitoriness."

Among his best friends for a time was another outcast, one at the other end of the social scale from the Jewish boys. This was Count Hans Kaspar von Rantzau, whose memory is preserved in Mann's portrait of Hanno Buddenbrook's friend Kai Mölln:

> Kai was a lad of about Hanno's height, dressed not in a sailor suit but in shabby clothes of uncertain color, with here and there a button missing and a great patch in the seat. His arms were too long for the sleeves of his coat, and his hands seemed impregnated with dust and earth to a permanent gray color; but they were unusually narrow and elegant, with long fingers and tapering nails. His head was . . . neglected, uncombed, and none too clean, but endowed by nature with

all the marks of pure and noble birth. The carelessly parted hair, reddish blond in color, waved back from a white brow, and a pair of light blue eyes gleamed bright and keen from beneath. The cheekbones were slightly prominent; while the nose, with its delicate nostrils and slightly aquiline curve, and the mouth with its short upper lip already had a definite character.[12]

Hans Kaspar remained Thomas's friend through the three years of preparatory school, Dr. Bussenius's Progymnasium on Fleischhauerstrasse (Butchers' Street). The friendship continued even through the five years in the Katharineum, as the Lübeck Gymnasium was called. There is no reason to doubt that the picture in *Buddenbrooks* is essentially autobiographical: a picture of two boys linked by mutual understanding of an imaginative world closed to their fellows, by early attempts at artistic expression, and by a shared hatred of school. To an extent, the Kai of the novel, who as a small child makes up romantic tales and as an adolescent tries his hand at writing fantasies, springs from a fission of the author's personality. His is the role of the writer, as Hanno's is that of the potential musician that Mann became only in the fictional alter ego of Adrian Leverkühn. Since Hanno is destined to die in the novel, this splitting of the author's mind, this withdrawal of the author's consciousness from his character before the end, was a psychological necessity. But in physical appearance—recollected with the precision of a writer who in his boyhood must already have been a keen observer—Kai was fully modeled on Count Hans Kaspar.* It can surely be said that the intensity of the emotional bond between the boys was taken from life.

Even more intense, and consequently of briefer duration, was the bond with Armin Martens, the object of Thomas Mann's "first love." Writing of this at the very end of his life to his former Lübeck schoolmate Hermann Lange, Thomas Mann said: "And a more delicate, more blissfully painful love was never again to be granted me. Something like that is not forgotten, even if seventy eventful years pass over it. It may sound ridiculous, but I cherish the memory of this passion of innocence like a treasure."[13]

---

* Mann paid tribute to his boyhood friend in choosing the name Hans Castorp for the hero of *The Magic Mountain*. He disguised the name Kaspar by resorting to another autobiographical borrowing: Castorf was the name of the village where Mann's uncle and godfather, Nikolaus Heinrich Stolterfoht, had an estate.

To Armin, son of a merchant and sawmill owner on that same Fleischhauerstrasse where Dr. Bussenius's institute was located, Thomas addressed his first love poems; and one day he confessed his love to the boy. Armin did not know what to make of it; and this classically Freudian manifestation of pubescent homosexuality soon faded, giving way in the course of a year to an infatuation with a tawny-haired, pigtailed dancing partner, who likewise became the object of lyrics. To both these passions, and to the boy and girl who had stirred them, Thomas Mann "erected a monument" in *Tonio Kröger*. Armin Martens, who as Hans Hansen was destined to become the symbol of healthy normality and competence, was in fact the first of Mann's classmates to fall into one of the many pitfalls laid by *das Leben*—Life writ large. "In real life he took to drink and made a melancholy end in Africa."[14]

In *Tonio Kröger* Thomas Mann describes how Tonio tries to inspire stolid, unimaginative Hans Hansen with some of the excitement that Schiller's *Don Carlos* had stirred in him. "For the queer thing was," Mann remarks, "that Tonio, who after all envied Hans Hansen for being what he was, still kept on trying to draw him over to his own side, though of course he could succeed in this at most only at moments and superficially. . . ."[15]

But there were other friends whose inclinations ran rather more in a literary direction. Some of them were several years his senior, such as Korfiz Holm, his squad leader in the hated gymnastics class, who as editor of *Simplicissimus* became an important figure in Thomas Mann's life during the early Munich years. Another was Ludwig Ewers, a classmate of Thomas's brother Heinrich, who was to become a well-known journalist and critic. A third boy, the same age as Thomas and sharing with him a gift for mockery of "the whole thing"—meaning school and the teachers—was Otto Grautoff, the local bookseller's son and a future art historian.

For these and other schoolmates, among whom "the little count" was included, the Mann brothers jointly gave parties that featured good food and readings from Schiller's *Wilhelm Tell*. If nothing else, the Katharineum, or rather one of its teachers, had awakened in Thomas Mann an enthusiasm for Friedrich von Schiller that was to persist into the last year of his life. Thirty-five years later, when he visited Lübeck for the seven hundredth anniversary of the city's founding, he met this teacher, Dr. Ludwig

Hermann Baethcke. To the delight of the "snowy-haired emeritus," Mann still remembered the teacher's set phrase when he spoke of Schiller: "This is not just any reading you are having; it is the very best reading you could have!"[16]

At those parties, Ludwig Ewers recalls, Senator Mann himself gladly accepted roles in the plays. He would urge the youngsters on, but maintained enough of a dignified presence throughout the long afternoons—the readings often lasted into the evening—to keep the boys from falling into their favorite subject: savage criticism of the school and its teachers. Critics they nevertheless remained, and under the influence of Naturalism, then in its heyday, they freely discussed literature past and present.

B U T how tenuous were all these friendships with schoolmates and neighbors compared to the one relationship that was not friendship, nor yet hostility; not love, nor yet rivalry; that was compounded of awe, admiration, affection, anger, and envy: the relationship of the little to the big brother. Heinrich, four years older, was always taking the lead, showing the way; and the younger brother scrambled to keep up, catch up, hold on.

Heinrich had a box of watercolors, some grainy paper, bottles of colored inks, and a rather considerable talent for drawing; before he settled down to his profession, he thought he might become a painter. Thomas, naturally, also practiced drawing and developed a certain gift for caricature. But he would fly into a rage when people asked him: "Who is it supposed to be?" Almost weeping, he would exclaim his reply: "It's a man, can't you see, a drawing I've made, made up of outlines, good grief!"[17] Was his anger due to the artist's early resentment of "identity hunting," as he would have us believe? Or was it due to the peculiarity that behind all his caricatures, according to a friend's testimony, Tommy's own features could always be discerned?[18] There is indeed a rather charming self-portrait he included with his first preserved letter of 1889, showing him as a mustachioed man-about-town, with side-whiskers, a monocle, a choker collar, and a comic look of maturity. But if he drew only himself in boyhood, he had widened his repertory somewhat a few years later, when he and Heinrich produced the *Bilderbuch für artige Kinder*. There could be no doubt, however, that Heinrich wielded pen and brush with the authority of talent as well as age. The younger brother could imitate, playfully at first, with determination as he grew older; but he could never catch up.

In school the difference was equally marked. The brothers agreed in hating the entire process of schooling, and Heinrich rebelled against the tyranny of those schoolmasters he would later portray with such devastating wit and insight. But although he spent most of his spare time reading or painting, as Thomas spent his reading, writing poems, or dreaming, Heinrich was able to fend off the suspicions of the masters and conform to their requirements. Unlike his younger brother, he went straight through the course with grades mostly of 1's and 2's (equivalent to A's and B's). He completed the Gymnasium and successfully passed the *Abitur*, which entitled him to attend the university, in 1889. Meanwhile, Thomas was being "left back" twice; his promotions, moreover, were always by the skin of his teeth. Small wonder that his admiration for his elder brother was mingled with envy and despair.

Heinrich led the way into literature; but even before that he had led the way into life, by way of travel. For in the summer of 1884 the thirteen-year-old visited Uncle Gustaf Sievers—the husband of Senator Mann's younger sister Olga—in St. Petersburg. Heinrich assiduously kept a journal of the trip, noting his daily routine: life in a dacha, accompanying Uncle Gustaf to the office and the stock exchange, visiting churches. He noted that "everywhere you see images of the saints and the Virgin; and people throw themselves down before each, cross and bless themselves."[19] He toured the Hermitage and the Winter Palace, where Peter the Great in wax sat upon his canopied throne. Such were the tales Heinrich brought home to tell his smaller brother; and they so fired Thomas's imagination that when he began reading adult novels he turned to the Russians. Heinrich himself preferred the French writers for reading and for models.

The desire to emulate, the rancor of smallness, the anguish of inadequacy—these are characteristic emotions of younger siblings. To them must be added, in the middle-class family of late-nineteenth-century Germany, rivalry for maternal love and dread of paternal reproof. Given two boys of such extraordinary sensitivity and intense will as Heinrich and Thomas Mann, the resulting "fraternal constellation"[20] entailed hatred as well as affection. Thomas

Mann's treatment of the tensions between Christian and Thomas Buddenbrook sprang from a deep experience with the inner nature of relations between brothers. Inevitably, the greater force, the greater agony, had to be on the side of the younger. There was a period during the childhood of Thomas and Heinrich when the boys, living in the same room, did not speak to each other for more than a year.[21]

But there were those other times, more frequent, when they talked exuberantly: in earlier childhood about the fairy tales of Andersen, Grimm, and Perrault that their mother read to them; later, as the heroic past moved more into the focus of knowledge, about historical personalities. In adolescence they argued about the relative merits of Napoleon and Bismarck. Anyone familiar with the brothers' future work and mentality would assume that conservative, German-oriented Thomas favored Bismarck, while progressive, Francophile Heinrich would have revered Napoleon. But it was the other way round, and an understanding of this paradox will lead to the heart of the differences and likenesses of these brothers. There would be many years of bitterness and suffering from *das brüderliche Welterlebnis*, the fraternal constellation; but all conflicts between the brothers took place within the framework of *das kindliche Gefühl*, the emotional ambience of childhood. No coarsening of the sensibility by real life, no degree of habituation to fame and the world, could alter that sense of shared childhood. "Being brothers means: being small boys in a dignifiedly provincial corner of the Fatherland and making fun of that dignified corner; it means sharing the freedom, irreality, purity of living, the absolute bohemianism of youth."[22]

Each of the boys was to become the author of a vast oeuvre. Yet the shared trait of their youth was indolence, a voluptuous craving for idleness that contrasted strongly with the active spirit of their commercial ancestors. Thomas has spoken of this in the essay mentioned above, "Sweet Sleep": "I have a good deal of Hinduism in myself, a heavy and sluggish craving for that form or nonform of perfection that is called Nirvana or Nothingness, and although I am an artist I have a highly unartistic inclination toward Eternity, expressing itself in a disinclination toward structure and standards. What opposes that, believe me, is . . . discipline; is . . . morality."[23]

The difference between the two boys lay in the degree of their rebellion. Thomas's whole nature needed that indolence and dreaminess which provided the matrix for the conception of works of art. But he also had a strong sense of conformity, a bourgeois "tameness" that prompted him to agree with his father's work ethic rather than his mother's romantic inclination toward Art. Not that his mother encouraged his literary leanings. On the contrary, she scolded him for his attempts to write and refused to believe in his talent—out of disappointment at his failures at school, as she later admitted. But the older brother bore the brunt of family disapproval; that is inevitable in such situations. Heinrich Mann suffered the sting of public condemnation in his father's will.

Heinrich had resisted all his father's efforts to draw him into the family business. Quarrels over the boy's future embittered Senator Mann's last years—quarrels that are curiously transmuted in *Buddenbrooks* into conflicts between the brothers Thomas and Christian. The father could neither force nor induce Heinrich to take an interest in grain; the young "dandy" was bent on a career in literature, which the senator saw as a certain road to failure in life. A compromise was finally reached, and in October 1889—Thomas was then a few months past his fifteenth birthday—Heinrich entered the Dresden book shop of Jaensch & Zahn as an apprentice. A book shop at least provided a passionate reader with books, and Heinrich apparently read more than he worked. After half a year his employers wrote to Senator Mann charging Heinrich with apathy, indolence, and truculence. "Their whole description makes me anxious about your future,"[24] his father wrote to Heinrich in May 1890. In reply Heinrich defended himself vigorously, complaining about Herr Jaensch ("His principle is to treat the apprentices as badly as possible, using swear words"), and praising Herr von Zahn as a "highly cultivated and therefore naturally amiable" man with whom he unfortunately had much less to do than with his partner.[25] In spite of his unhappiness Heinrich stuck it out in Dresden for another year. In April 1891 he had had enough, and after an apparently explosive scene with Herr Jaensch that brought his father hastening to Dresden, he left the book shop and Dresden behind and went to Berlin.

It was with this painful experience in mind that Senator Heinrich Mann, drafting his will in June 1891, wrote:

I wish the guardians of my children to consider it their duty to influence these children toward a *practical* education. Insofar as they are able, they are to oppose my eldest son's leanings toward so-called literary activity. In my opinion he lacks the prerequisites for sound, successful work in this direction, namely sufficient study and broad knowledge. The basis of his proclivities is dreamy self-indulgence and inconsiderateness toward others, perhaps from lack of reflection.

The senator had more confidence in the good sense and docility of Tommy, for he continued: "My second son is responsive to calm admonishments; he has a good disposition and will find his way to a practical vocation. I feel justified in expecting that he will be a support to his mother."[26]

The second son can at least be credited with having the more skillfully concealed his intentions from his father. Only the year before, the whole city had helped to celebrate the hundredth anniversary of the firm of Johann Siegmund Mann. The city and port were decked out with flags, the lines of congratulators endless. And Thomas Mann watched his father, whom he admired and loved with timid affection, "prudently representing a century of bourgeois competence; and my heart was heavy. . . . I knew at the time that I would not be my father's and my fathers' successor, at least not in the way that was tacitly required of me, and that I would not lead the old firm into the future."[27]

But although he thought with relief of his second son's turning to some practical vocation, Senator Mann knew that Tommy also would not and could not carry on the firm. Nor, it would seem, did the senator any longer wish it. Disappointment with his children and with his own failure to adapt to the new era of "imperial capitalism" had soured his pleasure in commercial enterprise. In his will he provided for the liquidation of the family business. Then, as if the will were a ticket of departure to be eagerly grasped, only a few months after drawing up the testament he came down with a mortal case of blood poisoning.

Thomas, sixteen, stood in the room as the pastor of St. Mary's in his clerical garb knelt beside the dying senator's bed and engaged in long prayers. But Senator Heinrich Mann did not have the faith of his forefathers: Thomas could recall him sitting on the beach at Travemünde, his gold pince-nez clamped on his nose, reading a novel by none other than Emile Zola. The boy watched his father turning his head restively and finally interrupting the pastor's flow of pieties with a vigorous "Amen!" The pastor went on undisturbed "and even made laudatory mention of the Amen in his funeral sermon, although, as was immediately apparent to me, the adolescent boy, it had meant no more than 'get it over with.' "[28] *Schluss*—the German word expresses a finality that, in the opinion of one critic, may have suggested to Thomas Mann the portentous scene in *Buddenbrooks* in which Hanno draws a double line under his own name in the family tree. The end came on October 13, 1891, less than a year after the death of Grandmother Elisabeth Mann.

Although the mayor of Lübeck had just suffered a tragic loss in the suicide of his daughter, who "in a fever threw herself out of the window,"[29] the sympathies and mourning of the city concentrated upon the decease of Senator Thomas Johann Heinrich Mann. The mayor ordered the flags to be flown at half mast from the town's buildings and the ships in the port. The *Lübeckische Blätter* devoted its entire front page and an additional one and a half columns to the senator's obituary. It recalled the prestige of his firm, stating that Senator Mann had made it "the most important grain house in our city." It mentioned his place on the boards of directors of several shipping companies, banks, and a life insurance company; his service as a member of the finance and tax departments of the municipal government; and his high position in the Chamber of Commerce. With his multitude of offices, Senator Mann had directly affected the lives of many of his fellow citizens. He had actively promoted the Lübeck-Büchen Railroad and at the time of his death was chairman of its executive board. He had supported the improvement of the roads and pushed the project for a canal linking the Elbe with the Trave.[30]

Absorbed though he had been in administration and in the encouragement of industry and commerce, Senator Mann had not forgotten the welfare of his poorer fellow citizens. He had been a member of the Society for the Promotion of Charity and had helped to found an Association for Vacation Colonies to provide recreation for the poor. As he once remarked wryly, "You'll find me everywhere where there's no money to be made."[31] And in fact he seems to have spent as much of his time on the affairs of his city-state as on his own business. Although he had headed his firm for a quarter of a century, Senator Mann had not really succeeded in notably increasing its capital. With his son Heinrich at his side he had driven out to the villages to introduce his putative successor to the farmers who sold him their grain. The farmers would come to the gate to meet the senator in his hired carriage, and the bargain was struck without any examination of the grain—for there was mutual trust. These personal calls were intended solely to strengthen the friendship on which the business relationship was founded. A sense of personal rectitude, of ambition modified by concern for the commonweal, and of pride in position balanced by patrician skepticism—these were as much part of Senator Mann's bequest as the firm's capital.

After the funeral—"which in size and pomp surpassed anything that had been seen in Lübeck for many years"[32]—the Mann family had to face the prospect of what were then called "reduced circumstances." The need to economize was patent; it was also accompanied by a certain guilt and shame, as if wealth were a personal merit and its loss or absence proof of a frivolous disposition. Julia Mann, a widow with five children, and at forty still attractive, no longer felt at ease in Lübeck. Perhaps she never had; but now the city seemed to her constricting.

Financial pressures and the desire to escape the too familiar faces of neighbors prompted her first action: sale of the stately town house that Senator Mann had so hopefully built only ten years before. For the children, the wrench may have been no greater than the sale of their grandmother's house on Mengstrasse the previous year. The widow Mann and her brood moved into a rented house outside the Burgtor, at Roeckstrasse 9. Her two sons were nearly grown, and one was already out in the world; the two girls, Julia (Lula) and Carla, were fourteen and ten; and the "Benjamin" of the family, Viktor, was barely two. Julia Mann, an independent-minded, spirited person who from early childhood had nevertheless been controlled and directed by others, now had to work out a new pattern for her life.

In the spring of 1892 she made her bid for freedom. With the two girls and the baby she left the town that had been her home since she was seven. In a city where she was unknown it would not be demeaning for her to live in an apartment. Traveling with her husband, she had once seen Munich, the city of artists, and had fallen in love with the city and the surrounding mountains. On the slender basis of one encounter she removed to Munich, where she found for herself and the three younger children an eight-room apartment with a terrace, stone steps, and a walled garden. In Berlin Heinrich was working as a "volunteer"* for the progressive publishing house of S. Fischer, which was to figure so largely in his brother's life. Thomas was boarded with one of his teachers, Dr. Hupe, and left behind in Lübeck to complete his studies at the Katharineum. For him, too, a period of relative freedom began. With his family's departure from Lübeck, his childhood ended.

---

* It was quite common for the sons of the middle class to spend a year or more as unpaid apprentices in some practical trade which they expected to pursue.

3

Adolescence

D R. HUPE, a tall, broad-shouldered man with a slightly
stooped appearance, straw-blond beard and hair, and large,
sea-blue eyes behind gold-rimmed glasses, taught English
at the Katharineum. Not at all the model for the unfortunate Candidate Modersohn of *Buddenbrooks*, Dr. Hupe laid a foundation in
speaking and writing English that was to serve his pupil in good
stead nearly half a century later, when exile in America imposed
upon Thomas Mann in his sixties the necessity of relearning the
almost forgotten language. With kindness and enthusiasm the English teacher had accomplished something of a miracle with his sluggish and unresponsive pupil. When Hupe read, or rather chanted,
English poems in his rapturous manner, Thomas listened attentively
and respectfully, which he could not always manage to do in his
other classes. English, French, even Latin—these were after all literature, therefore pertinent to the self-image he had already formed.
And Dr. Hupe had responded to his interest with kindness. Unlike

the rest of Thomas's teachers, he had conceived a strong affection for the boy and a conviction of his potentialities. It was out of that affection that he had offered to board Thomas during the school year, when Julia Mann decided to leave for Munich. He was counting heavily on his ability to encourage a dreamy and recalcitrant youngster to use his gifts in school as well as outside.

The details of what followed are obscured by our informant's discretion. We hear only that Dr. Hupe had overestimated his powers, that he had taken in the boarder "on unfavorable conditions," and that the task "consumed his nervous strength."[1] Does this mean simply that he was not charging enough, had not reckoned with unexpected expenses, or that Thomas was truly "recalcitrant" and Dr. Hupe failed to encourage him to do better at school? At any rate, Thomas had to move, "for the second time losing a loving home," as Ludwig Ewers puts it in his reminiscences, and spent the next Gymnasium year boarding with a Professor Timpe.

Timpe ran a regular boardinghouse for a number of students. The others were young nobles from country estates in Holstein and Mecklenburg who came to Lübeck for their schooling. These boys were already practicing for their future roles as beer-drinking university students, and Thomas—high-spirited despite his failures at school—got along well with them and occasionally joined their parties. Professor Timpe dutifully made efforts to control his band of young aristocrats. He tried to establish curfew hours, and a former schoolmate recollects that Thomas had difficulty obtaining permission to go out. But Thomas himself later recalled only the gaiety and freedom of that period, when the "institution" had virtually given him up, expecting no more of him, and he was left pretty much to his own devices after school hours.

With or without permission from Professor Timpe, Thomas contrived to make his almost nightly way to the city opera house on the same street as his boyhood home, the Beckergrube. His violin teacher, Herr Winkelmann, played in the small and not always tuneful string section, and in earlier days the conductor, Alexander von Fielitz, had been a welcome friend in his parents' home. Fielitz composed "modern music," and Thomas had often heard his mother singing and playing the conductor's song cycle *Eiland*. Thomas had loved music from the time he had sat, as a small boy, listening to his mother pour her longings into Chopin études and nocturnes, or singing the poems of Eichendorff, Heine, and Storm in the settings of Schubert, Schumann, and Franz. He himself played the violin passably, and as he grew older was able to accompany his mother. In those days, before recording, the passion for orchestral music that so often develops in late adolescence could be indulged only by attendance at concerts and the opera. The normal musical fervor of an eighteen-year-old conjoined, in the case of Thomas Mann, with the enthusiasm for Wagner that, as Nietzsche would have it, was sweeping Europe like a contagion.

The cheapest place in the city opera house (aside from standing room) was a seat that had no number; it was marked by the letter A and presumably was one of those little seats at the end of rows in European theaters that can be snapped down. This was Thomas's favorite seat; the old ticket seller who crouched "in a kind of unventilated cave illuminated by a gas flame"[2] would on successive evenings sell him the same greasy bits of cardboard which were collected at the entrance to be sold again. Thomas unfailingly attended when young Emil Gerhäuser, the dramatic tenor—"in the Maytime of his voice"—sang Lohengrin or Tannhäuser or Walther in *Meistersinger*. In spite of the defects of the orchestra, the weakness of the chorus, and the general provinciality of the production, Thomas was "as the French say, *transporté*"; he heard *Lohengrin* so many times that for the rest of his life he knew it virtually by heart. Surely, he declared, the opera house could not have held a more receptive or absorbed listener than himself. In after years he was willing to call this encounter with Richard Wagner "one of the principal artistic events of my life."[3]

What did the adolescent hear in these Wagnerian operas that so enchanted him? And what did the incipient artist find that so enormously instructed him? Young Thomas sat in his folding seat with his nerves quivering and his intellect afire, stirred by insights into as yet unexperienced emotions and by glimpses of portentous meanings. In his later life he acknowledged that he could never forget all the felicity Wagner had given him.

Thomas Mann was coming to consciousness as a youth and as a writer in the fin de siècle, and it seemed to him that Wagner provided a summation of the nineteenth century's monumental achievement; that Wagner was the perfect expression of the century itself. To think this was enthusiastic exaggeration; but years would pass before Thomas Mann, seeing his world and history as a mature artist, really came to grips with the century of his birth. At seventeen, however, he was already aware, although dimly, of how vastly the world had changed in the past ninety years. In 1800 the condition of ordinary life had been still fairly close to the traditional patterns of civilized society. Railroads, steamboats, gaslight, photography, and a thousand other inventions and innovations still lay in the future. So did the overwhelming abundance of nineteenth-century music, the enormous achievement of the novel, the discoveries of historiography, sociology, anthropology, chemistry, physics, astronomy—the list grows too long. By 1890 life could be called "modern," even by the standards of nearly a century later. Those ninety years had seen the consummation of the Industrial Revolution, the consolidation of the social and political consequences of the French Revolution, the impact of the innovative thought of Darwin, Marx, and James Clerk Maxwell. Those years had seen upheaval upon upheaval in all the realms of human endeavor, from the way people moved about, to the way they built their houses, grew their food, and thought about their nature and destiny. A boy with a sensitive nervous system, filled with vague ambitions and enjoying his first taste of independence, trying to reach out beyond the confines of what seemed to him a smug, narrow, provincial town, could try to grasp the world only through literature and music. And those arts had turned lovingly toward the past. For even as the nineteenth century was ferociously wiping out the past, it was unearthing fairy tales and sagas, was inventing folklore and linguistics, was developing archaeology and history into sciences, and was passionately preserving and collecting.

Richard Wagner followed the lead of his Romantic predecessors in dredging history for his materials. But he was bolder, more passionate, and more egotistic than the Romantics; he wanted to embrace everything in the totality of his *Gesamtkunstwerk*. And so he seized upon the new historical subjects that the Romantic scholars had unearthed, that the Romantic poets had played with, and, like young Siegfried forging his sword out of fragments, converted them in the fire of his art into authentic myth. Or at least it sounded authentic to the young listener, who never thought of laughing at the posturings or the alliterations of Wagner's woeful wanderers. The ironic view came later. Preadolescent ("adolescence hangs on with me,"[4] he wrote at twenty-six), young Thomas had willingly succumbed to the cloudy emotions of his beloved Romantic poets. With the loss of his father, the departure of his brother and then of his mother and sisters, and with the persistent growing sense of his own difference from his fellows came a preoccupation with isolation, death, and sex to which the works of Wagner spoke directly.

The fin de siècle was discovering psychology, then only just emerging from under the mantle of philosophy. In Richard Wagner Thomas found the gift for analysis, the psychological naturalism, that he also came to admire in Paul Bourget. Sigmund Freud, who would initiate the twentieth century's total reassessment of values to a far greater extent than Nietzsche, was still working with Breuer on experiments in the hypnotic treatment of the neuroses and had not yet published. Soon Freud would be ready to strike out on his own. But his perception of the central role of sexuality in the psychic life had already been intuitively anticipated by Wagner. Wagner was capable of such shattering defiances of convention as his statement "Love in its fullest reality is possible only within sex."[5] All love, he insisted, was derivative from the sexual feelings; and as if he were determined to hammer the point home, he devoted an entire opera to carnal love.

In that last decade of the nineteenth century, carnality, the liberation of sexuality from the repression of the past half-century, was in the air. In any case, sexual liberation is always an issue for the young. Thomas Mann speaks only in very general terms of his own sexual awakening, placing it not in his eighteenth year, when the vicarious experience of operatic sex served adequately, but in his twentieth—"a belated and violent outbreak of sexuality."[6] But he could not fail to observe, even before acquaintance with psychoanalysis had provided him with the words in which to describe it, such manifestations as the "erotic mother-complex" in *The Valkyrie* and *Parsifal*, or the incestuous passion of Siegmund and Sieglinde— which he later parodied in one of his most daring stories, "The Blood of the Walsungs," as well as in *The Holy Sinner*, his novel of grace and redemption. For Wagner, too, sexuality was bound up with the idea of redemption; and Thomas Mann paid tribute to Wagner's Kundry, the seductress who is also the vessel of Grace, as the boldest and strongest of the composer's conceptions. Scarcely ever is an echo unintentional in Thomas Mann's later work. The very title of *The Holy Sinner* in German, *Der Erwählte*, alludes to the Jewish brother-sister pair in "The Blood of the Walsungs"; in German the Chosen People are *das erwählte Volk*. While writing *The Holy Sinner*, the seventy-five-year-old Mann was playing with ideas and engaging passions he had first encountered in the works of Richard Wagner more than half a century before.

Wagner towered above his contemporaries, a godlike creator who simmered together in one magic cauldron religion, sex, historical memory, and a collective unconscious not yet named but already sensed. Back in the dawn of civilization theater and music had sprung from myth; but by now both had descended into triviality. Wagner redeemed opera (the man had a passion for redemption, as Nietzsche observed) by discovering that it could be used for the embodiment of myth. Or to put it another way, the pretentiousness and triviality of musical theater combining with the deep seriousness of myth begot music drama. The historical and mythological plots of Wagner's music dramas, when regarded as purely literary productions, seem today quite as bombastic and silly as most of the libretti of grand opera. The music by itself does not satisfy the stringencies of modern music criticism—although its time may come again. But taken together, and lavishly staged in the manner demanded by Wagner's theory, the "total work of art" remains a unique phenomenon, one of those monuments of nineteenth-century giantism that, like *War and Peace*, is still loved as well as respected, is still, in the jargon of today, "relevant."

It was altogether relevant to young Thomas, who, having surrendered his greasy ticket, surrendered himself to the tempests of orchestra and voices as if he were alone in the theater, blissfully experiencing "hours of nervous and intellectual transport and rapture."[7] In the Stadttheater, Lübeck's opera house, he could relive the delights of his solitary childhood performances with the puppet theater. Had he not in a sense invented the *Gesamtkunstwerk* himself when he manipulated his puppets while chanting or ranting his own texts in front of the scene he himself had set? By now he knew enough to understand that his own bent was more restricted, that if he could write, that would be enough. For him, anything more would be dilettantism. Yet before him on the stage, Wagner, master dilettante, the rather clumsy poet, the unskilled painter, the amateur actor, and the imperfectly trained musician created a composite that overwhelmingly surpassed the sum of its parts. And Thomas worshiped, admired with only occasional misgivings, and learned whatever he thought could be useful for purposes only dimly defined.

From the first, Wagner's theory left him cold. He could scarcely believe that anyone had ever taken seriously the notion of all-embracing totality, of combining music, poetry, painting, and acting. That was indeed, he now knew, child's play. "Art is whole and perfect in each of its forms; we do not need to add its various branches together in order to make it perfect,"[8] he later wrote. What Wagner could teach him was technical and exemplary. He absorbed, at first unconsciously, later consciously, the possibility of employing musical structure as the framework for prose. The idea quickly went beyond the mere use of the leitmotif as an identifying device. It comprehended variations on a theme, hidden quotation, recapitulation and development, false starts and false endings, returns to earlier themes and earlier keys, and final resolutions. To construct a novel that would sound like, and essentially be, a musical piece in prose became one of his ambitions. He ultimately realized it most effectively in the tetralogy of *Joseph and His Brothers*, which he frequently compared to Wagner's *Ring* cycle, and perhaps less effectively in the novel specifically devoted to a musician's life, *Doctor Faustus*.

BY HIS eighteenth year Mann had reached only the lower second form at the old Katharineum. He had changed "homes" again, was boarding with a Professor Hempel, and consorted with a group of seniors, some of whom had distinctly literary inclinations. He himself was emerging from the shadow of the school. Not that he was doing significantly better; but "the institution no longer expected anything more of me; it was leaving me to my fate."[9] And he himself, older, no longer felt the helplessness he attributed to Hanno Buddenbrook. He no longer accepted the school's opinion of him as the just condemnation of all his ways. On the contrary, he had become rather cocksure and cheerful, convinced that his mind was sound and sharp. Instead of worrying about lessons undone, and dreaming of vague future glories, he had already settled down in seriousness to learn his craft.

Even more important than the writing, which he had after all been practicing since his fourteenth year, was the excitement of first publication. Thomas had joined with Otto Grautoff, Korfiz Holm, and a few of his older friends at school to carry out a plan common to groups of aspiring young writers: they had founded a magazine. It was printed, moreover, and with a flowery border. The contents were largely provided by the editor, one Paul Thomas—these were Thomas Mann's two given names. (He never afterward made use of the "Paul.") The magazine was called *Der Frühlingssturm* (Spring Storm), perhaps in deliberate reminiscence of Frank Wedekind's *Frühlingserwachen* (Spring's Awakening), perhaps by sheer coincidence. Wedekind's drama of adolescent sexuality and of children crushed and betrayed by the adult world had appeared only two years before. The small edition, paid for by the author and published in Zürich, had made little impression upon the public. But it was the talk of the tightly knit literary world, and had already made a reputation for its author. It is not impossible that Thomas Mann or some member of his circle had read the play or heard gossip about a work that was destined to stimulate a whole literature on the pathos of childhood (the subtitle of *Frühlingserwachen* was *"eine Kindertragödie"*), from Gerhart Hauptmann's *Hannele's Ascension* to Hermann Hesse's *Beneath the Wheel*. Certainly, in its cynical presentation of the Gymnasium teachers Wedekind's play was not without influence upon *Buddenbrooks* as well as Heinrich Mann's *Professor Unrat*. *Frühlingserwachen* also touched on the theme of pubescent homosexuality that is threaded lightly through Thomas Mann's work.

Young Thomas Mann was, however, no antiauthoritarian like Wedekind. A mediator by nature, he balanced the revolutionary promise of the magazine's title by the sobriety—not to say the presumption—of its subtitle: "A Monthly Journal for Art, Literature, and Philosophy." The program of *Revolution mit Massen*—in moderation—was set forth in the editorial that opened the first issue. This first of the writer's pieces ever to see print is a curious document, *in ovo* already containing Thomas Mann's characteristic technique of mingling narrative and essay. The initial sentences are short, almost fragmentary, in marked contrast to the elaborate periods of the later style and even of the last two paragraphs:

> It was afternoon. After school. Between one and two o'clock. I did not feel like going home yet and strolled, my Caesar under my arm and a bostanjoglo* between my lips, in the streets and out through the city gate. . . . It was a remarkably warm spring day. So warm that all the budding and blossoming about me visibly suffered. Everything looked thirsty and tired. . . . And not a breath of air. Not the slightest noticeable life in this slack aridity.[10]

The schoolboy was giving himself airs, with his cigarette and his Caesar; but he was also seeing himself with just a touch of irony (the word, so overused in connection with Thomas Mann, is unavoidable). As he was to do so often, so successfully, and sometimes so irritatingly, he placed himself in the foreground. Yet it was not quite himself. That sophisticated schoolboy strolling among the parched buds and blossoms was neither Paul Thomas nor Thomas Mann. To use a term that had then not yet been applied in the modern sense, he was a persona. As a writer must, young Thomas was already trying on various masks.

At this point most schoolboy editorialists would have fallen into the pathetic fallacy of conjuring up a spring storm to sweep away the dust and bring welcome moisture to greening shoots. But Thomas Mann is already truthful and accurate. He invokes the storm—so effectively that one of his early admirers, the critic Arthur Eloesser, reads a bit carelessly and imagines that he has "very neatly arranged this symbolic natural event."[12] But it is invocation, not evocation:

> Our worthy Lübeck is a good town. Oh, an altogether excellent town! But it often strikes me that it resembles that grassy square, covered with dust and needing the spring storm that vigorously shakes life out of the smothering husks. For life is there! Certainly—you can see it in the single green blades that are breaking freshly through the

---

* ". . . one of those sweet, cheap Italian cigarettes to which I was addicted to the point of gluttony. . . ."[11]

layer of dust, full of youthful strength and valor, full of unbiased views and radiant ideals!

Spring storm! Yes, like the spring storm sweeping through dusty nature we want to sweep with words and ideas into the plethora of mental dustiness and ignorance and limited, puffed-up philistinism that confronts us. That is our magazine's aim; that is the aim of *The Spring Storm*.[13]

Unfortunately for its mission of kicking up the dust in Lübeck, the magazine expired after two issues. The spring storm that would sweep through Lübeck, upsetting old families if not old prejudices, did not arrive for another seven years. Along with the new century, it blew in when *Buddenbrooks* was published and an excited citizenry, persuaded that the book was a roman à clef, passed lists of "identified" characters from hand to hand. But *Der Frühlingssturm*, although it created no more of an upheaval than the aborted revolution of 1848 so wittily described in *Buddenbrooks*, at any rate opened its friendly columns to the editor's first published poem and a first story—or rather, sketch—that has in recent years, after long omission from the canon, been included with the collected shorter fiction. The poem "Zweimaliger Abschied" (Double Farewell) has all the laboriousness and lack of sharp originality that characterized Thomas Mann's verse throughout his life—as he well knew in later years, when he used verse chiefly for playful purposes, to heighten an unbearably dramatic moment in *Joseph*, to lighten the description of combat in *The Holy Sinner*. "Zweimaliger Abschied," essentially Theodor Storm with a dash of Schiller, fortunately made no attempt at rhyme, for in those days Thomas inadvertently turned anything in rhyme into an echo of Heinrich Heine's *Buch der Lieder*. At least this tale of parting forevermore was told in sturdy blank verse:

> We walked along in silence with the sea—
> Upon my shoulder lay your dear blond head
> And the soft fragrance of your dampened hair
> Caressed enticingly my very nerves. . . .

The Biedermeier sentiment gives way, for a moment, to a touch of naturalism at the railroad station:

> A noise and flurry,
> A sodden and a dirty gray confusion
> Of suitcases—people—steam.
> I looked at a bouquet—I carried it—
> And at your parents—also looked at you—

Then the sentiment returns, romanticism in the guise of realism:

> Both of us knew what the sea had heard
> On that damp and dusky summer night . . .
> "Never—never again . . ."[14]

In some respects Mann's first published story, which likewise appeared in *Der Frühlingssturm*, is far more juvenile than this poem. Its title was "Vision"; it is essentially what American editors call a short short story or a mood piece, and again it opens with the proud new accomplishment of cigarette smoking. The smoke forms bizarre letters. Suddenly all is agitation. The language is highly charged, excessive and melodramatic: "Wild movement in all my senses. Feverish, nervous, insane. Every sound screeches." And a vision arises of something seen once before. It is described in elaborate, nervous, fragmented language that reminds one rather of Heinrich than of Thomas Mann: a vision of a girl's hand, pulse, a bubble rising in a glass of champagne ("pale gold"). The bubble reaches the surface, the vision vanishes, and as the writer-narrator leans back wearily, "pain twitches." Even two or three years later Thomas Mann would not have permitted himself that kind of false note. Now, however, he capped it by the banality of his ending: "But I know it now as surely as I did then: You loved me after all . . . And that is why I can weep now."

The parts are superior to the whole; there are phrases and bits of observation and description that would do credit to any mature writer. The tone is that of a school exercise by an unusually gifted pupil. And it was in fact as a pupil that Mann still regarded himself, for with youthful frankness he dedicated the story to Hermann Bahr. Very likely his brother Heinrich had called his attention to Bahr, who had been connected with S. Fischer's publishing house. Heinrich's employment as an unpaid apprentice with S. Fischer Verlag came shortly after Bahr's departure from *Die Freie Bühne*, the magazine that Bahr had attempted to make the voice of the modern movement, *die Moderne*. Already the influences of Schopenhauer and Nietzsche, combining with currents from the French painters and the writers of the *Décadence*, were stimulating in Germany a fashion for jarring juxtapositions of sense impressions, colors, and psychological states. Hermann Bahr formulated and exemplified the ideals of literary Impressionism; he also put himself forward as the discoverer of Hugo von Hofmannsthal, whose close friend he became. A member of the circle of Viennese innovators that included Arthur Schnitzler and Richard Beer-Hofmann as well as Hofmannsthal (the latter, like Thomas Mann, still a schoolboy, but already published), Bahr himself was a somewhat facile novelist. Primarily he was what the Germans refer to as a "publicist"—an editor, critic, and literary impresario with remarkable antennae. He wrote the manifestos of the new Symbolism before that literary movement became conscious of itself. And he overthrew the idols of Naturalism even before they had been enshrined in the temple. Thomas Mann was undoubtedly thinking of Bahr's *Die Überwindung des Naturalismus* (1891) when he dedicated his little story to "the writer of genius Hermann Bahr." And although it is doubtful that Bahr ever saw "Vision" in print, the Viennese littérateur reciprocated Mann's regard, in after years becoming one of his steadfast admirers.

DER FRÜHLINGSSTURM also provided evidence of young Thomas's admiration for Heinrich Heine. There was a poem in the magazine that perfectly mimicked the rhythms and rhymes of the *Buch der Lieder*:

> *Nun will ich noch einmal singen*
> *von Lust und Liebe und Mai*
> *und wenn die Saiten zerspringen*
> *dann ist das Ganze vorbei.*

> *Noch einmal lass wild dich umschlingen*
> *o Leben, du blühende Fey* . . .
> Oh let me once more sing the praises
> Of joy and of love and of May.
> By the time the strings will have broken
> It will all have vanished away.

> Once more let me wildly embrace you,
> Oh Life, you exquisite Fay . . .

There was also a short prose essay entitled "Heinrich Heine the 'Good,' " a review of a "defense" of Heine that had been published in the *Berliner Tageblatt* by a Dr. Conrad Scipio. With an air of thoroughly mature judgment, Mann reprimands Scipio for his condescending, "philistine" efforts to prove Heine an orthodox Lutheran and a good man who had returned to the fold of religion on his deathbed. Mann approvingly quotes that Heine witticism beloved of adolescents—*"Dieu me pardonnera, c'est son métier"*—and announces firmly that "Heinrich Heine was not a 'good' man. He was only a great man."[15]

In his enthusiasm for Heine, in trying his hand at verse, fiction, and criticism, Thomas at this time was faithfully following in the footsteps of his elder brother. His youthful revolt against society, natural though it was for his age, seems also to have been borrowed from his brother, who was bohemian by instinct, a born "gypsy in a green wagon." Burdened by the knowledge that he could not conform to his father's wishes and carry on the family business, Heinrich conceived an antagonism to the "bourgeois" world of Lübeck that was expressed in savage denunciations. Heinrich Heine, the intellectual and racial outcast to whom the Germans refused to erect a monument, was likewise the subject of Heinrich's early poems, written in 1888 when *he* was seventeen. Heinrich, too, had a gift for mimicry:

> *Ihr wollt Ihm kein Denkmal setzen*
> *Ihr lieben, braven Leut'?*
> *So dumm, wie ihr wart, als Er lebte,*
> *So dumm seid ihr noch heut.*[16]

> No monument for him, you say,
> You dear good upright folk.
> As stupid as he found you,
> So stupid are you still.

And in a letter to Ludwig Ewers, the friend of both Mann brothers, Heinrich wrote in 1890: "The only poet who is so fortunate as to satisfy all my demands is Heinrich Heine. I love him as a writer, and as a human being at least cannot despise him; for his weak-nesses spring from hot blood and a bold imagination; and long, pa-tiently endured suffering has ennobled him."[17]

Heinrich was sending a good many poems to his friend Ewers that year when he himself was not so patiently suffering in the Dresden book shop. Ludwig had on at least one occasion read some of the poems to the Manns, and Heinrich asked him to be more discreet in the future, until he could surprise his father ("pleasantly, I hope") with his first poem in print. "And leave out my brother also, who alarmed me, after your reading the poems aloud, by an enthusiastic outburst of admiration."[18]

Heinrich's first published poem appeared in print by November 1890 in *Die Gesellschaft*, the magazine he regarded as the most modernist of the German periodicals. It published, he advised Ewers, "all the real realists, the whole movement."[19] Thomas, too, had the pleasure of his first publication in the same magazine: the poem "Zweimaliger Abschied." This time he signed the poem "Thomas Mann." Heinrich, who had been roaming around Ger-many, Switzerland, and France on the small income his father had left him, visited Lübeck in May and early June 1893, and may well have used his new connections with the world of literature to help Thomas break into the magazine. Heinrich must have brought his admiring and grateful younger brother news of the great world. Probably Heinrich confided that he was working on a novel (*In einer Familie*) in which a young man facing a choice between two women chooses the one who represents the harmonious, ordinary, unpretentious life "in a family." In this novel Heinrich was trying to do for Germany what Paul Bourget with his "learned and deli-cate psychology"[20] was doing for France.* In October of that year Heinrich dedicated the completed novel (which was printed the following year with financial aid from his mother) to Bourget. There can be little doubt that the two brothers discussed Bourget at length. Forty years later Thomas still recalled Heinrich's en-thusiasm for the conservative French novelist and essayist, and

---

* Thomas Mann's "delicate psychology" appears to be an echo of Nietzsche's phrase for Bourget, "delicate psychologist"—which rather suggests that whatever major influence Bourget may have had upon the younger Mann was filtered through the philosopher, his acknowledged mentor. Bourget himself was strongly influenced by German philoso-phy and psychology.

twitted his brother: "On the whole your conservative period was in your youth."[21]

On Heinrich's urging, Thomas read Bourget, and it is quite possible that he began with *Le Disciple*, which had just been published in Paris. Even though Thomas never set out, as Heinrich was doing, to reproduce Bourget's effects, he may well have allowed certain passages to affect him unconsciously. Unlike Heinrich, who seemed to have an instinctive affinity to French, so that he was already keeping parts of his diary in that language, Thomas read French with some difficulty. The very effort may have impressed certain phrases on his memory. There is, at any rate, a passage in *Le Disciple* that may have suggested the famous play on *l'amour* and *la mort* in the Walpurgis Night chapter of *The Magic Mountain*.* Bourget's comments on *dédoublement*, the splitting of the personality into participant and observer, actor and student of the action, may have stimulated Mann's own meditations on the problem of "the Artist" and "Life." Likewise, Bourget's grand vision of the potentialities of science[23] may have persuaded Mann of the usefulness of such materials for the novelist's art. But it is hard to believe he would not have hit on the same ideas of his own accord.

H E I N R I C H , the future committed socialist, had decided that he wanted to become the novelistic analyst of high life. That meant the *haute vie* of Paris; later he turned his thoughts more successfully to the *Herrenleben* of Berlin. But to understand high life one had to live high, and that was scarcely possible on the modest income from a liquidated grain firm that had been sold at a loss and divided into many portions. Heinrich recalled his father's story about the famous actor who had said that he could not play Hamlet, prince of Denmark, if he had eaten potatoes and herring for supper. All very well to lead the cosmopolitan life as best he could with limited means. But that meant sticking to small, middle-class boarding-

---

* *Cette idée de la mort sortie des profondeurs intimes de ma personne, cet obscur appétit du tombeau dont je me sentis possedé comme d'une soif et d'une faim physiques, vous y reconnaîtrez, mon cher maître, une conséquence nécessaire de cette maladie de l'Amour si admirablement étudiée par vous. Ce fut, retourné contre moi-même, cet instinct de destruction dont vous signalez le mystérieux éveil dans l'homme en même temps que l'instinct du sexe."*[22]

houses; and he believed that all the imaginative powers he could summon up would not raise him above the level of "the more or less empty pockets." Once he had received his small inheritance, he decided, he would put aside a sum sufficient to let him live an *existence supérieure* for a month. Five thousand francs ought to suffice. From the viewpoint of his 5-franc boardinghouse, that "ought to suffice" sounded almost blasphemous, but from the other point of view it would be quite natural. He would take a small apartment near the boulevards—unfortunately a furnished flat, since the glory would be brief. He would have a first-class Paris tailor dress him afresh from head to foot. Silk shirts and silk dressing gown. *"J'insiste sur ces détails, ils ne sont point ridicules au fond."* Then he would "quickly take as elegant a woman as is attainable for the money" he had to offer.

The quotations are from an entry in Heinrich's diary that bore the heading "My Plan."[24] It is a curious document, full of delighted anticipations, avowals to himself that the whole plan is in the interests of a literary project, propitiatory reassurances to the ghost of his father that he really is not a wastrel. Heinrich also wondered whether he would be seeing the authentic fashionable world. Would not the woman guide him only into the demimonde?

It is impossible to know whether, on his visit to Lübeck, Heinrich said anything to his younger brother about this "plan." It seems likely that he at least dropped hints about it—he had, after all, come straight from Paris, and it is often an older brother's feeling that he must introduce the younger to "life." In those early days the brothers confided rather freely in each other, as the surviving letters make plain; and surely something fixed in Thomas's mind the notion of Heinrich as a spendthrift, which was often to trouble their relationship in future years. Their experience of living together in Italy would not have done it, for in the small matters of daily existence Heinrich inclined to be cautious and tightfisted, rather distinctly "bourgeois."

AFTER Heinrich's visit in May and June of 1893—the very months that saw the publication of *Der Frühlingssturm*—Thomas settled down to his last year at the old Katharineum. In *A Sketch of My Life* he makes light of this end of his formal schooling: "I have glad memories of this period. . . . The uncertainty of the future did not oppress me."[25] We should not allow ourselves to be deceived by this optimistic appraisal, which Mann wrote in the year after he received the Nobel Prize, looking down from one of the summits of his life. The melancholic note of his early work, the heaviness of spirit to which he frequently refers, certainly sprang in part at least from the pain of failure in school. For all that the Gymnasium expected no more of him, and that he was inwardly convinced of his own intelligence, he was, like other schoolboys, hardly able to pit himself against the standards of the institution. In *Buddenbrooks* he describes with acumen and humor how Hanno and his classmates agree with the reproofs of their tyrannical teachers and principal, how they accept their punishments as deserved, and believe the authorities' predictions of a bleak future. When in March of 1894 he received his *Abgangszeugnis*, the school-leaving certificate, he could not help being humiliated. He had just skated by with a "partly satisfactory" or "barely satisfactory" in all his subjects: religion, German, Latin, French, English, history, geography, mathematics, science. Even in Conduct his one mark of "good" was crossed out and revised to "on the whole good." He was, moreover, leaving school in the lower second form, with two years still to complete. He had remained only long enough to receive the One Year Volunteer's certificate, that privilege for the sons of the bourgeoisie which exempted them from the obligatory two years in the German army; they had to put in only one year of so-called voluntary service. The school year ended on March 16, 1894. He promptly left Lübeck to join his mother, his two sisters, and his four-year-old brother in Munich. Heinrich, at this time, was in Florence.

4

Rambergstrasse 2

THERE was a walled garden with a brown canvas pavilion in which the family often took their tea. Stone steps ran up to the terrace that linked the garden and the eight-room ground-floor apartment at number 2 Rambergstrasse. The dining room held an enormous sideboard with lion's-paw feet. From the wall the Ancestors, Statius Brage and his wife, looked down upon the family from portraits painted on wooden panels in the Dutch seventeenth-century manner. Julia Mann would often comment laughingly that her three boys had inherited the Brage features, especially nose and brow. More recent ancestors hung in the living room, with its rather old-fashioned, green-upholstered furniture: portraits of Maria da Silva, Julia Mann's mother, shoulders bared in her Biedermeier dress; and of Great-Grandfather Marty. But the heart of the apartment was the salon, which faced the street. Here stood the black Bechstein grand piano on which Julia Mann played almost every day. And here, too, stood the walnut desk at which she wrote her memories of her Brazilian childhood. The desk also served her for the more mundane chores of keeping household accounts.

In the Rambergstrasse apartment, "filled with the leftovers of a once-prosperous middle-class household,"[1] Thomas found a merry familial atmosphere, considerably freer than it had been in Lübeck. There, even after the death of Senator Mann, the obligations of mourning and the Manns' social position had inhibited Julia Mann's natural sociability. Here in Munich she could enjoy playing the attractive young widow. She had gathered around her a circle of friends and admirers who would soon pay court equally to mother and daughters—a situation that Heinrich Mann used in his early novel, *Zwischen den Rassen*, and that appears again, rather heavily freighted with mythological references to Demeter and Persephone, in Thomas Mann's *Felix Krull*—that is, in the continuation written in his last years. The sisters were not yet grown; but Carla was a stagestruck thirteen, Julia ("Lula") a soberer and more conventional seventeen. Little Viko was a rambunctious, charming boy of four who already had a perfect command of the (to these northerners) ludicrous Munich dialect.

Rambergstrasse was a short street off Türkenstrasse, one of the main arteries of what was then suburban Schwabing, the artistic and literary quarter of Munich, and within walking distance of the university. As a boy of nineteen, Thomas could not yet quite venture to enter the literary life of the Schwabing cafés, although he did not have long to wait. And as a student who had retired rather shamefully from the Gymnasium without obtaining his *Abitur*, he could not enroll in the university for any regular course of studies. But there was nothing to prevent him from attending lectures as an auditor, and it would seem that he resolved to do so almost from the time of his arrival in Munich in April 1894.

His mother, who strongly opposed his literary ambitions even as she was furthering Heinrich's by financing the publication of *In einer Familie*, had other plans for him. She had obtained a post for him as an unpaid apprentice with the South German Insurance Bank. Obediently, as Heinrich had done, Thomas gave it a try. He had not the slightest intention of remaining in the insurance business, but was unwilling to quarrel seriously with his mother immediately after coming to Munich. And so began what he subsequently described as "a singular interlude."[2] For six months he sat at a slanting desk, like a clerk out of a Dickens novel, copying out memoranda packed with facts and figures, inventories of insured objects. At the same time he secretly wrote his first short story, "Gefallen" (Fallen). He sent it, of course, to *Die Gesellschaft*, the magazine that had already published his poem. This was only natural; but the poem had been dispatched from distant Lübeck to this very city, for the magazine was published in Munich. Moreover, Thomas could even meet the editor, Michael Georg Conrad, of whom he later wrote: "He was really the man of this city, and it was like him: at once folksily rustic and cosmopolitan, European—the ideal man, the ideal city."[3]

"Gefallen" was omitted from Thomas Mann's collected works throughout his life, and he himself dismissed it as "crashingly immature, although possibly not unmelodious."[4] For the age of the writer, however, the story is remarkably poised, adroit, sophisticated in technique, stylistically assured. Only the somewhat deceptive air of philosophical consistency strikes the note of immaturity. That it shows the influences of Goethe, Bourget, and Turgenev, as a number of critics have pointed out,[5] is hardly surprising; the remarkable thing is that it is already recognizably Thomas Mann. The intrusion of a self-conscious narrator, so frequent in the later works, makes its appearance here in this first extended work of fiction. The narrator serves a vital function in enlisting the reader's empathy; at the same time his tone suggests that the doctor who actually tells the story is not to be taken fully at his word.

"Gefallen" is worth lingering over for a moment, since it has never been published in English. It is the story of a "decent young man"—*der gute Junge*—who becomes a cynic after his first experience with love. But it is also a didactic story centering on a discussion and, not incidentally, a good meal—like so much of Mann's later work. Four young men meet for dinner in the studio of one of them, a painter (already the atmosphere of Schwabing has been put to fictional use). The studio is described with precision, from its Etruscan and Japanese vases to its thick Oriental rugs and faded embroidered silks "arranged in clashing combinations that seemed to be pointing their fingers at themselves."[6] The young men dine well and address themselves enthusiastically to the wines. "Over the Roquefort" Laube, the passionate advocate of women's rights, begins riding his hobby. He denounces the double standard of morality. Dr. Selten, who is older than the others, offers to tell a story that is applicable to the argument. And he describes his first love for a virtuous young actress whom he succeeds, by the very purity of his passion, in seducing—only to find her shortly afterward betraying him. The double standard, that is, is legitimate after all. "The woman who falls for love today will fall for money tomorrow,"[7] the doctor concludes.

Cynical philosophizing on the nature of womankind ill suited the young man of nineteen; and the writer's deliberate separation from the content by the device of double narration suggests that no personal experience of Thomas Mann's underlay the story. It was Heinrich who all his life had a tendency to fall in love with actresses, Heinrich who in his novel *Im Schlaraffenland* showed the depths of cynicism he was capable of, and Heinrich also whose features correspond with the sparing physical description of the doctor in the story. Moreover, Heinrich was in Munich during those crucial months from April to October in which Thomas was undergoing the same ordeal Heinrich had experienced at the Leipzig book shop. The story Thomas wrote surreptitiously at the insurance company's slanting desk might very well have been based on an experience of Heinrich's. The two brothers were very close at this period, in which the younger was rapidly catching up with the elder. As yet, no public successes or failures had introduced the note of jealousy.

Publication of "Gefallen" brought Thomas Mann the first of those respectful if not reverential letters from fellow writers that, in the course of his long life, were to become honor and onus in equal measure. The poet Richard Dehmel, at the age of twenty-seven already an established writer and editor and a man who had likewise done his stint of work in an insurance company, wrote: "I have just read your wonderful story "Gefallen" in the *Gesellschaft*, and then read it again aloud to my wife, and I must tell you how delighted and moved I am. Nowadays there are so few writers who can portray an experience in simple, heartfelt prose that you must permit me this somewhat importunate expression of my pleasure and admiration."[8] Dehmel added that if Thomas Mann had any other manuscripts "of equal maturity" (an indication that he had some inkling of the writer's age), he would be glad to have them submitted for the magazine *Pan*, which was just being launched.

Dehmel's letter was dated November 4, 1894. On that same day

Thomas registered at the University of Munich as an auditor. He had gained his freedom already, after the briefest of trials in the workaday world. Publication sufficed to persuade his mother that he could, like his older brother, become a writer. Years later she confessed: "Strange how I ranted against Tommy's efforts! At the time very great disappointment with his schoolwork must have robbed me of all belief in his talent. Or else, in an effort to imbue him with more eagerness for study, I tried to block his urge to become a writer."[9]

It is not unlikely that Julia Mann was acting out of a guilty conscientiousness, playing the father's part for her now fatherless son, all the while secretly pleased that he reflected her own leanings toward "the finer things." At any rate, a man's word sufficed to sway her; she gave her consent when her lawyer, whom Thomas had won over, proposed that the young man attend the university and study "journalism." Writing with a practical end in view seemed a suitable compromise to Julia Mann; and Thomas made of these studies what he wished. The boy who had hated school registered as an auditor for courses that covered a wide range: political economy, general world history and the history of culture, German mythology, fundamentals of aesthetics, and Shakespeare's tragedies. It was a heavy program, but with no examinations to fear, no class recitations to prepare for, no weary pedants to crack the whip, Thomas thoroughly enjoyed his education. In his single year at the university he laid the foundations for that wide learning that was to earn him the reputation of being one of the most "intellectual" of writers. As he rather proudly confessed in later life, there was an element of superficiality and fraudulence about his apparent scholarly achievements, since he would "work things up" only for the purpose of his fiction:

> I sometimes notice with embarrassment that on the basis of my books people regard me as a virtually universal mind—a man of encyclopedic knowledge. What an illusion! In reality I am, for a (forgive the phrase) world-famous writer, almost inconceivably ill-educated. In school I learned nothing but reading and writing, the multiplication table, and a little Latin. I resisted everything else with dull obstinacy and was considered a hopeless lazybones. This was premature, for later on I did develop into a hard worker when it became necessary to supply the scholarly foundation for a work of fiction, that is, to collect

information in order to play literary games with it—or, strictly speaking, to scandalously misuse it. Thus I became in turn an expert in medicine and biology, a firm Orientalist, Egyptologist, mythologist, and historian of religions, a specialist in medieval culture and poetry, and so on. But the worst of it is that as soon as I finish the book for whose sake I run up such expenditures of scholarship, I forget with incredible speed everything I have learned and go about with an empty head, in wretched awareness of my total ignorance.[10]

As so often with Thomas Mann, this confession can be taken at face value and can simultaneously be regarded as purest fiction, a case of the author's adopting the pose of his character Felix Krull. Throughout his literary career Mann knew when he needed to lean upon experts, and he never hesitated to turn to them for technical advice. But he had somehow acquired, in a year at the university and in desultory reading, the intellectual framework into which bricks of knowledge could be fitted to make exactly the kind of structure he desired. Nor was he all that forgetful. For example, he was particularly fascinated by the course he took in the summer semester of 1895 on the Courtly Epic of the Middle Ages—it was taught by Wilhelm Hertz, the poet and translator of Middle High German. More than half a century later, while writing *The Holy Sinner*, Mann consulted frequently with a medieval expert. But he was still adept enough at reading *Mittelhochdeutsch* to make his own translations of poems with only a little help.

"Living like a student without formally being one,"[11] he frequented the cafés where contemporary writers and future politicians foregathered—one published story served to make him a writer also. Nor was it a betrayal of his clear sense of vocation when he joined the Academic Dramatic Club and took part as an actor in Ibsen's *The Wild Duck*.

> The principal event while I was a member was the German premiere of Ibsen's *The Wild Duck*, which the club put on under the direction of Ernst von Wolzogen. It was a literary success in spite of the protests of a conservative public. Wolzogen himself played the part of old Ekdal; the writer Hans Olden was Hjalmar; and I, wearing Wolzogen's fur coat and glasses, took the part of Werle, the wholesale merchant. When we met in later years the author of *Lumpengesindel* [Wolzogen] used to joke that he had "discovered" me.[12]

Baron Ernst von Wolzogen, bearded, mustachioed, bespectacled, would have looked every inch a Prussian army officer but for his artistically wild tousle of hair and his lighthearted addiction to all the Muses. In Berlin he had founded the famous literary café Das Überbrettl; in Munich he led the way in staging the dramas of such radicals as Gerhart Hauptmann and Henrik Ibsen. Nearly forty at the time he lent Thomas Mann his fur coat, he was a thorough professional of the theater, and it speaks well for Thomas's acting ability that Wolzogen was willing to assign him an important if rather brief part that would be demanding for a trained actor. The puppet theater of childhood and the dramatic productions of the Lübeck schoolboys had given Thomas a measure of experience. Those who knew him, and especially those who heard him read aloud in later life, have testified to his ability to dramatize. Carl Zuckmayer once declared that if Thomas Mann had not been a great writer, he would have been a great actor.[13]

There is no evidence that Thomas ever seriously considered a career as an actor. But his part in Wolzogen's production brought him into the world of Ibsen more deeply than casual reading or theatergoing ever would have done. Out of the rehearsals, discussions, and efforts at identification that constitute the normal work of an acting company comes a unique, if sometimes also peculiarly slanted, understanding of the play and playwright. Later Mann would assert that Ibsen's dramatic work had made as great an impression upon him in his youth as the art of Richard Wagner. When Mann was working on *Royal Highness*, so he informed Hugo von Hofmannsthal, he "referred back to the dialogue in [Ibsen's] *The Pretenders* between Skule and the skald" to see whether it would justify the scene between the prince and the poet Martini (in *Royal Highness*) where "reality suddenly appears and converses with its own symbol."[14]

There is a touching scene in *The Wild Duck* in which Hjalmar betrays his lack of worldliness by his ignorance in regard to the Tokay; he does not know that vintage year is a factor in the quality of wines. By the time he has reached home he has reshaped his humiliation into a triumph; he displays his newly acquired knowledge to his wife and repeats as his own the words that were addressed to him. The duality of the scene, the conjunction of sophistication and naiveté in the character, and of subtlety and obviousness in the

author's use of the leitmotif, sounds "Mannian." The reader is irre-
sistibly reminded of Tony Buddenbrook quoting Morten Schwarz-
kopf on social problems, or of Hans Castorp citing his mentors,
Settembrini and Naphta.

In the Munich of Thomas Mann's young manhood Ibsen was a
living tradition. A voluntary exile from his native land (as Mann
was to be in later life), Ibsen had spent a number of years in Dresden and moved to Munich in 1875, the year of Mann's birth. Munich became his second home; he felt far more at ease there, as he
wrote to the great critic Georg Brandes, than he did in Norway. The
children of Munich, respectfully mocking, referred to him as "the
white tomcat," in reference to his mane of white hair and his white
beard. Children would follow him about as he took his walks in the
Englischer Garten. Thomas Mann had missed the living presence of
Henrik Ibsen by three years, but his new acquaintance Michael
Georg Conrad, the editor of *Die Gesellschaft*, could describe the
dramatist as he had seen him in the Café Maximilian, where he appeared daily "in all weathers, always at the second table to the right
from the entrance, generally alone, a mug of beer, a glass of cognac,
and a bottle of water before him. He had a newspaper in his hand,
but often looked over it, for the people going in and out were them-
oelvee a chronicle, a living collection of newspapers at least as important and interesting as the printed paper of the dailies."[15] Often,
as Conrad described him, Ibsen sat like a statue, meditating, his
fingers curved as if he were holding a pen. Then, after a while, he
would stand up quietly, take his cane, his top hat, and his gloves,
and go out with somewhat tripping footsteps.

What Ibsen had to give young Thomas Mann, particularly in
The Wild Duck, was surely not awareness of the discrepancy between appearance and reality. Thomas knew all about that; it had
formed the basis of the antic humor he shared with Otto Grautoff
during his school years. But Ibsen taught him the possibility of exploiting the ironic note for literary purposes. All the characters in a
work may be flawed, as they are in *The Wild Duck*, where all are
living their life-lie, even Dr. Relling, who propounds the theory of
it. The young idealist Gregers ruins lives by his moralistic view of
human nature; but after having destroyed the child he refuses to
recognize his own guilt. At most he will admit to suffering from bad
luck; his destiny is to be thirteenth at table. Hjalmar is weak, self-

indulgent, deliberately self-deluded. Werle, sounder than most of the other characters in acceptance of reality, is morally indifferent. His imminent blindness symbolizes his inability to see that he has built his fortune on another man's disgrace. Ibsen casts a cold eye on all his characters; and his example was not lost on Thomas Mann. Such minor technical matters as Ibsen's use of dialect and malapropism for humorous effect and for characterization count for little compared to the overall lesson.

Thomas Mann was always generous in acknowledging his literary debts, and unfortunately his critics have tended to follow his lead too dutifully. With any writer of strongly original bent the whole question of "influences" becomes perplexing and full of dubieties. Nevertheless, it is possible to argue that the example of Ibsen's objectivity may have saved a young writer, already inclined to think that he had but to speak of himself to include the world from indulging himself too soon or too naively in too many *Tonio Krögers*. Ibsen's detachment earned him many enemies in Norway; a similar quality in Thomas Mann's early works baffled and disturbed even his friendly critics (such as Kurt Martens). Detachment accorded with Mann's instincts, and it reassured him to see that same coolness present in one of the major writers of his time. But the early stories are also full of regret that the attitude of detached observation must be the enemy of spontaneity. The theme runs through all his work to reach a culmination in *Doctor Faustus*, where the obligation imposed on the artist to remain detached and "cold" becomes a pact with the devil. Incidentally, the scholars have discussed a multitude of sources of *Doctor Faustus*; but surely Ibsen's *The Master Builder* deserves a mention. Halvard, the problematical artist with his power to inspire devotion, his trolls and servitors, his ruthless ambition and apocalyptic end, must have lingered in the mind of the writer who conceived Adrian Leverkühn. Thomas Mann knew the play by the time he was nineteen, for the schoolboy "Paul Thomas" contributed a review of *The Master Builder* to *Der Frühlingssturm*.

But a young man is affected above all by what his contemporaries are doing; and the closest, the most intimate contemporary was Heinrich Mann. Heinrich, leading the way as always, had already, at the age of twenty-five, fulfilled a young writer's dream by becoming editor of a magazine pompously and progressively titled

Das Zwanzigste Jahrhundert (The Twentieth Century). The magazine's publisher and his associates, however, looked fixedly backward rather than forward. During its short life *Das Zwanzigste Jahrhundert* acquired a certain notoriety as Germany's principal organ of conservatism, nationalism, pan-Germanism, anti-Semitism, and black reaction in general during the closing years of the nineteenth century. The critic and biographer Klaus Schröter has made much, rather too much, of the Mann brothers' contributions to this magazine, and of their having passed over their association with it in complete silence ever afterward.

Far from being fin de siècle aesthetes, these sons of the Lübeck "tax senator" (*Steuersenator*) turned quite easily and naturally to political thought. Senator Mann had not hesitated to comment in his letters to Heinrich on the unfortunate outcome of elections in which some sixty socialists had been returned to the Reichstag. "God preserve the emperor and Bismarck"[16] had summed up Senator Mann's position shortly before his death. Five years later, with his father no longer there to incite him to opposition, it became possible for Heinrich to take a similar stance of straightforward monarchism and nationalism. In the works of Paul Bourget, still his favorite writer, he found an ideological substructure for these instinctive ideas. And so we find Heinrich Mann writing in *Das Zwanzigste Jahrhundert* praises of "the class of honorable wholesale merchants"—at the very time that his younger brother Thomas was playing the part of the perhaps dishonorable but nevertheless praiseworthy wholesale merchant, Werle, in *The Wild Duck*.

The political opinions of young men in their early twenties are by no means unimportant—indeed, they often change the world. But they are also highly changeable, and it would be almost unnatural if they were not subject to revision under the pressures of experience, superior arguments, or altered conditions of life. It is doubtful that Heinrich and Thomas Mann could ever really have embraced the intense chauvinism and rabid anti-Semitism that became the nightmare of Germany and the world for some decades of the twentieth century. Both the Mann brothers would later seek out Jewish wives, and the attraction, for whatever reason, must have been there from the start in Heinrich as well as in Thomas: the attraction of *Geist*, as we have earlier seen. Anti-Semitism, moreover, was inconsistent with the admiration for Heine both brothers had repeatedly professed and exhibited. Not all criticism of Jews is necessarily anti-Semitic; and there can be no doubt that when Heinrich Mann satirized wealthy Jews he was directing his scorn at wealth rather than Jews. That is evident from one of his earliest poems: "Outside the Exchange I see them strolling, / Jews of both denominations. . . ."[17] In *Im Schlaraffenland* he portrays Jews savagely, but no more savagely than he does the other inhabitants of his rather "strange aquarium"—to borrow a remark Thomas Mann made when it was suggested that his portraits of Fitelberg and Breisacher in *Doctor Faustus* might be taken as anti-Semitic.[18]

Nevertheless, both young men succumbed to the opportunistic impulses that Heinrich would also unsparingly analyze in *Im Schlaraffenland*. Both brothers trimmed their coats to fit the cloth; both sacrificed principle for publication. Heinrich, as the responsible editor, had to make the greatest concessions to the general tendency of the magazine; and it may be that with his passionate temperament he convinced himself that he believed what he wrote. Thomas, contributing reviews of ephemeral books of verse, could easily be less committal. The regular publication of minor pieces certainly consolidated his sense of himself as a real writer, not just an aspirant. But it is difficult to tell whether he is subscribing wholeheartedly to the conservative principles of the magazine's backers and readers, or only pretending, perhaps even making fun of those earnest ideologues. This possibility satisfies a psychological requirement: that ideas "tried on for size" must ultimately be worn in earnest, whereas those who hold certain ideas in earnest for a while can later readily and guiltlessly discard them. Thus twenty years afterward, when he was writing *Betrachtungen eines Unpolitischen* (Reflections of an Unpolitical Man), Thomas Mann adopted as his own some tenets of the conservative and nationalistic creed. Heinrich, on the other hand, put conservatism behind him after his year of editing *Das Zwanzigste Jahrhundert*, and thereafter aligned himself consistently with the more liberal if not necessarily radical movements of the actual twentieth century.

There was a hidden irony, and perhaps a degree of disavowal of his public stance, in Heinrich's choice of residence during the year of his editorship (April 1895 to March 1896). For Heinrich spent most of that period in Italy. He edited his arch-German, chauvinistic periodical, which was printed in Berlin, largely from Rome—the city in which, by his own testimony, his talent was born: "In Rome, Via Argentina 34, talent overpowered me."[19] The yield of this "eruption of talent," as he also called it later on, was a group of novellas that were subsequently brought out by Albert Langen, the Munich publisher of Frank Wedekind and of the magazine *Simplicissimus*.

Rome had overwhelmed Heinrich from the very first. As he wrote at the time, he felt as if he were "in a wonderland" of "invincible strangeness." As he had recorded his boyhood impressions of St. Petersburg, he now kept a journal of his encounter with Rome: "I feel like the sailors in the *Arabian Nights* who enter a mysterious, deserted city. . . . For three weeks here I have been encountering new surprises every single day, a fountain, a ruin, a church that I had not seen or not paid attention to. For it is ridiculous, all the things one does *not* pay attention to here. The first three days I did not consciously look at the column in the Piazza Colonna. If it stood in any other city, one would see nothing but it."[20]

The exultation of the diary must have been repeated in his letters home, and to his brother Thomas, which unfortunately have not been preserved. The outcome was predictable, sensible, and practicable, since the small income from their inheritance that both young men enjoyed would go much farther in inexpensive Italy. In July Thomas joined his brother, and to escape the summer heat of Rome they went to the ancient town of Palestrina in the nearby mountains—to talk, to read Nietzsche, to absorb the colorful, vivacious, passionate life of "the little town," as Heinrich subsequently entitled his novel set in Palestrina. As Thomas later said, they were biding their time. Thomas devoured Russian and Scandinavian novels "in the reek of countless three-centesimi cigarettes."[21] Heinrich read French novels and sketched. Both worked on short stories, reviews, occasional pieces. As Heinrich later recalled rather sententiously, in penetrating other languages and literatures they experienced their own, in print and orally, to the point of despair, to the point of bliss. "In his early twenties my brother was devoted to the Russian masters; half my life consisted of French sentences. Both of us learned how to write German—largely for that reason, so I think."[22]

Neither, in recollection, ever sentimentalized the youthful bond: the pact of two gifted apprentices.

5

Italy

A NONDESCRIPT blend of farmland and urban sprawl stretches under a smoky sky for some twenty miles from Rome to the foot of the Sabine Hills. From the plain, the road winds up an escarpment to the small town of Palestrina, which climbs the steep slope in a series of terraces. Palestrina, birthplace of the composer, is as old as Rome itself. The streets connecting successive levels of the main thoroughfare are flights of stairs, and among these is one great wide staircase with steps of white marble. Its majesty contrasts with the plain façades of the low houses that line both sides of the stairs. In the ancient Roman town of Praeneste those marble steps, as well as the foundations of many of the present buildings, formed parts of a gigantic temple of Fortuna. The temple, which in antiquity must have been visible under clear skies as far away as Rome, rose up the hill on at least five terraces. At the top, some of the columns may still be seen, incorporated into a medieval palace of the Colonna family. It later became the property of the Barberinis, and is now a museum.

In the last decade of the nineteenth century, when Thomas and Heinrich Mann stayed in Palestrina, the air was limpid over the Campagna, and the lofty site of the town guaranteed cool breezes. Citizens of Rome came to Palestrina to escape the capital's summer heat, just as Romans had come to Praeneste as long ago as the fifth century B.C. In later times the emperor Hadrian was attracted by the beauty and salubriousness of the mountains. He built a so-called villa nearby—in fact a tremendous complex, a veritable palace, the vast remains of which may still be seen.

Thomas and Heinrich Mann would have arrived in the mail coach that daily dashed up the steep, winding street to the post office, the horses' furious pace stimulated by loud cracks of the whip. In *The Little Town* Heinrich has lovingly described the approach of this diligence, which seated eight persons inside and one outside on the box beside the coachman. It brought passengers and goods; watching its arrival was the major event of the day for the Palestrinans. Otherwise there was little to do in Palestrina besides visiting the "acropolis" at the crown of the hill, taking a walk to the garden of the Capuchin monastery, and spending an idle hour or two at the café in the piazza. The small black pigs noted in *Doctor Faustus* have vanished from the streets, although their grunts can still be heard behind walls in the more outlying parts of the town, as can the cackling of whole henyards somewhere behind the façades. But the laden donkeys remain, trotting nimbly up the steps and still, with their wide loads, pressing inattentive pedestrians against the walls of the houses.

Thomas Mann spent two summers in Palestrina, in 1895 and 1897. In his later recollection they had blended into one "long, scorching Italian summer"[1]; and it is neither rewarding nor necessary to try to separate the components, even where this can be done. Actually, very little record of the first summer has survived; most of what we know about Thomas and Heinrich in Palestrina dates from 1897.

In the summer of 1895 Thomas left Munich with some regrets, for there was a girl in the picture. "The departure from Munich is going to be hard for me for several reasons, but she means to write to me,"[2] he informed Otto Grautoff in the rather teasing tone characteristic of his letters to this old schoolmate. He was looking forward with enthusiasm to "shady tranquility in silent groves" that would "favor my creative work."[3] Rather boastfully, he declared that he counted on conceiving, if not writing, at least a dozen novellas. At this time, what he meant by "novella" was a moderately long short story rather than the ampler type of narrative, almost a short novel in proportions and ambition, that *Tonio Kröger* and *Death in Venice* were to be. No project so formidable as a novel seems to have occurred to him.

As always, Heinrich had scouted out the terrain and found a place for them to stay. In April he had visited Palestrina with his friend Heinrich Lehmann and had stayed at the Casa Bernardini, on the public stairway now called Via Thomas Mann.* The *pensione* was run by Signora Pastini. Adaptably, Heinrich Italianized his name, signing the guest book "Enrico Mann." Thomas, when he entered his own name, also flaunted his meager Italian, but with the conceit of his twenty years insisted on his vocation: "Thomas Mann, *poeta di Monaco*" (poet from Munich). Only six years had passed, after all, since he had signed a letter "lyric-dramatic author."

Idyll of alternating shade and bright sunlight, the town and the countryside filled with animated, carefree, talkative folk given to ready dramatization—that is one aspect of Palestrina as both brothers experienced it. There was also a darker side: the dirt of narrow streets and the shadow of illness (both brothers had delicate lungs), the long penumbra of a history soaked in blood, and the tragedy of brotherhood: love and envy, admiration and emulation, affection always mingled with inadmissible feelings. This was the Palestrina of the cold stone floors where, in Heinrich's *The Little Town*, betrayals, murders, and suicide take place; where, in Thomas's *Doctor Faustus*, the pact with the devil is sealed—perhaps.** Like Rüdiger Schildknapp and Adrian Leverkühn in their Casa Manardi, Heinrich

---

* The town has not publicly expressed gratitude to Heinrich, who watched its animated street life more closely than his brother did and set a whole novel in Palestrina. Perhaps someday there will also be a Via Heinrich Mann. The Casa Bernardini was destroyed by bombs during the Second World War.
** The devil has the last word in this momentous scene, but Adrian never voices assent, although thereafter he behaves as if he had. Unlike Goethe's *Faust*, there is no wager; there are no specific words constituting a pact, although there are suggestions that a pact was made in the past. But this will be discussed in greater detail later.

and Thomas occupied a huge living room with two large windows, simply furnished with wicker chairs and horsehair sofas. There was ample space for two to work or read without interfering with each other. The child who in *Doctor Faustus* repeats "*Spiriti? Spiriti?*" was taken straight from the life of the Casa Bernardini. So was much of the family that ran the pensione—Thomas remembered each individual with precision when, half a century later, he came to the writing of *Doctor Faustus*. But then he also had the benefit of Heinrich's novel, if he needed reminding.

We catch a glimpse of the two brothers together in their room at the Casa Bernardini in one of Thomas's letters to Grautoff: "My brother, who sees me writing, asks about your brother."[4] (Ferdinand Grautoff, Heinrich's classmate, was already launched on the literary career to which Otto Grautoff desperately aspired. Thomas turned upon Ferdinand some of his incipient hostility toward his own brother.) While Thomas wrote letters or drafts of stories, Heinrich often sketched. In spite of considerable writing and publication, he had not yet definitely settled on his vocation. He thought he might become a painter; but the kind of sketching he did was literary in its conception and purpose: an endless series of portraits of every imaginable type and condition of humanity. The brothers called this rogues' gallery "The Social Order." Later, when Heinrich was preparing the sprawling canvases of his novels, he had his characterizations ready to hand in pictorial form; and what he so effectively depicted was truly a panorama of the social order.

During that first summer in Italy neither brother was so indolent as Thomas Mann suggests in his brief autobiographical sketches. In addition to choosing articles for *Das Zwanzigste Jahrhundert*, polishing them, and determining the magazine's makeup, Heinrich contributed over thirty signed articles of his own, and a good many unsigned pieces in addition. He enlisted his brother for half a dozen book reviews and a pair of longer mini-essays. These were Thomas's first ventures (since his schoolboy writing for *Der Frühlingssturm*) into utilitarian prose, *Schriftstellerei* rather than *Dichten*—that is, literary work as opposed to fiction or poetry. One piece, published in the August 1895 issue of the magazine, discussed Oskar Panizza, an older author whom Thomas had met in the literary coffeehouse associated with the Academic Dramatic Club in Munich. Panizza had published a book, *Das Liebeskonzil*, that a Bavarian prosecutor found blasphemous. In the 1890s blasphemy was a penal offense. The author was tried, convicted, and sentenced to a year in jail. A Swiss publisher brought out Panizza's address to the court; and it was on this rather than the book itself that Thomas Mann wrote a commentary. The fledgling writer, in keeping with the tendency of the magazine and his own inclinations to swim against the stream, supported the court decision, which was being denounced as an outrage by the "modern" (today we would say "liberal") writers. Dr. Conrad, the editor of *Die Gesellschaft*, had testified for the defense and had been forced to admit that certain of the allegedly blasphemous passages were at any rate "tasteless." Thomas, who was indebted to Conrad but much too young to play literary politics, argued: "In that case, can we not agree with the verdict from the artistic standpoint also? Or are those who still demand a little good taste in art really nothing but retarded clods?"[5]

With the callousness of youth, Thomas wasted no sympathy on the poor middle-aged author languishing in jail. There is no indication that Thomas thought a sentence of a year a rather considerable penalty for "tasteless" language, or even for some ninety separate instances of minor blasphemies. As polemic, his squib was rather amateurish. It prejudged the issue by declaring apodictically that "the court is obliged to represent other than artistic interests; practical interests."[6] But the tone of patrician haughtiness harked back to his origins; here was the tax senator's son speaking. The schoolboy had called in vaguely revolutionary terms for a fresh wind to sweep away the accumulated dust of old ways and institutions. The apprentice writer, footloose in Italy and working for a conservative periodical, preferred to support constituted authority against its victim. Years later we will find him for a time negotiating with the Munich police censors and seeing their point of view even as he tried to help his brother's friend Frank Wedekind—who also had once served time in a German prison, not for blasphemy but for the evidently more heinous crime of lese majesty.

Perhaps Thomas would not have been so hard on the author of *Das Liebeskonzil* if he had been able to anticipate the good use he was to make of Panizza's writings. Panizza, like Friedrich Nietzsche, had the most ambivalent feelings about the work of Richard Wagner. Panizza's "Bayreuth und die Homosexualität" was published in *Die Gesellschaft* in 1895, and Thomas undoubtedly read it there. In this essay, and in an earlier "epistolary novella"[7] published in the same magazine, Panizza discussed the temptations and perils of Wagnerian music. He invented a village schoolmaster in Bayreuth who has been gradually converted from his love of "classical" music—Haydn, Mozart, and Beethoven—to the "beloved poison" of Wagner. The argument might be regarded as a popularization of Nietzsche's *The Case of Wagner*, which Thomas by his own account had read at the age of nineteen—that is, just before leaving for Italy. Nietzsche and Panizza made him aware, or more probably reinforced his existing awareness, of the musical and moral ambiguities in Wagnerian theory and practice. A few years later we find him putting their views on Wagner as symbol of decadence into the mouth of Edmund Pfühl, the organist whom Gerda Buddenbrook coaxes into capitulating to Wagner. Pfühl is modeled somewhat on Panizza's Bayreuth schoolmaster; but Thomas Mann has given his character fuller life and greater eloquence:

> Gerda Buddenbrook was an impassioned admirer of the new music. But Herr Pfühl was so savagely and indignantly opposed to it that in the beginning she had despaired of winning him over.
>
> On the day she first laid some piano arrangements from *Tristan und Isolde* on the music rack and asked him to play them, he sprang to his feet after twenty-five bars, and began pacing back and forth between the bow window and the piano with every sign of extreme disgust.
>
> "I will not play this, my dear lady! I am your obedient servant, but I won't play this! This isn't music—do believe me! I have always fancied I know a little about music. This is chaos! This is demagogy, blasphemy, insanity! This is perfumed fog with lightning flashing through it. This is the end of all morality in art. I won't play it!" . . .
>
> But . . . this music was less alien to him than he had thought at first. . . . Irresistibly growing stronger, a love for this art began to stir in him.[8]

Once again in a musical context, but far more subtly, allusively, secretly, Thomas Mann was to show indebtedness to Panizza. That was fifty years later in *Doctor Faustus*. Panizza's *Das Liebeskonzil* dealt with the sudden appearance of syphilis in Europe at the end of the fifteenth century. As Panizza presents it, the devil has been assigned by God the task of punishing mankind, and invents syphilis as the most effective means of poisoning man in body and soul. After considering many of the famous beauties of history, the devil finally selects Salomé as his "carrier" to bring "the pox" into the world. The association of the devil with the dread disease had certainly been suggested to Thomas Mann by other sources as well; and critics have not been lax in tracking these down. But one critic[9] has cleverly penetrated the "forms and masks"[10] behind which, in *Doctor Faustus*, Mann concealed a reference to Panizza's book. Adrian Leverkühn, in connection with his meeting with Esmeralda which results in the fateful infection—the pivot of the novel's "plot"—attends or plans to attend the Austrian premiere of Richard Strauss's *Salomé*. It is characteristic of Thomas Mann's wit in the writing of his mature years that he even manages an unforced association between the first performance of the opera (a historical fact incorporated into the novel) and the "premiere" of syphilis.

THE impressions of Thomas Mann's youth served him for a lifetime of fiction. One other experience of that first summer in Palestrina was visual rather than literary. Palestrina had been, we have mentioned, a temple of Fortuna; and the privately owned palace at the top of the hill preserved a Roman mosaic which may still be seen there. It is believed to be of the first century, and it is a highly unusual and arresting example of its kind. The waters of some great river appear to have risen so that many animals are caught on rocks projecting above the flood. At the top, huntsmen in kiltlike white aprons are perched on a rocky escarpment. They are aiming arrows at deer and birds. The wide river winds past lions, baboons, hippopotamuses, gazelles. Elephants bathe in the water, and a crocodile slithers across the foreground. Large boats with cabins amidships, and a multitude of smaller, canoelike craft, are plying the stream. On the shore stand temples, palaces, and loggias. A sense of a rich and bustling life in a hot climate pervades the scene.

There is indirect evidence that Thomas must have seen this mosaic. Heinrich, in his *Zwischen den Rassen*, brings his heroine Lola to Palestrina. "She let him show her the Roman mosaic. 'Is it a flood on the Nile?' she asked."[11] Obviously, the Roman mosaic was one of the tourist sights of Palestrina in 1895, as it still is today.

Beyond noting the existence of this wonderful mosaic, Heinrich made meager literary use of it. For him it remained merely background for the passions of his characters. But in all probability his brother accompanied him on the day he saw the mosaic, since in Palestrina they took their daily walk together. At any rate, the reader of *Joseph and His Brothers* who visits what is now the Museo Nazionale in Palestrina cannot help associating *Il Mosaico del Nilo* with "the monkey land of Egypt," as in the novel Jacob contemptuously calls the land of the Nile. Thomas Mann himself recalled that the immediate inspiration for *Joseph* had indeed been pictorial—a portfolio of illustrations for "the story of Joseph, the son of Jacob"[12] shown to him by an artist who wanted him to write an introduction to the pictures. Buried under this allusion may be an unconscious memory of the mosaic as the mysterious source that flowed underground for thirty years until it rose to the surface again in the great mythological epic of Mann's maturity. The source would have watered already fertile soil, for we have Thomas Mann's own testimony that from his early youth he was as familiar with Egyptian lore as he was with the gods of Greece and Rome. Even in Dr. Bussenius's Progymnasium he knew that the proper Egyptian form for the name of the bull god was Hapi, not the Hellenized Apis.[13]

There is no way of proving definitely that a line of descent exists between the Nile mosaic seen by the twenty-year-old and the vast fresco of Joseph and the early civilization of the Near East that Thomas Mann created in the sixth and seventh decades of his life. But we do know that the summers in Palestrina, and the whole time in Italy with Heinrich, were crucial to Thomas Mann's development. There is also some possibility that *Doctor Faustus* was likewise first suggested to him in Palestrina. Karl Kerényi, friend and mentor in matters mythological of Mann's later years, carefully assembled a number of hints that all point in one direction.

Kerényi, who went to Palestrina to study its archaeological remains, held that the ancient temple was not really dedicated to Fortuna but to Venus, the brighter but also the more dangerous goddess. He found the atmosphere of Palestrina rather uncanny, perhaps because he was seeing it with *Doctor Faustus* in mind. But as a classical philologist he was also aware that the people of Palestrina had been associated in ancient times with the denizens of Hades. In his essay "Thomas Mann und der Teufel in Palestrina" (Thomas Mann and the Devil in Palestrina), he cites the seventh book of the *Aeneid*, in which Virgil pictures the ancient inhabitants of Praeneste as walking with the left foot unshod—the sign of those consecrated to the gods of the underworld. The black pigs in the streets remind him that in the New Testament demons enter into a herd of swine. And then, in the guest book of the Antico Albergo Bernardini he finds that someone else had sensed chthonian vibrations in Palestrina. Some Englishwoman, venturing the joke because she felt sheltered by her language, had repeatedly invoked the devil in her comment in the guest book. Much of the writing had become illegible, but Kerényi was able to make out such phrases as "from hell," "the devil," "go plumb to hell," and the absurd signature "Moll Doodle." "How the brothers must have laughed at this," he speculates[14]—for Thomas, if not Heinrich, had managed to learn a good deal of English in the Katharineum. Kerényi himself does not venture to assert with any assurance that the genesis of *Doctor Faustus* goes back to Thomas Mann's twentieth year. But that the germ of the novel came to Mann early in life is explicitly stated in *The Story of a Novel*; the only question is, how early?

Palestrina was also, for both brothers, a unique opportunity to practice the insights and to discuss the problems of their craft. Half a century later Heinrich recalled:

> After the heat of the summer day we descended from our Roman hill town . . . down to the highway. Before us, all around us, we had a sky of massive gold. I said: "Byzantine icons are on a gold ground. That is not meant figuratively, as we can see; it's an optical fact. All that is lacking here is the Virgin's narrow head, with her far too heavy crown, gazing down indifferently from her three-dimensional zenith." My brother disliked the sanctimonious tone. "That is the outward aspect," he said.[15]

As so often, Thomas also made use of this experience; the same spectacular sunset is mentioned in *Doctor Faustus*, in the chapter in which Serenus Zeitblom describes his visit to Palestrina:

> We looked towards the sunset as we returned to the little town, and I have never since seen anything resembling that splendor of the evening sky. A layer of gold, laid on with oily viscosity and bordered by crimson, floated on the western horizon. The sight was so extraordinary and so beautiful that it might well make the soul spill over in

wanton high spirits. Still, I was slightly annoyed when Schildknapp, pointing to the wonderful spectacle, shouted his "Sightsee that!" and Adrian burst into his grateful laughter.[16]

The anecdote, and its two versions, tells much about the tie between the brothers, which even then was somewhat brittle. There must have been many other unrecorded occasions on which the brothers responded in opposite ways. But these mild disagreements were, for the time being, taking place within the general framework of brotherliness, of sharing free exchanges of opinions and learning to recognize again in manhood the differences they had already observed in their common childhood. Thirty years later, reflecting on those differences, Thomas Mann generalized about visual and aural artists— "those who experience the world mostly through their eyes, and others who relate to it chiefly with their ears."[17] Clearly, he assigned Heinrich to the former class, himself to the latter. And he came to the perhaps surprising conclusion that the first type of sensibility was that of the South, the second that of the North. Here we have again the Latin and Nordic antithesis to which both brothers referred so frequently. And Heinrich responded with far more sympathy than his brother to the Latin world of Italy. While Thomas had carefully written down in his notebook how to ask for a timetable at the railroad station, Heinrich immersed himself in Italian life, learned to speak the language fluently, and exploited in his fiction the colorful personalities and vibrant visual qualities of the South. With his painter's disposition he saw richness of pattern, boldness of line, and exuberance of color all around him; and his works are full of lavish descriptions of paintings, landscapes, architecture, sculpture, artifacts. Unlike Thomas, he often described the material world for its own sake, rather than for its symbolic value— with the consequence that in his early works set in Italy his writing often became lush to the point of absurdity. But he also developed immense skill in sheer physical description. If we wish to know what Lübeck looked like, we must turn not to Thomas Mann's *Buddenbrooks*, but to Heinrich Mann's *Professor Unrat*.

The difference between North and South may also be felt in terms of temperature as well as temperament. The South is warm, the North cold; and Thomas Mann's devil in *Doctor Faustus* is distinctly a being of the North, for he emanates ultimate coldness.

In the novel Adrian Leverkühn seems to commit himself to the coldness of feeling the devil demands as his price: "Thou shalt not love." Certainly it would be reading the novel crudely to imagine that in Palestrina Adrian's creator arrived at anything so definite as that terrible acceptance, that abandonment of all hope of human feeling. But clues to something akin to Adrian's experience are scattered throughout Mann's works and letters; and what we know of his manipulation of the autobiographical elements in his fiction justifies our feeling that Palestrina was the scene of crucial, shattering emotions, and that these were connected with Heinrich, with the love and hatred, the admiration and envy, he felt for his elder brother. The negative feelings seemed to him sinful; his desire to use them as the substance of stories evidently struck him as wicked. *Doctor Faustus* was essentially a confession of this emotional complex. More than once Thomas Mann spoke of the peculiar excitement that had seized him while he was writing *Faustus*, of his sense of having stripped himself to the skin. But if *Faustus* was confession, it was also in itself a continuation and elaboration of the very "crime" to which it confessed: the fullest possible exploitation of all human relationships for the sake of art.

A fuller discussion of this whole complex must be set aside for the present; the many issues posed by *Doctor Faustus* cannot be raised at this point without gross violation of chronology. And the book can be seen in its full truthfulness only against the background of seventy years of Mann's life. Yet chronology also has required some mention of it here. For our present purposes it is enough to suggest that something like a dialogue with the devil did take place in Palestrina. It is implicit in one of the early stories and directly alluded to in *Buddenbrooks*, where the experience is attributed to Christian Buddenbrook. *Spiriti, Spiriti!* indeed.*

The content of Mann's Palestrina experience was to be the obses-

---

* We also have the story reported by Peter de Mendelssohn, who had it from a Munich artist named Fabius von Gugel, who averred that he had it from Thomas Mann himself. The testimony dates from the year 1953, when Thomas and Katia Mann were visiting Rome. The young Municher, who was living in Rome at the time, called on the Manns at their hotel to show the novelist a portfolio of his work. Mann took great interest in the surrealist and visionary drawings and reciprocated by describing a vision he had had, many years ago when he was young and staying in Palestrina. He then related essentially the vision of the devil as Adrian Leverkühn experiences it in *Doctor Faustus*. The artist, who at the time had not read *Faustus*, made notes on what he had

sion of his early and middle years, and may be summed up in the phrase "the tragedy of brotherhood." The transformations of the brother theme in Thomas Mann's art will necessarily engage our attention from *Buddenbrooks* through *Joseph and His Brothers* (the theme multiplied by twelve, so to speak) and on even to that biting portrait of Hitler so succinctly entitled "A Brother." Sometimes brotherhood meant, to Thomas Mann, the reverse of brotherliness; sometimes, as in *The Transposed Heads*, he saw it as a virtual exchange of identities.

Before leaving for Italy in the spring of 1895 Thomas had completed a novella which at the time bore the title "Walter Weiler." With assumed carelessness he informed Grautoff in a postscript that the story was accepted for the magazine *Pan*, and that *Pan*'s editor, Richard Dehmel, had paid him a call. Dehmel must have asked for revisions, and the story was rewritten in 1897, probably in Palestrina, under a new name that showed Italian influence, "Der Bajazzo."* No manuscript of "Walter Weiler" exists; we know the story only in the revised version that was ultimately published not in *Pan* but in S. Fischer's magazine *Neue Deutsche Rundschau*. It is not inconceivable that in Palestrina Thomas gave the story a twist that, in conscience-stricken moments, might have seemed to him treachery to an elder brother still beloved and deeply admired. And the sense of that treachery may have given rise to the "interview with the devil," if such there was. In April 1897 Thomas wrote to Grautoff that some time ago he had completed the revision of "Walter Weiler," and that it now had "more style, superiority, and taste,"[19] but that he thought the arrangement and composition had been more artistic in the earlier version. This seems to imply that the essential content of the story remained the same, but that it gave him some cause for dissatisfaction.

"Der Bajazzo" may be regarded as the second (if "Little Herr

---

been told. In view of how often Thomas Mann drew on the occurrence, we can well believe that he did have some such vision, though perhaps the finer details of the apparition were worked up novelistically. It is interesting that the figure described—red-haired, tilt-nosed, scrawny, shabby, audacious—is a recurrent physical type in the Mann *oeuvre*. He is the desperate man outside the ballroom in *The Hungry* and the wayfarer outside the cemetery in *Death in Venice*.[18]

* The title has been variously translated as "The Clown," "The Joker," and "The Dilettante." *Bajazzo*, a loanword in German, probably derives from the Italian *pagliaccio*, the "Punch" in Neapolitan popular comedy.

Friedemann" is the first) short story in which the autobiographical elements that were to form the background of so much of Thomas Mann's early work plainly appear on the surface. Here we meet the small old town, with its narrow, gable-overhung streets, its Gothic churches and fountains, from which Walter Weiler comes—although in the revised version the hero remains nameless. His ancestors are four generations of merchants; his mother is an idealized version of Julia Mann, his father "a powerful man of great influence in public affairs."[20] A puppet theater is his favorite toy, and with it he gives those elaborate performances of self-composed music dramas mentioned earlier. Among his schoolmates he wins respect and popularity by his skillful imitations of the teachers, but he is too busy watching the petty tyrants of the classroom for comic gestures to pay close attention to their lessons. Vaguely artistic, the boy writes poems, draws, explores on the family grand piano the laws of harmony and the secrets of modulation (like Adrian Leverkühn in the novel written half a century afterward). He never really learns to play the piano, but he improvises "expressively" on it. His mother encourages this "dilettantism"; his father scornfully dismisses it as a buffoon's accomplishments.

In the last decades of the nineteenth century and the first decade of the twentieth, the concept and phenomenon of "modern dilettantism" fascinated a good many writers. The traditional sense of *dilettante* as a dabbler in the arts persisted; but to this use of the word such writers as Paul Bourget added overtones of aestheticism and bohemian disregard for the conventions and demands of society. Nietzsche defined dilettantism as a "dangerous delight in intellectual tasting"; Bourget spoke of it as "less a doctrine than a disposition of the mind, at once highly intelligent and highly voluptuous." While admitting a difficulty in exactly defining the word, Bourget spoke of the dilettante as an "intellectual epicurean" and saw him as the surest manifestation of decadence and nihilism. The idea was taken up by Hermann Bahr, by Hugo von Hofmannsthal, and most emphatically by Heinrich Mann. These writers elaborated on the idea of the dilettante as an aesthete who experienced all of nature in terms of art. By the end of the nineties the notion of "dilettantes of life" who are unfit for the serious business of living had already filtered down into the popular novel—and was consequently soon thereafter abandoned by serious novelists.[21]

The dilettante in Thomas Mann's story thus derived significantly from its literary models, from the portraits of dilettantes in Bourget's novels, and from the descriptions of the hero in Heinrich's *In einer Familie*. The specific details of the story, especially at the beginning, were borrowed from the lives of both brothers, and also from Thomas's view of a potentiality that lay in both their natures. But the autobiographical vein slides almost imperceptibly into the biographical; and as the story proceeds, more and more of the crude facts and the subtle psychological insights seem applicable to Heinrich rather than to Thomas. It was Heinrich who was sent off to work as an apprentice during his father's lifetime—not, to be sure, in a lumber company down by the river, but in a Dresden book shop. It was Heinrich who would subsequently say of himself, "I read a great deal, read everything I could lay my hands on."[22] It was Heinrich who was always sitting with a book on his knees; Heinrich who soon after his father's death used his inheritance to go traveling; Heinrich who seemed so proud and aristocratic that by instinct he despised the dry and unimaginative people around him;[23] Heinrich who escaped being called up for military service; Heinrich whose ambitions for high life contrasted so oddly with his carefulness about money, his prudent insistence on living within his means in modest pensions. Even the age ascribed to the protagonist of the story—twenty-seven—corresponds to that of Heinrich rather than that of Thomas: in the early summer of 1897, when Thomas was revising "Der Bajazzo," Heinrich was already well into his twenty-seventh year.

Along with many references to Heinrich, genuine autobiographical elements are interspersed—and there are enough of these to have thrown critics off the track, so that this story has been universally interpreted either as strictly based on Thomas Mann's own life, a kind of warning to himself, or as a literary exercise under the influence of Bourget. There is one passage in the story, for example, that alludes to Thomas's friendship with Otto Grautoff: "I had friendly relations with only one of them, a gifted and cheerful young man of good family whom I had known at school. . . . Like me, he made fun of everyone and everything. . . ."[24] Thomas was to speak of Grautoff in much the same terms in *A Sketch of My Life* (1930); at the time he was writing "Der Bajazzo" the passage was clearly intended as a generous tribute to Grautoff, who would surely read the story.

After some three years of travel the "dilettante" realizes that he is running through his capital and must settle down. He chooses a middle-sized city that in a general way resembles Munich, sets himself up in a bachelor apartment with a few pieces of the family furnishings, including the portraits of the Ancestors (Statius Brage and his wife—portraits Thomas in fact kept for himself), and proceeds to lead the life of the perfect aesthete, neither needing nor seeking employment, devoting himself to appreciation of the finer things of life, and for quite a while complacent about his escape from the banality of ordinary existence.

> Henceforth my days passed in reality in accordance with the idea that had always been my goal. I rose about ten o'clock, breakfasted, and spent the time until noon at the piano or reading a literary magazine or a book. Then I sauntered up the street to the little restaurant I regularly patronized, dined, and then set out on a longer walk through the streets, took in a gallery, strolled to the outskirts of town, to the Lerchenberg. I returned home and resumed the morning's occupations: read, made music, sometimes even amused myself with what might pass for drawing, or carefully indited a letter. If I did not go to the theater or a concert after supper, I lingered in the café reading newspapers until bedtime. I regarded that day as good and beautiful, as one that had yielded some happiness, if at the piano I had succeeded in finding a motif that seemed to me new and lovely, or if reading a story or looking at a painting had produced in me some delicate but persistent mood.[25]

This idyll is not destined to last. Boredom creeps in, and then reality crashes in, taking the form of a pretty girl driving a carriage. The dilettante falls in love and discovers that he has nothing to offer. He has his appreciations, his fastidious aesthetic judgments; but he is neither creative artist nor self-satisfied bourgeois. In his aesthete's life he has somehow squandered his heritage of culture and good family and has forfeited his self-respect, which inevitably means also forfeiting the respect of others. The story ends in sheer disgust. Even "to end it all" would be too heroic for a dilettante, a buffoon. He will go on living, eating, sleeping, finding things to do, and gradually resigning himself to cutting "an unfortunate and ridiculous figure."[26]

In "Gefallen" Thomas had, as we have seen, probably borrowed an experience from Heinrich, almost certainly availed himself of a cynicism that did not come naturally to him. In "Der Bajazzo" he went further, exploiting Heinrich's precocious incursions into life. Ten years later Heinrich was to turn the tables, but more generously, assigning to the character Arnold in *Zwischen den Rassen* a number of his brother's attributes. But he also used Arnold as a vehicle for autobiographical confession, just as Thomas used the dilettante partly for such purposes. Thus, in *Zwischen den Rassen* Heinrich could write:

> As soon as I was free, at twenty, I withdrew into the solitude of a life of travel. . . . Had I not, in walks on the city wall, suffered visions of my future greatness which sent such giddy surges of madness racing through my head that my knees shook? Had I not, for the sake of several women, stood rigid as if filled with hot sand . . . and regained my life only to expose it once more to the fevered air of love?[27]

If "The Dilettante" is to be regarded as a sketch of a potentiality in Heinrich's nature, it is a cruel sketch. For the rest of his life, of course, Thomas was to be "guilty" of ruthlessly using casual acquaintances, friends, or relations for literary purposes. Early delicacy eventually gave way to an assured conviction that "indiscretion loses all sting as soon as it is also (and primarily) directed against the author's own person. In my work I expose myself with such passion that by comparison the few indiscretions against others scarcely matter."[28] But at the time he was satirizing Heinrich in "Der Bajazzo" he may well have felt as if he were committing spiritual fratricide—*Brudermord*. The intensity with which he ever afterward reacted to the charge of casting a cold eye on the human scene suggests a strong sense of guilt; and much of his fiction deals in more or less disguised form with aspects of this problem.

A F T E R a brief excursion in southern Italy—Salerno and Porto Anzio, where Thomas wrote another short story, called "Encounter," of which nothing is known but the title, the two brothers returned to Heinrich's lodgings in Rome, an old palazzo with a view of the Pantheon and a magical name, Via Torre Argentina 34. The number was magical also; years later Thomas assigned to Hans Castorp room number 34 in the Berghof, and it is possible that his playful fascination with the number 7 began thus early in Rome. "I am enthusiastic about Rome,"[29] he wrote to Grautoff. What it was he especially liked he did not say, at least in any of the letters that have been preserved. In fact the overrich blue sky got on his nerves, and he despised the palm trees. This we know from his comments years later in *Betrachtungen eines Unpolitischen*, into which he incorporated a piece on "Wagner in Rome" that he had evidently written at the time. The one experience in Rome that made him "weak in the knees from enthusiasm"[30] was, of all things, a performance of the music of Richard Wagner—or rather, a demonstration for and against Wagner—in the Piazza Colonna. Maestro Vessella, conductor of the municipal orchestra, was a fanatical Wagnerite, determined to import the new German music over the opposition of many of his fellow countrymen. Amid cries of *bis* and *basta*, amid whistling and shouting, the orchestra played on:

> The twenty-year-old stranger—as alien here as this music, part of this music—stood wedged in the crowd on the pavement. He did not shout because he was choked up. Peering toward the podium, which furious Italianissimi were trying to storm and which the musicians were defending with their instruments, his upturned face smiled in awareness of its pallor and his head pounded in tempestuous pride, in youthfully morbid sensibility. . . . Pride in what? Love for what? Only for a controversial taste in art? Quite possibly he thought of the Piazza Colonna twenty years later, in August 1914, and of the nervous tears that suddenly overflowed his eyes and ran down his cold face at the victory of the "Nothung" motif, and which he had been unable to dry because the press of a foreign throng prevented him from raising his arm. Still, I am not mistaken. Even though the fervent experience with this art might have become a source of patriotic emotions for that youth—still it was an intellectual experience that I had shared with the best minds of Europe, just as Thomas Buddenbrook had shared his [discovery of Schopenhauer].[31]

It would seem significant that Thomas Mann's most powerful impression of Italy came from something he had brought with him;

that he should in foreign surroundings have become so intensely conscious of his Germanness, of his own cultural baggage, slight though that still was when he was twenty. The same blue skies and semitropical vegetation, the same formal gardens and magnificent fountains, the same antique, medieval, and Renaissance monuments, the same density of history and colorful modernity, the same temperamental, engaging, complex populace, presented themselves to both brothers, both young men. Heinrich embraced and adapted; Thomas resisted and rejected. Perhaps the difference was partly one of age; for later Thomas yielded somewhat, tried to learn what Italy could teach him, and was for a time in love with Florence. But we may suspect that Thomas, like Adrian Leverkühn, "did not want to see anything."[32]

Sightseeing, as Rüdiger Schildknapp knew, is an art that must be learned. And as Schildknapp also knew, there is inevitably something ridiculous about it. At a certain point every traveler feels he has had enough of it. At the end of October 1895 Thomas returned home—which still meant Rambergstrasse 2—to Munich.

6

Forms and
Masks

BETWEEN the brief visit to Italy in the summer of 1895 and the longer stay from the autumn of 1896 to the spring of 1898, Thomas spent the better part of a year in Munich. He had been thinking of going to Berlin, ostensibly to attend the university there. But that would have meant once again following in the footsteps of Heinrich, who five years earlier had worked for S. Fischer in Berlin and audited some lectures at the university.

At the end of October Thomas returned to Munich with Heinrich, and he then changed his plans for unknown reasons. Perhaps his mother opposed his departure; perhaps he consciously wanted to break the pattern of imitating each phase of Heinrich's career. In any case he was writing, and that alone would have been sufficient motive for him to stay quietly at home during the winter months. In November he completed "On the Psychology of the Sufferer," presumably an essay, of which no trace remains. In December 1895 he incorporated his Italian experiences into a story, "Der Wille

zum Glück" (The Will to Happiness). The title alone showed that
he had been reading Nietzsche; the form betrayed another influence.
What that was he confessed to his friend Grautoff: "At the moment
I am reading exclusively French, which I must at last learn thoroughly, and I am already finding few pleasures so subtle as that of
reading Maupassant's novellas, these daring little stories that are
untranslated and untranslatable."[1]

The burden of "The Will to Happiness" is simple enough: star-
crossed lovers. Paolo Hoffmann, a young painter, suffers from severe
heart disease. He obviously has not long to live. When he falls in
love, and his love is reciprocated, the girl's parents refuse consent to
the marriage on grounds of his hopeless illness. Her father has made
plain that he has the highest esteem for Paolo, but that he is obliged
to be concerned for his daughter's lasting happiness. But five years
pass, the girl's feelings remain unchanged, she refuses an advantageous marriage, and at last the parents relent. The marriage takes
place, and Paolo dies the morning after the wedding night. The
narrator, his former schoolmate, concludes: "I asked myself whether
he had acted badly, deliberately so, toward her whom he had wedded. But I saw her at his funeral, as she stood at the head of his
coffin; and I recognized in her face also that expression I had seen
in his: the solemn and intense earnestness of triumph."[2]

It is rather amusing to find young Thomas, a short while after
ending his story on so banal a note and in such patent imitation of
the French school, giving a lecture to Grautoff on the technique of
short-story writing:

> I have read *your* latest work, "On the Hill," with pleasure. The lan-
> guage is improving, becoming more agile, more accurate, more trans-
> lucent—again I cannot say more than that. I rather wish that you
> would have some little inspiration once in a while. All these grue-
> somely profound thoughts conceived on nocturnal walks are things you
> really ought to save up for your diary; there they would be safe and
> sound, it seems to me. Really, you still lack everything that makes the
> *storyteller*, above all *invention, plot*. Do try to see whether you can
> tell a *tale*, some kind of outward event in which various people act and
> talk.[3]

Of greater interest than the feeble "plot" of "The Will to Happiness"
is the use the young writer makes of semiautobiographical back-

ground, and of his most recent experiences. Paolo Hoffmann comes
from a town in North Germany; his father had made his money
as a planter in South America and had married a "native woman
of good family."[4] After the rebuff from his sweetheart's father, Paolo
travels in Italy and—a note we have heard before—crosses from Sicily
to Africa, carrying out in fiction a plan that Thomas and Heinrich
had conceived for their future travels.

For the reader alert to the facts in the lives of the brothers Mann
it is a delight to observe the deftness with which the youthful author
weaves the fraternal strands together to make the single character
of Paolo Hoffmann. *Mann* is contained in the surname. Paolo is the
Latin form of Thomas's given name, Paul—but it was Heinrich who
bore the foreign, Latin-American name of Luis. Paolo spends some
time boarding with an old professor so that he can finish his schooling—like Thomas. He and the narrator are bosom friends who have
"secretly read Heine at fifteen"[5] and pronounced their verdict upon
the world and men—like Thomas and Grautoff. Paolo wants to be a
painter, his health is delicate, he is capable of falling headlong in
love—all attributes of Heinrich. On the whole it is Heinrich who
preponderates; and this may be taken as either exploitation or tribute. For the story as a whole, with its rather crass effects, its pronouncements on Bernini, its somewhat florid descriptions, owes a
good deal to the style of Heinrich's early work. Yet even at twenty
Thomas Mann was already making subtle points by the use of quotations, hidden and otherwise. Aside from the allusion to Nietzsche in
the title, there is a direct quotation from Heine's poem "Unterwelt."[6]

But the real surprise of this story lies in the appearance and
treatment of Thomas Mann's first Jewish characters—the first in a
long line. The father of Paolo's beloved is a Baron Stein, a retired
broker. "Is he a Jew?" the narrator promptly asks when Paolo
mentions the name. Here indeed is a picture to gladden the heart
of an inveterate reader of, or writer for, the conservative magazine
to which Thomas was contributing. But if any loyal readers of *Das
Zwanzigste Jahrhundert* came upon "The Will to Happiness"
(hardly likely, since they would not have read *Simplicissimus*,
where the story was published), they would have thought that
Thomas Mann was—to use a phrase not yet invented—"soft on Sem-
ites." For Mann ironically reverses the standard situation, and in so
doing implicitly parodies the ideology of the magazine that, a year

and a half later, he was to call "the simpleminded little rag."[7] The plutocrat with the purchased title does not conform to the stereotypes. He is not a Jew who has bought himself a beautiful Aryan wife, nor is he an innocent Aryan who has succumbed to the charms of a lovely Jewess. Rather, it is his wife who is Jewish, and ugly, although she wears diamond earrings. Their daughter, the product of *Rassenschande* (mixed marriage, a betrayal of racial purity), is beautiful; and all three Steins are depicted as persons of sterling character. It would seem that the experience of working on *Das Zwanzigste Jahrhundert* had only served to intensify the philo-Semitism which, so Thomas Mann later asserted, was his basic attitude toward Jews. Heinrich, too, soon underwent either a change of heart or a reversion to earlier feelings. For in April 1897, announcing to Grautoff that the magazine had "peacefully expired," Thomas commented that Heinrich was quite pleased to have it go under, since he had always run it with some reluctance and solely for the salary's sake.[8]

Even before *Das Zwanzigste Jahrhundert* perished without ever having seen the dawn of the twentieth century, a new periodical had sprung up to provide a place in which Thomas Mann's writings could reach a considerably wider and certainly more quick-minded audience. The new magazine turned to the past for its name, choosing the title of Germany's great satiric novel of the seventeenth century, *Simplicissimus*. In its sardonic, questioning spirit, its challenge to convention and to the institutions of society, its willingness to print the forerunners of the twentieth century's sexual and social revolutions, it belonged very much to the coming age.

Shortly after his return from Italy, Thomas received a postcard from a Herr Otto Erich Hartleben asking him to meet in some tavern "in connection with *Simplicissimus*."[9] Had Thomas been home somewhat longer, he would undoubtedly have noticed the advertisements for the new magazine. The symbol of *Simplicissimus*, a red bulldog drawn by Thomas Theodor Heine, who was to make his reputation as the magazine's illustrator, snarled at the public from a thousand posters all over Munich. In his innocence, Thomas thought the postcard must be some mistake—all the more likely since it was addressed to "Theodor" Mann. He ignored the invitation. When he at last caught up with the gossip of literary Munich—this by the middle of January 1896—he felt, chagrined, that he had foolishly thrown away an opportunity. But he got in touch with the publisher directly and offered his story "The Will to Happiness." It was promptly accepted and printed in three installments in the August and September issues of the weekly. With that publication, Thomas Mann became at once identified with *"Der Simpl,"* as the magazine was called by its many friends and well-wishers. A bolder change of fronts, from *Das Zwanzigste Jahrhundert* to *Simplicissimus*, can scarcely be imagined. Thomas Mann had taken a giant leap from the extreme conservative to the extreme liberal position, at least insofar as having his work printed in a magazine served to define his politics. That is a questionable assumption. There can be no question, however, about his sharing many of the attitudes of *Simplicissimus*, above all its mockery.

The new magazine became almost from its inception the rallying point for young rebels and slightly older radicals who found the jingoistic, bombastic, imperialistic posturing of Wilhelmine Germany insufferable. It was a very youthful magazine (like its contemporary and rival *Jugend* [Youth], which had burst upon the literary scene just four months before the first issue of *Simplicissimus*). That is scarcely surprising, for "the wealthy publisher Albert Langen"[10] who so promptly accepted "The Will to Happiness" was a man of twenty-seven, only two years older than Heinrich Mann. The son of a Rhineland sugar refiner, he came into a sizable inheritance after his father's death. Langen was a prime candidate for the mantle of "dilettante": He went to Paris to become a painter, found he had insufficient talent, then tried to write, made a similar discovery, and ultimately satisfied his love affair with the arts by founding a satirical illustrated weekly whose artists became as famous as its writers. He embarked on another love affair with Dagny, daughter of the Norwegian novelist, dramatist, and poet Bjørnstjerne Bjørnson. Bjørnson, who in his time had been expelled from his native land for "high treason"—that is, for stating frankly his views on monarchy and social questions—advised his new son-in-law on Scandinavian literature and helped to give the new magazine its highbrow level and its radical political cast.

After the founding of *Simplicissimus*, Langen, who had already done some small publishing in Paris, used the magazine as a proving ground for his rapidly expanding publishing house, which started with Scandinavian and French writers but soon acquired a sizable list of young Germans. In this dual enterprise of magazine and book publishing Langen was following the example of Samuel Fischer, whose magazine, *Die Freie Bühne*, had become the *Neue Deutsche Rundschau* in 1894. There was, however, a vast difference between the sober, formal *Neue Deutsche Rundschau* with its strictly literary content, small format, and dignified tone, and the brash, oversized, and above all illustrated *Simpl* with its savage cartoons, its whimsy, its anecdotes, ballads, and jokes. The *Neue Deutsche Rundschau* was all good writing; the fine stories and incisive political commentary of *Simplicissimus* needed to be searched out from amidst a welter of caricatures and advertisements.

The latter leaned heavily to bicycle, health, and potency ads. Typewriters "with visible writing" could be purchased on convenient monthly installments—*bequeme Monatsraten*—of 10 to 20 marks. Devices were offered for those cases where "for medical and anatomical reasons it is absolutely essential to prevent conception." Readers concerned with ethics as well as technics could find guidance in a heavy volume entitled *Means for the Prevention of Conception Examined as to Their Value and Moral Justification*. Another serious problem of the day was alluded to in advertisements for Dr. Franz Müller's sanatorium, which offered treatment for addiction to alcohol, morphine, opium, and cocaine. An American company offered the German amateur photographer its "Brownie Kodak"; meanwhile German industry was taking a lead over America in producing a "motorcar for three persons." Its 3 horsepower enabled it to attain a speed of 30 to 35 kilometers per hour.

The jokes, interspersed wherever there was space for them, often verged on disrespect for the monarch. "Hey, Xaverl, do you like our emperor?"—"Sure, on a 20-mark piece." Or: "What's that shoe doing there under the glass, Mr. Mayor?"—"That's a precious relic to me. Our Most Noble Royal Highness most amiably deigned to expectorate on that shoe on the occasion of His Sublime Majesty's recent visit to our city."

In the narrow columns squeezed between advertisements and caricatures appeared stories by, say, a Norwegian named Knut Hamsun, a Bavarian regionalist named Ludwig Thoma, or a young Jew from Fürth whom Ernst von Wolzogen had introduced to Albert Langen. Thomas Mann met this young writer, temporarily employed as an editor of *Simplicissimus*, on a momentous occasion.

Thomas had gone in person—"I must have been in a great hurry"—to the magazine's offices to collect his remuneration for "The Will to Happiness." The editor, as if he understood the importance of these first earnings for literary work, paid the smartly dressed author in gold marks—"alas, we shall probably not see their like again,"[11] Mann commented in the post-Inflation period thirty-five years later. He was twenty-one; the editor who "benevolently" handed him those gold pieces was Jakob Wassermann, all of twenty-three, who had so far published one slender novel and a few short stories. The look Thomas Mann took as benevolent might simply have expressed Wassermann's sheer physical pleasure in handling coin of the realm, which came his way seldom enough. At the moment he was barely keeping body and soul together while working on his novel *Die Juden von Zirndorf*. Like Thomas, Wassermann was a member of the Academic Dramatic Club; very likely the two writers would have met sooner or later either there or in one of the other literary groups of Munich.

That encounter in the offices of *Simplicissimus* marked the beginning of a lifelong amity between the two writers—friendship may be too strong a word, although Thomas Mann used it in speaking of his relations with Wassermann, and was on occasion Wassermann's houseguest. A moralist who aspired to treat grand subjects, Wassermann had a gift for spellbinding narration. In joking tribute to him Mann remarked that he "would be able to sit in the Orient to this day and tell stories—stories—and the people would stand around him listening wide-eyed and openmouthed."[12] But the flair for storytelling was Wassermann's blessing and his curse. At his best he could produce fine tales like "Adam Urban," haunting novels like *Caspar Hauser*; but his work verged on kitsch and often went over the brink. His popular touch made him one of Germany's most successful novelists; his editions and his earnings were huge. Moreover, Thomas Mann actually read Wassermann—whereas his usual way was only to dip into the books of his fellow novelists. In fact, he paid Wassermann the tribute of an unconscious borrowing: the name of Frau Stöhr, the Mrs. Malaprop of *The Magic Mountain*, may well be a reminiscence of Fräulein Stöhr, a minor character in Wassermann's *The World's Illusion*.

This would not be the first time that a useful name stuck in Mann's memory. *Buddenbrook* appears as the name of a second in a duel in Theodor Fontane's *Effi Briest*, which Thomas read early in 1896. Nor was *Stöhr* his first borrowing from Wassermann. A few months after their meeting we find Thomas apologizing, in a letter to Korfiz Holm, his former Lübeck schoolmate and gymnastic squad leader who was now an editor of *Simplicissimus*, for the "dastardly plagiarism" he had unwittingly committed upon Jakob Wassermann. The apology is followed by the remark: "I suppose his influence is generally in the air of Europe."[13] This is strange, because Wassermann had published so little up to this time, and certainly had no reputation outside Germany. Probably Thomas Mann was joking and took it for granted that the recipient of his letter would understand that the entire apology was meant humorously. For at this time, and later, Mann had very definite ideas about literary borrowing. An article on that subject, entitled "A Plagiarism," appeared in the July 1896 issue of *Das Zwanzigste Jahrhundert*, signed simply "M." Since it referred to a borrowing by D'Annunzio, the author was probably Heinrich rather than Thomas Mann; but the viewpoint was shared by both brothers. The writer, the argument ran, has a right to incorporate a passage from another's work into his own as a "building block." In taking this view both brothers were following the lead of their beloved Heinrich Heine, who had written: "But nothing is more foolish than this charge of plagiarism. In art there is no Sixth Commandment; the writer has the right to reach out and take wherever he finds material for his work. He may even appropriate whole columns with carved capitals, if only the temple in which he uses them as supports is truly magnificent."[14]

The point was one Thomas would have occasion to make repeatedly in defense of what he later called his "montage" technique. Korfiz Holm, who had shared with him the editorship of *Der Frühlingssturm*, would almost surely catch the allusion. For "Heinrich Heine der 'Gute,' " that brief defense of Heine in their schoolboy magazine, had cleverly incorporated lines from Heine himself— Thomas Mann's earliest use of the technique of hidden quotation which he was to make his hallmark.

Simplicissimus also opened its pages to that colorful writer whose *Frühlingserwachen* may, as we have mentioned, have suggested the title of *Der Frühlingssturm:* Frank Wedekind. Or rather, Frank Wedekind imparted to the periodical his own satiric spirit, his political liberalism, and his social and sexual radicalism. By sheer coincidence a story of Wedekind's also dealing with a *Liebestod* from a weak heart was published in several issues of the magazine immediately before the appearance of Thomas's "The Will to Happiness." But Wedekind's point was the power of sexuality to triumph over death, rather than the identity of love and death. His sexual frankness and political daring meant that he was constantly running afoul of the censors, so that he had difficulty getting his plays performed or his stories and articles published. Unable to earn his living by his writings alone, he became a strolling singer and player. He wrote poems about love and sex, composed the music himself, and sang them in public, accompanying himself on the guitar. He also acted in his own plays.

Wedekind was eleven years older than Thomas Mann, and the gap in age and life styles seems to have been too great for more than a cool mutual respect to develop between them. Between Heinrich Mann and Wedekind, however, a genuine friendship formed. Wedekind's café was the noisy Torgelstube; there he wrote, and later in the evening went to a quieter back room to preside over his *Stammtisch*, as the reserved table for regular guests was called. Heinrich Mann sometimes sat in this back room, off to one side, drinking the sourish Tyrolean wine. One day Wedekind abruptly came over to him and said: "We aren't put on this earth to go prowling around each other forever." Heinrich promptly moved over to Wedekind's long table, and the two men were friends at once, as if they had always known each other. In his old age Heinrich recalled:

> In my recollection there is no one who so completely discarded his public manner in order to come closer to me. It did not lie in my nature to change my outward behavior; but his tormented mind, which could well use calm and security, understood and was sure of the feelings at the root of that behavior. I never challenged him. He never attempted to humiliate me. Without any special prearrangement, we left these delightful manifestations of friendship unused.[15]

By "outward behavior" Heinrich Mann meant that aristocratic coolness and remoteness which contrasted so strongly with his bohemian impulses. Wedekind had in fact recognized a kindred soul. Heinrich

Mann in his personal life was a "gypsy in a green wagon"[16] but his public manner remained unbending. Thomas also had a good deal of that stiffness, which arose partly from the shock of contact between North German primness and Bavarian laxity.

With each other, the brothers could still be easygoing, and in their leisure hours they forged travel plans for the autumn. This time their ideas had some of that romantic boldness which Thomas had presumably already assigned to "Walter Weiler." They would go by train only as far as Genoa, there take ship for Corsica, and spend some time in the Corsican capital of Ajaccio. Sicily, and possibly Africa, were on the itinerary, then Naples, Rome, and eventually some place in French Switzerland—Thomas was evidently concerned with improving his French. The plan was "not to see the . . . esteemed Fatherland again" before 1898. "Then, to be sure, unless the army surgeon has a heart, there awaits me the gruesome Moloch of 'militarism.' But I don't much like to let my mind dwell on that, and it crouches, gray and horrible, a puffy-eyed monster, behind the colorful, attractive games of the immediate future."[17]

Before those attractive games could begin, however, there was the task of consolidating, as far as that was now possible, the bridgehead Thomas had established in the literary world. He was already beginning to think about a volume of short stories, and to that end cultivated Albert Langen and Korfiz Holm. He also entered a contest. *Simplicissimus* was offering a prize of 300 marks for the "best novella in which sexual love plays no part."[18] Perhaps, after the Wedekind and Mann stories, Albert Langen wished to show the authorities that his publication was not given over exclusively to racy fiction. Thomas submitted a sketch entitled "Der Tod" ("Death"); it was accepted for publication, although the prize went to Wassermann. In diary form, this sketch recorded the last few weeks in the life of a nameless count (a "Herr Graf" was almost de rigueur in German and especially in Austrian literature of the period). Years earlier the count had become convinced that he would die on October 12 of his fortieth year. "A prophecy is in itself inconsequential," the diarist remarks; "what counts is whether it gains power over you. But if it does that, it is already proved and will be fulfilled."[19] Here was a thought Thomas would repeat many times, adding the variation that prophecies tend to fulfill themselves in a somewhat inexact way. From the vantage point of twenty-one, forty can seem a remote age, barely attainable or worth attaining; and Thomas Mann seems always to have had a half-playful, half-serious superstition that the important events in his life had to happen in years ending with a zero or a five. At the time he wrote "Death" he may have had a similar conviction that he would die at forty; we do know that he later planned to have Felix Krull "stop writing" his memoirs at that age.[20]

"Der Tod" employs the moods of the sea to express symbolically the approach of death. For the sea as portal to eternity Mann was drawing equally upon childhood memories of the beach at Travemünde and the affirmations of death in Heinrich Heine's North Sea cycle. But to the romantic anticipations of Heine and his own youth, Mann added ironic disillusionment. For when Death at last pays his visit to the expectant count "he behaved like a dentist. . . . So jejune, so boring, so bourgeois."[21]

"Death" strikes some Mannian notes; but the twenty-one-year-old writer had not yet found his tone or shown what he could do. At some time before September 27, 1896, he had also written the first short story that was to become part of the "canon," that would be the title story of his first book, and of which he afterwards said that it represented his "breakthrough":[22] "Little Herr Friedemann." Quite possibly a revision of a story called "The Little Professor" which he had written in 1894 and submitted to Richard Dehmel, "Friedemann" is set squarely in the world of the Buddenbrooks, the world of the ancestors, which was already taking on larger-than-life dimensions in Thomas Mann's mind. Bits and pieces of the mythologizing of Lübeck and the psychologizing of its inhabitants can be traced in many of Mann's early short stories. The novel was unconsciously forming even before he dreamed that he could work in the larger form like his contemporary and fellow North German, Theodor Fontane.

Thomas Mann read Fontane's "new novel, *Effi Briest*, which is absolutely first-rate"[23] in February 1896. It has been persuasively argued that one of the figures in that novel decisively influenced the characterization of the unfortunate hunchback in Mann's story.[24] Certainly the love of Alonzo Gieshübler, the small, crooked-shouldered pharmacist, for Effi Briest parallels in some respects Johannes Friedemann's hopeless passion for Gerda von Rinnlingen; but what remains latent in Fontane's novel is the source of tragedy in

Mann's story. Moreover, early and late Thomas Mann found physical disability, a weak heart, unsound lungs, a crippled arm, convenient outward symbols for the inner malaise of those who were not on an easy footing with "Life." From this tendency arises a corollary that, perhaps, has not been adequately recognized by the critics, or by Mann himself in his lifelong valiant efforts at self-interpretation. The corollary is that for fictional illness to be fully believable it must generally end in death; only then is a reader inclined to take it seriously. Thus the preoccupation with illness as symbol, and in the later writings as the source of art and thought, inescapably led by the very laws of fiction to Mann's apparent infatuation with death. We must resist the temptation to read too much, biographically, into the fatalities that end such stories as "The Will to Happiness," "Death," and "Little Herr Friedemann." A mortal outcome was also a convention of the period, as well as the easiest solution for an unpracticed writer. Thomas Mann was not drowning in melancholy or contemplating suicide; he was merely learning the craft of fiction. His letters to his friend Grautoff at this period reflect a consistently humorous bent and a growing confidence in his ability to cope with the task he has set himself: learning how to bring out in his writing the insights he had already achieved into the complexities of experience.

Munich was beginning to pall. "My last few weeks, since I returned from Austria, have passed very quietly: too quietly, for my nerves demand a change. I am glad that my Munich days are numbered."[25] The mention of Austria refers to a brief visit to Vienna and the Salzkammergut at the end of July. During the summer he had reached his majority, which brought him the proceeds of a small insurance policy—200 marks. Somewhat in the style of Heinrich's "My Plan," he resolved to blow the entire sum on one visit to Vienna —which to Germans of the nineties represented the imperial capital of gaiety and light loves. Arthur Schnitzler's *Anatol* (published in 1893) had explored erotic cynicism; his *Liebelei* had been the sensation of the previous year's theatrical season. There is no evidence that Thomas Mann went to Vienna looking for a "süsses Mädel" ("sweet young thing"); but there is a slight evasiveness—or perhaps only wonder—in his recollection that he managed in four days to squander a sum that would handily have lasted a month in Italy. In a tribute to Vienna written many years later he relates only that he stayed "at the good old Hotel Klomser on the Herrengasse" and witnessed the arrival at the imperial palace of "some semioriental deputation in national costume which was to be received by old Franz Joseph." But what else he did there in the security of his "deepest youthful incognito,"[26] what it was that made him love Vienna as a city where he had been happy from the time of his first encounter with it, we do not know.

Heinrich had business in Zürich, and the brothers arranged to meet in Rome. During the second week of October 1896 Thomas departed for Venice. He spent some three weeks there, perhaps seeking something of that "semioriental" atmosphere which seems to have attracted him at this time. There are no surviving letters from Venice, nor any later recollections of those weeks. The first letter we have is from Naples, November 8, and is addressed—like most of the extant letters of this time—to Grautoff. Thomas reports that he has been trying to escape as far as possible from Germanism, German ideas, and German *Kultur*, to the "remotest, most alien South." And once again he mentions the Orient:

> While my brother remained in Rome, I went to Naples, from which I promised myself a select and sensational mixture of Rome and the Orient.
>
> I was not disappointed. The oriental note sounds audibly here—although that almost excludes the proud aristocratic distinction that is characteristic of Rome, that majestic city par excellence. Naples is more plebeian, but with a naive, lovable, gracious, and amusing vulgarity. It does not have the bold and imperial Caesarean profile of Rome; its physiognomy has a somewhat turned-up nose and puffy lips, but very beautiful dark eyes. . . . I have been closely studying this physiognomy for four days; its sensual, sweet southern beauty grips me more and more.

These are suspiciously equivocal terms for the description of a city, especially when we learn that the young letter writer is "a little weary from loneliness," and so we are already prepared when he continues:

> I think of my suffering, of the problem of my suffering. What am I suffering from? From knowledge—is it going to destroy me? What am I suffering from? From sexuality—is it going to destroy me?—

How I hate it, this knowledge which forces even art to join it! How I hate it, this sensuality, which claims that everything fine and good is its consequence and effect. Alas, it is the *poison* that lurks in everything fine and good!—How am I to free myself of knowledge? By religion?—How am I to free myself of sexuality? By eating rice?

. . . Here and there, among a thousand other peddlers, are slyly hissing dealers who urge you to come along with them to allegedly "very beautiful" girls, and not only to girls. They keep at it, walk alongside, praising their wares until you answer roughly. They don't know that you have almost resolved to eat nothing but rice just to escape from sexuality! . . .[27]

Rice, he continued, at least had the advantage of cheapness, and that was just as well, since he would have to live a full two months on slightly more than 400 lire. One way to escape both financial stringencies and physical urgencies was to stay at the desk; and in a mood of penance he wrote another of his sketchlike stories. Entitled "Disillusionment," it is a monologue set against the background of Venice. Later, Thomas Mann would be capable of waiting forty years for the right moment to make use of "material," but at this time he was young enough and impatient enough to want to turn experience promptly into literature. Thus the stranger encounters the narrator in the Piazza San Marco, which the author had seen for the first time only a few weeks before. But the story itself criticizes the very tendency to which the author willingly succumbs. Even at his simplest and most youthful, Thomas Mann was complex and mature.

"Disillusionment" is a companion piece to "Death"; the monologuing stranger has found that the poets are liars, that all grand words are deceptive. Art, experience, do not come up to his expectations. To beauty, love, suffering, his response is: Is that all? Now he waits for death, but like the count in "Der Tod" he fears that it, too, will be only the last great disappointment.

There is a measure of self-irony in this sketch; perhaps it was the earliest of those many warnings Thomas Mann issued to himself (and to his readers) throughout his life: that literature, the artists, must not be taken too seriously. Such warnings were influenced by his readings in Nietzsche, whom he was avidly studying at this time. That philosopher, who was master of language as were few Germans among his contemporaries, feared the shaping influence of language upon thought. In borrowing this idea, Mann characteristically modified it.[28] For he had no desire to deny or betray his vocation. But thus early he was saying, as he was to repeat often in the future, that fiction could be a serene and cheerful game, even a sacred game, but it was still a game.

Short, evocative sketch though it was, "Disillusionment" supplied a felt practical need of the moment: to assemble enough stories for a slim volume. Once before, Thomas had missed an opportunity: That time Richard Dehmel had asked to see his other work and he had had nothing to send. Now the hoped-for invitation had come from a far more important quarter, and this time he meant to behave like the professional writer he already was.

It is difficult to say what fortunate chance or instinct had restrained him from offering "Little Herr Friedemann" to *Simplicissimus*. Perhaps he had not wanted to send it there while "Death" was entered in the prize contest; perhaps Albert Langen's editors had made him too keenly aware of the magazine's space limitations; perhaps he was moved by ambition to conquer another field. In any case, from Italy he sent "Little Herr Friedemann" to the *Neue Deutsche Rundschau*, which in the four short years under its new name had established itself as virtually *the* literary magazine of Germany. Oskar Bie, editor of the *Rundschau*, accepted the story immediately and wrote that he wished to see all the author's other writings. With that letter from Bie began Thomas Mann's lifelong relationship with S. Fischer Verlag. Whether Heinrich's previous employment there and his somewhat better-known name smoothed the path for Thomas cannot be determined. In the event, the *Neue Deutsche Rundschau* printed "Little Herr Friedemann" in its issue of May 1897, "The Dilettante" in September of the same year, and a new story, "Tobias Mindernickel," the following January.

Thomas returned to Rome at the end of November; but this time he did not share a room with Heinrich at Via Torre Argentina 34. He lived nearby in the Via del Pantheon; but the brothers evidently saw a good deal of each other, especially at meals, which they took together at a little restaurant called Genzano. Here they drank good wine and ate *crochette di pollo*. "Evenings we went to a café, played dominoes, and drank punch. If we heard German spoken, we fled."[29]

Dominoes was not their only amusement; they also collaborated on a work of "art." Their sister Carla was to be confirmed in the spring of 1897, and the two brothers decided to give her a joint confirmation present. They worked together in happy harmony, drawing and rhyming, on a whimsical and extravagant *Bilderbuch für artige Kinder* (Picture Book for Well-Behaved Children). Thomas Mann later observed that the *Bilderbuch* anticipated the fantastic and pessimistic humor of *Simplicissimus;* but the probability is that his memory was playing him false and that in fact he and Heinrich were carrying the mood and techniques of *Simplicissimus* to a point of delightful absurdity. The gay ballad meters, the preposterous distortions to achieve whimsical rhymes (*Schrette* and *Stemme* for *Schritte* and *Stimme*), help to correct any misconception of these two young writers as preternaturally mature and grave.

The one copy of the *Bilderbuch*, hand-lettered and hand-colored, unfortunately disappeared in 1933, along with many precious mementos of the Mann family. But Viktor Mann, who inherited it, and Thomas Mann's children, to whom Viktor gave it, remembered in whole or in part many of the sardonic and mock-heroic verses. And at one time or another some of the drawings were reproduced, so that these were preserved and provide some notion of the vanished *Bilderbuch*. One of these is the famous "Mother Nature," a sketch of an obese, lewd female with tousled hair and porcine features, grinning sadistically and licking her lips. So deeply embedded in Thomas Mann's mind was this drawing in his youth that he alluded to it half a century later in *Doctor Faustus* where the devil, explaining his involuntary changes of appearance, speaks of "the mummery and hocus-pocus of Mother Nature, who always has her tongue in the corner of her mouth."* That allusion serves as one more confirmation of the intimate psychological relationship between the stay in Italy and the conception of *Doctor Faustus*.

Preparation of the *Bilderbuch* did not interfere with more serious literary pursuits. Throughout the winter both Thomas and Heinrich worked on novellas. Heinrich's "Das gestohlene Dokument" (The Stolen Document) was accepted by *Simplicissimus;* thus encouraged, he wrote four more novellas in three months. Albert Langen agreed to publish these as a book in his Langen's Little Library

---

* H. T. Lowe-Porter, unfortunately unaware of the picture Thomas Mann had in mind, translated this as "tongue in her cheek."[30]

(Kleine Bibliothek Langen); and Heinrich's first book after *In einer Familie*, his first commercial publication (since the novel had been subsidized) appeared in April 1897. Thomas now got up his courage to propose that Fischer publish a similar collection of his stories in book form. To "catch up" with his brother was alluring; but he was by no means immodest about what he had accomplished thus far. (He had already eliminated "Fallen" from the list of stories he submitted to Fischer; the volume would consist of "Little Herr Friedemann," "Death," "The Will to Happiness," "Disillusionment," and "The Dilettante." (Later "Tobias Mindernickel" would be added.) As he wrote to Grautoff in April 1897:

> So perhaps a slender volume will be put together, or perhaps not—I really don't even know whether I may hope for one. It would certainly mean an encouragement for me, but it is another question whether it would be helpful to my reputation. For my scribblings hitherto all seem to me gray and boring in comparison with the strange things I have in my head. . . .
>
> Truly, it seems to me that I may look forward to my future with pleasure and confidence. For some time I have felt as if fetters have dropped away from me, as if only now have I obtained space in which to develop myself artistically, as though only now have I been given the means to express myself, to communicate. . . . Since "Little Herr Friedemann" I am suddenly able to find the discreet forms and masks in which I can walk abroad among people with my experiences. Whereas formerly, if all I wanted to do was communicate from myself to myself, I needed a secret diary. . . .[31]

This expression of growing assurance was matched by an enormously encouraging affirmation from the outside world. At the end of May, S. Fischer wrote that he would be glad to publish the novellas in his Fischer Collection, a pocketbooklike series of much the same type as Langen's Little Library. Fischer's terms were scarcely generous—he offered only 150 marks for the volume, and that sum included the right to publish "The Dilettante" in the *Neue Deutsche Rundschau*. The books in the collection series were priced so low, Fischer apologized, that he could not pay more. But he could do much better if his new author would give him the opportunity to publish a larger prose work, perhaps a novel.

The suggestion struck home, struck fire; how could it not with a born novelist who up to this time had failed to recognize his true vocation? It came, moreover, just at that time of year when a young man's spirits would naturally revive. The weather was wonderful, the sky deep blue; it was already warmer than it would be in Munich in July; and Thomas and Heinrich took long walks out into the Campagna, stopping in an *osteria* for a glass of wine, or sat over a vermouth in an outdoor café on the Corso, watching the people pass, and "for ten minutes able to persuade oneself that life is a very pleasant affair."[32]

Any latent antagonism between the brothers evaporated in the warmth of anticipated worldly success. Yet there must have been occasional outbreaks of bad feeling. This is indicated by a passage in a letter that Heinrich drafted in 1918, in the midst of their wartime quarrel: " '*In inimicos*,' you said, twenty-two years old, sitting at the piano in Via Argentina *trenta quattro*, your back turned to me."[33] If Heinrich was accurate in giving Thomas's age, this could have happened anytime after June 6, 1897. The brothers stayed in Rome until nearly the end of July, and the scorching heat of that summer in Rome could easily have made tempers run short. That brotherliness held some ambiguities is likewise suggested by a curious slip on Thomas's part. It seems reasonable to assume that the title of a series in which a writer's first book is to appear would be burned into his memory. Yet in a letter dated on his birthday—written, that is, only a day or two after Fischer's letter of May 29 arrived in Rome—Thomas tells Grautoff that Fischer will be publishing the volume of novellas "in his Little Library."[34] That, of course, was the series in which Heinrich's book was appearing. Clearly, now that Thomas was overtaking Heinrich, his sense of rivalry was growing keener. But at this time such bouts of jealousy must have been brief, and he seems to have fought them. Perhaps that is what he meant by his obscure remark to Grautoff that he was employing his leisure "cleaning out a little the Augean stable of my conscience."[35]

By August both brothers were installed once more under Signora Pastini's care in the Casa Bernardini in Palestrina, and Thomas had plunged into preparations for his first major literary enterprise.

7

Buddenbrooks

The latest news is that I am making preparations for a novel, a big
novel—what do you say to that? . . . Until recently I thought I
would never find the courage for such an undertaking. But now, rather
suddenly, I have discovered a subject, taken a resolve, and intend to
begin writing in the near future, after reflecting a bit longer. The
novel . . . may be called something like *Downhill*. . . .[1]

T H E letter in which Thomas Mann thus announced his
plans to Otto Grautoff also mentions that he has recently completed two stories, "Luischen" ("Little Lizzy") and "Tobias
Mindernickel." These stories, studies in cruelty and grotesquerie,
are connected by deliberate and perhaps somewhat arch similarities
of names and backgrounds with each other and with earlier stories.[2]
Thus Frau Jacoby's lover in "Luischen" has some of the qualities of

the Bajazzo; and two men outwardly so strikingly dissimilar as Attorney Jacoby and Tobias Mindernickel share the same abject attitude toward the world. Both new stories can be regarded as elaborations on a higher literary plane of the kind of exuberant distortion that characterized the *Bilderbuch;* Heinrich was to develop it further in the devastating social satire of *Im Schlaraffenland.* Flashes of similar caricature occur in *Buddenbrooks;* but Thomas instinctively knew that the mode would be inappropriate for a work of any considerable length.

The "subject" that he had mentioned to Grautoff was the area in which he felt at home, which lay nearest to hand: the background of his own life and that of his family. He had already experimented —as has been mentioned—with using parts of that background in the short stories and novellas of the past two years. But the idea that he could or would want to attempt a larger form had not occurred to him. But then in Rome:

> I read a French novel, *Renée Mauperin,* by the Goncourt brothers. I read it again and again, with sheer delight in the lightness, the felicity, and precision of the book, which was composed in a succession of extremely brief chapters. My admiration proved to be productive; it made me think that after all it should be possible for me to do this sort of thing. Thus it was not Zola as has been widely assumed—at the time I had not even read him—but the far more artistic Goncourts who set me going.[3]

This explicit statement has been little regarded, perhaps because *Renée Mauperin* is no longer widely read. But as is always the case with Thomas Mann, his self-interpretations must be taken seriously in two ways: at their face value and also as possible examples of the "forms and masks" under which his real messages, his most intimate concerns, may be concealed.

The outward aspect of *Renée Mauperin*—its succession of extremely brief chapters—unquestionably affected the composition of *Buddenbrooks.* Here, clearly, was the solution for a writer who felt that he suffered from shortness of breath; and the early chapters of *Buddenbrooks* are in fact extremely short. As the book moves on and the writer's hand grows surer—and likewise, as the influence of the French model waned with the passage of the years during which he worked on the novel—the chapters tend to increase in length. Even where they do not, there is a feeling of wider scope and longer breath. At the very end there is a reversion to the brief, staccato chapters of the beginning—did he once more reread the concluding chapters of *Renée Mauperin* in preparation for his own final chords?*

But Thomas Mann did not read the Goncourt brothers' novel repeatedly only to observe how short scenes could be worked by accretion into a larger composition. On his own he had in fact already mastered this technique in "Little Herr Friedemann," which is gracefully divided, relatively short though the story is, into fifteen smaller units, most of them only a page and a half or two pages in length. He had done the same in "The Dilettante," although there the segments are not so fully developed as scenes; and "Death" also was broken up into a succession of small sketches disguised as dated diary entries. Thus *Renée Mauperin* could at most have served the young writer as confirmation of a method already congenial to him, and as evidence that the method could be extended from a thirty-page novella to the novel of approximately two hundred and fifty pages that he initially conceived.

If the comment on the "succession of extremely brief chapters" is, therefore, somewhat misleading, the tribute to the "lightness, the felicity, and the precision of the book" is not. These were the qualities he aimed for, these were the qualities he achieved, so that the bulky novel never seemed heavy—greatly to the surprise of readers who expected to be bored and could not understand why they were not. But there were some other aspects of *Renée Mauperin* that Mann did not mention, perhaps because he wished his readers to make the discoveries for themselves, perhaps because he was not himself conscious of how pervasively he had been guided by the French novel.

Renée Mauperin closes with a magnificent and protracted description of dying which must have persuaded Thomas Mann that in literary terms as much could be done with the close of life as with its events. The celebrated death scenes of *Buddenbrooks* surely owe

---

* It is amusing that, as T. J. Reed has pointed out, the first French critic to comment on *Buddenbrooks* complained that the novel was "a confused succession of rapid scenes, brief visions . . . an incoherence painful to our Latin mind."[4]

something to the example provided by the Goncourts. Nor should it be forgotten that *Renée Mauperin* depicts, among other things, the extinction of two families, one noble and one bourgeois. The noble family has reverted to savagery and ignominy; its fate is sealed by one last flash of the ancient code of honor. The bourgeois family perishes from the corruption brought on by social climbing, the pursuit of money, and the vapidity of social mores. It would not have escaped the young reader's intuition that the Goncourts were telling the story of their own forebears, that Monsieur Mauperin was a portrait of their father. Perhaps Thomas had even been made aware of these matters by retrospective essays or respectful obituaries; for Edmond de Goncourt had died only a year earlier, in July 1896.

Careful realism in the depiction of everyday life, extraordinary observation, and a willingness to describe in detail the artifacts and customs of society—such attitudes were natural to Thomas Mann, and the Goncourt novel could only have confirmed his innate sense that scrupulous attention to detail was essential to the credibility of longer works of fiction. The portrait of a spirited, unconventional young woman whose misfortunes wring the heart (there is little else in common between Renée Mauperin and Tony Buddenbrook) was already familiar to him from Fontane's *Effi Briest*; these figures may have influenced the nuances but certainly not the conception of Tony.

Perhaps the reason *Renée Mauperin* affected him so strongly, although this remained forever unspoken, was the novel's joint authorship. That exemplified an ideal association between two brothers very different in gifts and temperament but united in their devotion to literature. Perhaps the loneliness of creation, the enforced isolation of the writer's life ("Literature is death,"[5] Thomas would write to Heinrich a few years later), could be mitigated by some such collaboration as the Goncourts had practiced. Heinrich had been having similar thoughts, for he recalls: "In the first half of our working lives my brother and I informed each other of the same secret thought. We wanted to write a book together. I was the first to speak, but he was prepared. We never came back to that. Perhaps it would have turned out something altogether amazing. Not for nothing does one have this earliest companion, born to accompany one."[6]

Heinrich, they had decided, would do the historical sections and

Thomas the parts dealing with "modern life." The subject was apparently to be the crime and punishment of Aunt Elisabeth Mann's son-in-law Guido Biermann—who by a simple transmutation of beer into wine became, in *Buddenbrooks*, Tony's son-in-law Hugo Weinschenk. The whole "jabber novel"* would be cast in the mock-heroic tone the brothers had already practiced in the *Bilderbuch*. But Heinrich had plans of his own—his novel of Berlin literary life, *Im Schlaraffenland*, was already germinating—and the idea was soon dropped. Heinrich continued to contribute reminiscences of family history; there were things that he, as the elder brother, would be privy to, past events and scandals that had escaped Thomas or been deliberately concealed from him. And other members of the family could also be tapped for information.

"I found I did not know enough."[7] This is the eternal plaint of the novelist, and Thomas drew up long lists of questions. One such list was sent to Consul Wilhelm Marty, his father's cousin. Thomas asked about the general atmosphere in Lübeck before the establishment of the Empire, about the old and new currencies in the city, about business cycles and the rise and fall of grain prices, about the possible reasons for the decline of a grain firm, and even about the kind of street lighting Lübeck had had before Thomas's birth.

Many of the "preparations" that Thomas mentioned to Grautoff have survived all vicissitudes and are preserved in the Zürich Archives, where they have been exhaustively studied. Among the items is Consul Marty's reply, typed on stationery bearing the letterhead of the vice-consulate of Portugal in Lübeck. Marty painstakingly supplied the requested information, and Thomas incorporated most of it into the novel. The story of Thomas Buddenbrook's ill-omened purchase of standing grain—one of the significant stages in his ethical as well as his financial decline—is directly based on Marty's statements about the practice, and the author weaves Marty's very words into the fabric of the narrative. At this earliest stage in his career Thomas Mann was already employing the "montage" technique that he later discovered, or pretended to have discovered, during the writing of *Doctor Faustus*.

---

* *Gipper-Roman*. The verb *gippern* and the noun *Gipprigkeit* were schoolboy slang words shared by Otto Grautoff and the Mann brothers. *Gippern* meant something like "to babble on in a sardonic fashion," and may just possibly have derived from, or been formed in imitation of, the English *jabber* or *gibberish*.

Another family member who helped in a major way to fill the gaps in Thomas's knowledge was his sister Julia. Still pursuing the Biermann-Weinschenk story, Thomas wrote to her asking for all the information she could supply on their Aunt Elisabeth, her two husbands, her daughter Alice, and her son-in-law, the insurance man Biermann who had been convicted of fraud. Julia's reply has been preserved; it is a remarkable document for a young woman of twenty with the conventional habit of mind that Julia Mann later displayed. The vividness with which she organized and related the facts Thomas needed testifies once again to the literary gift that all the Manns appear to have shared.* Her twenty-eight-page letter provided much of the background for the story of Tony Buddenbrook; the realistic details were there, and "all" the author had to invent was the total configuration, the artistic placing and weighing of the facts, the emotions of the participants, and the structuring of emotions and ideas into a narrative. Above all, he had to sort out his own feelings and his own understanding of these facts of family history, had to learn to see them with sympathy as well as with irony—which the young so naturally feel toward elderly kin—and had to fit them into an intellectual framework. What did it mean to be a businessman—and to be brother, sister, son, and grandson of businessmen—in a small North German city in the nineteenth century? Even with so many material facts provided, writing the novel was no easier.

Twenty years later, reflecting on the work that had grown under his hands without a preconceived theoretical basis, a far more speculative Thomas Mann expressed some astonishment at the degree to which he had unconsciously anticipated the arguments of Ernst Troeltsch, Werner Sombart, and Max Weber on the role of the Protestant ethic in the rise of capitalism. He conjectured that this agreement was not coincidental, that the source from which novelist and social scientist alike derived was Nietzsche. But in those early days in Palestrina, when the novel was assuming form, the idea of *Leistungsethik*, the ethic of achievement, had not yet come to the fore. If it was present in his mind at all, then it was so only as an un-

---

* But then, we have Viktor Mann's testimony that both sisters—"whether it was the example of their brothers or the atmosphere of this artistic city [Munich]"—also wrote. Julia in particular went in for "melancholy verse."[8]

fulfillable mandate. He was not, at this stage, thinking of rendering "an aspect of the psychological history of the German bourgeoisie in general."[9] What he was primarily concerned with, in the initial stages of the novel's conception, was only what could be done from recent memory, "the story of the sensitive latecomer Hanno and, at most, of Thomas Buddenbrook."[10] In the light of this statement it is remarkable to find that the first name to be set down in the notes for the novel was Christian. Although Thomas Buddenbrook holds his place at the moral center of the novel, his brother and potential double, the Bajazzo that Tom might have become had he been less imbued with *Leistungsethik*, is there from the start.

It would be vulgar error to accept what Mann called "the tactless interpretation that, for example, Thomas and Christian Buddenbrook 'mean' my brother and myself."[11] There was, moreover, a "model" for Christian in real life: Thomas's uncle Friedrich Mann, his father's brother—who many years later was to protest publicly against his "portrait." But for an understanding of the relationship between brothers, of the similarities and differences that can flow out of the same background, Thomas did not need to look to the older generation. That is what we must keep in mind when we think about such fraternal pairs as Christian and Thomas Buddenbrook, or for that matter Jean and Gotthold Buddenbrook. In his own life Thomas Mann was experiencing, and simultaneously seeking to understand through his writing, an archetype of the human condition. Ultimately he grasped this quite well, for the aesthetic and temperamental disparity between himself and Heinrich grew upon him in the course of the work. As he later summed it up:

> What a school of experience—of objective and subjective experience— a first work is for a young artist! For the first time I learned the true nature of the epic element, for it carried me along on its billows. In the course of *writing* I found out what I myself was, and what I wanted and did not want—namely, not southern aesthetic posturing, but the cooler North, ethics, music, humor. I discovered my own attitudes toward life and death.[12]

There is a reverberation in this passage of recently concluded wars with Heinrich. And in the stress on the novel's organic growth there is a good measure of stylization, as there is also in Mann's repeated statements that the work expanded beyond his wildest dreams because of his instinct to begin everything *ab ovo:*

> But everything I had thought I could treat as a mere preliminary to the principal story assumed a highly independent, highly self-assertive form. In my anxiety over this development I was somewhat reminded of Wagner's experience with the *Ring* cycle, which had grown from the initial conception of *Siegfried's Death* into a tetralogy with an intricate fabric of leitmotifs.[13]

Actually, as the preliminary sketches make plain, something close to the full scope of the novel must have been in Thomas Mann's mind at least from a very early stage. Once launched on the kind of realistic precision he had admired in *Renée Mauperin*, he assiduously pursued facts. He had the courage, or impudence, to check with Aunt Elisabeth herself. She showed no alarm, resentment, or suspicion; a letter of hers on "Biermann's misstep" has been preserved. He asked his mother for the old family papers, and with the help of these he began drawing up genealogies and chronological tables, so that the multitude of characters who were, in his head, already peopling the unwritten novel would make their entrances and exits in the proper years, displaying neither extreme precocity nor miraculous longevity. Most of the characters were eventually fitted into the novel; a few were discarded and their personalities or their names (for instance, Rodde) reserved for use fifty years later. In notes written on scraps of paper or in his notebooks Thomas began setting down cue phrases that already gave hints of the events of the novel. The "downhill" theme was elaborately worked out in a table showing the dispersal and diminution of the Buddenbrook firm's capital. And in one of the early chronologies the dates run from the founding of the firm in 1764 (later corrected to 1768) to the death of "little Johann" (Hanno) in 1877. Under the heading "prehistory" the birth and marriage of the Consul, the births of Thomas, Antonie (Tony), and Christian, are listed in tabular form. Then follows:

NOVEL

1835—Beginning of narrative
1836—Birth of Marie [This name is later changed to Clara.]

1845—Death of old B and his wife [This date is corrected to 1840,
 then to 1842.]
 48—Revolution
1847—Antonie's first marriage [This date is changed several times.]

 . . .

1859—Antonie's second marriage ends in divorce.
 End of 50's; gas lighting.[14]

The full chronological table, of which the above is only a sampling, indicates that most of the main subjects of the novel were conceived before a line had been written. With equal care, not to say pedantry, the twenty-two-year-old author even authenticated the menus for the novel's festive occasions. He wrote to his mother for recipes and an old family cookbook. She was as helpful as the other members of the family, and her instructions proved useful to Thomas in a double sense. For what was eaten could also supply material for conversations; and in fact the ladies at Buddenbrook parties quote almost word for word from some of Julia Mann's recipes. In this respect Thomas may even have gone too far in the direction of naturalism, at least in the minds of contemporary critics. Only a few years after publication of the novel he commented rather bitterly: "In fairly wide circles I am esteemed, I think, as the describer of good dinners."[15]

The early notes for *Buddenbrooks*, on loose sheets and in notebooks, testify to an extraordinary diligence during that long, scorching Italian summer. Thomas's preliminary work consisted not only in "sketching out chronological patterns and detailed family trees, accumulating psychological points and factual material."[16] Sometimes he slipped from outlining to elaborating whole scenes, setting down bits of dialogue. In his notebooks the character of Tony can be seen moving steadily to the forefront.

In October the brothers returned to Rome, and this time both of them stayed in Heinrich's *pensione*, Via Torre Argentina, "three flights up."[17] The first page of the manuscript of *Buddenbrooks* is dated "end of October 1897"; and the untried novelist thereafter made astonishing progress. By the eleventh of December he was writing away at "the fifteenth chapter of my novel" and was at the same time "drunk with subjects for novellas."[18] The fifteenth chapter is that tour de force, for a young man who had never had a head for business, in which Johann Buddenbrook, Jr., explains to his wife how the capital of the firm has suffered attrition, so that they really cannot afford to hire a manservant. The Consul's reckoning for his wife's benefit follows item for item one of the notes that Thomas drew up during his preparatory work in Palestrina.

Thomas's health had been somewhat troublesome during this period, particularly the nerves of his teeth, as he mentioned in a letter to Grautoff. Perhaps that was the reason he ascribed sensitive teeth to Hanno and hit upon the extraction of a tooth as the precipitating cause of Thomas Buddenbrook's death. It makes for a nice novelistic touch that Hanno, standing outside the door while his father is making his will, feels with his tongue for a doubtful tooth.

In the course of the summer in Palestrina Thomas had acquired a dog, first in a long line. He and Heinrich had come upon it on a haystack, and Thomas found the cheerful little stray a corrective to his bouts of melancholia, so Heinrich testifies. Whenever the brothers went for a walk, if the dog was not on the spot Thomas would invariably ask: "Do you really think we ought to go alone?"[19] Titino, a short-haired hound of playful disposition and clumsy movements, accompanied Thomas back to Munich and eventually became a member of his mother's household, much to the delight of Viktor Mann, then eight years old.

By April both brothers could look back upon an almost uncannily productive winter, as if they had bartered their souls for creative powers. Thomas had written at a pace he would seldom equal again. Heinrich experienced what he later called an "eruption of talent": "I did not know what I was doing. I thought I was going to make a penciled draft but wrote almost the complete novel."[20] *Im Schlaraffenland* was rapidly becoming a devastating satire with a strong tendency toward grotesque caricature. Subtitled "a novel of elegant people," it dealt with far more sophisticated characters and subjects than Thomas's growing *Buddenbrooks*. Heinrich reached out beyond literary life into the world of finance, the theater, society, the corrupters of talent and those they corrupted.

At the end of April Thomas set out for Munich with the considerably swollen manuscript of *Buddenbrooks* in his baggage. There was room enough, for his clothes were apparently down to a minimum after his year and a half away from home. (One of his first acts in Munich was to visit his tailor; he did not want to call on friends or acquaintances until he could once more "offer a reasonably respectable aspect.")[21] His mother had moved—she was growing restless and was to change apartments frequently during the following years. There was no longer room for him at home, physically or psychologically. He quickly found the first of a series of bachelor flats, and by May 1, 1898, had installed himself at Theresienstrasse 82, ground floor, right. From there he promptly made an effort to resume his contacts with the literary world by writing to his old schoolmate Korfiz Holm at the offices of *Simplicissimus*. He invited Holm to drop in on him in his new quarters some afternoon, and then added casually—although of course this was the point of the letter—"I will then slip a copy of my volume into your pocket, so that at least one person reads it."[22]

The volume of stories, *Der kleine Herr Friedemann*, was in truth pocket-sized and could be bought for 2 marks. It had been postponed repeatedly, but at last had come out, with its attractive but scarcely appropriate jacket showing a young woman with a great feathered hat leaning on one elbow and reading. Thomas's eagerness to have his friend Holm read the book was no doubt compounded of pride in this first bound product of his pen and the practical hope that *Simplicissimus* might print a review. There was still time for that, since *Der kleine Herr Friedemann*, along with five other items in the Fischer Collection, was not going to be distributed until the end of the month. Apparently, advance copies had already been sent abroad, however, for Thomas Mann later recollected that while still in Rome he had seen copies of the book in the book shops.

Disappointments in first publication are not uncommon. After a year and a half, 1,587 copies of an original edition of 2,000 were still in S. Fischer's stockrooms—which meant, if a reasonable number of review copies had been sent out, that fewer than 400 copies had been sold. The young author's eagerness to present copies may well have sprung from forebodings that this was to be the fate of his first book. At any rate, "the literary success of your book was greater than its sales would suggest,"[23] Samuel Fischer wrote to him at the time he sent this reckoning. And in fact the few reviews that have been preserved indicate that the publication of *Der kleine Herr Friedemann* had at once placed Thomas Mann among the noted young German writers of the day. A few reviewers spoke loudly, clearly, and enthusiastically; but on the whole not much fuss was made about the book. Nevertheless, consensus was arrived at among

the arbiters of taste by some mysterious process that escapes examination. The reviews of *Buddenbrooks*, when the novel was published three years later, confirm that recognition had already been
accorded to the author of a book of stories that scarcely reached the
general public. Probably magazine publication was a force very
much to be reckoned with.

T H O M A S had been back in Munich no more than two
weeks when he had to cope with one of the crises that occurred periodically in his relationship with Otto Grautoff. This son of the once
bankrupt Lübeck bookseller had all along harbored exaggerated notions of how wealthy the rich tax senator's son was. During his stay
in Italy Thomas frequently complained because Grautoff made a
practice of sending him letters and manuscripts postage-due. Now
that Thomas was back in Munich, no longer subject to the expenses
of travel and, moreover, a successful author with one book published and a contract for another, Grautoff asked him for a loan of
2,000 marks. Since only Thomas's reply to this request has survived,
we do not know what purpose Grautoff had in mind. But probably
he hoped for a loan that would enable him to attend the university
for a while.

Thomas managed the rather difficult task of refusing without
offending by candidly revealing his own financial situation. Not
only was he in no position to advance such a sum, he wrote, but in
his young life he had not yet had the good fortune to see so much
money all at once.

The honorable and in every respect excellent Herr Krafft Tesdorpf
"administers" my father's legacy in Lübeck—to the extent that it has
not already gone down the drain because of this same gentleman's
idiocy (I intend to take subtle revenge on him in my novel). Herr
Tesdorpf sends my mother the interest every quarter, and she gives
us our share of it. But not a penny of the capital may be drawn on
under any circumstances, so Herr Tesdorpf maintains, although any
paragraph to that effect in the will escapes any normally constituted
human eye. My brother has asked the administrator—who quite incidentally receives 2 percent of the whole—for capital; I asked for some
capital when I wanted to relieve my mother of the cost of equipping

me, in case I have to do my military service. We met with a mild but sober rebuff; and God knows what is going to happen with my sisters' dowry if they should wish to marry. In short, you can see that I would be spending 10 pfennigs for a stamp quite needlessly if I attempted to ask this fierce man for 2,000 marks.[24]

Thomas's revenge upon Herr Krafft Tesdorpf came in his depiction of the administrator of the Buddenbrook estate, Herr Stephan Kistenmaker, who is in such haste to liquidate the firm that the heirs suffer severe losses. When Gerda Buddenbrook wishes to sell her house to the broker Gosch for 85,000 marks, Herr Kistenmaker swears that he can easily get much more. "He continued to swear this until he was forced to dispose of the property for 75,000 marks to an elderly bachelor who had returned from extended travel and decided to settle in the town."[25]

The remark to Grautoff about revenge is one more indication of how elaborately *Buddenbrooks* had been planned from the start. The passage just cited occurs in Chapter 1 of Part Eleven, close to the end of the novel. It would take Thomas another two years or more to reach that point. Yet even such details as Herr Kistenmaker's 2 percent commission for the "service" of dissipating Gerda Buddenbrook's fortune were evidently planned at the time of this letter to Grautoff in May 1898.

A week earlier, in giving Grautoff his address, Thomas had praised his new quarters on Theresienstrasse as "very pleasant."[26] But he quickly became dissatisfied and moved into what he later called his "expensive bourgeois and banker's apartment"[27] on Barerstrasse. This must have proved either too expensive or too inconveniently situated, for by October he had moved again, this time farther out into Schwabing and closer to his mother's new apartment, so that he was able to take his meals with the family. His two small rooms at Marktstrasse 5 were on his favorite floor, three flights up. Either he liked climbing stairs or, more likely, the cheaper and quieter apartments were in the loftier regions. In any case, the ascent provided useful exercise to one of sedentary habits.

A spirit of improvisation and practicality pervades any artists' colony, for painters and sculptors are forever stretching canvas, making frames, devising armatures, carpentering studios, and dabbling in crafts. Even the patrician and somewhat dandified young man that Thomas Mann was at this time succumbed to the influence of his surroundings—Schwabing, a still half-rustic and only recently incorporated suburb, was Munich's, and indeed Germany's, bohemia. The new flat on Marktstrasse was unfurnished. Thomas took over some of his mother's surplus furniture, including the massive mahogany bed in which he had been born. But he also bought a number of wicker chairs and spent days on his knees painting them with red enamel. There is a brief description of this apartment in the short story "The Wardrobe."

This story provides a kind of counterpart to the vision of the devil in Palestrina, and is also thematically related to the sketch "Death." Albrecht van der Qualen wakes as the Berlin-Rome express stops in some middle-sized German station. He does not know the name of the town or whether it is morning or evening; he has no watch and ignores the calendar, for he has been trying to lose his awareness of time and space ever since the doctors told him that he has only a few months to live. Although he has a ticket to Florence, he leaves the train and begins a walk through the cold, damp city. He crosses a bridge and looks down at a long, decaying boat sculled by a man in the stern. The mythological reference is plain; the river is the Styx, the boatman Charon.*

On the outskirts of town he comes upon a For Rent sign. On impulse, he takes the offered rooms, wretched and bare though they are. In the bedroom the only furniture besides the massive mahogany bed, a few chairs, and a washstand, is a wardrobe.

> It was squat, stained brown, slightly rickety, with a naively ornamented top. It stood in the middle of the right-hand wall, exactly filling the niche of a second white door which must lead into the rooms entered by the main and middle doors on the landing. . . . The wardrobe was completely empty. It had several rows of hooks on its ceiling, but it seemed that this solid piece of furniture had no rear wall. It was closed at the back by a gray cloth, a piece of coarse, common burlap that was fastened at the four corners with nails or tacks.[29]

The lovely nude girl who later appears in this wardrobe addresses Albrecht van der Qualen with the pronoun of intimacy. "Shall I tell you a story?" she asks, and proceeds to tell sad stories. Then she lifts

---

* Henry Hatfield called attention to this point in 1950.[28]

the lower right-hand corner of the burlap at the back of the wardrobe and disappears. But she returns the next night, and the next. Sometimes, when Albrecht van der Qualen cannot control himself and reaches out for her, she does not resist; but then she does not appear for several nights.

This "story full of riddles," as the subtitle calls it, has been much puzzled over by critics. Its surrealistic note, its teasing mystification, set it apart from the rest of Mann's early tales. So does the swiftness of composition; Mann's notebook indicates that it was written between November 23 and November 29, 1898. The naked girl may be (and has been) taken as the Muse, the lonely, tormented (*Qualen* means "torments") man as another of Thomas Mann's artist figures who must restrain himself and "eat rice" if he is to hear his Muse's voice. But Albrecht van der Qualen in fact eats rather well, and the very imagery of the story emphasizes that. Both before and after his elegant dinner we are reminded that the room's three red-enameled chairs "stand against the white walls like strawberries in whipped cream."[30] Strawberries—overripe, tainted ones—would come into Thomas Mann's mind again fifteen years later in connection with another story.

Albrecht is a significant name; in *Royal Highness* it will be given to the elder brother, the reigning sovereign who abdicates in favor of his younger brother. Even earlier, in notes for *Die Geliebten*, a novel never written but absorbed into other works, an Albrecht was intended to incorporate characteristics of Heinrich Mann and Gabriele D'Annunzio. In "The Wardrobe" there is one sentence, separated from the rest of a paragraph by ellipses and thrown into the story as a curious non sequitur, that must be intended as a clue. It reads: "Incidentally, his dark hair was smoothly parted on the side."[31] This was the way Heinrich Mann wore his hair.

During 1898 Heinrich Mann stayed in Italy, but he paid several visits to Munich. It is possible that "The Wardrobe" was written under the immediate impact of one such visit. Heinrich was wont to say of himself: "I am a neurasthenic. That is my profession and my fate."[32] And during this and the next several years he was compelled to return repeatedly for long stays to Dr. Christoph von Hartungen's sanatorium, Villa Cristoforo, on the Lago di Garda in Riva. It may be that van der Qualen's unspecified illness reflects Thomas's anxiety about his brother's health.

Thomas had the same tendency to neurasthenia—his early letters are full of references to the parlous state of his "nerves"—and he instinctively combatted it by fresh air and exercise. He acquired a "velocipede"[33] which he had to carry up his three flights of stairs. In those days, he later recalled, "I was such an impassioned bicycle rider . . . that I scarcely went a step on foot, but even in pouring rain went on all my errands, in loden cape and rubber overshoes, on my machine. . . . Mornings, after my work, I used to stand it on its saddle and clean it."[34]

He was not alone in this passion. At this same time his near neighbor Frank Wedekind, who lived on Türkenstrasse, was writing to a friend: "In recent days I began cycling again and found to my alarm that I had completely forgotten how. It is true, though, that in the old days they did not have the kind of machines they have now. But since everybody here who can draw breath is cycling, I want to take it up again."[35] Pot-bellied Wedekind was soon attracting considerable attention as he rode around Munich on his white bicycle.

At this time, it so happened, Frank Wedekind's work impinged upon Thomas Mann's life and significantly affected the course of his next two years. Wedekind was, in fact, responsible for Thomas Mann's only regular employment, aside from those few months he had spent as a bored insurance clerk.

At the end of July 1898 Otto von Bismarck, architect of the German Empire, died in Friedrichsruh. Eight years earlier he had received his reward: the title of Duke of Lauenburg and rough dismissal by Kaiser Wilhelm II. But even in his sulky retirement Bismarck had remained the Kaiser's conscience; the old chancellor's very existence, and the occasional articles he published, had somewhat restrained Wilhelm's follies. No sooner was Bismarck dead than Wilhelm planned and carried out a pompous voyage to Palestine that called attention to Germany's new navy and her interests in the Near East. These needless affronts to Great Britain were undertaken even while Germany's diplomats were discussing a defensive alliance with their British counterparts.

Simplicissimus commented sarcastically, in picture and word, on all the fanfare over the Kaiser's visit to Jerusalem. The magazine created a sensation with its caricature of the Kaiser by Thomas Theodor Heine, alongside a poem entitled "In the Holy Land," signed by one Hieronymus. In the poem King David rises from his grave and reaches for his harp to sing the praises of "the Lord of Nations" and his large retinue of police officials.

The circulation of *Simplicissimus* shot up; but orders went out to seize the issue of the magazine and to arrest the publisher, the artist, and the poet on charges of lese majesty. Heine, the cartoonist, was caught; Albert Langen, the publisher, fled to Zürich and from there went on to Paris. The author, Frank Wedekind, could not make a quick getaway. He lingered to attend the premiere of his *Erdgeist*. Then, as he himself told the story,

> all of Munich knew that I was the author of the poem. . . . After the end of the performance the police sent a detective to me to let me know that they would need only another two days to discover the author of the poem. Thirty of us celebrated all night long in the most questionable restaurants. In the morning two friends took me to the railroad station . . . and next morning at eight [I was] here in Zürich, where I met Langen two days later. It was the collapse of a whole large building that I had constructed for my future; and there remained for me the task of using the rubble as best I could. On my second day here I began a new play. . . . The reason I evaded arrest was chiefly that the police suggested that as my natural course. I thought: they must know best.[36]

Half a year later Wedekind decided to surrender to the authorities rather than risk permanent banishment from Germany. He was tried, at first sentenced to prison, then had this sentence commuted to incarceration in a "fortress," where he spent some six months under conditions he found quite tolerable, since he was permitted to write.

Wedekind's problems proved to be Thomas Mann's opportunity. *Simplicissimus*, its circulation booming as a consequence of the scandal, was left without its publisher, its chief cartoonist, and one of its principal contributing editors. Korfiz Holm was overwhelmed; when he ran into Thomas Mann on the street, he at once thought of hiring his colleague from *Der Frühlingssturm* to work on *Simplicissimus*. Thomas Mann served as reader and editorial assistant for both the magazine and the Langen publishing house at a salary of one hundred marks a month. This princely remuneration would have been scarcely enough to live on; but as a supplement to Thomas Mann's inherited income it made for considerable comfort, if not luxury.

Of even greater importance was the opportunity to read the works of his contemporaries who were submitting their manuscripts to the magazine or the publishing house. He was inclined to be charitable, for he responded to stories as a writer rather than as a critic, which meant that he could see the possibilities in even an inept narrative. In after years he recalled that he had wanted to accept most of the novellas that were submitted, and that his superior, Dr. Geheeb, often had to cross out the "yes" he had written on the envelope of a manuscript and set down a firm "no." But this may be exaggeration; Mann later prided himself on his capacity for admiration, which he regarded as a virtue and a necessity for a young writer.

During the first months on *Simplicissimus* the new job must have slowed the writing of *Buddenbrooks*. Thomas Mann complained about the "stupid editorial work (you would not believe how time-consuming such nonsense is!)."[37] Nevertheless, he managed to save out two hours a day in which to roll his novel a little way along, as he put it. He had already formed the habit, which remained for his entire life, of reserving the morning for writing. It may be, however, that when he first began working for the magazine he went to the office at regular hours. That might account for his having written "The Wardrobe" in the evening and what is more "entirely contrary to my habit . . . with the assistance of cognac grog." And half in apology for the fantastic tone of the story, he adds: "It is noticeable."[38]

Whether or not "The Wardrobe" showed that it had been written "under the influence," it was the first work by Thomas Mann to cross the Atlantic. The New York German newspaper *Volkszeitung* picked up the story immediately after its publication in the *Neue Deutsche Rundschau*, and without so much as a by-your-leave reprinted it in its issue of June 25, 1899. Thomas Mann was not quite sure whether to be annoyed or flattered by this pirating. "Apparently that can be done over there without any more ado," he remarked. "At any rate, the American people are to be sincerely congratulated."[39]

The person to whom these lines were addressed was a new friend, Kurt Martens. He, too, was a writer, and one of a number of new literary acquaintances whom Thomas Mann, hitherto rather solitary, met as a result of his work for *Simplicissimus*. Martens had submitted a novella, "The Fiddler John Baring," to the magazine. Thomas Mann signed the letter of acceptance (delicately calling the piece a "sketch"), and Martens was delighted, for he recognized the name. He had already noticed Mann's contributions to *Die Gesellschaft*, had sensed in them a personality akin to his own.

> I at once asked him to visit. He came. Exceedingly modest, almost shy, but bearing himself well, a grave, slender youth crossed my threshold. His sensible, reflective conversation, bathed in mild melancholy, enchanted me as no man's speech had ever done before. From then on we visited each other more and more frequently. . . . The feeling of friendship for him became for me a source of quiet, gentle happiness that has lasted. From the first word on I loved him, voluntarily subordinated myself to him, the younger man, because he was the greater and at the same time all too modest. I believed in his singularity and his future when he himself was still hesitantly groping his way forward. It gave me satisfaction that I was never jealous of him, but hailed his rapid rise as a victory of my own cause.[40]

A native of Leipzig, five years older than Thomas Mann, Martens had the wit, the social graces, and the journalistic fluency that Mann respected, lacked, and sometimes wished for. Martens was involved in everything; he made a point of knowing all the prominent literary personalities of Munich. During Thomas Mann's absence in Italy, Ernst von Wolzogen had founded the Munich Literary Society. Martens became a member and persuaded Thomas Mann to join. In the early days of their friendship Martens frequently tried to coax Mann more into life—"he smilingly called it 'crude' life"[41] —but he met with an obstinate, perhaps instinctive resistance. Martens himself had both feet planted rather squarely in "life"; he had a wife, child, and summer home. Perhaps it is significant that the two men began using the intimate *du* five years after they first met, and just around the time that Thomas Mann began courting Katia Pringsheim. During that difficult courtship he sometimes leaned rather heavily on the older man for sympathy, advice, or simply a willing ear. Mann later commented that Martens "belonged among the few people—I could count them on the fingers of one hand— whom I ever addressed as *du*."[42]

Mann sometimes read sections of *Buddenbrooks* to Martens and another new friend, Arthur Holitscher, a novelist, journalist, musician, and egotist. Martens was overcome with admiration; Holitscher attempted to take some credit for the book. In his memoirs Holitscher claimed that it was he who brought about the publication of *Buddenbrooks*. He made much of his intervention, as also he made much of his closeness to Thomas Mann. He could not resist embroidering a story and told one that will probably prove as enduring in the biography of Thomas Mann as the story of the cherry tree in the life of George Washington—if only because one must tell it in order to deny it. According to Holitscher, he one day visited his friend Mann in Schwabing. There was a small piano in the study, a portrait of Tolstoy on the desk, a sizable heap of manuscript in front of the picture. Mann "fiddled splendidly, and I accompanied him as best I could."[43]

Before the music, Mann read him the scene of Thomas Buddenbrook's visit to the dentist. They talked well that afternoon, and Holitscher left with a feeling that their friendship had deepened. Then, in the street, he glanced up. "At the window of the apartment I had just left I saw Mann, armed with an opera glass, looking after me. This lasted for only a moment, however; in the next minute the head vanished with lightning rapidity from the window."[44] This story—Holitscher's revenge for what he regarded as a cruel portrait of him in *Tristan*—was meant to show Mann's ruthlessness in exploiting his friends for the purposes of his fiction. The story persists, has been quoted again and again, although the probability that the incident ever took place is exceedingly small. Katia Mann has called the story an absurd fabrication. She concedes that Thomas Mann did indeed have Holitscher's appearance in mind when he described Detlev Spinell in *Tristan*. But Mann never watched Holitscher through opera glasses, because "he had no need to."[45] Katia Mann has testified that her husband had only to glance at a person to take in his whole appearance, and to remember it indefinitely. Actually, literal, journalistic description was never Mann's concern; in his works description always has an import beyond itself, a symbolic, narrative, or characterizing function. Mann had above all the gift that Henry James described in *The Art of Fiction:*

> . . . the faculty which when you give it an inch takes an ell, and which for the artist is a much greater source of strength than any accident of residence or of place in the social scale. The power to guess the unseen from the seen, to trace the implication of things, to judge the whole piece by the pattern, the condition of feeling life, in general, so completely that you are well on your way to knowing any particular corner of it—this cluster of gifts may almost be said to constitute experience.[46]

Experience in this restrictive sense was, for the time being, all that Thomas Mann seemed to require. He could not, of course, fail to be attracted by the glittering social, musical, and theatrical life of Munich, and he sometimes joined the *Simplicissimus* crowd at the Odeon Bar. He was only twenty-three, and the sacrifice of "life" to "literature" was gradually becoming a major problem for him. But for the present he resisted the efforts of friends like Martens and Holitscher to draw him into the extracurricular activities of young intellectuals. He would play music with them, and he accepted Martens's invitation to his country cottage in Gmund, for there it was quiet, and he found long tramps with Martens entertainment enough. But on the whole he seemed to have the feeling that he must avoid involvements with people or causes, that he must conserve his strength. As he once remarked to Kurt Martens: "Genius is getting enough sleep."

8

The Army

IN JUNE of 1899 Thomas Mann moved again, this time to Feilitzschstrasse. Here he was even closer to the bicycle paths of the Englischer Garten, and once again he had to carry his wheel up three flights of stairs. Kurt Martens called the building "a poor folks' home" and spoke of Mann's quarters as "a paltry little room."[1] Arthur Holitscher saw the same place as an apartment with a "study."[2] Presumably there was a bedroom also. Thomas Mann mentions that he kept his bicycle in the kitchen—which adds still another room. Perhaps the older Martens (he was all of twenty-nine) arrived at the top of those stairs out of breath and out of sorts. It seems unlikely that the apartment was as mean as it looked to Martens. Thomas Mann always had an instinct for dignity and solidity; he would not have chosen quarters that reeked of the garret poet.

He was, however, indulging himself in poetry in those days, seeking relief from the interminable accumulation of the pages of *Bud-*

denbrooks. In one poem he solemnly pronounced: "Cognition is the worst of agonies."[3] In another he spoke of his dreams of a slender laurel wreath that might one day adorn his brow as a reward for one thing or another that he had done rather prettily:

Ein Traum von einer schmalen Lorbeerkrone
Scheucht oft den Schlaf mir unruhvoll zur Nacht,
Die meine Stirn einst zieren wird zum Lohne
Für dies und jenes, was ich hübsch gemacht.[4]

I often toss and turn at night
With dreams of a slender wreath,
Seeing it placed upon my brow—
Reward for this or that nicely done.

Any error in prediction was surely on the side of modesty; in after years no one could speak of his laurel wreath as slender. Or rather, only the author himself could, and shortly before his death he wryly commented: "Ah yes, I did finally make it to that 'slender laurel wreath.' "[5] Nevertheless, the poem was a first manifestation of that tendency toward matter-of-fact self-congratulation which irritated some of his contemporaries. There was a paradox at the heart of such seeming egotism. With all his ambition, he was clear-eyed enough to "see through" fame. Yet even as he perceived how often fame was the product of manipulation, he set to work manipulating his own reputation. He clearly felt that this fundamentally ironic attitude justified his so doing. But the effort of assuming a pose undermined the irony, so that at times he could become woefully humorless about himself or his work. In speaking of writing as "a consoling game"[6] he was already confounding pose and principle. In "Monolog," the poem quoted above, he was in effect writing his own review (as in fact he was virtually to do later on) and asking to be taken at his own evaluation.

But he was young, and he might properly be allowed a little boasting. For he knew he was hiding a pearl of great price. Most of his creative energies were going into *Buddenbrooks*; as far as the world knew, he had stopped writing, was lost in indolence. In the August 1899 issue of *Simplicissimus* he did have something published, a sketch entitled "Gerächt" (Avenged); but he was rather embarrassed about it. To Martens he apologized, saying that he was just trying to keep his name before the public until the novel was completed. And in writing to Richard Dehmel to ask him for a contribution to *Simplicissimus* he went out of his way to remark that the publication of such stories as "Gerächt" must be regarded as evidence that "the periodical is in desperate straits."[7] His opinion on this remained fixed; the story was not reprinted during his lifetime and was included in his collected works only after his death.

"Gerächt" is indeed of greater biographical than literary interest. In it for the first time appears a young woman of Russian background and emancipated ideas with whom a young man has a platonic relationship. The Dunya Stegemann of "Gerächt" was to be reincarnated as the Lisaveta Ivanovna of *Tonio Kröger*. "Gerächt" may in fact serve as a clue that Tonio's Lisaveta means more to him than a kindly listener, that the relationship described in the novella could have taken a more serious turn. In his autobiographical lecture "On Myself" Thomas Mann made a point of remarking that Tonio's Russian friend Lisaveta was "entirely fictional."[8] Perhaps so—yet the liberated Russian or Russo-German woman occupied a singularly important place in Mann's psychic life. Any number of women in turn-of-the-century Munich could have served as models for Dunya or Lisaveta. All we know, however, is that "Gerächt" and *Tonio Kröger* were conceived almost simultaneously. For the key event that gave rise to *Tonio Kröger* actually happened to Thomas Mann during the summer of 1899.

In September Mann set out to pay his first visit to Lübeck since his departure five years earlier—by no means the thirteen years mentioned in *Tonio Kröger*. But there was psychological truth in the longer interval given in the novella. He had left Lübeck as a schoolboy; he returned a grown man who chose to arrive incognito. Although he had many relatives in the city who would have welcomed him, he put up at the Hotel Stadt Hamburg. Perhaps his newly refurbished wardrobe was a shade too fashionable, or perhaps he walked about with a furtive air prompted by the fear of meeting people who might recognize him. At any rate, the police, on the lookout for a certain confidence man, briefly detained and interrogated him in the manner unforgettably described in *Tonio Kröger*. This farce of mistaken identity confirmed, if it did not implant, that notion of the artist as swindler that Thomas Mann later so fruitfully elaborated.

For Mann himself in later years, and for his critics as well, the interest of this first return to the city of his birth lay in the famous novella that emerged from the experience. But there was an aspect of the native's return that has been overlooked. He had been so eager for this trip to Lübeck that he turned down an earlier invitation from Kurt Martens to visit him at his cottage in Gmund. The reason may well have lain in a need to see once more the "Buddenbrook house," the home of his grandparents at Mengstrasse 4. In the writing of *Buddenbrooks* he had at this time arrived at the death of Senator Buddenbrook's mother and the subsequent sale of the old house. It may be that he wanted to pay a visit to the house on Mengstrasse (such a visit is actually described in *Tonio Kröger*) in order to see for himself the room in which he wished to place Elizabeth Buddenbrook, née Kröger, upon her bier. To write of selling the Buddenbrook house was in a sense re-enacting the actual sale of his grandparents' home, with himself in the role of his father. That was maturity, to be sure—an early maturity at the age of twenty-four—but it was also painful. He now needed to see through Tony Buddenbrook's aging eyes the home where he had played as a child, so that he could render her grief at losing her childhood home. Ultimately he decided to repress most of the outward signs of her emotion, in keeping with the prevailingly cool tone of the novel. After her first tears Tony agrees to be "sensible," and reveals her anguish only by the high valuation she places on the house: "A hundred thousand marks would be the least, wouldn't it, Tom?"[9] In the novella, written three years later and far more lyrical in tone and intent, Tonio Kröger is permitted to express freely his estrangement from the past and his nostalgia for it.

From Lübeck Mann went on to Copenhagen, and then to the seaside resort of Aalsgard—"near Elsinore,"[10] he later noted, as if he wished to suggest a connection between Tonio and Hamlet. Though he stayed less than a week in Aalsgard, that was time enough for him to witness a dance at the hotel. Dance and near-arrest coalesced; while he read Goncharov's *Oblomov*, "unbeknownst to myself I sketched out *Tonio Kröger*."[11] In a sense he was already looking beyond *Buddenbrooks*—in part, as he admitted, because he was weary of the long toil on the novel. But perhaps he was also seeking a way to evade its foreordained conclusion. Hanno Buddenbrook was doomed; that had been the premise with which the novel began. But to the degree that Hanno stood for his creator, that creator must find a way to resurrect him from his premature grave and show him entering the profession that Thomas Mann had actually chosen. For the author had innate toughness; he had qualities of perseverance and endurance he had denied to his surrogate. *Tonio Kröger*—the name came straight out of the *Buddenbrooks* complex—would provide the continuance that fiction denied but life permitted. The point would have been emphasized if Thomas Mann had carried out his original intention and given the novella "the ugly but thrilling title *Literature.*"[12]

Shortly after his return home from his northern vacation Mann had a reading experience that he was to make much of, perhaps too much. At a bookseller's sale he had at one time bought the Brockhaus edition of the works of Arthur Schopenhauer. The volumes stood on his shelves for a long time, their pages uncut. But one day in the fall of 1899 he fell to reading them "as one probably reads only once in a lifetime."[13] He later spoke of this as a "tremendous spiritual experience—I mean the experience of Schopenhauer, whose work Thomas Buddenbrook reads toward the end of his life and as a result of which he is made ripe for death."[14] Mann himself became, or thought he became, "a disciple of Schopenhauer" who "did not love the optimistic emphasis on progress."[15]

The section of *Buddenbrooks* that was written under the immediate impact of this reading was Chapter 5 of Part Ten. It runs to unusual length compared to the staccato, short-winded chapters characteristic of the novel. Obviously this chapter was written in one breath, out of a single impulse. At the beginning of Chapter 5 Thomas Buddenbrook feels that both his wife and his life are slipping from him—his wife alienated by a musical lieutenant, his life sapped by the effort of meeting the ordinary demands of his position, and by a deeply hidden guilt. He begins to be conscious of his imminent end, to think about making arrangements before it is too late. And in such a mood he takes up a book he bought a long time ago and sits in the garden reading for a full four hours "the second part only of a famous metaphysical system"[16]—Arthur Schopenhauer's *The World as Will and Idea.*

He did not understand it all. Principles and premises remained unclear, and his mind, unpracticed in such reading, was not able to follow certain trains of thought. But the very alternation of light and darkness, of dull incomprehension and sudden perception, thrilled him, and the hours vanished without his looking up from his book or even changing his position in his chair.[17]

Recalling his first reading of the philosopher in after years, and probably making a bit of a legend of it, Thomas Mann declared that he had ascribed to Thomas Buddenbrook his own sense of having experienced a revelation. Yet it is quite clear from his own account that he too "did not understand it all." He was not, and never would be, a professional philosopher. He had not read Kant, without whom, as Schopenhauer repeatedly warns his readers, an understanding of the philosophy of the will was impossible. Even Mann's "days and nights" of "metaphysical intoxication"[18] are probably phrases that rather deliberately stylize and exaggerate the experience. In that early bout of excitement in the autumn of 1899 Thomas Mann may have read little more than he permitted Thomas Buddenbrook to read, and like his character he was stirred chiefly by the chapter "On Death and Its Relation to the Indestructibility of Our Essence."[19]

Mann's preoccupation with death, and his feeling that death rightly constituted one of the fundamental subjects of literature, certainly did not derive from any philosopher. It was pre-existent in Thomas Mann, as his earliest stories show—those written before his reading of Schopenhauer. It was rooted in the very nature of a family novel such as he was writing; it sprang from the experience of a boy who in adolescence lost a strong father; it had literary antecedents in such novels as *Renée Mauperin* and the works of the German Romantics; and above all it was an essential aspect of the zeitgeist. But Schopenhauer's pessimistic view that it would be better never to have been born, and that the will to live perpetually seeks to cancel out the results of its own blind strivings, helped to form that zeitgeist. Mann did not have to have read Schopenhauer to be a Schopenhauerian; he was one before he read him, as he remarked. But those days or hours in the autumn of 1899 that he spent stretched out on the sofa in his bachelor apartment (not seated in the garden pavilion like Senator Buddenbrook), cutting pages and passionately reading the gloomy misogynist's perversely soaring prose, did have a temporary impact. The reading confirmed the skepticism with which he already regarded life. It somewhat accentuated the

half-love for easeful death that he later ascribed to some of his characters. It contributed to a flirtation with the idea of suicide. This was
a tendency whose perils he recognized, in himself and in others.
Germans were all too susceptible to it.

In later life Thomas Mann repeatedly paid tribute to Schopenhauer as one of the major sources of his approach to the world, as a
nourisher of his thinking and his emotional life. He usually linked
Schopenhauer with Goethe, Wagner, and Nietzsche as formative
geniuses. Yet compared to his enthusiasm for the latter three, his
appreciations of Schopenhauer are rather cool in tone. "He really
was a tremendous writer and his system remains an admirable work
of art. . . . He anticipated Freud before Nietzsche, who always remained his disciple."[20] So Mann commented toward the end of his
life when a defense of Schopenhauer seemed called for. Yet in the
one major essay he devoted to Schopenhauer his explication of the
philosopher consists of little more than direct paraphrase or quotation. In the case of Schopenhauer there is little evidence in Mann's
works of that abundance of reference and cross-reference which
testifies to the fructifying influence of the trinity who summed up
German culture for him. Nietzsche may have been Schopenhauer's
disciple, but it was Nietzsche whom Thomas Mann loved. For Schopenhauer he seems to have felt respect and that affection one reserves for the foibles of youth. The metaphysics, the mysticism, and
the pessimism that attracted him as a young man struck him as more
questionable while he was wrestling with the German soul during
the writing of *Doctor Faustus*. "Poor fellow," he wrote of Schopenhauer in 1946, "much good he did humanity with his particular
song of life."[21]

It is not altogether surprising that at this period he was rather
preoccupied with death. The blame should not be laid wholly at
Schopenhauer's door. He was now facing the necessity (though one
long foreseen) of ending *Buddenbrooks* on the highly symbolic note
of three different types of death in rapid succession: death in extreme
old age, in middle life, and in youth (the Frau Consul, Senator
Thomas, Hanno). Changes in his own life, in his family, in his
career, were impending. And change, like travel, strengthened an
awareness of mortality that was never far from his thoughts.

At the beginning of the year 1900 he received his statement from
S. Fischer, mentioned earlier, and learned that his first book, *Der*

kleine Herr Friedemann, had sold just over four hundred copies. That hardly seemed to augur well for *Buddenbrooks*. At the end of June he commented wryly in a letter to a relatively new friend, Paul Ehrenberg: "My novel . . . will probably be finished next month, whereupon I shall probably have to throw it into my publisher's maw for a song. Money and mass applause are not to be won with such books; but even if it should again turn out to be only a small literary success, I'll be proud and grateful."[22]

His prediction of the literary future of the book was certainly faulty, but he was right about the date of completion—which suggests that by now, after his three years of laboring on the novel, he was thoroughly in command of the creative process. On July 18 he informed his old friend Grautoff: "Today I wrote the last line of my novel."[23]

The completion of *Buddenbrooks* might have left him at loose ends for a while—but for another major change in his circumstances. The long-suspended threat of army service at last became a reality on his twenty-fifth birthday, June 6, 1900. He had previously been twice rejected on medical grounds (narrow chest, nervous heart), and indeed it is difficult to see what the military expected to do with this slight young man who had been unable to perform the simple gymnastic exercises required in a German secondary school. Perhaps the international situation was regarded as graver—at the beginning of the year German suspicions of England flared when the British confiscated a number of German ships, allegedly for carrying contraband to the Boers. Or perhaps Mann's passion for bicycling and third-floor apartments had physically strengthened him more than he knew. At any rate "their lordships of the Higher Reserve Commission . . . classified me as fit for all branches of the services, whence it follows that on October 1, to the consternation of the enemies of the Fatherland, I shall shoulder a gun."[24]

His friend Kurt Martens regarded the drafting of Thomas Mann as a cultural atrocity on the part of the military authorities. But Thomas himself was not so certain. His ambivalence is mirrored in the letters he wrote at the time. "I am completely acquiescent (believe it or not). . . . Only in this way can those nervous crotchets of mine be exorcised." That was the affirmative mood—to be promptly corrected by a prediction that in fact proved quite accurate: "Of course it is possible that I won't be able to stand up to it, and that they will have to release me again after a few weeks. . . ." To which he added, his mood again reversing: "But I hope for the best."[25]

Certainly Thomas Mann had never looked forward to anything resembling a military career. He had doggedly stayed on in Gymnasium until he completed *Sekunda* because that was the legal requirement for obtaining the One-Year-Volunteer's certificate—the great loophole in the German system of universal military service. Inherited from the Prussian army of the Napoleonic era, the system of One-Year Volunteers was extended to the entire German Reich after the unification of Germany in 1871. It provided that young men of *Bildung* (education or culture) who were able to supply their own rations, uniforms, and equipment at their own expense, would be conscripted for only one year, with the prospect of promotion into the officer class if they wished to continue on in military service. In other words, those who could afford secondary education and the cost of their own keep for an entire year could avoid the otherwise mandatory three years of military service followed by more years in the reserve army.

This frankly class-oriented system actually represented a step toward rather than away from democracy. It was fairer than the previous systems of conscription, prevalent even in the United States during the Civil War, which permitted the well-to-do to pay for a substitute. There were even alleviations built into the German system, so that poor youths who qualified educationally could obtain a kind of military scholarship; they would not be obligated to pay for their own maintenance. One of the great advantages of the system, its advocates believed, was that it persuaded young men to stay in school longer and work harder at their lessons. Certainly it had the former effect on Thomas Mann; he would surely have dropped out of the Katharineum before reaching second form (or, in American terms, the junior class) had it not been for dread of that three-year term of compulsory military service.

Having been found fit this time, he was scheduled to begin his military service on October 1, 1900. Meanwhile there were the revisions of *Buddenbrooks* to attend to. He expected these to take his full energies throughout the summer: "I see it coming that whole chapters at the beginning, which now strike me as repulsively stupid, will have to be reworked."[26] But his recollection had played him false; the chapters were not so bad after all. Less than a month after the last lines were written he was ready to send the whole bulky manuscript to S. Fischer in Berlin. He had intended to recopy it, for it was written on both sides of the page in his curiously sloping and sometimes difficult Gothic script. But he could not face the labor; besides, the book looked shorter this way. Nevertheless, this was the only copy of the work on which he had so long labored —a later age would marvel at his confidence in the postal system. He wrote "manuscript" on the wrapper and insured the parcel for 1,000 marks. "The post office clerk smiled."[27] The same day, August 13, 1900, he wrote to Grautoff to announce the event: "I have just burned myself fearfully with wax while sealing my novel. Apparently I am capable of writing such a book, but sending it to Berlin is an art in itself."[28]

Two weeks later he gave himself a severe psychological burn at his first meeting with his publisher. Samuel Fischer was on vacation, and the letter that Mann sent along with the manuscript was forwarded to him. He responded promptly that he was looking forward to reading the novel, and meanwhile would be happy to make the author's acquaintance and if possible spend a few days with him. Would Mann care to join him and their mutual friend Arthur Holitscher in the Tyrol? Or if that was not practicable, could they meet in Munich? Fischer would be passing through that city at the end of the month.

Holitscher was something of a busybody, with a rather inflated sense of his own importance. Although he had spoken favorably of *Buddenbrooks* to Fischer, Thomas Mann had little inclination to spend a few days with Fischer as Holitscher's quasi-protégé. Moreover, for reasons having to do with his new friendship with Paul Ehrenberg, his self-confidence was at a low ebb. He believed he made a poor impression in person; he dreaded several days in the company of the awesome head of S. Fischer Verlag. And so it was arranged that he would meet the Fischers in Munich and dine with them on August 29. Given his nervousness, it is scarcely surprising that the occasion went off "as inconsequentially as possible,"[29] and that nothing definite came of it. He would have to write to Fischer, he told Grautoff, and try to make his literary personality come to the fore once again in his publisher's imagination, dispelling the unfortunate impression of his physical and social being.

Such was the inauspicious beginning of one of the longest and most fruitful associations between author and publisher in the history of letters. One would have expected an instant affinity between Thomas Mann and this man with a seemingly infallible instinct for greatness, whose roster of major writers included Ibsen, Hauptmann, Hofmannsthal, Schnitzler, Wassermann, Hesse, and George Bernard Shaw. Thomas Mann later spoke of him as one of those who, like Jacob, were blessed in the Lord. But along with the blessing went a "religiously colored melancholia, so that he had to struggle against moods of depression."[30] It is clear that the dinner must have been a rather tense affair; but perhaps that was due to a publisher's normal caution. Here Fischer was meeting a man startlingly young, for all his rather distinguished appearance, who had just completed an enormously long novel, and whose earlier book had sold hardly at all. Until he had a chance to read the novel, Fischer could scarcely be expected to show warmth and enthusiasm. But that was precisely the response for which the author had hoped, and he attributed its absence to his own unattractive personality. Hardly surprising that after the meeting Thomas Mann could only wonder: "What will become of my novel—that is the ominous problem."[31]

F O R the moment the even more ominous problem of his military service obtruded. His efforts to volunteer for the field artillery ("I have no objection to riding and shooting")[32] proved fruitless; that branch of the service had no openings. His choice was restricted to the Guards Infantry Regiment, which at least had the merit of being conveniently garrisoned in Türkenstrasse. But Martens had warned him against the gymnastics associated with infantry training.

There was no way out, however; and since he would have to face it, Mann ordered a resplendent blue dress uniform. Its red collar with silver strips, its gleaming buttons and shiny black belt would let him look the soldier and cut a dashing figure at his sister Julia's wedding. That notable family event took place on October 9, just one week after he became a recruit in the Guards Regiment.

With her marriage to the banker Josef Löhr, Lula was the first among the five Mann children to wed; and the wedding was accordingly celebrated with great pomp. The reception at the Hotel Vier Jahreszeiten was a glittering occasion, enlivened by ten-year-old

Viktor Mann's becoming quite tipsy. Thomas did not appear, as he had jokingly threatened, as a "romantically costumed and brutalized mercenary who steals the silver . . . , drinks immoderately, spits on the floor. . . ."[33] He thought well of Löhr, who at thirty-eight was already director of the Bavarian Bank of Commerce. Lula, who was twenty-three—an age at which, in those days, girls began to fear they would never find a husband—did not seem to be madly in love with her fiancé. But her brother observed that Jof, as the family called him, was a "good, kind, cultivated person" and that "with all due respect for 'love,' one does get further without it."[34] Not everyone shared that view. His friend Paul Ehrenberg, the painter, had implored Lula to reject Löhr's suit—Ehrenberg was attracted to both Mann sisters. Carla scornfully described Löhr as a man who always wore tails and a London top hat. Heinrich detested Löhr and condemned Lula for choosing this husband; he did not come to the wedding, and soon Lula and he quarreled. Thereafter Heinrich centered all his brotherly affection upon Carla. These intimate familial complications were not without their effect upon Thomas Mann's fiction; but forty-five years were to pass before he felt free to make full use of the material.

The Guards Regiment was something else besides an opportunity to wear a fine blue uniform. Just as Thomas had feared, it was endless drill in the deadly sport of Prussian goose-stepping. The willing spirit with which he had viewed the prospect of a year in the army was quickly dissipated. Indeed, how could he, the born outcast, observer, outsider, have endured the rough tone and enforced companionship of a barracks? The shouting, the appalling waste of time, the insistence on "iron snappiness,"[35] were sheer torture to him. The antiauthoritarian streak in his nature, which had turned him into a rebel in school, made him incapable of meeting the requirements of military service. Indeed, he saw the whole thing as school all over again. He found the life he was being forced to lead "ridiculous and abominable,"[36] and almost immediately began to speculate on ways to obtain his release.

After a little drill in "that ideal and masculine gait known as parade marching,"[37] he developed tenonitis—inflammation of the tendon of the heel. The pain became so extreme that he was sent "to the infirmary, then to the hospital; and after I had lain for two weeks with a water-glass poultice, I had dropped too far behind in the training—just as it had been in school."[38] The army doctors were skeptical; if they recognized his pain, they also thought him determined to exaggerate it, and they were right. At the time he denounced the doctors as incompetent for having overlooked his flat feet when they gave him his original physical examination. But later he called their accepting him as fit "a psychological mistake"[39]—a curious and revealing phrase. In fact he appears not to have had flat feet at all—at any rate, no such defect showed in a print of his ailing foot made on charcoaled paper.

A weary cycle began: from hospital back to infirmary back to garrison, and after a few steps of drill back to the infirmary. The latter struck him as the most unhealthful and abhorrent place he had ever seen, and he became desperate with the desire to escape. Clearly, strings would have to be pulled, private connections enlisted; and so he consulted his mother's doctor, Hofrat May. In title-mad Germany a Hofrat automatically commanded respect; and fortunately Hofrat May knew the chief medical officer of the regiment. The doctor might be an "ambitious ass,"[40] but he procured Thomas Mann's discharge before Christmas. It was, Mann admitted a dozen years later, a "most amusing example of corruption."[41]

Brief though it was, that army experience found its way into literature in a variety of ways. Heinrich Mann, who seems to have been exempted readily from military service, requested and drew upon his brother's recollections when he was writing his novel *Der Untertan*. Thomas himself intended to save the general atmosphere of the army ("the sensation of being hopelessly cut off from the civilized world, subject to a terrible, overpowering external pressure")[42] for the penitentiary episode in *The Confessions of Felix Krull, Confidence Man*. But that episode was never to be written; and what he ultimately created in *Felix Krull* was a magnificent alternative: an extension into the parodistic and comic realm of what must be the conscript's universal fantasy—how to deceive the draft board. The priceless scene of Felix Krull's simulating "epileptoid" symptoms possibly goes back to the reveries of an unhappy One-Year Volunteer as he sat cleaning his rifle in barracks while whistling a melody from *Tristan*.

In one of his letters to Heinrich, Thomas admitted that he had reported sick even when his foot did not hurt too much, in order to force the authorities to release him. In a jaunty autobiographical fragment entitled "In the Mirror," written in 1907, he acknowledged that "the body is to a certain degree subject to the mind and if there had been the slightest liking for the business within me, the ailment probably could have been overcome."[43] Yet he reacted with extreme indignation when Herr Tesdorpf, the administrator of the Mann estate who kept the whole family on such a short rein, wrote to Julia Mann suggesting that her son had freed himself from military service by malingering. Thomas promptly fired off a letter so angry and spiteful that "the old donkey is now threatening to sue."[44] The trivial contretemps suggests a certain self-righteousness and blindness about the way his behavior might look to the outside world. That inability to see himself as others saw him was to afflict him in increasing measure as time passed. It was strange, since in all other aspects of human psychology he was so penetrating. And in later years it cost him dearly, for he made enemies and could not grasp why.

Little or no guilt seems to have attended his half-deliberate escape from army service. Creative artists, *Dichter*, had no business marching in rank and file; an oversensitive patrician senator's son obviously must be spared the all too democratic life of the barracks. These assumptions suffered something of a shock after the outbreak of the First World War, when poets in their fifties (and Thomas Mann was then forty) like Richard Dehmel went to the front. At that time a certain embarrassment appeared in Mann's correspondence with men serving in the army, such as Dehmel and Paul Amann. He began rather lamely to speak of doing war service with his pen, a phrase that must have brought wry smiles to the lips of those who read it in the trenches. But what guilt feelings he had would not be explicitly admitted until, nearly half a century later, he came to the writing of Chapter 30 of *Doctor Faustus*.

It is of coincidental interest that a writer who was later to be his friend, Hermann Hesse, came up for military service that same year, within a month of Mann, and in July 1900 was rejected because of nearsightedness.

THE ordeal of barracks, infirmary, and hospital was all the harder to bear because of uncertainty over the fate of *Buddenbrooks*. Two and a half months had passed without a word from Samuel Fischer. Had he made such a poor showing at that wretched dinner with the publisher? He brooded over that. Would the novel be left on his hands? The waiting was all the more agonizing because he felt cut off from the literary world.

The letter that finally came from Fischer was almost as bad as a rejection. Fischer thought the book too long. He did not believe that in this day and age many people would find time and concentration to read a novel of nearly sixty-five signatures. What was more—and this was the closest Fischer came to direct criticism—there was perhaps too much lingering over matters of secondary importance. In short, could the author see his way clear to cutting the novel by about half?

A critical moment. Thomas Mann afterward took pleasure in recalling it, retelling it, stylizing it. Lying on his back in the army hospital, he courageously answered Fischer that "large size was an essential characteristic of the book and that cutting it would botch the whole design."[45] Length did not necessarily imply tedium, he argued. But although he flatly refused to cut, he took a conciliatory and resigned tone on all business matters. He would sign any kind of contract that at least preserved appearances, for he did not want it to look as if he were simply giving away the labors of three years. To his brother he confided that he had finished the novel by the utmost exertion of will and did not have the strength to work on it again. He wanted to turn to other things. But if *Buddenbrooks* went unpublished, further writing would come hard.

There was a special edge to his concern over the fate of his novel, for Heinrich had just published his *Im Schlaraffenland*. That short, sparkling satire of Berlin literary and social life was being widely advertised by its publisher, Albert Langen—as Thomas reported to Heinrich the moment he was released from the army. Heinrich, who was still under treatment at Dr. von Hartungen's sanatorium in Riva, was urging Thomas to join him in Italy once again. We do not have the earlier letters, but evidently the brothers had discussed this possibility for some time. Thomas was eager to visit Florence. He already had in mind a Renaissance drama dealing with Lorenzo and Savonarola, provisionally entitled *The King of Florence*. In addition, ideas for all sorts of stories were running through his head, and he thought it quite possible that he would have a volume of tales ready before the drama on which he had set his heart.

T H E fate of *Buddenbrooks* was not settled until the beginning of February. Then, at last, "a letter from S. Fischer blew in telling me that come spring he wanted, first, to bring out a second small volume of my stories and then, in October, *Buddenbrooks*, uncut, probably in three volumes. I shall have my picture taken, right hand tucked into the vest of my dinner jacket, the left resting on the three volumes."[46]

The contract came somewhat later. It offered the impressive royalty of 20 percent of the retail price; but Thomas Mann was somewhat upset to find that no advance was to be paid. He was feeling like "a church mouse"[47] because his mother had subtracted taxes from his quarter's income; and in addition he rather urgently wanted money for his trip to Florence. The quarterly 160 or 180 marks had been all very well for the life of an impecunious student living in Italy; and at home in Germany his earnings from the editor's job at *Simplicissimus* and the sale of an occasional short story had provided a margin of comfort. But he had quit the magazine when he entered military service, and he had no intention of returning to it. As a writer, he wanted to be able to live from his writing. Fischer's conditions provided no immediate cash: "I shall see nothing at all until September 1902. . . . If the edition sells out . . . I shall be receiving 2,000, for the bookstore price will probably have to be around 10 marks. But who is to say that even as many as one hundred copies will be sold."[48]

But at least there would be publication, and there was some assurance in the publisher's insisting on an option on his future production. This good news, combined with a beneficent if curious upturn in his personal life, brought him out of the nearly suicidal depression into which he had plunged during the earlier part of the winter.

9

Friendship

When spring comes, I shall have behind me a terribly turbulent winter. Really dreadful depressions with quite serious plans for self-elimination have alternated with an indescribable, pure, and unexpected inner joy, with experiences that cannot be told and the mere hint of which would naturally sound like boasting. But these highly unliterary, very simple and vital experiences have proved one thing to me: that there is something sincere, warm, and good in me after all, and not just "irony"; that after all everything in me is not blasted, overrefined, and corroded by the accursed scribbling. Ah, literature is death! I shall never understand how anyone can be dominated by it *without* bitterly hating it. Its ultimate and best lesson is this: to see death as a way of achieving its antithesis, *life*. I dread the day, and it is not far off, when I shall again be shut up alone with my work, and I fear that the egotistic inner desiccation and overrefinement will then make rapid progress.[1]

S O T H O M A S M A N N wrote to Heinrich in the middle of February 1901; and the exact point at which warmth and sincerity turn into posturing, phrasemaking, and "accursed scribbling" can be heard in the very rhythms of the prose. What follows the semicolon after "irony" is already literature rather than simple confession. The elder brother, who had been accustomed since their father's death to acting somewhat *in loco parentis*, responded at once to the hint about suicide, and to Thomas's allusion, in his next letter, to the fate of Hanno Buddenbrook: "At bottom I want nothing better for myself than a respectable case of typhoid fever."[2] Heinrich was in the Tyrol at the time, staying at Dr. von Hartungen's sanatorium in Riva and hoping to meet Thomas in Italy before too long. His anxious reply is lost; from Thomas's next letter it is clear that Heinrich begged his brother not to commit any "follies." Perhaps he offered to come to Munich, for Thomas reassures him: "You can leave for Italy without the slightest worry."[3]

What was the cause of the emotional turmoil that can be traced in the notebooks as well as the letters of this winter, and that continued, though with diminishing intensity, for another two years? Undoubtedly Thomas was suffering from the aftershock of his army experience. He had endured the physical pain with a good deal of stoicism; but the toll that barracks and infirmary had taken on his nerves is betrayed by his remark to Heinrich that he did not know whether, given his obsession with death, he "could go through the next bout of military service."[4] He also was having difficulty with his writing, in particular with *Tonio Kröger*. He was feeling a certain jealousy of Heinrich's apparent success, which came out against his will even as he congratulated Heinrich on the translation into French of his *Im Schlaraffenland:* "In a word, you are flourishing while at the moment I am going to pieces."[5]

But none of these matters accounted for the intensity of his emotional state, for the rapid shifts from depression to exaltation, for his "excessive suffering" followed by "profoundly joyful astonishment."[6] This whole emotional complex was connected with Paul Ehrenberg, whom Thomas had met some time toward the end of 1899. Paul Ehrenberg and his younger brother, Carl, were the sons of a Dresden painter and art professor at the academy in that city. Their mother died while they were still young; they grew up as more or less adopted brothers of Hilde and Lilli Distel, who had connections in Lübeck and were distantly related to the Manns. Hilde Distel was a friend of Lula Mann, and it was through his sister that Thomas Mann met first Paul and later Carl Ehrenberg. Hilde Distel also enjoys an honorable place in the footnotes to literature, for it was to her that Thomas Mann addressed a request for the details of "a wonderfully melancholic love story"[7] that he was to incorporate into *Doctor Faustus* more than forty years later. She became a singer.

Music, in fact, provided the binding energy that held this coterie of young people together. Paul Ehrenberg had become a painter like his father, and was in Munich to study at the academy there. He soon won a considerable reputation as a portraitist, but he was also an excellent violinist and for a time wavered between painting and music. His brother, Carl, pursued a distinguished career as a conductor, professor of music, and composer. Under the Ehrenbergs' influence Thomas, who had neglected his violin during the past few years, began to practice again. He played trios with Paul and Carl; and as a counterbalance to too much masculine company, perhaps, he also played with a young woman. She was Ilse Martens, sister of that blond schoolmate who reappears in his works in various guises. Paul Ehrenberg bore a rather striking physical resemblance to Armin Martens, that "beloved friend who under the name of Hans Hansen in *Tonio Kröger* acquired a certain symbolic life, though in person he later took to drink and came to a sad end in Africa."[8] Ilse was another member of what almost amounted to a colony of Lübeckers in Munich. She was a close friend of Lula Mann and therefore in and out of the Mann household a good deal.

With the Ehrenbergs Thomas Mann enjoyed the pastimes of youth—apparently for the first time since his school days with the young aristocrats of Professor Timpe's boardinghouse. Music took first place, of course, but the three young men also went cycling, gave suppers for each other, went together to the many festivals that the Schwabing artists provided. The lively Ehrenbergs coaxed and prodded the rather stiff, withdrawn young man into taking part in "ordinary" amusements. Fifty years later Thomas Mann remembered with gratitude the "cheerful patience" they showed to him, who had been so shy and difficult to get along with. He recalled that Carl's bicycle had been dubbed "the cow" because its underside was always filthy, and that after coffee the three young men would throw stones at empty beer bottles. "With you two I could be high-spirited."[9]

There was no question of standoffishness with either Paul or Carl; from the first he addressed them as *du*. They took him out of himself. There was also that element of reciprocal education that so often characterizes the friendships of young men. Thomas tried to interest Paul in Nietzsche, as Tonio Kröger tries to interest Hans Hansen in Schiller. And he was willing to learn about painting from Paul. When Paul was away from Munich, Thomas wrote to him at length about what was going on at the galleries. He went so far as to work up elaborate descriptions of individual paintings—descriptions that were more literary exercise than friendly communication.

Here, perhaps, lay the contradiction of which he was well aware. All along, the literary impulse seems to have warred with his craving for simple experience. Even as his relationship with Paul assumed what he was soon calling "a character of somewhat excessive suffering,"[10] he was filling notebooks with bits of dialogue, fragments of psychological analysis, elements of plot, names—with, in short, the raw materials for a novel to be entitled *Die Geliebten* (not, be it noted, *The Lovers*, but *The Loved*). *Die Geliebten* was ultimately abandoned, although Thomas Mann later thriftily tucked most of the elements of the unwritten story into his other works.

Geliebt was the adjective that Mann used in referring to Armin Martens. The question arises: Is the word to describe his feeling for Paul Ehrenberg to be *love*? The question arose right at the outset, and in writing to Heinrich Mann, Thomas made an effort to answer it:

> What is involved is not a love affair, at least not in the ordinary sense, but a friendship, a friendship—how amazing!—understood, reciprocated, and rewarded. . . . According to Grautoff, I am simply going through an adolescent infatuation; but that is putting it in his own terms. My nervous constitution and philosophical inclination have incredibly complicated the affair; it has a hundred aspects from the plainest to the spiritually wildest.[11]

What are we to make of this ambiguous confession? What, especially, are we to make of it in conjunction with the recurrent allusions to homoerotic relationships in the works of Thomas Mann? Certainly there was no suggestion of anything remotely resembling a physical relationship between these two young men. Paul Ehrenberg later married. Thomas Mann wrote of himself in 1920: "I am a family founder and a father by instinct and conviction. I love my children, deepest of all a little girl who very much resembles my wife—to a point that a Frenchman would call idolatry."[12] With friends like Kurt Martens, Mann could discuss the whole question of homoeroticism with no embarrassment or suggestion of personal involvement. And the ease with which he introduced the theme into his writing, the candor with which he confessed his early attachments to Armin or Paul, suggests that he felt himself firmly rooted in heterosexuality. But he saw no "effeminacy" in attraction to the same sex, and he had a notion that homoeroticism, although neutral in matters of culture, was nevertheless peculiarly related to *Geist*, to the things that belonged properly to the realm of mind.

Many years later he wrote of *Death in Venice:* "Passion as confusion and as a stripping of dignity was really the subject of my tale."[13] The confusion applied not only to the nature of the emotion but also to the sex of the object; and here we discover a pattern that was apparently fixed early in Thomas Mann's boyhood. In the fictional works the pattern is exemplified again and again. Tonio Kröger's attachment to Hans Hansen is shortly afterward transmuted into his love for Ingeborg Holm—although his absorption in her scarcely betters the sexual confusion; on the contrary, it earns him only the dancing master's insult, "Fräulein Kröger." Hans Castorp's memories of Pribislav Hippe are very quickly diverted into his infatuation with Clavdia Chauchat, and he cannot even say which is cause and which effect: "Is that why I am interested in her? Or was that why I felt so interested in him?"[14] Adrian Leverkühn's trip to Hungary, during which his intimacy and his relationship *"per du"* with Rudi Schwerdtfeger is established, is followed directly by his decision to marry Marie Godeau.

In these cases Thomas Mann was recording in his fiction, in disguised and transmuted but basically faithful form, what he consciously or unconsciously recognized as the patterns of his own life. He destroyed his early diaries in a solemn auto-da-fé that he reported to his friend Grautoff with a recommendation, perhaps not entirely disinterested, that Grautoff do the same. Consequently, we have tantalizing hints but few hard facts about Mann's adolescent years and young manhood. We do know of at least one other early episode of infatuation with a boy, because the letters to Grautoff allude to another schoolmate named Willri Timpe—Professor Timpe's son. That attachment was almost but not quite strong enough to make bearable his classes with Johann Carl Schramm, the gymnastics teacher at the Katharineum. Now in February 1901, writing to Grautoff of his urge to dedicate his new collection of stories to Paul Ehrenberg, Mann suddenly became aware of how his behavior must look to others: "It's crazy and ridiculous! I'm already writing nothing but 'he' and 'him'; all that's left is to write it in capital letters and draw a golden frame around it, and the 'Timpe' era will be resurrected in all its glory."[15] This passage is followed immediately by a cry to escape from these emotional straits, to get on with his plans for a drama about Savonarola and Lorenzo de' Medici: "If I only knew how things would turn out with Florence, with you, with my brother. Do everything you can to be able to travel in April!"[16]

Never for a moment was there any question of Paul Ehrenberg's accompanying him to Italy, where, amid a foreign scene, the constraints of ordinary life might have been lifted. Had there been a "real" homoerotic relationship, such a trip together would surely have been longed for. But on the contrary, when he thought of traveling companions, his mind turned above all to his brother, and if Heinrich was to be unavailable he would make do with Grautoff, or even Holitscher, whom he did not really like but who might be useful for literary purposes. He was already at work on *Tristan*.

The erotic pattern noted above had been operative in Munich, where the music-making with Paul Ehrenberg was balanced by duets with Ilse Martens. It was played out again almost as soon as Mann rather reluctantly left Munich, where Paul was painting his portrait, for Florence. There Heinrich had found—in consideration of his brother's limited funds—a "cinque-lire pension."[17] It was located on the Via Cavour; and there the two brothers encountered two sisters, Miss Edith and Miss Mary Smith. The pairs formed naturally, and communication was evidently no great problem. English had been one of Thomas's few good subjects at the Katharineum, and the girls were evidently cultivated, at any rate knew enough German to ask to read the books of the two young authors. The four played cards together, flirted, talked, and Thomas thought that Miss Mary could have stepped out of a painting by Botticelli. He was strongly attracted to her, and while Heinrich was away for a short time the two apparently talked seriously about marriage. At least that seems the plausible interpretation of a passage in a letter to Heinrich:

> Miss Edith and Miss Mary send their regards. The former would like to read your *Schlaraffenland*. She had been waiting, incomprehensibly, for you to offer it to her. Miss Mary had her birthday day before yesterday and I gave her a basket of candied fruit. She has been a true joy. But now I am becoming too melancholic for her taste, I think. *She is so very clever** and I am so stupid as always to love those who are *clever,** although in the long run I cannot keep up with them.[18]

In later life Thomas Mann seems to have wondered what became of Mary Smith, perhaps even hoped that despite the passage of thirty years she might write to him, as all the world was doing in the aftermath of his receiving the Nobel Prize. For in *A Sketch of My Life* he flung a wide net by devoting a whole paragraph to this affair of a few brief weeks:

> In a pension in Florence I had made friends with two of my tablemates, English sisters; the elder, who was dark, I found sympathetic, but the younger, who was blond, delightful. Mary, or Molly, returned my feelings, and there followed a tender relationship and talk of marriage. What held me back were certain misgivings; perhaps it was too soon to marry, perhaps the difference of nationality would be a bar. . . . At any rate, the friendship came to nothing.[19]

But a poignant memory lingered, and after his return to Munich he dedicated to her the short story "Gladius Dei," which he wrote that summer. Again he tried out his English; the dedication read: "To M. S. in remembrance of our days in Florence."[20] Altogether, a passion for dedicating had seized him during this period. It was a novelty to dedicate a short story; even more unusual, perhaps unprecedented, to dedicate sections of a novel. The early printed editions of *Buddenbrooks* bear dedications of Parts Three, Eight, and Nine

---

* In English in the original.

to his sister Julia, to his brother Heinrich, and to Paul Ehrenberg. In a letter to Paul he maintained that there was no special connection between the particular text and the individual, that the chapter was chosen only because Paul already knew that part of the book—which among other things included the quarrel between the two brothers, Christian and Thomas. A close reading of the parts in question leads to some interesting speculations on why these parts are associated with Julia, Heinrich, or Paul, but to no definite conclusions.

Miss Mary Smith had not exorcised the attachment to Paul. But Paul was away from Munich, the proofs of *Buddenbrooks* were arriving, and the young author was eager to finish *Tonio Kröger*. Since *Buddenbrooks* was being set from the original handwritten manuscript, "it was for me and the compositors a nasty piece of work."[21] The proofs were finished by early July, and Heinrich and Thomas decided to spend some weeks at the summer resort of Mitterbad, near Meran, where Doctor von Hartungen served as the *Kurarzt*. Thomas had been having digestive and gastric difficulties —perhaps the result of serious dental infections earlier in the spring —and felt the need of a cure. Anyhow, all his problems seemed to settle in his stomach, he commented whimsically.

On July 10, 1901, the brothers departed from Munich and arrived that evening in Bolzano (Bozen) in the Tyrol—"a picturesquely situated, hot little town that is full of tourists and therefore quite entertaining."[22] They spent the night there, and the next morning, after a short trip on the Meran local railroad, they stopped at Lana, a small station, from which they had a three-hour ride into the mountains on horseback. Mann reported: "I rode a kind of charger of fabulous build but with the temperament of a sloth and the whims of a donkey short on sleep."[23]

Dr. von Hartungen, who in later years had Franz Kafka under his care, strongly believed in the body's own curative powers. That summer was the only period recorded during which Thomas Mann participated in what might be called athletic activities. The good doctor insisted on morning gymnastics and some ten hours in the open air—the stimulating, aromatic air at a thousand meters. He also led his patients in mountain climbing, and promised that by the end of the summer they would tackle a glacier. Riding was probably not included in the program; it seems to have been a one-time affair of essential transportation, and Thomas Mann mentioned it only because Paul Ehrenberg was involved with horses, either riding them or painting them. And climbing, after all, was only a more strenuous form of his usual exercise, walking. Otherwise, his distaste for physical activities (except for cycling) seems to have prevailed; and it was with overwhelming relief that he heard he was finally finished with military life. He reported to Paul in the somewhat facetious tone he reserved for this friend: "I have not exactly been 'mustered out,' but the High Commission on Reserves has appointed me a militiaman. Therefore, if some day the Fatherland should be sorely in need, it will take me as its last resort. Until then I can continue to devote myself undisturbed to cultural tasks. I regard that as quite in order. Don't you?"[24]

Dr. von Hartungen did try to lure Thomas into a new form of physical exertion, rowing; but the "neurasthenic" writer seems to have spent much of his time lying back in the rowboat and reading while his "Lohengrin skiff"[25] drifted on the Lago di Garda. That was in Riva, in the late fall and early winter, when he went to the doctor's sanatorium for the formal cure. The intimate knowledge of sanatorium life—reinforced by a famous three-week stay in Davos —was to stand Thomas Mann in good stead many years later. But the story *Tristan*, whose locale is a sanatorium, was completed before his visit to Mitterbad—which suggests some unrecorded visit to Riva in earlier years, probably on his way to or from Italy in the late nineties. It is also possible that he was drawing on descriptions by Heinrich.

Tristan was Mann's first completed work since "The Way to the Churchyard," a short story he had written in the spring and summer of 1900 and dedicated to Holitscher. Hard to say whether this dedication was an apology in advance for what he meant "to do" with Holitscher in the near future or an expression of gratitude to Holitscher for interceding with Fischer on behalf of *Buddenbrooks*. Perhaps both. The short story was another "grotesque," tailored in the manner of *Simplicissimus* (where it appeared in September 1900). The jesting tone in which the writer comments on his own storytelling has a clear purpose: The reader is being warned not to take too seriously the painful fate of Lobgott Piepsam, whom life has beaten long before he meets the blond cyclist on the path to the cemetery. This story, almost unbearably cruel despite its humor, offered one more guise of Mann's consistent theme of "chandalaism"

—the state of being an outcast—and yet another confrontation of life with death. Piepsam's paroxysm of rage at the cyclist who "came on like Life itself"[26] resembles the fury of Tobias Mindernickel as he kills his helpless small dog.

In *Tristan* the same sardonic manner and the same antithesis of life and death are employed to make a point that had become central with Mann, though originally borrowed from Wagner and Nietzsche: the joining of death and eros in the *Liebestod*. He had already struck this note in the novel: when Hanno Buddenbrook wildly "improvises" on the piano before he comes down with typhoid fever. In fact, it is the "Liebestod" that Hanno plays; Mann offers his readers the clue by using almost exactly the same working to describe the music in *Buddenbrooks* and in *Tristan*.[27]

Was he appropriating the plot device from Heinrich, who had used it in a story entitled "Dr. Biebers Versuchung," written in 1898? That story is set in a sanatorium, and Dr. Antonius Bieber marks the crisis of the story by playing from *Tristan and Isolde* on the piano. The brothers kept an eye on each other's work, and the similarities in this case could scarcely have been accidental or a matter of unconscious recollection. The three-year interval seems too short for Thomas Mann to have forgotten his brother's tale. It would, of course, be futile to attempt to assign priorities in these matters. The brothers talked, they traded enthusiasms; and who can say whether some common boyhood experience underlay a given motif in their work? The same theme would be handled by each in a strikingly different way. *Tristan* was one more item in a continuing dialogue, one that for Heinrich still seemed in the nature of a pleasant conversation, while for Thomas it was an emotionally exhausting swing between rancor and remorse.

In many ways *Tristan* anticipated *The Magic Mountain*, though that novel was conceived more than a decade later. But in its technique and theme it remained very much in the orbit of *Buddenbrooks*, for which it served as one of those shorter pendants that Thomas Mann liked to write after his major works "as a relaxation from strain and a gesture of self-satisfaction at having brought to an end an arduous task."[28] There is the same method of short, numbered chapters, the same antithesis between artist and burgher, the same proposition that a family of sturdy businessmen "declines" into weakness and art. Herr Klöterjahn, the insensitive businessman in *Tristan*, comes from a commercial city on the Baltic coast which, though it goes unnamed, is clearly Lübeck. His lovely and ailing wife is a fine pianist who in her girlhood played duets with her father, even as did Gerda Buddenbrook. But the chief character in the story is the neurasthenic literary man, Detlev Spinell, who is at the sanatorium for some largely imaginary complaint. There is nothing imaginary about the tuberculosis of fragile Frau Klöterjahn, though her husband takes persistent comfort from the fact that it is the trachea that are affected, not the lungs. Spinell falls in love with the young woman. Model wife though she is, under the writer's influence she begins to take another view of herself and to feel vague stirrings of dissatisfaction with her married life. One afternoon the writer coaxes her into playing a piano arrangement of Wagner's *Tristan and Isolde*. Spinell listens with profound emotion. This is the nearest the two come to declaration and consummation. Soon afterward Frau Klöterjahn's condition worsens and her husband is summoned. Spinell writes a rash and impossible letter to the husband, denouncing him for his crudeness of soul and identifying him with the crudeness of life itself, "the everlasting antipodes and deadly enemy of beauty."[29] Whereupon Herr Klöterjahn comes to have it out with the writer, who, brave enough where the written word is concerned, makes a miserable showing vis-à-vis the angry husband. In the midst of their encounter, the patient has a severe hemorrhage and dies.

Though the sick young woman is drawn with utmost tenderness, the dominant figure is Detlev Spinell. The writer is described so carefully that he was immediately recognizable as the spit and image of Arthur Holitscher, who could not but feel that he had been cruelly ridiculed. Nevertheless, Mann's Flaubertian defense that there was more of himself than Holitscher in the portrait was honestly meant. *Tristan* parodies what Mann knew from self-insight to be the weaknesses of the artist's temperament and especially his own form of it. It is Mann who, like the preposterous Spinell, feels called upon "to explain, express, and make self-conscious"[30] all the unseeing, unknowing, uncomprehending life around him. It is Mann who feels menaced by the robust bourgeois spirit as personified by Herr Klöterjahn. It is Mann who spends his best energies polishing phrases and who cares more about his language's being quoted correctly than about the subject at hand. It is Mann who smiles engagingly at his antagonist and is ready to take back whatever he may have said to offend.

Yet there is still another identity lurking in the caricature of the literary man: that of Heinrich. To be sure, Detlev Spinell has a solitary book to his credit, whereas Heinrich was all too prolific. Heinrich had just dashed off his new novel, *Diana*, which he announced as the first of a trilogy. It was set in Italy and dealt with a high-spirited young woman, one Duchess of Assy, beautiful, gifted, a fighter in the cause of liberty, and ultimately a wanton. In choosing such a subject, Heinrich was carrying out his youthful dream of chronicling the *"haute vie."* But he was perhaps also replying to his brother's *Buddenbrooks*, whose characters by comparison might seem a plodding and middle-class lot. Thomas felt the need to even the score.

The allusions to Heinrich are fairly covert. We are told of Spinell's small, neat handwriting—Heinrich's handwriting was also small and neat. The name Spinell itself contains some hidden meanings. When, for example, the writer is first introduced, we are told that his name is "like some kind of mineral or precious stone."[31] There is indeed an oxide of magnesium and aluminum called Spinell in German. It has a red variety which resembles and is often found with the ruby. It is as if Mann were saying: This writer looks like, but is not, a precious stone. The name also has a vaguely Italian cast, so that Frau Klöterjahn asks whether the writer's name is Spinelli. She is corrected: "Spinell, not Spinelli, madame. No, he is not an Italian; he only comes from Lemberg [i.e., Lübeck], I believe."[32] The joke here is on Heinrich's Italian airs. The name might also carry associations with the Italian painter Spinello, whose frescoes Thomas might have seen on his recent visit to Florence. Spinello was not a painter of the first rank; it was generally agreed that his flamboyant conceptions were not matched by skill of execution. This was the very criticism Thomas would have leveled against Heinrich's writings, especially the latest manuscript, whose fevered scenes, rhapsodic descriptions, and torrent of esthetic judgments were bound to offend Thomas's taste. Lastly and more generally, Thomas pokes fun at his writer for his "esthetic" attitudinizing. This was the same fault Heinrich was guilty of, in his brother's eyes, in his whole relationship with reality.

Yet over and beyond these innuendos, the figure of Detlev Spinell is a grand comic creation, with, moreover, a good dash of nobility. Spinell may be ridiculous and ineffectual, but the portrait in the end is a magnanimous one. Nor would Thomas have long to suffer from the sense of being hopelessly outdistanced by his brother. While he was finishing *Tristan*, the proofs of his novel were arriving. And in October 1901, shortly after his return from Mitterbad, he at last held in his hands the two volumes of his *Buddenbrooks* (rather than the three and four volumes Fischer had at various times threatened). No photograph of him has survived with his right hand tucked into the vest of his dinner jacket and his left resting on the volumes, as in his comic vision of the successful author.[33] But he was soon to be one.

10

Fame

T HOMAS MANN'S painful uncertainty over the fate
of *Buddenbrooks* had lasted from the middle of August 1900
to the end of March 1901, when he at last received a draft
contract from Samuel Fischer. He had seen something of the first
(unfavorable) and the second (favorable) reader's reports to Fischer;
and the misunderstandings had taught him an important lesson. He
realized that his art could be too subtle, that the forms and masks
could conceal his intentions so thoroughly that they might not be
recognizable. If a highly intelligent reader like Fischer's editor
Moritz Heimann, a noted "finder and liberator of young talent,"[1]
could initially fail to see the quality of *Buddenbrooks*, it might be
both necessary and prudent to offer explanations. We will recall that
upon receiving Fischer's doubtful letter with its proposal that the
novel be cut in half, Mann had stood his ground, replying that
length did not necessarily imply tedium, and so on.[2] He must have

been surprised and pleased to find the publisher, in a letter of acceptance, echoing his words:

> Although as a consequence of reading the book at long intervals I do not have a wholly clear and sharp view of its outlines, I have been so strongly impressed by details that I can only congratulate you on your work. As soon as the book is printed I shall read it again to get out of it all that lies within this rich work. I have also realized now that the size of your book has necessarily resulted from the whole constitution of the work and the special nature of your talent, although as a publisher I am not exactly delighted with this unusual bulk.[3]

When the book was finally published at the end of 1901, Thomas Mann applied the lesson he had learned. Although he maintained that the book's prospects were dim, he at once set about guiding its fortunes. *"Habent sua fata libelli* [Books have their own destiny]," he was fond of quoting in later life; but he himself was scarcely ready to leave the reception of his books to fate. As an editor of *Simplicissimus* he had seen something of how reputations were made; if he needed more instruction, Heinrich's *Im Schlaraffenland* would have taught him much about the art of self-promotion. And although Heinrich might be too proud to apply what he knew, Thomas was not.

It was, then, not by chance that his friends Otto Grautoff and Kurt Martens were among the first reviewers of *Buddenbrooks*, or by chance that at this time he availed himself of whatever literary contacts he had. When, for instance, Richard Dehmel sent him an invitation to contribute to an anthology for children, Mann took occasion to inform the older writer of the publication of his novel and to flatter him: "I am very eager to hear your opinion of the book. You know, you really 'discovered' me. . . ."[4] To the submissive, only occasionally mutinous Grautoff, Mann frankly issued instructions, for he had a rather low opinion of his schoolmate's literary gifts.

Grautoff had nevertheless succeeded in escaping from the dreaded vocation of bookselling in which his father had gone bankrupt. Following in the footsteps of his brother Ferdinand, he broke into journalism, found a job on the magazine *Jugend*, the rival of *Sim-*

plicissimus, and by the time *Buddenbrooks* came out had attained the dignity of feature editor on the *Münchner Neueste Nachrichten*. In spite of the psychological battering that Thomas Mann's frank criticism of his writing and personality inflicted on him, he had remained a loyal friend who could be trusted to review the novel in the "right" way.

Grautoff was in Florence—"think of me occasionally in 'Fiorenza,' my sublime stage, the scene of my symbols,"[5] Mann wrote to him—so it was not possible to discuss the review with him orally. And by the time Grautoff returned, Mann had himself left for his overdue cure at Dr. Hartungen's Villa Cristoforo in Riva. To these circumstances we owe the good fortune of a letter to Grautoff requesting him, first of all, to take in hand personally the reviewing of Kurt Martens's book *Die Vollendung*. Mann actually did not think very well of it, but Martens had been obliging in all kinds of ways and would be reviewing *Buddenbrooks* for *Das literarische Echo*. "This is my first opportunity to repay him a little," Mann remarked to Grautoff. Then followed:

> A few more hints about *Buddenbrooks*. In *Der Lotse* [a Hamburg newspaper in which Grautoff also reviewed the novel] as well as in the *Neueste* please stress the *German* character of the book. Mention as two truly German ingredients . . . *music* and *philosophy*. Granted, the author . . . has not found his mentors in Germany. For certain parts of the book Dickens, for others the great Russians, may be named. But truly German in its whole mode (intellectual, social) and in the subject itself: in the relationship between the fathers and the sons in the different generations of the family (Hanno and the senator). Censure a little (if you will) the hopelessness and melancholy of the end. Say a certain *nihilistic* tendency can sometimes be detected in the author. But his affirmativeness and strength is his *humor*.[6]

The instructions—a more neutral word would hardly be justified— continue in this vein. Grautoff should speak of the book's very bulk as a sign of unusual artistic energy, of the *epic* tone, of the epic effect of the leitmotif, of Wagnerian influence, and so on. And Grautoff, in the review that was published in the *Münchner Neueste Nachrichten* a month later, dutifully rattled off the very phrases: "artistic energy . . . certain nihilistic tendency . . . highly original humor . . . musical and philosophical . . . Wagnerian . . .

epic . . . leitmotif . . . Dickensian influences in certain parts, in others Tolstoy, Dostoevsky, and Turgenev . . . truly German." He did rather well in tacking together the prescribed phrases into a plausible paragraph—although Thomas Mann must have winced at the style when Grautoff took off on his own and produced such sentences as: "Hanno appears as a last, belated, preciously overripe blossom in the fall."[7]

Kurt Martens was older, more solidly established in life, and a writer of some reputation; it would not do to give him orders, although a year or two later Mann would feel assured enough to set him straight about certain misconceptions. But Martens could be relied on to convey a proper sense of the novel's importance, and he had more space at his disposal, because he was writing for a literary journal rather than a newspaper. He took occasion to mention Thomas Mann's other book, *Der kleine Herr Friedemann*, and to slip in a mention of Heinrich's *Im Schlaraffenland* by warning the reader against confusing Thomas with his brother. *Buddenbrooks*, the reviewer declared, fulfilled all the hopes that readers of the stories had placed in the young writer. Martens caught and summed up an essential quality of the novel: "His characters, his situations, the everyday events he describes, unimportant and ordinary in themselves, take on a unique charm solely by becoming for a creative writer, for Thomas Mann, intense experience."[8] Mann differed from beginners with lofty goals and inadequate command of means, Martens argued, by his mature and sure technique: "He does without all complications, thickens no plots, constructs no conflicts, conceals his own ideas and hopes, makes it his ambition to portray calmly but emphatically the way life unrolls before his mind's eye, as the inescapable destiny of poor, guiltless, mostly ridiculous people whom one loves all the more deeply, the more one must disdain them."[9]

Martens was careful to distinguish Thomas Mann from the regionalists—*Heimatkünstler*—who specialized in local color and laid it on thick and without perspective. "Much more important to him are the souls of people and their relations to eternal laws, to birth and death."[10]

Some ten deaths occurred in the novel, Martens noted, many of them described in careful detail and each one deeply moving. Here was a writer for whom death in all cases meant release, salvation, but dying was attended by all possible torments and represented the peak of horror in human life. "The manner in which Thomas Mann depicts physical sufferings and their effect upon the mind . . . testifies to both the intensity of his feeling and the flexibility of his style."[11] A few reservations were made at the close of the review. Martens was afraid that his friendship for the author might lead him to overestimate the book. There was a certain shallowness of philosophic outlook, he noted, which stood in the way of the novel's achieving "universal importance." Readers, however, proved not to mind this so much. As time showed, *Buddenbrooks* was to be the most read, the most universal, of Mann's novels.

As reviewers, these two friends were more or less reflections of the author's own opinions about his work, and as such their testimonials lacked that aura of a grace conferred that every writer craves: the total stranger's spontaneous acclaim, response, understanding. That came to Mann from a young writer his own age who had not yet made a name that was to rank beside Mann's own: Rainer Maria Rilke. At this time the poet was living in a picturesque village near Bremen that had become something of an artists' colony. Rilke had recently married Clara Westhoff, and in his vain efforts to support wife and child he was taking on any literary work he could find. Very likely his review of *Buddenbrooks* was done simply on assignment from the *Bremer Tageblatt*, the newspaper in which it was published. But it is possible that Friedrich Huch,* a friend of his Munich days who was also a friend of Thomas Mann's, had alerted him to the new novel.

Right at the outset Rilke stated flatly: "Without any doubt we shall have to take note of this name." He recognized what was unique about the novel's structure: Most modern writers wishing to show the decline of a family would have contented themselves with showing the last stage of the decline, the last heir dying of inner weakness; but Mann had had the patience to start "when the family's fortunes have reached their peak." This required telling the lives of four generations; and Rilke marvels over the fact that the two weighty volumes can be read "without tiring or skipping any-

---

* A writer of considerable gifts and morbid disposition, Huch was introduced into the Mann family by Viktor Mann, who tells an engaging story about their meeting in *Wir waren Fünf*. He died young; Thomas Mann spoke movingly at his funeral.

thing, without the least sign of impatience or haste." That was one of the qualities Mann himself was often to refer to in future years, with no small pride.

Rilke perceived what Mann had put into the novel as his contribution to "sociology": "The story shows the calm, unselfconscious life of an older generation and the nervous, self-observing haste of its descendants; it shows . . . how the decadence of the family manifests itself above all in the fact that the individual members have changed the direction of their lives. . . . The tendency toward introversion becomes more and more apparent."

Rilke even seemed to divine the writer's very procedures: "One is wholly involved . . . as if one had found in some secret drawer old family papers and letters in which one slowly read ahead, to the limit of one's own memories." The poet goes on to praise the "colossal labor" and "noble objectivity," and he concludes with a ringing phrase that Thomas Mann was to use and Albert Schweitzer to make famous: "an act of reverence toward life—life that is good and just in its enactment."[12]

Thomas Mann never forgot this review, but otherwise his path and Rilke's seem never to have crossed, although they lived in Munich at the same time and had many mutual friends and acquaintances. Mann was sufficiently familiar with Rilke's work to detect its influence upon that of other poets; but he apparently never felt any warmth toward him. Many years later, writing to Agnes Meyer in the highly personal and candid vein of his correspondence with her, he spoke of Rilke as "the Austrian snob": "Although there is no denying that he attained extraordinary heights in poetry . . . his aestheticism, his aristocratic airs, his sanctimonious preciosity, were always an embarrassment to me and made me feel that his prose was quite unbearable."[13]

A few days later Mann half apologized for these remarks:

> I am afraid we shall each cut a poor figure with posterity on the score of our critical confessions. For after all, the man of the *Duino Elegies* was unquestionably a kind of lyric genius. . . . Ah well, you and I don't have to be as wise as posterity; they must pardon us if as Rilke's contemporaries we are somewhat irked by the weaknesses of— not his person, but his personality. . . . Incidentally, you probably

don't know that Rilke wrote one of the first and best reviews of *Buddenbrooks*.[14]

F O R the purposes of biography, *Buddenbrooks* may be regarded principally as an instrument through which Thomas Mann came to grips with "the world of the father"[15]—that is to say, with the family constellation. The author was seeking to arrive at an understanding of why, how, a family seemingly so solidly rooted in life should have produced such mutants as his brother and himself. It must have been, he seems to have presumed, that the seeds of "decline" had long lain quiescent, waiting for the favorable psychological—or could it possibly be sociological and historical?—moment in which to germinate.

The older generation, the hearty Johanns, stable inhabitants of a stable world, are from the beginning shown as not untouched by the virus of the French disease *décadence*. But their resistance is high. They believe firmly in the sound middle-class virtue of money-making, in pursuing it by honest methods according to the principles that a later time would call "the Protestant ethic." They can speak dialect with the *Volk* and command respect from the workers who come along with newfangled, ill-digested ideas of social revolution. These forebears had not originally engaged Mann's interest; but what he called a pedantic inclination to plumb the origins of everything drove him to seek more and more information about them in the family chronicles, in the recollections of Consul Marty and others, and in his own memories and imagination.

In the course of his search he paid such scrupulous attention to the material facts of existence, to the births, christenings, weddings, and funerals of the life from which he had sprung, to the rise and fall of grain prices and real estate values, and even to the obscure borderline where ordinary business practice shaded over into unethical conduct, that he produced a rendering, easily mistaken for naturalistic, of Hanseatic life in the nineteenth century. Beyond that, for all that his novel was so German in form and content, as he then liked to stress, it had become "a supra-German, pan-European book, a fragment of the psychological history of the German bourgeoisie in general."[16]

One of Mann's key perceptions, which unlike the initial idea of "decline" surely came to him in the course of the book's working out, was his recognition of the part played by women in sustaining the bourgeois ethos. Tony Buddenbrook, patterned after the Aunt Elisabeth whom young Thomas hardly knew, gradually becomes the heroine of the novel. She sacrifices herself for the family by entering into loveless marriages, and after she has ceded all her chances for acting she constantly speaks up for the family's traditional values, for the preservation of its property and its patrician distinction, its *Vornehmheit*—throughout the novel *vornehm* is one of Tony's favorite words. Endlessly brave in the adversities that she partly brings on herself out of a sense of family loyalty, Tony has remained for millions of readers the best-loved character in the novel. In the end, even her sacrifices are vain; her seemingly advantageous matches bring only further financial loss to the house of Buddenbrook. Yet she *is* the Buddenbrooks. Introduced in the first scene, she is present in the last; through her the author succeeded in linking the four generations.

But the nature of woman is ambivalent. The other female protagonist of the novel is Tony's antithesis, embodiment of an alien, destructive element that is the family's undoing. Gerda, Tony's former schoolmate, is depicted throughout as cool, remote, and above all intensely musical. And music stands for a dangerous instability entering into the solid and stolid world of the grandfathers. Music bespeaks a potential otherworldliness, the allure of nirvana, the longing for extinction. There is enough of the burgher in Thomas Buddenbrook to make him virtually tone-deaf, so that his wife can tell him condescendingly he will never understand music. Yet he craves it, though he can possess it only imperfectly, through her. When he first hears Gerda Arnoldsen play her Stradivarius, tears nearly come to his eyes. He brings her home as his bride, thus introducing into his staid bourgeois existence the romance he longed for.

Almost everyone in town agrees that Gerda is strange; and by the subtlest hints the author suggests that there is something of the mermaid about her. When we first meet her in Therese Weichbrodt's pension she is combing her hair with an ivory comb. Thomas must go to Amsterdam to fetch her from the sea, as it were. And like the little sea-maid of a later novel, she introduces the mortal infection of music into the Buddenbrook household, as well as the poison of possible adultery. She never shows any sign of aging, and when her changeling son falls sick and dies—returning to the palace at the bottom of the sea, so to speak—she remains unmoved. At the end, unaffected by a lifetime that has passed, she returns whence she came, to play duets with her father. Her whole life with Thomas Buddenbrook seems like a sea-goddess's brief sojourn among mortals. And this indeed is what Tony Buddenbrook senses when, with a knowing look at Gerda and Tom, she quotes the lines of the town poet, Hostede, about "Venus Anadyomene" and "Vulcan."[17] The young novelist, fearing that his readers might miss the point, widens his references (and succeeds only in confusing the matter) when he introduces a medley of female mythological figures: "What a woman, gentlemen! Hera and Aphrodite, Brunhilda and Melusina all in one!"[18]

In short, in dealing with the world of his forebears Thomas Mann had already devised, within the shell of a naturalistic novel, the kind of mythological and symbolic substructure that was to become more prominent in his later works. But for all his skill, he had also experienced what he later came to call the "self-will on the part of a work."[19] For example, Christian Buddenbrook seems to have assumed far more importance than originally intended. It is true that Christian was the first character to be sketched in Mann's preliminary notes,[20] but it seems unlikely that Mann intended so lively a portrait from the outset. In the course of writing he must have realized that he was not yet done with the "Bajazzo" theme; perhaps he also realized that he would never be done with the brother theme. But in elaborating it, he gave to it the additional structural function of a classical, mythological element that was also pertinent to his own situation: the archetypal theme of hostile brothers, *die feindlichen Brüder*.

In the novel the antagonism between the Consul and his brother Gotthold serves to anticipate the conflict between Christian and Thomas. Christian makes a fool of himself by his self-display, by his lack of "seriousness," by his fondness for the stage and for actresses. But Thomas Buddenbrook himself has not always been a paragon of moral purity, as his affair with the little flower girl shows. He does not dream of marrying her, because he has early recognized that his brother is a kind of alter ego, that only by keeping the tightest hold on himself will he be able to resist those impulses toward disintegration that he hates in Christian. And Thomas's son Hanno sees all too clearly that his father's whole life is like that of an actor, that his public conduct, his speeches, his "representation," are not naive and natural but the products of deliberate, artificial effort. And here, suddenly, Thomas Buddenbrook also steps beyond himself, becomes a metaphysical concept, a manifestation of Schopenhauer's blind striving of the will.

In writing this long novel—and perhaps this is its larger significance biographically—Mann had provided himself with a body of work, an opus, that already expressed a formed personality. Hereafter he could and often did reflect back upon that work, seeking to determine the nature of his own art. Like his readers, he himself could find ever greater depths in it. The consequence was an even more powerful autobiographical preoccupation; but he consistently strove to use autobiography for the ends of art.

B E C A U S E of its relatively high cost, the two-volume first edition of *Buddenbrooks*—6 marks a volume—sold rather slowly at first. But in Lübeck it went quite briskly under the counter; it was regarded as a roman à clef, and the city buzzed with gossip about it. The subtitle, "Decline of a Family," seemed to promise scandal, and for the mores of the time that promise was fulfilled in the account of Tony Buddenbrook's two divorces and Hugo Weinschenk's dereliction. Lübeck was a city of eighty thousand by this time, but the people who counted formed a small, closely knit coterie. Here was a novel that appeared to be about the business aristocracy of the city. And since Thomas Mann had filled his story with founders, successors, children, and grandchildren, with business acquaintances and rivals of the Buddenbrook family, with the usual dignitaries of small-town life such as the pastor, the doctor, the dentist, and the broker, those citizens who looked at his cast of characters with an eye to detecting the persons behind them were not disappointed. Identifiable originals were easy to find, especially with the aid of lists more or less inaccurately and crudely matching characters in the novel and their presumed models. Several such lists circulated in Lübeck and may be seen to this day in glass cases in the Thomas Mann Room now established in the Schabbelhaus, the home of what may be loosely translated as the Lübeck Chamber of Commerce. Indeed, the tradition has not died in Lübeck; the booklet describing the collection in the Thomas Mann Room contains seven pages pairing the characters in the novel with the persons on whom Thomas Mann supposedly modeled them.

The very existence of such a collection indicates that the dust has long since settled. But at the time of publication Lübeck was reportedly up in arms against the author of *Buddenbrooks*. Many of the townspeople are said to have regarded the book as an act of outrageous impudence or cheap revenge by a ne'er-do-well who had turned his back on the city that had nurtured him. A teacher at the Katharineum spluttered: "That's supposed to be an important writer? I had him in German. He was never able to write a decent composition."[21]

It is difficult to measure the extent of Lübeck's outrage. Contemporary written records are few, and later accounts by such persons as Otto Anthes, who became a resident of Lübeck shortly after the publication of *Buddenbrooks*, may well have been influenced by the author's own recollections—which certainly contained an element of stylization. Anthes thought that what affronted Thomas Mann's former fellow citizens was chiefly the book's tone, the air of objectivity which to the unliterary sounded like superciliousness. Significantly, the one person of literary stature in the city, the prolific novelist and journalist Ida Boy-Ed, vigorously defended both the novel and its author. But to Thomas Mann himself his near-arrest in Lübeck two years *before* the novel was published set the tone of his relations with the city of his birth. It suited the self-image he was then conceiving and working up in *Tonio Kröger* for him to believe that the citizens of Lübeck were shocked and offended by the use he had made of them in his novel. That there was some adverse comment cannot be doubted. Yet only two years after publication of the novel Ida Boy-Ed thought she could invite Mann to give a reading in Lübeck. He rather nervously declined her first invitation, but such a reading actually took place in December 1904. It was politely received; there is no record of riots in the streets against the presence of a bird who was "befouling his own nest" and dragging "his closest relations into the mire."[22]

The earliest reports from S. Fischer about the sales of *Budden-*

brooks were not encouraging. But within nine months after publication the atmosphere had changed. Author and publisher met in Munich during the summer, when Fischer passed through the city on his way to his vacation resort in the Tyrol. The novel had begun to sell, Fischer told Mann. Public recognition had by now gone beyond the carefully orchestrated initial reviews; the novel had evidently taken hold.

Perhaps the clearest evidence of this for both author and publisher was the review by Samuel Lublinski that was published in the *Berliner Tageblatt* in the middle of September. Lublinski had read some of the earlier reviews and went out of his way to counter the criticism that the novel had no structure, or that there was not enough dialogue. On the contrary, he pointed out, only the writer's admirable composition allowed him to contain such a vast span of time within two volumes; and the novel's dialogue was ample, wonderfully subtle, and uncannily effective. This heartwarming review by a poor, crippled Jewish man of letters ended with the amazingly accurate prediction "that the book would grow with time and be read by many generations."[23]

Fischer now believed that he had made a mistake in setting too high a price on the novel. If the public could afford it, the public would buy it. He offered the author 1,000 marks at once, and held out the possibility of a second, cheaper edition in the near future. At the beginning of the following year this one-volume edition came out at half the price of the first edition; and before the end of that year more than ten thousand copies had been sold. *Huset Buddenbrook* (The House of Buddenbrook), a translation into Dano-Norwegian, was published in two volumes in 1903; a translation into Swedish, in 1904.

Summing up this experience from the perspective of a Nobel Prize winner thirty years later, Thomas Mann exaggerated for literary effect: "It was fame. I was snatched up in a whirl of success. . . . My mail was swollen, money flowed in streams, my picture appeared in the illustrated papers, a hundred pens made copy of the product of my secluded hours, the world embraced me amid eulogies and congratulations."[24]

But since reflection upon his own life was Thomas Mann's way of approaching an understanding of his world, he did not rest content with this analysis. A decade later, once more taking measure of the same experience, he gave an entirely different view of it:

> It was fame. . . . One need not go so far as to say that success is a misunderstanding, but the element of misunderstanding undoubtedly attaches to any influence that spreads far and wide. The success of *Buddenbrooks* is a very vivid example of that principle. The novel was interpreted as a product of regionalism, as a narrative of North German bourgeois life along the lines of the German humorous tradition established by Fritz Reuter. These features—which were undeniably present—helped my book in spite of its gloominess to win the approval of the German reading public. For the time being, at any rate, that public overlooked all the supranational, European influences that had flowed into the novel and that, even more important, pointed outward to what was characteristically European. Today, I imagine, it can be fittingly said that in this book the German novel first laid claim to acceptability by the rest of the world. This was the German novel's breakthrough into world literature. . . .[25]

How greatly the emphasis has shifted between this "objective" comment on his own work, written nearly forty years after the novel's publication, and those suggestions that Grautoff so sedulously parroted. On the one hand, "Stress the *German* character of the book," and on the other hand an underlining of the international aspects of *Buddenbrooks*. Thomas Mann's whole political evolution is summed up here. In 1940 he wanted to see himself as a German writer who even in his beginnings had introduced a leavening of Europeanism into a somewhat ponderous German tradition. But in fact there was no real inconsistency. Early and late he did not want *Buddenbrooks* mistaken for a regionalist novel; the chief difference was that by 1940 he detested Nazi exploitation of *Heimatkunst* and therefore did not wish to be identified with it for political rather than literary reasons. Even during his most nationalistic period, the years of the First World War, he stressed the international aspects of *Budden-brooks*. In the *Betrachtungen eines Unpolitischen* he spoke of the book's "totally European literary atmosphere" and called it "artistically international,"[26] even as he once again emphasized its German character. He looked both ways because greatness—by which he meant universality—had been his "secret and painful ambition throughout the work."[27]

T H E winter of 1901–02, after the publication of *Budden-brooks*, found Thomas seemingly once more wrapped up emotionally with Paul Ehrenberg. "He is his old self. . . . I too am my old self,"[28] Mann wrote to his jealous confidant Grautoff. In fact, changes in the relationship had already taken place, although Mann underwent relapses into the passive attitudes of an earlier period. His concentration upon Paul alone was coming to an end; letters were addressed to Paul and Carl Ehrenberg jointly, and the twosome was imperceptibly becoming a threesome. The balance had shifted from emotions experienced for the sake of living to emotions entertained for the sake of literature. That is evident from Mann's confession to Kurt Martens at the beginning of the summer: "I haven't worked this winter, I have merely lived, simply as a human being, and assuaged my conscience by filling a notebook with observations."[29] By the time he wrote these lines he was already working again, and it might have been closer to the truth to say that his thoughts had not really strayed far from literary projects at any time during the winter. The notebooks that have been preserved also testify to this. Although under the Ehrenbergs' influence he had been listening to a great deal of music—in the middle of March he went to concerts three nights out of four—he was also writing slowly and painfully away on *Tonio Kröger*, steeping himself in Renaissance reading for his *King of Florence* (as *Fiorenza* was then called), and keeping an eye open for fresh subjects. It was at this time that he wrote that letter to Hilde Distel inquiring about the incident in the Dresden streetcar that had caught his fancy.

During the summer he solidified his friendship with Kurt Martens by staying with him and his wife at their summer place in Bad Kreuth. He became "uncle" to Martens's small daughter, Hertha; the two literary men walked and talked; and in a whimsical bread-and-butter note Mann begged Martens not to go to any trouble returning the nightshirt, the "very worn" pair of slippers, and the bottle of mouthwash he had left behind. "I am accustomed to such losses; they happen on every journey, and the things are easily replaced."[30] Later in the year he told Martens he would like to dedicate *Tonio Kröger* to him. At this time the novella was still unfinished, but nearing completion.

His health was not good, or he had persuaded himself that it was not—his chief complaint seems to have been an upset stomach, which may have been due simply to a bachelor's irregular eating habits. He had also, it is clear, developed a taste for sanatorium life, so that by late spring he had already made up his mind to return to Riva in the autumn for a stay of six weeks or so.

At the Villa Cristoforo, where he stayed from the beginning of October to the middle of November 1902, he followed a soothingly monotonous regimen. His day began at seven with gymnastics; then came breakfast. At eight o'clock he sat down at his desk—he had persuaded Dr. von Hartungen to relax the previous year's rule against writing. But he wrote no more than a few lines, so he claimed. At half past eight the mail interrupted, and by nine o'clock his morning "work" was over. He then thrust a book into his pocket and strolled down to the lake, which could be reached from his room in two minutes. The boatman unchained his blue-and-white row-boat, rented for 10 gulden a month, and he rowed vigorously out into the lake. As he wrote to Paul and Carl Ehrenberg:

> I have . . . tried to give a picture of how lovely it is to glide about in the gently breathing and plashing sunlit stillness of the lake, walled in by stern mountains. But at times the picture is different, more sinister. The clouds hang low and menacing and the wind howls gruesomely above the angry waters, which race with savage force upon the naked breast of the fissured cliffs. But I feel no fear! Erect and solitary amid the fury of the elements, my sturdy figure stands in the rear of the boat and with sinewy hands clenched, peering keen-eyed around me, I defy the waves that foam raging about the delicate bow of my slender vessel. The thunder roars, the frail skiff groans fearfully, and in the sulfurous glow of lightning flashes—no, thank God it isn't all that bad, most of the time quite gentle and contemplative, and when I tire of rowing I let myself drift, read a bit, and think about this and that. So the hours pass, and on the stroke of one lunch begins, a very good, very ample lunch that does not pass in the twinkling of an eye. . . .

There follows a detailed description of the company at table, each member of which is filed away in the writer's notebook, just in case

he may someday want to write another short story about a sanatorium. Lunch—a heavy midday meal, in keeping with Central
European custom—was followed by a nap. At half past three the
doctor came round to administer massage. A two-hour walk—the
day's real exercise—filled out the rest of the afternoon. That left only
a short time for violin practice before the supper bell rang. After
the meal came a brief social period, an evening stroll, a few more
pages of Frenssen's *Jörn Uhl*, and it was already time for bed. A
mystery, as he remarked, how even a letter such as he was writing
could be squeezed into such a day. "For the rest, I am sometimes in a
good, sometimes in a bad mood, sometimes full of high hopes and
sometimes on the verge of despair. But that has always been so and
probably always will be so."[31]

He returned to Munich on November 15, bringing with him the
nevertheless finished manuscript of *Tonio Kröger*, and moved into a
new and "very pretty little apartment."[32] It was attractive enough
for him to cease his restless moving around; he stayed at Konradstrasse 11 for the next two years. Moreover, his present status as an
author with sizable royalties was signaled by his coming down to
earth. No more carrying his bicycle up endless flights of stairs; his
new address was *parterre*—on the ground floor.

1 1

A Wider
World

W HILE he was still in Riva, Thomas Mann had
written to Carl Ehrenberg to express his regret that "you
so thoroughly disliked (don't deny it!) my latest, namely
'The Hungry.' That vexed me because after all I am more eager to
kindle people like you than the Maximilian Hardens. Of course I'm
not saying that the piece can lay claim to importance as a coherent
work of art. It is not meant to be anything more than a psychological
study. . . . Well, perhaps you will take a look at it again when it is
printed."[1]

"The Hungry" appeared in print in Maximilian Harden's magazine, *Die Zukunft*, at the end of Janurary 1903—one month before
the publication of *Tonio Kröger* in the *Neue Deutsche Rundschau*—
but was excluded from the collection of stories published later in the
year under the title of *Tristan*. The reason for this exclusion was obvious: "The Hungry" was a mere chip from the workshop in which
Tonio Kröger was being slowly hammered out. In "The Hungry"

Detlef, the artist who believes in redemption by the Word, watches his friends at a carnival ball with feelings of being forever the outsider—just like Tonio Kröger standing on the glass veranda of the Danish hotel and looking into the lighted ballroom at reincarnations of Hans Hansen and Ingeborg Holm. In the long novella Tonio's crush is explicit: "The fact was that Tonio loved Hans Hansen, and had already suffered a good deal on his account."[2] While Mann worked on *Tonio Kröger* his attachment to Paul Ehrenberg revived memories of his boyhood infatuation with Armin Martens, and he had the courage to treat the theme openly. In "The Hungry" a conventional disguise is still preserved; the real-life situation is inverted. As Lilli dances with "the little painter"[3] and Detlef lets the moving stream of revelers carry him away, he hopes that she (rather than the unnamed painter who stands for Paul) will notice his departure. But the partners are absorbed with each other and their pleasure in the dance. Detlef goes out into the darkness, where the cabs stand in a long line, the horses covered with blankets, their heads drooping, the well-bundled coachmen stamping about in the hard snow. He lights a cigarette, and as the match goes out he sees a man with "red-bearded, hollow-cheeked, lawless face, with wretchedly inflamed, red-rimmed eyes that stared with savage scorn and a certain greedy curiosity into his own."[4] The derelict eyes his fur coat, his opera glasses, his patent-leather shoes, and snorts con temptuously. Detlef is momentarily abashed at the sight of one even more an outcast than himself. Then he recovers his balance, assures himself that no sympathy is necessary, that both of them are hungering, their fates basically the same. *"But we are brothers."*[5]

It is hardly surprising that neither Carl Ehrenberg nor his brother Paul liked this story, which so explicitly set down on paper a shared experience at a Munich carnival ball, and even used the name of their adoptive "sister," Lilli Distel. Neither young man could have been pleased at being identified with mute, unreflective life; they did not consider themselves ignorant of the transfigurations that mind and art can confer. What Thomas Mann regarded as a tribute often could not help striking the innocent victims of his art as offensive.

"The Hungry" was consciously constructed as a bridge between "Tristan" and *Tonio Kröger*. The writer Detlev of "Tristan" has undergone a minimal change to Detlef. But where Detlev Spinell despised and was worsted by the crude life-force of the Klöter-jahns, father and son, the Detlef of "The Hungry" shares Tonio Kröger's longing to embrace the simple-hearted blond and blue-eyed ones. There is an irritating naiveté about "The Hungry," a heavy-handedness that only here and there afflicts the otherwise far subtler *Tonio Kröger*. In the letter to Carl Ehrenberg cited above, the author apologized for the facile ending of "The Hungry," calling it "not abreast of the times and inconsequential to the point of triviality."[6]

Heinrich Mann must have snorted when he read "The Hungry." For Heinrich, the onetime editor of the reactionary *Das Zwanzigste Jahrhundert*, had devoted the entire first volume of his newly published *Die Göttinnen* to his heroine's pursuit of *Freiheit*—freedom for the inarticulate, fiery Dalmatian people as well as a woman's freedom to violate convention. In his fiction and thought Heinrich was working his way from aristocratic neoromanticism toward social conscience. He too was writing of the artist's isolation, the artist's inability to live simply and directly. But he would not accept the artist's excuses. "Comedian" was his savage epithet—borrowed from Nietzsche perhaps—for the posturings of artists who thought they could be Renaissance men. "A comedian who has forgotten his lines,"[7] he called his writer, Mario Malvolto, in "Pippo Spano." The notion that psychological suffering might be equivalent to suffering from real hunger and cold, or from the real pain of a mortal wound, struck him as preposterous. And he may have wondered, as we must wonder, what ironies underlay the use of the word *brother* in that apostrophe to the derelict: "But we are brothers." Relations between Heinrich and Thomas were no longer so warm as they had been during that stay in Florence when the two young men courted two English sisters.

Their differences in temperament and in approaches to the obsessive tasks of novel writing were accentuated after *Die Göttinnen* came out in December 1902. This novel, with its vast canvas, its multitude of characters, and its geographic range over half of Europe, was built around the successive passions of the Duchess of Assy. In the first volume, "Diana," she is involved with revolution; in the second, "Minerva," she becomes a devotee of the arts; and in the third, "Venus," she consecrates herself to sex. Heinrich Mann himself spoke of the novel as "exotic, adventurous, full of movement and suspense," and emphasized its "fantastic events and moods rare in modern novels" as well as its "intense eroticism" and "pagan view of life."[8] He intended this novel as a major work, a counterpart to *Buddenbrooks* in impact and in its survey of a whole lifetime and period. His deliberate distortions of the normal rules of German syntax, and the tempestuousness of his imagery, roused the enthusiasm of younger German writers. Erich Mühsam was to call *Die Göttinnen* "the most gigantic enterprise that any German novelist has ventured on."[9] Gottfried Benn henceforth numbered Heinrich Mann among his "gods," placing him in the same august company as Nietzsche and Taine.[10]

And Thomas Mann? He was appalled.

Thomas Mann saw fit to express his reaction to Heinrich's novel indirectly, in a review of another novel—apparently the first review he had written since his days as a contributor to *Das Zwanzigste Jahrhundert*, seven years before. He chose to discuss a novel by Toni Schwabe, a young woman whose writing he had discovered while he was working as an editor for *Simplicissimus*. Novel and novelist would be forgotten today but for Thomas Mann's review, in which he took occasion to aim a few darts at his brother: "I read—and was fascinated. By what? Oh, in the gentlest fashion. No trace of breathlessness. No furious and desperate assaults upon the reader's interest. . . . The delicate emphasis with which its effects are achieved is, to be specific, exactly the opposite of that bombast which for several years past has been imported into our parts from the beautiful land of Italy."[11]

There were more such thrusts. The review appeared in the March 21, 1903 issue of *Freistatt*, a Munich literary and political weekly, and Thomas may have hoped that Heinrich, down there in the "beautiful land of Italy," would never see it. But by the end of the year some oversolicitous friend had provided Heinrich with a copy. Private disagreements were one thing, well understood and accepted between brothers. But such a public slur from Thomas stung; Heinrich remembered it fifteen years later.

During the summer of 1903 the brothers had the opportunity to talk at length, for the first time since their stay in Florence. Heinrich returned to Germany and spent the summer at the Schweighart farm in Polling, where Frau Julia Mann was taking up residence. Polling had been a Benedictine monastery that was founded by a Duke of

Bavaria in the early Middle Ages. Eventually secularized, it had been divided into two large farms. Ultimately the buildings of the monastery proper were bought by the Dominicans and converted for use as a girls' boarding school, a school of domestic science, and a kindergarten. The former administration building of the monastery was turned into a residence by the Schweigharts, the present owners of one of the farms. It was a Gothic structure with pointed arches, filled with fine old baroque and Biedermeier furnishings as well as paintings, sculptures, and books salvaged from the monastery. Like many European farmers, Max and Katharina Schweighart supplemented their income by taking summer boarders, and Thomas's brother-in-law, Josef Löhr, had apparently discovered the beautiful, tranquil summer retreat, so conveniently close to Munich, even before his marriage to Lula. He had invited his future mother-in-law to come there with little Viktor in the summer of 1899. The boy in particular found the farm a second home where he spent many of the happiest years of his youth.

Frau Julia returned to Polling summer after summer, and eventually decided to leave Munich altogether and make Polling her permanent home. Her interest in society, her coquetry, her élan, seem to have subsided after she reached the age of fifty. Young Viktor was also something of a problem, and he had taken to farm life with such enthusiasm that she may have thought it wise to let him have his head.

More than forty years later Thomas met Viktor in Zürich after the long wartime separation. Viktor reports that his brother soon brought the conversation around to Polling. "You will find the Schweigharts in my *Doctor Faustus*," he said, adding reflectively: "Polling had atmosphere."[12] At the time his thoughts were full of *Faustus*; he had completed the book only six months earlier and was going about Switzerland giving readings from it. It is hardly surprising, therefore, that the meeting with Viktor should have brought to mind the Pfeiffering of his latest novel, and the Schweigestill family whom he had lovingly modeled on the Schweigharts.

That summer of 1903 the entire family, except for sister Lula and her husband Jof, were together for the first time in years. Carla had made a rather inauspicious debut in the theater—at the beginning of October Thomas would go to Düsseldorf to see his sister on the stage, and the stay at the grand hotel in Düsseldorf provided him with material he ultimately used in *Royal Highness* and *Felix Krull*. Carla also made a contribution, a more direct one, to Heinrich's fic tion. Evidently she described her experiences to Heinrich in detail, and he promptly used them in his new novel, *Die Jagd nach Liebe*— he had begun it during the winter in Florence, interrupted it in the spring to set down the flashy "Pippo Spano," and now finished it in the course of the summer. The pace alone left Thomas aghast. Yet for all the speed of its composition, *Die Jagd nach Liebe* is one of Heinrich's better novels; but Thomas was not prepared to see that. Probably he heard some pages read aloud during the summer, but Heinrich must have kept the more shocking passages to himself. When the novel came out, Carla seemed in no way offended by her portrait in it. "I find Ute extraordinarily interesting," she wrote to her brother, "especially since I resemble her artistically more than you imagine."[13]

During the summer Thomas Mann was not altogether idle or engaged in literary disputes with his brother. He continued to work on *Fiorenza*, although he was having difficulty with the "unaccustomed dramatic form."[14] That he was influenced by Heinrich in his choice of Florence as his setting, and dialogue as his medium, can scarcely be doubted; but he was also using his Renaissance drama to write a kind of covert "anti-Heinrich."[15] (This was the title of an outburst he set down in his notebook two years later.) He was never to master either the form or the conflicting emotions that went into this drama, and it may be regarded as Thomas Mann's lone egregiously unsatisfactory work. The more trouble he had with it, the more he labored over it; but despite brilliant passages it remained neither a playable play nor a readable closet drama.

This same summer saw him visiting once again the Martens family in Bad Kreuth. Thomas Mann was drawing closer to Kurt Martens, partly out of gratitude for Martens's unswerving allegiance to his literary self. The older man freely acknowledged Mann's superior gifts as a writer. Here was a basis for friendship quite different from the postadolescent crush on Paul Ehrenberg. "I believed in his exceptional talent and in his future while he was still hesitantly groping his way forward,"[16] Martens later wrote. Martens's review of *Tristan* in *Das literarische Echo* spoke of "stories of such noble purity that all the younger writers of fiction will no doubt acknowledge Thomas Mann without envy as a master of their art."[17]

Otto Grautoff of course added his laudation, in a lengthy review that was published in the magazine *Die Gegenwart*. He recapitulated his friend's brief career and hailed *Tonio Kröger* in language that was almost certainly suggested by the author. What is more, a newly acquired friend, to whom one of the stories ("Little Lizzy") was actually dedicated, had the temerity to review *Tristan*. He was Richard Schaukal, who had courted both Mann brothers for some time. "Schaukal is a queer bird," Thomas had commented several years earlier upon receiving a batch of Schaukal's poetry. He had leafed through it just enough to come to the conclusion that, as he told Heinrich, "it is obvious that he is much closer to you."[18] At this time Thomas knew only that Schaukal had married rich and held some government post in Moravia. But in September 1902 he at last met Schaukal and was quite taken with him. His comment reveals something of his standards at this time: "To my surprise he was enormously likable. At any rate no man of letters [*Literat*] but a poet (although sometimes a rotten one, but that is not so bad). Moreover, he has good manners, is well dressed, modest out of cultivation, and gratifyingly bourgeois."[19] The friendship did not last; it ended a few years later on a bitter note. But for the present Schaukal went so far as to call Thomas Mann "perhaps the finest German prose writer of the present."[20]

Unfortunately, Schaukal belonged to the nationalistic school that Heinrich Mann's magazine *Das Zwanzigste Jahrhundert* had represented. Consequently, Schaukal took occasion to hail Thomas Mann as Germanic and Nordic, and to condemn Heinrich Mann for having fallen prey to French and Italian influences. It is somewhat startling to encounter in Schaukal's review, dated August 1903, the ominous term "racially pure" (*rassenrein*) as his highest compliment to Thomas Mann. Praise of this kind was hardly better than blame, and Thomas Mann hastened to write to his brother about it:

> I want to assure you explicitly that I have never given the author reason to imagine I could take pleasure in or in any way approve of a disparagement of your achievements, especially where I am under discussion. . . . Since he takes occasion to call himself my friend, in the public eye . . . I must partly bear responsibility for this stu-

pidity and am very tempted to inform the editors of my annoyance. At any rate, Schaukal need expect no warm thanks from me for this service of friendship.'[21]

But Thomas Mann made no public protest on his brother's behalf. Three years later Heinrich was more militant when his brother needed defending against this same Richard Schaukal.

No such strains troubled the relationship with Martens; in fact, sometime between the end of 1903 and April 1904 there took place between Mann and Martens the momentous (for Mann) step from the formal *Sie* to the familiar *du*. In view of the time, it probably happened during the Munich Fasching season of 1904. And since there were so very few friends, aside from former schoolmates, with whom Thomas Mann ever arrived at this intimate footing, the reason probably sprang from Mann's need for a male confidant at this particular juncture, preferably one who could guide him through the intricacies of courtship. There may also have been some impulse on Mann's part to express gratitude to Martens for providing him with material for a story. On one of their walks at Bad Kreuth the older man had told an anecdote that Mann turned into a short story before the end of the year: "Ein Glück" (published in English as "A Gleam"). "I am very glad you approve of my treatment of your tale," Mann wrote to him after Martens had read and complimented him on the story. "At the time you told it to me I recognized it at once as belonging to my own realm of ideas and feelings."[22]

By this Mann meant that it fitted into the patterns of love and jealousy that he was exploring in his voluminous notes for *Die Geliebten*. "A Gleam" is chiefly remarkable for the novel way in which the narrator introduces himself in the first paragraph as a kind of corporeal "spirit of narration"[23] who is pausing between "Florence of the old days" and "perhaps a royal castle"[24]—that is, between *Fiorenza* and *Royal Highness*—to tell his tale. That striving for the mythic dimension which informed all his work here prompted Thomas Mann to mythologize himself, since the anecdote he was relating would not bear any heavier freight. More and more frequently at this time, jottings for a novel about a prince began to appear in Mann's notebooks. The prince was to stand for the lonely existence of the artist whose very success sets him apart from humanity as effectively as the artistic mission did. Mann experimented with the same theme in another of those sketches that had become virtually his hallmark: "The Child Prodigy." Written almost to order for the Christmas issue of Vienna's *Neue Freie Presse*, it made fun of the infantile, sexless artist who is at once an authentically inspired performer and a charlatan catering to his audience. The audience comes off no better: the money-minded businessman who reckons the evening's "take," the martinet of a piano teacher who would put a coin on the back of the prodigy's hand, and the supercilious music critic are briefly drawn with acid humor. In fact, the story betrays the influence of Heinrich's satiric manner—Thomas must have been reading *Die Jagd nach Liebe* at the time he wrote it—and a half-conscious awareness of this must have produced his feeling that "The Child Prodigy" had "slipped completely off the rails"[25] so that it would be better if it were never published.

The end of older friendships was already being foreshadowed. In the middle of the summer Mann could still write a long and chatty letter to Paul Ehrenberg, whose chair and rug he was keeping in his apartment during Paul's absence from Munich. That letter closed with a rare piece of verse that tells a good deal about Thomas Mann's view of himself in the summer of 1903. Dedicated "to my dear Paul Ehrenberg," it ran:

> Here is a man with warts and all
> And full of passions great and small,
> Ambitious, love-starved, and conceited,
> And touchy, jealous, easily heated,
> Excessive, factious, hardly stable,
> Now far too proud, now miserable,
> Naive and so sophisticated,
> World-fleeing, world-infatuated,
> Nostalgic, weak, a wind-bent reed,
> Half seer, half moron, blind indeed,
> A child, a fool, a writer too
> In fantasy and will entwined,
> But with the virtue that to you
> With all his heart he is inclined.[26]

But thereafter letters to Paul Ehrenberg cease for a considerable time, although in the notebooks references to P. continue. Letters and friendly relations are for a while restricted to Carl Ehrenberg.

We even hear, a few months later, of "confusions and furious disputes"[27] with Paul. The reason for these outward and inner changes appears to have been Thomas Mann's meeting with Katia Pringsheim.

1 2

Courtship

T HE STORY of Thomas Mann's wooing and winning of Katia Pringsheim was long ago romanticized by the
parties concerned, in particular by Thomas Mann himself.
And why not? Since the end of the era of arranged matches, most
marriages have been the culmination of a romance, and romances
are pre-eminently the stuff of literature. For a writer to make literary use of his own romance is surely one of his prerogatives.
Thomas Mann set about the task fairly promptly, using the vehicle
of his already planned novel about a prince. "An attempt to seal a
pact with 'happiness,' "[1] he called that novel, first conceived as a
symbolic tale of the artist's necessarily isolated and "representative"
existence. *Royal Highness* went beyond his original intentions, because between conception and execution the lonely prince unexpectedly found his princess. Or was it so unexpected? Perhaps we
may equally well say that his playing prince made him look
around for the princess.

The romance, as Thomas Mann liked to call it, "begins in far-away old Lübeck," where a boy of fourteen saw the reproduction of a popular genre painting in an illustrated magazine.

> Anyone who has lived through some part of the nineteenth century will recall that painting in those days had the amiable ability to produce, from time to time, a sensational picture that sent thrills of delight through the whole of bourgeois society. Such a painting, aimed directly at the heart of bourgeois taste, traveled from city to city, and everybody wanted to see it.[2]

The magazine reproduction so pleased young Thomas Mann that he cut it out and tacked it above his desk. Its title was *Children's Carnival;* it depicted five black-haired children in harlequin costumes, long black stockings, tall white hats, in poses of innocent sauciness. Four of the children were boys—Pierrots—and one a large-eyed, sweet-faced Pierrette, "presumably the twin sister of the almost equally pretty little fellow at her side with his melancholic naughty-boy look."[3] Who can say whether it was the subject, the whimsy, the poses, the charm of the children, or simply the fame of the painting that so captivated the schoolboy Thomas Mann? In any case he used the magazine illustration as a pinup and thus had before his eyes for many months a picture of his future wife at the age of five. For it so happened that the models for *Children's Carnival* were the five children of Professor Alfred Pringsheim and his wife, Hedwig.

Alfred Pringsheim's father had made a fortune in Silesian coal mines and the early railroads. But the same law of "decline"—from solid moneymaking to music, art, and literature—that Thomas Mann was to describe in *Buddenbrooks* applied to these newly emancipated Jewish families. The tycoon's son turned his back on business and became a mathematician. He attended the universities of Berlin, Heidelberg, and Munich, and from 1886 on taught mathematics at the University of Munich, where he became *ordentlicher Professor* (that is, full professor and member of the faculty) in 1901. His books on mathematics were esteemed by those able to understand them. But he had other strings to his bow. In the words of his grandson, Klaus Mann:

> He collected paintings, tapestries, majolica, silverware, and bronze statuary—all in the Renaissance style. His collection was so important

that Kaiser Wilhelm II, as a sign of his appreciation, conferred upon him the Order of the Crown, second class. . . . IIis fourth passion—along with mathematics, his beautiful wife, Hedwig, and the Italian antiquities—was the music of Richard Wagner. The young professor was one of the first contributors to and promoters of the Bayreuth festival, and remained an enthusiastic adherent of the Wagner cult all his life. But his personal contact with the Master came to an abrupt end when the Master, in the presence of his "non-Aryan" admirer, let slip an anti-Semitic remark. The genius was tactless and ungrateful and the professor had a choleric temperament.[4]

This anecdote may have been invented by Klaus Mann, who at the time he wrote the above was keenly conscious of the anti-Semitic side of Richard Wagner. According to Katia Mann, her father "had once fought a duel in Bayreuth on Wagner's account" and as a consequence had so embarrassed the Wagner family that he "had forfeited his personal relationship with the people at Wahnfried."[5] Nevertheless, Alfred Pringsheim's love for Wagner's works was not diminished; he prepared and published arrangements of Wagnerian pieces for one and two pianos.

His wife, Hedwig Dohm, the mother of Katia, was the daughter of two eminent writers, Hedwig and Ernst Dohm. Both were the children of Jewish families that had converted to Protestantism—the first half of the nineteenth century saw many such conversions in Germany. Ernst Dohm studied philosophy and theology, and for a time considered going into the ministry. He became a writer instead, an editor on various magazines, and participated in the founding of the humorous Berlin weekly *Kladderadatsch** in 1848. In 1849 he became editor in chief, and he continued in that post for the next thirty-four years. He was regarded as one of the wittiest political satirists in Germany. In spite of his sharp criticism of the government on many occasions, he managed to keep the goodwill of Bismarck, whom he esteemed. Like Alfred Pringsheim, his future son-in-law, he was a passionate Wagnerian and became president of the Wagner Association. In addition he was mad about the theater

---

* *Kladderadatsch* is a North German exclamation used to indicate a heavy fall accompanied by the sound of breaking glass or crockery. The magazine was one of the spiritual ancestors of *Simplicissimus*.

—as was his wife—and wrote a number of comedies. He also translated the fables of La Fontaine into German.

His wife, Hedwig Schleh, was the daughter of a wealthy tobacco manufacturer. An unusually beautiful, intelligent, and high-spirited girl, she threw herself wholeheartedly into the struggle for the emancipation of women. Thomas Mann has described her in "Little Grandma" as exceptionally small, vivacious, and opinionated. In her younger days she conducted a Berlin literary salon that was a worthy successor to the famous salon of Rahel Varnhagen. "Survivors of that circle, Varnhagen himself and Alexander von Humboldt, came to her house." So did Franz Liszt. After her children were grown she began to write, and published a number of books with such titles as *The Scientific Emancipation of Women* (1874) and *The Rights and Nature of Women* (1876). She also wrote comedies, like her husband, and novels on which her grandson-in-law commented: "Well, they were not exactly highly important, although as documents of Berlin and Munich social life they will undoubtedly retain their value."[6]

Hedwig and Ernst Dohm's daughters married men of prominence, and they or their children continued the literary tradition of the family as translators or critics. The oldest daughter, likewise named Hedwig, went on the stage, and with considerable success. Tiny and exquisite like her mother, she played Juliet in Meiningen. There the wealthy young mathematician Alfred Pringsheim saw her, resolved to marry her, and carried it off. For his bride he built "a princely house in the finest district of the beautiful city of Munich"[7] and filled it with his Renaissance collections.

> The palatial house on Arcisstrasse resembled a museum, but it was equipped with all modern comforts. The Pringsheims were among the first people in Munich to acquire a telephone and electric light. Their house soon became a center of the intellectual and fashionable world. . . . The social style of the house was simultaneously informal and opulent. The most famous painters, musicians, and writers of the era there met princes of the House of Wittelsbach, Bavarian generals, and traveling bankers from Frankfurt and Berlin. The hostess . . . contrived always to be amusing and original—whether she chattered about Schopenhauer and Dostoevsky or about the latest soirée at the

crown princess's. Among her admirers were artists such as Franz von Lenbach, Kaulbach, and Stuck, to whom she sat for portraits. . . .[8]

The name Kaulbach brings us back to the *Children's Carnival*. Friedrich August von Kaulbach was director of the Munich Academy of Art and one of the most notable portraitists of the day. At a children's masquerade ball he happened to see Katia Pringsheim and her four brothers in their harlequin costumes, and as a friend of the family he asked the parents for permission to paint the children. They were delighted, of course, and the children sat for the artist. The painting caught on in the manner described by Thomas Mann; evidently it was "aimed directly at the heart of bourgeois taste." It was reproduced everywhere; friends of the Pringsheim family who had been to St. Petersburg brought back paper napkins with the five Pringsheim harlequins decorating one corner. The original oil hung in the resplendent Renaissance living room of the Pringsheim mansion on Arcisstrasse, and there Thomas Mann must have seen it on his first visit. Sooner or later he made the association between the dark-eyed child in the picture and the daughter of the house. But he never said, and Katia never asked, at what point recognition came.

Katia Pringsheim and her twin brother Klaus were tutored at home—an hour a day sufficed for the elementary subjects of the first three years. Then Klaus went on to Gymnasium; but since in those days there was no Gymnasium for girls, several Gymnasium teachers came to the house on Arcisstrasse to tutor Katia in their subjects. Her father's position made it possible for her to take the *Abitur*. She passed this examination with ease, and thus qualified for the university. There she studied experimental physics with Röntgen, the discoverer of X-rays, along with calculus and the theory of functions with her father. She also read widely—she had read *Buddenbrooks* before the author of that long novel crossed her path. She learned French from her governess, and during her childhood thought in that language rather than Bavarian German. She could read the New Testament in Greek. So it is hardly surprising that Thomas Mann, a mediocre scholar, to put it mildly, should have exclaimed that Katia was "a wonder, something indescribably rare and precious whose mere existence outweighs the cultural activities of fifteen writers or thirty painters."[9]

But his enthusiasm had been kindled even before he met this prodigy, for he had watched her from afar. The Pringsheim family were music lovers; so was Thomas Mann. In those days the "cause" of music lovers in Munich was the precarious financial state of Kaim Hall. Franz Kaim, wealthy son of a German piano manufacturer, had recently built this hall to house the "Kaim concerts," a subscription series he had founded. Even back then building costs could exceed estimates, and when the hall was completed the entrepreneur discovered that he was on the brink of bankruptcy.* The music lovers of Munich rallied to the builder's support by taking subscriptions to concerts long in advance. Wealthy Professor Pringsheim bought five subscriptions at once so that all of his children could attend together. The five beautiful young people in their orchestra seats, chattering and joking in their private language, made a striking sight. And the writer in the cheaper balcony, sweeping the audience with his opera glasses, early took note of them. Perhaps the unconscious image of *Children's Carnival* prompted him to hold his glasses in lingering contemplation of the five. As he wrote to Katia during the courtship:

> It is almost always in the Kaimsaal that I see you, for I often watched you there through my opera glasses before we knew each other. I see you coming in from the left, up front, with your mother and your brothers, see you going to your seat in one of the front rows, see the silver shawl around your shoulders, your black hair, the pearly pallor of your face, your expression as you try to seem unaware that people's eyes are on you—it is impossible to say how perfectly and how wonderfully in detail I see you! . . .[10]

According to Katia Mann, the decisive impulse came from an incident in the streetcar. Thomas Mann has given a transmuted version of it in the changing-of-the-guard scene in *Royal Highness*. As Katia Mann tells it:

> When not using my bicycle, I always went to classes by streetcar in the morning and again in the afternoon, and Thomas Mann often took the same car. I had to get out at the stop at the corner of Schell-

---

* Heinrich Mann made use of this "material" in *Die Jagd nach Liebe*, assigning Kaim's misfortunes to his hero, Claude Marehn.

ing and Türkenstrasse and walk the rest of the way, with my brief-case under my arm. Once, as I was about to get off, the conductor came up and said, "Your ticket."

I say: "I'm getting off here."

"I gotta have your ticket."

I say: "But I tell you that I'm getting off. I've just thrown it away because I'm getting off here."

"I gotta have your ticket. Your ticket, I said."

"Just leave me alone," I said, and jumped off in a rage.

He called after me: "Beat it, you fury!"[11]

In the original television interview on which her memoirs are based, Katia Mann imitates with vivacity and delight the conductor's dialect and his pronunciation of the highfalutin German word *Furie* as *Furche*. As she tells the anecdote, her face at nearly ninety still holds much of the loveliness and liveliness that Thomas Mann discerned in the girl of twenty.

The anecdote is revealing in another way. For if what impressed the young writer was the princely tone of the Pringsheims, what Katia seems to have prided herself on was her independence and her familiarity with plebeian reality as represented by the streetcar. Perhaps this combination of high privilege and a roguish down-to-earth quality was the essence of that patrician spirit which Thomas Mann had known from childhood.

There were other combinations. As the only girl among four brothers, Katia grew up something of a tomboy, and her boyish ways could have been more appealing to Thomas Mann than the careful manners of more conventional young ladies. The merry child of the harlequin picture was now a striking beauty. A painting of 1899 shows her with a mass of dark hair falling over her shoulders in a romantic tumble. Her features are firmly chiseled and harmonious; her eyes especially have an intense keenness and gravity. This particular look in the eyes is also to be recognized in the photograph of the seventeen-year-old taken when Katia and her twin brother Klaus were about to enter the university. She wears a white sailor costume with a white cap tilted rakishly over her forehead. But the expression is of the utmost seriousness. It is that of a girl looking deep into her unknown future.

T H E man who was to give that future its shape had by now seen her frequently, was determined to meet her, and fortunately found himself in a position to arrange a meeting. For he was no longer the unknown young scribbler from Lübeck. The steady sale of *Buddenbrooks*, the acclaim for *Tristan*, the increasing number of public readings, had transformed the shy young man into something of a social lion. He had gone as far afield as Königsberg in East Prussia to read to the Literary Society there, and had followed this by a reading at the Press Club in Berlin. There he had been invited to the home of Samuel Fischer, where he had met Germany's foremost dramatist, the dominant literary personality of the day, Gerhart Hauptmann. That was "a momentous experience"[12]—the comment comes from his bread-and-butter note to his publisher. And Fischer, with his instinct for bringing his writers together, probably put Mann in touch with the firm's Munich author Ernst Rosmer.

The name Ernst Rosmer concealed a woman who in private life was Elsa Bernstein. It is to Frau Justizrat Bernstein that both Katia and Thomas Mann always gave the credit for promoting the match. Elsa Bernstein and her husband, Max, a distinguished Munich lawyer, were both writers and both S. Fischer authors. Ernst Rosmer wrote a number of highly successful plays; the Bernsteins entertained on the kind of scale that made their home a notable gathering place for the artists, writers, and musicians of Munich. A woman of forty at this time, Elsa Bernstein loved young people and enjoyed introducing younger artists to those who were already established. Felix Weingartner and Hugo von Hofmannsthal frequented her salon; so did a novelist whom Thomas Mann greatly admired, though he never met him: Theodor Fontane; so did the painters Stuck and Kaulbach. And the Bernsteins, for their part, were members of the circle—a very wide circle it was—that received invitations to the home of Professor Alfred Pringsheim.

Frau Bernstein apparently procured Thomas Mann an introduction to the Pringsheim household. Some time in February 1904 he paid a formal call there, was briefly introduced to the daughter of the house, and was invited to the grand ball—no fewer than one hundred and fifty guests—that the Pringsheims were giving the next day to celebrate Fasching. As both a newcomer to the house and "a famous man,"[13] Thomas Mann found himself the object of much curiosity.

He was stared at, introduced around, listened to. *Buddenbrooks* had reached the eighteenth thousand (as he noted in a rather tactless letter to Heinrich), and he found himself having to put on a public persona "in the most strenuous way."[14] His usual self-irony returned when he remarked to Heinrich (who would certainly catch the allusion to the plan for *Royal Highness*): "Basically I have a rather princely talent for 'representation' when I am in fairly good form."[15]

That evening of the grand ball he really met Katia Pringsheim—that is, he had some opportunity to talk with her. His lady at table was none other than Elsa Bernstein, and perhaps it was on this occasion that he confessed to her his interest, so that her matchmaking instincts were aroused. Katia Mann recalls that shortly after their first meeting Elsa Bernstein invited the two of them to dinner and thoughtfully seated them side by side. But by then, it would seem, Thomas Mann had already made a considerable impression on his own. He had cleverly borrowed a book from Frau Hedwig Pringsheim, and a week after the ball he called on her, on the excellent pretext that he was returning the book. "I found her alone. She . . . she called Katia down, and the three of us chatted for an hour. . . . The prospect of an invitation to lunch was held out."

Hedwig Pringsheim had understood at once what was afoot, and Thomas Mann—who after one evening with Katia had fallen head over heels in love—sensed that the mother was well disposed toward him. That is hardly surprising. Both of Frau Pringsheim's parents had been literary people; a writer must have seemed to her an eminently acceptable and natural suitor for her daughter. And here was a young writer, handsome in his rather stiff way, who moreover had been connected with a satirical magazine, just like Ernst Dohm. And so two days after Thomas Mann returned her book, Frau Pringsheim sent her son Klaus to reciprocate the call. Mann noted:

> He brought me a card from his father who, alas, was too busy to call on me himself. I had met Klaus briefly at the ball: a highly prepossessing young man, soigné, informed, amiable, with North German manners. Not a suggestion of Jewishness arises in connection with these people; one is aware of nothing but culture. We chatted freely about art, about his music, his sister. . . .[16]

At the end of February 1904, Mann's imagination had already outstripped reality. Seeing himself as good as married to Katia Pringsheim, he exclaimed: "The possibility has dawned on me and makes me burn."[17] His brother's potential objections came to his own mind: the question of race, and above all the question of wealth. He could see Heinrich, with his antibourgeois sentiments, sneering at his ambition to marry into the upper bourgeoisie. And he answered the potential charge by pointing out in his letter to Heinrich that he already had more money than he knew what to do with—again a tactless thing to say to his struggling brother. In any case he was above material things: "Whether I warm my feet at night by a kerosene stove or a marble fireplace does not affect the degree of my comfort."[18]

When Elsa Bernstein invited Thomas Mann and Katia Pringsheim to dinner, she kindly made sure that the young writer would shine as the guest of honor: she asked him to give a reading. Thereafter his calls at Arcisstrasse 12 became more frequent. When Thomas Mann arrived, the servant Ignatz—who came from the eastern provinces of Austria and was given to the kind of Slavic termination that Mann later made use of in *Death in Venice*—would whisper conspiratorially: "Fräulein Katiu is in the garden."[19] Klaus Pringsheim played nearly as active a matchmaking role as Elsa Bernstein; he served as a chaperone who knew how to look the other way, and lent his support to a suit that Katia at first did not take very seriously. Probably he also invented the nickname by which the Pringsheim brothers referred to Mann, "the liverish cavalry captain."[20]

''I SUFFER a great deal, but also enjoy quarter hours of unimaginable happiness; and when I of all people chose K.P. of all people for love and marriage, I could not expect that everything would run as smoothly as between Hans Müller and Käthchen Schulze."[21] So Thomas Mann wrote to Kurt Martens after three trying months during which he had striven to persuade Katia Pringsheim to consent to marry him.

The grand ball "in the Italian Renaissance salon with the tapestries, the Lenbachs, the doorjambs of *giallo antico*,"[22] had taken place after the first week in February. One lovely day in March Thomas Mann boldly turned up at Arcisstrasse 12 and invited Katia to accompany him on a bicycle tour, claiming that she had promised to go. She had promised nothing of the kind, but the warmth and sunlight were so enticing that she went along anyhow—only to punish him for his brazenness by racing away on her "very good, fast American Cleveland bike."[23] With the vulgar bicycle transmogrified into a blooded steed, the scene ultimately was played out between the American heiress Imma Spoelmann and Prince Klaus Heinrich in *Royal Highness*.

Perhaps even for Hans Müller and Käthchen Schulze—or for Jack and Jill—the course of true love never runs so smoothly. Professor Pringsheim was not eager to see Katia's studies interrupted, and he apparently had a father's usual reluctance to lose a daughter. But his displeasure did not go so far as active opposition. Frau Pringsheim indicated that she favored the suit of this highly presentable young man, concerning whom the family bookseller, Herr Buchholz, gave such a favorable testimonial: "Thomas Mann? Oh, yes. He will certainly make at least as much of a name for himself as Gottfried Keller."[24] A mere six weeks after Mann formally met the Pringsheims he was already risking, in Hedwig Pringsheim's presence, references to "Katia" instead of the "Fräulein Katia" or "your daughter" that etiquette prescribed. This audacity is alluded to in the lighthearted story—essentially another of his "sketches"— that he wrote during the spring of 1904: "At the Prophet's."

The story was based on a reading that Mann attended on Good Friday (April 1), 1904. Perhaps it was the date that prompted the author to indulge himself in a little numerological foolery: he mentions "the novelist" seventh among the guests. Ultimately an even dozen arrive for the reading of Daniel's "Proclamations," and at the last minute this number is increased, by the arrival of "the wealthy lady," to thirteen—the number of persons present at the Last Supper. It is difficult to see any really serious purpose in these references to the Easter story—probably Mann merely wished to set up reverberations in the reader's mind. On this occasion, at any rate, there is no question of any supper; the fierce, humorless disciple goes on and on with his reading until the novelist is famished.

The model for the prophet Daniel (resurrected as Daniel zur Höhe in *Doctor Faustus*) was Ludwig Derleth, a poet of some reputation who was a member of the Stefan George circle. Daniel's sister, Maria Josefa in the story, was modeled on Derleth's sister, who was acquainted with both the Manns and the Pringsheims. Katia Mann in her memoirs speaks of her as "the beautiful Anna Maria Derleth," and remarks: "They both had a way of trying to turn every-thing into something remarkable and marvelous and intense."[25] If Thomas Mann noticed Anna Maria's beauty, he prudently kept all reference to it out of his story.

"At the Prophet's" was probably written during Mann's stay in Riva from the middle of April through the first week in May. Mann calls the story a "harmless tribute"[26] to Frau Professor Pringsheim, who figures in it as the rich and beautiful lady who attends such bohemian functions "out of curiosity, out of boredom, out of craving for something different, out of amiable extravagance, out of pure universal goodwill, which is rare enough in this world."[27] The portrait was flattering enough, and he could not imagine that she would be angry with him. Yet he took the precaution of showing the manuscript to her. In it he openly admits his love for the lady's daughter, so that this was also a way of making his suit explicit without having to offer the embarrassing declaration of intentions which might otherwise have been requisite. Thus "At the Proph-et's" fulfilled a function in the courtship. Its wonderfully humorous depiction of the garret artist—"strange regions there are, strange minds, strange realms of the spirit, lofty and spare"[28]—served Mann as a means of distancing himself, in the eyes of the Pringsheims, from bohemian extremes. Only recently he had shown Tonio Kröger as an habitué of artists' studios, as a strayed bourgeois. Now he was taking pains to portray the narrator in "At the Prophet's," who is almost undisguisedly Mann himself, as a bourgeois returning to the fold, who after exposure to genius, to "the isolation, the freedom, the spiritual passion, the magnificent vision," thinks chiefly of his sup-per and deplores the absence of "a little feeling, a little yearning, a little love."[29] At the very beginning of the sketch Mann defines his own position in the phrase that thirty-three years later he chose for the title of his magazine: *Mass und Wert*. The suitor affirms his be-lief in moderation and established values.

While he was in Riva Mann received a book that helped to raise his spirits at this critical juncture and to give him the courage to pursue his arduous courtship. The book was *Die Bilanz der Moderne* by Samuel Lublinski—the reviewer who had predicted that *Budden-brooks* would be read by generations to come. Now, in a book that aimed to be a definitive study of contemporary literature, Lublinski was calling Mann "the most important novelist of the modern movement." Lublinski neatly summed up the ideas behind *Buddenbrooks:* the theory of heredity "discreetly hinted at" in the background, combined with observation of social change. "An originally robust family of merchants that has risen to high station slowly goes to pieces, because along with cultural refinement the crude and even somewhat stupid instincts begin to crumble, and because this process of disintegration unfortunately reaches its climax in the seventies, when the boom engendered by finance capital and industry was literally crying out for robust brutes." With astonishing empathy, for he knew nothing of Mann's highly private identification with the image of St. Sebastian, Lublinski spoke of the "clear and cold lines drawn with a firm and subtle hand" and of "the intellectual manliness of a youth who clenches his teeth and stoically stands while the swords and spears pierce his body."[30] This endurance of the slings and arrows of fortune, Lublinski continued, also characterized the novel's protagonist, Senator Thomas Buddenbrook. Mann expressed his deep sympathy with his characters only by way of a melancholic irony, Lublinski pointed out, and this had caused many critics to misunderstand him altogether and charge him with coldness.

Mann promptly wrote to Lublinski expressing his warmest thanks for the book. Only five or six persons in Germany knew what irony was, he declared, and understood that it was not necessarily the result of coldheartedness. He was so pleased with this formulation that he soon afterward repeated it in letters to others, including Katia.

He was writing to Katia now. The stay in Riva produced the first of those letters which played so large a part in his successful wooing. For lovely, twenty-year-old Katia Pringsheim was by no means flattered out of her wits that a distinguished writer, who seemed older than his twenty-eight years, had fallen desperately in love with her and wanted to marry her. "I was twenty and quite happy with my existence, with my studies, my brothers, the tennis club, everything. I was content and really didn't see why I should leave it all so quickly."[31] She did not at all want to marry so young, and to her suitor's pleas kept replying: "But we don't know each other well enough yet."[32] It was a heavy campaign Thomas had to mount, and he encountered the usual difficulty of lovers in the early years of the twentieth century: that young men and women were seldom left alone. "All these little amusements that fill the evening mean wasted time, an almost wicked waste of time, while we—you and I—would have so many more important things to talk about," he complains. "You must know, must see from my face, how intensely, how painfully that keeps coming back into my mind. If only we were alone more! Or if I knew how to make better use of the brief minutes that are sometimes given to me!"[33]

By the end of April he had told her "in plain words" how much he loved her. In his letters he pleads for understanding, blames himself for any awkwardness she feels with him:

> You know that I could not develop myself personally, humanly, as other young people do. . . . You know what a cold, impoverished existence mine has been, organized purely to display art, to represent life; you know that for many years, *important* years, I regarded myself as nothing, humanly speaking, and wished to be considered only as an artist. . . . Only one thing can cure me. . . .[34]

By his twenty-ninth birthday he had learned how to make better use of the brief minutes alone with her that were sometimes given, could speak of "the inexpressible bliss of the seconds in the dark garden when I felt your sweet, sweet head against my cheek." And although on that occasion he left with "mortal sadness," he could still declare: "I have no reproaches for you. Only love! Only love!"[35]

That experienced paterfamilias and man of the world Kurt Martens, who by now had completely replaced Otto Grautoff in the role of intimate, advised him to get away from Munich and Katia's benumbing presence, to stop acting like a lovesick mooncalf and assert himself, to insist that Katia stop putting him off. "What kind of weakling are you anyhow?" Martens wrote (or so Mann quotes him). "Everyone knows that you are wooing her, everyone is talking about it. And she continually sets you trials of patience, puts you off, plays with you. Is that a proper part for you? Show yourself a man! Give her an ultimatum! You cannot help seeming less and less desirable to her, the longer the thing drags on. . . ."[36]

Mann retorted that he was grateful for the friendly intention, that Martens saw the matter the way every impartial person had to see it—and that nevertheless he was wrong:

To manifest manly strength by confronting the girl with the decision would mean forcing her to say no, to the sorrow of both of us; for right now, due to the unusual nature of her whole development, she cannot yet persuade herself to say yes. To play the vexed lord and master on that account, and with dignity throw the whole thing up, must strike me as the height of folly as long as I have reason to believe that it would be doing her an ill service. And she has given me reason for believing that. As far as people are concerned—well, they are entitled to have at last some reason for gossiping about me. I've been a reserved eccentric long enough and not very generous about feeding people's craving for sensation. Their talk can scarcely harm us, after all, for since when has it been a disgrace for a man to pay court openly to a girl?[37]

Katia continued to hold that everything was happening too quickly; her suitor declared that he was exercising "superhuman patience and tenacity."[38] He understood her reluctance better than she herself understood it. She enjoyed being with him, felt easy and uncomplicated with him—so long as he did not speak of marriage. But she could not see herself married, to him or to anyone else. He was, after all, not her first suitor—there had been a professor; there had been a young man from Silesia, likewise named Pringsheim; there had been other young men of no importance; and there had been the distinguished theater critic of the *Berliner Tageblatt*, Alfred Kerr—a man of thirty-seven at this time—who never forgave Thomas Mann for snatching the prize he had had his eye on. Katia had never taken these suitors seriously, since marriage was not on her mind, as it was for most girls of her class at that time. It was, however, on her mother's mind. Hedwig Pringsheim must have urged it on her daughter; perhaps this was one reason that whenever the issue came up, whenever Thomas Mann asked Katia to be his wife, she looked at him "like a hunted doe."[39]

The tension was relieved by chance. During the summer Katia's father fell gravely ill. Katia went to Bad Kissingen in Lower Franconia to help her mother, who had accompanied the professor to this noted *Kurort*. Thomas Mann saw Katia off:

I went to the train, brought her flowers, and since Klaus took a touchingly long time to pay the porter, I had the opportunity to tell her how sad I felt. Did she, too, feel a little sadness? A little, yes. Very careful. But at any rate she pressed my hand for a long time, and looked only at me while the train pulled out of the station. I feel like death. This is a parting for an almost indefinite time. She will stay three weeks in Kissingen, then stop only briefly in Munich on her way back; and she is going to Switzerland with her mother for the rest of the summer. In the autumn she will be with relatives in north Germany. Isn't it enough to drive one to despair? On the twenty-first of this month I am supposed to read to the Göttingen Literary Society, and I wanted to be in Bayreuth on the thirty-first for *Parsifal*, but I'll give that up if I can see her here for fifteen minutes. . . . You cannot imagine how I love this creature. I dream of her every night, and wake with my heart all sore. I have tasted too much of her to be able to surrender now. Death seems to me far less a surrender than living without her.[40]

There followed many letters to Katia, only a few of which have been preserved. In Munich, Mann noted, two or three days without Katia had seemed an eternity, and yet he managed to live for almost three months without her "in a tolerably good state of mind. Man is a remarkably tough vertebrate!"[41]

The separation, as he must have realized sometime during the summer, had been a godsend, because it allowed him to write frequently. In letters he was in his element. In letters he could create the intimacy that Katia fended off in their encounters. As she somewhat wryly remarked no fewer than seventy years later, "He *did* know how to write."[42] In letters he could say, as the courtship approached its climax: "Do you know why we suit each other so well? . . . Because you are, as I understand the word, a *princess*. And I —you may laugh now, but you must understand me—I have always seen myself as a kind of prince, and in you I have found, with absolute certainty, my predestined bride and companion."[43]

One cannot help wondering whether he was not confounding himself with one of his characters, one still only partly formed in his mind. Here, so close to the end of his courtship, this bit of posturing suggests that he was regaining some of his normal objectivity, was no longer so transcendently in love. If this is so, then he would have benefited by the rule he had set down in *Tonio Kröger:* "The one who is more deeply in love is at a disadvantage—life had already taught his fourteen-year-old soul this simple and harsh lesson."[44] Perhaps this subtle shift in his feelings may explain the suddenness of his victory once Katia returned home from the Baltic coast, where she and her twin brother had been vacationing with relatives. She was happy to see him after the long separation; they had some time alone together ("that you—immortal phrase—showed me your books"),[45] and in the very next letter, written at the end of September, the pronoun of formal address disappears and with an ecstatic *du* the lover writes: "Oh, you amazing, painfully sweet, painfully tangy creature!"[46] Hardly a conventional tribute, this; but its sharpness of definition makes clear how intensely felt it was.

On October 3, 1904, Thomas Mann became engaged to Katia Pringsheim. The romance had come to its predestined happy ending.

1 3

Marriage

"THE last half of the courtship—nothing but intense psychological stress. The engagement—no laughing matter either, believe me."[1] The sudden plunge from the contemplative to the active life imposed novel strains which Mann tried to deal with in his usual manner. On the one hand he played the Steadfast Tin Soldier of Andersen's fairy tale ("fundamentally it is the symbol of my life");[2] he wore his light-gray velvet vest with its silver buttons along with his dress coat and took pride in assurances that he was becoming more worldly. On the other hand he kept looking over his shoulder at himself, so to speak, trying to see what was happening to him. "Representation" was harder now, because he believed he had to *be* rather than to *seem*. The problem was to accommodate himself to a wholly new mode of existence. He had now officially entered the realm of happiness, and it behooved him to look around, to determine what the laws and ordinances were and where room could be found, in this hitherto unknown country, for writing.

The painful ambivalence with which he conducted these explorations may have been expressed in the persistent physical symptom he suffered from—"frightful constipation."[3]

His announcements of the engagement in letters to various friends reflect his tangled emotions. Public readings in Berlin and Lübeck had been arranged for the end of October. He had been looking forward especially to the appearance in Lübeck with eagerness and trepidation. Now the social obligations that followed from his engagement, combined with the necessity that he finish *Fiorenza* in time for its promised publication in the *Neue Deutsche Rundschau*, forced him to postpone both readings. In writing to Ida Boy-Ed in Lübeck to explain the reasons for the delay, he characterized his state of mind as "an incredible mixture of distraction, blissfulness, and exhaustion," and spoke of his twinges of conscience springing from "the artist's half moralistic, half ascetic suspicions of 'happiness.' "[4]

Ida Boy-Ed, his motherly Lübeck friend, was a fellow writer to whom he could confide such scruples. She would understand his defense of "indiscretion" followed by an indiscreet reference to his cool literary relations with his brother. The ideas that he would soon try to work out in an essay on "Mind and Art" were already germinating. At best he regarded Heinrich as a determined aesthete, a principled devotee of beauty—which Thomas was apt to call *Schönheit* when he wanted to express a certain respect for it; when he was particularly angry or disgusted with the cult of beauty he would scornfully refer to it by the Italian word *bellezza*. Yet even in anger he carefully weighed his words, as in this confession to Ida Boy-Ed:

> We almost broke off relations with each other over his last book. Nevertheless, the feeling that his artistic personality awakens in me is as far as possible from contempt. Rather, it is hatred. His books are bad, but they are so in such an extraordinary way that they provoke passionate opposition. I am not referring to the shamelessness of his eroticism, which is merely boring, or to his sensual haptomania, which is both mindless and soulless. What outrages me is the aestheticistic iciness, the funereally cold wind, that blows from his books. It is repugnant to me in the same way as the atmosphere in Hofmannsthal's *Elektra*. The art of these people is provocative but lacks inner

strength; it pierces dreadfully to the bone without leaving anything at all behind spiritually . . . but don't you know that I am more or less counted one of them! I am a "cold artist"; that has been said in more than one magazine. Because of an exaggerated adoration of art I have supposedly lost all relationship to feeling and to living life. Truly, I sometimes wish it were so. . . .[5]

Much might be said about the rightness or wrongness of this interpretation. As so often, Thomas Mann was rejecting in Heinrich the very tendencies he found in himself and considered harmful. To the superficial eye, the chief fault in Heinrich's writing of this period would seem to be an excess of heat rather than coldness. Certainly Heinrich often ruthlessly manipulated his characters; but the color, the sensuous detail, and the sensuality in his books made them read as if they had been written in a fever. Yet by the artistic standards that Thomas had worked out for himself, he was right about Heinrich. For he could see that his brother created his works out of observation and intelligence, whereas he, Thomas, invested much of himself in each of his characters.

Nevertheless, Heinrich was still the beloved brother to whom alone he could confide, with assurance of being understood, the ambiguities of his new situation. In a Christmas letter he apologized for not writing earlier and assured Heinrich that he had by no means ceased "to fret over the not altogether simple problem of our relationship." As if he felt the need to justify himself before this most intimate of critics, he elaborated on the question of happiness, which he had raised with Ida Boy-Ed. "I have never regarded happiness as something light and bright, but always as something earnest, grave and austere as life itself."[6] Moreover, this present happiness was not something he had either sought out or received as a gift. Rather, he had submitted to it out of a sense of duty, out of a sort of morality, obeying an innate imperative:

"Happiness" is a form of service—its opposite is incomparably more comfortable; and I stress that not because I assume that you are feeling anything like envy, but because I suspect that on the contrary you may be regarding my new existence and personality with some contempt. Don't. I have not made things easier for myself. Happiness, *my* happiness, is to a great extent experience, movement, insight, torment, it is akin not so much to peace as to suffering, and therefore could not possibly become a permanent danger to my art.[7]

By this time his readings were already behind him—Berlin, he told Heinrich, had been "a lush adventure, Lübeck a farcical and touching dream."[8] Katia and her mother accompanied him to Berlin so that he could meet some Pringsheim relatives—Katia's aunt and uncle Elsa and Hermann Rosenberg, Professor Pringsheim's parents, and "Little Grandma," Frau Hedwig Dohm. Throughout all these encounters he did his best, played the Steadfast Tin Soldier, but all the while remained conscious that adjustment to his new family required of him "absorbing efforts."[9] He did not try to make it wholly clear to Heinrich—and maybe it wasn't even clear to Thomas himself—whether the strangeness of these highly cultivated people sprang from their Jewishness or from their wealth; and perhaps his feelings of uneasiness were not much different from those of any prospective son-in-law being introduced to his bride's relations. But he was more conscious of these matters than the ordinary fiancé.

The dream of Lübeck was both touching and farcical, because he received from his native city, which he had not seen for five years, an actual wreath—was it of laurel?—for his readings from *Fiorenza* and "The Child Prodigy." A dinner followed the readings, and at table Mann could not resist—like any triumphant lover—speaking of his secret in public:

> Some of you know that I stand at a significant turning point in my life, as far as its outward and personal aspect goes. I was accompanied as far as Berlin by the girl who has consented to be my wife, and a wholly new chapter in the novel of my life is about to begin, a chapter that was conceived in a lovely delirium and that now must be shaped with love, art, and faithfulness.[10]

In Lübeck he did not venture to stay again at the Hotel Stadt Hamburg—for fear, as he jokingly remarked, of another attempt to arrest him. Instead he accepted Ida Boy-Ed's invitation to be her guest. He might well have preferred to stay with his sister Lula's friends the Kulenkamps, for he regarded Natalia Kulenkamp as "lovely in the tenderest meaning of the word."[11] The previous year she had come to Munich on a visit, and he had seen a good deal of her then and found that "much mutual sympathy"[12] existed between them. Natalia and Ida Boy-Ed had both invited him to stay in their homes whenever he came to Lübeck; he left it to them to decide between them, and the older woman was awarded the privilege. He did, however, see something of the Kulenkamps, for he had occasion to borrow a pair of rubber overshoes from Natalia's husband—he had brought none, although he should have remembered that it always rained in Lübeck in December. Perhaps there was something symbolic in his walking off with the overshoes and forgetting to return them. The previous year he had already observed that Herr Kulenkamp reminded him somewhat of one of his own characters, the Herr Klöterjahn of *Tristan*. In any case, the Lübeck reading went off without a hitch; there was a large audience, and "The Child Prodigy" was well received, although the scenes from *Fiorenza* were not so successful.

B A C K in Munich, he set to work, in the face of many social distractions, to prove to himself that the impending marriage and his establishment in "burgher" life would not destroy him as a writer. *Fiorenza* had been promised for an early issue of the *Neue Deutsche Rundschau*, so that it would be published in the fall. He had vowed to himself that he would finish this venture into drama before the wedding. With what he sometimes thought of as his last remaining energy, he succeeded in carrying out his intention. By the end of January 1905 *Fiorenza* was sent off to Berlin.

Inevitably, some of the preoccupations of this hectic period in his life entered into the play, in small matters and large. There is, for example, an allusion to one of Alfred Pringsheim's collections in Lorenzo's mention of "the bright objects of majolica."[13] Lorenzo's mistress, Fiore, had originally been conceived as a mythic being, ageless like Gerda Buddenbrook, skilled in magic arts, and bearing on her beautiful shoulders a heavy freight of allegory, for she was meant to represent all at once the city of Florence, Art, and Woman. Now, however, she took on some of the fleshly reality and sauciness of Katia Pringsheim: "She says the cheekiest things in so adorable and lovely a way that it sounds like the music of the angels."[14] The doubts that trouble almost every bridegroom beset the successful suitor. His ambivalence found expression in epigrams of renunciation: "One should not possess. Longing gives one a giant's powers; possession unmans."[15] Mann puts this sentiment into the mouth of the dying Lorenzo, who does not really mean it; the words are spoken under the shadow of illness and fear of death. And Mann, too, does not really mean such abnegations. They are not to be understood literally as philosophical positions. Rather, they are fancies he is playing with, notions engendered by the conflicts in his feelings.

Ideas held and not held, advocated and not advocated, are of the essence in what the world would later recognize as characteristic Mannian irony. But the intellectual content in *Fiorenza* could not be presented with that mastery of ironic detachment, that elegant equilibrium, that Mann ultimately achieved. In part he was hampered by the dialogue form, which limited the omniscient narrator's observations to brief stage directions. In part he had not yet worked his ideas out with sufficient clarity—a fact he well knew and confessed to Heinrich. The earnest correspondence he had been having with Heinrich over the means and ends of art has not been preserved. But the "brother problem"[16] found its way into the portraits of the two antagonists in *Fiorenza*. Again and again in the climactic final scene, stress is laid on the fraternal relationship. Lorenzo several times addresses Savonarola as "brother," and at one point he exclaims: "If we are enemies, so be it, but I tell you that we are enemy brothers." (Mann uses the phrase *feindliche Brüder*, which harkens back to the title of Schiller's tragedy *Die Braut von Messina oder Die feindlichen Brüder*.) The monk angrily repudiates this suggestion: "I hate this contemptuous fairness, this lewd condescension, this depraved tolerance of opposition."[17] Lorenzo is no portrait of Heinrich, any more than Savonarola is a portrait of the author. But the sensitive reader will detect, in the speeches of each, aspects of the two brothers, the characteristic timbres of their different voices. It is a measure of Thomas Mann's self-doubt, and of his fundamental respect for his elder brother, that he concedes Lorenzo the victory, insofar as any victor emerges from the confrontation: "You hate the age and the age understands you. Which is the greater?" Lorenzo asks. And although the prior savagely replies, "I am! I am!"[18] we do not believe him.

The antagonists find common ground in their disdain for the crowd. But Lorenzo's scorn is that of the haughty ruler who naturally despises the masses. In Savonarola's eager echoing of Lorenzo, on the other hand, there is a note of hypocrisy. "Fame teaches us the lesson of contempt," the prior says in one of those lines of blank verse that are scattered liberally throughout the play. The words fit well enough into the scene. But we somehow feel the author looking over his character's shoulder. Momentarily, we sense, Mann has lost his grip on the historical reality of the monk and the Medici. Such lapses are rare in Mann's work, for he had already learned how to use research to stimulate his imagination and to provide the necessary factual background for his fictional structures. For *Fiorenza* he had studied Vasari's *Lives of the Painters*, Jacob Burckhardt's *Civilization of the Renaissance*, and Pasquale Villari's works on Florence and Savonarola. For dates and data, for the characters of Pico della Mirandola or Piero de' Medici, he relied on these authorities. For his depiction of the Florentine artists as greedy, vain, jealous, superstitious, squabbling children, he could draw on his own observations on the art world of Munich, which he had earlier described in a brilliant offshoot of *Fiorenza*, the short story "Gladius Dei." But all his faithfulness to detail did not suffice to make of *Fiorenza* the kind of artistic triumph his readers had already come to expect.

One of the difficulties, surely, lay in the change in the author's intentions during the five years he had been occupied, on and off, with the drama. In the course of those years he had learned from experience something about fame and ambition, and what he learned must have changed his perspective on Savonarola. Villari, his principal authority, showed Savonarola in a highly favorable light, as a sincere reformer, devout, moderate in victory, so little the destroying angel that he saved Lorenzo's library at the expense of his own monastery. Under Villari's influence, Mann initially accepted the friar's own view of himself: "So far there is nothing of the *King of Florence* but the psychological points and a formless dream: the rest is yet to come. The ambiguity of the title is of course intentional. Christ and Fra Girolamo are one: weakness become genius dominating life."[19]

These words were written in 1900. In the completed *Fiorenza* there is little Christlike about Savonarola. His kingdom is very much of this world, and it is based on hatred rather than love. As Mann shows him, Savonarola is motivated by something akin to the prophetic fury of Praisegod Piepsam in "The Way to the Churchyard." In his confrontation with Lorenzo the friar raves that he will break the city's great wings. At that threat to his beloved Florence, Lorenzo cries out in anguish and refuses absolution. The final scene is replete with Mannian ironies: Lorenzo, the exponent of art and life, is dying; the spokesman for mortality and death is momentarily victorious. And the final scene, with its rapid shifts of emotions, its locking of wills, and its passionate discussion of Mind and Art, almost rescues the work as drama. Almost.

Mann himself was too astutely self-critical to believe he had carried it off. Although he was enormously relieved to have finished, to have sustained the discipline of the dutiful writing stint while engaging to the full in what he still ironically referred to as "Life," he also recognized that he had suffered "a grave defeat."[20] And he saw what the major difficulty was: his "effort to fill an intellectual construct with life" had resulted in a "fiasco."[21] Ever since the writing of *Tonio Kröger* he had excessively confounded the concepts of Mind and Art, he told his brother; and in the play he had set them up as hostile opposites. Now he had learned his lesson, and his only hope was to turn back, to return to the "naiveté" of *Buddenbrooks.* The play was plainly too long and too lacking in dramatic intensity for stage performance. It needed the detachment and subtlety that an author's commentary could provide, but the dialogue form ruled that out. *Fiorenza* would remain, he sadly acknowledged, "a mongrel."[22] He was steeled for a rough reception—but then, he expected the same for all his works immediately upon finishing them. It had been a pleasant surprise, therefore, when Oscar Bie, editor of the *Neue Deutsche Rundschau,* termed the play "something extremely choice."[23] Bie was well disposed toward Mann; it was he who had first welcomed the young author of "Little Herr Friedemann" to the Fischer Verlag, and had thrown his support behind *Buddenbrooks.* The two men had met at last during Mann's December visit to Berlin. Yet Bie's praise of *Fiorenza* might seem to imply that the play was caviar to the general. Whatever Bie meant,

Mann took his words as highly affirmative, and possibly found in them some needed encouragement as his wedding day drew near.

T H E wedding took place at the civil registry on February 11, 1905, followed by a family reception at the Pringsheim home on Arcisstrasse. The Mann family was represented by Mother Julia, Sister Julia and her husband, Josef Löhr, and the somewhat scapegrace younger brother, Viktor, who was not quite fifteen. Viktor consumed lobster mayonnaise and Moët et Chandon 1898 to excess and relates—but he is not always a trustworthy reporter—how Thomas got around the frightful custom of a formal speech by invoking the nicknames of all the important members of the Pringsheim family: "Ladies and gentlemen, have no fear—I shall be brief. Mimchen, Muhne, Puhne, Fink, and Fei—hurrah!"

Neither Carla nor Heinrich Mann was present, and years later Thomas saw to it that he was unable to attend Heinrich's precipitate wartime wedding. Carla's reason or pretext was legitimate: she was under contract in a distant provincial theater of the sort described in Heinrich's *Die Jagd nach Liebe*. And Heinrich was unwilling to leave Florence, because he had at last been successful in his own "pursuit of love." He had met and fallen in love with Ines Schmied, a girl who resembled his mother in her origins—she was the daughter of a German who had become an Argentine planter—and his sister Carla in her ambitions: she wanted to be an actress or singer. Ines was the same age as Katia, like her a beauty, but in disposition far more bohemian. Heinrich Mann would ultimately commingle traits of Ines and his mother to create his remarkable Lola, the heroine of *Zwischen den Rassen*. Unlike his brother, Heinrich seemed in no hurry to explore the "bourgeois" condition of formal marriage. Ines was bent on a career, and on Heinrich's part the financial basis for marriage in the style then required scarcely existed.

For Thomas it was otherwise. Immediately after the wedding he and Katia set out for an elegant honeymoon in Switzerland. A week after the wedding Thomas at last had the leisure to write to Heinrich, to thank him for the wedding present that he had sent jointly (without ever seeing it) with Carla, and to express his own astonishment at "what I have gone and done in real life."[24] At the moment, he somewhat abashedly admitted, he and Katia were living "on the lushest scale" in Zürich's finest hotel, the Baur au Lac. And with for once a tactful awareness of Heinrich's sensibilities he declared that his conscience was not always untroubled by this life in a fool's paradise—*Schlaraffenleben*, he called it, as a kind of bow to Heinrich's Berlin novel, *Im Schlaraffenland*.

FATHER-IN-LAW Pringsheim's wedding gift to the young couple—and a way of easing the loss of his daughter for himself—was a completely furnished apartment. Located at Number 2 Franz-Josephstrasse, it was conveniently near to Arcisstrasse, so that the schoolgirl abruptly transformed into housewife could easily drop in on her parents or brothers anytime she pleased. In keeping with Mann's fondness for height above the street, the apartment was three flights up, and during her pregnancy Katia found those stairs toilsome. Except for the altitude, the young husband's wishes seem to have been consulted to the minimum extent consistent with good manners. Alfred Pringsheim took pleasure in selecting fine pieces of antique furniture; and Mann clearly felt a certain irritation at the high-handed way the father-in-law went about making decisions even in regard to the writer's study and desk.

Whatever dissatisfaction the new tenant may have felt about the appointments of that study, however, he did not let it go unused. Although toward the end of the year we find him complaining about how little he had produced, he seems to have settled into a habit of regular work during the early months of his marriage. His morale depended upon it; the example of Heinrich certainly spurred him (his brother had still another novel coming out in the spring!); and circumstance made it incumbent upon him to deliver something. The hundredth anniversary of Schiller's death was approaching, and *Simplicissimus* was planning a special issue in honor of Germany's great dramatist, poet, and historian. Thomas Mann, the magazine's former assistant editor, was naturally asked to contribute something. Only recently he had written of Tonio Kröger's enthusiasm for *Don Carlos*. Now something different was required—but he did not attempt the sort of essayistic appreciation to which, a full half century later, he would devote almost the entire last year of his life.

Instead, he took a few morsels from his personal life, especially from his latest experiences, together with a few morsels from Schiller's biography, and mingled them to perform that act of the imagination for which in later years he came to use the phrase *unio mystica*. During the composition of a short, enchanting, slightly mysterious sketch entitled "A Weary Hour," he became Friedrich Schiller arriving at an impasse in the writing of *Wallenstein*—as he himself had so often arrived at impasses while laboring over *Fiorenza*. The time of the story, given in careful clues, is December 1796. The unnamed writer, seated at his desk, shivers and snuffles, then gets up to go over to the tile stove. But it is after midnight, the household sleeps, and the stove is cold. The writer broods on his work— why not acknowledge that it is a defeat, a misguided undertaking? "The design was wrong and the language was wrong; it was a dry and lifeless history lecture, slow paced, uninspired, useless for the stage."[25]

We know, of course—*we* being Mann's readers of 1905—that *Wallenstein*, that unplayable monster of a drama, ultimately became a classic of the German stage, even though it had to be performed on two or three successive nights. Despite his candid confession of defeat in his letter to Heinrich, Mann had evidently not entirely abandoned hope for his *Fiorenza*. Perhaps the world would once more prove to him that he had wrought better than he knew.

"A Weary Hour" may be read both as a sincere homage to Schiller and as a statement of some of Mann's deepest concerns at this juncture in his life, immediately after his marriage. The story's charm lies in the tension between the authentic biographical elements that refer to Schiller and the autobiographical passages in which Mann speaks with remarkable candor of his own concerns. He engaged in research, but he used the results with considerable freedom. Thus he described the study in Jena from a photograph of Schiller's study in Weimar. He pieced together fragments from the writer's letters in order to compose much of Schiller's interior monologue; but he also intermingled a fragment from a letter of his own, which he had written to Katia the previous August. Early in his married life he had asked Katia for permission to excerpt some of his letters to her. He copied the passage in question into his notebook, and immediately afterward jotted a reminder to himself to purchase a book, *Schiller: Intimes aus seinem Leben,* by Ernst Müller.[26] The passage from his letter ran:

> . . . because my work is causing me much trouble. This is of course quite in order and in itself not a bad sign. It has never yet "effervesced," and would make me suspicious if it did. It effervesces only for ladies and dilettantes, for the easily satisfied and the ignorant who do not live under the pressure and the discipline of talent. . . . For the greatest, the most insatiable, their talent is the harshest scourge.[27]

Almost every individual element in "A Weary Hour" points in two directions, toward Friedrich Schiller and toward Thomas Mann. Schiller's near-invalid condition is feelingly described, but some of the symptoms are Mann's own, not Schiller's. The writer's youthfulness is stressed, and his weariness. The sentences about the artist's egotism apply equally to the story's subject and its author: "To be great, to be extraordinary, to conquer the world and win an imperishable name! . . . To be known, known and loved by the peoples of this earth! Babble all you will of egotism, you who know nothing of the sweetness of this dream and this drive. Everyone who is out of the ordinary is egotistic. . . ."[28]

A magical blending of subject and author takes place in the closing passage, where the writer stands over his sleeping wife, looking down at the dark ringlet of hair curling over her cheek. Simultaneously he avows his love and begs her forgiveness for his need to wrestle with his self-imposed task. He warns her that he may not be wholly hers, never wholly happy in her, because of his commitment. Then, after stooping to kiss her, he tears himself away from the lovely warmth of her slumber and returns to his desk.

We, the readers contemplating this moving scene, must be careful not to project every single detail upon the author himself. The sum is truer than the parts. Thomas Mann never wrote after midnight, and in his well-ordered household, sustained by the servants his substantial income and Alfred Pringsheim's subsidy made possible, the stoves never grew cold in December. During the time of his struggles with *Fiorenza*, Mann had not yet been married. Rather than carry that uncertain literary project into the uncertainties of the married state, he had finished the play all in a rush, contrary to his habit and convictions. Strictly speaking, therefore, the ending of

"A Weary Hour" refers only to Schiller. But the emotion informing those final paragraphs would have been inaccessible to Thomas Mann a scant two months earlier.

Neither Katia nor Thomas has recorded the subtle adjustments that householding requires of a newly married pair, the assignment of roles that follows the formation of a partnership. But it is clear that the high-spirited young woman who had grown up surrounded by four brothers soon took over the management of those departments of daily life for which her husband seemed inadequately equipped. She began at once to edit his business letters, and in later years she took over the writing of them. She began also to serve as sensitive listener to readings from works in progress.

A new work was initiated almost immediately after the completion of "A Weary Hour." Mann's experiences with Katia's Berlin relatives, the Rosenbergs, had inspired a story that he thought of as the "Tiergarten novella"[29]—the Rosenbergs lived in the Tiergarten section of Berlin. While Katia went through the stages of her first pregnancy, Mann worked away through the summer and early fall on "The Blood of the Walsungs," trying to distill his impressions of the new milieu into which he had been plunged. What was characteristically Jewish, what characteristic of wealth?

While he was working on the story, chance provided him with a further opportunity for studying the Rosenbergs at home. He and Katia had decided to vacation in Zoppot, on the Baltic coast, during August. They had considered Travemünde, but Katia had been shy of exposing herself, six months pregnant, to the curiosity of her husband's fellow townsmen. Otherwise she seemed to take pregnancy very well; in Zoppot they went for two- and three-hour walks without her tiring. Altogether, the beginning of their seaside stay was exhilarating. But then the weather turned rainy and windy, the paths softened to muck, word came that there was cholera in nearby Danzig, and the two decided to cut their stay short by a week. They fled to the Villa Rosenberg in Wannsee,

> where we intend to stay another week before our return to Munich, as guests of my wife's relatives; here we lead a sheltered, superior life. Ah, say what you will, wealth is a good thing after all. I am enough of an artist, corruptible enough, to be enchanted by it. And besides, the contradictory tendency to asceticism on the one hand and

luxury on the other hand is probably part and parcel of the modern psyche. One can see it on the grand scale in Richard Wagner.[30]

Back home at his mahogany desk Mann ingeniously combined the material of his observations with a *jeu d'esprit*—the potentialities of twinship. He performed a kind of thought experiment upon his characters, using for his model of twins some traits of his wife and her brother Klaus, such as their habit of holding hands. Further in the background, as a contributory source of "The Blood of the Walsungs," may be Poe's "Fall of the House of Usher," a tale that was one of Mann's earliest impressions. Rereading it in September 1933 he noted "details that I have imitated: the Lady passing through the background of the room is the same as Frau Pastor Höhlenrauch in 'Tristan.' "[31] Though Mann speaks of imitating "details" in the plural, he mentions no other instances. But it is worth remembering that the brother and sister in Poe's story are presumably incestuous, twins who understand each other by the merest signs—"sympathies of a scarcely intelligible nature had always existed between them."[32] Of course the incest motif was also openly borrowed from Wagner; the romantic mélange formed an excellent cover for the story's realistic observation. Mann's use of *Die Walküre*, that arch-Aryan drama by the anti-Semitic composer, as the template for his Jewish Siegmund and Sieglinde must surely be ranked among the richest ironies in his fiction.

The incest motif admirably served the purpose of disguise. The shock effect on the reader of his bringing into the open the traditionally taboo relationship between brother and sister served to distract attention from his real subject: the mores of wealthy Jews, among whom he was now cast by marriage and by his profession. "The Blood of the Walsungs" is a novella of manners; Mann minutely sets down the decor of wealth: the rugs, the eighteenth-century *boiserie*, the tapestries with their pastoral idylls, the orchids in a glass vase at each table setting. The table conversation is unlike anything to be found among the dullards of northern Germany, and poor Beckerath, the stolid Hunding of the tale, the intruder into this closely knit family and inbred race, cannot keep up his end. The wit, the displays of logic-chopping among the young people, their condescension toward their father—all these half-racial, half-familial traits are recorded with the precision and impartiality of an outsider

become insider. Not all the observation reflected the Berlin Rosenbergs; the Pringsheim atmosphere also made its contribution. For
that reason Mann took care to introduce superficial camouflage.
Frau Aarenhold is described as emphatically ugly; there would be
no confounding her with his mother-in-law, who was still noted for
her beauty. Herr Aarenhold is made a businessman, not a professor.

As a further precaution, Mann enlisted his father-in-law's aid,
partly because he needed it, partly because he wanted a pretext to
inform him. At table one day he came out with his request. He had
written a story with a Jewish character and needed a Yiddish word
for "cheat," a strong word that if possible expressed contempt for
the victim. After due thought, and some professorial divagations on
the difficulty of taking words out of context, Alfred Pringsheim offered a suggestion. But he asked no question about the events in the
story; this lack of curiosity was in keeping, so his son Klaus attests,
with his lack of interest in fiction. It was in keeping also with the
cool, though only occasionally chilly, relationship between the professor and his son-in-law—throughout their lives they addressed each
other "with the accepted form employed in the educated countries
of the West, the third person *pluralis*"[33]—that is, the formal pronoun
Sie.

To be on the safe side, Mann invited his mother-in-law and
brother-in-law Klaus to a reading of the story he loved opportunities to read his works aloud in any case. Afterward, Hedwig Pringsheim congratulated him on his handling of so delicate a subject in
so artistic a manner. Klaus Pringsheim, by his own testimony, felt
flattered rather than uneasy at finding certain of his own phrases
and characteristics attributed to the hero of the tale. He agreed with
his mother that there could be no objection to publication of "The
Blood of the Walsungs." The "cleared" story was promptly sent off
to the *Neue Deutsche Rundschau;* and it was in the editorial offices
of the magazine that the first objections were raised. Oscar Bie, the
editor, thought the Yiddish words in the last line ("we've began-
effed him—the goy!")[34] too coarse. He pleaded with Mann to change
the ending, to handle it as discreetly as he had the rest of the story.

The request produced something of a crisis of conscience, which
was interrupted but in no way alleviated by the birth of the Manns'
first child on November 9, 1905. It was a shaking experience for the
father. Thomas wrote to Heinrich:

Unexpectedly, the birth was frightfully difficult, and my poor Katia had to suffer so cruelly that the whole thing became an almost unendurable horror. I shall not forget this day for the rest of my days. I had a notion of life and one of death, but I did not yet know what birth is. Now I know that it is as profound a matter as the other two. Immediately afterwards, all was idyll and peace (the counterpart to the peace after the death throes), and seeing the child at the breast of its mother, who herself is still like a lovely child, was a sight that transfigured and sanctified the atrocious agonies of the birth (which had gone on for almost forty hours). The little girl, who will be named Erika at her mother's wish, promises to be very pretty. For brief moments I think I see just a little Jewishness showing through, and every time that happens it greatly amuses me.[35]

The matter of "Jewishness" brought him to the point of the letter. He enclosed a copy of "The Blood of the Walsungs"—whose milieu, after all, was the same as that of Heinrich's *Im Schlaraffenland*—and reported Bie's objections. Could Heinrich advise him? "How would you conclude? If you have any inspiration—don't withhold it from me!" He was, he confessed, already beginning to doubt the ending as he had it, with its "foreign words." Heinrich, who was in any case fond of just such shock effects in plose, urged him not to give way. "To sacrifice typicality to propriety is kitsch."[36]

In the end, Thomas disregarded the advice and eliminated the words that had offended Oscar Bie. He was doing so only for the magazine publication, he told his brother in a subsequent letter, and would restore the original ending when the story appeared in book form. (In fact, this promise was kept only for the French translation, "Sang réservé," which was published in 1931 and revived the whole "scandal" described below.)

The new ending ("Beckerath . . . ought to be grateful to us. His existence will be a little less trivial, from now on.")[37] was sent to Oscar Bie. Mann then set off on a lecture tour that took him to Prague, Dresden, and Breslau. He found Prague beautiful beyond his expectations, and since the trip carried him through the lands of the Seven Years' War, he kept his eyes open. For he was thinking of a novel about Frederick the Great to follow *Royal Highness*. He clearly enjoyed his readings, enjoyed the applause he received and the easy platform manner he developed as the tour progressed. He also enjoyed visiting his Aunt Elisabeth, the original of Tony Buddenbrook,

in Dresden. But on his return, in the best of spirits, a dashing surprise awaited him.

Somehow—the most likely explanation is that gossip flowed from
the Berlin editorial offices of S. Fischer to Munich literary circles—
a manifestly distorted version of the interchange between Oscar Bie
and Thomas Mann had reached Munich. Thomas wrote to Heinrich:

> Returning from my December journey I found the rumor here that I
> had written a violently "anti-Semitic" (!) story in which I terribly
> compromised my wife's family. What should I have done? I looked at
> my story in my mind and found that in its innocence and independ-
> ence it was not exactly suited to quashing this rumor. And I must
> acknowledge that humanly and socially I am no longer free. So I
> sent a couple of imperious telegrams to Berlin and succeeded in hav-
> ing the January issue of the *Rundschau*, which was printed and ready
> to go, published without "The Blood of the Walsungs." . . . The
> people are cheated of their scandal, and I, who at first foamed at the
> mouth somewhat, am by now fairly calm about it. The piece wasn't
> all *that* good, and the thing that is valuable about it—the description
> of the milieu, which I really consider very new—can probably be
> used elsewhere sometime.[38]

But words are winged, and once they are printed it is not easy to sup-
press them. The story saw the light of day after all, and that very
soon. The pulped January issue of the *Neue Deutsche Rundschau*
was thriftily used as packing paper. A shipment of books from
S. Fischer Verlag, packed in such crushed pages, was sent to a Munich book shop, where an apprentice began smoothing out the pages
and reading them. He became fascinated by the story, though it began in the middle, and he soon connected it with gossip overheard
at a literary tea party. After another shipment of books, similarly
packed, had arrived, the apprentice managed to piece together a
complete copy of the suppressed story, with title page and author's
name. He must have made copies also, for Mann angrily protested to
Fischer that "The Blood of the Walsungs" was circulating in Munich in clear disregard of his wishes.

This contretemps prompted the writer to consider the whole
question of the relationship between literature and its underlying
reality. He remembered only too well the fuss over *Buddenbrooks*,
Holitscher's resentment over "Tristan," the uneasiness that Hein-

rich's *Die Jagd nach Liebe* had stirred in Munich and in his own family. And now in Lübeck the name of Thomas Mann had actually been dragged into court by way of example. The time had come for him to take a public stand—and to clarify his own ideas as well. The matter also bore on his next novel. He had no wish, after completing *Royal Highness*, to be haled into court on a charge of lese majesty, for all the world like such a radical as Frank Wedekind. It was essential to establish once and for all his right as a literary man to make any use he pleased of the people who passed through his life or remained in it. As a preliminary, he embodied his thoughts in a brief note entitled "Ein Nachwort" ("A Postscript") which was published in the *Lübecker General-Anzeiger* of November 7, 1905. He followed this with a short essay, "Bilse un ich" ("Bilse and I"), which appeared in the *Münchner Neueste Nachrichten* in two installments, on February 15 and 16, 1906.

"A Postscript" commented on a court case in Lübeck. A writer named Dose was sued by a cousin for allegedly libeling him in a novel; the writer denied that he knew anything at all about his cousin or had intended to portray him. The prosecutor brought in references to Thomas Mann's *Buddenbrooks* and to a then notorious, best-selling novel that within two years of its publication had become virtually synonymous with the concept of the roman à clef: *Aus einer kleinen Garnison*. The author, Lieutenant Fritz Oswald Bilse, had been sentenced to six months' imprisonment for his novel's revelations of corruption in a small garrison town in Lorraine. The prosecutor's references stung Thomas Mann for two reasons: he did not like his work demeaned in his native city, and he did not want to be named in the same breath with a trashy amateur. He gave no thought to the fact that Lieutenant Bilse's book had also been banned —and that, accordingly, it should have been to every serious writer's interest to defend it. At this time, as Thomas had written to Heinrich, he had no use for "freedom" and could not understand what was meant by it.

"A Postscript" was directed chiefly to the citizenry of Lübeck. He knew none of the parties, he said, and had not read Dose's book. But if he had been called to testify, or if he himself had been similarly prosecuted for writing *Buddenbrooks*, he would not have answered as Dose did that he was unconscious of similarities to any living person. That sort of reply struck him as unworthy evasiveness.

On the contrary, when he wrote *Buddenbrooks* he had "looked at the realities with full consciousness,"[39] and shaped his work on the basis of them, although adding what was most intimately his own. This was only what all writers did; the greatest works of world literature portrayed living persons who were the author's contemporaries. Had Lotte and her husband tried to sue Goethe for writing *Werther?* On the contrary: "They realized that it would have been petty to hold a grudge against the writer who in his book had conferred upon them a life a thousand times superior, more intense and lasting than they were leading in their ordinary, respectable reality—and they held their peace."[40]

There follows a curious paragraph that illustrates once more Mann's growing skill at managing his reputation, at persuading the public to see him as he wished to see himself:

> "Perfect," my fellow townsmen will say, "he's comparing himself with Goethe." Heaven forbid, no. But Goethe was not always the genius far above all libel suits, as he now is. He too was once present, a contemporary, modern, just a young man from Frankfurt who "wrote," who put his life into poetry and fiction, who formed in books the impressions he garnered from the world and people, just like me. And if I am asked to which of them I feel more closely akin, to Goethe or to Bilse, I shall answer wholly without megalomania: to Goethe.[41]

The modest disclaimer implanted the claim: here was a writer who naturally associated himself with the greatest. Few besides Thomas Mann himself could then believe in the possibility that time would justify such aspirations. And he himself doubted as often as he believed; indeed, his very doubts, his crises, his failures of nerve, what he then called his "neurasthenia," possibly provided the tension that made possible his achievement. But whatever his inner state, he knew instinctively that it was necessary to make outward show of pride and confidence, to assert that he was already breathing the more rarefied air of those Olympian heights he hoped someday to scale. Meanwhile, he appealed to local patriotism; he asked his fellow townsmen not to despair of him, not to think ill of him, to remember that "without love of family and native soil, books like *Buddenbrooks* are not written; and those who know me, those who have read certain of my works that followed upon that book, know how deeply I have remained, for all my artist's libertine notions, a burgher of Lübeck."[42]

The same kind of assertiveness and self-advertisement can be discerned in the foreword Mann wrote for "Bilse" when the article was published as a small brochure later in 1906. He spoke of the artist-egotist's conviction that he is serving only himself, "raising his own heart as a monstrance,"[43] and the gratifying discovery that he is speaking for many others: "To stand for many in standing for oneself, to be *representative*, that too, it seems to me, is a small kind of greatness. It is the austere happiness of princes and poets."[44]

He took secret pleasure in phrases such as this which embodied the prospectus for a novel not destined to be published for another three years. "Austere happiness" (*strenges Glück*) would form the last words of *Royal Highness*. He had borrowed the phrase from Heinrich's *Die Jagd nach Liebe*.

In the notebook he was keeping at this time he summed up the whole complex: "Representative vocation in any sense, whether in the Napoleonic or Klaus Heinrichian sense, whether great or small, necessarily makes one egotistic. One naturally makes much of one's personality if one sees in it a *symbol*, an incarnation, a collecting point, a microcosm."[45]

In "Bilse and I" Mann pursued the same trend and the same argument—by implication comparing himself to (in addition to Goethe) Turgenev, Schiller, Wagner, and Shakespeare. Great writers do not invent their characters but find them in their surroundings, he maintained—in German the assertion provides opportunity for a neat play on the words *erfinden* and *finden*. What matters is not where the writer's material comes from, but what he does with it, how he animates it, "fills it with his breath and being."[46] Mann's language becomes so daring here—he uses an archaic, poetic word for "breath"—that the phrase might almost be translated: "fills it with his pneuma and essence." Then, in one of those abrupt shifts of mood that form one of the great delights of his style, he shrugs off the pose of divinity and talks about the time he began writing *Buddenbrooks* in Rome, Via Torre Argentina *trenta quattro*, three flights up. At that time and in that place his native city had little reality for him; he had made it into his own dream. He labored away at the book for three years, and then was profoundly amazed when he heard that it was stirring a scandal in Lübeck, and that people resented it. "What did today's real Lübeck have to do with my . . . work? Foolishness. . . . If I make a sentence out of a thing, what does the thing still have to do with the sentence? Philistinism. . . ."[47]

It rapidly becomes clear that he is thinking of "The Blood of the Walsungs." The first allusion is circumspect: the reality that a writer uses for his purposes may be the person nearest and dearest to him; he may borrow every last detail and mark (*Merkmal*; the same word is used in the final sentence of "Wälsungenblut") of that person; and yet there will remain an enormous difference, for him, between the reality and his creation. The second allusion is plainer; Mann meets the rumors head-on. An identity exists between the author and all his characters even where the reader does not sense it, where the reader would swear that the writer was motivated by nothing but scorn and disgust as he created his character: "Is not Shylock the Jew a repugnant and horrible creature? Shakespeare, to universal delight, sees to it that he is terribly cheated and crushed. And yet there comes more than one moment in which we are prompted to surmise a profound and fearful solidarity of Shakespeare with Shylock."[48]

This was the best he could do by way of apology to the Pringsheims. The language, with its odd excess of strong words, so contrary to his usual style, suggests that the matter was far more disturbing than he ever admitted. For he knew he would go on committing the offense in one way or another. With more or less success in disguising his originals, inflicting more or less pain upon his models, he would continue to do what every writer does more or less openly: convert the raw materials of life into the refined products of art. Perhaps it was not denuding that the victims so much feared, but declassing. In his next narrative there should be no problem about that, because he was elevating the social station of his nearest and dearest.

1 4

Theater and
Novel

EVERY writer knows those periods of fallowness and shallowness when hopes are soon dashed, when outside irritations conspire with inner irritability to sap confidence and hamper production, when tributes turn sour and the success of others rankles. For Thomas Mann the fourth decade of his life had something of that character. He conceived grandiose projects and struggled to complete the most minor of them. In his troubled state he sought and found those distractions that a steadily growing family and expanding household bring. Inevitably, there were moments in which he blamed the family for his difficulties; but it was only to his brother (who was himself part of Thomas Mann's problems) that he dared to confess this feeling. To Heinrich he confided that he sometimes felt as if he were chained with a golden ball on each leg, that the comforts of bourgeois luxury threatened him with stagnation and flabbiness. Using the language of *Royal Highness*, he declared: "I admit that I cannot shake off a feeling of unfreedom that in hypochondriacal periods becomes very oppressive, and you'll surely call me a cowardly bourgeois. Easy for you to talk. You are absolute. I, on the other hand, have deigned to give myself a constitution."[1] At this time of seeming triumph he seriously feared for his artistic future—though we must also recognize that such comments were partly intended to deflect those feelings of envy that, Thomas sensed or believed, sometimes bedeviled his brother.

Relations between the brothers fluctuated like the thermometer of a patient with quartan fever. After the publication in 1905 of Heinrich's magnificent Lübeck satire, *Professor Unrat*—the novel that was subsequently to become famous as the basis of the motion picture *The Blue Angel*—Thomas Mann was outraged. He took as stuffy an attitude toward the book as the teachers at his and Heinrich's old Gymnasium, the Lübeck Katharineum—whom Heinrich ridiculed far more fiercely than Thomas had done in the "Hanno's school day" sections of *Buddenbrooks*. Like so many of Heinrich Mann's contemporaries, Thomas failed to see the greatness of *Professor Unrat*. In one of his notebooks he set down, under the heading of "Anti-Heinrich," a list of objections to the novel. He took issue with petty faults of style and flaws in construction, dubbed Heinrich's expressionistic language "a godforsaken kind of impressionism,"[2] and burst out: "I consider it immoral to write one bad book after the other from fear of the anguish of idleness."[3] On the other hand he would shortly afterward assure Heinrich: "I am obsessed by the necessity of our sticking together."[4] And a few months later, while telling his brother about his ambition to write a historical novel on the life of Frederick the Great, he candidly remarked: *"The brother problem always stimulates me."*[5]

Heinrich displayed a far steadier fraternal loyalty in spite of provocation. He quickly came to his brother's defense in a literary skirmish of a kind that was to recur often in the future. Richard Schaukal was that minor literary man who had thrust himself into the lives of both Heinrich and Thomas in 1900 by sending them his works. At the time he was a young writer with a few books of verse to his credit; subsequently he had written one of the earliest reviews of *Buddenbrooks*, and a highly favorable one. When Schaukal and Thomas finally met in person in September 1902, good relations developed, and Mann dedicated the story "Little Lizzy" to him. Schaukal might have thought he would endear himself by praising

Thomas and denigrating Heinrich. Thomas had to assure Heinrich that he had had nothing to do with the attack and would not thank Schaukal for it. Either at this time or somewhat later Heinrich broke off relations with Schaukal. Thomas's turn came in October 1905: "Now he has exhausted my patience too."[6]

Schaukal had sent Mann a bulky manuscript and asked him to recommend it to Fischer. At the same time he commented, recklessly in view of the favor he was asking, that he had read the first two acts of *Fiorenza* in the *Neue Deutsche Rundschau* and found them poor, and so had refrained from reading the third act. Mann took this as a piece of outrageous impudence; he wrote to Schaukal to say that they had reached a parting of ways. Schaukal threw himself with obvious pleasure into a public battle: the *Berliner Tageblatt* of March 5, 1906, carried his savage review of *Fiorenza*. Without recanting his earlier praise of Thomas Mann, rather emphasizing it and identifying himself as an "admirer," he argued that the drama was a stillborn child, a purely literary product into which the author had put too little of himself. Its fault was not lack of drama, but lack of life breathed into the work. And he concluded: "Mann is not one who will surprise us again and again; he is not protean, not versatile."[7] But although the review was an act of personal revenge, in fairness it must be said that Schaukal's criticisms of *Fiorenza* were not unfounded—even if his analysis of the cause of the play's failure was absurd. Had not Thomas Mann himself admitted that *Fiorenza* was a fiasco? Why should he be incensed at someone's saying so?

But incensed he was. He was pained, furious, and also frustrated because he felt that he could not reply. As he explained to Heinrich, he could not stand the agitation. Moreover, Schaukal would promptly produce the grateful and appreciative letters Mann had written him in the past.

No, I can do nothing, much as the article in the *B.T.* may harm me. But that no one has turned up, that none of all my "friends and admirers" has felt sufficiently stirred to give this limited and self-righteous coxcomb his comeuppance publicly, or at least privately— that hurts me. You cannot do it, for then it will be said: That's his brother. . . . He calls Wassermann (who by this time is a master) a Jewish journalist; but so far he has never said it publicly. And publicly he has also remained silent about your books, which he regards as brazen hackwork. That *Fiorenza* is hackwork, and moreover bad hackwork, he declares openly in the *Berliner Tageblatt*. And the *brutality* of it is that he *knows* how much pain the book caused me.[8]

Heinrich took the hint; he also rose to the bait, for the article he wrote, and which Thomas placed in Maximilian Harden's *Die Zukunft*, dwelt on the theme of "hackwork." It was a splendid piece of literary swordplay, in the course of which Heinrich defended himself, Thomas, and Wassermann, stabbing Schaukal in several places. First he remarked on the feebleness of Schaukal's talent, which hardly qualified him to present himself as a serious critic; then he set forth his brother's "official line" on *Fiorenza*. He pointed to the parallel between the declining bourgeois of *Buddenbrooks* and the dying Lorenzo Medici:

> These dukes were bourgeois, and degenerated like bourgeois: not the way knightly families usually degenerate, with atavistic relapses into murderous ferocity, with hunting as their ultimate passion, to the point of idiocy. The Medici succumbed to sensual and moral over-refinement, to aestheticism, to a weakening of self-confidence as the consequence of too varied and subtle insights.[9]

Heinrich concluded his piece with a sentence that spoke from his brother's as well as his own heart: "A writer . . . uses people who have been hallowed by distance in time, and by illustrious names, in order to make known with greater solemnity his own, always nothing but his own destiny."[10]

A response by Schaukal and an *ad hominem* rebuttal by Heinrich brought the battle to an end. Thomas, delighted and grateful, wrote to his brother: "It's like among small boys: somebody did something to me and big brother comes along and avenges me."[11]

Heinrich had dealt doughtily with the "distortions" of an enemy; Thomas himself felt he had to correct the well-meaning "mistakes" of the literary man who was perhaps his best friend. Kurt Martens had published an article in the *Leipziger Tageblatt* entitled "The Mann Brothers." Although it was generous in its praise of both Manns, Thomas felt he had to set the record straight. He was determined to be taken on his own terms, even if that meant reproving this friendliest of critics. And so when Martens sent a copy of his essay, Thomas responded with a letter long enough to be an article. Martens was not the finest of writers, and Thomas's scorn for his sometimes inept phrases repeatedly breaks through the superficial effort to remain polite and grateful:

> Many thanks for your kindness in sending your essay. A fine dual portrait that testifies to your talent as a critic. Certainly it contains minor distortions, exaggerations, misunderstandings, premature judgments— but the important thing is that you say something definite. And after all, what does "a likeness" matter? Everything is viewed interestingly and said interestingly; that is the main point.
>
> Nevertheless, I should like to note for you personally a few things that I shook my head over.[12]

Five years earlier Mann had instructed Otto Grautoff to refer to a certain nihilistic tendency in the author of *Buddenbrooks*, but now he took issue when Martens spoke of the novel as "destructive." Critical and sardonic, perhaps, but not destructive. "Must one write dithyrambs to establish oneself as an affirmer of life?" And certainly it was not fair to attribute to him "icy misanthropy" and "lovelessness toward everything of flesh and blood."[13] Was he not, like the narrator in "At the Prophet's," on good terms with life?

The defense continues, page after page. It is not true that in "Bilse und Ich" he "would like to put creative imagination on the same level with dime-novel ingenuity," as Martens represents. On the contrary:

> I say that writers who have nothing but "inventiveness" are not far from the dime novels. I say that very great writers did not invent anything in their whole lives, but merely poured their souls into traditional materials and reshaped them. I say that Tolstoy's work is at least as strictly autobiographical as my humbler product. . . . I don't say: The novelist has the right to do portraits of people. Such a right cannot be proved. I do say: Important writers through the ages have assumed that right. I should like to present a few reasons for this. I should like to point out the error inherent in making a literal identification between reality and its artistic image. I should like to have a work of art regarded as something absolute, not subject to everyday questions of right and wrong. I note a misunderstanding and I undertake to analyze its origins; if possible to decrease its harmful effects.

That is all. Is this unworthy, useless, megalomaniacal? Have I not acted in the interests of society as well as those of art? I had counted on plain gratitude and I hear people shouting: Yes, yes! or No, no! The world is odd.[14]

In this epistolary essay Mann keeps coming back to the one point that had stung him most: the idea that he was a "cold artist."[15] The term had been applied to the Mann brothers by a friendly critic named Karl Muth; he had borrowed it from an eighteenth-century writer who had used it of Goethe. But despite the flattering association Mann fiercely resented it, and when he found Martens giving another variation of the "charge," he protested vehemently. It was simply not true that his books would receive more cool respect than heartfelt affection, but he feared that this statement would become a self-fulfilling prophecy:

If you represent me a few more times as embittered, icy, mocking, and rootless, your prediction will probably come true. So far it has been otherwise. . . . Since I am neither frivolous nor crotchety nor tart nor stiff, I do not see, if I should somehow prove lasting, why Germans should refuse me love in the future. What aspects of my humanity would they take exception to? I was a quiet, well-behaved person who won a measure of prosperity by the work of his hands, took a wife, begot children, attended first nights, and was so good a German that I could not stand being abroad for more than four weeks. Is it absolutely necessary to go bowling and drinking on top of that?[16]

At the very end of his long letter Mann tried to propitiate: "I hope you won't find this reply ungrateful or preposterous. But I thought: Why shouldn't I gently steer right my most intelligent and best-informed critic where he seems to be going wrong or distorting?"[17]

We do not have Martens's reply; but it stands as testimony to Mann's psychological ascendancy over the older writer that the friendship continued. In fact, Martens immediately afterward sent him one of his books, a novel entitled *Kreislauf* (Circulation). Mann read it in Oberammergau, where he and Katia had rented a place for the summer, and brought the book back "read quite to pieces and all marked up with pencil."[18] In spite of his best efforts he could do little more than damn with faint praise; his congratulations sounded insincere, and he became aware of this himself in the course of writing the letter, so that he had suddenly to check himself and tell the truth:

> It is certainly superfluous sincerity, and therefore no doubt clumsy bluntness, if I admit to you that your book does not meet my ideal. The language is correct, but sublimity is lacking. Examples of stylistic laxness and slackness occur. It is not a prose poem but an extraordinarily competent novel. That is not what I am longing for—but why should my longing matter to you! When I carp you must consider that I have by now come around to applying a desperately exacting standard, which one of these days will presumably hinder me from producing anything at all.[19]

That was a note he was to strike repeatedly during the next years.

IN MAY 1906 Thomas Mann went to give a reading in Dresden and took the opportunity to spend three weeks at a noted sanatorium nearby, the Weisser Hirsch. For his health was by no means the best. Every eight to ten weeks he would have spells of illness, during which he felt so wretched that he was incapable of the slightest effort. These periods would begin with depression, eye-strain, restlessness, and sleeplessness. He would feel nauseated, would gag and throw up, all the while suffering from a kind of continual abdominal pain which he thought was "a purely nervous condition."[20] Next day, feeling utterly vacant, unable to think or even to read, he would doze away the time, subsisting on a little soup, wondering what was going to become of him. "Then the following day I am very weak and gentle, as it were transfigured; and then I slowly get going again."[21] The illness attacked him at all seasons of the year. At the time it was called neurasthenia; it is now considered to be the relatively rare deficiency disease coproporphyric anemia.* It recurred at intervals throughout Mann's life; attacks were often brought on by stress, so that in this sense he was right in referring to its nervous origins.

The stay at the sanatorium helped not at all, and it was followed by the sort of social occasion at which he was required to play the Steadfast Tin Soldier: a visit to Samuel Fischer's new home in the

---

* I am indebted to Dr. John Olson of Colrain, Massachusetts, for this diagnosis.

Grünewald section of Berlin. He returned to Munich half dead with fatigue, convinced that the effect of the sanatorium had been entirely negative. Possibly he was still shaken by a minor train derailment he experienced on the way to Dresden; that might well have been a severe shock, although he made light of it when he described it in a short story three years later.

In the depression induced by illness he blamed his troubles on his new family. He would have been better off without a wife and child and retinue, he told Heinrich; he should not have let himself in for human attachments, because he simply did not have the strength for them. Even though he seemed the happier of the two, his life was immeasurably harder than Heinrich's. Heinrich was lucky, he wrote, not to have tied himself down, to have devoted himself more stringently and faithfully to his art.

Another characteristic symptom of the illness was *Verstimmung*[22]—feeling altogether out of sorts, in constant bad temper. In that state, and with the guilty awareness of how slowly *Royal Highness* was moving forward, he was obliged to respond to Heinrich's latest book of fiction, *Stürmische Morgen* (Stormy Mornings). It contained four stories, one of which had been published in *Simplicissimus* at the beginning of the year with a dedication "to my brother Thomas."[23] This was "Abdankung" (Abdication), the tale of a schoolboy named Felix who dominates and humiliates all his schoolmates by sheer force of will. He succeeds in keeping them down, despite occasional murmurs of revolt, until he falls in love with Hans Butt, the sluggish fat boy, the most lumpish and servile of them all. Then he is seized by a passion for submissiveness as strong as his passion for dominance had been. He makes the boy his lieutenant, then forces him at first to command and after a while to humiliate his leader. When Felix has achieved an ultimate self-abasement, and can find no way out of the tangle of his emotions, he chooses to interpret a flash of exasperation on Butt's part as an order to commit suicide.

When Thomas first read this story in the magazine, he had exclaimed that this "perverse tragedy of genius" was the most extraordinary thing Heinrich had written. This was, he admitted, the judgment of a person deeply involved, who felt so close to the story "that I almost feel as if it were by me."[24] Since a story by himself was invariably about himself in one way or another, in saying this he was acknowledging the sharpness of Heinrich's observation and its truth. Heinrich not only saw his brother's fierce ambition to excel—the quality Thomas was beginning to call *Leistungsethik*, the ethic of achievement—but also identified its link to homoerotic impulses. "Abdankung" was a minor masterpiece in which this whole complex brings death to a schoolboy; some years later Thomas would approach the same theme in a major masterpiece, and show the complex bringing death to a writer of mature years.

Reading the story in *Simplicissimus*, Thomas failed to notice that Heinrich's intention was satiric as well as descriptive. Heinrich was showing what sheer will could accomplish but implied that its object could be unworthy if not debased. The story suggested also that infatuations of this kind—as Heinrich remembered only too well from Thomas's "Ehrenberg era"—were potentially suicidal. On second reading of "Abdankung" Thomas must have become aware of these further meanings. Small wonder that vexation, combined with the general malaise of his illness, led him to produce one of the most sarcastic statements he had sent to Heinrich in their years of correspondence: "a brilliant book that displays all your virtues, your rushing tempo, your famous verve, the delightful pungency of your language, all your amazing virtuosity, which one surrenders to because it undoubtedly comes directly from passion."[25]

Far from answering in kind, Heinrich read Thomas's letter as a cry for reassurance, and responded with that elder brother's sympathy which came so readily to him whenever he sensed a need. He moved Thomas deeply—"your sympathy has given me a tremendous lift"[26]—and moved him still more by confiding his involvement with Ines Schmied. Thomas had heard about the affair, of course, and chose to see the relationship as resembling his own with Katia: "You are united, you are sure of yourselves . . . —that really is a more favorable situation than ours was before our marriage."[27] Rather delicately, he suggested that Heinrich marry Ines, and expressed the hope that they would spend part of the year in Munich. Heinrich's society would provide relief on those occasions when he found his wife's family too much for him. (The nature of these in-law stresses is not clear.) He was going to be lonely, for Grautoff was leaving; this oldest friend had decided he was getting nowhere in Munich and planned to go to Paris in the fall, there to set up as a freelance writer on art, and if necessary to live by shining shoes.

"That is perhaps an act of great stupidity, and yet I will watch him depart with a certain yearning."[28] There was a great deal the two of them had to straighten out about life, and he hoped Heinrich would carry out his plan of visiting during the summer in Oberammergau. He, Thomas, was counting heavily on this forthcoming stay in the country.

O B E R A M M E R G A U did not fail him. It was, he told Samuel Fischer, good, blessed, praiseworthy. "For I am working, working, working here. Daily. With pleasure, with good hope, putting black on white, and making progress—a joy I had almost ceased to know, and which is so necessary for me."[29]

Mann's use of the phrase "good hope" is a curious and revealing stylistic slip on the part of this great stylist. *Guter Hoffnung* is a German euphemism equivalent to the English "expecting"; Mann uses it in that sense in *Royal Highness*.[30] Obviously the phrase came to his mind because Katia was once again, so soon after the birth of Erika, "in good hope." The mountain air of Oberammergau and the moderate social pace of the country—only family visits from Carla and Heinrich during the latter part of the summer—obviously did her as much good as they did Thomas. The birth of their second child had about it none of the appalling circumstances that had attended the birth of Erika. The child born on November 18, 1906, was a boy, to the delight of both husband and wife ("I was always annoyed when I had a girl, I don't know why,"[31] Katia Mann admitted in her old age). The child was baptized Klaus Heinrich, presumably after the brothers of both parents; but it surely could not have been accidental that the initials K.H. appeared so frequently in Mann's notebooks and letters at the time. They stood both for *Königliche Hoheit* (*Royal Highness*), the title of the "novella" he was working on, and for the hero of the story, long since given the name Klaus Heinrich. Erika and Klaus were the first of those matched pairs into which the children of Katia and Thomas Mann so symmetrically fell.

M A N N ' s fiction had all along been accompanied by reflection on the nature of the enterprise itself. Since *Royal Highness* was partly meant to deal with the artist in the guise of prince, such reflection came all the more naturally to him at this time. Even in casual personal letters he tended to set forth his theories rather obsessively:

> The artist is akin to the prince in that, like the latter, he leads a *representative* existence. What etiquette is to the prince, the lofty obligation to create form is to the artist. The artist, as I know him, is never the man who can "let himself be seen" freely and without more ado. He needs prudence in passion, idealization in self-depiction, or in short: art. That is his human weakness.[32]

Early in 1907 the magazine *Nord und Süd* sent Mann a questionnaire on his opinion of the contemporary theater. What was its cultural value, what did his own general culture and artistic development owe to it? As it happened, his thoughts were in any case dwelling on the theater, for there was talk of a production of *Fiorenza*. Carl Heine, the director of the Schauspielhaus in Frankfurt am Main, had the play in rehearsal, but kept postponing it—in January Mann wrote asking him not to put it off till April, as he seemed to intend, since by then the season would be over. The questions posed by *Nord und Süd*, therefore, seemed to accord with Mann's concerns of the moment.

The writing of essays fell into that slightly déclassé category which Mann called *Schriftstellerei* or *Schriftstellern* as opposed to *Dichtung* or *Musizieren*—literary activity as against creative writing, fiction, poetry. The distinction hardly exists in English, but much was made of it in the Germany of Mann's day, and he simultaneously went along with the idea and rejected it. German writers found it easy, in literary guerrilla warfare, to score hits by dismissing a colleague as a *Schriftsteller:* not the sublime, almost deified poet (which term include the highbrow prose writer), but a common pen-pusher. Mann himself was all too often the target for this kind of sniping. The elaborate ironies of his style, the involved periods which by their very complexity mocked their ostensible message, and the cool omniscience of his narrative tone invited the charge that he had none of the poet in him. But as was his wont, he also anticipated this criticism, assimilated it into his legend. The desire to analyze, to reason, to set forth ideas, could sometimes become his strongest literary passion, he confessed. He quite well knew that dealing with complex questions cost him "a disproportionate amount of time and nervous energy,"[33] and he could not shake off the feeling that he was merely compromising himself to no good purpose. Yet the craving to explicate repeatedly overpowered him, for at bottom it sprang from the same impulse to explain himself that governed his fiction. And he contrived, in his articles on general problems or on other literary figures, to talk a great deal about himself, overtly or covertly. The products of his pen as a *Schriftsteller* were also fragments of a great confession, to use Goethe's famous phrase.

The queries from *Nord und Süd* initially struck him as a challenge, and he decided to interrupt his work on the novel just for a few days in order to work up a brief response. "I wrestled with it for weeks, not days; more than once I was sick of the business to the point of desperation. More than once . . . I was on the verge of throwing up my hands. But I had committed myself and obeyed my categorical imperative: Stick it out."[34]

The essay on the theater actually set up the same kind of cleavage between theater and drama as that between poet and man of letters. The theater, Mann argued—in passages that revealed recent reading of Nietzsche—is virtually independent of literature, self-contained and self-concerned, an art of simplification, an art of spectacle, an art for the masses. The theater is "the most naive, the most childlike, the most popular form of art."[35] Drama, on the other hand, is a form of literature; it may provide the basis for an effective theatrical piece, but in itself it must be regarded as discredited, compromised, if it turns out to be too effective on the stage. In the classical drama it is the language, not the plot, that matters; this is also true of Racine and Corneille. "The Greeks, the Frenchmen of Racine's day, did not attend the theater to see an adventure represented, but to enjoy beautifully chiseled speeches."[36]

All this was patently argument on behalf of *Fiorenza*. He wanted desperately to believe that his hopelessly talky and untheatrical work fell within the canons of classical drama. Granted, it did not meet the theater's requirements of naiveté and staginess. He knew well enough—had learned it from "the modern art"[37] of Richard Wagner—that the essence of theater was its direct appeal to the senses, its sensuousness if not its sensuality. But it was only a step from sensuality (*Sinnlichkeit*) to symbolism (*Sinnbildlichkeit*); presumably the step could be taken in either direction. It was possible to hope, therefore, that if you placed symbols on the stage, the very weight of their symbolic existence might give them the palpable reality (*Sinnfälligkeit*) that would assure survival in the theater.

To hang an argument on such verbal jugglery might seem reckless; but the graceful movement of Mann's prose and the underlying *pro domo* passion make the essay more persuasive than strict logic would allow. It soon becomes clear that Mann is wrestling with the problem that had obsessed him ever since his first consciousness of what Wagner must mean to an artist like himself. If you wanted to know anything about our times, you had to understand the art of Wagner, he acknowledged. And how that art captivated! But the very intoxication of the music brought with it shame and doubt. Could an art so popular, an art for the multitude, really be good? Could it be high art? He himself, Thomas Mann, had found his way to the heart of the crowd; his *Buddenbrooks* evidently appealed to the discriminating and the indiscriminate masses alike. And having tasted the sweets and the fruits of popularity, he certainly wanted more; but he had continually to justify himself before his own extraordinarily sensitive artistic conscience. This conflict emerged privately in his letters to Heinrich, and publicly in a short article that he wrote during the summer in answer to still another inquiry sent to him by the Bonn Society for Literary Criticism.

Before the summer began, however, there was an opportunity for a family reunion in Italy. Early in May 1907 Katia and Thomas traveled to Venice, where they met Heinrich and Carla. Thomas was dissatisfied with the Grand Hotel they stayed at on the Lido; he called it "a pretentious dive."[38] There is no other record of the stay; but if we may judge by the quickened pace of correspondence with Heinrich afterward, and by Thomas's friendly reaction to Heinrich's fine new novel, *Zwischen den Rassen*, something of a rapprochement between the brothers took place during those weeks in Venice. Unfortunately Katia and Thomas could not linger; in Venice came the sudden news that the premiere of *Fiorenza* was to be given in Frankfurt on May 11. For the sake of staying longer with Carla and Heinrich, Thomas decided to miss it; he and Katia finally attended the sixth and last performance on May 23. The performance was inadequate, the Lorenzo miserable, but the audience respectful; there were repeated curtain calls for the author after the second and third acts. All this prompted Thomas to declare the play performable

—and in fact performances of it have repeatedly been tried for seventy years. But if it has never entirely disappeared from the boards, it has never really won a place for itself. And *Fiorenza* remained Mann's first and last venture in the theater.

For the summer the family rented a house in Seeshaupt, at the southern end of the Starnberger See, a charming vacation region much favored by royalty. The empress Elisabeth of Austria often stayed at her ancestral castle in the neighborhood, and King Ludwig II of Bavaria, having escaped his warders, had met his end in the lake. The Villa Hirt, as the Manns' cottage was called, must have lacked a guest room, or else the family preferred not to expose guests to two small children. Thomas invited Heinrich to spend some time with them, but carefully indicated that there was a good country inn nearby. He was now working on the novel with some consistency, but was appalled at what small steps he kept taking. And Katia was chafing; this earnest, spirited young woman, plunged all too soon into child rearing and the administration of a sizable household, felt she needed intellectual occupation. Thomas had somehow gained the impression that Heinrich was editing Flaubert in German translation for a publisher, and wondered whether Katia might not be entrusted with the translation of one of the volumes. "She is eager and would in all probability do it as well as, in fact better than, the average."[39] Nothing came of this, because someone else was actually in charge of the project.

The Manns moved up to Seeshaupt in the second week of June. At the end of the month the distinguished literary critic Professor Berthold Litzmann of Bonn University asked Mann to contribute a manuscript to a special issue of the literary publication he had created, the *Mitteilungen der literarhistorischen Gesellschaft Bonn.* Litzmann, who after his retirement would move from Bonn to Munich and become a neighbor of the Manns in Herzogpark and a friend of the family, was planning an issue containing statements by writers on their aims and methods. Mann felt obligated to make some kind of contribution, since he was a member of the literary society, and since Litzmann intended to devote an entire issue to his work. But recent experience with the essay on the theater had served as a warning—if he responded to every inquiry, he would never finish his novel. Therefore he gave himself a deadline of two weeks, and determined to keep his reply short. Even so, the four pages of his

"Communication to the Bonn Society for Literary Criticism" did not get done for some three weeks—probably because he turned it into a rather significant statement of his method of work. This early piece of self-revelation may well have given rise to the legend of his machinelike steadiness. That was not his intention; in fact he was really apologizing for weakness when he wrote:

Every morning a step, every morning a "passage"—that happens to be my way, and it has its justifications. . . . It is not a matter of timidity nor of laziness, but of an extraordinarily lively sense of responsibility that demands perfect freshness, so that after the second hour of work I would rather not undertake any important sentences. But which sentence is "important" and which one is not? Does one ever know beforehand whether a sentence or a fragment of a sentence may not be destined to recur, to serve as a motif, parenthesis, symbol, quotation, reference? And a sentence that is going to be heard twice must have something to it. It must—I am not speaking of "beauty"— possess a certain elevation and symbolical mood which makes it worth being sounded again in any future novelistic situation whatsoever. Thus every passage becomes a "passage," every adjective a decision, and it is clear that working in this way one cannot shake pages out of one's sleeve. I glance at this or that well-received work of fiction and I say to myself: "Oh, yes, I'm willing to believe this went briskly!" As for myself, the watchword is: clench the teeth and take one slow step at a time. The watchword is: practice patience, idle through half the day, go to sleep, and wait to see whether things may not flow better next day with the mind rested. To bring to a conclusion anything of fair size, to keep the faith with something already started, not to run away, not to reach out for something new that is tempting in its youthful radiance—given the way I work, to stick to it requires a patience, or rather an obstinacy, a stubbornness, a discipline, and a repression of one's will that is almost unimaginable and that, believe me, stretches the nerves to the screaming point. All judgment of the novelty and possible effectiveness of the work has been lost in the course of time. Faith in it becomes artificial, becomes a galvanic twitching. The greater part of one's nervous energy is consumed in simulating that faith; and ultimately one asks oneself whether the whole struggle stands in any reasonable proportion to the dignity and importance of what one is struggling for. The outcome will tell—this time, too.[40]

Some readers would see in this a self-serving document, a pretentious excuse for low productivity, for the exhaustion of a rich but thin creative vein. The envious—and Mann's rapid rise to fame guaranteed him a steady supply of ill-wishers—could use confessions of this sort to charge him with posturing, with self-importance, and with contempt for his fellow writers. But he was in fact telling the honest truth about himself and baring the painful doubts that assailed him while he worked—the doubts that his assured public manner concealed. The barb directed at Heinrich's rapid production was only the inverse of his own anguish, and an expression of his bewilderment: that the brother whom he knew so well, whose background was the same as his, many of whose ideas and characters sprang from the same sources, should treat the problems of literary composition in a manner so fundamentally different from his own. Where did Heinrich get his éclat, his confidence, his apparent disdain for the conventions of literature and of life? Heinrich too felt anguish—over his own relative failure compared to his brother. His many books had attracted less critical attention than Thomas's few, and their total sales probably did not equal those of *Buddenbrooks* alone. Yet Heinrich seemed to suffer from few of the rancors that rose up in Thomas the moment he even considered Heinrich's productivity. In Arnold, the German protagonist of *Zwischen den Rassen*, Heinrich had created a demi-portrait of his brother that was as eminently fair as it was sharply observed—and it is the hesitant, overly philosophical Arnold who in the end becomes the hero of the novel. Thomas did not indicate directly that he recognized the likeness, but he called *Zwischen den Rassen* "your mellowest, most humane, at the same time your most controlled and artistic book—and certainly this combination is the reason I have been so deeply moved."[41]

The improved relationship between the brothers, characteristic of this period, also influenced Thomas's portrait of Grand Duke Albrecht in *Royal Highness*. In spite of the mild mockery with which he describes Albrecht's neurasthenia and hypochondria, the tone of the younger brother's relationship to the elder is clearly one of affectionate respect. And Thomas indicates his belief that his own feelings are reciprocated: "And at this moment it could be seen that he [Albrecht] loved Klaus Heinrich." Albrecht wishes his brother happiness, but not too much of it, and hopes that he will have the love of the people but not bask too comfortably in it. To which Klaus Heinrich responds: "Neither happiness nor the love of the people will ever make me stop being your brother."[42]

A SYMBOLIC fiction must be provided with the most realistic of foundations—this was an article of faith with Thomas Mann from the outset of his career. For all of his novels he "read up" beforehand, and in addition he usually found one or more informants to provide him with specific data. He particularly prized concrete details. They stimulated his imagination; they were the framework upon which he hung his story and his meaning. It might be said that this practice was in keeping with his early devotion to the great realistic novels of the Scandinavians and Russians. But Heinrich Mann, the disciple of Latin esprit, likewise did a great deal of reading and clipping in his preparatory work—even though his conception of fiction called for a far greater overlay of "invention" and grotesquerie.

The origins of *Royal Highness* go back to 1903 at least; its evolution can be traced through Thomas Mann's notebooks.[43] With this project in mind, Mann read memoirs and novels of court life in Denmark. In addition, some of his continuing reading on the life of Frederick the Great came in handy for *Royal Highness*. From histories and collections of letters he extracted those details that lent verisimilitude to his fable. In addition, the scandals touching royalty in the middle of the decade came as a stroke of luck to a writer planning a novel of court life. Royal Highnesses were much in the news in Germany, although not always in the most favorable sense. And even if he had not been interested in such gossip, Thomas Mann could not possibly have overlooked the biggest scandal of all. For it was set in motion by a friend of the Pringsheim family, a powerful literary man whom Mann had met and with whom he had corresponded: Maximilian Harden, editor of *Die Zukunft*. Harden, a onetime actor, was generally regarded as Germany's most brilliant journalist.

Harden began with dark hints about a clique that was allegedly exerting undue influence upon Kaiser Wilhelm, a camarilla whose morals were as unsound as its politics. At the end of April 1907 he came out in the open: In an article in *Die Zukunft* he charged several of the monarch's intimates with homosexuality. The principal target was Prince Philipp von Eulenburg und Hartefeld, the German ambassador to Vienna. For a full week the exposé caused endless tongue-wagging everywhere in Germany except at the Imperial Court—where no one had the courage to tell Kaiser Wilhelm about it. At last Crown Prince Wilhelm was persuaded to show his father the issues of the magazine. Kaiser Wilhelm, much against his will, was forced to act on the "Caesar's wife" principle. Most of the individuals involved were removed from their positions of trust, although they may well have been innocent of moral and political transgressions. One of them, Count Kuno von Moltke, sued Harden for defamation.

Thomas Mann followed the progress of this case, which was tried in the courts of Munich, with keen interest, and with displays of surprising sympathy for Harden, for whom he felt a rather unpleasant fascination: He admired the man's brilliance as a journalist, kept in mind Harden's friendship with Katia's Berlin relatives, but also rather detested him for his libertarian attitudes, his assaults against Germany's institutions, his inconsistencies, and his obsession with politics. Mann's sympathies swung more strongly toward Harden when the writer became the person attacked rather than the attacker. When the Berlin weekly *Der Morgen* asked Thomas Mann for his views, he replied that he had "no doubt of Harden's political seriousness, his sense of responsibility, and his affirmative intentions." He described Harden as a man of "extraordinary talent and passion."[44]

Harden's legal defense in Munich was conducted by none other than Max Bernstein, to whose wife Thomas Mann was indebted for her effective matchmaking not too long before. During the following year, in which the suit dragged on through the courts, Bernstein kept Katia and Thomas informed about the trial; he complained of the judge's obvious bias for the aristocratic plaintiff and against the bourgeois scribbler. Nevertheless, Harden was acquitted.

Aside from the keen interest that Thomas Mann took in this political sensation of the day, he also profited from the incidental revelations, in newspaper and magazine articles, of the lives of royalty and the idiosyncrasies of a monarch's entourage. He accumulated folders of clippings with material that might prove useful. He must

have been specially pleased by the Crown Prince's role in the Eulenburg affair, for Crown Prince Wilhelm of Hohenzollern was constantly, if unwittingly, providing the author of *Royal Highness* with
the kind of realistic background he needed to flesh out his "fairy
tale," as he was wont to call the novel. Above all, Crown Prince Wilhelm had had the good taste to celebrate his wedding with his own
fairy princess, Cecilie, on June 6, 1905, Thomas Mann's thirtieth
birthday. For a writer who made much of birthdays, and even more
of "round-numbered ones," the date alone would have established a
link—even if he had not already been at work on his novel. He must
have clipped accounts of the royal nuptials, for in *Royal Highness*
the wedding of Imma and Klaus Heinrich follows step by step the
elaborate Berlin ritual—even to the brilliance of the weather, the
civil marriage preceding the ceremony in the royal chapel, and, as
the final act of an eventful day, the nocturnal torchlight procession
of the students. In fact, the whole idea of Klaus Heinrich's marriage
to an American may have been suggested by the same Crown Prince
Wilhelm's earlier romance with Gladys Deacon, a young lady from
Boston whom Wilhelm met while on a visit to England.

In addition to his reading and clipping of newspaper and magazine articles, Thomas Mann relied on informants to guard him
against errors of fact or tone in his handling of life in a small provincial court. Which cabinet ministers controlled the ducal finances?
What sort of budget would be assigned the various members of the
royal family? What procedures would be followed in introducing an
American into court society? Questions of this sort were answered by
one such informant, whose name appropriately enough was Dr.
Printz. He threw himself into his task with something of the same
zest, the same eagerness to suggest ideas and even possible twists of
plot, that Theodor Adorno would manifest forty years later when he
acted as Mann's musical consultant during the writing of *Doctor
Faustus.* Such underservants of the Muse were able to enjoy the
pleasures of contributing to works of fiction without the daily drudgery of creation.

Thomas Mann, who faced the drudgery, tried to resist the distractions the world was only too willing to offer. Often his efforts
were in vain. At the end of the year 1907 he found time to dash off,
in a rather devil-may-care mood, a humorous autobiographical
fragment called "In the Mirror" ("Im Spiegel"). He described his

dark and shameful past: a failure at school, a failure in the fire insurance business, a dilettante at the university, a vagabond in Italy, where he smoked too many of those sweet, cheap cigarettes sold by the Italian government, a failure in the military service, and finally an editor of *Simplicissimus*—anyone could see that he was sinking lower and lower. Surely he would end up sitting glassy-eyed, a woolen scarf wrapped around his neck, in an anarchists' café. Or lying in the gutter—which was only right, wasn't it?

Was that the case? Not at all. He was on top of the world, with a princess for a wife, two promising children, a large apartment in the best part of town, equipped with electric light and other modern conveniences, magnificently furnished. He was the lord and master of three buxom servant girls and a Border collie, and ate sugar buns with his morning tea! What is more, he was in the habit of going on triumphal tours, and people would applaud as soon as he entered the hall. And all this for doing nothing useful—it was enough to make the guardians of his youth doubt everything they had believed in.

This sort of spoofing, with himself just as much the target of good-natured mockery as society's *idées reçus*, lay precisely within the orbit of *Royal Highness*, where he was trying for the same light tone. But that was not easy to achieve, and he was already warning friends that he would be spending at least the rest of the winter on the novel. To his brother he announced that he had at last reached the love story—"but there are still great difficulties in composition."[45]

He certainly underestimated the world's potentialities for distraction. Throughout the fall and winter of 1907 he was more involved than he would have wished in the plans for a production of *Fiorenza* in Munich. The "Frankfurt experiment"[46] had only whetted his appetite for further productions, and he now took an interest in the casting and even the acoustics and visual qualities of the Munich theater. The rehearsals again went on far longer than anyone had anticipated. Heinrich proposed that Carla be given the part of Fiore; Thomas brushed the suggestion aside. Carla was under contract elsewhere and probably could not come. Besides, he did not wish to risk "additional experiments in so experimental a matter."[47]

The performance of *Fiorenza*, postponed from October to November, finally took place in the middle of December. Mann evidently attended both the dress rehearsal and the opening, for he reported that the rehearsal had been much better. He learned, from comments in out-of-town newspapers, that he occupied a "literary position in Munich" and that this was the reason the play had not been hooted off the stage. In the *Münchner Neueste Nachrichten* it was attacked as an anti-Catholic, even anti-Christian work; and Mann was constrained to defend it. In his "Letter to a Catholic Newspaper" he pointed out that the general tendency of "these dialogues" was just the opposite, that "the monk Girolamo Savonarola is their real hero." Although Savonarola appears on the stage only toward the end of the play, Mann points out, "from the very first word he is nevertheless present on the scene in spirit." The monk's character and fate had engaged the artist's "most intimate psychological sympathy," and if Lorenzo de' Medici is made to appear at times superior to Savonarola, that is solely "an expression of the [author's] effort to achieve poetic justice."[48]

Given the world's distractions and those of Mann's bustling household, it is perhaps surprising that he made as much progress on the novel as he did. In February 1908 he tried to combine a visit to his mother with a major surge on the novel. Even in the tranquillity of Polling he found writing conditions not very favorable, but he stuck to his desk for those two hours every morning and managed to push his tale somewhat ahead. Yet he complained: "Everything always demands much more space and time than I thought."[49]

This was to be a recurrent theme throughout the years. Progress on *Royal Highness* was scarcely aided by the Manns' decision, after summering in Bad Tölz, to build a vacation house there. Thomas Mann had his father's instincts for burgher solidity. A third child was on the way, summers in the country had become a necessity, and a parcel of land in Tölz was for sale at a reasonable price. The building of the "cottage" began on September 28, 1908; by November 1 Mann could write "the shell is almost finished."[50]

If only a novel could be completed at such a pace.

1 5

Highness

A T T H E beginning of November 1908, Thomas Mann wrote hopefully that *Royal Highness* was "finished or as good as finished."[1] In fact he did not complete the novel until the middle of the following February. This laggard pace and inability to forecast contrast with his certainty eight years earlier, when he was approaching the end of *Buddenbrooks*. Now family life consumed some of his energies. Now, whenever he felt too dispirited to write, or whenever his delicate digestive system troubled him, there were always distractions: letters to answer, people to meet. Even so, eight years was a long interval between novels. The comparison with brother Heinrich was always painful enough; but what about such old friends as Jakob Wassermann, who steadily published novel after novel? Wassermann's work was uneven, to be sure, but Thomas respected it and had read his recent *Caspar Hauser* with sincere enthusiasm. Although Wassermann was an S. Fischer author, this novel had not been published by Fischer, and Mann could therefore feel free of that somewhat incestuous taint attaching to writers of the same publishing house who praised one another's books. He reviewed *Caspar Hauser* for the *Münchner Neueste Nachrichten* in laudatory language, despite reservations about the novel's style and consistency of tone. Kurt Martens, too, had recently treated the theme of Caspar Hauser, in a play; in his review Mann took occasion to mention Martens's work—but only to say that "its literary qualities did not quite equal its theatrical effectiveness." On the other hand, he called Wassermann's novel "a literary work of great and grave beauty . . . so sure, dignified and artistically tranquil, so successful."[2]

One consequence of this friendly review was a reading in Vienna arranged by Jakob Wassermann, who was eager to introduce Mann to his Viennese peers, Arthur Schnitzler and Hugo von Hofmannsthal. Mann had met Hofmannsthal years earlier at the home of Samuel Fischer, but the contact had been brief. He had also recently corresponded with Schnitzler, for he had sent the Viennese doctor a copy of "The Blood of the Walsungs"; in spite of his voluntary suppression of this story he was eager to know what a Jewish writer would think of it. When Schnitzler asked permission to pass the story on to Wassermann, Mann consented, but indicated that he did not want the "Walsungs" to circulate any further.

Believing though he did that such distractions could only hold up his work on *Royal Highness*, that his literary fame was interfering with his concentration on his primary task, he accepted Wassermann's invitation. At the end of November 1908 he traveled to Vienna and gave his reading: a chapter from *Royal Highness*. Two days later Schnitzler, Wassermann, and Mann set out together for the popular resort at the Semmering Pass. Here they met Hugo von Hofmannsthal and his wife. What the four writers talked about is not recorded, but this first meeting was followed by half a day's visit to Hofmannsthal's "little old baroque palace with the appropriate furnishings"[3] in Rodaun. Well into the next year Mann kept referring to the impression Hofmannsthal's choice surroundings and supple Viennese charm had made upon him. At least part of the visit was spent on what really counted: Hofmannsthal read aloud from a comedy he was working on. In the course of that half day the two men had established a friendship—if that is the proper word for a relationship that remained unfailingly formal but consistently cordial—that lasted for the next twenty years, until Hof-mannsthal's death. For Christmas Hofmannsthal sent his poems to Thomas Mann—who read them with care and admiration. And when half a year later Hofmannsthal rather stringently questioned certain aspects of *Royal Highness*, Mann answered the criticism thoughtfully and did not take offense.

For *Royal Highness* had at last been brought to its long-planned conclusion. As a family man with three children, Thomas Mann now took a smilingly wry rather than a romantic view of marriage. The third child, Angelus Gottfried Thomas Mann, later to be called Golo, was born on March 27, 1909. Once more Katia did not have an easy confinement; the seventeen hours of labor, which Thomas spent at her side, exhausted both of them. "The child is again rather the Mucki type—slender and somewhat Chinese,"[4] Thomas wrote to Heinrich. (Mucki was an early nickname for Erika.)

This item of familial chat came as a postscript to a long letter to his brother that attempted to deal with the social stresses between Lula (their sister Julia Mann-Löhr) and Ines Schmied, Heinrich's fiancée. In point of fact there was no longer much prospect that Ines and Heinrich would ever marry, and the proper Lula could not abide the ambiguous relationship. Ines, for her part, could not abide Lula.

The two women had quarreled over what Thomas dismissed as "bagatelles." And although he urged upon Heinrich that "sensible people need not worry their heads over such female antipathies,"[5] he took Lula's side, for it was after all the side of decency and convention against the laxness and looseness of gypsies in green wagons. He wondered whether Heinrich had not put too much into Ines's head about Lula's philistinism and narrowness. The comical part of the whole story was that Ines was offended over, of all things, a breach of etiquette: She had paid a call on Lula and the call had not been returned. The bohemian of 1909 might despise bourgeois niceties, but she wanted them observed toward herself.

Thomas concluded with a plea for more candor and brotherliness: "I have always thought that there could not be a falling out among siblings. They laugh at each other or shout at each other, but they do not ominously bid each other good-bye."[6] And rather nervously, he begged Heinrich not to misread the games he had played with their family relationship in *Royal Highness*. What he no doubt had in mind was the seeming ruthlessness with which the novel arranges for the elder brother's abdication in favor of the younger. What a pity if Heinrich were to apply this innocent twist of a fictional plot to their own rivalry in the domain of literature—where the younger brother had in fact already displaced the elder.

Heinrich's reply (which has not been preserved) must have been reassuring, for Thomas wrote: "Your letter has greatly relieved me."[7] Nevertheless, the plan for a joint vacation in Italy was canceled. Thomas's old intestinal ailment was still troubling him; Heinrich also was not too well, and perhaps did not care to spend time with his brother at this juncture. Instead, Thomas went for a month to the already famous Bircher-Benner Institute in Zürich—"a hygienic penitentiary whose successes are being highly praised now."[8] Dr. Maximilian Bircher-Benner's Lebendige Kraft (Vital Strength) Sanatorium on the Zürichberg was strictly vegetarian: The regimen stressed raw fruits, nuts, and vegetables, as well as sunbathing and fresh air, gardening, hot and cold baths, and gymnastics. The view of sparkling Zürich, its lake, and the more distant, snow-covered Alps, offered some compensation; but during the first few days Mann was on the verge of packing his suitcase and taking French leave. He spoke wryly of himself as "a grass-eating Nebuchadnezzar going on all fours in the air-bath."[9] But his digestion improved so remarkably that he stayed, despite the severities. Later he would consider drawing upon his experiences at the Bircher-Benner Institute for a chapter (never to be written) on Felix Krull's life in prison.

Royal Highness had been completed on February 13. Almost immediately after finishing, Mann dashed off a short story, "Railway Accident," making use of the train derailment he had experienced three years earlier. He treated with light irony the plight of the young writer, a persona of himself, who fears that his sole manuscript of a novel, which is in his suitcase in the baggage car, has been destroyed in the wreck. What, he asks himself, will he do in that case? And his answer, given more in a tone of mockery than of boast, is that he will write it all over again: "My beehive, my artful web, my clever fox's burrow, my pride and travail, the best of me." The story is one of Mann's minor works, but the perfect little scherzo can now be read as a many-sided jest on the pride of Wilhelmine Germany. The tale was also written out of that elation Mann always experienced after the completion of a longer work. With *Royal High-*

ness now in proof he could afford to recall how close he had come to losing the one existing copy of the manuscript, together with all the "hamster's hoard" of notes and studies he had acquired over the years by "eavesdropping, stealth, suffering."[10]

The novel had been finished under pressure of chapter-by-chapter publication in the *Neue Deutsche Rundschau* from January to September. (In book form *Königliche Hoheit* finally appeared in October 1909.) The consequence of this procedure was somewhat unfortunate: opinions were formed before the entire novel was accessible, thus before all the leitmotifs and tags could be seen in the light of the author's full intentions. The topical allusions and the probable "happy ending" were fairly obvious from the outset, so that *Royal Highness* almost at once came to be regarded as something "lightweight" among Mann's works, fit for serial publication but not to be taken quite seriously between hard covers. Although this novel fits logically into the corpus, embodies characteristic attitudes, and makes use of many of Mann's favorite literary devices, it was woefully misunderstood at the time of publication and has been largely neglected since.

The plot of *Royal Highness* appeared to be fable pure and simple, and Mann fostered that impression by repeatedly referring to the novel as his "fairy tale."[11] Yet he employed all the methods of realism he had so thoroughly tested in *Buddenbrooks* to set his scene: a small German principality with a million inhabitants and few natural resources, inexorably slipping ever deeper into financial ruin. Neither the lithium salts of the baths, nor the tourist trade, nor the revenues from the fields and forests, suffice to keep the state afloat —and the spendthrift habits of past generations of rulers have imposed a heavy burden of debt upon their descendants. The many palaces are slowly decaying; there are no funds for even essential repairs. The country's forests—its sole capital resource—are being sacrificed for temporary reprieves from bankruptcy. All this Thomas Mann describes with cool expertise in a mere eleven pages. A political economist might well envy the sharpness of the chapter entitled "The Country."

When Samuel Spoelmann, a prodigiously wealthy American of mixed German and Creole background, decides to buy a run-down castle and settle in the capital city, vague hopes are stirred in the dogged, overtaxed populace. An old tale is recalled, a gypsy's prophecy that someday a prince with one hand will lead the country out of its woes. And although not one-handed, Prince Klaus Heinrich was born with an atrophied arm. When he begins to court Imma Spoelmann, daughter of the American tycoon, the people's dim anticipations turn to certainties and demands. The novel ends with the prince's accomplishing, despite his handicap or because of it, his duty to the state and the mandate to forge his own happiness and that of his beloved—to be sure, an "austere happiness."

In courting and winning the daughter of a millionaire, Thomas Mann himself had for a while played his part in such a fairy tale. And he would have been the first to admit he had borrowed some of his wife's traits, and some details of his own courtship, for his portrait of Imma Spoelmann. But even as he grounded his story in reality, he was at pains to emphasize the purely symbolic, representational, formal existences of his hero and heroine, who never have anything real to do. Guided by his "princess," whose wealth has isolated her much as royalty has him, but whose instincts are earthier, Klaus Heinrich finds his way to the realm of facts, of things, of tasks. He studies economics with Imma, and together—when they are married—they save the country. So while the whole thing was a fairy tale, it offered satisfactions of a realistic sort.

In drawing a German principality that could be seen as paradigmatic for all of Germany, Mann had taken the risk of offending public opinion. Moreover, he had given his fictional prince the crippled arm of the reigning monarch of the German Empire, Wilhelm II. In some quarters, therefore, the story was regarded as a satire directed against the Hohenzollerns. The novel was also seen as vaguely suspect, as though any humorous treatment of royalty were seditious. And there were still minor princes within the German empire. One such prince protested that this mere commoner had the whole picture wrong: Mann had distorted life at court, had garbled the details of ceremonies, and had caricatured the upbringing and education of a prince. Mann felt obliged to offer an apologia in the pages of a Munich periodical.

It was a relief to him, therefore, when he learned that a writer so well disposed as Ida Boy-Ed was going to review the novel for the Lübeck papers. He thanked her warmly in words that revealed and perhaps even somewhat exaggerated his attachment to his native city: "It is incredible how concerned I am about Lübeck. Would you like a bold comparison? Napoleon once said that after every act, every battle, every victory, his first thought was: What will the Faubourg St. Germain say about it? Lübeck is my Faubourg St. Germain. I always think: What will Lübeck say about it?"[12]

If Ida Boy-Ed could be considered representative of what Lübeck would say, Mann had every reason to be gratified. Her long review in the *Lübeckische Blätter* paid gracious tribute from a practiced and popular elder writer to a younger master of the craft. She pointed out that "the improbability of a prince's existence in the framework of modern life" was a theme that hitherto had been missing from the contemporary German novel. No writer had yet dealt with "the artificially engendered and preserved loneliness of royalty, its deepest alienation from the simplest realities." Only a lonely man could describe "the latent tragedy of such loneliness" while at the same time smiling ironically at its perversities. In his newly published "monumental" novel Thomas Mann had produced a document of importance to cultural history, one which at the same time was permeated with poetry. In addition he had "for the second time created a form of his own for a subject uniquely his own."[13]

Ida Boy-Ed had read the book not only as a fellow novelist who could appreciate its technical virtuosity, but as a friend who could trace the provenance of many of its details. She praised the birth scene when the grand duchess is delivered of the prince and recognized such minor characters as the half-wit with a rose in his buttonhole who goes to the station when the train starts and waves when the guard blows the whistle, in the conviction that his waving makes the train start. "All of us elderly Lübeckers well know the character the writer had in mind," Ida Boy-Ed commented. "But the most amazing thing is that Thomas Mann was a small boy when he had the opportunity to observe him."[14]

The allusion to Katia's confinements, the reference to Mann's Lübeck childhood, pleased the author immensely. He wrote effusively to thank the older writer for her kindness:

> Your study of my book seems to me among the very best, most brilliant, warmest, and finest things you have written, and proud as I am of your praise, I am equally proud that my work was the occasion of your writing this fine piece. . . . How sensitive is your remark that the vitality of a work of art consists less in superficial liveliness than

in that organic coherence which is a function of memory, of circumspection, and of conscientiousness. I shall certainly not hear anything better, hardly anything as good.[15]

Another older woman writer, Gabriele Reuter, repaid Mann's earlier good words for her work with a review praising the "rare delicacy" of Mann's handling of the relationship between the prince and the American heiress: "It will not be easy to find a comparable love story in contemporary literature."[16] Another review initiated a correspondence that was eventually to develop into a friendship. Hermann Hesse, to whom Mann had been introduced six years earlier by Samuel Fischer, reviewed the novel for the bimonthly *März*, of which he was co-editor. Hesse concerned himself largely with novelistic technique, and like any writer reviewing a fellow craftsman's work he instinctively defended his own approach to the art. In later years Hesse was to learn much and borrow much from Thomas Mann; but at this time he objected to *Royal Highness* as too intellectual, too contrived, too manneristic, too conscious of the reader. He condemned Mann's caricatures and contrasted the artificiality of *Royal Highness* with the naive and natural power of *Buddenbrooks*. He concluded nevertheless on a respectful note: Mann's poorest work would always be superior to the average.

No sooner was the review printed than Hesse began to feel that it had been too carping. He hastily sent Mann an apology. Mann replied that "critical understanding" in no way displeased him. But he earnestly defended himself against Hesse's charge:

> I sometimes think that what you call my "playing up to the public" springs from my long, passionately critical enthusiasm for the art of Richard Wagner—that art, as exclusive as it is demagogic, which may have permanently influenced, not to say corrupted, my ideals and artistic strivings. Nietzsche speaks of Wagner's "shifting perspective," meaning that he appeals sometimes to the crudest, sometimes to the most refined tastes. This is the influence I have in mind, and I don't know whether I shall ever summon up the willpower to shake it off completely.[17]*

---

* After this letter the Hesse-Mann correspondence lapsed for six years, so far as we know. At any rate no letters from this period have been found. Hesse went to India in 1911, and the resultant psychological upheaval may have turned him away from literary courtesies. In the middle of the war he wrote briefly to Mann again in connection with a humanitarian cause.

When it came to reviewing *Royal Highness*, even so well-disposed a critic as Hermann Bahr proved disappointing. Mann had long felt the warmest affection and gratitude toward Bahr; he remembered that at the outset of his career "Bahr's first symbolistic prose colored the style of the nineteen-year-olds."[18] While still in school Mann had copied Bahr's style "with slavish delight,"[19] finding artistic satisfaction precisely in his ability to reproduce it. But now, in the long-awaited review for the *Neue Deutsche Rundschau*, Bahr found that Mann's prince and heiress lacked all individual character, that they were merely representatives of their classes, their economic conditions—and he implied that Mann's approach was that of a Marxist.

Mann was somewhat disconcerted by Bahr's rambling article; for although it was friendly enough, it identified him with a literary movement with which he felt he had little in common. Writing to Kurt Martens, Mann commented:

A certain didactically anti-individualistic note in the book cannot be denied, and my brother, a passionate democrat of the newest stamp (his latest novel is extremely interesting as a topical work) was *delighted* with Bahr's interpretation of *Royal Highness*. Doesn't that strike you as significant? Politically, democracy is certainly on the march in this country, and belles lettres are unmistakably taking some part in it. Haven't you noticed that almost all our "intellectuals" signed the appeal . . . in favor of electoral reform in Prussia? Granted, they'll write their names on practically anything that's put in front of them; but it's still a sign of the times that the politicians are trying to recruit them. The increasing interest is mutual. . . . It is certainly a misunderstanding to regard *Royal Highness* as a book of social criticism; and what you call the "altruistic"—and Bahr and my brother the "democratic"—element in it is only one of its implications. Although its artistic merit is not based on that, perhaps its intellectual or ethical merit is, and if the book is read at all in the future it may possibly be for the sake of this element. . . . At any rate you are perfectly right in saying that henceforth "democratic" books cannot seriously be expected from me.

He concluded this highly revealing letter, which reflects the essayistic tasks that were engaging him at the time, with a mention of his newest fictional concern: "I am now collecting, noting, making studies for something long planned, something quite unusual: *The Confessions of the Confidence Man.*"²⁰

I F to be called a democrat was mildly disturbing, to be denounced as "a champion of Jewish racial policy"²¹ was painful, baffling, and in its viciousness and idiocy sickening. That accusation came in a review by a *völkisch* writer named Otto Schmidt-Gibichenfels, who saw the whole of *Royal Highness* as part of a plot to undermine Aryan racial purity. The matter was embarrassing also, and not only because Thomas Mann had a Jewish wife and Jewish relations by marriage. There was a sense of being tarred with the same sort of brush he and Heinrich had wielded, though reluctantly and rather gingerly, during their brief association with *Das Zwanzigste Jahrhundert.*

Of course no reader of *Royal Highness* could overlook Mann's sympathy and respect for Dr. Sammet, the Jewish physician who is present in the life of Prince Klaus Heinrich from the day of his birth. In one of its aspects *Royal Highness* is an *Erziehungsroman*, and in that sense a forerunner of *The Magic Mountain.* Like Hans Castorp after him, Klaus Heinrich encounters a series of preceptors and is molded by them. Dr. Sammet is not the least important of these. But whether Otto Schmidt had even read the book sufficiently to discover Dr. Sammet remains doubtful; his attack seems to be based largely on Gabriele Reuter's review. He jumped to the conclusion that the billionaire Spoelmann was Jewish, while the "heroine" united within herself "*all four different human races, no less!*" Obviously "the dullest bonehead cannot help catching on to the point of the whole story." The "Jews and their henchmen" are trying to persuade good honest Germans that racial mixing will lead them out of the degeneracy into which they have fallen through "inbreeding, prosperity, and long-lasting urban culture" and will help them rise to new heights both economically and racially. But no Jew was going to persuade Otto Schmidt-Gibichenfels to take fool's gold for coin of the realm.

> Let them [the Jews] drag the cities financially, morally, and racially into the bog. As long as an authentic German peasantry tills the fields, an authentic German sovereign sits upon the throne, and an

authentic German nobility stands at his side, sword in hand—just so long will the cunning and deceptions practiced against our people by all the Jews and Jew hirelings come to naught.[22]

Thomas Mann would hear this tone again, all too frequently, in subsequent decades. He had in fact already heard it in the remark by another race-obsessed critic, Adolf Bartels, that he was "most probably" Jewish. This was an awkward allegation, for it would be most unbecoming for him to expostulate that he was not. He managed to combine public denial with forthright affirmation:

I . . . represent not a Jewish but only a Latin mixture of bloods. Still, I have neither the right nor the desire to engage in any kind of racial chauvinism. I am, though not otherwise richly blessed with wholly un-equivocal convictions, a convinced and unequivocal "philo-Semite," and I firmly believe that an exodus such as Zionists of the strict per-suasion dream of would amount to about the greatest misfortune that could befall our Europe.[23]

That statement surely reflected the attitudes of his wife and her family. Totally assimilated, they had little interest in Zionism. Thirty-five years later, under the impact of the systematic extermi-nation of Europe's Jews, Mann had changed his mind about Zionism. In a tribute to Chaim Weizmann he then wrote (in English):

The Zionist idea proves to possess a steadily growing persuasiveness and power. . . . It is a spiritual fact which must be respected, and it will overcome every resistance that opposes its realization. This re-sistance arises largely from the misunderstanding that Zionism aims to repatriate in Palestine all the Jews of the world. Aside from the fact that this is physically perhaps not possible, it may also not cor-respond with the wishes of many Jews who have been rooted for many centuries in the civilization of the West, nor would it be in the interest of those so-called "host" countries which owe so deep a debt of gratitude to the civilizing stimulus of the Jewish people.[24]

Philo-Semitism certainly need not involve approval of every Jew, and it in no way forbade Mann's taking the part of one Jew against another in those feuds that were a feature of German literary life. Along with enemies like Bartels in the German racist camp, Mann could count on the malice of people like Alfred Kerr. Reviewing other works, Kerr would go out of his way to sting Mann with a barbed comment, often one that revealed inside knowledge of the writer's personal circumstances. He liked to hint that Mann, who he had once thought showed promise, had let his artistic gifts atrophy because he was no longer driven by necessity, having married a millionaire's daughter. Or he referred to Mann as "an old sanatorium client" whose dearest wish was "to describe himself in a high social position and novelistically cover up his Achilles heel."[25] That allusion to the inglorious end of Mann's military career was enough to make the supersensitive writer "sick for days."[26]

One hostile critic like Alfred Kerr was almost more than Mann could stand. And now of his own accord he had brought down on himself the spite of another former friend of the family, Theodor Lessing. He provoked the quarrel partly out of frustration because he could not do anything to protect himself against Kerr. But when he spoke of his motivation as "a just emotional upheaval of an entirely unselfish kind,"[27] he was being truthful. The whole imbroglio resulted essentially from Mann's sense of loyalty toward the critic who had first reviewed *Buddenbrooks* with such keen understanding: Samuel Lublinski.

In the eyes of a later generation the whole affair had somewhat comic-opera overtones. But it also had a racial aspect, complicated by the fact that Lublinski was a man who had heroically overcome physical and racial disabilities and by sheer force of intellect won a place for himself as a spokesman for "the modern" in literature. The philosopher Martin Buber, a close friend of Lublinski's, described him as one whom nature had brought into the world "crippled, paralyzed, diminished in all his senses, moreover in the most unfavorable, the most merciless environment. Nature had left him only the will to desire the utmost, the impossible."[28] And Lublinski, Buber added, had used this powerful will to create a world of the mind.

This was the man whom Lessing chose to attack. Lessing thought of himself as a polymath; others regarded him as a dilettante. His interests and expertise ranged from medicine and philosophy to literature and mathematics. A baptized Jew, he had returned to Judaism under the influence of Zionism. He was nearly the same age as Thomas Mann, whom he had met in Munich, probably during Mann's brief attendance at the university. He also knew Carla Mann and the Pringsheim family. In 1906 Lessing had published a book on Schopenhauer, Wagner, and Nietzsche which Thomas Mann read, or at least dipped into; in a letter to the author he called it admirable. Such adjectives came to him the more readily when he had merely leafed through a book.

Lessing's totally unprovoked, savage ad hominem satire on Samuel Lublinski was published in the weekly magazine *Die Schaubühne* in January 1910. Curiously, the tone was that of the anti-Semites of a later generation of Germans—the very generation that murdered Theodor Lessing in Marienbad in 1933. The nastiness of the article, the despicable allusions to Lublinski's physical handicaps and Jewish accent in German, aroused general indignation in those comparatively innocent times. Thirty-three German writers of note signed a statement denouncing Lessing's article. Thomas Mann was asked to join the signatories, but chose instead to publish an independent statement of his own.

He wrote his piece, "Der Doktor Lessing," with a vigor, an inventiveness, a delight in the cut-and-thrust of insult, that must have come as something of a surprise to himself. A few years earlier he had had to appeal to Heinrich for help against the assaults of Richard Schaukal. Now he revealed a capacity for polemics that foreshadowed the literary activist of the war years and the Nazi era. He proved to be adept at ridicule, referring to "the gruesome anecdote that he [Lessing] along with a few other Schwabing ecstatics once danced stark naked around a fire." He called Lessing a "disadvantaged dwarf who ought to be glad that the sun shines on him also."[29]

That allusion to the naked dancing evidently struck home, for in his rejoinder Lessing spoke of Mann "with boyish hand destroying the airily dancing cordax of a harmlessly playful little satire."[30] For him to call his vicious lampoon "harmlessly playful" was disingenuous, to say the least; but the key word was *cordax*. A cordax is the wanton dance of bacchantes; the use of this farfetched word was perhaps an inadvertent confession. In any case, the absurdity of the image must serve as a sample of Lessing's preposterous style. And of course the one exchange was not the last of the affair. Lessing printed the entire controversy in a pamphlet entitled "Tommy Milks the Cow of Morality," full of the kind of strained language and pseudo-sophistication that Alfred Kerr had popularized. As the affair wore on, Mann became thoroughly sick of it; he was, as he complained in one of his replies, "like the man in the fairy tale carrying a dwarf on his back." And although he managed to shake off the dwarf by dint of steadfastly refusing to go on with the quarrel, he never forgave or forgot. Twenty-three years later, when he learned that Lessing had been killed by the Nazis, he noted the fact in his diary without a flicker of sympathy.

I T would have been a relief to turn from such ugly literary feuding to summer in the country and the joys of domesticity "under our grand-brand-new roof."³¹ But just this year, when he badly needed the rest, departure for Bad Tölz had to be delayed until the middle of July. On June 7, 1910, the day after Mann's own birthday, Katia gave birth to their second daughter, Monika, afterward called Moni. Four children in five and a half years of marriage struck Thomas Mann as perhaps excessive. Much as he enjoyed the little ones' drolleries, much as he was steadied by the sense of having taken his proper role in the world, he apparently felt that enough was enough. "God willing no more will come along," he commented ruefully. "It already verges on the ridiculous."³²

"Landhaus Thomas Mann," the stationery now read, and Thomas Mann was proud enough of the new country home to invite acquaintances, friends, and even his publisher. It was a substantial villa in Bavarian country style, located in a lively resort town outside Munich, with a pond in walking distance. The children felt that Bad Tölz was their true home, although they spent only a small part of the year there. It was the landscape of childhood.

Paradise is imbued with the bittersweet fragrance of conifer, tonic herbs, and raspberries, fused with the scent of moss that has become warm in the sun—the vast, powerful sun of a summer day in Tölz. The clearing where we spend the morning picking berries lies in the midst of a stately forest, the beautiful wood of fir trees which commences right behind our house. . . . And here are the children with the dog, and Mother wearing a summer dress, a pretty garment made of heavy linen, with wide, puffed sleeves and lavish embroideries. . . . Mother is bareheaded, offering the dark richness of her hair to the caress of the sun. . . . [Father] appeared at twelve o'clock on the dot to walk with Mielein [the children's nickname for their mother] and the rest of us, across the meadows to the marshy pond where we had our swim before luncheon.[33]

That is how Klaus Mann recalled it in the autobiography he wrote in English thirty years later. He goes on to describe a somewhat monotonous idyll of long, lazy summer afternoons that blended together to form one of "the myths of childhood."[34] But the Manns had been in Bad Tölz barely two weeks when the idyll was blasted by tragic news.

1 6

Tragedy in Polling

"*JE T'AIME. Une fois je t'ai trompé, mais je t'aime.*"[1] This was the note that Carla Mann left behind before she took "enough potassium cyanide to kill a company of soldiers."[2] The news reached Thomas Mann in Bad Tölz by telephone, Heinrich and Viktor Mann by telegram. For the rest of his life Heinrich believed that he had heard Carla call him in her last moment:

> When I was nearing forty the person I loved most in the world died, far from me. My mind would have accompanied her anywhere rather than to her death. I should have known and did not even guess. Toward noon I was strolling in a denuded garden, the only one on this South Tyrolean mountain. All was still; then I was called: from the house, I thought. So little prepared was I, that in the first moment it did not occur to me: No one here calls me by my given name. Later in the day came the telegram with the news.[3]

This was the first death in the family in twenty years. What made the shock harder to bear was that Carla had been a beautiful young woman, not yet thirty, who unfortunately blurred the distinction between her performances on the stage and her playacting in her own life. "You are a writer," she had once said to Heinrich. "Those who read you see people. I want to be seen myself, really present myself to them. What you are with your mind alone, I am with my whole body."⁴ So she had spoken in the confidence of twenty; but the following nine years of bit parts and small theaters had left her with ambition undimmed but with the growing realization that she did not have the talent to achieve fame.

Both her elder brothers sadly watched her posturings at home and lukewarm successes in the provinces with an objectivity that in no way compromised their affection. Thomas saw that Carla lacked the innate vitality of the true actress, lacked "theater blood." Heinrich provided Carla with a mirror in the Ute of his *Die Jagd nach Liebe*; and perhaps after a while this had helped her to recognize that her hopes of a great career on the stage would never come to fulfillment. She looked around for a way out, grasped at "a way back into the bourgeois realm,"⁵ and decided upon marriage to a young manufacturer from Mulhouse. Already delighting in her fantasies of raising French-speaking children, she ignored the opposition of her fiancé's family and his own uncertainties.

At this point the story assumes the hue of a second-rate thriller or an opera plot, except that it was played out in deadly earnest and ended with a real corpse lying on the chaise longue, hands and face showing dark spots from the abrupt suffocation caused by cyanide. There was a former lover in Carla's life, a doctor, who now used the threat of disclosure for erotic blackmail. Fearing that he would destroy her chances for marriage, she yielded to him. Nevertheless he exposed her, sending an anonymous letter to the young man from Mulhouse. Her fiancé came to Polling, where Carla was staying with her mother for the summer, to question her.

"Coming from an interview with him, the unhappy creature hurried past her mother with a smile, and locked herself into her room, and the last that was heard from her was the sound of her gargling with water as she tried to cool the caustic burning in her throat."⁶ Such was Thomas Mann's account of his sister's last moments, written nearly twenty years later. There is a faint coldness in it, a touch of anger at the wound Carla's act had inflicted upon their mother. That same reproachful note was sounded openly in the letter he wrote to his one-time intimate friend Paul Ehrenberg less than two weeks after his sister's suicide. Paul had sent condolences. Thomas replied:

> Many, many thanks for your sympathetic lines. Yes, poor Carla. There is hardly any satisfactory explanation for her death; at least none that can be couched in a few words. You probably knew that she was engaged to a young manufacturer from Mühlhausen, and quite happily so. Nevertheless, there were inner conflicts which made it impossible—subjectively—for her to go on living. She imagined she saw her hopes collapsing, thought her chances for life were exhausted. And so she took some of the potassium cyanide which she had had around for a long time. She must originally have bought it as a sort of aesthetic caprice and idiosyncrasy—you know, the way she kept a skull on the dresser as a young girl. And then she played too long with the idea, grew used to the thought of taking it at the first provocation. . . . What she would do to all of us, what a blow it would be to our lives when she smashed her own life, apparently never entered the poor child's mind. You can imagine our Mama's grief. It happened in Polling—in Mama's apartment. She is here with us now and is gradually returning to a tolerable state of mind.[7]

There is also a touch of old rancor in this account. Thomas was well aware of Carla's disdain for his own marriage. Five years ago she had scorned him for grasping at bourgeois security and wealth—though she, too, had come round to these values before her drastic finale. The children of the family had split: Thomas and Julia on one side, Heinrich and Carla on the other. Thomas's grief was interlaced with some bitter memories. But Heinrich truly mourned Carla, and immediately after Carla's death he wrote his brother a letter that Thomas called "feverish and reprehensible," containing "much that must be strictly and firmly dismissed." Thomas refrained from answering it on the grounds that "in your present state of nerves it would do more harm than good."[8]

Heinrich's state of nerves sprang from an anguish that Thomas did not feel. When at last Thomas felt ready to relate the story of his sisters' lives and deaths in the guise of the Rodde sisters of *Doctor*

Faustus, he devoted more space and novelistic intensity to Inez Rodde, modeled on his sister Julia, than to Clarissa. In fact he told Carla's story in much the same manner, and at times using the very same dry phraseology, that he had employed earlier in *A Sketch of My Life* (written in 1929).

Heinrich's suffering, on the other hand, brought him to an even closer understanding of his sister. Under the immediate impact of Carla's death he set down in his notebook, under the heading of "Carla," a sketch of his sister that rings with absolute truthfulness—even as it also sounds like the scenario for the play he was soon to write.

> She was an actress. Render unto the body what is the body's. Spasms of passion that she basically despises. Exaltation in which she does not fully believe. Awareness of incompatibility with another human being, and of artificiality. Pride in this, contempt for self-deception, for weakness, for sentiment; disengagement from *life*. Also *cheerful* out of disengagement.
>
> At twenty-seven, disgust. It is time to bring warmth into life, to seek a shelter before the haughty powers of resistance are entirely lost. (The career has brought disappointment.) She chooses her first love in a new world, a French one, speaks her first true words of love in a new language. . . .

Heinrich recounts in detail how Carla is slandered for being an actress and a girl of loose morals, how she manages to win over her fiancé's mother, how the former lover intervenes. But Heinrich blames Carla, too, for her faulty choices: "She had chosen a weak man in order to live; that was her actress's instinct, hostile to life. This time once more she held herself back when she thought she was finally giving herself." Instead she succumbs to the scoundrelly doctor, succumbs, Heinrich believes, because of the poison in her drawer, which represented a way out for her whenever she might need it. And she confesses to her fiancé what she has done.

> She could simply have continued to say no, there was no truth to it. But instead she offers up a clumsy fiction. Why? At bottom she wishes to betray herself, although that will be the end. She despises herself too intensely for lying. Earlier, lying was unnecessary; she was free.

Her deepest instinct is still to be free. Lies unite people; the truth sep-
arates them. One must be able to lie if one wishes to live. Carla is not
capable of living.[9]

In Heinrich's drama *Schauspielerin* (Actress), written almost immediately after Carla's death and published in 1911, the heroine is
pictured as being driven to her death by the diabolic doctor, who
even provides her with the cyanide he has obtained, under false pre-
tenses, from her fiancé, the manufacturer. The involved plot made
for effective theater; but Heinrich also put it to use as a vehicle for
extraordinary flights of psychological penetration. *Schauspielerin*
had its premiere in November 1911 and thereafter was performed
frequently in theaters all over Germany. And as often happened, by
the time Thomas Mann came round to dealing with his sister's death
in *Doctor Faustus*, he had consciously or unconsciously absorbed his
brother's play and made it his own. He borrowed from Heinrich
the name Seiler, but assigned it to Clarissa's teacher; in *Schauspielerin* it is the name of the fiancé. And he likewise borrowed Heinrich's interpretation: that the "specter from her past" had virtually
murdered the girl. "In my opinion the scoundrel, aside from satisfying his lechery, had actually aimed at her death. His infamous
vanity demanded a woman's corpse along his way; he lusted to have
a human being die the death, if not exactly for his sake, at any rate
because of him."[10]

Carla's death cast its shadow over the entire summer. So it was
with mixed feelings that Mann helped to celebrate his father-in-
law's sixtieth birthday on September 2. The party was held at Bad
Tölz—and a university professor ranked so high in Wilhelmine
Germany that the whole small town threw itself into doing honor
to Alfred Pringsheim, who was not even a resident. The band from
the baths gave a concert, vast numbers of telegrams arrived, Thomas
"managed to deliver a speech" at dinner, and "in the evening there
was a torchlight procession and singing by the schoolchildren." But
the celebration awoke bitter reflections in Thomas:

Yes, life goes on, and as long as one is not also lying in a black, rec-
tangular pit in the ground, interlaced by tree roots, one must go along
with it a little.
My feelings have been in sad disorder all this while. If Carla had

been able to imagine what her deed would do to the rest of us, I think she would not have committed it. But gradually we regain our balance, and already I can think without disgust of the toilsome and passionate playing that is called artistic work.[11]

The artistic work in question consisted of *Felix Krull*, the fiction he found hard to sustain, and an offshoot of his reading for "Old Fontane." He was to abandon it in mid-course and return to it only at the end of his life. Now he interrupted it for the sake of another assignment. In "Old Fontane," the first of his published essays on literary figures, Mann attempted a rather daring experiment in nonfictional autobiographic allusion—an experiment so successful that he repeated it frequently in future years. The occasion was a new volume of Theodor Fontane's letters. Fontane, whose life spanned the last three quarters of the nineteenth century, was a North German with a "Latin admixture" in his blood, whom Mann greatly admired and from whom he had learned. Instead of simply reviewing the new book, Mann chose to sketch Fontane's temperament and his attitudes toward his art. But from Fontane's letters and life Mann craftily selected those quotations, opinions, poses, and prospects most applicable to himself. The essay therefore can be read both as objective analysis and as confession. For example, Fontane's writing did not flow; it "dribbled." Fontane took so dim a view of the writer's occupation that he declared: "Only fools would boast of such a trade."[12] And Mann points up the quotation by a reference of his own that looks backward to *Tonio Kröger* and forward to his current work on *Felix Krull:* "In Munich a swindler was recently caught in a first-class hotel. After his signature in the register he had added as his profession the word 'writer.' "[13]

For the reader acquainted with the course of Mann's life during his first thirty-five years, the parallels come in a shower. Mann had failed to finish Gymnasium. He writes that Fontane felt himself to be so badly educated that he would not come to Weimar to receive an honor, for fear of being addressed with a Latin or Greek tag; whenever that sort of thing happened to him he wished the earth would open and swallow him. In Fontane's letters Mann even finds the very argument he himself had advanced in justifying his borrowings from reality, and he quotes Fontane quoting one of his own favorite lines from *Hamlet:* "I am particularly grateful to you for pointing out that I attack myself no less than others. And had I been able to follow my inclination, I would have come down even harder on myself. For despite all the vanities we cannot shake off, we ultimately come round to regarding ourselves as something highly dubious: 'Thou comest in such a questionable shape.' "[14]

With Heinrich ever on his mind, Mann cannot resist the chance to disparage his brother's rapid production by choosing an appropriate passage from Fontane: "Storm took more time to write a little lyric than Brachvogel did to write a three-volume novel. . . . An ordinary man writes down masses of stuff as it goes through his head. The artist, the true poet, often searches for the right word for a fortnight."[15]

Mann also quotes Fontane as saying that one of his favorite occupations is making fun of himself. But speaking on his own behalf he warns others not to make fun of him; Mann has no wish to give further stimulus to the Lessings and Kerrs. "The right to be ironic about the works of the mind and 'literature' (a fashion nowadays that is deplorably misused by trespassers in the realm of culture) has first to be won by great accomplishments."[16]

The essay on Fontane astonishingly foreshadowed the political convictions and contradictions that were to occupy most of Mann's time and thought during the second half of the decade. He was already deeply preoccupied—indeed always had been—with the nature of Germanism. But beyond that he was trying to understand the problem of the writer who is conservative by temperament but sometimes revolutionary by sentiment or logic. He sees Fontane as the admirer (and critic) of Bismarck who nevertheless had in mind to write a grand historical novel about the *Likedeeler*, the fifteenth-century buccaneers and communists who preyed on the maritime traffic of the Hansa towns. And with unmistakable reference to himself, Mann defends Fontane's right to apparent inconsistency: "As guardian of myth the writer is conservative. But psychology is the keenest sapper's tool known to democratic enlightenment."[17] And what is the writer's realm if not myth and psychology?

The article on Fontane was dispatched to Maximilian Harden on August 21, accompanied by a deprecating letter in which Mann remarked that it was probably too long and not altogether suitable for *Die Zukunft*. But despite the advance apologies he was taken aback by Harden's reply. The editor was surely familiar enough

with Mann's life and circumstances to recognize the personal allusions, and may have found these objectionable. But he chose to declare his dislike of the subject rather than the review—and it is
hardly surprising that Harden, the German publicist who came
closest to the spirit of the American muckrakers, should have been
hostile to Fontane's aristocratic Prussianism. He accused Fontane of
"duplicity" and seems also to have objected, inconsistently, to Fontane's ambivalence toward Bismarck. Mann found himself forced to
answer the charges on Fontane's behalf and his own ("Is it possible
to be so stern with the old boy?"). Harden was not to feel obliged to
accept the "thoroughly unimportant article" out of any "considera-
tions"—by which he meant obligations to Katia's Berlin relations.[18]
Either this oblique reminder sufficed or Harden was won over by his
arguments; in any case the essay on Fontane was published in the
October issue of *Die Zukunft*. Curiously, a new correspondent of
Mann's, Ernst Bertram, had also written a review of Fontane's
letters and sent a copy to Mann. Mann was delighted to find some of
his own insights corroborated by a full-fledged scholar: "I find that
our two essays splendidly complement each other—even in the quotations. In saying which I don't overlook the fact that mine needs
complementing far more than yours."[19]

T H E birth of Monika meant that the Munich apartment on
Franz-Josephstrasse became crowded beyond endurance. At the beginning of the Manns' married life only five years before, it had been
spacious, but their establishment had grown considerably. Room
had to be found for four children, a nurse, a governess, two servants;
and for the paterfamilias a secluded study was absolutely essential.
Moreover, the new house in Bad Tölz had already accustomed the
family to ampler space and more countrylike surroundings. Accordingly, the Manns rented two connecting four-room apartments in a
brand-new suburb, what had formerly been the village of Bogen-
hausen, across the river Isar from the Englischer Garten. Along the
river itself was still that wild and sometimes boggy country that
Mann would describe in *A Man and His Dog*. The district was
called Herzogpark, for the ducal park lay close by. The park might
have borrowed its name from *Royal Highness* (or lent its name to
the sovereign in that novel), for it was called Herzog Albrecht

Anlagen. In this neighborhood Thomas Mann settled in; the new apartment at Mauerkircherstrasse 13 was only a stone's throw from Poschingerstrasse, where he would later build his house. Here, in Herzogpark, the Mann family remained through war, revolution, inflation, and worldwide depression for nearly a quarter of a century. It is no wonder that the promenade along the river, now far more trimmed and tamed than it was in 1910, today bears the name Thomas Mann Allee. Beyond the bridge over the Isar the same promenade becomes the Heinrich Mann Allee.

The move to the larger quarters in Herzogpark coincided with the end of that period of isolation that almost every young family passes through when sheer pressure of time, the obligations of child rearing, and the adjustments to the increasing demands and delights of small children tend to stifle the social instincts. New acquaintances began to make their appearance, some of them to be taken into the household as friends of the family, among them the young writer Bruno Frank and the young critic Ernst Bertram. Soon Bruno Walter would move to Mauerkircherstrasse—the conductor met Mann around 1912—and the neighboring families would become close. For getting into town there was a convenient streetcar, line number 30, easily reached by a flight of stone steps; and chance meetings on the tram were common. The people who unselfconsciously rode "number 30" along with their servants formed a fairly coherent group, comfortably upper middle class, the gentry of a society still frankly nonegalitarian.

If there was no pressing business in town, it was always possible and pleasant to cross the bridge over the Isar to the Englischer Garten on foot, and stroll through this park to the very center, or to old haunts in Schwabing. The streetcars stopped running early, and in clement weather Mann made it almost a rule to walk home in the evenings after attending the theater, a concert, the opera, or a literary or political lecture. Walking was his only exercise, and he tried if possible to walk twice a day, regarding this habit as essential to his health. But these walks were essential also to his literary work; in their course he did much of the thinking and imagining that would be set down in a morning's writing session.

The "voice" that Thomas Mann had found for his confidence man had an altogether unique timbre; but it also had a brittleness, a quality of ingenuity for its own sake, that the writer found hard to sustain. He evidently looked for excuses not to work on the novel, although at the same time he frequently read from it, with great effectiveness, on lecture platforms. In November 1910 a lecture tour took him to Weimar, where he enjoyed the "touching hospitality of an old school friend, Count Vitztum von Eckstädt. He was delighted to discover that all the impressions he gathered of life at a petty court were "strict confirmations of my intuitions in *Royal Highness.*"[20]

The tour provided enough distraction to keep him from returning to *Felix Krull* immediately after his return. But the memories of boyhood evoked by this visit with his old friend stimulated him, on his return, to dash off a short story, "The Fight Between Jappe and Do Escobar." Contrary to his habit, he finished it so quickly that he was able to read it aloud in the family circle by December 11. In later years he referred to it as one of his "incidental sketches, which were humorous in conception, slighter in scope, and more superficial in treatment"[21] than his other attempts at comedy. In later life the story may have embarrassed him because of its emphasis on the androgynous physique and temperament of boys at puberty. Perhaps he was also inclined to disown it because it sounded more like a story Heinrich might have written. The milieu, in fact, is that of Heinrich's "Abdication." But Thomas enriched this story of adolescence with political overtones that critics have missed and of which he himself may have been unaware (though this is not likely). Certainly the simple story of an abortive fight between a Spanish and a German boy, with the French dancing master acting as referee and the narrator's English friend coolly looking on, reflects the international tensions of those years before the First World War. While he spun his fables of the artist's isolation and unhappiness, Mann did not ignore the ominous confrontation of Triple Entente and Triple Alliance that sent Europe reeling from crisis to crisis during the first decade of the new century. When the war came, Mann professed to be surprised; but he had already anticipated it in his fiction —in "The Fight Between Jappe and Do Escobar" and, more notably, in the portentous opening sentences of *Death in Venice* written the following year. He anticipated as well, out of deepest knowledge of himself, the painful ambiguities of his own position on the war. The fight is over, has come to no clear conclusion, although the Spaniard's nose has been bloodied. The boys are sitting around, disappointed. Someone calls out that others should fight, another pair of combatants. The narrator comments: "Nobody offered. But why at this summons did my heart begin to beat like a little drum? What I had feared had come to pass: the belligerence had spread to the onlookers. . . . Why was it that I had to feel personally challenged to conquer my nervous timidity, to make an unnatural effort and draw all eyes upon myself by heroically stepping into the ring?"[22]

The story as a whole harked back to the period of *Buddenbrooks* and *Tonio Kröger;* the setting is Travemünde, the seaside resort near Lübeck where the Buddenbrooks spend their holidays; and the dancing master of both earlier works even appears again. But there was an unaware looking-forward as well to a tale not yet conceived: the charm of Johnny Bishop in "Jappe and Do Escobar" strongly resembles that of Tadzio in *Death in Venice,* and the two boys in fact wear the same English sailor suit.

The productive vein lasted right to the end of 1910. For the Christmas issue of the *Berliner Tageblatt* Mann rapidly wrote a review of a new edition of Adalbert von Chamisso's classic *The Marvelous Tale of Peter Schlemihl.* He had been presented with a copy by another new friend in his widening Munich circle, Hans von Weber, editor of the influential magazine *Der Zwiebelfisch* and wealthy publisher of fine editions. For his new edition of *Peter Schlemihl* Weber had found a young illustrator named Emil Preetorius, soon to be an intimate of the Mann family. "Pree," as Mann called him, would go on to become one of Germany's foremost book illustrators, stage designers, and collectors of Far Eastern works of art. Though Mann had not yet met the illustrator, he was greatly taken by the edition itself. He praised the originality of the format, the excellent paper, the pleasing print, and especially dwelt on the wit and suitability of Preetorius's illustrations.

He gave way to the temptation to read Chamisso's immortal tale again—"for the first time, strictly speaking, for I was too young the last time it fell into my hands"[23]—and found that he was likewise enchanted by *Peter Schlemihl* itself. That is hardly surprising, for here in this nineteenth-century Romantic's story Mann found his favorite themes, his own perplexities, his own disguised autobiographical approach to art. A pact with the devil, no less, is the principal plot element in this story of the man who sells his shadow in exchange for a sack that produces an unlimited supply of gold coins.

But everyone notices the lack of a shadow, and poor Schlemihl is jeered at and hounded wherever he goes, so that he is condemned to keep out of the sun and emerge only after dark, for all the world like one of Thomas Mann's "outsider" characters. "In *Peter Schlemihl* the shadow has become the symbol of all bourgeois solidity and human affiliation."[24]

The following year Mann's own publisher, S. Fischer, decided to include *Peter Schlemihl* in its popular Pantheon editions, and what could be more natural than that Mann should be asked to write an introduction. The result was an essay on Chamisso, into which Mann thriftily incorporated large sections of the *Berliner Tageblatt* review, and to which he added a section on Chamisso's life and work and a peroration directed straight at his own preoccupation of the moment: the forever simmering conflict with Heinrich. As he went over Chamisso's life, he more and more assimilated it—as he had done with Fontane—to his own concerns: the differences between the French (i.e., "Latin") and German spirit and the nature of concealed autobiography in works of fiction. ("Writers who give of themselves at bottom want others to understand them, for they are concerned not so much with the fame of their works as with the fame of their lives and suffering.")[25]

It is curious to see how this essay, compact and elegant though it is, ends abruptly on a petulant note betraying inner tensions:

> It is the good old story. Werther shot himself, but Goethe remained alive. Schlemihl, shadowless, proudly strides in his seven-league boots over hill and dale, a naturalist "living for himself alone." But Chamisso, after he had turned his sufferings into a book, hastened to outgrow the problematical pupal state. He settles down, becomes a paterfamilias, an academic, is revered as a master. Only everlasting bohemians consider that boring. It is not possible to remain forever interesting.[26]

Death in
Venice

THOMAS MANN'S irritability may have sprung from his sense of being overburdened, for the year had been strenuous in every respect. Family concerns and responsibilities seemed to multiply. He had come to a standstill on *Felix Krull*, largely from the sense that he could not keep up the high standard set by the opening chapters. Moreover, after the Weimar reading he had committed himself to a more extended tour, which would take him through the Ruhr district and Westphalia, where he would read the choicer bits from his work in progress and from earlier novellas. Tours of this sort had become a significant aspect of his literary activity. He rather enjoyed the platform appearances. The hero of that earlier story of his, "Railway Accident," is a writer on his way to just such a performance, though he is keenly aware of the humorous side of the enterprise: "I was on my way to Dresden, whither I had been invited by some friends of letters: it was a literary and artistic pilgrimage, in short, such as from time to time I undertake not unwillingly. You make appearances, you attend functions, you show yourself to admiring crowds—not for nothing is one a subject of Wilhelm II."

The expenses were paid; the fees were welcome; and the writer who would otherwise tend to stay close to his study perforce saw more of the world. He made valuable contacts with the cultural elite of each German city, and was thrown in with a wide variety of human types in the haphazards of travel. Above all, these readings were a way to extend and maintain a loyal audience. Mann must have been a masterly reader, for throughout his career he could be assured of strong attendance and hearty applause.

Nevertheless, such tours took their toll on his delicate constitution, for in March he complained of stomach trouble and headaches, which might require another stay at the Bircher-Benner Institute. But, although its regimen had helped him two years ago, he could not quite face another term there. Katia, too, was ailing and could use a holiday. They decided, therefore, to take a trip together in the spring. Heinrich was also to come along. Whatever ill feeling the death of Carla had brought to the surface had by now been overcome on both their parts. They were making conscious efforts to strengthen family links. The plan was for the three of them to stay on the island of Brioni, off the coast of Dalmatia.

From the very start the trip was marked by dissatisfaction. Brioni, highly recommended by friends, proved to have been overpraised. The weather was rainy. The island, picturesque enough with its rugged cliffs, had no sandy beach to allow for that intimacy with the sea which Thomas Mann always found stirring. Nor were they delighted with conditions at their hotel—the best on the island, to be sure, where an Austrian archduchess was staying. Every time this lady entered or left the dining room, the rest of the guests had to rise and remain standing a moment. Katia, always the enemy of empty formalities, found this particularly irksome.[1]

Nevertheless, the Mann party stuck it out for ten days, then made an impulsive decision. They went to Pola and took a steamer for Venice, "the incomparable, the fabulous, the like-nothing-else-in-the-world." They knew the city well; they had previously always reached it from the north, by train. On their boat now was a bizarre figure: an old fellow dressed in oversmart clothing, his face touched up with rouge, his goatee and mustache with dye. He was surrounded by a band of young men in their twenties, apparently clerks on an excursion, who behaved boisterously throughout the voyage. At the steamer's landing pier in Venice, the Manns transferred to one of the waiting gondolas to be taken to the Lido. They had reserved rooms at the Hotel des Bains. They were delivered there safely enough, but when they disembarked and prepared to pay their gondolier, the man did not wait for his fare. One of the bystanders remarked that the man was unlicensed and unreliable; he had evidently been frightened off by the sight of some harbor police. Grateful that their luggage had been put ashore, the Manns had it trundled to their hotel.

The hotel attracted a well-to-do, cosmopolitan crowd. Among the American, English, German, French, and Russian guests were two Polish families, whose flock of children were supervised by a governess. At the very first meal in the dining room, Thomas's eye was caught by one of the children, a boy of about thirteen, dressed in a sailor suit and of unusual beauty.

It was now Heinrich's turn to be repelled by the atmosphere of a grand hotel. Moreover, the wind from the mainland was giving him headaches—both brothers were acutely sensitive to weather and had the habit of referring their inner ups and downs to atmospheric conditions. Heinrich kept urging that they go to the mountains. In an obliging spirit, the Mann party set off for a place in the Apennines. But this, too, proved a bad choice; they left in a hurry and turned back to Venice. In the course of the latest moves, one piece of luggage was indeed lost; it was Heinrich's suitcase and would have to be traced. They returned, with some gratification on Thomas's and Katia's part, to their previous hotel and prepared to stay a couple of weeks. As was his custom, Thomas hired one of the little cabins on the sands and spent most of the day there, reading, writing letters, and surveying the beach scene, "the sight of civilized society giving itself over to a simple life on the edge of the element,"[2] a spectacle that reminded him of childhood holidays and continued to give him keen pleasure to the end of his life. One evening the uneventful course of the holiday was broken when a street singer entertained the hotel guests with a little concert of current hit tunes, which he performed with lewd gestures and suggestive vocal effects. Rumors were going round that there was cholera in the city, but the Manns scarcely paid heed. The hotel, however, was conspicuously emptying out. When the Manns went to the offices of Cook's to see about return tickets, the English clerk advised them not to put off their reservation for a week, but to leave as soon as possible. There really was an epidemic brewing, but the authorities had hushed it up for fear of the effect on tourism. The Manns took the warning and left the next day. Their entire stay at the Hotel des Bains amounted to a week.

Many of these small incidents from a faraway vacation of the Manns have a familiar ring. For they are all incorporated, almost literally, in a story that has become a classic of twentieth-century literature. Mann, in his *Sketch of My Life*, fully acknowledged his debt to happenstance, which had put before him all the components, even in the right order, from which he could construct his *Death in Venice:*

> Nothing is invented in *Death in Venice*. The "pilgrim" at the North Cemetery, the dreary Pola boat, the gray-haired rake, the sinister gondolier, Tadzio and his family, the journey interrupted by a mistake about the luggage, the cholera, the upright clerk at the travel bureau, the rascally ballad singer, all that and anything else you like, they were all there. I had only to arrange them when they showed at once and in the oddest way their capacity as elements of composition. Perhaps it had to do with this: that as I worked on the story—as always it was a long-drawn-out job—I had at moments the clearest feelings of transcendence, a sovereign sense of being borne up such as I had never before experienced.[3]

Other elements he would need for his tale also came to hand with almost uncanny convenience. Earlier in that month of May, Gustav Mahler lay dying. The newspapers provided frequent bulletins on his condition and later published reverential obituaries. Thomas Mann, ill at ease in Brioni and ever an avid newspaper reader, followed the drama with particular interest. He knew Mahler personally—in that close-knit world of the arts, that went without saying—and had been forcibly impressed at his first meeting with the composer by Mahler's appearance and manner: Here was someone who had the genuine aura of a "great man." He would have met Mahler again at the Pringsheim house on Arcisstrasse, where Mahler was a prized guest whenever his affairs brought him to Munich. There had been such an occasion only recently, when Mahler had come to

Munich to conduct the premiere of his Eighth Symphony—a concert Mann had attended. So as the story began forming, Mann borrowed Mahler's physical features for his aging artist figure, and even christened him with the first name Gustave. In age, too, he modeled his hero on Mahler, who was fifty-one when he died; Aschenbach is in his fifties. Aschenbach's life, however, was drawn as lonelier and more austere than the composer's. In the mock biography, Aschenbach is allowed marriage and a child, but these are disposed of in a single paragraph. Aschenbach is almost entirely without human relationships. He lives exclusively for his art. The art, however, is not music but literature. And here Mann abruptly drops Mahler as model and turns to a writer he knows well—himself.

He lent to Aschenbach many of his intimate personal habits: the three morning hours devoted to writing, the essential midday nap, the indispensable teatime, the afternoon walk that would refresh him for his evening bout of letter writing, and even one of his favorite routes through the Englischer Garten. He also allotted to Aschenbach his special tenderness for prepubescent boys. It was a theme he had sounded before in works from *Buddenbrooks* to *Tonio Kröger* to "The Fight Between Jappe and Do Escobar," but it is here given a central and more portentous place.

In creating an elderly author plausible enough to appear in any encyclopedia, Mann gave him a Collected Works made up of a number of subjects he himself had been tempted by at one time or another. These castaway titles included a novel entitled *The Abject* and a biography of Frederick the Great.[4] He also drew up a literary profile of the kind he was master of—a blend of criticism, biography, and novelistic insight—such as he had already executed for Schiller and Fontane. He went to pains to point out the underlying theme of his imaginary author's body of work. His voice here, in its special eloquence, is very like the accents he would use in connection with himself, in all those explanations he would give his whole life long, to critics or especially intelligent readers, of the "true" theme, the hidden meaning and consistencies, binding together his seemingly disparate writings.

The boy by whom the aging Aschenbach is gradually enthralled is likewise not invented. His actuality was verified many years later, when the author was already ten years dead. While Erika Mann was editing the collected letters of her father in the early 1960s, she received a note from Poland from one Count Moes, who introduced himself as the real-life equivalent of Tadzio. The Polish translator of *Death in Venice*, asked to investigate the claim, sought out Count Wladyslaw Moes in his home in Warsaw. He met a man of sixty-eight who produced undeniable proof, in the form of photos and recollections, that he was indeed the ravishing boy of the story. He remembered vividly all the particulars of that holiday at the Hotel des Bains, even to his sisters' demure dresses, his own striped linen suit and beloved blue jacket with gilt buttons. His mother, too, had been described with great fidelity, and their governess of the time. The formality with which the children had filed into the dining room was also after life.

Even the last tussle between Tadzio and the brawnier Jaschiu had taken place, for Count Moes's playmate on that holiday had been another Polish boy, named Janek Fudowski, who was sixteen and played very rough. The two boys had even been conscious of "an old man" who was always watching them out on the beach. Wladyslav Moes had thought little of that at the time. He was a winsome boy and used to admiration. Women would stop him on the promenade and ask to kiss him, and he had often been painted and sketched. His family had left the resort in a hurry, because of the cholera scare.[5]

Thomas Mann was always to affirm emphatically his good luck, both human and literary. Fortune gave him what he needed and just when he needed it. Certainly this was so in the case of *Death in Venice*. Yet the story might have taken another form altogether. It was related to literary ideas the author had been nurturing for a considerable time—he had long been intrigued by the concept of an older man who has given himself singlemindedly to high achievements, only to be seized late in life by love of an inappropriate object who will prove his downfall. Later on, in 1920, by which time *Death in Venice* was firmly established in its place in literature, he provided an interesting gloss for it. Writing to Carl Maria Weber, poet, critic, and declared homosexual, Mann parries some of the implications of *Death in Venice* by offering what might be considered an alternate version:

> What I originally wanted to deal with was not anything homoerotic at all. It was the story—seen grotesquely—of the aged Goethe and

that little girl in Marienbad whom he was absolutely determined to marry, with the acquiescence of her social-climbing mother and despite the outraged horror of his own family, with the girl not wanting it at all—this story with all its terribly comic, shameful, awesomely ridiculous situations, this embarrassing, touching, and grandiose story which I may someday write after all. What was added to the amalgam at the time was a personal lyrical travel experience that determined me to carry things to an extreme by introducing the motif of "forbidden" love. . . .[6]

We may remember that the theme of love as a dangerous force undermining a life of too strict propriety had already been explored "within the family." Heinrich had taken up the very subject in his *Professor Unrat*, where an upright Gymnasium teacher falls in love with a woman of easy virtue, an entertainer in a low tavern. Under her spell he goes quickly downhill. Dismissed from his post, he opens a night spot together wih his mistress. This club, The Blue Angel, lures the respectable people in town, so that immorality spreads in ever widening circles. But the book had been published back in 1905, and except for enjoying some notoriety among Lübeck schoolboys, who passed it along in secret, it had had no success. Much had happened to both of the brothers since then, and many literary works had intervened. In all probability, Thomas Mann had forgotten the whole matter and saw no kinship between his illustrious writer and his brother's humble schoolmaster.

In any case, Thomas returned from Venice with the lineaments of one particular story in his mind. By July he was already at work, as he wrote to Philip Witkop, "on a quite curious thing I have brought back from Venice: a novella, serious and pure in tone, concerning a case of pederasty in an aging artist. You will say: Hum, hum. But it is very decent."[7]

IT IS WORTH noting that the German word Mann uses is *Knabenliebe*, whose overtones are somewhat different from our clinical *pederasty*. The disposition was neither rare nor unmentionable in Wilhelmine Germany. In fact, at this time it was enjoying a vogue in artistic-intellectual circles, under the banner of Stefan George. Notable first for bringing the new poetry from France to

Germany by his translations of the Symbolists, George had launched himself as a leader of a literary movement. He gathered a band of disciples. His magazine *Blätter für die Kunst*, with its *Jugendstil* typography and its message of art for art's sake, was soon a powerful force on the literary scene. In addition to the magazine, George had other means to make his influence felt. His poetry readings—carefully staged affairs, solemn in tone and open only to invited guests—had an impact out of proportion to the attendance. The sacerdotal atmosphere, the special reading style George had developed, were imitated by his followers. Those attracted to George were chiefly eccentric young men, fanatics of various sorts, visionaries, worshipers either of classical antiquity or of the pagan Germanic past, united in their contempt for the mediocre present. Women were excluded; they had nothing to offer the new order, though the wives of a few older married members were tolerated at the circle's readings. Most of the circle's ideas were drawn from Nietzsche: the polarity between Apollonian and Dionysiac elements, the scorn for faith in progress, the call for a return to myth, the theme of civilization's downfall, the need for a new morality and for exceptional people who could usher in the new order, the heralding of the Superman. George's personality held the diverse members together. The locus of the circle was indefinite, since George had followers throughout Germany. He liked to travel and stay with favored friends while keeping his real habitation a mystery. Nevertheless, his chief outpost was Munich, where the most prominent of his followers lived.

Literary Munich would have known of George's liaison with a boy of that city, one Max Kronberger, whom the poet had celebrated under the name of Maximin. The story was a curious one. The boy had been fourteen when the poet had approached him out on the street and by degrees won his trust. According to outside testimony, the boy had been in no way remarkable, either for looks or for gifts: Physically a slim, dark-haired Mediterranean type, he came from a decent middle-class background, was direct, natural, intelligent, unassuming. But love, and particularly love at first sight, has little to do with such outward qualities. George liked to compare the boy to the Beatrice who had inspired Dante. The poet's behavior toward the object of his love was scrupulously correct: He introduced himself to the boy's family, attended the boy's confirmation, encouraged him to be diligent in his schoolwork. Over the next two years he supervised the boy's development, went for walks with him, discussed literature, and criticized the boy's first verses, which he reciprocated with some poems of his own. He introduced the boy to the circle and gradually unfolded to his young mind some of their artistic and philosophic doctrines. The boy was included in the circle's masquerades at Fasching. Cast as a Roman youth, wearing a tunic and a wreath of laurel or violets, the boy acted as attendant on George, who would appear at these revels as Dante, in flowing robe and headcloth.

This blameless relationship, which conformed closely to Plato's prescription for ideal love, continued for two years. Shortly after the second of these Fasching celebrations, the boy took sick and died suddenly of meningitis. George's grief was intense. It found expression in a series of poems dedicated to the dead boy, the Maximin poems. The boy was transformed into a cult figure, intercessor and savior, half Hermes, half Christ, by whom the poet and the age itself would be redeemed. The myth of Maximin, a glorious boy in the sweetest moment of youth, the personification of beauty, and the possessor of simple and superhuman wisdom, became the keystone of the Georgian creed.[8]

There were other components—a strong streak of anti-Semitism, for instance, though some of the prime members of the circle were Jewish. There was an emphasis on sacrifice and dedication, on leadership and subordination. Nor did the passage of time mellow the Georgian outlook. On the contrary. It grew fiercer and more uncompromising and widened its scope to rule not only over poetry but over questions of culture and the social order.

George's aggressive and autocratic temperament was the farthest possible from Mann's own. Even as a young man living in Schwabing, Mann had never been comfortable with the mood of the George people. He had painted a definitive picture of the Georgian milieu in that earlier story "At the Prophet's" (1904), which, incidentally, can now be read as an example of Mann's own brand of second sight, for in it he showed himself fully aware of the frightening potentialities of the movement. After his marriage Mann had moved even farther away from the rarefied idealism George represented. Within the Mann family certain lines of George's poetry became family jokes; certain words served in the family vocabulary to denote silly, false spirituality.[9] Serious as Mann was about art, he had a keen sense of the fallibility of the artist's nature. He deeply distrusted prophetic poses.[10] Moreover, as a writer who made his living by his pen, he was inclined to a "low opinion of artists who were interested only in speaking to a coterie."[11] Nevertheless, he took a careful tone publicly toward George and what George stood for, including the homoerotic aspect of the cult.

In fact there existed a link between the two writers in the form of Ernst Bertram, the new friend who had come into Mann's life early in 1910. Ernst Bertram's own life-partner was a young man named Ernst Glöckner, who was an orthodox Georgian in every respect. He served as official calligrapher to the group, transcribing their poems in Old Gothic script in accord with the master's preference for the handwritten over the printed. Bertram himself was not so strongly marked with the Georgian stigmata. In 1910 he was an *Assistent* at the University of Bonn (what we would call a teaching fellow) and was engaged in writing his book on Nietzsche, which would take him ten years and finally in 1922 procure him his appointment at the University of Cologne. In addition, he wrote stories and poems in the manner of Stefan George. He moved back and forth between his mother's house in Bonn and the more stimulating city of Munich, where he lived ascetically in quarters on Ohmstrasse—he had no means of livelihood beyond a small family allowance and occasional literary earnings.[12]

A gentle, weak young man of twenty-seven, widely read and deeply musical, he first impressed Mann by the piercing insights he had shown into the meanings of *Royal Highness*. Correspondence led to a meeting. The friendship ripened quickly. Thomas found the younger man highly congenial. Did Thomas Mann, thirty-five, possessor of a literary reputation, husband and father, proprietor of a town dwelling and a country house, say: "There but for the grace of my talent go I?" Did their intense discussions ever touch on the subject of *Knabenliebe?* It is most unlikely. For the first eight years of the friendship, Thomas Mann continued to address his letters "Lieber Herr Doktor." The content of the letters remained on the highest intellectual plane. Nor would Thomas Mann have willingly given up the dominance he had through age and status by admitting to what he felt to be a defect in his nature.

Never in his whole life was he to admit openly to that defect, except in the deep privacy of his diaries. Yet he nursed this secret as a source of pleasure, of interest, of creative power. Perhaps he exaggerated the strength of the inclination in himself, as he exaggerated all the little ailments, the headaches and incipient colds, he recorded in his diary. Be that as it may, an understanding of the homoerotic urge formed a secret bond between him and the respectful, highly intelligent, and equally reticent Bertram. The secret did not have to be articulated for it to ease and warm their relationship. A visit or a letter from Bertram brightened the day for the older man. In years to come, they played Beethoven sonatas together, went for walks, attended concerts, discussed culture, politics, and above all Nietzsche, whose ideas held unending interest for them both. During the war years, Mann was to thresh out the problems of the *Betrachtungen eines Unpolitischen* in long dialogues with Bertram, who used this opportunity to guide Mann's thoughts along his own fervently pro-German path. How much overt or underground influence Bertram had on Mann's thinking is hard to estimate. But there is an entry in the diary of 1919 implying that the influence was considerable and that it had emotional roots. The *Betrachtungen* had just come out and was having a great success with conservative elements in Germany. Mann basked in that success, which compensated somewhat for the struggle he had had with the writing of that book. He thought of himself for the nonce as a righteous rightist. And as events developed in the wake of Germany's defeat, he insisted: "I do not regret a single word of the *Betrachtungen*." Yet in the diary he wrote, "For myself, there is no doubt in my mind that even the *Betrachtungen* is an expression of my sexual inversion." A startling admission, and one we might expect him to enlarge on. But he said no more on the subject.

After those war years of intellectual intimacy, Mann began addressing his letters *"Lieber Bertram."* He also tried to draw the younger man into his own emotional sphere, which was, after all, deeply familial. When Bertram was in Munich, he saw Mann frequently, dropping in without ceremony and often being asked to stay to family meals like a relative. To make him even more so and to seal his connection with the family, Mann was to ask Ernst Bertram to be godfather to the newest Mann baby, the little Elisabeth, born in the dark war year of 1918. Bertram was also to cast his influence on Mann in still another way, for he had a considerable part in the writing of the "Gesang vom Kindchen," "a family idyll," as Mann described it, written to celebrate Elisabeth's birth. The "Gesang" was a poem, Mann's one and only attempt in that genre since his early verses. It was a rash experiment, and Mann needed Bertram's constant encouragement with its hexameters. They went over these together line by line.

B U T all this was still to come. There are hexameters woven into the rich texture of *Death in Venice*, but for the most part it is honest prose. Nor was the war yet in anyone's mind in that summer of 1911. The Manns were installed in their country house in Bad Tölz with their four merry, original little ones. Katia was delighted to be back with the children. As always after a spell of idleness, Thomas was eager to get to writing. The plot of a story and its most telling details had been handed to him on the proverbial silver platter in golden Venice. It was a light "improvisation" which might do for *Simplicissimus*. He began to make his customary notes, blocking out the essentials of the story. He included two newspaper clippings: one a photo of Mahler and the other an account of a cholera epidemic in Palermo.

Since his disciplined work habits allowed him to combine writing with a good deal of everyday stir, it was no interruption when Samuel Fischer came on a visit in July. The publisher would be seeing for the first time the house built on the proceeds of *Buddenbrooks* and *Royal Highness*.

The visit was cordial, as always. Moments of it were captured by Frau Hedwig Fischer, who had recently taken up photography.[13] The photos show author and publisher conversing over a well-set tea table. Mann is slim, youthful, with a dark mustache and almost unseamed brow. He bears not the slightest resemblance to the deteriorating character his mind is dwelling on. Fischer's wise and patient bald-domed face looks unusually benign. He surely approved of the conditions and the spirit in which Thomas Mann was living. A talented author with few family problems and a keen sense of the need for productivity made the heart of any publisher glad.

But there were problems, for the health of Katia, which had borne up well during their recent vacation trip, was once again causing anxiety. She ran high temperatures of unknown cause. The use of X-rays was still a fairly arcane matter; they were not yet available to the family doctor as a diagnostic tool. The standard remedy was mountain air. So early in September Katia left with her parents for a two-and-a-half-week trip to Sils Maria in the Swiss Engadine. Thomas remained alone with the children, their nanny, and a housekeeper. Once Katia returned, "relatively recovered but still needing to be careful," Heinrich came for a visit.

He brought with him his play *Schauspielerin*, based on the recent tragedy of their sister Carla. He read the play to Thomas, who not only saw no fault in using such intimate material for literary purposes, but even exerted himself on the play's behalf. Heinrich was encountering difficulties in having the play produced. Hence Thomas wrote to his friend Arthur Schnitzler in Vienna, who had excellent connections. Thomas urged the merits of the play and even suggested the actress who might find the part of Leonie (Carla) to her liking. The letter had its effect. By November of the same year the play was given its premiere in Berlin, with the actress suggested by Mann in the star role, and subsequently went on tour through German cities, including Munich. There both the playwright and his brother attended the premiere and applauded vigorously, to the scandalization of those in the audience who recognized the play's background. But both brothers were on principle immune to such philistine prejudices. As far as they were concerned, the personal was given its highest value when it was converted to literature. Carla herself would have shared this view, Thomas thought. As he later wrote to Heinrich, "she who is at peace" would have found the play beautiful and have pronounced it good. The only question was whether their mother, living in seclusion in the Bavarian village of Polling, knew of it. Was it safe to speak of the play to her, who had been, of all the family, the one most cruelly stabbed by Carla's desperate act?[14]

Thomas had a highly "personal" little thing of his own in the works. During the same visit, Thomas read the beginning of the story to Heinrich, who, after all, had been present when much of it happened. But Thomas had not come far with the tale. As so often with ideas of his, it was showing a will of its own and revealing dimensions he had not suspected. He was already referring to it as an "impossible conception." But his creative strategy had always been to "hold fast" and count on winning through by patient application.

On the grounds of hard work he excused himself from a gathering in Berlin to celebrate the twenty-fifth year of the Fischer publishing house, with whose success his own was so related. Nevertheless, he gave some readings; he went to Brussels in November and in January to Heidelberg and Bremen.

On wintry railway journeys, in hotels of uneven quality, he brooded on the problems and possibilities of his current work. In the course of that year, he read Goethe's *Elective Affinities* five times over—or so he claimed afterward, when he liked to represent the story as a disguised treatment of the Goethe episode. More to the point, he looked into Plato's dialogues, especially the *Symposium* and *Phaedrus*, and the *Republic*.

Of course, this was not his first exposure to them. Literate people were presumed to have a good acquaintance with the classics. Their education began early, usually with an illustrated book on mythology given them as children. Mann vividly remembered his mother's volume with the picture of Pallas Athena on the cover and the games it had inspired.[15] To be sure, by the time he was in Gymnasium this enthusiasm for classical studies had faded, or at least it had not been equal to the rigors of Greek and Latin grammar.

But now that Attic world of gods and heroes came vividly back to him. In his rough notes for the story he at once set down such names as Eos, Ganymede, Hyacinthus, and Eros, and such phrases as "a divine face that mirrors the greater Beauty."[16] The Polish boy in the Edwardian sailor suit was only another embodiment of all those youths the Olympian gods had, in the mild words of those bowdlerized mythologies for children, "conceived a fondness for." Beautiful mortals "kindled love in the hearts" of the gods. They were "stabbed by the darts of Eros"—pictured as a nude young winged male. But what was this Eros? What was this power of love which for the Greeks represented cosmology itself, and later swayed both gods and mortals? A mysterious power—to what might it be likened? In the beginning was the Word—could Eros, then, be the same as that Word? In his first notes Mann dashed down this perhaps dubious analogy: "Eros is the Word." And Aschenbach was a man of the Word, as he himself was. He saw, or was beginning to see, what sort of lofty themes he would have to deal with.

But good disciple of Naturalism that he also was, he gathered notes on Venice and found out what he could of its sanitary arrangements. He also read up on cholera, both from the historical and medical angles.

The story, then, in its finished form is a consummately skillful fusion of myth and reality. Its plot is slight: hard to believe that so slender a framework can support such weighty content. Every scene, even the smallest, is drawn with surpassing artistry. It can be read and reread, analyzed endlessly, without uncovering its secret deep enchantment. The critic Erich Heller has summed it up well, for even his one-paragraph précis suggests some of the tale's complexities:

> The story is as well-known as it is simple: the writer Gustave von Aschenbach . . . tired by years of uninterrupted work, decides to travel. His journey . . . leads him to Venice. Guests at the same Lido hotel are a Polish family. The youngest child, a boy of about fourteen called Tadzio, strikes Aschenbach as possessing perfect beauty. His admiration gradually grows into passion. As he keeps the secret of his love, so Venice seeks to guard its own: a spreading epidemic of Asiatic cholera. Yet Aschenbach discovers it. Instead of warning the Polish family and departing himself, he yields to the hypnosis of his passion. Staying on, he joins with his own the sinister secret of Venice. With his moral will broken and his soul deranged, he dies on the beach in the sight of Tadzio, who stands Hermes-like on the fringe of the sea, silhouetted against the blue horizon.[17]

ASCHENBACH dies of the more merciful form of the disease. The medical description is not the least powerful passage in this story. Mann always excelled at such medical scenes. Sickness, its stealthy onset and its muted threat, fascinated him. Now it came near him personally. Katia was once more having fevers; this time the doctors no longer made light of the symptoms. They spoke of a pulmonary catarrh, which was the then current euphemism for early-stage tuberculosis. A mere mountain vacation would no longer fit the bill. Katia was sent to a sanatorium not far from Munich, favorable for family visits. When her condition did not improve, she went on, in the middle of March, to Davos. Her mother saw her safely there. The railroad line went no farther than Chur, so the twenty-nine-year-old dark-haired little invalid was transferred to a sleigh and wrapped in furs and robes for the journey into the snowy heights.[18]

High in the Alps, the village of Davos was noted for its pure and bracing air. It had been a health center since the 1870s, and was by now studded with sanatoria housing what was practically an industry—the care of the tubercular. The lung-sick were known to benefit from high altitudes, cold air, rest, ample meals. There was not much else that could be done for them, though the disease was carefully monitored and there was a vogue for arsenic injections. Against the advice of their family doctor, Katia submitted to a series of these, in the hope of speeding up recovery and getting back to her children. The injections did no good and had severe side effects on her nervous system.[19]

Halfway through her stay at the Waldsanatorium operated by Dr. Friedrich Jessen, her husband came for a three-week visit. This was in May. He had been writing daily to his absent wife, keeping her informed of everything at home, while she in her turn described the singular world she was inhabiting. Keen-witted as Katia was, with an eye for human foibles and the self-confidence of a well-loved wife, she must have written some sprightly letters. So Thomas Mann had a good introduction to the customs and the cast of characters he would encounter when he came to Davos in May.

He had to report ruefully to Katia that the novella was still not finished. The precise ending eluded him. But now he had already done enough to be sure it was something important. The impossible conception had its name now. He had already discussed its publication in a luxury edition—hand set and limited to a hundred copies—with Hans von Weber, whose Hyperion Press specialized in such collectors' items. Of course, he would still have to clear the matter with Samuel Fischer, who normally did not care for such private arrangements on the part of his authors. But the novella was still an unknown quality, and a hundred copies, for subscribers only and not even reviewed in the press, could not interfere with the trade edition. Fischer gave his consent.

That change of air Thomas Mann would seek whenever his writing needed new momentum once more proved beneficial. For in June, back in Tölz with the children, and with his own mother presiding over the household, he brought the difficult task to its conclusion. That summer's visitors were entertained by evening readings in their host's little study. Their sympathy and enthusiasm, he later noted in that impersonal tone which was one of his many voices, might have prepared him for the almost stormy reception the story was to have at its publication.[20]

Afterword

by

CLARA WINSTON

IT WAS in 1970 that Richard Winston formally began a full-length biography of Thomas Mann. We had only recently completed our translation of the selected *Letters* of Mann. To this Dick thought to add an introduction supplying background that might not be familiar to present-day readers. For Thomas Mann (1875–1955) already belonged to another age—several other ages, one might say, given the sharp discontinuities of those eighty years of German history. In addition, the letters, always elegant, discursive on the highest level, and shunning the prosaic out of courtesy to Mann's correspondents, were not entirely self-explanatory. It would be helpful, Dick thought, to supplement them with some direct biographical data.

In compiling the data and writing the introduction, Dick made a startling discovery. And it was not he alone who was surprised; others who had been closely associated with the career of Thomas Mann were equally so. The short biography brought into view a Thomas Mann who only slightly resembled the figure they knew, the Thomas Mann to whom they had always paid honor, but who had always held himself at a distance. To be sure, the newly discovered Thomas Mann was still the great novelist, devoted to his calling, vastly productive. But there was so much more to him that fame had screened.

For the way had not been easy, the triumphs not as self-evident as they had appeared. The sources of the works, and the works themselves, were more curious than had been noted: The paradoxes were sharper, the psyche more endangered, the stage more peopled, the emotional involvements more critical. Thomas Mann created two artist figures whose names are by now classic. These two—Gustave Aschenbach of *Death in Venice* and Adrian Leverkühn of *Doctor Faustus*—had as their outstanding traits an aloofness from the human condition, an austere dedication to their art, and a lack of simple "feeling," that, Mann seemed to imply, marked the true character of the artist. Readers, critics, and scholars of Thomas Mann had taken these figures for self-portraits, and there was enough in Mann's public demeanor to support this interpretation. "I am inwardly tired and skeptical, outwardly as disciplined and affable as possible," he described himself in a letter of his last year.

But as the biographical sketch revealed, Thomas Mann was no Aschenbach or Leverkühn. He had not starved his life to feed his art. In fact, he was bewilderingly caught up in life, for where, one could now ask, had there been the time or the detachment for that row of great works? He had fought with great energy on literary and political battlefields. Several times over he had seen the stable world around him crashing to pieces. He had had more than his share of acquaintances, alliances, loves, hates, tragedies. In fact, Mann's personal history had all the elements of a great novel. Dick expected to spend many years piecing the story together and telling it.

An ambitious project, but Dick thought he had a head start. We had, after all, been entrusted with the English version of Mann's letters. We had also translated three of Mann's *Last Essays*, as well as that flight into autobiography, *The Story of a Novel: The Genesis of Dr. Faustus*. We had rendered into English an exchange of letters with Paul Amann, an uncelebrated intellectual serving in the Austrian army with whom Mann kept up a correspondence both during the First World War and later. (These letters of Mann's were marked by a rare comradely tone—perhaps out of guilt at his own civilian status.) And we had translated the correspondence with Erich Kahler, published as *An Exceptional Friendship*. In the course of these assignments we had read thousands of letters and become familiar with all the shades of Thomas Mann's personal voice and alert to the changes the years had brought to the letter writer. And Dick had done considerable research toward a biography when, in the mid-1960s, he had lectured throughout Germany on "Thomas Mann in America" under the auspices of the U.S. Information Service.

But over and beyond all of this, Dick could draw on a preoccupation with Thomas Mann that went back to his own youth. Dick had reached adulthood in the late thirties; he was seventeen when Mann made his first visit to the States, twenty-one when Mann moved here to stay. From the very first the distinguished novelist was treated as a celebrity of the first rank, his doings and pronouncements regularly reported by the press, his standing in literary circles unequaled. His books were widely read, were in fact best sellers. At his public appearances he spoke to packed houses. Mann was at that period (how unlikely it seems now!) a kind of guru, and his German accent and Germanic stiffness only added to the force of his emanations. To a young man with literary leanings and a passion for the German language, the figure of Thomas Mann loomed very large. Dick had already devoured all his fictional works from *Buddenbrooks* on, and he hurried to get hold of each new book as it appeared with that sense of partisanship and possessiveness specific to the young. For to the young, discovering a favorite author is more than defining one's literary taste; it belongs rather to the order of religious experience. Thomas Mann opened the world to Dick, guided his thoughts, set his standards—as he did for innumerable others. Like many others, Dick could have testified: You have formed my mind.

What is more, Dick's devotion was not a passing phase. It continued into the 1950s, by which time the name of the novelist, at least among the knowing, was more apt to arouse impatience than adulation. Reviews, particularly in the more advanced journals, were beginning to strike a sour note. Continual praise becomes monotonous; clever people have better ways of displaying their keenness. But Dick had a loyal nature and was not particularly concerned with self-display of that sort. Now and then he would re-

read a Mann work and be astounded at the artistry and meaning that
had escaped him earlier. He found new favorites: *A Man and His
Dog, Disorder and Early Sorrow*—which corresponded, in their acute
and loving picture of family life, with his own current experience.
And as soon as our own children were at all ready for grown-up
reading, he urged Mann upon them. Two more disciples were added
to the fold.

Whenever we were in Europe we tended to fetch up in Mann territory. Place is a strong element in Mann's work, and we searched
for him in places. Venice conformed remarkably to description.
Davos had changed, and we had to find other equivalents, less fashionable Alpine villages. In Munich, street names recalled the addresses of a young man who went about on a bicycle and diffidently
submitted short stories to the magazines of the day. The rough path
along the Isar where the dog Bashan had romped was now a paved
promenade called Thomas Mann Allee. We walked long in wind
and rain in Lübeck. In Palestrina, donkeys clattered up the Roman
marble staircase that forms that remarkable town's chief artery,
just as they might have done in the late 1890s, when the two Mann
brothers, Heinrich and Thomas, holed up there for a spell of writing.
The Barbarini palace which crowns the height is now a museum,
and in it we came upon what was doubly a treasure: a vast mosaic
(Roman, first century A.D.) of the land of the Nile, extraordinary in
itself for vividness and delicacy of detail. But as Dick construed it,
this panorama of Egypt must also have been the germ for the Mann
masterpiece *Joseph and His Brothers*, begun thirty years after that
sojourn in Palestrina.

Zürich was thick with Mannian associations. The Mann Archives
are located in a seventeenth-century house overlooking the Old
Town. The spot, with its garden, can easily be transposed to a more
rural setting, for the gigantic old tree almost blocking the front path
evokes the courtyard of the Schweigestills. Inside the thick-walled
building, the modest home of an eighteenth-century Swiss poet, are
located not only literary materials on the twentieth-century writer
but such memorabilia as his desk and reading chair. In fact the entire study is installed there, complete to the bibelots on the writing
desk. A few scholars are usually settled in the sunny reading room.
The mood is highly professional, though one day a week is set aside

for school visits, when parties of Swiss children are led through to be taught respect for "our" Thomas Mann.

A far less official atmosphere reigned at 39 Altelandstrasse, Kilchberg. From the outside the house had a chill, disused look, for it was indeed Thomas Mann's "last address," as its illustrious owner had predicted. Frau Katia in her early eighties was tiny, wore a floor-length dress of dark-blue heavy ribbed wool, served tea. The electric kettle came from the States, of which she had, in general, good memories. Age had pared her face back to its childhood lines: A very bright child with a talent for mockery took measure of the visitors. How many journalists and professors she had served tea to over the years. Translators—her husband had been close friends with several. We knew. We knew a great deal. A false position, we felt—but once launched on this ceremonial visit, we had to go through with it. She proved skillful in parrying questions about her husband—seemed even displeased with the topic. In her deep voice she grumbled over some point in someone's recent monograph. What nonsense. It should not be allowed. She preferred to speak of her grandchildren, of the difficulties of finding a way to a vocation nowadays. Of course her husband had not had that worry—he had wanted to be a writer and he had become one.

It was strange to be chatting with someone whose past one knew so intimately, whose childhood pictures had made one catch one's breath—what a lovely girl. One knew the nicknames of her children, the kind of games they had played, and what had become of each. Somewhere upstairs in that still house lay Erika, "who was looking forward to seeing you but unfortunately does not feel well today." Also, with a mischievous glance, "The hairdresser failed to come when she was supposed to. You know how ladies are about their hair." Her own was white, and bobbed in the fashion of the twenties.

The next time we came the ritual and even some of the remarks were the same. She hobbled, explaining that she had recently fallen off a ladder. She was rather proud of the accident, which testified to her basic sprightliness. She volunteered the story of her first encounter with Thomas Mann: She was returning to school on the streetcar and had talked back to the conductor, who had called her a fury, in Bavarian dialect moreover. Thomas Mann had chanced to be on the tram and had overheard the exchange; the incident had made a favorable impression on him. Later on we recognized this as a stylized anecdote offered to many—Frau Katia related it with much the same zest in the film made of her for German television. It had probably been a family joke. But when we were leaving, her face creased with tears as she went over the clinical details of Erika's recent death. And she herself had reached this great age, which she had never wanted, and was outliving even her children. It was nonsense, and should not be allowed.

So the personal encounter can yield something, but perhaps not enough to justify its basic offense against tact. That was how Dick felt about it. He trusted more in traditional methods of research. He read, learned to see meanings between the lines, or meanings, clear enough in context, that had become blurred with time. He found secrets in unexpected places—the occasional pieces, for instance, that Mann, his whole life a hardworking man of letters, produced in great numbers (they fill five volumes of the *Collected Works*). Then the long-sealed diaries were opened and became available—a whole new stratum of revelation. The richest? Well, yes and no. They did not cover the early years, but they would help immensely with later periods.

All in all, the biography was going to take longer than had been counted on. There was no point hurrying it, Dick thought, so long as he was content with the way it was going. How often it had happened with Thomas Mann that a slight idea had grown to vast proportions and had taken many years. Dick would jokingly tell friends that he expected to spend the rest of his life on the biography. He was cheerful, sustaining his faith in the project even when not directly at work on it. For often time had to be set aside for the translation that was our livelihood. Thomas Mann had also done his writing amidst much other business.

Dick was troubled, though, in his last year, by how slowly reading went. It was age, he supposed; he was now two years over the line of sixty, though such chronology seemed scarcely to matter. There was no lapse in his vitality or his confidence that he could do what he meant to. In a rainy spell in mid-August he caught some kind of cold, began to cough. It seemed only a summer flu, but it hung on and there was a good deal of pain. By the end of September it was diagnosed as cancer of the lungs. So common a phrase, so hard to comprehend. Chemotherapy was begun; and though the doctors warned that it could only be palliative, they suggested that if it worked at all, it might give him six to nine months.

The treatment seemed to work well. Dick reasoned that with his sound constitution and his will, he could extend the period long enough to finish the book, which now of course would have to be far more summary. But perhaps it would be more vivid that way. He was even glad of having such a good reason to let other responsibilities go, to practice a singlemindedness that had normally seemed too great a luxury.

He lay upstairs in his sunny room and went on with the reading of *The Magic Mountain*, which he was now attacking "with a pencil," as Thomas Mann would have said. I would find him smiling with pleasure. He even sat at his desk and continued smoothly, with seeming imperturbability, from the previous section. He outlined to me where he was going. In his writing he had reached the point of *Death in Venice*, which was the place to deal with a delicate, perhaps crucial, biographical question. Of course it was, like much else in Thomas Mann's life, ambiguous. But Dick thought he could put the matter in perspective, for he had evidence from all the periods in Mann's life that had to be balanced. But he was never to muster these arguments. The medical promises, which had also been ambiguous, were suddenly withdrawn, and we were left with our own special cause for tears—"Those clear drops flowing in such bitter abundance every hour of the day all over our world."

Duino Farm
September 19, 1980

Notes
Index

Notes

All quotations of the German version of works by Thomas Mann are taken from the thirteen-volume edition of Mann's collected works, the *Gesammelte Werke* (Frankfurt/M.: S. Fischer, 1974). Translations are the author's except where otherwise indicated.

Dates in parenthesis following works by Thomas Mann indicate the original date of publication, or, in some cases, composition of a given work.

Chapter 1: FOREBEARS AND CHILDHOOD

1. Thomas Mann, "Lübeck as a Way of Life and Thought" (1926), trans. Richard Winston and Clara Winston, in *Buddenbrooks* (1901), trans. H. T. Lowe-Porter (New York: Alfred A. Knopf, 1964), p. xx.

2. Thomas Mann, *Doctor Faustus* (1947), trans. H. T. Lowe-Porter (New York: Alfred A. Knopf, 1948), pp. 57–8.

3. Thomas Mann, *A Sketch of My Life* (1930), trans. H. T. Lowe-Porter (New York: Alfred A. Knopf, 1960), p. 54.

4. Thomas Mann, "Lübeck," p. xv.

5. Ulrich Dietzel, ed., "Dokumente zur Geschichte der Familie Mann," *Sinn und Form: Sonderheft Thomas Mann* (Berlin: Aufbau, 1965), pp. 10 ff.

6. Ibid., p. 50.

7. Viktor Mann, *Wir waren Fünf* (Konstanz: Südverlag, 1949), p. 9.

8. Thomas Mann, *The Magic Mountain* (1924), trans. H. T. Lowe-Porter (New York: Alfred A. Knopf, 1944), p. 22. Translation amended.

9. Viktor Mann, *Wir waren Fünf*, p. 15.

10. *Letters of Thomas Mann, 1889–1955*, sel. and trans. Richard Winston and Clara Winston (New York: Alfred A. Knopf, 1971), p. 3.

11. Thomas Mann, "Lübeck," p. xiv.

12. Thomas Mann, *A Sketch of My Life*, p. 3.

13. Julia Mann, *Aus Dodos Kindheit: Erinnerungen* (1903) (Konstanz: Rosgarten, 1958), p. 65.

14. Ibid., pp. 71–2.

15. Ibid., p. 76.

16. Thomas Mann, "Lebenslauf 1936," in *Gesammelte Werke*, vol. 11 (Frankfurt/M.: S. Fischer, 1974), p. 450.

17. Thomas Mann, *A Sketch of My Life*, p. 4.

18. Thomas Mann, *Letters*, p. 680.

19. Ibid., p. 88.

20. Ibid., p. 594.

21. Thomas Mann, "Kinderspiele" (1904), in *Gesammelte Werke*, vol. 11, p. 327.

22. Ibid., p. 328.

23. Thomas Mann, "The Dilettante" (1897), in *Stories of Three Decades*, trans. H. T. Lowe-Porter (New York: Alfred A. Knopf, 1936), pp. 30–1. Translation amended.

24. Thomas Mann, "Kinderspiele," p. 328.

25. Klaus Mann, *Der Wendepunkt* (1942) (Munich: Nymphenburg, 1969), p. 31.

26. Thomas Mann, "Kinderspiele," p. 329.

27. Thomas Mann, "Lebenslauf 1936," p. 451.

28. Ibid., p. 452.

29. Thomas Mann, "Lübeck," p. xiv.

30. Thomas Mann, *Buddenbrooks*, pp. 507–8.

31. Ibid., p. 510. Translation amended.

32. Thomas Mann, "Süsser Schlaf" (1909), in *Gesammelte Werke*, vol. 11, p. 334.

33. Thomas Mann, *Buddenbrooks*, p. 511.

Notes

Chapter 2: SCHOOL

1. Thomas Mann, "Zur jüdischen Frage" (1921), in *Gesammelte Werke*, vol. 13 (Frankfurt/M.: S. Fischer, 1974), p. 467.

2. Ibid., p. 468.

3. Thomas Mann, *Tonio Kröger* (1903), in *Stories of Three Decades*, trans. H. T. Lowe-Porter (New York: Alfred A. Knopf, 1936), p. 88. Translation amended.

4. Thomas Mann, "Zur jüdischen Frage," p. 469.

5. *Letters of Thomas Mann, 1889–1955*, sel. and trans. Richard Winston and Clara Winston (New York: Alfred A. Knopf, 1971), p. 31.

6. Thomas Mann, "Die Lösung der Judenfrage" (1907), in *Gesammelte Werke*, vol. 13, p. 459.

7. Klaus Schröter, ed., *Thomas Mann im Urteil seiner Zeit: Dokumente, 1891–1955* (Hamburg: Christian Wegner, 1969), p. 95.

8. Thomas Mann, "Zur jüdischen Frage," p. 472.

9. Ibid., pp. 471–2.

10. Ibid., p. 475.

11. Thomas Mann, *A Sketch of My Life* (1930), trans. H. T. Lowe-Porter (New York: Alfred A. Knopf, 1960), p. 4.

12. Thomas Mann, *Buddenbrooks* (1901), trans H. T. Lowe-Porter (New York: Alfred A. Knopf, 1964), p. 420. Translation amended.

13. Thomas Mann, *Briefe, 1948–1955*, ed. Erika Mann (Frankfurt/M.: S. Fischer, 1965), p. 387.

14. Thomas Mann, *A Sketch of My Life*, p. 6.

15. Thomas Mann, *Tonio Kröger*, p. 89.

16. Thomas Mann, *A Sketch of My Life*, p. 7.

17. Thomas Mann, "Bilse und ich" (1906), in *Gesammelte Werke*, vol. 10, p. 17.

18. Ludwig Ewers, "Die Gebrüder Mann," *Bonner Zeitung*, no. 348 (18 December 1909).

19. Sigrid Anger et al., eds., *Heinrich Mann: Werk und Leben in Dokumenten und Bildern, 1871–1950* (Berlin: Aufbau, 1971), p. 12.

20. Thomas Mann, *Letters*, p. 88.

21. Katia Mann, quoted in the introduction to Hans Wysling, ed., *Thomas Mann— Heinrich Mann: Briefwechsel, 1900–1949* (Frankfurt/M.: S. Fischer, 1968), p. xviii.

22. Thomas Mann, "Vom Beruf des deutschen Schriftstellers in unserer Zeit: Ansprache an den Bruder" (1931), in *Gesammelte Werke*, vol. 10, p. 306.

23. Thomas Mann, "Süsser Schlaf" (1909), in *Gesammelte Werke*, vol. 11, p. 336.

24. Anger, *Heinrich Mann*, p. 44.

25. Ibid., p. 46.

26. Ulrich Dietzel, ed., "Dokumente zur Geschichte der Familie Mann," *Sinn und Form: Sonderheft Thomas Mann* (Berlin: Aufbau, 1965), p. 54.

27. Hans Bürgin and Hans-Otto Mayer, *Thomas Mann: Eine Chronik seines Lebens* (Frankfurt/M.: S. Fischer, 1965), p. 11.

28. Thomas Mann, "Fragment über das Religiöse" (1930), in *Gesammelte Werke*, vol. 11, p. 423.

29. *Eisenbahnzeitung*, no. 242 (15 October 1891).

30. "Senator Thomas Johann Heinrich Mann," *Lübeckische Blätter*, vol. 33, no. 82 (14 October 1891), 489–90.

31. Heinrich Mann, *Ein Zeitalter wird besichtigt* (1945) (Berlin: Aufbau, 1973), p. 234.

32. Thomas Mann, *A Sketch of My Life*, p. 8.

Chapter 3: ADOLESCENCE

1. Ludwig Ewers, "Die Gebrüder Mann," *Bonner Zeitung*, no. 348 (18 December 1909).

2. Thomas Mann, "Erinnerungen ans Lübecker Stadttheater" (1930), in *Gesammelte Werke*, vol. 11 (Frankfurt/M.: S. Fischer, 1974), p. 418.

3. Ibid.

4. *Letters of Thomas Mann, 1889–1955*, sel. and trans. Richard Winston and Clara Winston (New York: Alfred A. Knopf, 1971), p. 24.

5. Thomas Mann, *Leiden und Grösse Richard Wagners* (1933), in *Gesammelte Werke*, vol. 9, p. 370.

6. Thomas Mann, *A Sketch of My Life* (1930), trans. H. T. Lowe-Porter (New York: Alfred A. Knopf, 1960), p. 25.

7. Thomas Mann, *Sufferings and Greatness of Richard Wagner* (1933), in *Essays of Three Decades*, trans. H. T. Lowe-Porter (New York: Alfred A. Knopf, 1947), p. 314.

8. Thomas Mann, *Leiden*, p. 374.

9. Thomas Mann, *Lebensabriss* (1930), in *Gesammelte Werke*, vol. 11, p. 101.

10. Thomas Mann, "Frühlingssturm!" (1893), in *Gesammelte Werke*, vol. 11, p. 545.

11. Thomas Mann, "Im Spiegel" (1907), in *Gesammelte Werke*, vol. 11, p. 331.

12. Arthur Eloesser, *Thomas Mann: Sein Leben und sein Werk* (Berlin: S. Fischer, 1925), p. 41.

13. Thomas Mann, "Frühlingssturm!" p. 545.

14. Thomas Mann, "Zweimaliger Abschied" (1893), in *Gesammelte Werke*, vol. 8, p. 1102.

15. Thomas Mann, "Heinrich Heine der Gute" (1893) in *Gesammelte Werke*, vol. 11, p. 713.

16. Sigrid Anger et al., eds., *Heinrich Mann: Werk und Leben in Dokumenten und Bildern, 1871–1950* (Berlin: Aufbau, 1971), pp. 32–3.

17. Ibid., p. 33.

18. Ibid., p. 39.

19. Ibid.

20. Thomas Mann, "Vom Beruf des deutschen Schriftstellers in unserer Zeit: Ansprache an den Bruder" (1931), in *Gesammelte Werke*, vol. 10, p. 307.

21. Ibid.

22. Paul Bourget, *Le Disciple* (Paris: Alphonse Lemarre, 1893), p. 278. Cf. Thomas Mann, *The Magic Mountain* (1924), trans. H. T. Lowe-Porter (New York: Alfred A. Knopf, 1944), p. 342.

23. Bourget, *Disciple*, pp. 257 ff.

24. Anger, *Heinrich Mann*, pp. 55–6.

25. Thomas Mann, *Lebensabriss*, p. 101.

Chapter 4: RAMBERGSTRASSE 2

1. Thomas Mann, *Doctor Faustus* (1947), trans. H. T. Lowe-Porter (New York: Alfred A. Knopf, 1948), p. 195. Translation amended.

2. Thomas Mann, *A Sketch of My Life* (1930), trans. H. T. Lowe-Porter (New York: Alfred A. Knopf, 1960), p. 9.

3. Thomas Mann, "Dem Andenken Michael Georg Conrads" (1927), in *Gesammelte Werke*, vol. 10 (Frankfurt/M.: S. Fischer, 1974), pp. 447–8.

4. Thomas Mann, *Lebensabriss* (1930), in *Gesammelte Werke*, vol. 11, p. 101.

5. Herbert Lehnert, *Thomas Mann: Fiktion, Mythos, Religion* (Stuttgart: W. Kohlhammer, 1968), p. 230, note 67.

6. Thomas Mann, "Gefallen" (1894), in *Gesammelte Werke*, vol. 8, p. 11.

7. Ibid., p. 42.

8. Klaus Schröter, ed., *Thomas Mann im Urteil seiner Zeit: Dokumente, 1891–1955* (Hamburg: Christian Wegner, 1969), p. 12.

9. Schröter, p. 11.

10. *Letters of Thomas Mann, 1889–1955*, sel. and trans. Richard Winston and Clara Winston (New York: Alfred A. Knopf, 1971), p. 627.

11. Thomas Mann, *Lebensabriss*, p. 102.

12. Ibid., pp. 102–3.

13. Carl Zuckmayer, in conversation with the author.

14. Thomas Mann, *Letters*, p. 54.

15. Hanns Arens, *Unsterbliches München* (Munich: Bechtle, 1968), p. 190.

16. Sigrid Anger et al., eds., *Heinrich Mann: Werk und Leben in Dokumenten und Bildern, 1871–1950* (Berlin: Aufbau, 1971), p. 43.

17. Klaus Schröter, *Heinrich Mann in Selbstzeugnissen und Bilddokumenten* (Reinbek b. Hamburg: Rowohlt, 1967), p. 26.

18. Thomas Mann, *The Story of a Novel: The Genesis of Doctor Faustus* (1949), trans. Richard Winston and Clara Winston (New York: Alfred A. Knopf, 1961), pp. 201–2.

19. Schröter, *Heinrich Mann*, p. 43.

20. Anger, *Heinrich Mann*, p. 59.

21. Thomas Mann, *Sketch of My Life*, p. 13.

22. Heinrich Mann, *Ein Zeitalter wird besichtigt* (1945) (Berlin: Aufbau, 1973), p. 231. p. 231.

Chapter 5: ITALY

1. Thomas Mann, *A Sketch of My Life* (1930), trans. H. T. Lowe-Porter (New York: Alfred A. Knopf, 1960), p. 11.

2. Thomas Mann, *Briefe an Otto Grautoff, 1894–1901, und Ida Boy-Ed, 1903–1928*, ed. Peter de Mendelssohn (Frankfurt/M.: S. Fischer, 1975), p. 58.

3. Ibid., p. 59.

4. Ibid.

5. Thomas Mann, " 'Das Liebeskonzil' von Oskar Panizza" (1895), in *Gesammelte Werke*, vol. 13 (Frankfurt/M.: S. Fischer, 1974), p. 367.

6. Ibid.

7. Hans Vaget, "Thomas Mann und Oskar Panizza: Zwei Splitter zu *Buddenbrooks* und *Doktor Faustus*," *Germanisch-Romanische Monatsschrift*, vol. 25, no. 2 (1975), p. 233.

8. Thomas Mann, *Buddenbrooks* (1901), trans. H. T. Lowe-Porter (New York: Alfred A. Knopf, 1964), pp. 407-8. Translation amended.

9. Vaget, "Thomas Mann," pp. 231–7.

10. Thomas Mann, *Grautoff und Boy-Ed*, p. 97.

11. Heinrich Mann, *Zwischen den Rassen* (1907) (Frankfurt/M.: Fischer Taschenbuch, 1977), p. 353.

12. Thomas Mann, *A Sketch of My Life*, p. 66.

13. Thomas Mann, "On Myself" (1940), in *Gesammelte Werke*, vol. 13, p. 163.

14. Karl Kerényi, *Tessiner Schreibtisch* (Stuttgart: Steingrüben, 1963), p. 103.

15. Heinrich Mann, *Ein Zeitalter wird besichtigt* (1945) (Berlin: Aufbau, 1973), p. 216.

16. Thomas Mann, *Doctor Faustus* (1947), trans. H. T. Lowe-Porter (New York: Alfred A. Knopf, 1948), p. 214. Translation amended.

17. Thomas Mann, "Lübeck as a Way of Life and Thought" (1926), trans. Richard Winston and Clara Winston, in *Buddenbrooks* (1901), trans. H. T. Lowe-Porter (New York: Alfred A. Knopf, 1964), p. xvii.

18. Peter de Mendelssohn, *Der Zauberer* (Frankfurt/M.: S. Fischer, 1975), p. 292.

19. Thomas Mann, *Grautoff und Boy-Ed*, p. 89.

20. Thomas Mann, "The Dilettante" (1897), in *Stories of Three Decades*, trans. H. T. Lowe-Porter (New York: Alfred A. Knopf, 1936), p. 29.

21. See Hans Vaget, "Der Dilettant: Eine Skizze der Wort- und Bedeutungsgeschichte," *Jahrbuch der deutschen Schillergesellschaft*, vol. 14 (1970), pp. 131–58.

22. Thomas Mann, "Dilettante," p. 34.

23. Ibid., p. 32.

24. Ibid., p. 33. Translation amended.

25. Thomas Mann, "Der Bajazzo" (1897), in *Gesammelte Werke*, vol. 8, p. 121.

26. Thomas Mann, "Dilettante," p. 50. Translation amended.

27. Heinrich Mann, *Zwischen den Rassen*, p. 194.

28. Thomas Mann, *Grautoff und Boy-Ed*, p. 150.

29. Ibid., p. 60.

30. Thomas Mann, *Betrachtungen eines Unpolitischen* (1918), in *Gesammelte Werke*, vol. 12, p. 80.

31. Ibid., pp. 81–2.

32. Thomas Mann, *Doctor Faustus*, p. 211.

Chapter 6: FORMS AND MASKS

1. Thomas Mann, *Briefe an Otto Grautoff, 1894–1901, und Ida Boy-Ed, 1903–1928*, ed. Peter de Mendelssohn (Frankfurt/M.: S. Fischer, 1975), p. 62.

2. Thomas Mann, "Der Wille zum Glück" (1896), in *Gesammelte Werke*, vol. 8 (Frankfurt/M.: S. Fischer, 1974), p. 61.

3. Thomas Mann, *Grautoff und Boy-Ed*, p. 64.

4. Thomas Mann, "Der Wille zum Glück," p. 43.

5. Ibid., p. 44.

6. T. J. Reed, *The Uses of Tradition* (Oxford: Clarendon, 1974), p. 23.

7. Thomas Mann, *Grautoff und Boy-Ed*, p. 93.

8. Ibid.

9. Ibid., p. 61.

10. Ibid.

11. Thomas Mann, "Tischrede auf Wassermann" (1929), in *Gesammelte Werke*, vol. 10, p. 450.

12. Ibid., p. 452.

13. *Letters of Thomas Mann, 1889–1955*, sel. and trans. Richard Winston and Clara Winston (New York: Alfred A. Knopf, 1971), p. 7. Translation amended.

14. Volkmar Hansen, *Thomas Manns Heine-Rezeption* (Hamburg: Hoffmann und Campe, 1975), p. 54.

15. Heinrich Mann, *Ein Zeitalter wird besichtigt* (1945) (Berlin: Aufbau, 1973), pp. 209–10.

16. Thomas Mann, *Tonio Kröger* (1903), in *Stories of Three Decades*, trans. H. T. Lowe-Porter (New York: Alfred A. Knopf, 1936), p. 88. Translation amended.

17. Thomas Mann, *Grautoff und Boy-Ed*, p. 75.

18. Thomas Mann, *Letters*, p. 7, note 2.

19. Thomas Mann, "Der Tod" (1897), in *Gesammelte Werke*, vol. 8, p. 72.

20. Hans Wysling, "Archiavalisches Gewühle: Zur Entstehungsgeschichte der *Bekenntnisse des Hochstaplers Felix Krull*," in Paul Scherrer and Hans Wysling, *Quellenkritische Studien zum Werk Thomas Manns* (Berne: Francke, 1967), p. 245.

21. Thomas Mann, "Der Tod," pp. 74–5.

22. Thomas Mann, "On Myself" (1940), in *Gesammelte Werke*, vol. 13, p. 135.

23. Thomas Mann, *Grautoff und Boy-Ed*, p. 69.

24. Hans Vaget, "Thomas Mann und Theodor Fontane: Eine rezeptionsästhetische Studie zu *Der kleine Herr Friedemann*," *Modern Language Notes*, vol. 90, no. 3 (April 1975), pp. 448–71.

25. Thomas Mann, *Grautoff und Boy-Ed*, p. 77.

26. Thomas Mann, "Verhältnis zu Wien" (1926), in *Gesammelte Werke*, vol. 11, p. 399.

27. Thomas Mann, *Grautoff und Boy-Ed*, pp. 79 ff.

28. Cf. T. J. Reed, *The Uses of Tradition* (Oxford: Clarendon, 1974), p. 275.

29. Thomas Mann, *A Sketch of My Life* (1930), trans. H. T. Lowe-Porter (New York: Alfred A. Knopf, 1960), p. 14.

30. Thomas Mann, *Doctor Faustus* (1947), trans. H. T. Lowe-Porter (New York: Alfred A. Knopf, 1948), p. 228. Translation amended.

31. Thomas Mann, *Grautoff und Boy-Ed*, p. 90.

32. Ibid., p. 94.

33. Hans Wysling, ed., *Thomas Mann—Heinrich Mann: Briefwechsel, 1900–1949* (Frankfurt/M.: S. Fischer, 1968), p. 116.

34. Thomas Mann, *Grautoff und Boy-Ed*, p. 95.

35. Ibid., p. 91.

Chapter 7: *Buddenbrooks*

1. Thomas Mann, *Briefe an Otto Grautoff, 1894–1901, und Ida Boy-Ed, 1903–1928*, ed. Peter de Mendelssohn (Frankfurt/M.: S. Fischer, 1975), p. 100.

2. Herbert Lehnert, *Thomas Mann: Fiktion, Mythos, Religion* (Stuttgart: W. Kohlhammer, 1968), pp. 45–6.

3. Thomas Mann, "Lübeck as a Way of Life and Thought" (1926), trans. Richard Winston and Clara Winston, in *Buddenbrooks* (1901), trans. H. T. Lowe-Porter (New York: Alfred A. Knopf, 1964), p. x.

4. Maurice Muret, quoted by T. J. Reed, *The Uses of Tradition* (Oxford: Clarendon, 1974), p. 72, note 45.

5. *Letters of Thomas Mann, 1889–1955*, sel. and trans. Richard Winston and Clara Winston (New York: Alfred A. Knopf, 1971), p. 23.

6. Heinrich Mann, *Ein Zeitalter wird besichtigt* (1945) (Berlin: Aufbau, 1973), p. 236.

7. Thomas Mann, "Lübeck," p. xiii.

8. Viktor Mann, *Wir waren Fünf* (Konstanz: Südverlag, 1949), p. 38.

9. Thomas Mann, "Lübeck," p. xiii.

10. Ibid., p. xi.

11. Hans Wysling and Marianne Fischer, eds., *Dichter über ihre Dichtungen: Thomas Mann, Teil I: 1889–1917* (Munich: Heimeran, 1975), pp. 47–8.

12. Thomas Mann, "Lübeck," p. xi.

13. Ibid.

14. Paul Scherrer, "Thomas Manns Vorarbeiten zu den *Buddenbrooks:* Zur Chronologie des Romans," in Paul Scherrer and Hans Wysling, *Quellenkritische Studien zum Werk Thomas Manns* (Berne: Francke, 1967), pp. 14–15.

15. Wysling and Fischer, *Dichtungen*, p. 38.

16. Thomas Mann, "Lübeck," p. x.

17. Thomas Mann, "Bilse und ich" (1906), in *Gesammelte Werke*, vol. 10, p. 15.

18. Thomas Mann, *Grautoff und Boy-Ed*, p. 101.

19. Heinrich Mann, *Zeitalter*, p. 216.

20. Klaus Schröter, *Heinrich Mann in Selbstzeugnissen und Bilddokumenten* (Reinbek b. Hamburg: Rowohlt, 1967), p. 43.

21. Thomas Mann, *Briefe, 1889–1936*, ed. Erika Mann (Frankfurt/M.: S. Fischer, 1961), p. 8.

22. Thomas Mann, *Letters*, p. 9.

23. Peter de Mendelssohn, *S. Fischer und sein Verlag* (Frankfurt/M.: S. Fischer, 1970), p. 280.

24. Thomas Mann, *Grautoff und Boy-Ed*, p. 103.

25. Thomas Mann, *Buddenbrooks*, p. 560. Translation amended.

26. Thomas Mann, *Grautoff und Boy-Ed*, p. 102.

27. Ibid., p. 105.

28. Henry Hatfield, "Charon und der Kleiderschrank," *Modern Language Notes*, vol. 65, no. 2 (February 1950), pp. 100–02.

29. Thomas Mann, "Der Kleiderschrank" (1899), in *Gesammelte Werke*, vol. 8, p. 157.

30. Ibid.

31. Ibid., p. 153.

32. André Banuls, *Heinrich Mann: Le poète et la politique* (Paris: C. Klincksieck, 1966), p. 592.

33. Thomas Mann, *Grautoff und Boy-Ed*, p. 105.

34. Thomas Mann, *A Sketch of My Life* (1930), trans. H. T. Lowe-Porter (New York: Alfred A. Knopf, 1960), p. 19.

35. Frank Wedekind, *Prosa* (Berlin: Aufbau, 1969), p. 496.

36. Ibid., pp. 497–8.

37. Thomas Mann, *Letters*, p. 10.

38. Thomas Mann, "Über den Alkohol" (1906), in *Gesammelte Werke*, vol. 11, p. 718.

39. Thomas Mann, *Letters*, p. 11.

40. Klaus Schröter, ed., *Thomas Mann im Urteil seiner Zeit: Dokumente, 1891–1955* (Hamburg: Christian Wegner, 1969), p. 14.

41. Ibid., p. 15.

42. Thomas Mann, *A Sketch of My Life*, p. 20.

43. Schröter, *Thomas Mann*, p. 16.

44. Ibid., pp. 16–17.

45. Katia Mann, *Unwritten Memories*, ed. Elisabeth Plessen and Michael Mann, trans. Hunter Hannum and Hildegarde Hannum (New York: Alfred A. Knopf, 1975), p. 57. Translation amended.

46. Henry James, *The Art of Fiction and Other Essays* (New York: Oxford, 1948), p. 11.

Chapter 8: THE ARMY

1. Klaus Schröter, ed., *Thomas Mann im Urteil seiner Zeit: Dokumente, 1891–1955* (Hamburg: Christian Wegner, 1969), p. 14.

2. Ibid., p. 16.

3. Thomas Mann, *Briefe an Otto Grautoff, 1894–1901, und Ida Boy-Ed, 1903–1928*, ed. Peter de Mendelssohn (Frankfurt/M.: S. Fischer, 1975), p. 109.

4. Thomas Mann, "Monolog" (1899), in *Gesammelte Werke*, vol. 8 (Frankfurt/M.: S. Fischer, 1974), p. 1,106.

5. Hans Wysling and Marianne Fischer, eds., *Dichter über ihre Dichtungen: Thomas Mann, Teil I: 1889–1917* (Munich: Heimeran, 1975), p. 140.

6. Thomas Mann, *Grautoff und Boy-Ed*, p. 109.

7. *Letters of Thomas Mann, 1889–1955*, sel. and trans. Richard Winston and Clara Winston (New York: Alfred A. Knopf, 1971), p. 11.

8. Thomas Mann, "On Myself" (1940), in *Gesammelte Werke*, vol. 13, p. 144.

9. Thomas Mann, *Buddenbrooks* (1901), trans. H. T. Lowe-Porter (New York: Alfred A. Knopf, 1964), p. 473.

10. Thomas Mann, *Lebensabriss* (1930), in *Gesammelte Werke*, vol. 11, p. 115.

11. Thomas Mann, "Lübeck as a Way of Life and Thought" (1926), trans. Richard Winston and Clara Winston, in *Buddenbrooks*, p. xi.

12. Thomas Mann, *Letters*, p. 24.

13. Thomas Mann, *Lebensabriss*, p. 111.

14. Thomas Mann, "On Myself," p. 142.

15. Thomas Mann, "Quotations" (1944), in *Gesammelte Werke*, vol. 13, p. 208.

16. Thomas Mann, *Buddenbrooks*, p. 524.

17. Ibid., p. 525.

18. Thomas Mann, *Lebensabriss*, p. 111.

19. Thomas Mann, *Buddenbrooks*, in *Gesammelte Werke*, vol. 2, p. 1,240.

20. Thomas Mann, *Briefe, 1948–1955, und Nachlese*, ed. Erika Mann (Frankfurt/M.: S. Fischer, 1965), p. 335.

21. Thomas Mann, *Letters*, p. 517.

22. Ibid., p. 16.

23. Thomas Mann, *Grautoff und Boy-Ed*, p. 110.

24. Thomas Mann, *Letters*, p. 13.

25. Ibid., pp. 13–14.

26. Thomas Mann, *Grautoff und Boy-Ed*, p. 110.

27. Thomas Mann, *Lebensabriss*, p. 112.

28. Thomas Mann, *Grautoff und Boy-Ed*, p. 112.

29. Ibid., p. 113.

30. Thomas Mann, "In Memoriam S. Fischer" (1934), in *Gesammelte Werke*, vol. 10, p. 473.

31. Thomas Mann, *Grautoff und Boy-Ed*, p. 113.

32. Ibid., p. 115.

33. Thomas Mann, *Letters*, p. 14.

34. Ibid., p. 16.

35. Thomas Mann, *Lebensabriss*, p. 112.

36. Thomas Mann, *Grautoff und Boy-Ed*, p. 124.

37. Thomas Mann, "Im Spiegel" (1907), in *Gesammelte Werke*, vol. 11, p. 331.

38. Thomas Mann, *Lebensabriss*, p. 112.

39. Ibid.

40. Thomas Mann, *Letters*, p. 60.

41. Ibid., p. 61.

42. Ibid., p. 60.

43. Thomas Mann, "Im Spiegel," p. 331.

44. Hans Wysling, ed., *Thomas Mann—Heinrich Mann: Briefwechsel, 1900–1949* (Frankfurt/M.: S. Fischer, 1968), p. 8.

45. Thomas Mann, "Lübeck," p. xii.

46. Thomas Mann, *Letters*, p. 23.

47. Wysling, *Thomas Mann—Heinrich Mann*, p. 8.

48. Thomas Mann, *Letters*, p. 26.

Chapter 9: FRIENDSHIP

1. *Letters of Thomas Mann, 1889–1955*, sel. and trans. Richard Winston and Clara Winston (New York: Alfred A. Knopf, 1971), p. 23.

2. Hans Wysling, ed., *Thomas Mann—Heinrich Mann: Briefwechsel, 1900–1949* (Frankfurt/M.: S. Fischer, 1968), p. 15.

3. Thomas Mann, *Letters*, p. 25.

4. Ibid.

5. Wysling, *Thomas Mann—Heinrich Mann*, p. 15.

6. Thomas Mann, *Letters*, p. 25.

7. Ibid., p. 28.

8. Thomas Mann, *Lebensabriss* (1930), in *Gesammelte Werke*, vol. 11 (Frankfurt/M.: S. Fischer, 1974), pp. 99–100.

9. Thomas Mann, *Briefe, 1948–1955, und Nachlese*, ed. Erika Mann (Frankfurt/M.: S. Fischer, 1965), p. 110.

10. Thomas Mann, *Letters*, p. 25.

11. Ibid.

12. Ibid., pp. 104–05.

13. Ibid., p. 105.

14. Thomas Mann, *The Magic Mountain* (1924), trans. H. T. Lowe-Porter (New York: Alfred A. Knopf, 1944), p. 123.

15. Thomas Mann, *Briefe an Otto Grautoff, 1894–1901, und Ida Boy-Ed, 1903–1928*, ed. Peter de Mendelssohn (Frankfurt/M.: S. Fischer, 1975), p. 136.

16. Ibid.

17. Mann, *Letters*, p. 25.

18. Wysling, *Thomas Mann—Heinrich Mann*, p. 22.

19. Thomas Mann, *A Sketch of My Life* (1930), trans. H. T. Lowe-Porter (New York: Alfred A. Knopf, 1960), p. 35,

20. Wysling, *Thomas Mann—Heinrich Mann*, p. 255.

21. Thomas Mann, *Briefe, 1948–1955*, p. 429.

22. Ibid., p. 428.

23. Ibid.

24. Ibid., pp. 428–9.

25. Letter to Paul and Carl Ehrenberg, 22 October 1902. Handwritten original in Thomas Mann-Archiv, Zürich.

26. Thomas Mann, "The Way to the Churchyard" (1900), in *Stories of Three Decades*, trans. H. T. Lowe-Porter (New York: Alfred A. Knopf, 1936), p. 81.

27. Thomas Mann, *Buddenbrooks* (1901), trans. H. T. Lowe-Porter (New York: Alfred A. Knopf, 1964), pp. 595–7, and *Tristan* (1903), in *Stories of Three Decades*, pp. 154–5.

28. Thomas Mann, preface to *Stories of Three Decades*, p. vi.

29. Thomas Mann, *Tristan*, p. 161.

30. Ibid., p. 160.

31. Ibid., p. 134.

32. Ibid., p. 140.

33. Thomas Mann, *Letters*, p. 23.

Chapter 10: FAME

1. Thomas Mann, "Moritz Heimann zum fünfzigsten Geburtstag" (1918), in *Gesammelte Werke*, vol. 13 (Frankfurt/M.: S. Fischer, 1974), p. 819.

2. Thomas Mann, "Lübeck as a Way of Life and Thought" (1926), trans. Richard Winston and Clara Winston, in *Buddenbrooks* (1901), trans. H. T. Lowe-Porter (New York: Alfred A. Knopf, 1964), p. xii.

3. Peter de Mendelssohn, *S. Fischer und sein Verlag* (Frankfurt/M.: S. Fischer, 1970), p. 292.

4. Thomas Mann, *Briefe, 1889–1936*, ed. Erika Mann (Frankfurt/M.: S. Fischer, 1961), p. 30.

5. Thomas Mann, *Briefe an Otto Grautoff, 1894–1901, und Ida Boy-Ed, 1903–1928*, ed. Peter de Mendelssohn (Frankfurt/M.: S. Fischer, 1975), p. 137.

6. Ibid., pp. 139–40.

7. Ibid., pp. 249–50.

8. Klaus Schröter, ed., *Thomas Mann im Urteil seiner Zeit: Dokumente, 1891–1955* (Hamburg: Christian Wegner, 1969), p. 19.

9. Ibid., pp. 19–20.

10. Ibid., p. 22.

11. Ibid., pp. 22–3.

12. Rainer Maria Rilke, "Thomas Mann's *Buddenbrooks*," trans. Henry Hatfield, in Henry Hatfield, ed., *Thomas Mann: A Collection of Critical Essays* (Englewood Cliffs, N.J.: Prentice-Hall, 1964), pp. 7–9.

13. *Letters of Thomas Mann, 1889–1955*, sel. and trans. Richard Winston and Clara Winston (New York: Alfred A. Knopf, 1971), p. 374.

14. Ibid., p. 375.

15. Henry Hatfield, "Thomas Mann's *Buddenbrooks:* The World of the Father," in Hatfield, *Thomas Mann,* pp. 10–21.

16. Thomas Mann, "Lübeck," p. xiii.

17. Thomas Mann, *Buddenbrooks,* p. 243. Cf. Herbert Singer, "Helena und der Senator: Versuch einer mythologischen Deutung von Thomas Manns *Buddenbrooks,*" in Helmut Koopmann, ed., *Thomas Mann* (Darmtstadt: Wissenschaftliche Buchgesellschaft, 1975), pp. 247–56.

18. Thomas Mann, *Buddenbrooks,* p. 243.

19. Thomas Mann, "Lübeck," p. xi.

20. T. J. Reed, *The Uses of Tradition* (Oxford: Clarendon, 1974), p. 46.

21. Quoted by Otto Anthes in Schröter, *Thomas Mann,* p. 23.

22. Schröter, *Thomas Mann,* dust jacket facsimile of a contemporary newspaper clipping.

23. Thomas Mann, *A Sketch of My Life* (1930), trans. H. T. Lowe-Porter (New York: Alfred A. Knopf, 1960), p. 19.

24. Ibid., p. 30.

25. Thomas Mann, "On Myself" (1940), in *Gesammelte Werke,* vol. 13, p. 141.

26. Thomas Mann, *Betrachtungen eines Unpolitischen* (1918), in *Gesammelte Werke,* vol. 12, p. 89.

27. Hans Wysling, ed., *Thomas Mann—Heinrich Mann: Briefwechsel, 1900–1949* (Frankfurt/M.: S. Fischer, 1968), p. 19.

28. Thomas Mann, *Grautoff und Boy-Ed,* p. 137.

29. Thomas Mann, *Letters,* p. 29.

30. Ibid., p. 30.

31. Letter to Paul and Carl Ehrenberg, 22 October 1902. Handwritten original in Thomas Mann-Archiv, Zürich.

32. Thomas Mann, *Briefe, 1889–1936,* p. 35.

Chapter 11: A WIDER WORLD

1. Hans Wysling, "Dokumente zur Entstehung des *Tonio Kröger,*" in Paul Scherrer and Hans Wysling, *Quellenkritische Studien zum Werk Thomas Manns* (Berne: Francke, 1967), p. 56.

2. Thomas Mann, *Tonio Kröger* (1903), in *Gesammelte Werke,* vol. 8 (Frankfurt/M.: S. Fischer, 1974), p. 272.

3. Thomas Mann, "Die Hungernden" (1903), in *Gesammelte Werke,* vol. 8, p. 264.

4. Thomas Mann, "The Hungry" (1903), in *Stories of Three Decades,* trans. H. T. Lowe-Porter (New York: Alfred A. Knopf, 1936), p. 171. Translation amended.

5. Ibid., p. 172. (Italics added.)

6. Wysling, *"Tonio Kröger,"* p. 56.

7. Heinrich Mann, "Pippo Spano" (1905), in *Der Unbekannte und andere Novellen* (Munich: Deutscher Taschenbuch Verlag, 1973), p. 52.

8. Sigrid Anger et al., eds., *Heinrich Mann: Werk und Leben in Dokumenten und Bildern, 1871–1950* (Berlin: Aufbau, 1971), p. 93.

9. Ibid., p. 96.

10. André Banuls, *Heinrich Mann: Le poète et la politique* (Paris: C. Klincksieck, 1966), p. 593.

11. Thomas Mann, "Das Ewig-Weibliche" (1903), in *Gesammelte Werke*, vol. 13, pp. 383–4.

12. Viktor Mann, *Wir waren Fünf* (Konstanz: Südverlag, 1949), p. 182.

13. Anger, *Heinrich Mann*, p. 97.

14. Thomas Mann, *Briefe, 1948–1955, und Nachlese*, ed. Erika Mann (Frankfurt/M.: S. Fischer, 1965), p. 445.

15. Hans Wysling, ed., *Thomas Mann—Heinrich Mann: Briefwechsel, 1900–1949* (Frankfurt/M.: S. Fischer, 1968), p. xxxiv.

16. Klaus Schröter, ed., *Thomas Mann im Urteil seiner Zeit: Dokumente, 1891–1955* (Hamburg: Christian Wegner, 1969), p. 14.

17. Ibid., p. 26.

18. *Letters of Thomas Mann, 1889–1955*, sel. and trans. Richard Winston and Clara Winston (New York: Alfred A. Knopf, 1971), p. 18.

19. Thomas Mann, *Briefe, 1889–1936*, ed. Erika Mann (Frankfurt/M.: S. Fischer, 1961), p. 36.

20. Schröter, *Thomas Mann*, p. 28.

21. Wysling, *Thomas Mann—Heinrich Mann*, p. 23.

22. Thomas Mann, *Briefe, 1889–1936*, p. 41.

23. Thomas Mann, *Der Erwählte* (1951), in *Gesammelte Werke*, vol. 7, p. 10.

24. Thomas Mann, "A Gleam" (1904), in *Stories of Three Decades*, trans. H. T. Lowe-Porter (New York: Alfred A. Knopf, 1936), p. 273.

25. Thomas Mann, *Briefe, 1948–1955*, p. 448.

26. Hans Wysling, "Thomas Manns 'Maja'-Projekt," in Scherrer and Wysling, *Quellenkritische Studien*, p. 30.

27. Ibid.

Chapter 12: COURTSHIP

1. Thomas Mann, *Lebensabriss* (1930), in *Gesammelte Werke*, vol. 11 (Frankfurt/M.: S. Fischer, 1974), p. 118.

2. Thomas Mann, "Katia Mann zum siebzigsten Geburtstag" (1953), in *Gesammelte Werke*, vol. 11, p. 522.

3. Ibid., p. 523.

4. Klaus Mann, *Der Wendepunkt* (1943) (Munich: Nymphenburg, 1969), p. 13.

5. Katia Mann, *Unwritten Memories* (1974), ed. Elisabeth Plessen and Michael Mann, trans. Hunter Hannum and Hildegarde Hannum (New York: Alfred A. Knopf, 1975), p. 6.

6. Thomas Mann, "Little Grandma" (1942), in *Gesammelte Werke*, vol. 11, p. 473.

7. Klaus Mann, *Der Wendepunkt*, p. 12.

8. Ibid., p. 13.

9. Hans Wysling, ed., *Thomas Mann—Heinrich Mann: Briefwechsel, 1900–1949* (Frankfurt/M.: S. Fischer, 1968), p. 26.

10. *Letters of Thomas Mann, 1889–1955*, sel. and trans. Richard Winston and Clara Winston (New York: Alfred A. Knopf, 1971), p. 34.

11. Katia Mann, *Unwritten Memories*, p. 15. Translation amended.

12. Thomas Mann, *Letters*, p. 31.

13. Wysling, *Thomas Mann—Heinrich Mann*, p. 26.

14. Ibid., p. 27.

15. Ibid.

16. Ibid.

17. Ibid., p. 28.

18. Ibid.

19. Katia Mann, *Unwritten Memories*, p. 17. Spelling amended.

20. Ibid., p. 20. Translation amended.

21. Thomas Mann, *Letters*, p. 36.

22. Wysling, *Thomas Mann—Heinrich Mann*, p. 27.

23. Katia Mann, *Unwritten Memories*, p. 17.

24. Ibid., p. 18.

25. Ibid., p. 26.

26. Thomas Mann, *Letters*, p. 25.

27. Thomas Mann, "At the Prophet's" (1904), in *Stories of Three Decades*, trans. H. T. Lowe-Porter (New York: Alfred A. Knopf, 1936), p. 286.

28. Ibid., p. 283.

29. Ibid., p. 289.

30. Klaus Schröter, ed., *Thomas Mann im Urteil seiner Zeit: Dokumente, 1891–1955* (Hamburg: Christian Wegner, 1969), pp. 28–30.

31. Katia Mann, *Unwritten Memories*, p. 19.

32. Ibid.

33. Thomas Mann, *Letters*, pp. 34–5.

34. Ibid., p. 35.

35. Ibid., p. 36.

36. Ibid., p. 38.

37. Ibid., p. 37.

38. Ibid., p. 39.

39. Ibid.

40. Ibid., p. 40.

41. Ibid., p. 42.

42. Katia Mann, *Unwritten Memories*, p. 19.

43. Thomas Mann, *Letters*, p. 45.

44. Thomas Mann, *Tonio Kröger* (1903), in *Gesammelte Werke*, vol. 8, p. 273.

45. Thomas Mann, *Letters*, p. 45.

46. Ibid.

Chapter 13: MARRIAGE

1. Hans Wysling, ed., *Thomas Mann—Heinrich Mann: Briefwechsel, 1900–1949* (Frankfurt/M.: S. Fischer, 1968), p. 31.

2. *Letters of Thomas Mann, 1889–1955*, sel. and trans. Richard Winston and Clara Winston (New York: Alfred A. Knopf, 1971), p. 677.

3. Thomas Mann, *Briefe, 1889–1936*, ed. Erika Mann (Frankfurt/M.: S. Fischer, 1961), p. 59.

4. Thomas Mann, *Briefe an Otto Grautoff, 1894–1901, und Ida Boy-Ed, 1903–1928*, ed. Peter de Mendelssohn (Frankfurt/M.: S. Fischer, 1975), p. 153.

5. Ibid., p. 150.

6. Wysling, *Thomas Mann—Heinrich Mann*, p. 30.

7. Ibid., p. 31.

8. Ibid., p. 32.

9. Ibid., pp. 31–2.

10. Ibid., p. 34.

11. Thomas Mann, *Briefe, 1948–1955, und Nachlese*, ed. Erika Mann (Frankfurt/M.: S. Fischer, 1965), p. 445.

12. Ibid., p. 445.

13. Thomas Mann, *Fiorenza* (1905), in *Gesammelte Werke*, vol. 8 (Frankfurt/M.: S. Fischer, 1974), p. 1,038.

14. Ibid., p. 995.

15. Ibid., p. 1,040.

16. Wysling, *Thomas Mann—Heinrich Mann*, p. 44.

17. Thomas Mann, *Fiorenza*, p. 1,063.

18. Ibid.

19. Thomas Mann, *Letters,* p. 20.

20. Wysling, *Thomas Mann—Heinrich Mann,* p. 34.

21. Ibid.

22. Ibid.

23. Ibid.

24. Ibid., p. 33.

25. Thomas Mann, "Schwere Stunde" (1905), in *Gesammelte Werke,* vol. 8, p. 373.

26. Hans-Joachim Sandberg, *Thomas Manns Schiller-Studien: Eine quellenkritische Untersuchung* (Oslo: Universitetsforlaget, 1965), p. 32.

27. Thomas Mann, *Letters,* p. 42.

28. Thomas Mann, "Schwere Stunde," p. 376.

29. Wysling, *Thomas Mann—Heinrich Mann,* p. 38.

30. Thomas Mann, *Grautoff und Boy-Ed,* p. 156.

31. Thomas Mann, *Tagebücher, 1933–1934,* ed. Peter de Mendelssohn (Frankfurt/M.: S. Fischer, 1977), p. 165.

32. Edgar Allan Poe, *The Fall of the House of Usher* (1839), in *The Complete Works of Edgar Allan Poe,* vol. 3, ed. James A. Harrison (New York: AMS, 1965), p. 289.

33. Thomas Mann, *The Magic Mountain* (1924), trans. H. T. Lowe-Porter (New York: Alfred A. Knopf, 1944), p. 328.

34. Wysling, *Thomas Mann—Heinrich Mann,* p. 265.

35. Ibid., p. 40.

36. Ibid., p. 42.

37. Thomas Mann, "The Blood of the Walsungs" (1906), in *Stories of Three Decades,* trans. H. T Lowe-Porter (New York: Alfred A. Knopf, 1936), p. 319.

38. Wysling, *Thomas Mann—Heinrich Mann,* pp. 45–6.

39. Thomas Mann, "Ein Nachwort" (1905), in *Gesammelte Werke,* vol. 11, p. 546.

40. Ibid., pp. 546–7.

41. Ibid., p. 548.

42. Ibid., p. 549.

43. Thomas Mann, "Bilse und ich" (1906), in *Gesammelte Werke,* vol. 10, p. 10.

44. Ibid., p. 11.

45. Volkmar Hansen, *Thomas Manns Heine-Rezeption* (Hamburg: Hoffmann und Campe, 1975), p. 116.

46. Thomas Mann, "Bilse und ich," p. 15.

47. Ibid., pp. 15–16.

48. Ibid., p. 16.

Chapter 14: THEATER AND NOVEL

1. Hans Wysling, ed., *Thomas Mann—Heinrich Mann: Briefwechsel, 1900–1949* (Frankfurt/M.: S. Fischer, 1968), p. 46.

2. Ibid., p. xxxv.

3. Ibid., p. xxxiv.

4. Ibid., p. 38.

5. Ibid., p. 44.

6. Ibid., p. 37.

7. Klaus Schröter, ed., *Thomas Mann im Urteil seiner Zeit: Dokumente, 1891–1955* (Hamburg: Christian Wegner, 1969), p. 42.

8. Wysling, *Thomas Mann—Heinrich Mann*, pp. 51–2.

9. Schröter, *Thomas Mann*, p. 48.

10. Ibid., p. 49.

11. Wysling, *Thomas Mann—Heinrich Mann*, p. 52.

12. *Letters of Thomas Mann, 1889–1955*, sel. and trans. Richard Winston and Clara Winston (New York: Alfred A. Knopf, 1971), p. 48.

13. Ibid.

14. Ibid., pp. 49–50.

15. Schröter, *Thomas Mann*, p. 37.

16. Thomas Mann, *Letters*, p. 51.

17. Ibid.

18. Thomas Mann, *Briefe, 1889–1936*, ed. Erika Mann (Frankfurt/M.: S. Fischer, 1961), p. 65.

19. Ibid., p. 66.

20. Thomas Mann, *Briefe an Otto Grautoff, 1894–1901, und Ida Boy-Ed, 1903–1928*, ed. Peter de Mendelssohn (Frankfurt/M.: S. Fischer, 1975), p. 158.

21. Wysling, *Thomas Mann—Heinrich Mann*, p. 54.

22. Thomas Mann, *Grautoff und Boy-Ed*, p. 158.

23. Wysling, *Thomas Mann—Heinrich Mann*, p. 270.

24. Ibid., p. 50.

25. Ibid., pp. 54–5.

26. Ibid., p. 56.

27. Ibid.

28. Ibid., p. 57.

29. Thomas Mann, *Briefe, 1948–1955, und Nachlese*, ed. Erika Mann (Frankfurt/M.: S. Fischer, 1965), p. 451.

30. Thomas Mann, *Königliche Hoheit* (1909), *in Gesammelte Werke*, vol. 2 (Frankfurt/M.: S. Fischer, 1974), p. 135.

31. Katia Mann, *Unwritten Memories*, ed. Elisabeth Plessen and Michael Mann, trans. Hunter Hannum and Hildegarde Hannum (New York: Alfred A. Knopf, 1975), p. 22.

32. Thomas Mann, *Briefe, 1889–1936*, p. 67.

33. Thomas Mann, "Mitteilung an die literarhistorische Gesellschaft in Bonn" (1906), in *Gesammelte Werke*, vol. 11, pp. 713–14.

34. Ibid., pp. 714–15.

35. Thomas Mann, "Versuch über das Theater" (1908), in *Gesammelte Werke*, vol. 10, p. 35.

36. Ibid., p. 49.

37. Ibid., p. 37.

38. Wysling, *Thomas Mann—Heinrich Mann*, p. 58.

39. Ibid., p. 62.

40. Thomas Mann, "Mitteilung," pp. 716–17.

41. Wysling, *Thomas Mann—Heinrich Mann*, p. 60.

42. Thomas Mann, *Königliche Hoheit* (1909), in *Gesammelte Werke*, vol. 2, p. 347.

43. Hans Wysling, "Die Fragmente zu Thomas Manns 'Fürsten-Novelle': Zur Urhandschrift der *Königlichen Hoheit*," in Paul Scherrer and Hans Wysling, *Quellenkritische Studien zum Werk Thomas Manns* (Berne: Francke, 1967), pp. 64–105.

44. Letter to the editor of *Der Morgen*, undated [December 1907], summarized in Hans Bürgin and Hans-Otto Mayer, eds., *Die Briefe Thomas Manns: Regesten und Register*, vol. 1 (Frankfurt/M.: S. Fischer, 1976), p. 91.

45. Wysling, *Thomas Mann—Heinrich Mann*, p. 64.

46. Thomas Mann, *Briefe, 1889–1936*, p. 70.

47. Wysling, *Thomas Mann—Heinrich Mann*, p. 63.

48. Thomas Mann, "Über Fiorenza" (1908), in *Gesammelte Werke*, vol. 11, pp. 560–2.

49. Wysling, *Thomas Mann—Heinrich Mann*. p. 65.

50. Thomas Mann, *Briefe, 1889–1936*, p. 73.

Chapter 15: HIGHNESS

1. Thomas Mann, *Briefe, 1889–1936*, ed. Erika Mann (Frankfurt/M.: S. Fischer, 1961), p. 73.

2. Thomas Mann, "Jakob Wassermanns *Caspar Hauser oder die Trägheit des Herzens*" (1908), in *Gesammelte Werke*, vol. 10 (Frankfurt/M.: S. Fischer, 1974), p. 553.

3. Letter to Ludwig Ewers, 13 January 1909, quoted in Peter de Mendelssohn, *Der Zauberer* (Frankfurt/M.: S. Fischer, 1975), p. 756.

4. Hans Wysling, ed., *Thomas Mann—Heinrich Mann: Briefwechsel, 1900–1949* (Frankfurt/M.: S. Fischer, 1968), p. 76.

5. Ibid., p. 74.

6. Ibid., p. 76.

7. Ibid.

8. Ibid., p. 77.

9. Postcard to Walter Opitz, [?] May 1909, summarized in Hans Bürgin and Hans-Otto Mayer, eds., *Die Briefe Thomas Manns: Regesten und Register*, vol. 1 (Frankfurt/M.: S. Fischer, 1976), p. 1,060.

10. Thomas Mann, "Das Eisenbahnunglück," in *Gesammelte Werke*, vol. 8, pp. 423–4.

11. Thomas Mann, *Briefe an Otto Grautoff, 1894–1901, und Ida Boy-Ed, 1903–1928*, ed. Peter de Mendelssohn (Frankfurt/M.: S. Fischer 1975), p. 162.

12. Ibid., p. 163.

13. Ibid., p. 251.

14. Ibid., p. 253.

15. Ibid., pp. 165–6.

16. Klaus Schröter, ed., *Thomas Mann im Urteil seiner Zeit: Dokumente, 1891–1955* (Hamburg: Christian Wegner, 1969), p. 51.

17. Anni Carlsson and Volker Michels, eds., *The Hesse-Mann Letters: The Correspondence of Hermann Hesse and Thomas Mann*, trans. Ralph Manheim (New York: Harper and Row, 1975), p. 1.

18. Thomas Mann, "Peter Altenberg" (1920), in *Gesammelte Werke*, vol. 10, p. 423.

19. Thomas Mann, "On Myself" (1940), in *Gesammelte Werke*, vol. 13, p. 132.

20. *Letters of Thomas Mann, 1889–1955*, sel. and trans. Richard Winston and Clara Winston (New York: Alfred A. Knopf, 1971), pp. 55–6.

21. Schröter, *Thomas Mann*, p. 50.

22. Ibid., p. 52.

23. Thomas Mann, "Die Lösung der Judenfrage" (1907), in *Gesammelte Werke*, vol. 13, p. 459.

24. Thomas Mann, "An Enduring People" (1944), in *Gesammelte Werke*, vol. 13, pp. 506–7.

25. Wysling, *Thomas Mann—Heinrich Mann*, p. 83.

26. Ibid.

27. Thomas Mann, "Der Doktor Lessing" (1910), in *Gesammelte Werke*, vol. 11, p. 730.

28. Martin Buber, *Briefwechsel aus Sieben Jahrzehnten* (Heidelberg: Verlag Lambert Schneider, 1972), p. 282.

29. Thomas Mann, "Der Doktor Lessing," p. 724.

30. Schröter, *Thomas Mann*, p. 55.

31. Thomas Mann, *Grautoff und Boy-Ed*, p. 167.

32. Ibid., p. 170.

33. Klaus Mann, *The Turning Point* (London: Victor Gollancz, 1944), pp. 30–1.

34. Ibid., p. 15.

Chapter 16: TRAGEDY IN POLLING

1. Thomas Mann, *Lebensabriss* (1930), in *Gesammelte Werke,* vol. 11 (Frankfurt/M.: S. Fischer, 1974), p. 121.

2. Ibid., p. 120.

3. Heinrich Mann, *Ein Zeitalter wird besichtigt* (1945) (Berlin: Aufbau, 1973), p. 205.

4. Ibid., p. 227.

5. Thomas Mann, *Lebensabriss,* p. 120.

6. Thomas Mann, *A Sketch of My Life* (1930), trans. H. T. Lowe-Porter (New York: Alfred A. Knopf, 1960), p. 140.

7. *Letters of Thomas Mann, 1889–1955,* sel. and trans. Richard Winston and Clara Winston (New York: Alfred A. Knopf, 1971), p. 58.

8. Ibid., p. 57.

9. Sigrid Anger et al., eds., *Heinrich Mann: Werk und Leben in Dokumenten und Bildern, 1871–1950* (Berlin: Aufbau, 1971), pp. 461–4.

10. Thomas Mann, *Doktor Faustus* (1947), in *Gesammelte Werke,* vol. 6, p. 508.

11. Thomas Mann, *Letters,* p. 58.

12. Thomas Mann, "The Old Fontane" (1910), in *Essays of Three Decades,* trans. H. T. Lowe-Porter (New York: Alfred A. Knopf, 1947), p. 290.

13. Ibid., p. 293.

14. Thomas Mann, "Der alte Fontane" (1910), in *Gesammelte Werke,* vol. 9, pp. 17–18.

15. Thomas Mann, "The Old Fontane," p. 295.

16. Thomas Mann, "Der alte Fontane," p. 19.

17. Ibid., p. 33.

18. Thomas Mann, *Briefe, 1889–1936,* ed. Erika Mann (Frankfurt/M.: S. Fischer, 1961), p. 86.

19. Thomas Mann, *Thomas Mann an Ernst Bertram: Briefe aus den Jahren 1910–1955,* ed. Inge Jens (Pfullingen: Neske, 1960), p. 9.

20. Hans Wysling, ed., *Thomas Mann—Heinrich Mann: Briefwechsel, 1900–1949* Frankfurt/M.: S. Fischer, 1968), p. 92.

21. Thomas Mann, preface to *Stories of Three Decades,* trans. H. T. Lowe-Porter (New York: Alfred A. Knopf, 1936), p. vii.

22. Thomas Mann, "The Fight between Jappe and Do Escobar" (1911), in *Stories of Three Decades,* pp. 338–9. Translation amended.

23. Thomas Mann, "Peter Schlemihl" (1910), in *Gesammelte Werke,* vol. 13, p. 399.

24. Thomas Mann, "Chamisso" (1911), in *Gesammelte Werke,* vol. 9, p. 56.

25. Ibid., p. 54.

26. Ibid., p. 57.

Notes

Chapter 17: *Death in Venice*

1. Katia Mann, *Unwritten Memories*, ed. Elisabeth Plessen and Michael Mann, trans. Hunter Hannum and Hildegarde Hannum (New York: Alfred A. Knopf, 1975), p. 61.

2. Thomas Mann, *Death in Venice* (1912), in *Stories of Three Decades*, trans. H. T. Lowe-Porter (New York: Alfred A. Knopf, 1936), p. 400. Translation amended.

3. Thomas Mann, *A Sketch of My Life* (1930), trans. H. T. Lowe-Porter (New York: Alfred A. Knopf, 1960), p. 46.

4. Katia Mann, *Unwritten Memories*, pp. 65 ff.

5. Peter de Mendelssohn, *Der Zauberer* (Frankfurt/M.: S. Fischer, 1975), p. 873.

6. *Letters of Thomas Mann, 1889–1955*, sel. and trans. Richard Winston and Clara Winston (New York: Alfred A. Knopf, 1971), pp. 103–4.

7. Thomas Mann, *Briefe, 1889–1936*, ed. Erika Mann (Frankfurt/M.: S. Fischer, 1961), p. 190.

8. See Franz Schonauer, *Stefan George in Selbstzeugnissen und Bilddokumenten* (Reinbek b. Hambug: Rowohlt, 1960).

9. Thomas Mann, *Briefe, 1889–1936*, p. 293.

10. Katia Mann, *Unwritten Memories*, p. 50.

11. Anni Carlsson and Volker Michels, eds., *The Hesse-Mann Letters: The Correspondence of Hermann Hesse and Thomas Mann, 1910–1955*, trans. Ralph Manheim (New York: Harper and Row, 1975), p. 1.

12. Peter de Mendelssohn, *Der Zauberer*, p. 841.

13. Ibid., p. 884.

14. Hans Wysling, ed., *Thomas Mann—Heinrich Mann: Briefwechsel, 1900–1949* (Frankfurt/M.: S. Fischer, 1968), p. 95.

15. Thomas Mann, "Kinderspiele" (1904), in *Gesammelte Werke*, vol. II (Frankfurt/M.: S. Fischer, 1974), p. 329.

16. De Mendelssohn, *Der Zauberer*, p. 879.

17. Erich Heller, *Thomas Mann: The Ironic German* (Boston: Little, Brown, 1958), p. 100.

18. De Mendelssohn, *Der Zauberer*, p. 888.

19. Thomas Mann, *Letters*, p. 59.

20. Thomas Mann, *A Sketch of My Life*, p. 46.

Index

"Abdankung" (H. Mann), 223–4
Academic Dramatic Club, Munich, 59–60,
    69, 90
Adorno, Theodor, 234
ambition, *see* reputation and ambition of
    TM
Anthes, Otto, 162
"anti-Heinrich," 173, 217
anti-Semitism, 63–4
    in Lessing's attack on Lublinski, 248–9
    in Stefan George circle, 272
    of Wagner, 180
army service, *see* military service of TM
astrology, 12–13
"At the Prophet's," 188–9, 272
Aus einen kleinen Garnison (Bilse), 212

Bad Tölz, 236, 250–1, 275, 279
Baethcke, Ludwig Hermann, 28–9
Bahr, Hermann, 47–8

on dilettantism, 78
review of *Royal Highness*, 245
"Bajazzo, Der" ("The Dilettante"), 77–81
    Elisabeth Mann's home described in, 18
    published in magazine, 98, 100
    puppet theater in, 15–16
    short scenes in, 104
    title translations, 77 *n.*
Bartels, Adolf, 24, 25, 247
"Bayreuth und die Sexualität" (Panizza),
    70–1
Benn, Gottfried, 171
Berliner Tageblatt (newspaper):
    TM's review of *Peter Schlemihl*, 262–3
    review of *Buddenbrooks*, 163
    review of *Fiorenza*, by R. Schaukal, 218
Bernstein, Elsa, 185, 186
Bernstein, Max, 185, 233
Bertram, Ernst, 259, 260, 273–4

Betrachtungen eines Unpolitischen
  (*Reflections of an Unpolitical Man*),
  64, 82, 164, 274
Bie, Oskar, 98
  on "Blood of the Walsungs, The," 209,
  210
  on *Fiorenza*, 202–3
Biermann, Guido, 106, 109
Bilanz der Moderne, Die (Lublinski), 189–
  90
Bilderbuch für artige Kinder (Picture
  Book for Well-Behaved Children), 29,
  99
Bilse, Lieut. Fritz Oswald: *Aus einen
  kleinen Garnison*, 212
"Bilse and I" ("Bilse und ich"), 212, 214–
  15, 220
Bircher-Benner, Dr. Maximilian, 240
Bircher-Benner Institut, Zürich, 240, 265
birth of TM's children:
  Angelus Gottfried Thomas ("Golo")
    (1909), 239
  Elisabeth (1918), 274
  Erika (1905), 209–10
  Klaus Heinrich (1906), 225
  Monika (1910), 250
Bismarck, Prince Otto Eduard Leopold von:
  death of (1898), 117
  and (Ernst) Dohm, 180
  and (Theodor) Fontane, 258, 259
  and Mann brothers, 31
Blätter für die Kunst (periodical), 271
"Blood of the Walsungs, The"
    ("Wälsungenblut"), 207–11
  incest in, 41–2, 208
  TM's defense of, 215
  and TM's philo-Semitism, 25
  and (Arthur) Schnitzler, 238
Bonn Society for Literary Criticism, 228,
  230
"borrowing," literary, 90–1
  in *Buddenbrooks*, 212–13
  see also quotations in TM's work
Bourget, Paul:
  and dilettantism, 78, 79
  Disciple, Le, 51
  and (Heinrich) Mann, 63
  and TM, 51

  psychology of, 41, 50 and *n*.
Boy-Ed, Ida:
  TM's letter to, on H. Mann, 196–7
  and TM's reading (1904) in Lübeck, 162,
    196, 198–9
  review of *Royal Highness*, 242–3
"Brother, A," 77
"brother problem," *see* "fraternal
  constellation"
Bruhns, Julia da Silva, *see* Mann, Julia
  (née Bruhns)
Bruhns, Ludwig, 10
  letter to Julia (1869), 11–12
Bruhns, Maria da Silva, 10
Buch der Lieder, Das (Heine), 46, 48
Buddenbrook house (Mengstrasse, Lübeck),
  12, 126
Buddenbrooks:
  autobiographical elements of, 158–60
  background and writing of, 102–13, 119,
    127–30
  basis in reality, 212–13
  characters: Betsy Buddenbrook, 19;
    Christian Buddenbrook, 31, 108,
    160–1; Consul Buddenbrook, 7, 160;
    Edmund Pfühl, 71; Gerda Budden-
    brook, 71, 159–60; Hanno Budden-
    brook, 15, 20, 148; Hugo Weinschenk,
    106; Ida Jungmann, 18; Johann
    Buddenbrook (the Founder), 6; Kai
    Mölln, 26–7; Lebrecht Kröger, 7;
    Stephan Kistenmaker, 114; Thomas
    Buddenbrook, 31, 108, 111, 127–8;
    Tony Buddenbrook, 10, 11, 61, 105,
    107, 126, 159
  chronologies, 109–10
  fraternal tensions, 30–1, 108, 160–1
  Lübeck in, 4
  Lübeck's response to, 46, 161–2
  Mann family as models for, 6–9 *passim*,
    106–8
  name, source of, 90–1
  and *Renée Mauperin*, 103–5
  reviews of, 153–7, 163
  revision, submission to Fischer, 131–2
  sales record, 162–3
  Schopenhauer's influence, 127–9
  uncertainty over fate of, 136–8

Carlebach, Ephraim, 22
Casa Bernardini, Palestrina, 68 and *n.*, 69,
  101
Caspar Hauser (Wassermann), 237–8
Chamisso, Adelbert von: *Marvelous Tale
  of Peter Schlemihl, The*, 262–3
childhood of TM, 14–19, 26; *see also*
  school experience of TM
"Child Prodigy, The," 176, 198, 199
children of TM, *see* Mann, Angelus
  Gottfried Thomas ("Golo"); Mann,
  Elisabeth; Mann, Erika; Mann, Klaus
  Heinrich; Mann, Monika
Children's Carnival (magazine illustration,
  by A. von Kaulbach), 179, 182, 183
cholera, 266–7, 269, 275, 278
coldness attributed to TM, 81, 190, 197,
  220–1; *see also* detachment
*Confessions of Felix Krull, Confidence
  Man, The:*
  and (Julia Bruhns) Mann, 55
  notes and background for, 173, 245–6
  prison sequence (unused), 240
  writing of, 164, 257, 260–1
Conrad, Michael Georg:
  on Ibsen, 61
  TM's description of, 56
  and Panizza trial, 70
courtship of TM and Katia Pringsheim,
  176–94

Da Silva family, 9–10, 24–5
Davos, Switzerland, 278–9
death (theme):
  in *Buddenbrooks*, 155–6, 126–9 *passim*
  and illness, 95, 278
  and Schopenhauer's influence, 128–9
  and sleep, 24
  in "Tod, Der," 94, 95, 97
  in *Tristan*, 148
  see also suicide
"Death" ("Der Tod"), 93–4, 97, 104, 115
Death in Venice, 77 *n.*
  Aschenbach, 268
  background and notes for, 265–70, 275,
    277–8
  completion of, 279–80
  homoeroticism in, 143, 268, 269–70

TM reads aloud to H. Mann, 276
  setting for (Venice), 4, 265–7, 277–8
  Tadzio, 262, 266, 268–9, 277
dedications of TM's work, 145–6
  Buddenbrooks (in sections), 145–6
  "Little Lizzie," to R. Schaukal, 174, 217
  Tonio Kröger, to K. Martens, 166–7
  "Vision," to H. Bahr, 47
  "Way to the Churchyard, The," to A.
    Holitscher, 147
Dehmel, Richard, 98, 125
  and *Buddenbrooks*, 153
  on "Gefallen," 57
  and "Walter Weiler," 77
  in World War I, 136
Derleth, Ludwig, 188
detachment, literary, 62; *see also* coldness
  attributed to TM
devil:
  in *Doctor Faustus*, 68 *n.*, 73–4, 75–6,
    76 *n.*, 99
  in *Liebeskonzil, Das* (Panizza), 71–2
  in *Peter Schlemihl* (Chamisso), 262
  and syphilis, 71–2
Diana (H. Mann), 150, 170
"Dilettante, The" ("Der Bajazzo"), 77–81
  Elisabeth Mann's home described in, 18
  published in magazine, 98, 100
  puppet theater in, 15–16
  short scenes in, 104
  translations of title, 77 *n.*
dilettantism, 78–9
  and (Albert) Langen, 88
Disciple, Le (Bourget), 51
"Disillusionment," 97–8
Distel, Hilde, 141, 165
"Dr. Biebers Versuchung" (H. Mann), 148
Doctor Faustus:
  black pigs in, 67, 74
  characters: Adrian Leverkühn, 27, 68,
    72, 76, 143; Rodde sisters, 254–5;
    Schweigestill family, 172
  detachment portrayed in, 62
  devil in, 68 *n.*, 73–4, 75–6, 76 *n.*, 99
  and (Hilde) Distel, 141
  guilt expressed in, 136
  Italian influences on, 68–75 *passim*, 99

Doctor Faustus (*cont.*)
  Jewish characters in, 25, 64
  Lübeck in, 5, 15
  musical structure of, 43
  pensione in, 68–9
Dohm, Ernest, 180–1
Dohm, Hedwig, *see* Pringsheim, Hedwig
  (*née* Dohm)
Dom, Hedwig (née Schleh), 180, 181, 198
"Doktor Lessing, Der," 249
drama and theater, 226–8

education of TM, *see* school experience of
  TM
Effi Briest (Fontane), 91, 94, 105
Ehrenberg, Carl, 140, 141, 165, 168, 170,
  176
Ehrenberg, Paul, 140–4, 146, 165
  and (Julia Mann) Löhr, 134
  TM's letters to, quoted, 130, 166, 254
  TM's poem for, quoted, 176
  and *Tonio Kröger*, 169
Elective Affinities (Goethe), 277
Eloesser, Arthur, 45–6
"Encounter," 81
engagement of TM and Katia Pringsheim,
  194–202
English language fluency of TM, 37, 74,
  144, 145
Ewers, Ludwig, 28, 29, 38, 50
exploitation of people for literature, 81,
  121–2, 169, 220

fame, *see* reputation and ambition of TM
Faust (Goethe), 68 *n.*
Fehér (schoolmate), 23
Felix Krull, see *Confessions of Felix Krull,
  Confidence Man, The*
"Fight Between Jappe and Do Escobar,
  The," 261–2, 268
financial situation:
  of (Heinrich) Mann, 51–2
  of TM, 95, 113–14, 118–19, 138, 187
Fiorenza (*The King of Florence*), 199–202
  background, research for, 165, 201
  idea for, 137
  TM's defense of, 227
  productions of, 226, 228–9, 235–6

Schaukal's review in *Berliner Tageblatt*,
  218
  writing of, 173, 196, 199
Fischer, Samuel:
  letters on *Buddenbrooks*, 137, 138, 153
  TM's meetings with, 132–3, 185, 222–3,
  275
Fischer (S.) Verlag, publishers:
  and (Heinrich) Mann, 36, 47
  and TM, 98, 100, 101
  see also *Neue Deutsche Rundschau*
Florence, Italy, 137, 144
Fontane, Theodor:
  and (Elsa) Bernstein, 185
  Effi Briest, 91, 94, 105
  TM's essay on, "Old Fontane," 257–8
Frank, Bruno, 260
"fraternal constellation" (TM and
  H. Mann): artistic differences, 75–7
  passim, 170, 171, 196
  and *Buddenbrooks*, 30–1, 108, 160–1
  in childhood and school days, 13, 15,
  29–31
  in *Fiorenza*, 200–1
  in TM's "Chamisso," 263
  in TM's letter to (Ida) Boy-Ed, 196–7
  in *Royal Highness*, 231–2
  tension over literary success, 101, 217
Freie Bühne, Die (periodical), 47–8, 89;
  see also *Neue Deutsche Rundschau*
Freistatt (periodical), 171
Freud, Sigmund, and Wagner, 41
Friedemann, *see* "Little Herr Friedemann"
Frühlingserwachen (Wedekind), 44
Frühlingssturm, Der (periodical), 44–9
  TM's editorial, in first issue, 44–6
  TM's review of Ibsen's *Master Builder*,
  62

"Gefallen" ("Fallen"), 56–7, 81
Gegenwart, Die (periodical), 174
Geliebten, Die (*The Loved*), 116, 142, 175
George, Stefan, 270–3
"Gerächt" ("Avenged"), 124–5
"Gesang vom Kindchen," 275
Gesellschaft, Die (periodical), 50, 56
"Gestohlene Dokument, Das," (H. Mann),
  99

Gipper-Roman ("jabber novel"), 106 and *n.*
"Gladius Dei," 145, 201
"Glück, Ein" ("A Gleam"), 175
Goethe, Johann Wolfgang von:
  Elective Affinities, 277
  Faust, 68 *n.*
Goncharov, Ivan Aleksandrovich: *Oblomov*,
  126
Goncourt brothers:
  Renée Mauperin, 103–5, 128
Gosslar (schoolmate), 23–4
Göttinnen, Die (H. Mann), 170–1
Grautoff, Ferdinand, 69
Grautoff, Otto:
  friendship with TM, 28, 69, 79–80, 143,
    165, 191
  and *Frühlingssturm, Der*, 44
  leaves Munich (1906), 223–4
  TM's letters to, 95; quoted, 67–8, 85, 96,
    100, 102, 111, 130, 132
  requests loan (1898), 113
  review of *Buddenbrooks*, 153–5
  review of *Tristan*, 174

Harden, Maximilian, 232–3, 258–9; see also
  Zukunft, Die
Hartleben, Otto Erich, 87
Hartungen, Dr. Christoph von, 116, 137,
  140, 146–7, 166
Hauptmann, Gerhart, 185
health:
  of (Heinrich) Mann, 116, 240
  of (Katia) Mann, 265, 275–6, 278–9
  of TM, 111, 117, 133–4, 146–7, 166, 196,
    222, 240, 265
Heine, Heinrich, 48–50
  Buch der Lieder, Das, 46, 48
  on plagiarism, 91
  "Unterwelt," 86
Heine, Thomas Theodor, 87, 117, 118
"Heinrich Heine the 'Good,' " 49
Heller, Erich, 278
Hesse, Hermann:
  correspondence with TM, 244 *n.*
  military service, 136
  review of *Royal Highness*, 244
Hofmannsthal, Hugo von, 78, 238–9

Holitscher, Arthur:
  attempts to socialize TM, 122
  and *Buddenbrooks*, 121, 132
  on TM's Feilitzstrasse quarters, 123
  as model for Detlev Spinell, 149
  as traveling companion, 144
Holm, Korfiz:
  and *Frühlingssturm, Der*, 44
  TM's letter to, on Wassermann, 91
  as schoolmate, 28
  as *Simplicissimus* editor, 91, 93, 112, 118
Holy Sinner, The, 15, 41–2
homoeroticism/homosexuality:
  in "Abdankung" (H. Mann), 223–4
  and *Death in Venice*, 143, 268, 269–70
  and (Paul) Ehrenberg, 142–4
  and *Frühlingserwachen* (Wedekind), 44
  of (Stefan) George, 270–3
  in "Hungry, The," 169
  and Kaiser Wilhelm's associates, 233
  and TM, 273–4
  and (Armin) Martens, 27–8
Huch, Friedrich, 156 and *n.*
"Hungry, The," 77 *n.*, 168–70
Hupe, Dr., 36–8

Ibsen, Henrik, 59–62
  Master Builder, The, 62
  Wild Duck, The, 59–60, 61–2, 63
illness as theme/symbol, 95, 278
Im Schlaraffenland (H. Mann), 57, 64,
  103, 106, 111, 137, 153
"Im Spiegel" ("In the Mirror"), 136, 234–5
incest motif, 41, 208
In einer Familie (H. Mann), 50, 79
"In Praise of Transitoriness," 26
"In the Holy Land" (by Hieronymous,
  pseud. of F. Wedekind), 117–18
"In the Mirror" ("Im Spiegel"), 136, 234–5
irony, 200, 226
isolation of the writer, 105, 139, 170

Jagd nach Liebe, Die (H. Mann), 173,
  176, 183 *n.*
  (Carla) Mann as model for Ute, 253
  TM's borrowing from, 214
Jews:
  in "Blood of the Walsungs, The," 207–11

Jews (*cont.*)
in *Doctor Faustus*, 25, 64
in *Royal Highness*, 246–7
as schoolmates, 22–4
in "Will to Happiness," 86–7
see also anti-Semitism; philo-Semitism
of TM; Zionism
Joseph and His Brothers, 43, 73

Katharineum (Gymnasium), Munich, 27,
131
Kaulbach, Friedrich August von, 182
Children's Carnival (magazine illustration), 179, 182, 183
Kerényi, Karl, 73–4
Kerr, Alfred, 192, 248
King of Florence, The, 199–202
background, research for, 165, 201
idea for, 137
TM's defense of, 227
productions of, 226, 228–9, 235–6
Schaukal's review in *Berliner Tageblatt*,
218
writing of, 173, 196, 199
Kladderadatsch (periodical), 180 and *n*.
Kleine Herr Friedemann, Der (collection),
100, 112, 129–30
"Kleine Herr Friedemann, Der" (short
story):
autobiographical aspect, 77–8
and *Effi Briest* (Fontane), 94
illness as theme, 95
publication in *Neue Deutsche Rundschau*,
98
Königliche Hoheit, see *Royal Highness*
Kulenkamp, Natalia, 199

Langen, Albert, publisher, 88–9, 93, 99,
118
TM as reader for, 118–19
Leipsiger Tageblatt (newspaper), 219
Lessing, Theodor, 248–50
"Letter to a Catholic Newspaper," 236
Liebeskonzil, Das (Panizza), 69–70
Literarische Echo, Das (periodical), 173
"Little Grandma," 181
"Little Herr Friedemann" ("Kleine Herr
Friedemann, Der"):
autobiographical aspect, 77–8

and *Effi Briest* (Fontane), 94
illness as theme, 95
publication in *Neue Deutsche Rundschau*,
98
"Little Lizzie" ("Luischen"), 102–3, 217
"Little Professor, The," 94
Little Town, The (H. Mann), 67, 68
Litzmann, Berthold, 229
Loewenstein, 24–5
Löhr, Josef ("Jof"), 133, 134, 172
Löhr, Julia (née Mann), 107, 141
birth (1877), 13
and (Ines)Schmied, 239
wedding (1900), 133–4
Lübeck, 3–5
in *Doctor Faustus*, 5, 15
Holstentor, 4
TM's departure from (1894), 53
in TM's early short stories, 94
TM's public reading in (1904), 162
TM's visit (1899), 125–6
"Postscript, A" addressed to, 212–14
in *Buddenbrooks*, 4
reaction to *Buddenbrooks*, 46, 161–2
and *Royal Highness*, 243
in *Tristan*, 149
and Venice, 3–4
see also residences of TM: Lübeck
"Lübeck as a Way of Life and Thought,"
14
Lübeckische Blätter (newspaper): review
of *Royal Highness*, by I. Boy-Ed, 242–3
Lublinski, Samuel, 163, 248–9
Bilanz der Moderne, Die, 189–90
review of *Buddenbrooks*, 163
"Luischen" ("Little Lizzie"), 102–3, 217

Magic Mountain, The:
characters: Castorp family, 7; Frau
Stöhr, 90; Hans Castorp, 27 *n.*, 61,
143, 246; Rüdiger Schildknapp, 68
and *Disciple, Le* (Bourget), 51
and *Tristan*, 148
Mahler, Gustav, 267–8
Mann, Angelus Gottfried Thomas
("Golo"): birth (1909), 239
Mann, Carla:
and *Bilderbuch für artige Kinder*, 99
birth (1881), 13

death and after-effects, 252–7
and (Heinrich) Mann, 134, 173, 252,
  254–6
and TM's wedding, 203
and theater, 172–3, 253
Mann, Elisabeth: birth (1918), 274
Mann, Elisabeth (née Marty), 7–8
death, 34
and Mann children, 18
Mann, Erika:
birth (1905), 209–10
and Count Moes, model for Tadzio, 268–9
Mann, Friedrich, 108
Mann, "Golo" (Angelus Gottfried
  Thomas): birth, 239
Mann, Heinrich (TM's brother):
For individual literary works, see titles
birth (1871), 12
as book-shop apprentice, Dresden, 32
education, early travels, 30
and father, 32–3
and (S.) Fischer Verlag, 36, 47
health of, 116, 240
on (Heinrich) Heine, 49–50
in Italy, 64–83 *passim*, 101, 110, 137,
  144, 228, 265, 266
and (Carla) Mann, 133
and TM, *see* "fraternal constellation"
and TM's marriage, 203
"My Plan," 51–2, 95
physical appearance of, 14
poetry of, 49, 50
political views of, 63–4
and (R.) Schaukal, 174–5, 217–19
and (Ines) Schmied, 203, 224, 239
and (Edith) Smith, 144–5
at *Zwanzigste Jahrhundert, Das*, 62–3,
  69
see also "fraternal constellation"
Mann, Heinrich (TM's father), 9–10,
  12–13
death, funeral of (1891), 33–5
and Heinrich (son), 32
and TM (son), 33
wedding of (1869), 11
Mann, Joachim Siegmund, 6
Mann, Johann, 6
Mann, Johann Siegmund, 6
Mann, Johann Siegmund, Jr., 6–8

Mann, Julia (née Bruhns) (TM's mother):
and Carla's death, 253–4
engagement and wedding, 11–12
family, background, 9–11
and TM's literary talent, 32, 55, 58
in Munich, 35–6, 54–5
in Polling, 171–2
public role, 18
and *Schauspielerin* (H. Mann), 276
as widow, 35, 55
Mann, Julia ("Lula"), *see* Löhr, Julia (née
  Mann)
Mann, Katia (née Pringsheim):
and childbirth, 209–10, 225, 239, 250
courtship by TM, 120, 177–94
education, 182
engagement to TM, 194–202
health, 265, 275–6, 278–9
as model for Fiore, in *Fiorenza*, 199–200
physical appearance, 183
wedding (1905), 203
Mann, Klaus Heinrich:
on Bad Tölz, 250–1
birth (1906), 225
on his childhood, 17
on (Alfred) Pringsheim, 179–80
Mann, Luiz Heinrich, *see* Mann, Heinrich
  (TM's brother)
Mann, Lula, *see* Löhr, Julia (née Mann)
Mann, Monika: birth (1910), 250
Mann, Thomas:
For individual literary works see titles
birth (1875), 12
education of, *see* school experiences of
  TM
and (Heinrich) Mann, see "fraternal
  constellation"
Mann, Thomas Johann Heinrich, *see*
  Mann, Heinrich (TM's father)
Mann, Victor ("Viko"), 13–14, 55, 99,
  107 n., 156 n., 203
birth (1890), 13
at Polling, 172
We Were Five, 14
"Mann Brothers, The" (K. Martens),
  219–21
Mann forebears of TM, 5–14
Martens, Armin, 141, 142, 169
early friendship with TM, 27–8

Martens, Ilse, 141, 144
Martens, Kurt, 120–1, 122, 165–6, 173–4,
    175, 191, 238
  Kreislauf, 221–2
  TM's letters to, quoted, 175, 245
  on TM's military service, 130
  "Mann Brothers, The," 219–21
  review of *Buddenbrooks*, 155–6
  review of *Tristan*, 173–4
  Vollendung, Die, 154
Marty, Elisabeth, *see* Mann, Elisabeth
    (née Marty)
Marty, Johann Heinrich, 8
Marty, Wilhelm, 106
Marvelous Tale of Peter Schlemihl, The
    (Chamisso), 262–3
Mass und Wert (periodical), 189
Master Builder, The (Ibsen): TM's review
    of, in *Frühlingssturm*, 62
military service of TM, 93, 130–1, 133–6,
    140
"Mind and Art," 196
Mitterbad, 146–7
"Monolog," 124
"montage" technique, *see* "borrowing,"
    literary; quotations in TM's work
Mühsam, Erich, 171
Münchner Neueste Nachrichten
    (periodical):
  TM's review of Wassermann's *Caspar
    Hauser*, 238
  review of *Buddenbrooks*, by O. Grautoff,
    154–5
  review of *Fiorenza* (production), 236
Munich:
  Kaimsaal, 183
  (Julia) Mann in, 35–6, 54–5
  TM in, 52–4; *see also* residences of TM:
    Munich
  Schwabing quarter, 55, 114–15
Munich Literary Society, 120
music:
  in *Buddenbrooks*, 159
  and Ehrenbergs, 141, 165
  and (Julia) Mann, 10, 54
  and TM, 38–9, 141–2, 144, 165
  structure of, and TM's prose, 43
  see also Wagner, Richard
Muth, Karl, 221

myths and mythology, 17, 277
  and *Felix Krull*, 55
  and Wagner, 42

"Nachwort, Ein"|("A|Postscript"), 212–14
Naples: TM on, 96
narrator in TM's fiction, 56, 175, 200, 226
Neue Deutsche Rundschau (periodical),
    89, 209, 211, 245
  TM's writing in: "Bajazzo, Der" ("The
    Dilettante"), 77, 100; *Fiorenza*, 196,
    199; "Little Herr Friedemann," 98;
    Royal Highness (serialized), 241;
    "Wardrobe, The," 119
  see also *Freie Bühne, Die*
Neue Freie Presse (periodical), 176
Nietzsche, Friedrich Wilhelm:
  Case of Wagner, The, 70–1
  influence on TM, 97–8, 107, 129
  and "Will to Happiness, The," 86
Nord und Süd (periodical): questionnaire
    on theater, 226–8

Oberammergau, 225
"Old Fontane," 257–8
"On Myself," 125
"On the Psychology of the Sufferer," 84

Palestrina, Italy: Mann brothers in, 65–81,
    101
Pan (periodical), 57, 77
Panizza, Oskar, 69–72
  "Bayreuth und die Homosexualität,"
    70–1
  Liebeskonzil, Das, 69–70, 71–2
  TM's article on, in *Zwanzigste Jahrhun-
    dert*, 69–70
Peter Schlemihl (Chamisso), 262–3
philo-Semitism of TM, 22–6, 63–4, 87,
    246–8
physical appearance of TM, 14, 29, 54, 275
plagiarism, *see* "borrowing," literary;
    quotations in TM's work
"Plagiarism, A" (H. Mann?), 91
Poe, Edgar Allan: *Fall of the House of
    Usher, The*, 208
poetry of TM, 123–4
  for (Paul) Ehrenberg, 176
  "Gesang vom Kindchen," 275

"Monolog," 124

"Zweimaliger Abschied," 46–7, 50

political convictions:

of (Heinrich) Mann, 63–4

of TM, 63–4, 164, 258, 261

Polling, 171–2

(Carla) Mann's death at, 253, 254

TM writing *Royal Highness* at, 236

"Postscript, A" ("Ein Nachwort"), 212–14

Preetorius, Emil, 262

Pringsheim, Alfred, 179–80, 181, 256

and TM, 188, 204, 209

Pringsheim, Hedwig (née Dohm), 180, 186, 188, 192

and "At the Prophet's," 189

and "Blood of the Walsungs, The," 209

Pringsheim, Katia, *see* Mann, Katia (née Pringsheim)

Pringsheim, Klaus, 182, 186, 187

and "Blood of the Walsungs, The," 208, 209

Professor Unrat (H. Mann), 75, 217, 270

puppet theater, 15–16, 60, 78

quotations in TM's work, 86, 91, 106, 200, 255; *see also* "borrowing," literary

"Railway Accident," 240, 264–5

Rantzau, Count Hans Kaspar von, 26–7

readings, public, 185, 210, 264–5

in Berlin (1904), 185, 196, 198

in Dresden (1905, 1906), 210, 222

in Lübeck (1904), 162, 196, 198–9

in Prague, Breslau (1905), 210

in Vienna (1908), 238

in Weimar (1910), 261

Renée Mauperin (Goncourt brothers), 103–5, 128

representativeness, 18 *n.*

of artist, 226

of (Julia) Mann, 18

of TM, 195–6, 214

in *Royal Highness*, 245

reputation and ambition of TM, 113, 124, 153–4, 163–4, 201–202, 206, 213, 228

research by TM for fiction, 58–9, 232; *see also under individual titles*

residences of TM:

Bad Tölz, 236, 250–1, 275, 279

Florence: Via Cavour, 144

Lübeck: Beckergrube, 18–19; Breite Strasse, 12; with professors, 36–8, 43; Roeckstrasse, 35

Munich: Feilitzstrasse, 123; Franz-Josephstrasse, 204, 259; Konradstrasse, 167; Markstrasse, 114, 115; Mauer-kircherstrasse, Herzogpark, 259–60; Rambergstrasse, 54–5; Theresien-strasse, 112, 114

Oberammergau, 225

Palestrina: Casa Bernardini, 68 and *n.*, 69, 101

Rome: Via del Pantheon, 98; Via Torre Argentina, 82–3, 110

resorts:

Bad Kissingen, 192–3

Mitterbad, 146–7

Seeshaupt, 229

Travemünde, 19–21, 262

see also Bad Tölz

Reuter, Gabriele: review of *Royal Highness*, 244, 246

Rilke, Rainer Maria, 156–7

TM on, 157–8

Riva, *see* Villa Cristoforo (sanatorium), Riva, Italy

Rome:

(Heinrich) Mann in, 64–5, 82–3, 101, 110

TM in, 82–3, 98, 101, 110

Rosenberg, Hermann and Elsa, 198, 207

Rosmer, Ernst (pseud.), *see* Bernstein, Elsa

Royal Highness:

background, notes for, 175–6, 178, 232–4

changing-of-the-guard scene, 183–4

characters: Albrecht, 116, 231–2; Dr. Sammet, 25, 246; Imma Spoelmann, 188, 234, 242; Prince Klaus Heinrich, 188, 225, 234

Düsseldorf hotel in, 172–3

final words of, 214

Ibsen's influence on, 60

and (Heinrich) Mann, 239–40

publication and reviews, 241–6

Royal Highness (*cont.*)
serialized in *Neue Deutsche Rundschau*, 241
sanatoriums:
Bircher-Benner Institut, Zürich, 240, 265
Villa Cristoforo, Riva, Italy, 116, 137, 140, 147, 166–7
Waldsanatorium, Davos, 279
Weisser Hirsch, near Dresden, 222
Schaubühne, Die (periodical), 249
Schaukal, Richard von, 174–5, 217–19
Schauspielerin (H. Mann), 256, 276
Schiller, Friedrich von:
"feindliche Brüder" borrowed from, 200
TM's early enthusiasm for, 28–9
TM's homage to, "A Weary Hour," 204–7
Schleh, Hedwig, *see* Dohm, Hedwig (née Schleh)
Schmid-Gibichenfels, Otto: review of *Royal Highness*, 246
Schmied, Ines, 203, 224, 239
Schnitzler, Arthur:
Anatol, 95
Liebelei, 95
and TM, 238
and *Schauspielerin* (H. Mann), 276
school experience of TM, 19, 27, 30, 43–4, 52–3
failure in, 30, 53, 55
at university, 58–9
schools:
(Dr.) Bussenius's elementary, 19
Katharineum (Gymnasium), 27, 131
University of Munich, 58
Schopenhauer, Arthur, 127–9, 161
World as Will and Idea, The, 127–8
Schriftsteller, 226–7
Schröter, Klaus, 63
Schwabe, Toni, 171
Schwabing quarter, Munich, 55, 114–15
Schweigert, Max and Katharina, 172
sea, the:
and TM, 20–1, 265
in "Tod, Der," 94
Seeshaupt, 229
self-promotion, *see* reputation and ambition of TM

sexuality:
and TM, 96–7
and Wagner, 41
see also homoeroticism/homosexuality
sickness as theme/symbol, 95, 278
Simplicissimus (periodical), 65, 87–90, 93, 99, 117–18
(Heinrich) Mann's writing in, 99, 223
TM as reader for, 118–19, 138
TM's writing in: "Gerächt" ("Avenged"), 124–5; "Tod, Der" ("Death"), 93; "Way to the Church-yard, The," 147; "Weary Hour, A," 204–5; "Will to Happiness, The," 86
Sketch of My Life, A (quoted), 52–3, 145, 267
on (Otto) Grautoff, 79
on (Carla) Mann's death, 255
Smith, Mary, 144–6
Springer, Idachen, 18, 20
Spring Storm, see *Frühlingssturm, Der*
Story of a Novel, The, 74
Stürmische Morgen (H. Mann), 223
suicide, 129, 138–40
"Sweet Sleep," 21, 31
Switzerland, and TM, 8

Tesdorpf, Krafft, 113–14, 136
theater and drama, 226–8
Thomas, Paul (pseud. of TM), 44
Thomas Mann Allee, Herzogpark, 260
time (theme), 26
Timpe, Professor, 38
Timpe, Willri, 144
"Tobias Mindernickel," 98, 102–3
"Tod, Der" ("Death"), 93–4, 97, 104, 115
Tölz (Bad Tölz), 236, 250–1, 275, 279
Tonio Kröger:
characters: Hans Hansen, 28, 151; Lisaveta Ivanovna, 125
homoeroticism in, 143
and "Hungry, The," 168–70
inspiration for, 125–6, 127
writing of, 140, 166–7
Transposed Heads, The, 77
Travemünde, 19–21
in "The Fight Between Jappe and Do Escobar," 262

Tristan, 147–51
    Detlev Spinell, 149–51, 169–70
    (Arthur) Holitscher portrayed in, 121
    reviews: by (Otto) Grautoff, 174; by
      (Kurt) Martens, 173–4; by (Richard)
      Schaukal, 174
    setting of, 147

unio mystica, 205
University of Munich, 58
Untertan, Der (H. Mann), 135

Venice:
    and *Death in Venice,* 4, 265–7, 277–8
    and Lübeck, 3–4
    TM's visits: October 1896, 96; May 1907,
      228; May 1911, 265–7
Via Thomas Mann, Palestrina, 68
Vienna: TM's visit (1896), 95–6
Villa Cristoforo (sanatorium), Riva, Italy,
    116, 137, 140, 147, 166–7
"Vision," 47

Wagner, Richard:
    and (Julia) Mann, 10
    and TM, 39–43, 228, 244
    music performed in Rome, 82
    Panizza on, 70–1
    and (Alfred) Pringsheim, 180
"Wälsungenblut," *see* "Blood of the
    Walsungs, The"
Walter, Bruno, 260

"Walter Weiler," 77, 93
"Wardrobe, The," 115–16
    pirated publication in New York, 119
Wassermann, Jakob, 89–91, 93, 218, 219
    Caspar Hauser, 237–8
"Way to the Churchyard, The," 147
"Weary Hour, A," 204–7
Weber, Carl Maria, 269
Weber, Hans von, 262, 279
Wedekind, Frank, 91–2, 117
    Frühlingserwachen, 44
    "In the Holy Land," 117–18
Wild Duck, The (Ibsen), 59–60, 61–2, 63
Wilhelm, Crown Prince, 233, 234
Wilhelm II, Kaiser, 117, 232–3, 242
"Will to Happiness, The," 84–6, 95
Wolzogen, Ernst von, 59–60, 120
World as Will and Idea, The (Schopen-
    hauer), 127–8

Zionism, 247
Zuckmayer, Carl, 60
Zukunft, Die (periodical), 168, 219, 232–3,
    258–9
Zwanzigste Jahrhundert, Das (periodical),
    62–3, 69, 87, 91
"Zweimaliger Abschied" ("Double Fare-
    well"), 46–7, 50
Zwischen den Rassen (H. Mann), 55, 79,
    81, 228
    Arnold, 231
    Lola, 10, 203

Grateful acknowledgment is made to the following for permission to reprint from previously published material:

Aufbau-Verlag Berlin und Weimar: *Heinrich Mann, 1871–1950. Werk und Leben in Dokumenten und Bildern*. Mit unveröffentlichten Manuskripten und Briefen aus dem Nachlass. Herausgegeben von Sigrid Anger. © Aufbau-Verlag, Berlin und Weimar, 1977. Heinrich Mann, *Ein Zeitalter Wird Besichtigt*. © Aufbau-Verlag, Berlin und Weimar, 1975. Translations made with the permission of the publisher.

Verlag Heinrich Ellerman KG: Excerpts from the autobiography of Klaus Mann, published in 1942 as *The Turning Point*, and in a revised edition in 1952 as *Der Wendepunkt*. Translation made with the permission of the publisher.

S. Fischer Verlag GmbH: Excerpts from the following works by Thomas Mann: *Briefe, 1948–1955, und Nachlese*, 1965 edition; *Briefe an Ida Boy-Ed, 1903–1928*, 1975 edition; *Autobiographisches*, 1960 edition; *Briefe an Otto Grautoff, 1894–1901*, 1975 edition; *Briefwechsel, 1900–1949*, 1969 edition; *Gesammelte Werke*, Volumes I, II, VII, IX, X, XI, XII, XIII; *Buddenbrooks*; *Essays of Three Decades*; *Stories of Three Decades*; *The Magic Mountain*; *A Sketch of My Life*; *Doctor Faustus*. Excerpts from *Unwritten Memories* by Katia Mann. Translations made or amended by permission of, and copyright in the name of, the publishers, S. Fischer Verlag GmbH.

S. Fischer Verlag GmbH and Christian Wegner Verlag GmbH: Excerpts from *Thomas Mann in Urteil Seiner Zeit* by Klaus Schröter, 1969. Translations made by permission of the publishers.

Alfred A. Knopf, Inc., and Andre Deutsch Ltd: Excerpts from *Katia Mann: Unwritten Memories* by Katia Mann, translated by Hunter G. and Hildegarde Hannum, edited by Elizabeth Von Plessen and Michael Mann. Copyright © 1975 by Alfred A. Knopf, Inc. Used by permission of the publishers; some translations amended by permission of Alfred A. Knopf, Inc., Andre Deutsch Ltd, and S. Fischer Verlag GmbH.

Alfred A. Knopf, Inc., and Martin Secker & Warburg Ltd: Excerpts from the following works by Thomas Mann: *Buddenbrooks*, translated by H. T. Lowe-Porter, Copyright 1924 by Alfred A. Knopf, Inc., copyright renewed 1952 by Alfred A. Knopf, Inc.; *Essays of Three Decades*, translated by H. T. Lowe-Porter, Copyright 1929, 1933, 1937, 1947 by Alfred A. Knopf, Inc.; *Stories of Three Decades*, translated by H. T. Lowe-Porter, Copyright 1936 by Alfred A. Knopf, Inc., copyright renewed 1964 by Alfred A. Knopf, Inc.; *The Magic Mountain*, translated by H. T. Lowe-Porter, copyright 1927 by Alfred A. Knopf, Inc., Copyright renewed 1955 by Alfred A. Knopf, Inc., Copyright 1952 by Thomas Mann; *A Sketch of My Life*, translated by H. T. Lowe-Porter; *Doctor Faustus*, translated by H. T. Lowe-Porter, Copyright 1948 by Alfred A. Knopf, Inc.; *Letters of Thomas Mann, 1889–1955*, selected and translated from the German by Richard and Clara Winston, Copyright © 1970 by Alfred A. Knopf, Inc. Translations used by permission of the publishers; some translations amended by permission of Alfred A. Knopf, Inc., Martin Secker & Warburg Ltd, and S. Fischer Verlag GmbH, Frankfurt-am-Main.

A NOTE ABOUT THE AUTHOR

Richard Winston, the author of CHARLEMAGNE:
FROM THE HAMMER TO THE CROSS (1954) and THOMAS BECKET (1967),
in the course of over thirty years translated
more than a hundred full-length books
from five European languages, including the works
of some of the foremost German writers.
He died in 1979. His wife and collaborator,
novelist Clara Winston, is the author of
THE CLOSEST KIN THERE IS (1952), THE HOURS TOGETHER (1962),
and PAINTING FOR THE SHOW (1969).

A NOTE ON THE TYPE

This book was set in Waverley,
a typeface produced by the Intertype Corporation.
Named for Captain Edward Waverley,
the hero of Sir Walter Scott's first novel,
it was inspired by the spirit of Scott's
literary creation rather than actually being
derived from the typography of that period.
Indeed, Waverley is a wholly modern typeface,
if not by definition, certainly by
association with the designs of the best
contemporary typographers.

Composed by American–Stratford Graphic Services,
Inc., Brattleboro, Vermont.
Printed and bound by American Book–Stratford
Press, Saddle Brook, New Jersey.

Designed by Margaret Wagner.